THE COMPLETE HEARTS SERIES

KALEIDOSCOPE HEARTS

TORN HEARTS

PAPER HEARTS

ELASTIC HEARTS

claire contreras

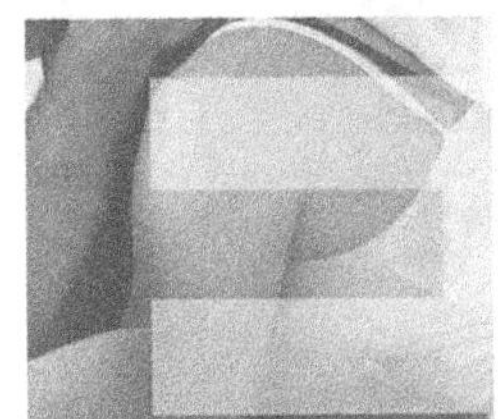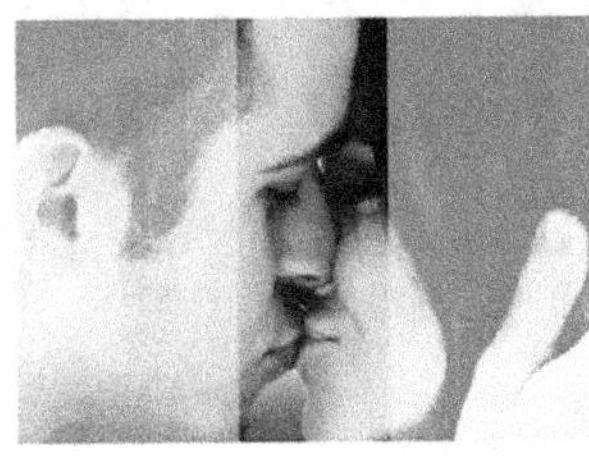

KALEIDOSCOPE HEARTS

claire contreras

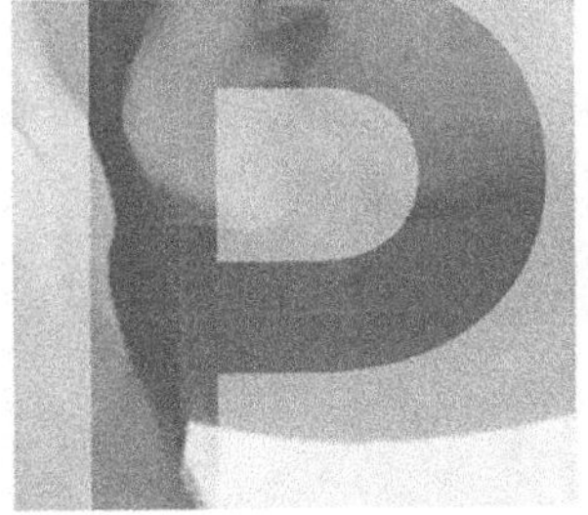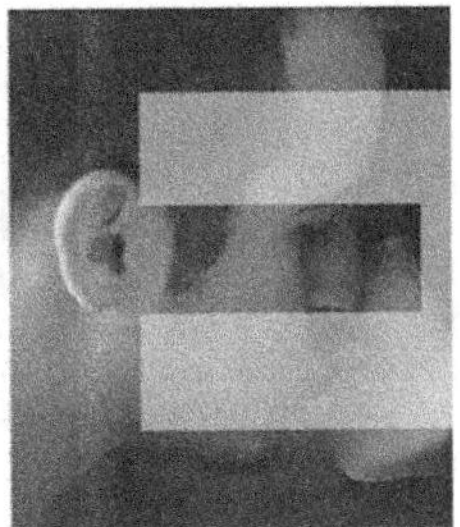

"and she always had a way
with her brokenness. She would take her pieces
and make them beautiful."

-R.M. Drake

Prologue

THE FIRST BOY I fell in love with used to regale me with stories about kings and queens and war and peace, and how he hoped to one day be somebody's knight in shining armor. I lived vicariously through his late night adventures, watching the way he swung his hands animatedly as he told his stories, and loving the way his green eyes twinkled when I laughed at his jokes.

He taught me what it feels like to be touched and thoroughly kissed. Later, he taught me the pain one feels at the loss of someone that you've grown attached to. The one thing he forgot to teach me was how to deal with the way my chest squeezed after he broke the ghost of what heart I had left. I'd always wondered if it had been a missed lesson. Now I wonder if maybe he'd been trying to figure it out for himself, or if he just never felt anything at all.

Chapter 1

THEY SAY THE best way to move on is to let go. As if letting go is the easy part. As if trying to dim or erase three years of memories, good and bad, is something you can do in one day. I know it's not, because in a couple of weeks, it will be one year, and the memory of him is as potent as if he was still here. His San Francisco Giants sandals are still in front of the sink, right where he left them. The smell of him lingers on some of his shirts—the ones I still haven't gotten around to wearing to bed. His presence is powerful even in his absence. As I walk around the house making sure everything is out of sight, I know that for me, this is a huge step in the letting go process.

I'm in the kitchen taping up the last of the boxes, when I hear the jingle of keys followed by heels on the hardwood. Another sound I'll miss, I'm sure, once I leave this place.

"Estelle?" she calls out in a soft melodic voice.

"Kitchen!" I wipe my hands over my jeans and make my way over to her.

"Hey. You got a lot done last night," she says, smiling sadly, her eyes glistening as she looks around the nearly empty space. She has the same wild curly hair and expressive caramel eyes her son had. Seeing her makes my heart hurt all over again.

I shrug and bite the inside of my cheek so that I won't cry. Anything not to cry over this again, especially since I haven't in so long. When Felicia pulls me into her arms, I let out a slow breath and try not to completely lose it. I try to be strong for her and Phillip. Wyatt was their only child and, as hard as his loss is on me, I can only imagine the emptiness they must feel. We usually don't cry when we get together—not even when she comes over here—but selling this place is more than just saying goodbye to a house. It's leaving Christmas mornings and Thanksgiving dinners behind. It's saying, "Wyatt, we love you, but life goes on." And it does, which is one of the reasons I feel guilty. Life goes on, but why does it have to go on without him?

"It's going to be fine," I say, wiping my wet cheeks as I pull away from her.

"It is. It is. Wyatt wouldn't want us to break down over a house."

"No, he would definitely think we're dumb for mourning a structure," I say with a small laugh. If it were up to Wyatt, people would live in tents and bathe in rainwater.

"Yeah, and he would have cut the electricity on this place two months ago since you've been eating takeout anyway," she adds.

We shake our heads, new tears forming as the laughter dies and silence settles around us.

"Are you sure you don't want to stay with Phillip and me?" she asks, as we walk from room to room, making sure nothing is left out. The realtor is going to start showing the house tomorrow, and it needs to be perfect for potential buyers.

"No. Victor would be highly offended if I didn't take him up on his offer. He would probably start bringing up my not wanting to go to the same college as him, not liking the same football team, and the fact that I never paid up and did his laundry for a year that time in high school. I think that's why he's so eager to have me move in with him, actually."

Felicia's shoulders shake as she laughs. "Well, tell him I said hello, and invite him to dinner with us on Sunday. We'd love to have him over!"

"Sure," I say, my smile disappearing as I notice the sandals on the floor.

"You want me to take those, or do you want to keep them?"

"I . . ." I pause to take a shaky breath. "Will you take them?"

I don't think I can bear to look at them every day in a new place. I'm already keeping all of Wyatt's t-shirts, and it's not like the sandals fit me— they're like five sizes too big for my feet—but they're his favorite. Were. They *were* his favorite. That's something my therapist had me work on—speaking of Wyatt in the past tense. Sometimes I cringe when I do it, but I've gotten better. For a while, I was living this false reality where Wyatt was away on a business trip or something. He loved to travel alone and let the different cultures inspire his paintings. After a month, I started accepting that he wasn't coming back. After three, at the request of my therapist, I started putting his things in boxes so that I wouldn't have the constant reminder.

Putting them away didn't do much. The house was a reminder, and our art studio couldn't be packed up either. It was something I had to learn to live with . . . being without him. After six months, I was able to walk in and out of both places without having my heart squeeze in my chest every time. And now, a year later, I think I'm ready to move on. If Wyatt's sudden death taught me anything, it was that life is short, and we need to live it to the fullest. It's something I understand, but still struggle to follow through with some days.

"Honey, everything he left behind is yours, you know that," Felicia says. I don't even realize that I'm still crying, until I taste the salt of tears on my lips. I try to thank her, but the words stay lodged in my throat under the boulder that's settled there.

After one last look around, we hug, and I promise to see her on Sunday. I glance over a shoulder as I walk to the car, letting my heart squeeze one last time before I get in and drive away. The memories . . . the comfort . . . the past . . . all become a distant picture in the rearview mirror as I head to my brother's house. I'm running through a mental checklist of things I have to do, when a ringing phone cuts into my thoughts.

"Hey, how'd it go?" Mia asks in greeting.

"It was okay. A little sad, but not terrible."

"Sorry I couldn't be there. Did Felicia come to pick up some of his things? How is she doing these days?"

"Good. She looks good."

"Are we still going out tomorrow night?" Mia asks slowly, treading water.

"As long as we stick to one bar, I'll go. I'm not in the mood for bar hopping and doing the college girl thing you like to do."

Mia never shed her wild side persona when we graduated and started living our "grown-up lives." As much as I love hanging out with her, replenishing my liver with an insane amount of water after drowning it in alcohol the night before isn't something I can do every week, like she does.

"Okay, no bar hopping. I have a brunch date on Saturday morning anyway and can't afford to look like crap, so we'll take it easy."

"A date?" I ask with a frown, as I pull into my brother's driveway.

"Blind date. His name is Todd. He's a curator at The Pelican. Maria seems to think we'd be perrrfect together," she says, rolling her R's exaggeratedly to imitate her Italian author friend.

"Hmm . . . I don't think I've heard of a Todd," I say.

Mia and I have known each other for as long as I can remember. Our mothers were best friends growing up and later, married men who were also best friends. Much to our mothers' dismay, we realized early on that history wouldn't repeat itself when Mia kept going for the bad boys, while I stuck to the quiet types.

"Damn. I was hoping you had. Don't you know everybody in the art world? Todd Stern?" she says, a hopeful note on her voice.

I laugh because it's not far from the truth. Wyatt and I opened up Paint it Back—a gallery-slash-art studio—a couple of years ago, and between our artist and gallery owner friends, and Mia's connections in the photography world, we pretty much did know everybody. Well, obviously not everybody.

"Nope. Rob doesn't know him?"

"I'm not going to ask him! You know my brother has a big mouth. He'll go and tell my mom, and they'll start planning a wedding over a guy I haven't even seen yet."

I laugh, knowing she's right. "Well, I've never heard of the guy."

"Maria said he just moved here from San Fran, so I figured you would know him. New guy in town and all that jazz."

"This isn't really like high school, Mia."

"Actually, it's exactly like high school, which leads me to believe that if we haven't heard anything about him thus far, he's probably ugly."

"You're probably right," I agree with a laugh.

"Shit. Stefano is here for his shoot. Let me know if you need me to come by Vic's later. Love you!"

She hangs up in the midst of my goodbye, so I put my phone away and switch off the ignition. I do a quick face check in the rearview mirror to make sure my mascara is still intact and run a couple fingers through my wavy brown hair, picking it up into a quick ponytail. The only sound, as I walk up to the house with the last of my clothes in the bag in my hand, is that of the gravel crunching below my flats, and the waves from the beach just steps away.

Anticipation buzzes through me as I crouch down and flip the welcome mat to get the spare key out and open the door. I call out my brother's name as I walk through the door and past the living room, assuming that his car is parked in the garage. I get no response. I head upstairs toward the spare rooms. His master bedroom is downstairs, which is convenient for a twenty-eight-year-old single male, since the kitchen and living room (complete with a ginormous television) are only a few feet away from his door. When I step into the room, I'm taken aback by what I see. Not only did he make my bed with the new sheets I bought and left here the other day, but he also painted my room a soft shade of gray that I love.

I leave my bag on the bed and head to the balcony right outside the room. The balconies are one of my favorite features of this house, and what I went crazy over when he was thinking of buying it. There's one in each upstairs bedroom, and they both face the beach behind the house. As I'm stepping out onto the balcony, the phone chimes with a text message from Vic, telling me he'll be here in a couple of minutes. As I'm responding, I walk into the back of an easel that wasn't there when I last visited. Walking around it, I read the huge letters in Vic's handwriting that say: "Welcome Home, Chicken" and below, a drawing of a chicken that only a five-year-old would be proud of. I erupt in laughter and snap a picture of it, sending it to Mia and my mom, since they're the only ones who would get it. My brother started calling me that when I was five and afraid of the dark—like most five-year-olds are—and for some reason, the name stuck. Probably because every time he called me that growing up, it was in the form of a challenge he knew I wouldn't back down from.

I turn the page of the large sketchbook and leave it on a blank page before turning my attention to the ocean. My eyes take in the different shades of blues that twinkle in the sunlight—the cerulean, aqua, and midnight blue. It's a view that can't be ignored. It's one that reminds me of how small I am in the grand scheme of things. How small we all are. I'm not sure how long I stand there, just staring. Just breathing. Just enjoying the taste of salt on my tongue that I seem to get from the smell alone. A hand lands on my shoulder and I jump, snapping me out of my meditation.

"Holy crap, Victor!" I say, pressing both hands to my heart.

"You like your present?" he asks with a laugh as he pulls me into a hug.

"Yeah, you asshole," I say, smiling as I slap his chest playfully.

"Asshole? I get you the best present ever, and you call me an asshole? It was the terrible drawing of the chicken, wasn't it?"

"You know I hate that nickname." I groan and step into the house, trailing behind him as he walks downstairs. "Where's the food? I'm starving."

"It should be here soon. Let me go change," he says. "I have to go back to work soon."

"You're going back?"

"The case I'm working on is a fucking mess. The guy's wife is trying to take everything he has in the divorce. I don't know when these athletes will learn that they need a goddamn prenup."

"Oh," I cringe slightly. It's something Wyatt and I discussed when we got engaged—and had a huge disagreement over—every time it was brought up. You would never think an artist would care about that, but Wyatt was successful and wealthy. By the time he turned thirty-three, he'd been selling to a very wealthy group of people for years. That same group of people talked him into thinking that marriage without a pre-nup was grounds for a messy separation.

A knock on the door has me pivoting on my heel. I'm in a daze as I walk over to answer it, thinking, in hindsight, about how stupid the disagreement had been. We weren't even married when Wyatt died, and his parents insist on me keeping everything. They're older—much older than my parents will be when I reach Wyatt's age of death—and they're wealthy in their own right. The way they see it, they're not going to do anything with that money, and it rightfully belongs to me since I was half-owner of Paint it Back when he died. But alas, that's in the past. I don't want to think about it more than I already have—this is my fresh start.

The thought brings a smile to my face, which stays put as I swing the door open, quickly transforming into a full gape at the man standing there in a pair of green scrubs and a white doctor's coat. He's looking down, trying to wipe scum off his sneakers, his sandy brown hair covering most of his face. I can only make out his strong jaw and the bottom half of his full lips, but I recognize him immediately. When he finally looks up, his green eyes soak me in as they travel up my body until they reach my own. He smiles that slow, uneven grin that always made my breath fall short.

"Bean," I whisper, making his lips twist even higher, revealing twin dimples.

"Hey, Elle," he says. I clutch the doorknob a little tighter. I haven't seen him for so long, I'd forgotten the sound of his voice. "Food's here."

My eyes drop to the bags in his hands, and I step backward, opening the door a little wider. "Oh! Yeah. I wasn't expecting you."

"It's been a while," he says, stopping in front of me as he comes in. I back up to the door and stop breathing completely when he dips his face into mine and lets his lips brush lightly against my cheek. I do everything in my power not to breathe in the familiar scent of him that used to make my head swim. "It's good to see you again," he says, as he pulls away. The way he says it and the twinkle in his eyes make my heart drop to my stomach. How is it possible that he still manages to do that to me? Even after Wyatt. I hate him for it.

"It's good to see you too," I whisper and follow behind him after closing the door.

It is so *not* good to see him, though. Over the years, I've learned a lot about Oliver Hart, but the only one worth remembering, is that he's bad for my health.

Chapter 2

"YOU LOOK FAB," Mia says when I step into view at the bar she picked for our weekly happy hour.

"As do you, my lady," I reply with a small bow that makes her snicker. She's wearing a Victorian-style dress with a bustier that makes her boobs look like they're going to pop out the top. Her long, blonde hair is curled loosely and pulled back in two sections at the front.

"You're silly. I talked my parents and Rob into a family Halloween shoot so that I can showcase them around the studio next month, and I didn't have time to change before coming over here." She turns to the waitress. "Two lemon drops, please."

"What in the world are you dressed up as? Queen Victoria?" I ask, looking under the table to see what the rest of her outfit looks like. When I straighten again, she's looking at me like I'm crazy, and I realize she has no idea who Queen Victoria is.

"No! I'm Cersei Lannister."

"Ooohhh . . ." I say, taking a sip of the drink the waitress places in front of me.

"Rob dressed as Jamie."

"What?" I ask, sputtering half of the gulp back into my cup.

The bubbled laughter that escapes her lips soon turns into full hysteria. "I swear," she says, gasping for air. "You should have seen my mom's face!"

Robert is Mia's brother. Twin brother. And . . . clearly, neither are normal.

"You guys are sick. What did they say?" I ask, laughing with her.

"Mom doesn't know what the hell Game of Thrones is. Dad was horrified when he figured it out. He didn't want my mom to send out the Halloween cards she said she was going to make, but it was the first time we'd taken Halloween pictures since Rob and I were, like, eight. Anyway, she dressed up as Mary Poppins and Dad was Bert."

"Aww that's cute . . . you two are so, so weird though," I mutter. "Tell me about this Todd guy. Did you find out anything?"

"His last name is Stern—"

"He sounds like a lawyer or something," I interrupt.

Mia rolls her eyes. "He's an accountant."

"I thought he was a curator?"

"I don't know what Maria was thinking. I swear, sometimes I think it's a language barrier thing."

"What is?" I ask, trying not to laugh.

"This is the fifth guy she's tried to set me up with, and he's a freaking accountant! Do I look like I would date an accountant?"

"Well, no, but you don't have the greatest taste in guys, so maybe this is a good thing."

"Anywayyyyy," she says, dragging it out before finishing off her drink and signaling for two more. "How was your first night at Vic's?"

I let out a long sigh . . . my first night at Vic's. Heartbreaking, lonely, weird, sad, happy, weird . . .

"It was fine." I shrug.

Mia places her hand over mine to stop me from drawing lines of water on the table, beckoning my attention. "It's okay to not be okay, Elle."

"I am okay, though," I answer with a frown.

"You don't need to be strong for every single person, you know? You're allowed to break down. The love of your life died, you're in the process of selling your house together, and you moved in with your brother. It's a lot to take in. It's okay to not be okay. It's okay to take a break from work if you need it."

"It's been a year. And I already took a break from work," I remind her. After Wyatt died, I took two months off work, but that meant being home all the time. I even went to live with my parents for a couple of weeks to get away from the house. I couldn't take the memories and being there without him, but you can't turn your back on your struggles and expect them to disappear on their own. It just doesn't happen. So, I went home and dealt with the fact that he wasn't coming back. I went to see a therapist and got to a good place, but not staying in the house any more feels like . . . it's really over.

"Sometimes I feel like a bitch for selling the house," I say, finally. "I feel like I'm erasing him from my life or something."

Mia squeezes my hand. "Oh, honey, nobody thinks you're trying to do that. You need to move on. You're young, you're smart, you're talented as hell, and you're fun. You can't stop living because of a ghost."

My eyes cut to hers. "I haven't stopped living. I just don't want to move on like that. If I find someone, I find someone—if I don't, I don't." Mia has tried to set me up on two blind dates in the past couple of months. Even Felicia tried to talk me into going on one, but I wasn't ready. I still don't think I am, despite what everybody thinks. Even my own mom is driving me up the wall about the dating thing, as if some man is going to magically take the pain away.

"Elle . . ."

"I'm just saying that I don't care to date right now. Besides, I don't need a guy. I love being alone."

"Elle . . ."

"I'm serious, I do. And now I come to Vic's house thinking that this is going to be like summer camp or something, and freaking Oliver comes over my first fifteen minutes there, so really it's exactly like—"

"You saw Oliver?" Mia shouts, effectively shutting me (and a couple of people around us) up.

I nod, taking a sip of my drink.

"What happened? Oh. My. God. What happened when he saw you there? Did he know you would be there? Did you know he was here? Victor didn't even warn you? Holy shit!" Mia says, practically squealing.

"This is why I didn't want to bring it up."

She shoots me a look. "Spill. Right now. I want to hear every single detail of what happened. Is he still hot as fuck?"

"What do you think?" I say, letting out a short laugh.

"I think he's aging like fine wine. Does he still have the long hair? His hair was so hot," she says, fanning herself with her hand.

"His hair was so hot? Yeah, it's still long. Not as long, but long enough," I say before I realize the way that sounds—not because of the actual words— but because of mental images of me threading my fingers through it.

"Well, the whole package was hot. What was it like though—seeing him again?" she asks.

"For him, I guess like old times. For me, I don't know. It was . . ."

"Like old times pre-Oliver or post-Oliver?" she asks in another interruption.

"Easy on the questions, Columbo."

"You can't tell me something like that and then hold back. Just humor me!" Mia whines.

"Fine. Seeing him was . . . uncomfortable. I felt like I was being ambushed, even though he was just standing there with food in his hands. He brought sandwiches and sushi."

Mia searches my face. "So he knew you'd be there."

I shrug. Obviously, he knew I'd be there if he brought enough food for me to sit and eat with them, but I don't know how far in advance he knew I'd be there. It's not like sushi is difficult to find in Santa Barbara, but still. Victor and Oliver don't really care for sushi. It's my favorite food. I can eat it all the time and anytime.

"I didn't question it," I tell her quietly. "We didn't really talk about much other than his residency and my sculptures."

"He asked about the hearts?" Mia asks in a whisper.

I nod.

"Did you tell him why you make them?"

"Of course not," I say, scoffing. "I'm not that brave."

We share a small, pathetic, commiserative smile before she drops the subject. "So, what are you up to this weekend?"

I start telling her what the rest of my weekend looks like, and we ease into a conversation about that instead. Anything to get away from the topic of Oliver Hart.

Chapter 3

I START PACING the studio, placing blank canvases on each easel, as I make my way around the room. Saturday night is Ladies Night here, and tonight I have a group of bachelorettes coming over as the first stop of their party. The maid of honor already came by earlier with wine she'd wanted me to chill for them, and a CD of music she wants to play. Aside from doing a presentation in the beginning of the party, I don't get involved with anything. They usually pay to have fun and talk shit with their friends. The last thing they want is for me to tell them what strokes to use on their creative masterpieces.

At seven o'clock, I go to the bathroom and check my make-up. I feel good. I'm wearing a red shirt with black bows on the sleeves, black pumps and ripped skinny jeans that I couldn't even dream of fitting my ass into this time last year. At the sound of footsteps, I pull myself away from the mirror and into the open space, walking toward the front of the gallery with a smile on my face, as I make ready to meet and greet. I stop dead in my tracks when I find Oliver standing in the room, looking at one of Wyatt's paintings.

He's not in his scrubs today, so I guess he has the day off. He's wearing jeans that hug his narrow hips perfectly and a blue button-down shirt. He's thrown on a charcoal gray suit jacket over it, and he looks totally GQ, as Mia would say. I guess he's on his way to the group date Vic mentioned. He'd said they were going to a sports bar tonight, which for them is code for: We're taking out the girls we're currently fucking so they don't accuse us of only wanting sex, and, let's do this as a group at a sports bar so they know we're not serious.

"Hey. What are you doing here?"

Oliver gives me a onceover when he turns to face me. "You look better every time I see you. How is that possible?"

I don't let myself react the way I know he wants me to. Instead, I focus on the painting he's looking at. The one with the dark eye with butterfly wings for eyelashes. The one that watches the way Oliver is looking at me, and eavesdropping while he flirts.

"I was in the area and wanted to stop by to see the place. I hope that's okay," he says, as he walks toward me.

"You've never wanted to see it before," I say, keeping my voice quiet, but the words scream inside of me. He's never made an effort to come see the studio—not even after I sent him an invitation for the grand opening of the gallery portion a few years back.

Oliver's gaze pins me with something serious and intense—something that makes my insides rock—but I push back against the current. I push back against everything that draws me to him like a magnet as he takes one last stride and stands directly in front of me.

"I should have," he says, his voice a low purr that begs for me to close my eyes. I don't give in, though. I turn my face to look away—back to the eye that's still staring at us, judging. I swallow before I speak again, to make sure my voice sounds steadier than I feel.

"Why'd you come now?"

"Are you almost done here?" he asks, looking around.

"Actually, I'm just getting started. I have a bachelorette party—" I'm not even finished speaking before I spot a blonde in a short black dress pulling the door open. Her five friends follow closely behind her, all wearing black except for one wearing a short white dress and a tiara. I smile at them. "There they are now."

"Hi!" Gia, the maid of honor I've been in contact with, smiles and greets me.

"Oh my God, does this come with eye candy?" one of the girls says. "Is he our muse for the night?"

Oliver chuckles and flashes them a smile that makes all but one blush ridiculously. On principle, I assume she's not into men, because that smile makes every female swoon.

"Unfortunately for you, he's not. This is my friend Oliver, and he's on his way to a date," I say, meeting his amused eyes. "You girls can go on to the next room, and I'll be with you shortly. Gia, your stuff is on the table."

"Thank you so much," she gushes as she walks past. All the girls follow, but their eyes never leave Oliver. I'm about to ask him to stand here as an exhibit one of these days. Maybe that'll get me the movement I've been lacking around here.

"So . . ." I say, turning to him again.

"I came by to see if you wanted to join us tonight," he says, dropping his voice an octave as he reaches out and twirls a loose curl around his fingers.

"Why would I do that?" I ask quietly, taking a step back so he has to drop the strand of hair he's holding.

"Because you need a night out," he says, as his eyes flicker from my eyes to my lips.

I take one more step back, suddenly needing more than just a little distance between us. "I had one yesterday."

"Not with me."

The memory of the last time he said those words to me floods my brain, and he smirks like he has front row seats to the show inside my head, where he has the lead role.

"I have to go. They're waiting."

Oliver nods, stuffing his hands in his pockets. He does this thing where he looks down at his feet and lifts his head just slightly so that he's looking at me through his lashes. It's sexy and alluring and makes me feel uncomfortable about the way my heart stirs at the sight. I look back at Wyatt's painting again in an effort to squash that feeling, but it doesn't leave. It stays there, marinating in my core between the slice of yearning and the dash of guilt that sit there.

"Maybe another time," he says, his gaze still on mine.

"Maybe."

"The place is really beautiful, Elle. You've done a good job."

"Thanks. It was mostly Wyatt's doing, though," I respond. Oliver's smile drops. I watch his Adam's apple bob as he swallows his pride and nods.

"You both did a great job," he says. "Did Vic give you my number like I asked him to?"

"I haven't really seen much of him," I say, which is a lie. I saw my brother this morning and last night, and he didn't mention Oliver's number either time.

"I thought maybe he gave it to you, and you just hadn't used it."

"Why would I use it?" I ask, looking back when I hear the girls erupt in laughter from inside the studio.

"It would be nice if you did for a change," he says, shrugging.

My mouth drops. "It would be nice if I did?" I repeat.

We stare at each other in silence, me waiting for him to correct himself, him waiting for me to challenge him about what he said. Neither of us bites. We both know this is too much to cover in just a couple of minutes, and personally, I'd rather not cover it at all. I remember the bachelorette party I have waiting for me in the other room, and clear my throat.

"Okay, well, I'm sure I'll see you around. Have fun on your date tonight." I give him a small awkward wave as I pivot to walk in the other direction.

"Would you be interested in coming by the pediatrics unit in the hospital once or twice a week?" He smiles when I turn back around and raise an eyebrow, urging him to continue.

"I was thinking maybe you could paint with the kids or something. I know you like that sort of stuff," he suggests. Visiting the hospital would mean being somehow connected to Oliver again. As if he senses the doubt in my thoughts, he soldiers on, "I'm busy finishing up my residency, so I wouldn't be able to help much, but I have a friend that can help you iron out details."

"Sure. Give me a call and let me know what day is good for me to drop by." I turn one last time as a grin splits my face, and walk into the room full of overly excited, buzzed girls. Then it hits me: Oliver put this smile on my face. Memories of all the previous times he put a smile on my face bombard me all at once, and suddenly, as I look around the room at the happy women before me who are celebrating life and love, I feel like crying. But I don't. Oliver doesn't have the right to make me cry. Not anymore.

Chapter 4

ON SUNDAY MORNING, I wake up to the sounds of metal clanging and groggily get out of bed to find the source of commotion.

"What are you doing?" I ask over a yawn.

"Shit! You scared me. I still haven't gotten used to having you around," Vic says as he bends to pick up a pan off of the floor.

"At least you're wearing clothes," I say, glancing at his white and blue basketball shorts. "What are you doing?" I repeat.

He sighs. "Okay, this is awkward." He lowers his voice to a whisper. "There's someone in my room, and I'm trying to make breakfast."

I cover my mouth to keep from laughing at the thought of Vic making any kind of food worth eating, and peek my head around the wall, looking toward his room.

"And I'm not sure if she'll be dressed," he adds.

My eyes widen. "Maybe you should tell her I'm here."

"Yeah, I'm thinking I'll have to . . . you're kind of cock blocking what I had planned," he says, looking around the kitchen.

I cover my ears. "Don't speak. I'm going to shower and go have breakfast with Mia."

Vic's eyes light up in laughter. "You don't have to."

"Shh! Don't speak."

I go upstairs and pick out my clothes before going into the bathroom and getting ready as fast as humanly possible. It hadn't really occurred to me what sharing a place with my brother would be like. I switch on my phone as I slip out of the house, thinking about the desperate email I'm going to write my real estate agent, and I see two new text messages from an unknown number.

This is my number- Oliver

I program it into my phone before I read the next one.

Jen wants to know if Tuesday is a good day for you to swing by the hospital. She was able to get you an empty room that you can use for art.

After looking at my calendar for the week, I'm able to move some things around—not that I have much going on these days.

I respond.

Tuesday is great. Tell her to give you a time and where I should go when I get there.

I don't expect a response from him because it's only nine o'clock, and most childless humans our age are asleep at this time, but my phone buzzes as I'm pulling into the coffee shop I frequent.

I'll ask her. Will I see you later?

I try to remember if I'm missing something, but can't think of anything.

See me?

At Vic's.

Didn't know you were coming over.

Football Sunday.

I frown over this, realizing how long it's been since I joined them on football Sunday.

Vic keeps forgetting I'm living with him temporarily.

Uh-oh . . .

Let's just say I got dressed and out of the house a lot earlier than I hoped to on a Sunday.

LOL. Sorry. Where are you now?

About to have breakfast.

Want to come over? You can sleep here.

I freeze and stare at the screen, expecting the words to switch up on me and say something else.

Not with me, by the way.

I start typing out a message, but delete it when his next one comes through.

Okay, this is awkward. If you don't respond, I'm going to call you.

The phone vibrates in my hand a moment later, and I pick up, clearing my throat.

"I didn't mean for it to come out like that," he says. His voice. God I love his voice. It's deep and rich, and always sounds like he just woke up.

"It's fine. I'm fine, though. Thank you."

"I don't think we've ever spoken on the phone," he says.

"No, I don't think we have," I respond, not adding the gazillion other things that seep into my thoughts—*because you're an asshole, because you left, because I'm your best friend's little sister, because you couldn't have a relationship if your life depended on it . . .*

"Well, now we have. Okay, I just wanted to make sure you didn't take that the wrong way. I mean, unless you want to, and that would be totally fine by me too." I groan at the smile in his voice.

"Oliver . . ."

His chuckle jumps through the speaker and ricochets through my body. I hate what he does to me. "I'm just playing, Elle. Anyway, are you making bean dip tonight?"

"Do you want me to make bean dip tonight?"

"Is the Pope Catholic?"

"If you ask nicely, I'll make you some bean dip, Oliver. If you're going to be a sarcastic asshole, I'm hanging up on you."

He exhales. "Estelle Reuben, my favorite person in the entire world, would you please make me some bean dip? With extra guacamole."

I smile at his words, even though I shouldn't. *I shouldn't.* He's dangerous, I remind myself. This is what he does to you. Every. Single. Time.

"Okay."

I hear a door slam wherever he is, followed by rustling and then more rustling, finishing up with a heavy sigh. "There's an empty spot on my bed for sleeping, in case you're tired."

"Thanks for the offer, but I'll see you later."

I hang up at the sound of his laughter and put my phone away, as I turn my attention to the now-cold egg sandwich that I'd ordered for myself. Once I'm finished eating, I take the short walk to my studio and lock the door behind me. Glancing around at the paintings on the white walls, I wonder if I should rearrange them. A lot of them are Wyatt's, but most of them are local artists' work that I've fallen in love with through the years. Some of mine are also there, but I don't display those in the front part of the gallery. The front of the gallery is reserved for items I have for sale, and the only creations of mine I sell are my kaleidoscope hearts.

I went to school to become an art teacher, but was unsure about it. When I told Wyatt I wanted to be an art teacher but couldn't see myself in such a demanding field, he presented me with the idea for Paint it Back. He said this way my creativity would stay alive, and if I wanted, I could start a program for kids. Through the studio, we were able to start a summer program where older kids come over after their day camp and work on paintings. It started as a way to get them off the streets and focusing their energy on something else, but once school started, they kept setting up appointments to come by in small groups.

I'm setting white sheets over the easels for my Monday afternoon class, when my phone rings.

"Elle," my brother says brightly, as if he hadn't practically kicked me out a couple of hours ago. "I forgot to tell you, some people are coming over later."

"Oh, yeah?"

"Yeah, around twelve. You think you can make some of your bean dip?"

It takes everything in me not to growl at his request. "Sure. How many people?"

"Hmmm . . . me, Bean, Jensen, and Bobby . . . that's it."

"So only four people are eating?" I ask.

"Yeah, four."

I blink rapidly, wondering if he's going to include me in there at all.

"Well, five, if you want to stick around," he says, clearing his throat as he corrects himself.

"Who's Bobby? That guy you work with?"

"Yeah, he's the new guy. You'll like him, he's cool."

"Cool like you, I'm sure," I mutter. My brother and his friends are undercover comic book nerds in the guise of jocks. He's had the same group of friends since he was in grade school, and it's not often he brings another one into the close-knit group they have. I imagine that Bobby must fit the same description as the rest of them.

"You can tell Mia if you want," he adds, as a selling point.

"Mia and Jensen in the same room? No, thank you."

Vic laughs. "She's not over it?"

"Over him leaving her to be with his ex-girlfriend? I doubt it." I raise a brow as I take new brushes out of their package and put them in the silver canisters that sit beside each easel.

"He's a dick," Vic says. "Then again, she's not very bright. I would never have let you date one of my friends."

I put down the supplies in my hand and brace myself on the edge of the counter. "And why is that, exactly?"

He laughs a deep, rich laugh that would have made me smile under other circumstances. "Come on, Elle. You know them."

His words make me cringe. I do know them. I know them well.

"Anyway, I'll see you later. They get here at twelve for the pre-show so . . ."

"Yeah, I got it, Vic. Your dip will be ready before kick-off. Did that girl leave already?"

"Yeah, she left. I invited her over for dinner on Wednesday. Oliver and Jensen are also coming over with some . . . female friends, so you'll meet her then."

I make a mental note to disappear on Wednesday night, and tell Vic I'll see him later. Walking back to the gallery section, I notice one of my kaleidoscope hearts is crooked in its holding place, so I tilt it back upright. A magazine that covered an event we held here once had described my hearts as "heartbreaking, poignant, beautiful pieces." This specific one is on display, but not for sale. It was one of the first ones I made, and Wyatt refused to get rid of it. I used a lot of purples for this particular piece, and every time the sun peeks in here, speckled beams of purple light bounce off the walls.

"If anybody comes in here trying to buy it, you tell them I'll match their price and double it," he'd said to me with a grin.

Tears begin to well in my eyes as I stand there, looking at the way the light reflects off of it, and thinking of Wyatt. I wipe my eyes, take a breath, and walk out, locking the door behind me. I make it back to Vic's and hear him in the shower. I pop open a bottle of wine while I work on the dip, pouring the mashed beans at the bottom, the avocado in the middle, and sour cream on top. Once I'm done making a large bowl of that, I take out the Crock-pot I bought my brother three Christmases ago that he clearly hasn't used, and begin to set up some meatballs. Taking one last sip of wine, I walk to my room and throw myself into the bed.

Chapter 5

I DON'T KNOW how long I sleep, but boisterous shouts coming from the living room downstairs wake me from my nap. I blink rapidly, trying to clear my eyes, as I drag myself out of bed and walk to the bathroom. My reflection is a mess, so I brush my elbow-length hair, and put drops in my eyes until the pink clears and they're back to bright hazel. After applying some make-up, I readjust my black *Elvis is King* shirt so that the loose part at the top falls off my left shoulder, and brush off my fashionably torn jeans before heading down to the living room. It isn't until I'm already there that I realize I'm still wearing my Darth Vader slippers. It's too late to turn around though, since I've already been spotted.

"Hey, Elle," Jensen calls out, making all heads turn my way.

"Hey, Jensen. Did you move back?"

"Nope, but I'll be around a lot for the next couple of months," he says.

"Cool. Hey guys," I say, looking around the room and waving at Oliver, Vic and some blonde guy I've never met.

"Hey," they all say unanimously.

"Elle, this is Bobby. Bobby, this is my sister, Estelle," Vic says, not taking his eyes off the television.

Bobby stands and offers me his hand, which I take. He's actually pretty good looking in a preppy, boy-next-door kind of way, which makes me smile because I was wrong—he's not like all of my brother's friends. He's not tall and athletic like Vic and Oliver. He doesn't have the bad boy thing going that Jensen has, but he flashes a huge Colgate smile as he shakes my hand, and I am treated to the charming vibe that they all share. It's one that makes women do a double take, regardless of what a man looks like.

"When you said little sister, I was picturing a teenager with braces," Bobby says as his eyes travel down my body.

I drop my hand from his. "I'm sure that's what he sees when he describes me."

"That's definitely not how I would describe you."

At the hint of flirting in his tone, I look over his shoulder to look at Vic's reaction, but instead my eyes land on Oliver's. It kills me that I can't tell what he's thinking. He doesn't look upset or jealous, or even curious; he's just staring.

"I'm not sure I want to know how anybody would describe me," I respond.

Before he can say anything else, I step away and walk to the kitchen to get the stuff I made and place it on the table, somehow managing to dodge the beer bottles that cover it.

"She's beautiful, and she cooks?" Bobby says, reaching for a chip. "I think I might keep her."

"Yeah, right," Jensen says, slightly bothered. My brother's friends have this thing. They think they're all supposed to protect me from outsiders, as if the danger lies beyond their lair. I think my engagement with Wyatt threw them over the edge since none of them saw it coming.

"You're not going to give Bobby the whole spiel about staying away from your sister?"

My eyes find Oliver's again, and I smile when he pats the space beside him. My body stirs, wanting to move toward him, but my brain zaps sense into me. I take a seat beside Victor instead.

"Drop it," Vic says in response to Jensen's comment.

"When we were young, we all got this huge lecture about it," Jensen explains. I lean forward to get a better look at him while he tells the story, since I've never heard this before. "When we were little, we didn't care because Elle was totally like our own baby sister . . . but then she grew up, and any time any of us would make a comment about it, Vic was all *don't look at her, don't touch her. If I find out you did, I'll break your arms, and you'll never be able to come over to my house again.*"

"For the record, I would have gladly gotten my arms broken," Bobby volunteers with a smile, as his blue eyes flick to mine.

"It wasn't the arm breaking that was the issue; it was the ban from the house! He had the best parents! We practically lived in that house." Jensen says, laughing and taking a swig from his beer, which he raises toward me. "And I had a good throwing arm, so I couldn't risk it for a girl. Sorry, Elle."

"Trust me, I'm not sorry." I sit back and stretch my legs while they chuckle.

"Elle knows to stay away from you idiots. None of you are good for her," Vic says, taking a handful of chips and going for the dip.

My eyes find Oliver in time to see him wince slightly at Vic's words. Our gazes stick, and a million things run through my mind—*was that the cause of what happened? Did Vic's approval mean more than mine?* They're questions I know the answers to. They're thoughts that shadowed me for years, despite my attempts to sidestep them.

"Serious question," Jensen says, jolting my attention back to him. "Growing up, who would you say was most your type?"

I try not to laugh at the question and the face my brother makes. Victor has always been a guy's guy—the one everyone wants to take to a game and hang out with at a bar. Junior, Jensen and Oliver are all pretty similar in that sense. Out of the four, Junior is the only one married with a family, while the other three are forever bachelors. Or so it seems. Jensen is the epitome of what you don't take home to your parents. He's good looking and has the whole tall, dark, and handsome thing going, but he also has that dangerous edge to him with his motorcycle, tattoos and bad boy persona.

I look at Oliver, who has always had this easy way about him, from the lazy smile to the disheveled, sandy brown hair that makes you want to run your fingers through it. He has a way of looking at you that makes you feel like you're the only female in the room. And those dimples . . . God, those dimples. All my friends wanted to date the unattainable Oliver. He has that magnetism that powerful men have. Even when we were young, charisma oozed out of him in bucketfuls.

"Yeah, Elle," Oliver says, giving me a slow, sexy grin as his eyes bounce from my mouth to my eyes. "Who was most your type?"

I shoot him a look before tearing my eyes away from his and toward Jensen, who's watching me with amusement.

"Honestly? Jensen," I say, shrugging.

"Boom!" Jensen yells. "I always fucking knew it! So you would have hooked up with me?"

"I didn't say that. I only said you were most my type," I say, laughing. I don't mention that he was pretty much every teenage girl's type at the time.

"And this is exactly why I had to threaten them," Vic says, looking at Bobby, who's shaking his head in amusement.

My eyes fix on the Cowboys-Forty-Niners game on TV, and I jump slightly when I feel a tap on my foot.

"Really?" Oliver mouths, placing both hands over his heart as if he's wounded. I smile and shake my head. "I like your shoes," he says, flashing that half-grin of his.

"I know you do," I respond with a wink, then mentally kick myself for winking at him. We're still looking at each other when Bobby speaks up, and this time Oliver's eyes narrow at the question.

"So has the ban been lifted? Am I free to ask her out on a date?"

"I don't date," I respond, dropping my eyes from Oliver's.

"Impossible. A girl like you definitely dates," Bobby says.

"A girl like me." I let out a scoffed chuckle. I'm about to leave it at that, but then think better of it and soldier on. "Even if I was interested in dating, I wouldn't date one of my brother's friends. All of you are trouble with a capital T. Didn't you hear the speech?"

"Trouble with a capital T?" Jensen asks.

"Do we really want to go there right now?" I say, glaring at him until he catches my drift, and his laughter fades away.

"No, you're right. You're right. Vic was right." Jensen concedes.

"Let's drop the *dating my sister conversation* and watch the game," Vic says, giving each of the guys a long, pointed look. After a couple of seconds of being elbowed by him every time he moves to get food, I get up and sit beside Oliver on the loveseat.

"Ah . . . you did miss me, after all," he says, as soon as I get comfortable.

"Well, for starters, I couldn't think with your eyes burning holes into the side of my face, and you were my second choice for most my type, so . . ." I shrug and flash him a smile. We look at each other for a long moment before his eyes drop to my mouth and finally away from me to the television. Another touchdown is scored, another kick is made, and a long string of curse words is thrown out by each of them. Just as I'm contemplating making an exit, Oliver shifts beside me.

"I seem to recall a different order of hierarchy," he whispers huskily in my ear, making me shiver.

"Of course you do," I whisper back, unwilling to acknowledge the way my heart is playing Double Dutch in my chest.

"It's true." He moves closer so that his arm is pressed up against mine.

"You have your memories; I have mine."

Oliver's expression changes from playful to serious. "Yeah, I guess so." He exhales. "So, you ready for Tuesday?"

"I am. I'm excited to see the space and get the ball rolling. Thank you for asking me," I say, hoping he understands how much something like this means to me.

"I couldn't think of a better person for the job." He bumps my foot again and my heart vibrates at the touch.

"Stop playing footsies with me," I whisper.

"Or what?" he whispers back, cocking his head in a way that makes his hair fall over his left eye and bounce over his lashes every time he blinks.

"Or Darth Vader will be forced to draw his light saber."

His chuckle vibrates the couch and into me. "Trust me; he doesn't want to compete with mine."

When the double connotation hits me, my mouth drops open, and he laughs.

"Some things never change," I say.

His eyes darken. "Sometimes they get better."

I look away and sit there for a couple more minutes before I go back to my room, using the excuse that I need to see Mia before I go to Wyatt's parents' for dinner. After I say my goodbyes, I keep thinking about Oliver's words. I swear, the man haunts me more than my dead fiancé. It's unnerving.

Chapter 6

I USED TO be that girl who was optimistic about everything, but then life slapped me in the face and forced me to become a realist. I'm not cynical or anything, but I've been through enough not to see the world through rose-colored lenses. The day started off normal enough—my mom called to try to set me up with this guy, Derek. She's been trying to set me up with him since I was, like, six. This time, I said yes. The shrieks of happiness that permeated through the phone lines were intense, to say the least. It was as though she was channeling her inner hyena. I recall it all went downhill from there.

The gallery was spotless when I got here, just the way I like it. Now, it looks like ten groups of toddlers tore through it. It all started when Finlay, a thirteen-year-old boy, asked Veronica out on a date. Finlay's best friend, Brett, had apparently wanted to ask her out, so when he overheard the conversation and she said yes, he lost it. LOST. IT. In my studio! He threw his paintbrush at Finlay, splashes of the blue he was using to paint an ocean went everywhere, and that started a paint fight, which resulted in me calling their parents to pick them up.

So here I am, an hour after I wanted to be here, wiping paint off every surface in the room. My one salvation is that the room is an enclosed space separate from the art outside, because if they'd gotten any of this mess on one of the local artists' work, or worse—Wyatt's—I would have died. My ass hits the floor when I get tired of bending over, and I look around once more. The canvases they are painting on are still on their designated easels, and I take a moment to look at the one Fin was working on. It's a gloomy day in his world. The gray sky makes the water below it hit the rocks angrily. The dark blue brush strokes on the ocean almost make me feel like I can hear the waves, and I decide I want to see the real thing. My studio isn't far from the beach, and I don't enjoy it as often as I could. I gather everything I need for the hospital meeting into one box and set it aside, next to the door. As I'm locking up, I see the splashes of paint on my arm from the paint fight. Damn kids.

The temperature usually drops around sundown and, like clockwork, when the sun begins to set, I feel a cool gust of wind hit me. I pull my light jacket closed, as I stroll toward the water.

I stop at the light a block away and listen for the waves, feeling lighter already. Aside from the other galleries in the area, the ocean was a huge selling point for us when we got the place. If I close my eyes and think hard enough, I can picture Wyatt running toward the beach with his board under one arm, his wet suit practically falling off his body. The memory makes me smile, even though it makes my heart squeeze in my chest. When I first came back to the studio, that was my first thought. Not the gallery, not the painting he was working on that I have put away in the back room, not our daily breakfast together, or the way he would smile when I walked in a room—but remembering the way he ran toward that water.

Surfing was quite possibly the only thing he had in common with my brother. When I first got together with Wyatt, my mom joked that I purposely brought home the artiest man I could find. Forget the fact that he was highly successful, older, and made the effort to wear a suit to their house the first time they met. My mom saw him beneath it all. Not in a bad way. She grew to accept Wyatt, as did my dad. Vic never really did, but didn't say otherwise. I think they all saw him as an extension of me. I was already kind of an outsider in their world anyway. I hated going to those pretentious parties and galas my parents attend annually. My dad's an orthodontist, and my mom's an English professor, so everybody assumed their kids would follow in their footsteps. Well, Vic became an attorney, and I became a painter. They're supportive of me, though. They love my work and cheer me on, so even though I know I'm the black sheep in some ways, I'm never made to feel like one.

When I reach the sand, I take a really deep breath and close my eyes, relishing the moment. *Every second counts. Live in this moment. This is life. This is what matters.* It's a simple thought, but it's so easy to forget. The ocean is there as a constant reminder though. The big waves crashing against the rocks are as cleansing as they are dangerous. I take a seat in the sand and watch the surfers, young and old, and let the sounds wash over me. Instead of drowning out my pent-up sorrow, it cuts me in half. The anniversary of Wyatt's death was a couple of days ago. It came and went without much remembrance, other than from me and his parents, via the phone call we had to check up on each other.

A little over a year ago, I was on this very beach for a completely different reason. I saw ambulances drive through the sand and followed them because curiosity got the best of me. God. What would I have done if I hadn't followed them? How would I have found out? I wore a frown as I walked closer to the water, recalling the small crowd of people—mostly surfers—watching the paramedics work on someone. It was like I was having an out-of-body experience as I reached them. It felt like something was pulling me closer to the chaos, but I instinctively knew I wouldn't want to see what was going on once I reached it, so I walked slowly. I caught a glimpse of the man on the ground and thought, "Holy shit, that looks like . . . but . . ." and glanced down at my phone in a panic. I looked in every direction—toward the gallery, the beach, and the little colorful wooden shack that sold drinks—all the while my heart pounded in my chest.

My feet drove me forward, closer to the paramedics . . . closer to the body. And then I saw him. Really saw him. His long, blonde hair fanned over the sand, his brown eyes were closed, and his wet suit was pulled down to reveal a thin torso. My vision began to blur, walls that weren't there, beginning to close in around me. I felt like I was fading. Like I was there, but not really, because I wasn't supposed to be looking at what I thought I was seeing. My knees began to buckle when I finally reached him and saw just how white his lips were and how pale his face was.

"Wyatt?" I heard myself say, but the shriek belonged to someone else . . . someone in a panic . . . someone who felt like she was losing the love of her life, and that person couldn't have been me. "What happened? He's my fiancé. What happened? Wyatt!" I screamed over and over as panic rushed through me.

One of the paramedics held my arms, as I watched them work on him. CPR . . . pumping his stomach over and over . . . Finally, they brought out that machine I'd seen a million times in movies—the one that "clears" and zaps people when they're dead and need to be revived. When I saw that machine, I fell to my knees with a scream. I clutched the warm sand below me as the paramedic tried to calm me down.

"Why isn't he waking up?" I sobbed. "Why aren't you letting me go to him?"

"I need you to stay calm—"

My pleas died out with a howl and the sound of the tide crashing behind us.

"He was just surfing," somebody behind us said.

"He was taking too long to come up after his last wipe out," another added.

"I called nine-one-one when I noticed he wasn't coming up," a third one said. "I hope he pulls through!"

The paramedic helped me get up as they put Wyatt on a stretcher, and I let her walk me into the back of the ambulance. I sat there beside Wyatt's feet, staring at his face.

"Will he be okay?" I asked, half sobbed, half shrieked.

Nobody answered. They just kept on tapping him, breathing into his mouth, and pumping his stomach. They pronounced him dead on arrival when we got to the hospital, before they even wheeled him in. I knew he was gone before he even made it onto the ambulance, but it hurt so much more to hear them verbalize it. For days, I felt lost. He was only thirty-five and an excellent swimmer. The only thing I could think about was that those brown eyes would never look at me again. Those hands would never paint again. Those lips would never smile again. And coming back to this beach now, always brings back the memories.

The autopsy said he'd had a heart attack while he was in the water and that there wasn't enough water in his lungs for him to have drowned. The only thing I kept thinking was—he was only thirty-five.

I no longer cry when I come here. It's not filled with bad memories anymore because I know Wyatt loved this place as much as he loved the gallery. Today, though . . . today I cry. Today I let myself remember the look on his smiling face when we had breakfast in the morning. I close my eyes and take a breath, hoping to smell dry paint and gloss on him and hug myself tight at the memory of being in his arms at night. I let those thoughts break me open and hope that, even from a distance, the waves can wash away my pain. Tomorrow I'll be okay, but today I let myself bleed, and that's okay too.

Chapter 7

THE THING ABOUT life is that you never know when it will show you something that touches you so deeply that you can't help but be grateful for everything . . . even the bad. That's how I feel when wheelchairs holding kids pass by me as I walk down the halls of the hospital with the box of supplies in my hand. I round the corner on my way to Jen's office and stop dead in my tracks when I see Oliver leaving a room, still talking to whomever is inside. Apparently, his residency keeps him in the hospital for endless hours, because every time Vic mentions his name, he's here. I'm still standing there when he closes the door and walks toward me. Those green scrubs and that doctor's coat really do nothing to diminish his good looks. If anything, it makes him look even better, but it's that confident stride of his and the lopsided smile on his face that makes my heart thunder.

"You're early," he says, stopping in front of me.

I frown. "No, I'm not. I'm on time."

Oliver grins. "On time is early for you. You're always fashionably late."

"I *used* to always be fashionably late. Now I'm on time."

"I'm impressed," he says, his green eyes playful, as they scan my face. My hands full with the box I'm carrying, I'm forced to blow out a breath to get a strand of hair out of my face. Oliver chuckles, grabbing the hair and tucking it behind my ear. It's a simple motion, but somehow he makes it feel intimate. His eyes are on mine, his hand still behind my ear, when he steps closer. I've never been happier to be holding a box in my life, because the way he's looking at me makes my heart trip, and I'm not sure what I would do with my hands if they were free.

"What?" I ask, my voice a whisper.

"You're so grown up," he says, dropping his voice to match my whisper. It ignites little butterflies in my stomach to take flight.

"You make it sound like you're so much older than me."

Growing up, Oliver loved reminding me that he was older. Sometimes he would say it in a lighthearted tone—other times it sounded like a curse—though the curse was only when it was paired with, *you're Vic's baby sister.* And then one time he said . . .

He smiles softly. "I'm old enough to know better."

My mouth pops open, and I take a step back so he's forced to drop his hand. *That.* He said that.

Oliver clears his throat, as he seems to recall the same memory.

"I have to go. I don't want to be irresponsibly late," I say, rushing off before he can stop me.

What is he doing?

What am *I* doing?

I stop in front of a sign that reads: Jennifer Darcia, Assistant Coordinator, and I knock on the door. She calls for me to enter and I do, bumping the door with my hip to close it. I place the box down on one of the empty chairs in front of her desk and smile.

"Hi. I'm Estelle," I say, letting out a heavy sigh.

"Take a seat. I'm Jen," she replies.

We shake hands, and I sit down in the chair beside the one that holds the box. She looks like everything I picture as being Oliver's taste—blonde hair, bright blue eyes, nice smile, and big boobs. The only thing that throws me off is that she's older. I'm pretty sure she has ten years on me, which would give his little statement a whole new meaning. Maybe that's his deal—he's into older women, and I'm too young for him.

"Thank you so much for doing this for us," she starts. "I'm always looking for new things to keep the kids entertained, but lately the clown shows and movies aren't cutting it. I just want them to do something different, or at least *with* someone different, you know? If they have to be here, they might as well have a chance to interact with people other than the ones giving them their medicines." Her eyebrows draw together as she speaks, and I can tell she's passionate about the kids. I decide I like Jen.

"I'll do my best to keep them happy," I say with a reassuring smile.

"Thank you." She pauses. "Oliver says you two go way back."

I startle at the sudden change of subject. "Yeah, he's my brother's best friend."

"I believe the term he used to describe you was his 'favorite person, ever,'" she says. She's smiling, and I get the impression she wants me to tell her something private about Oliver, but the thing is, her statement floors me to the point of speech loss.

"He said that?"

Jen nods. "He did."

"That's . . . interesting." *Considering everything,* I want to add, but don't.

"Let me show you your new work space. You said you are available three times a week, correct?" she says, standing up.

"I'm available upon request, kind of like a clown minus the face paint—unless you need me to face paint—but I can't promise you the stuff I work with will come off easily."

She laughs and puts her hands up. "No, thank you. I don't want to be held responsible for that disaster."

Jen takes me to the next wing and shows me where to go and who to speak to, before heading back to her office. As I walk the hallways, I take in the outdated murals that adorn the walls. The only contrast to the blue that covers the walls are the fish that swim in all different directions. Looking at it makes me feel like I'm suffocating. Who would paint a fish tank on the walls of a children's hospital? For a place that's supposed to be comforting to the children and parents that have to see this every day, this is unacceptable. I'm shaking my head in disgust when a laugh snaps me out of the moment.

"I take it you don't approve?" Oliver says, appearing beside me.

"Don't you have a job to do?" I ask, dishing out my annoyance at what happened earlier and at the hideous hallway in front of us. I move to brush past him, and I bump his arm slightly.

"I'm sorry," he says, making me stop dead in my tracks. I don't turn around. "I'm sorry about earlier," he continues. "It's just . . . seeing you and then you . . . I just . . . shit." He laughs.

I turn and face him. "It's okay. Apologies have never been your strong suit, after all."

He cringes, and this time I walk away for good.

Chapter 8

EVERYBODY HAS A different definition of *moving on*. For me, selling the house I shared with Wyatt is a way for me to move on with my life. For my mom, moving on means dating. So here I am, sitting across from Derek, who's actually a really nice guy. He's been attentive, holding the door open for me, waiting for me to take a seat before he does, and asking me about my day while listening intently. He's not bad looking either. He's in shape and has a good sense of style, but for some reason, I'm not really here with him. I keep zoning out as he talks about his job as an architect.

"I'm not boring you, am I?" he asks in a polite tone.

"No, not at all. Sorry! It's just," I sigh, "this is a little weird for me."

"I understand. My mom was telling me about, you know," he says, waving his hand in my direction.

"Yeah. I'm okay talking about it. It's just weird to be out with another guy." I offer him a small smile.

"It's your first date since you lost him," he says with an understanding smile.

"Yeah."

"Are you still . . . how do I say this . . . it sounds weird to say *hung up on him* because it's not like it's your ex-boyfriend and he's moved on . . . " he says, letting his words hang.

"No, I'm okay. I mean, I'm okay with everything, really. It's just I'm sitting here thinking about what will happen next—will you try to hold my hand or kiss me good night, or I don't know," I shrug and laugh as I look away from him. "I think I just made this weirder."

Derek laughs. "What if we just take this one step at a time? No holding hands if you don't want that, and no kiss if you don't want that. I mean, we haven't even gotten our entrees yet."

"You're right," I say, smiling and feeling a little bit less uncomfortable. It is just dinner. I have the bad habit of jumping ahead of myself in every aspect of my life. Sometimes I need to learn to rein in some of my anxiety and just breathe. I start to tell Derek about the hospital and the kids I worked with the other day. I tell him how much it opened my eyes to the things I have and take for granted. Dinner goes by quickly after that, and when we reach my brother's house, the sun has gone down.

"Looks like you have company tonight," Derek comments, as his headlights flash over the cars outside.

"Yeah, Victor loves having people over. It's a shame he can't remember to turn the porch light on," I say, making him chuckle.

"I'll walk you up and make sure you don't trip."

We reach the door and stand there awkwardly, not knowing what the right thing to do is.

"So . . . kiss or no kiss?" he asks. I can't see his face, but the smile in his voice makes me feel comfortable.

I take a moment to think about it. I haven't had a pair of lips on me since Wyatt, but I can't say I'm not curious to know what it would be like to kiss someone else. Kissing Wyatt always felt easy. It felt comfortable, familiar. Taking a deep breath, I lean forward. Derek's hands hold the upper part of my arms, and his lips press to mine. A moment later, the light turns on and the front door opens. My eyes pop open, and Derek and I jerk apart from one another like we've been caught doing a lot more than just kissing. It feels like ninth grade all over again. Our heads snap to Oliver, who's holding the door open, arms crossed over his black t-shirt. His green eyes bounce from me to Derek and back again.

"Sorry. I didn't know you were out here," he says, though he doesn't look sorry at all.

"A gentleman walks his date to the door," Derek says, smiling at me.

I return his smile. "Thanks for the date."

"It was my pleasure. I'll give you a call tomorrow. Maybe we can do it again soon?"

I glance at Oliver who's brazenly watching our conversation, and I glare at him before looking back at Derek. "Sure. Call me."

I wait until he's halfway to his car before I face Oliver again, narrowing my eyes. "Well? Weren't you leaving?"

"No, I just heard a noise outside and came to check it out."

His eyes are glinting with mischief, and it fuels my anger. I move to brush past him, but he grabs my arm and leans into my ear, his whispered growl making me burn from the inside out.

"When do I get to take you on a date?" he asks.

My heart begins to beat frantically, and I tear my arm away. "Never."

I hear him chuckling behind me as I run up the stairs like a scared little girl, and I realize I *am* scared. I'm fucking terrified of having Oliver in my life because the last time I let him in, I barely made it out with my heart intact. I wonder if he even knows it.

Chapter 9

BEING ON THE phone with my realtor all morning made me realize something: You can try to steer your life in a certain direction all you want, but ultimately, the wind is in charge of your sail. It's a sucky realization. I spend the rest of my morning painting the ocean from the balcony in my room, and then gather my stuff and head to the hospital. When I get there, I walk to Jen's office and knock once, even though her door is slightly parted.

"Come in!" she calls, so I peek my head in. Unlike most of the people in the hospital, Jen wears slacks and a blouse to work—at least that's what she's worn every time I've seen her. She looks up and smiles at me as she continues to wipe a stain on her white blouse. "Sorry. Damn coffee."

"That's what happens when you wear a white shirt," I say, as she laughs.

"Every single time. You would think I'd learn."

I look down at my own white shirt and shrug. "I'm a painter, so I can get away with it. Anyway, I came by to ask you a question."

"Of course. Take a seat." She signals to the chairs in front of her, and I plop down in the nearest one.

"I know this is probably impossible to do, but I have to ask—is there any way I can repaint the halls in the pediatrics wing?"

Jen's brown eyebrows pull into a thoughtful frown.

"I totally understand if it's not a possibility, but I had to ask."

"No, no, we actually have to move some patients to another wing temporarily to get some new equipment in, so I guess if you could take advantage of those days, it would be doable. I need to run it by my boss first, though."

I nearly squeal in delight. "The rooms will be vacant?"

Jen searches my face and smiles. "What do you have in mind?"

"Well," I start, wringing my hands together. I'm starting to feel like I'm taking advantage of this opportunity, even though I would be the one paying for all of it and spending my time here. "I would fund this one hundred percent. I don't want you to think I want to be compensated, but if I can get some of my friends in here, I think we could do something really nice."

She's quiet for a beat, pulling her sandy blonde hair into a ponytail. "So you would pay for the paint and compensate whoever helps you?"

"Yes, of course," I respond quickly.

Jen is quiet again, searching my face for a little longer than I'm comfortable with, but I stare back, holding my hands on my lap as I wait for her answer.

"You really want to do this," she says finally. "Why?"

A rushed breath tumbles out of my lips and my shoulders sag a little. "Do I need a reason?"

"I suppose not," she says with a shrug. "But not many people would do something like this pro bono."

"I'm not many people," I respond with a smile. "I can speak to your boss myself if you'd like."

She shakes her head. "I'll call him right now. I doubt he'll have a problem with this. He's been saying for years that wing needs a facelift. I'll text you as soon as I have an answer."

"Thank you so much. I look forward to hearing from you." I stand and head to the door.

"Estelle," she calls out, her words bringing me back into her office. I turn, and she gives me a small smile. "The world needs more people like you."

Her words make me smile proudly. My life may be chaotic and sticky, but most days I go to bed feeling comforted by the thought that maybe I made a difference in one person's life. It's nice to have somebody else recognize it. I thank her and head to the pediatrics wing before I make a fool of myself and start crying or something. When I get there, the first person I spot is Oliver. He's got his back turned to me, leaning his hip on the counter of the nurses' station.

I can't hear what he's saying, but judging from the giggles of the two nurses he's talking to, you would think it's a Jim Carey-worthy joke. I'm sure it's not. Oliver isn't a funny joke teller—though he tries—but the female species never seems to mind. Myself included, once upon a time. I cover the urge to roll my eyes with a huge smile and move along, passing the station with a small wave and a smile as I say good afternoon. I don't stay long enough to look at Oliver's face, but I catch his movement as he straightens and pushes himself away from the counter.

I scan the room I was assigned to, my eyes bouncing from easel to easel and to the containers beside them. Taking a large stack of white paper, I clip one to each board on the easels and look up when I hear the door open. Gemma, a plump, red-haired nurse, walks in pushing a wheelchair. I met the kids the other day when I was here, so I recognize the young boy as Johnny, a thirteen-year-old with cerebral palsy. I greet him and then Danny, Mae, and Mike—all in their early teens—all cancer patients.

"You guys ready?" I ask with a smile.

They each bob their heads, but none say anything. Of course, all but Johnny are on their phones. I sigh, knowing what's to come. This is something I deal with every time a new set of teenagers comes in for the after school program at the studio. Through this, I've come to realize that teenagers are a lot like new shoes—uncomfortable and a bitch to break in—but once you do, you don't regret a single blister they caused.

"Do you want to do the boring, sappy introductions or do you just want to start painting the shit out of these canvases?" I ask, gaining the attention of all of them at once. Their eyes widen as if they can't believe I just said that.

Mike tucks his phone into his pocket and finally, for the first time, looks at me. He's not shy about it either, he lets his gray eyes wander my body as if I'm some girl he's about to hit on.

"Do I get to paint you?" he asks. I shake my head and laugh. He's definitely ballsy. Mae does not seem impressed by his comment and rolls her eyes, putting her phone in her back pocket and crossing her hands over her chest.

"Okay," I start. "First of all, we're not painting people. Secondly, I can see you're going to be trouble," I say, pointing at Mike with a raised brow. "And I'm going to let it slide because I kind of like trouble . . . as long as you do not start hitting on me." My back is turned toward the door, so I don't know what other kids come in once I start talking, but I soldier on with my little speech even though I know I'll probably have to repeat myself various times.

"That's actually one of my rules. Yes, I have rules," I say when Mike groans. "Rule number one: No hitting on your teacher. Rule number two: Keep your hands to yourself," I look between Mike and Mae and am glad I said it when I catch her blush. "Rule number three: Respect everybody's creativity. We all draw differently, and let's be honest—not all of us draw well, me included. Please don't bash each other's paintings, or sculptures, or whatever else we do in here. And lastly, the art room is Vegas. In this room, we talk about anything and everything you want. We scream and throw paint at our canvas and nobody gets to judge us. Got it?"

All of them nod their heads slowly.

"I have a question," Mae says, sitting in one of the stools set up in front of an easel. She adjusts the machine she's carting around so that it's out of the way and then looks at my expectant face. "You said you're not a good drawer, but you're a painter. Is there a difference?"

I smile at her question. "Huge difference. I'm best at making things with my hands. I usually use broken glass to make small sculptures."

"Broken glass?" Mike asks, wide-eyed.

"Yup."

"What do you make?" Danny asks.

"Hearts."

"You make hearts out of broken glass?" Mae asks in a gasp.

I nod and turn around, my hands flying to my chest when I see Oliver leaning on the wall beside the door with his arms crossed over his chest. His green eyes light up in amusement as his mouth turns into a full-blown grin at the look on my face.

"What are you doing here?" I ask, still holding my thumping heart.

"All of my patients are in here right now." He drops his arms and shrugs as he slips his hands into the pockets of his white coat.

"Oh," I respond, blinking away from him and turning back to the kids. "Anyway, let me show you what I'm talking about." I walk over to the box I brought over the other day, which is on the table beside Oliver. My arm brushes the front of his body as I reach across him, and I hear him intake a breath, which makes me do the same. I need to get a fucking grip around this guy. I grab the small box and walk to the other side of the room so I'm facing the group and can see who walks in. Gemma comes in and tells Oliver something quietly. I watch him nod before she walks out.

"Bathroom break," he mouths in explanation when he catches me looking. I nod and open the box, carefully taking out the glass heart and the stand it's on before placing it on the table.

"Oh my God," Mae says, her blue eyes widening as they take it in. "You made that?"

"I did," I say, smiling proudly. My eyes flicker to Oliver, who has a smile on his face. It makes my heart skip a beat, because it's not the gorgeous one he uses to impress women. Instead, it's a warm, comforting one. This one, he only offers when he agrees with something you said, or is proud of something you did. I turn my attention back to the heart and pick it up. It's what we call a 3-D heart, since it's not flat and has a circumference.

"That's legit," Mike says.

"It is really nice," Danny agrees.

"Thank you. This is my specialty. Most artists have one thing that they're known for. Warhol used blotted ink to create his signature Campbell's soup and Marilyn Monroe images. Romero Britto uses eccentric colors, so when you look at one of his sculptures or paintings there's no question as to who made it. Even if they were to make something different, you would have a hint letting you know that it's theirs. My thing is hearts. I paint them . . . sculpt them . . . but this right here is my kaleidoscope heart. It's my specialty."

"Ohhh," Mae says, as if what she's been looking at just dawned on her. She reaches for it, but thinks better of it and drops her hands.

"Take it," I say.

"No, I don't want to break it. It's too pretty."

"Take it. You're keeping it anyway. You might as well get used to holding it."

Mae's eyes widen. "I can keep this?"

"Of course."

"But what if it breaks?" she asks, hesitantly lifting the heart from its stand. She turns it over and over, creating little rainbows of color throughout the room as the light bounces off of the glass.

"Well," I say, raising my eyes to Oliver, who's watching me intently. "It's a heart. They always break at some point. Sooner or later someone will come along and shatter it anyway—might as well be you." I pause, my heart beating wildly in my chest as Oliver's gaze turns serious, and I find myself mesmerized by it, and trying to back my way out of its intensity. "Besides," I continue, looking at Mae again. "I know the girl who made it. If it breaks, I can get you a new one." I wink and clap my hands together. "Now let's talk about paint!"

Oliver's eyes burn holes into me for the next hour, but I refuse to look at him again. The kids paint different things: Mae a heart, Mike the LA Lakers logo, Danny a fish. They all get comfortable with the brush and the canvas in front of them. I make my way around the room, helping them perfect their strokes and learn how to control the weight of their hands. When the time comes for them to go back to their rooms, they thank me, and each says they are looking forward to their next session. I feel relieved and warm inside, which lasts all of three minutes before Oliver pushes himself away from the wall and walks to where I am busying myself cleaning up the room.

"Shattering hearts," he comments, his teeth grinding. "It's fitting."

"They're not shattering hearts, they're kaleidoscope hearts," I correct him.

"What's the difference? You make them with broken pieces."

I inch forward, standing close enough to feel his warm breath on my face, when I tilt my head to glare at him, my hands making tight balls at my sides.

"The difference is that it's already broken, but I use the pieces to rebuild it. The difference is that the heart has a second chance, and maybe it'll get broken again, but it's already shattered, so maybe the fall won't be as bad."

His eyes search my face as if he's looking for another answer. We stare at each other for a long time—long enough for my breath to quicken and my heart to begin to burn. Long enough for him to cup the back of my neck with his nimble fingers and pull my face to his abruptly, smashing his lips to mine. My resolve leaves me quickly, as my hands thread through his hair. I pull, begging him to come closer, as our tongues dance around each other in a passionate tango. He groans deeply into my mouth, and I feel it travel down my body to my pelvis, where it simmers. I can't remember the last time I was kissed like this. I feel like I'm floating and drowning at the same time, taking a breath and being submerged with the next.

When we pull away, we're both breathing heavily, and my face feels flushed. For a beat longer, I look at him—at his disheveled dark hair and the five o'clock shadow he rocks like nobody's business. My gaze wanders over his plump lips and slightly crooked nose, to the shallow dimple on his chin and the intense green eyes that cast me under a spell so long ago. When the reality of our shared kiss catches up to me, it hits me quickly, like a foul ball out of nowhere, and I back away from him.

"That shouldn't have happened," I say, rushing past him before he can react. He doesn't come after me, and that's just as well, because even if a part of me wished he did, I didn't expect him to. He never does.

Chapter 10

Past

Oliver

THERE'S A LOT to be said about evolution and the way beauty sometimes blossoms from the most unlikely ducklings. That's how I felt about Estelle when I went home for summer break that year. I had just finished dropping off Jensen and Junior's drunken asses and had parked in front of Vic's house. He wasn't in much better shape than they were. I'd given up drinking that year after learning what it did to your liver. The guys had given me shit about it all night, taking bets as to how long my drinking hiatus would last, as I nursed the same beer I'd gotten hours before. While they were busy getting wasted and hitting on a few questionable girls that would, for sure, make them cringe tomorrow morning, I'd been making mental plans with Trish as her face bobbed between my legs. She was not a questionable hook up. She was a model, and practically every man's Playboy fantasy come to life.

I sighed and hoisted Vic up, knowing he wouldn't make it to his room without my help. It was annoying that I had to babysit three guys who normally knew how to handle their liquor, but that night, they'd all acted like the sloppy sorority girls we made fun of at keggers. I opened the door, Vic gave me a slurred thank you, and I watched as he walked to his room.

Shaking my head, I turned back around, locked the door, and put the keys inside one of the flowerpots his mom had outside. I trotted down the steps smiling at the thought of Trish—her big tits, firm ass, and the way she sucked my dick, still fresh in my mind. As I reached the edge of the house, I stopped and realized I would have to walk home. It was fine since my mom's house was only a few blocks down, but I still contemplated whether or not to go back into the house and stay the night. The brief sounds of crying caught my attention. For a moment, I thought nothing of it—it could have been anything. It was dark out, and way past the hours that any normal human being went to bed. But then, as I pushed my long hair back after a gust of wind tossed it into my face, I heard it again and stopped walking.

I looked around and realized it was coming from Vic's house. I froze for a moment, hoping it wasn't Mrs. Reuben. The last time I tried to comfort a friend's crying mother, she came on to me, and I had to get the hell out of Dodge. Begrudgingly, I looked up and saw a small figure sitting on the roof of the house. The sight almost knocked me on my ass, partially because I was craning my head so hard to look up, but mostly because I could have sworn it was Estelle—except it couldn't be. The girl sitting up there wasn't a girl. But then it hit me—*when was the last time I saw Elle?* I squinted, trying to get a closer look, but couldn't. I walked to the back of the house and climbed the oak tree I'd climbed a million times before for different reasons, and stepped onto the roof. She was sitting down, head bent, her long, wavy hair falling over her shoulders and blocking her face.

When I sat down beside her, she jumped and faced me with a yelp, surprise and fear on her otherwise grief-stricken face. I'd known Estelle since I was thirteen and I'd never, ever seen her look like this. Not even when she didn't get the leading role in the Nutcracker, a performance she'd rehearsed for months before the tryouts. Immediately, I assumed a break up was the reason for her tears, and my blood began to boil at the thought of some loser doing this to her.

"What's wrong?" I asked as she wiped her tears and shook her head. Her face was no longer wet, save for the dip over the top of her lips. I'd never noticed how full they were before then. I'd never noticed how rosy and defined her cheekbones were, or the way her eyebrows turned into a slight frown when she looked at me. I'd never paid attention to how ridiculously alluring her eyes were. The different shades made them look like the marbles I used to collect when I was a kid. My gaze drifted down to her neck, where I noticed her swallow, and then over her tits, which were now full—not like the last time I'd seen her in a bathing suit when she was still flat chested. Jesus Christ, this girl was hot.

The clearing of her throat made my eyes snap back to hers, putting an end to their voyeuristic journey down her now grown- up body.

"You're so grown up," I said before I could stop myself, cringing at the voice I said it in, all needy and husky and—fuck my life—desperate. I expected her to roll her eyes, the way she normally did when I said anything to her, but this girl—this freaking girl—looked at me and smiled the sexiest smile I'd ever seen. And I had just been at a party full of hot girls smiling, but Elle's was slow and sensual when she wasn't trying to make it be. It was just her smile, the one I'd been seeing for as long as I could remember. Putting that smile on this grown-up version of her should be downright illegal.

"Are you hitting on me?" she asked, using a sultry voice that surprised the hell out of me.

"That depends," I said, inching to sit closer to her, somehow completely forgetting that I was at my best friend's house, and this was his little sister. The thought of Vic finding us crossed my mind, but I pushed it down. In that moment, under a sky full of stars with a sad Estelle, all I could think about was making her smile.

"What does it depend on?" she whispered.

"Whether or not it's working," I whispered back, lifting my hand and running it down her back—a motion I shouldn't have done, because now I knew Elle wasn't wearing a bra under the oversized sweater she had on, and that knowledge woke up everything in my lower region.

She shook her head softly, her eyes flickering between my eyes and mouth like she was actually thinking about my lips on hers. I shouldn't have liked that thought as much as I did.

"It's not," she said finally.

"Why were you crying?" I asked, gathering her hair and pushing it behind an ear so that I could get a better look at her. The wiggle of one of her outstretched legs caught my attention, and I realized she was wearing a knee brace.

"What the hell happened?"

"I blew out my knee in dance practice the other day for the fourth time, and when I went to the doctor today—thinking they would tell me my brace would come off in a couple of weeks like the last time—he said I have a torn ACL and can't dance anymore," she said in a hoarse whisper. As she looked away, I saw new tears begin to gather in her eyes. "Ever. My Julliard dreams are gone, just like that. Not that I had a real chance of getting in, but now the possibility is ruined."

I had no words for that. The only things Estelle did with her life were dancing and painting, but dance was her passion. It was her light. You could see the way it made her feel and how much she loved it with every move she made.

"You still have a year of school, Elle. Don't rule it out. Like you said, it's happened before," I said, cupping her face and wiping a stray tear with the pad of my thumb. She looked at me again and shook her head, but didn't move away.

"Not like this, Bean," she whispered, licking the tears off of her lips. "This time it's over for me. I just know it."

I pulled her face to my chest and held her there, letting her cry all over my shirt, because that was all I could do.

"I'm so sorry, Chicken," I whispered, as I pressed a kiss to the top of her head. It would have been considered a brotherly thing to do if I hadn't closed my eyes and smelled her hair, picturing it draped over my pillow.

She leaned away from my chest, wiped her face, and looked up at me. Her eyelashes stayed stuck together as she blinked. "Why are you here, any-way? Aren't you supposed to be at one of those crazy parties you're always talking about?"

"I was. I came to drop off Vic and heard you crying."

She nodded once, averting her eyes for a beat before looking at me again. "So, I'm so grown up," she said, repeating my words and smiling with a twinkle in her eyes that made my chest squeeze and my jeans tighten.

"You are."

She leaned her face closer so we were breathing on each other. If either of us leaned in a centimeter, our lips would be touching, and God, how I wanted that to happen.

"What are you thinking about?" she asked in a whisper.

"Things I shouldn't be thinking about," I whispered back, my eyes on her mouth again, wondering how it would feel.

"Like what?" she asked, her breath falling over my lips.

I closed my eyes and leaned back just a little bit. "Like things a nineteen-year-old shouldn't think about a sixteen-year-old."

"You act like you're so much older than me." We were both still whis-pering, trying to keep, whatever this crazy thing was, a secret. I was sure the crackling in the air between us would alert everybody in the general vicinity of this house that something was going on.

"I'm old enough to know better," I responded, tilting my face and lean-ing into hers, letting my lips brush hers lightly, then dragging them until I reached the edge of her mouth. I dropped a kiss there.

"I always wondered what that would feel like," she said, releasing a long breath as my lips grazed over hers.

"You've never kissed a guy before?" I asked, rearing back. What the fuck was wrong with the guys in her school? I hadn't even kissed her. Not really, anyway.

Elle laughed quietly. She looked at me like I'd grown two heads. "I meant what kissing *you* would feel like." She smiled bashfully and looked down at the space between us where our hands touched.

"You've thought about it?" I asked, smiling, wishing her confession didn't make me as happy as it did.

"Often," she said, trying to smother a smile of her own.

I sighed heavily, ran a hand through my hair, and looked back at her open window. I needed to change the subject. I couldn't think about her dreaming of kissing me, or the way I suddenly wanted to do so much more than that with her. "I can't believe you got out here with that cast. Let me help you get back in."

I offered her my hands and helped her up, looking away into the distance and paying attention to the sound of the ocean behind us—anything not to look down at her. Our hands were still connected, and I could feel her gaze on mine. I knew if I looked down, I would kiss her—full-on kiss her—and plunge my tongue in her mouth while I suck that plump bottom lip. I knew it. I wanted to so damn bad. But I couldn't. That wouldn't be fair to her or Vic.

"Ready?" I asked with a heavy sigh, as I pulled her hands in the direction of her window. I watched as she climbed in without turning back to me. When I said goodnight and started to walk away, she called my name. I walked back and dipped my head, holding on to the edge of the window.

"Will you come back tomorrow?" she asked, her eyes wide and hopeful.

I looked up at the sky, hoping something would tell me what a bad idea that was, then I let out a breath and looked at her again. "I can't think of anything else I'd rather do." And the thing is, it was true. For that month, I went back every night after the guys and I went out, and then I told Elle all about our adventures. Most of my stories were filled with warnings of what girls shouldn't do at parties, so despite the attraction I felt, I was offering my older brother knowledge. Estelle made it difficult to stay away from her, so I kept going back nightly. I loved our easy conversations about everything and anything. I loved the way she thought my jokes were shitty and the way her eyes brightened when I finally said a good one. But some nights, she would lean into me and ask me if I would kiss her when she was eighteen and what I'd do if she was a stranger in one of my college classes. Those questions made it hard for me to think straight. I tried to dodge them by smiling and laughing.

I never told her that if she was a stranger in one of those classes, I'd be on her like white on rice. I never said that if she was eighteen, I would break my rule and face the consequences. I did, however, tell her that I usually dated older women because they were less complicated and didn't expect as much. I was way too busy focusing on school and the college experience to be tied down. She always gave me a small frown when I dropped those little hints, like she wanted to challenge me and change my aversion to a real relationship. I kind of wished she had taken up that challenge, just to see how hard she'd try, even though I knew the outcome would be the same.

Chapter 11

Present

"YOU DID WHAT?" Mia asks in a bewildered tone that makes me bury my face in my hands.

"I know," I say in a smothered mumble.

"Look at me! I want to see how you really feel about this whole thing, because let me just say, I am shocked."

I drop my hands and look at her, really trying to school my features and not start laughing at the expression on her face.

"Oh my God. You liked it. I thought he kiss attacked you and you were pissed off, but you obviously liked it! Are you insane, Elle?"

I frown.

"No, really," she continues. "I'm all for you moving on with your life, *but Bean?* There are a million other guys out there."

"I know. I know." I let out a frustrated growl. I can't believe I freaking kissed him. "At least I walked out on him this time."

"I guess," she whispers.

"You guess?" I prompt.

"It's just . . . you walked away last time too, and look at where that got you."

"A new boyfriend, and later, fiancé?"

"Wyatt was another terrible rebound, but I'm not here to talk crap about people who can't defend themselves."

I let out a breath and shrug, because I don't want to open that can of worms. When I met Wyatt, this older—much older than me—man, I traded in my friends and family for time with him. I became the girl I said I would never be for a guy, but he wasn't just a guy, he was so much more. He was my mentor, my friend, my lover, and even though he had a controlling aura to him, and I dealt with crazy mood swings at times, he loved me. He was good to me.

"I don't want to talk about Wyatt," I say.

"You never do," Mia counters, raising an eyebrow. I know she's trying to goad me—trying to get me to the place where I lose my cool—because her words resonate something within me that I can't argue with.

"I don't want to fight right now, Meep."

"Because you know you'll lose the battle."

"I can't do this right now," I say finally, taking the glass of Moscato and drinking what's left in one huge gulp before slamming it down with a clink. I take out a bill and toss it on the table.

"You're seriously leaving over this?" she asks, balking at me.

"I have to go get some stuff and get ready to go to Felicia's house for dinner tonight, and I'm not in the mood to argue with you right now."

"How are you going to move on completely if you're still eating dinner with his parents every goddamn week?"

My mouth pops open. I can't believe she's even going there right now, even after knowing how upset this is making me. I try to regain control of the blood simmering inside my body, but the longer I stand there, the more impossible it is.

"Next time I need your advice, I'll ask you. You shouldn't be dishing out so much of it anyway! Your ex-boyfriend left you to marry his ex-girlfriend, and you rebounded with his uncle! How's that for fucked up?" I practically shout.

"I didn't know it was his uncle!" She slams her palms over the table and stands up, so it looks like we're in a boxing ring with the table serving as our referee.

"I . . . I . . ." I put my hands on my head and squeeze the impending headache. "I have to go. I can't . . . I can't right now." As it is, I already regret what I said to her. She didn't deserve that and I know it, but dammit! She knows I hate it when she brings up Wyatt. Even when he was alive, I refused to talk about him with her after a while, because it would always end up turning into a huge argument.

By the time I get to Victor's house, I decide I hate everybody and can only pray nobody else gets in my way, because I feel like I have enough pent-up rage inside me to make a charging bull look tame. The door slams behind me in a thud, and I head for the stairs, ignoring the voices coming from the kitchen.

"Elle?" Vic calls out.

"Yeah. I'm just here for a moment. Picking something up," I shout back, reaching the bedroom door and closing it behind me. I sag against it, feeling like a teenager avoiding her parents, and I focus on collecting my thoughts before the inevitable footsteps come up the stairs. The knock comes shortly after and I sigh, conceding to open it. I regret it immediately when I find Oliver standing on the other side, wearing nothing but a pair of swim trunks and a smile. I refuse to give in to the urge to let my gaze travel the length of his naked torso. My eyes can burn in hell for wanting to do it. My hands can follow them and sit beside Satan himself for wanting to reach out to tame the mussed brown hair falling over his forehead.

"What do you want?" I ask, not even trying to hide my annoyance.

He stops smiling and starts frowning, crossing his arms over his chest. I refuse to look at his defined arms. Absolutely refuse.

"What crawled up your ass?" he asks, and I start closing the door on him, but he stops it with his hand. I exhale.

"I don't have time for this right now, Oliver. If you want to annoy me, come back after nine o'clock," I mutter, looking down at his naked feet. They're probably the least attractive thing on his body, but then, feet usually are.

"Okay," he says, pushing the door wider and letting himself in.

"What are you doing?"

"Annoying you."

"I said after nine. It's six-forty, and I have to go." I grab the bag I have on the floor, filled with pictures of Wyatt.

"Where are you going? Another date?" he asks, as he walks around the room, picking up everything and looking at it—even a pink bra that's draped over my chair. He stays fixated on that.

"I guess you can call it that." I turn to the closet and sift through clothes, looking for something more modest to change into. The black shirt I have on shows off my entire back, and it's not something I would wear to Wyatt's parents' house without him there.

"I like what you're wearing," Oliver says huskily into my ear, making me jump. I turn quickly, both palms up and ready to push him away, but get sidetracked when my nose ends up on his sternum and I can't help but breathe him in. He smells of salty water and a natural scent that's sweet, yet masculine. I only hesitated for half a second, but it's long enough for him to place his hands over mine. He presses them to his warm chest, and my breathing escalates.

"Look at me, Elle," he says, using the deliciously low, demanding voice that made my toes curl and my eyes roll back many moons ago. I have no choice but to tilt my head back and give him my attention. "Forget those lame guys you're dating. Let me take you out."

My heart, if possible, spikes even further in my chest, overriding all warning of the impending chaos that's sure to come. I try to turn my attention to the poster hanging beside us, but the image of a kissing couple has my eyes darting back to deep green eyes that burn into mine. My stomach does a flip-flop—the way it always does when he looks at me that way. I try to take my hands back, because these feelings are too scary for me to deal with right now, but he holds them tighter, bringing them up to his mouth and kissing the tip of my ring finger. Why did he pick that finger to kiss? I pull harder, and he finally lets my hand drop.

"I can't," I say, my voice raspy.

A myriad of emotions flash in his eyes before they settle on determination, and I'm forced to take a step back—away from his scent, away from his warmth.

"Why not?"

I sigh and finally look away, back down at his naked feet. "I just can't." He knows why not. He shouldn't ask me that question. "What's Vic doing, anyway?"

His body moves into mine so quickly that I don't have time to react, as his large hands clutch my arms and his face drops, bringing his nose to mine. I just stare, wide-eyed, waiting for his lips to close the distance, but they don't. He just looks at me . . . breathes on me . . . lets me breathe on him, and then he groans. And that fucking groan bridges the distance between us and crawls into the core of me, draping over every fiber of my being.

"What do you want, Oliver?" I whisper against his lips. "What do you want from me? You want to kiss me? You want to fuck me? You want to come into my life like the hurricane that you are and tear down everything I've rebuilt before you disappear again?"

His lips brush lightly against mine—just a breath of a touch—yet he's crowding me like he's about to devour me. He won't though. He never goes in for the kill. He just casts the lure, reels me in and then cuts the line. As expected, his hands drop, and he pulls away from me as quickly as he'd approached. I feel a pang deep inside me that I desperately wish wasn't there.

"I'm sorry," he says quietly, shaking his head in a movement that makes his hair sway back and forth. His eyes are soft on mine now, and I can almost hear his thoughts: *I should never have kissed her. I should never—*

My brows rise in surprise at the apology, though. There are so many things I can say to him, but the sudden, defeated look in his eyes keeps my mouth shut. Finally, I exhale and push off the wall to stand in front of him, keeping enough distance between us to discourage us from reaching toward the other.

"It's okay just . . . don't do it again. The kiss the other day was a mistake . . ." I stop talking and walk past him, putting the bra away and sorting through my underwear drawer, like I'm unearthing hidden treasure or something. This time when I feel him come up behind me, I drop my head and exhale. He really needs to stop sneaking up behind me.

"Oli—" I start, and gasp when I feel his lips on the back of my neck, soft and warm. My heart thunders and I freeze in place, my shaking hands still inside the drawer. I close my eyes and focus on breathing, as he drops another kiss right beside that spot. I never knew the back of my neck was so sensitive. The feeling sends a ripple of sensation down my arms and through my body.

"It wasn't a mistake," he says in a husky whisper that makes my flesh break out in goose bumps. "You've never been a mistake. You want me to tell your brother that I want to date you? Is that what it would take?"

I pull my hands out of the drawer to clutch the edge of the dresser, and a moan escapes my lips.

"That sound," he growls, as he pushes his body against my back. I can feel the hardness of his chest . . . of him . . . against me. "That fucking sound drives me crazy, Elle," he says, sucking the side of my neck. I'm starting to pant, and I don't even care. I don't know what I want anymore. I don't know what I need. I don't know if it matters—if anything matters—when Oliver is making me feel this way. I don't even have time to let guilt sink in, because even that's a foreign feeling right now. A storm of lust rises inside me, and my heart continues to trip over itself as his lips descend on me over and over.

"I can't do this again," I whisper shakily. "I can't . . . oh God, you need to stop." I moan as he drags his hands down my sides, the tips of his fingers grazing my already pert nipples.

He presses against me again, pushing me into the dresser. "Was I a mistake to you?"

"Oliver," I plead in a soft whimper. My eyes roll back as his hands begin a sensual tease—up and down, squeezing and kneading—unhurried . . . as if we have all the time in the world for his seduction. As if we both don't know that as soon as he walks out of this room, whatever we're doing is over . . .

like it always is.

"What do you want, Elle? You want me to kiss you? You want me to fuck you? You want to pretend that *I'm* the one who hurricanes through your life?" His voice is guttural as he grinds against my ass. Another moan escapes me.

Suddenly, his words sink in, and my eyes snap open. That's the moment I slip out of his hold and turn to glare at him. His eyes are hooded as he looks back at me, his hair all tousled and sexy. Hell, everything about him is sexy. Oliver Hart is the definition of sexy in my book, but I'm too pissed off to be distracted right now.

"I'm the hurricane?" I say, pointing at myself. "*Me?*" I glance at the clock on the dresser and realize I'm already late, thanks to this . . . whatever we're doing.

"You think you're not?" Oliver counters, now looking at me through narrowed eyes.

"You're delusional." I walk back to the closet and, with my back to him, I pull the shirt I'm wearing over my head. I hear his sharp intake of breath, and I don't relish it like I normally would. Right now, he's officially back on my shit list.

"No. You are delusional, Estelle," he says, stepping forward so he's behind me again, his voice near my ear. He doesn't touch me this time. "You are so damn crazy, and I want to touch you so bad right now and fuck the insanity out of you."

A shiver runs down my entire body as I pull another shirt over my head. "Not going to happen."

"Not right now, but it is going to happen. Don't go on this date," he says. The soft plea in his voice thaws me a little, and I turn to face him.

"Why? Why shouldn't I go on a date?"

"Because," he breathes, running a hand through his hair. His eyes scan my room quickly, as if he's looking for the answer on my goddamn walls. Just when my anger is bubbling up because this feels like déjà vu all over again, his eyes flash back to mine, and the look in them is so potent that it freezes me. "Because I don't want you to. Because it's my turn. Because I've let you go a million times before, and I don't want to miss this chance with you. Let me take you out. Let me show you how good I can be, and I'm not talking about fucking, I mean me. *One date, Elle.*"

When my heart starts beating again, I let out a rushed breath. "One date."

Oliver smiles. It's the one that makes me swoon—the wide grin that shows off his dimples. "One date."

"Our definitions of dates are wildly different," I say, looking around the room. My eyes glance over everything—anything—so that I don't have to look at Oliver, but then he moves closer, and my eyes snap to his so that he'll stop moving.

"Okay, we'll define it so we're both on the same page."

I let out a small laugh. "Okay, I'll think about it. But if I decide to say yes, I have rules."

He chuckles. "Text me the rules."

"I will."

When I head downstairs, I hear him and Vic in the kitchen and pop my head in to say goodbye. Oliver's eyes take me in slowly, as if I'm the slice of pizza he's about to dig into, and I look away quickly before I get lost in his gaze.

"You're going to Felicia's, right?" Vic asks.

"Yup. I'll be back early. Bye, guys."

"Felicia?" Oliver asks, when I'm already halfway to the door.

"Yeah, Wyatt's mom," Vic responds.

"What?" Oliver asks, bewildered.

I laugh all the way to my car, and when I get there, I see a text message from him.

You played me.

I laugh, but don't respond.

What are the rules?

1- No touching. 2- No kissing . . . If I think of any more, I'll let you know.

Is Friday good for you?

I haven't agreed to this yet.

But you will.

I don't respond. I wonder if he would really ask Vic if he could take me out. For some reason, it makes butterflies ignite deep in my belly. Then I groan, remembering where I'm going and why. Maybe Mia is right. Oliver is the last person I should play this game with. He invented the fucking game. I'm just a newbie hoping for a win.

Chapter 12

Past

Oliver

GROWING UP, THE friend I could relate to most was Jensen—we both came from broken homes. Our families weren't wealthy like Victor's or Junior's, and we had jobs by the time we were fifteen. Even though we had similar backgrounds, Jensen and I still had our differences. He always needed a girlfriend, whereas the last thing I wanted was to be tied down. My parents' divorce probably had a lot to do with it. That, and the fact that when my older sister and I stayed at my dad's house every other weekend, he would openly talk about the issues he had with my mother. His main issue, my sister would say, was that our parents married too young and didn't get to experience life without the other. She was sixteen when she said that to me. I was nine. For some reason, her words stuck with me. Probably because I was always looking for the "real reason" they couldn't work things out.

As much as I loved and respected my father, I always said I wouldn't end up like him. I wouldn't leave my family just because I had an adventurous itch I needed to scratch. When I was a teenager I had girlfriends, but none of them held my attention long enough to be long term. It wasn't that I wanted to screw around or sleep with someone else. It was as simple as having different interests or the fact that I couldn't stay on the phone long enough to have a conversation without falling asleep. Beyond that, I really liked women. I liked the smell of them . . . the taste of them . . . and I liked trying to figure them out. My sister, Sophie, would hassle me and tell me I was becoming our father—which I didn't appreciate—and then I'd remind her that I wasn't involved with anyone.

"That's the problem, Bean, you're not George Clooney. You can't be a lifelong bachelor."

"Clooney gets some serious ass. I wouldn't mind being him."

"Yeah, but I want my kids to play with your kids at some point," she would remind me.

"Well, I haven't found the right girl yet."

And that was the thing. I hadn't. Not that I was looking, but I'd like to think if I was fucking her, I would know she was the right one for me. It's not like I got women in my bed without having a conversation with them first. All of them made my blood go straight to my cock, but that was about it. The last time I'd been in love was when I was twelve, and according to Sophie, that didn't really count. I just needed to keep having fun while I was in college—everything else would fall into place.

That's exactly where my head was when Vic called to invite me to a party he and his fraternity brothers were throwing. He was attending UCLA, while I was in Cal Tech—which are really close—so we were able to hang out every weekend. I was already planning on going to the party, but when he mentioned Elle was visiting him for the weekend and would be there, I was completely sold. I showered and avoided the calls from Pam, the girl of the moment. I was determined to go to this party and relax with my friends, and taking Pam meant I'd have to babysit, because she was one of those girls who got drunk off of one drink, and then still had ten.

I pulled up to the party and greeted a couple of guys I knew before heading to the back where Vic always hung out playing darts. He came into my line of vision and I had to laugh, because he was guarding the keg like it was a shrine.

"What's up, douchebag?" I said, patting him on the back when I reached him. He backed away and turned to me with a lazy smile on his face that made me chuckle. "Bean! Grab a cup. Actually, grab two. I've been standing in front of this shit for an hour waiting for you to get here."

"You could've told me to bring more beer," I said, laughing, as I reached for a red cup.

"Nah, I got you, I got you." He poured me a beer and finally stepped away from the keg.

"Anyone else coming? Jensen? Junior?"

"Jensen's . . . I don't know what he's doing, but he's back home, and Junior went to visit Rose's family."

I let out a low whistle. "It's getting really serious now."

Vic nodded, his face looking as terrified as I felt at the time about getting serious with somebody.

"Whatever. As long as it's not me, I'm good," Vic said, shrugging.

I chuckled. "You and me both."

"I never thanked you the other day . . . for coming with me," he said, his voice taking a serious note. I clinked my cup to his and shrugged. I'd gone with him to get checked because some girl he'd been fucking called to tell him she had an STD. It wasn't like I went in the room with him or anything, but I could tell he was pretty messed up over the news, so I went for moral support. He didn't want to tell anybody else about it. I'm not sure he would have even told me if he hadn't taken her call while we were out surfing together.

"That's what brothers are for. Have you . . ." gotten the results, was my question, but it seemed too serious to speak aloud at a frat party, and I wasn't sure he was ready to answer.

"Negative," he said, throwing back the rest of his beer. "Everything came back negative."

I let out a long relieved breath. I wasn't sure what I would have felt if he'd had another answer. We weren't kidding when we called each other brothers. I couldn't remember a time when Vic wasn't in my life, which is a big deal nowadays when friends were as fickle as the weather. He was there when my parents divorced, when my dad got sick—and everything in between. His parents took me in for weeks on end in the summer, when my mom was away on work trips and Sophie was off in school. Not that an STD meant death, but it was serious enough to make me realize how lucky we were to have dodged that shit thus far.

"You need to use a condom every-fucking-time, dude," I said in a breath, taking a gulp of my beer.

"I know. I know."

I stood beside him, nodding and facing the yard, which was full of guys in purple shirts and girls drinking and laughing. There was an area to the far left where there was a makeshift dance floor set up with a DJ. Only a couple of people were actually dancing there, and one couple in particular caught my eye. The guy was mainly just standing there, moving in a two-step, while the girl had her hands up, running her fingers through her long, brown hair. She wore a short, tight, black dress that captured every curve on her body, and on her feet, black converse. I was completely mesmerized by her and the way she moved her body. It was like she was doing a striptease without the stripping. Somehow, her dress, as short as it was, covered her nicely shaped ass. I opened my mouth to say something about her to Victor, but then she turned around, smiling, her back facing the guy she was dancing with, and I realized I knew her.

"What the fuck?" I nearly growled.

"What?" Vic said, snapping his eyes to meet mine.

"You let Elle wear that to this party?" I knew I sounded like a jealous boyfriend and I had no right, but here was the girl we were all constantly warned to stay away from and grew up taking care of like she was our own sister, and then . . . whatever . . . and here she was . . . and here was Vic. "What the fuck?" I repeated, glaring at him.

He looked at me like I was crazy and laughed at what was probably a furious look on my face. "She's eighteen. I can't really tell her what to wear, and hello . . . have you ever known her to wear anything more? Besides . . . I've been standing here watching her like a freaking hawk all night just in case that asshole tries anything stupid."

I gathered the hair that had fallen out of the bun I'd put it in and thought about what he said. I hadn't really noticed. We spent that summer together, talking almost every night on her roof and she always looked clothed enough. Well, not really, now that I thought about it. She was always wearing loose shirts and tiny shorts, or pajama pants and tiny shirts. I'd never really seen her at a party, other than her own or Victor's. Those times, she didn't wear make-up or tight ass dresses that would make any breathing male want to bend her over by the bushes and fuck her.

"I haven't really noticed, no," I said, finally.

He laughed. "That's because she's like your sister."

I froze. She was like a sister at one point when we were young, before she grew up. Before that summer happened. I didn't think my heart could take watching another one of those dances, knowing it was her, and that I wasn't that guy.

"Who's the guy?"

"Uh, that's Adam. I think she said his name is Adam."

"She brought him?" Why did that bother me?

"Yeah. Something about Mia not being able to come, and she didn't want to come by herself to hang out with a bunch of horny guys and annoying girls she didn't know."

I laughed. Annoying girls. That sounded like something she would say, but what did I know? I didn't know this Elle.

"So they're dating?" I pointed at them. They finally pulled apart and walked away from the floor. As they headed in our direction, Elle pulled her hair up into a ponytail and then let it flow through her fingers to drift back down. She was laughing at something Adam said behind her, and I wondered if he was making a joke about her ass, because that's where his eyes were.

"Nah, I don't think so. She's not into the serious relationship thing."

I gaped at Victor, and he gave me a shrug. "You're okay with that?"

He shrugged again, drinking his beer. "What am I supposed to tell her? Go get married, Elle, you need to go get married right now? She's eighteen!"

The thought of Elle getting married right now didn't bode well for me, so I stayed quiet and glanced in her direction again. I could see her eyebrows pull together as she got closer and the smile on her face drop when she saw me. My chest squeezed a little. What had I ever done to her? Shouldn't she be smiling?

"Hey, Bean," she said as she neared me. In that moment, for the first time ever—as I watched her plump lips moving as she spoke—I hated that she used my nickname. The nickname my mother had given me, no less. Bean sprout, she used to call me. It kind of stuck, to the point that all my friends used it when they addressed me. It never bothered me when little girl Elle said it, but grown-up Elle? I wanted her to call me Oliver. I wanted her to *scream* Oliver. And on that note, I cleared my throat.

"Hey, Chicken," I said, my smile growing when she glared as I used her nickname.

Adam chimed in with a laugh. "Chicken?"

Elle groaned. "Long story."

"It's not really that long," Vic said. "She was scared of everything as a kid, hence the name Chicken."

She rolled her eyes and took the cup of beer Vic had just poured for himself, chugging it down quickly. And I stood there, gaping, completely-fucking-entranced by the way she wiped under her mouth using two fingers, and at the wide smile in response to whatever it was Adam was saying. I couldn't concentrate on his words—I could only hear her throaty laugh and see her face . . . her body . . . and I really needed to stop. I knew I needed to stop. Adam said something about the bathroom, Vic pointed, and I seethed as Elle watched him walk away.

"How's the basil?" she asked Vic, who shrugged.

"Your plant, not mine."

"You're kidding me. Victor, how do you expect it to stay alive if you don't care for it?" she asked. "I'm going to go look."

"What basil?" I asked, watching her ass sway as she walked away.

"She planted some basil on the side of my house because her apartment has no proper lighting or something, and she expects me to take care of it. I don't know." He shrugged.

"Huh. I'm going to go see it."

"Good, that way you can keep an eye on her," he said.

I cocked an eyebrow. "What happened to 'she's eighteen'?"

"Well, yeah, she can be eighteen with Adam and shit—not with my fraternity brothers. That's different."

I stared at him, waiting for him to elaborate. He let out an impatient breath and shook his head. "That's sacred. That's like if I make a move on Sophie or something. You just don't do that shit."

I didn't bother to point out to him that Sophie was older than we were, and married, because I understood where he was coming from. She was Elle, the baby sister, and we were Vic's dickhead friends, the ones who liked to sleep around and had STD scares. Not the kind of guys you want around your sisters. It hurt though. The realization of how he felt and how he expected it to be that way, warred with the fact that looking at Elle made me yearn for something I knew I couldn't have.

The loud sounds of the party died down with each step I took toward the side of the house—the direction she'd gone. I stopped when I found her. She was bent over, looking at the plant on the ground, and I took a couple of seconds to admire how good she looked in that position.

"When did you get into gardening?" I asked, walking closer.

Her head snapped up, and she straightened with a shrug and a smile. "It's new. I'm trying to eat healthy. I want to plant my own crops, but it's kind of impossible in my dorm."

I stood beside her and faced the plant. "It looks good."

"Yeah, it smells good, too," she said. I could hear the smile in her voice, and it made me smile.

"So, how has your first semester been?"

"It's been . . . good, actually. Fun."

I turned my body to face her, tucking my thumbs in the front pockets of my jeans. "It sounds like you're having too much fun."

Elle tilted her head to look at me, wearing that tiny frown she got when she was trying to figure something out.

"What makes you say that?"

"I don't know. Adam . . . you dancing . . . Vic saying you're not into relationships . . ." I shrugged.

She laughed, her eyes lit in amusement. "That's something, coming from you."

"What's that supposed to mean?"

"You've never been into relationships. You have all the fun in the world."

"That's different."

"Different how? Is it because I'm a girl?" she asked, crossing her arms over her chest.

"No," I said quickly. "It's not that." It wasn't. The women I fucked were all single and not into relationships—it was what we had most in common. But this was Elle. This was . . . *Elle.*

"So what is it?" she challenged.

I groaned, running my hand over my hair and leaving it there. "I don't know. I . . . don't know. You're right. You should do whatever you want."

"Your hair's gotten longer," she said, her eyes trailing from mine, to my bicep, and then my head. I smiled.

"You can braid it better now."

She smiled. "Turn around."

I did. My shoulders stiffened when I felt her hands on them.

"I can't reach. You're going to have to kneel down," she whispered against my neck. My eyes fell closed as I tried to contain the fire beginning to blaze through me. I turned and walked to a bench at the side of the house. It was gross, and Vic had been trying to get rid of it for years, but right now, I was glad it was there.

Elle sat beside me, and I turned my back so she could let my hair down. I cringed when she pulled on the rubber band.

"I told you to stop using these," she said, sighing heavily as she ran her fingers through my hair. She massaged my scalp as if she was washing it. I resisted the urge to moan at how good it felt. Women loved to pull on my hair, and I never complained about that, but there was something about the way Elle touched it that made a tingling sensation run through me. When she was finished combing it through, she dropped her hands. The pause was long enough for me to turn my body and face her.

"You're not going to braid it?" I asked, frowning as I took in the faraway expression on her face.

She shook her head, her eyes dropping to my chest. I moved closer, until our faces were inches apart, but she still didn't look at me.

"Elle?" I asked, my voice a whisper.

Her eyes snapped to mine and for a beat, I got lost in the way the different colors in them swirled. They always reminded me of a marble. My favorite marble—blue, green, and brown. The way she looked at me made my heart pound. It was like a world of wonder lived in those eyes. I wished I could see myself the way she saw me. Maybe I would be a different person if I could. Maybe I would be a one-woman man—a man who wanted to go visit her parents for the weekend and get serious right now. Looking at Elle—right there at that moment—made me want to be that guy.

"I was, but it brings back memories," she whispered. "Braiding your hair, I mean."

I nodded and swallowed, pushing my hands down over my thighs so I wouldn't touch her.

"Do you remember when I asked you if you would kiss me when I was eighteen?" she asked in a whisper. She reached out and tapped the tips of her fingers over my knuckles as if they were piano keys. It made my heart beat faster.

"Yeah," I matched her whisper, but mine sounded hoarse.

"Would you?" Her eyes bounced to each of mine, her hands stilling over mine. "Would you kiss me, Oliver?"

My heart was beating so fast, I couldn't think. My lips parted slightly, and I nodded. I was always the chaser—the one sweet-talking girls—but this girl always seemed to have me at a loss for words. She threw me off balance. We moved toward one another until the tips of our noses touched. We held each other's gaze and, a millisecond apart, we closed our eyes. Our mouths touched . . . my lips slid between hers . . . her tongue slipped into my mouth . . . and as soon as it touched mine, I felt the fire ignited earlier, roll through me at full blaze.

Kissing Estelle felt like what I could only imagine kissing a cloud was like—light and sweet, and all consuming. Our mouths moved together in sync, as if we'd been kissing since we were born. Our hands framed each other's faces, like we were scared to pull away because the moment would be over. I'd never wanted to melt and disappear into a girl's mouth as much as I wanted to right then. When I finally broke the kiss—because my hands were developing a mind of their own and I didn't want to do something I would regret tomorrow—her eyes popped open. She looked at me like she was just seeing me for the first time—or maybe that's just how I felt because I wanted her to look at me like that. I kissed her again, this time more urgently, and groaned into her mouth when her hands pulled my hair. We pulled apart one last time, our chests heaving, when we heard someone calling out her name.

"That's Adam. He probably wants to leave," she said, panting.

"Are you going to go have fun with him?" I asked, dipping my head and taking her bottom lip between my teeth. She moaned and pulled on my hair, readjusting so she could straddle my hips. My hands moved to her thighs of their own accord. Everything in me wanted her so bad—all of her. And for so much more than just a make-out session.

"I'm having fun with you," she said against my lips, grinding down on me.

"Fuck, yes," I said in a moan, when she did it again.

Our tongues met and, as Estelle moved, I guided her hips to meet my thrusts. It was crazy. We were crazy. Anybody from the party could turn the corner and find us there, dry humping on that dirty bench, but we didn't care. We weren't *really* having sex, anyway, even though I wanted to. I wanted to pull my dick out of my pants and slip inside her more than anything, but this was Estelle, she didn't deserve a quick fuck at a frat party. Her name got louder, and we tore away from each other quickly. She sat back beside me as we caught our breaths, and finally a figure appeared in the corner.

"Elle, I've been looking everywhere. You're still looking at that damn plant?" Vic said, walking over to us.

"Yeah, well, we were talking," she said, standing up and straightening her dress.

"Adam is throwing up everywhere. You might want to take him home," he said.

She sighed heavily. "Are you serious? I don't bring a girl with me because I don't want to babysit, and then the guy I bring acts like a drunk sorority girl?"

I chuckled. "You want help?"

She shrugged. "I guess. If you don't mind."

I stood and followed to where the guy was. We waited for him to finish puking and I helped him get to the car—a shiny black BMW, which apparently he owned. It happened to be parked beside my beat-up Maxima and, for some reason, this drunk little shit having this car and trying to make a move on Elle bothered me. She'd never been a materialistic girl. I knew she didn't need much, but it made me feel a little inadequate and reminded me why I was waiting to settle down. I wanted to be at a secure place in my life when I settled down. I wanted the car, the house—and anything else my mind could conjure up as a necessity—out of the way before that happened, and I knew it wouldn't happen any time soon.

When she got into the driver's seat and started the car, I walked to her window. We looked at each other for a long moment, and then she smiled shyly.

"I always wondered what it would feel like to kiss you," she whispered. I grinned and looked around the driveway. Everybody was inside the party, so I dipped my head into the window and kissed her again, not caring that Adam was sitting there. He was passed out anyway.

"And?" I asked when I backed away.

"It was . . . everything." Her face lit up when she said it. "But don't worry; I know it was a one-time thing."

My smile vanished. I wanted to tell her it could be more. We went to nearby schools. It could be more. Then I remembered who she was and that her brother would never approve of me dating his sister. With my track record, I wouldn't approve of me either. And she was only eighteen. It was her first semester of college, and I was about to graduate and go to medical school.

"You're the one who wants to have fun now that you're a college girl," I said jokingly, kind of hoping she'd say otherwise. Instead, she smiled brighter.

"That, I do. See you next time, Bean."

Adam groaned beside her, and we both froze and glanced his way. He stayed put.

"Yeah, next time," I said, as she drove away. I sighed. My heart felt heavy as the taillights disappeared around the bend. I wondered if it would ever again stagger and skyrocket the way it just had.

Chapter 13

Estelle

Present

I HATE FIGHTING.

I hate being wrong, but I hate fighting more than I hate being wrong. I'm just not good at the grudge-holding thing. I get mad, scream about it and let go. Mia, on the other hand, gets mad, screams about it, and clings on to her anger like a leech. Needless to say, we haven't spoken in a couple of days. I'd managed to avoid Oliver the past few days at the hospital, while I painted vinyl records and surfboards with the kids. I saw him a couple of times by the nurses' station, though, and once leaving Jen's office. I caught glimpses of what his life must be like—the flirting, the multitude of sexual partners, the late night rendezvous he probably has in the hospital during the night shift. They aren't things I necessarily want to imagine, but that's just where my mind automatically goes when it comes to Oliver.

Two of my friends, Micah and Dallas, are standing in the middle of the hallway of the pediatrics floor, both with the same disgusted looks on their faces that I had when I saw the walls. I could tell from the way Micah keeps running his hands through his long blonde hair that he's nervous about taking this project on. Dallas is just full-on gaping, as if the walls are taunting him. Micah turns first and shoots me a *what the fuck did you get us into* look that I have to laugh at.

"But for real," he says when I reach them. My arms swing around his middle, and I squeeze.

"Thank you, thank you, thank you," I say against his back and then do the same to Dallas.

"Honey, this thank you better come with a blow job," Dallas says as I pull

away, laughing loudly until I hear a throat clearing behind me. I turn to find
Oliver standing there with a strange look on his face. That makes me laugh
harder, because clearly, he'd heard Dallas.

"Hey," I say. "This is Micah and Dallas. Guys, this is Oliver, my brother's
friend—the one who got me into this whole thing."

As they nod at each other, Dallas, who's just slightly taller than me, gives
Oliver a quick onceover, and Micah throws out a "hey man" that makes him
sound like a stoner straight out of Woodstock. Oliver returns their greetings
politely before his eyes return to mine.

"May I speak to you for a moment?" he asks, the intensity in his eyes
making my stomach twist.

"Sure. Guys, the paint is in there. I think we should start with the room
on the far left first. I'll be right back," I say, pointing to the room before turning to follow Oliver with a frown. "Where are we going?"

He opens a door and signals for me to go inside, but I stand rooted in
place. This side of the hospital is vacant because of the paint project, but I
don't want somebody to see us and get the wrong idea.

"Come in."

"We can talk here."

Oliver closes his eyes and takes a deep breath as if he's trying to calm
himself down. When he opens them, they look more tired than before, if
possible. "Please, Elle. Just humor me."

I shake my head, but do as he says, because I don't want to leave the
guys alone for too long. He's invited me into some sort of storage room, with
a bunch of filing cabinets lined up along the walls.

"So?" I ask, turning to face him. He's leaning against the door with his
hands in the pockets of his white coat, just staring at me. "What?"

"I haven't heard from you. I haven't seen you, and then when I finally
do, some guy is talking about you giving him a blow job?" He doesn't sound
upset, just confused and maybe a little hurt, I think, which is ridiculous and
impossible—because this is Oliver we're talking about.

"And?"

"And I miss you."

My heart trips a little at his admission and the way he says it, all smooth
and low. Then I remember Wyatt and his "I miss you's," which weren't said
often, only when he was away on one of his many trips, and only after it'd
been a couple of days since we'd spoken. I never questioned him or what he
was doing. I never wondered if he'd been with another woman, and even the

times Mia planted that seed in my head, nothing grew from it, because for some reason, I didn't care. I always wondered if there was something wrong with me for not caring.

"You don't miss me, Oliver. Besides, aren't you dating someone?" I remind him with a glare.

He rolls his eyes. "It's just a thing, I wouldn't call it dating."

"Just fucking," I say, sounding more bitter than I intended. "Not that I care," I add quickly. Oliver smirks, and I feel my face growing hot. "I have shit to do," I say, finally coming to my senses and stepping forward, but he doesn't move away from the door.

"Are you having fun with him?" he asks, nodding his head toward the outside. Having fun with him. It's funny how I can straight-out ask him if he's fucking somebody, but when he asks me, he uses the term *having fun*. It reminds me of when we were teenagers, and Mia's mom would call her boyfriends her *little friends*. "Or is it the guy with the long hair that you like? I know you have a thing for that."

I take a step back. I do have a thing for guys with long hair, probably because of him. I should hate guys with long hair because of him. I should, but of course, I don't. Oliver's hair isn't long anymore, but it's still long enough to run your hands through and tug on if his head is between your legs. He has a sandy brown scruff going on over his jaw that isn't just a five o'clock shadow anymore. It would probably feel delicious against the inside of my thighs.

"Why are you looking at me like that?" he asks, the huskiness in his voice snapping me out of my fantasy.

"Huh?"

He takes a step forward so he's right in front of me, my eyes at the level of the Dr. Hart ID on the pocket of his left pec.

"Elle. Look at me," he says. A slow, curling desire winds its way around my belly. I have two options: push past him and leave, or look into his eyes and acknowledge the desire that heats the air between us like a blowtorch. I choose the latter because I'm a moron, and because clearly, I like to have my heart shredded repeatedly. "You want me. After all this time, you still want me."

"I don't have time for this right now. They're waiting for me," I whisper, trying to pull away from the electrical current that is his gaze.

"One date, Elle. One date. I'm keeping my word and not touching you, I promise."

"You're already fucking someone. Do you really need another?"

His eyes narrow slightly. "For your information, I'm not. Do you really think this is about fucking you?"

I don't know, I want to say. History tends to repeat itself, but I hold my tongue on that part.

"I don't know what it's about," I respond, dragging my eyes away. I feel like I'm suffocating in this tiny space with him. I try to brush past, but he grabs my arm.

"One date."

I close my eyes and shake my head, regretting it when I feel tears start to prick them. "I'm not ready."

He drops his hand, looking pained. He'll live; he always finds things to fill his time with. As I open the door, I look at him over my shoulder.

"By the way, Dallas, the blow job guy, is gay. Micah, the guy with the hair, was one of Wyatt's best friends, and he is *so* not my type."

"He's cute," Dallas says later, while we're priming the walls, and I know he's talking about Oliver, so I make a grunting, annoyed sound that makes him laugh. My eyes sweep over to Micah, who doesn't comment.

"I'm just saying, I would totally do him," Dallas adds.

"He would probably do you too if he swung your way. You're older, kind of good looking with your nerdy boy glasses and your bow tie . . . yeah, I think he would." My words make him smile and roll his eyes.

"What did he want to talk about?" Micah asks, and my heart starts thumping in my ears. His tone is always nonchalant, so I can't read him properly, and that kills me.

"Just stuff."

"You dating him?" he asks. I suck in a breath. In a sense, I feel like Micah is the string telephone between Wyatt and me, and as soon as I feel like I'm cutting the string, he tightens the knot so I can't.

"No, I'm not dating him! I'm not dating anybody."

Micah sighs heavily and puts the roller down before turning to face me. "He's not coming back, you know? He's not on one of his trips around the world where he'll be back next week. You have every right to move on."

"I'm not ready," I say, my voice cracking as I pick up a roller back and continue painting. I hear the metal roller handle he's holding clatter to the floor, followed by approaching footsteps. I know he's behind me, but I refuse to turn around. I know if I do, I'll cry. I know if he keeps talking, I'll cry. I don't want to cry in here. I want this project to be about hope and life, not pain and loss.

"That wall," Micah says, standing beside me as he points at the wall. "That wall is your life, Elle. The blue isn't ugly, and it's not sad, but we're painting over it because its time is over. The nurses who walk in here won't forget how it looked. The kids who stare at these walls all day won't forget, and maybe they'll miss it sometimes, but we have to give them something that makes them happy to look at. Life is short, and brutal, and painful, and it takes loved ones away from us as quickly as it brings them into our lives, but it's also beautiful. Wyatt would want you to move on and be happy. Date, get married, have kids, travel . . . do whatever makes you feel alive. The longer you mourn, the less you live, and you know how short our time here can be."

Imaginary fingers curl around my throat and squeeze so tightly that I can't even respond. I don't even realize I'm crying until Micah pulls me into his chest, and a loud, wet sob escapes me. I hear something drop on the other side of the room and feel Dallas' arms wrap around us so that we're standing there, all three of us crying for the missing pair of arms that would've covered us all. I call it a night shortly after that, because I can't look at the wall without crying. As I head out, I see Oliver leaning his elbows on the counter with his face buried in his hands. I wonder if he's tired or if one of his patients isn't doing well.

I keep thinking about the damn blue wall, and even though I have reasons not to, I want to comfort him. Sorting through the negative memories in the past, I focus on the good ones and cling to those. Without further hesitation, I walk up behind him and wrap my arms around his middle, laying my cheek over his back. His body stiffens.

"We go out as friends. No date," I say against him, and feel him let out a long breath. I drop my hands when he straightens and turns to face me, his eyebrows furrowing as he scans my face. "Okay?" I ask in a whisper. He doesn't respond. Instead, he brings one of his hands up to cup my cheek. I shiver, as he runs the pad of his thumb over it slowly.

"Okay. A friends date," he responds. He holds my gaze as dips his head. I start to lose composure. Oliver knows my date rules include no kissing, and we're not even on a date, friends or otherwise. But, when his breath falls over my lips, my eyes flutter closed. He doesn't kiss me though. His lips land on the very corner of my mouth, like they did so many years ago on the roof of my parents' house. You would think with the one-man band going on inside my chest, that he'd done something more risqué. My eyes open slowly as he backs away from me, his eyes examining me as if I'm some sort of ancient artifact.

"It's still a yes, right? I didn't break any rules."

I nod slowly, enthralled by him, despite inner thoughts screaming *NO*. If that was his friendly kiss, I don't think I would survive a real one from him, even now that I know better.

"You'll send me the rest of the rules? Even if we are just going out as friends?" he asks, with a sparkle in his eyes that makes me nervous.

I nod again.

"At a loss for words?"

"You caught me off guard," I whisper.

He tries to hide a smile, but I see the dimples deepen in his cheeks, so I know it's there.

"You just made a really bad day a whole lot better for me," he replies, cupping my face and running his thumb over my bottom lip.

"You want to talk about it?" I ask, leaning into his touch.

He shakes his head and smiles sadly. "This is enough."

I can't help it; I smile back. We stand like that for a moment, staring into each other's eyes, his finger on my mouth and my heart in his hands, until the hospital speaker calls out his name.

"I should go. You have work and, unlike some people, I need sleep."

Oliver nods, drops his hand from my face, and steps toward the patient rooms.

"Good night, beautiful Elle."

"Good night, handsome Oliver," I say with a smile.

He grins as I turn to walk away.

"Text me when you get home," he calls out. I leave the hospital feeling much lighter than I did when I walked in. When I get to my car and press a hand to the spot his lips touched, I swear I can feel it tingling. I close my eyes and try to remember if Wyatt ever made me feel that way. I loved him—I really did—but every time I'm around Oliver, it's something I question. It makes me feel terrible for even comparing the two. Maybe I just loved them differently. Maybe Oliver has been more of a familiar, teenage-hormones kind of love and Wyatt was more of an adult, predictably stable kind of love. I can't decide which is best, or if either of them are, really. Not that I have to. Wyatt is gone, and there's nothing I can do about that. So why does going on a just friends date with Oliver make me feel like I'm making the ultimate betrayal to his memory?

Chapter 14

I'M PACING THE gallery when a woman opens the door and makes me stop in my tracks. She smiles as she lifts her sunglasses into her hair. She's older—probably the same age as my mom—and carries herself with the grace of a prima ballerina.

"Are you the owner?" she asks, looking around once before settling on me again.

"Yes," I respond, and walk to her. "Estelle Reuben. Have you been here before?" I ask. She looks familiar, but I can't place her. In the past, Wyatt and I hosted painting reveals in our gallery, so I figure maybe she came to one of those.

"Actually, I haven't. I think we may have met once in New York," she says, tilting her face to examine mine. "You're Wyatt's . . ."

"Fiancé." I fill in the blank. Fiancé, ex-fiancé, fiancé before death, I never really know what to say to a stranger who knew of me.

"I'm sorry for your loss," she says, smiling sadly. Her face muscles don't move much when she smiles, and it makes her look a little more grim than it does compassionate, but I return it nonetheless.

"Thank you. Do you collect?" I ask, figuring she must, if we met in New York.

"Yes. I've had my eyes on that one for a very long time." She lifts a delicate hand and points at my main attraction, the eye that watches over the gallery.

"Oh," I say in a whisper.

"How much for it?" she asks. "I've tried to buy it in the past to no avail."

My eyes widen as realization washes through me. "Priscilla?" I say, turning to face her. Priscilla Woods has been calling—and has had her husband's assistant call—for almost a year now. I keep turning down their offers, although they're big sums, because she wants my two favorite paintings, and I haven't been ready to give them up.

"You remember," she says smiling. "I'm in town for a couple of days, so I figured I would stop by to see if you're ready to sell these pieces to me."

"That one isn't for sale," I say, clearing my throat to make sure I'm heard.

"And the other? The shattered hearts with wings?"

I look away from her, toward where the painting hangs on the opposite wall. "It's called Winged Kaleidoscopes," I reply, suddenly feeling a lump settle in my throat. Wyatt painted it shortly after we got engaged. He painted three, sold two, and kept one for the gallery. I was never sure if he would sell it, even though the meaning behind it always made me tear up and smile. Ultimately, it was his painting to do with what he pleased.

"It's beautiful," she says, and she walks to stand before it. "It reminds me of a rebirth of some sort."

I nod and swallow, hoping to stay put together enough to get through a conversation. "It's very much a rebirth." It's a rebirth of my heart, of my hopes of love, of my love life, and the birth of our relationship.

"It doesn't have a price tag," she says.

"Some things don't have a price."

She turns to me and tilts her head. "Nothing tangible is priceless."

"Maybe not, but the memories behind them are."

My response makes her nod in understanding. Her eyes dart away from mine and look back to the painting. "So you're not willing to let go of the memories it holds?"

I stare at the painting in silence. I know that no price will ever be enough to cover those memories, but they'll forever be embedded in my brain, so maybe I should stop thinking about his paintings in terms of that. In the past couple of weeks, I've managed to turn over a new leaf. I feel like I'm headed in the right direction, yet when I'm faced with something like this—the reality of letting go, *really letting go,* of the past three years of my life—I stall like a car switching gears. I take a long breath, inhaling the ever-present smell of wood and paint, and when I let it out, I have my mind made up.

"I'm ready to let go of it," I say, my voice steady and determined.

Priscilla turns around and claps her hands in front of her with a happy squeal—the exact opposite of everything she looks like—with her fine pearls and perfect bob. It makes me smile a little, and I feel less sad about selling the painting.

"I can deliver it to your house," I say, knowing it's sold, because when somebody with money sets their eyes on something, they don't walk out without it.

"I live in New York," she responds. "I wouldn't expect you to fly all the way over there to deliver something."

"We do it all the time. I wouldn't feel right shipping it to you. Not this one."

She offers me a small smile. "I'll be taking it myself. We own a jet, so it wouldn't even fly in a closet. It will be well taken care of."

The way she speaks about it—as if it was a child—makes me feel slightly better about the sale.

"I'll draw up the paperwork for you."

"Do I have time to run across the street? I'm supposed to meet my girl-friend for lunch," she says, looking at her watch.

"Of course. I just need some information from you. I'll have it ready and packed up by the time you finish."

"Perfect. I can't wait to hang this on top of my fireplace and show off my new painting," she says.

Her painting. I try not to let the words puncture me, but they do any-way. When she leaves and I finish the paperwork, I take down the painting, gripping the edges of the canvas as I set it down on the floor. I fold my legs beneath me and let my fingertips graze each shattered heart, colorful and beautiful, and the wings that lift them up. Tears slide down my face as I touch each one and say my goodbyes. I begin to cover it, one layer, two layers, three . . . stopping to wipe my face with each wraparound I make. I think about the serious look on Wyatt's face as he'd mixed the watercolors . . . the look of elation as he'd gotten to the ivory wings when his vision came together on the canvas.

"Do you like it?" he'd asked. His face had beamed when it became clear that I loved it.

"I never want to sell it," I said, as he laughed and wrapped his arms around me, squeezing me into him.

"One day we will. When we get sick of looking at it."

I hope he doesn't think I got tired of looking at it, because I'm not. I don't think I will ever tire of staring at his paintings, but this isn't about that. This is my goodbye, I say to myself as I stand up and, with a heavy heart, hand a piece of my past over to somebody else. She will never know the history behind it, but she will appreciate it nonetheless.

Chapter 15

ON DAY FOUR of Mia-hiatus, I call her, and after we've had a long conversation about things, I drive over to her studio. I push the door open when I get there and take a moment to admire the photographs she has hanging on the wall. She's changed them all since my last visit. To the right, there's a black and white photo of a woman lying in bed. She's facing away from the camera, and the white bed sheets are bunched up at her bottom, so all you see is the curve of her naked back and lush black hair covering half of her shoulder. The lighting and the pose create a photo that is absolutely stunning. The wall facing the door features a family: The dad is wearing brown corduroy pants, a navy blue, button-down shirt, and, on his head, a Chewbacca mask that covers his face. The small boy beside him is dressed similarly and wears a storm trooper mask. Mom stands on the other side of their son and wears tight brown pants, a white shirt, and has styled her brown hair like Princess Leia. As I laugh at how adorable it is, I startle when Mia rounds the corner to greet me.

I glance down and notice she's wearing a red wrap dress and no shoes, which is funny because I'm wearing the same dress in black. We give each other a quick onceover and laugh.

"Hi," I say sheepishly.

"I'm sorry I'm such an asshole, and I'm sorry I wasn't there when you sold that painting," she replies, repeating what she said in our phone call.

"It's okay. I was fine. I'm sorry I said what I said—it wasn't my place."

We both let out a breath and walk forward with our arms held out, wrapping the other in a tight hug.

"You're such a bitch sometimes," she says against my neck.

"It's why we're friends." We pull away from each other, and I look back at the wall in front of us. "I really love this picture."

Mia smiles. "Isn't it awesome? It's their Halloween card this year."

"That one is stunning," I say, nodding at the one of the woman's back.

"Yeah, boudoir shoot for her soon-to-be husband. Lovely girl." She turns her blue eyes to me. "When are you going to let me shoot one of those for you? You'd be perfect."

I make a noise. "I would suck at that. I don't know how to look sexy on purpose."

Mia laughs. "That's what makes sexy, sexy! If you try too hard, you end up looking like an idiot. I'll help you though—you know I know how to work my magic."

"Yeah, clearly," I say, waving around her studio.

"Hey, do you want to be in a shoot for me this weekend?"

"A shoot? I came to take you out to lunch and grovel for forgiveness, not schedule a sexy shoot!"

"I know, but I have this model I'm shooting, and the girl just canceled on us because she's too sick to do it, and to top it off, this is a major shoot for a local magazine, and I'm supposed to have these pictures to them by next week. This is huge, Elle. This could be my moment."

"Shit," I say, letting out a slow breath.

"Yeah, shit. Every model I've worked with has given me a 'maybe,' and I can't deal with maybe right now."

She looks like she's about to cry, and I hate to see her this stressed over a job.

"Okay. I'll do it," I say. I mean, I've done this for her before. How bad can it be?

"Ah! Thank you!" she says, giving a little jump and hugging me again.

"Is this . . . okay, remember that time you made me take pictures with a guy on the beach? Is this like that?" That wasn't so bad until Wyatt showed up. We'd been frolicking in the water and doing our best not to look at the camera and pretend we had chemistry—which is hard to do with a guy you don't know, no matter how cute he is.

By the time we got comfortable with each other—comfortable enough to go in for the make-believe "we're about to kiss" shot—Wyatt showed up. He made me so nervous, I couldn't get back to feeling natural with the guy. Needless to say, that was strike one for him in Mia's book. It was terrible.

Mia's laugh snaps me back from my thoughts. "No, this will be indoors and much more intimate, so it's a good thing you haven't found a boyfriend yet."

"Yeah, thank God for that," I say halfheartedly, before I let her get back to work and head to my own studio. I make a mental note to grab a sandwich along the way.

Later, as I'm setting up for the kids to arrive, I get a text message from Oliver that makes me frown.

Rule #1- no short dresses.

I stare at it for a long moment, look down at myself, then outside to see if he's stalking me.

Are you stalking me?

??

Are you watching me from somewhere right now?

The phone starts to vibrate with his name on the screen.

"Does that mean you're wearing a short dress right now?" he asks in a whisper.

"Yes, and from the sound of your voice, I'm guessing you're in the hospital."

"How short?" he asks, ignoring my statement.

"Friends, Oliver," I remind him.

"Just tell me how short it is, for the love of God. I need a visual."

"Just above my knees."

"What color?"

"Black."

I hear a door open and close before his breath is back on my ear. I shiver as if he's standing behind me.

"Is it tight?"

I laugh. "Are you going to try to have phone sex with me at three o'clock in the afternoon? From work?"

He exhales. "I sent you a text message to tell you not to wear a short dress to our friend date, and you're telling me you're wearing one right now, in plain sight, for everyone to see."

"And? You act like I'm wearing lingerie."

"No, but every male in Santa Barbara is going to be looking at those legs of yours and wishing they were wrapped around their waist, and seeing the tops of your tits and wishing they could pull the dress down to get a better look . . ."

"Oliver!" I interrupt, completely flustered. I'm starting to get hot flashes and breathe heavily, and he's not even there to do any of those things to me. "Friends!" I shout. "Friends! I'm not going out with you if you keep saying these things to me."

He doesn't speak for so long that I actually look at my screen to make sure he's still there.

"What does me saying these things do to you, Estelle?" he asks, his voice grating over me, making me shiver involuntarily.

"Nothing," I whisper.

"Nothing?" I close my eyes at the challenge in his voice, knowing I should have just ignored the question altogether. "It doesn't make you wish we were alone somewhere?"

"Why would I wish that?" I ask, hoping my voice sounds steadier than it feels.

"Because if we were, I'd slip my hand under your dress . . ." he pauses and drops his voice even lower. "Into your panties."

"Who says I'm wearing any?" I ask in a breath.

"Are you not wearing panties, naughty Elle?" The smile in his voice makes a blush creep over my face.

"Maybe."

"If I slip my hand under your dress and find that you're not, I wouldn't be able to resist. I'd have to pull the dress over your head and find out if you're completely naked beneath it."

"And what if I am?" I ask quietly. *Why am I playing this game? Why, why, why am I entertaining this? Why am I enjoying it?*

"You'd be in a lot of trouble," he says with a rough growl that makes my heart skip.

"Oh yeah? What kind of trouble?" I tease.

"First I'd want to taste you," he starts.

"No kissing on friend dates," I taunt with a smile.

"I wouldn't be kissing your mouth," he says in a voice that makes my heart lurch, before he continues, "I'd take my time, kissing my way down your body until I reach your ankles, and then I'd move back up slowly, my tongue tracing the inside of your thighs . . . tasting every inch of you . . ." His words are a purr, and I'm panting at the vivid picture he's painting for me as if I can feel his hot tongue on my sensitive skin. "I'll savor you until you beg for my lips and mouth to fuck that—"

"Oliver!" I snap, a moan escaping my lips. I totally asked for that—I know I did—but hearing the actual words from him make me feel too hot, too bothered, too . . . much. I take a breath and manage to squeak out, "Don't you have lives to save?"

"I'm on break," he responds nonchalantly, as if he hadn't just said all those things to me. "I do eat lunch, you know."

"You're phone-sexing on your lunch break?" My eyes pop open and blink rapidly to adjust to the light in my studio.

He chuckles. "I'm skilled like that."

"Okay . . . I'm going to let you go now so you can finish enjoying your lunch break."

"You don't have to. I have a raging hard-on right now, and I have to hide in this dark closet until I figure out what to do about it before I can go about my day."

I sigh, sagging down to the seat behind me. Images of him flirting with all the nurses flash through my mind before I can stop them. "I'm sure there are many willing nurses . . . and hospital execs willing to help you out with that."

Silence again, followed by a harsh exhale. "I wish you wouldn't think so poorly of me."

"I wish you wouldn't have put those thoughts there to begin with, but that's life, Bean."

"I hate it when you call me Bean," he whispers, his voice suddenly morphing into something deeper, something sadder.

"Why?" I whisper back, even though I'm completely alone.

"I have my reasons," he says, before clearing his throat. "Anyway, the problem is gone, so no need to call for backup. Not that I would have."

"Okay, well . . . have a good day," I say, not knowing what else to say.

"You too."

I put the phone down, and as I'm about to pick up a piece of broken glass to start on my sculpture, it vibrates again.

Next rule: no "Bean" on our friend date.

Okay.

No Chicken, either. Only Estelle and Oliver.

Winged creatures flutter inside me.

E & O

Thank u. It's been a rough week. I needed that smile today.

When he says things like this, he makes me want to cry. I know his job is hard, and the fact that he wants to continue with pediatrics once he finishes his residency is something I can't fathom. Seeing him looking so defeated the other day was so unlike him. And now this message? It breaks my heart.

::curtsies:: I'll be here all day.

In your dress?

LOL. In my dress!

Neither of us responds after that and, as I continue to make my usual shattered, kaleidoscope heart, I smile. He's the reason I started making these in the first place, even though Wyatt was the one who taught me how to perfect them so that the heart wouldn't fall apart. I can't help but wonder if that was a sign somehow, but I don't let that idea hang around for too long. There's no point in believing in destiny if you're too stubborn to give in to it.

Chapter 16

MY FRIEND DATE with Oliver ends up falling on a Saturday. We've only seen each other in passing since our last text message-slash-phone conversation, and I've mainly been focusing on painting the rooms with Micah and Dallas.

Oliver gave me three rules for our date: no short dresses, wear comfortable shoes, and no lipstick. I had to outright laugh at the last rule, and of course, I didn't abide by it. I dressed in jeans, low black boots, and a frilly, white tank top with a dark green jacket over it in case it gets cold later. I left my hair down and straightened it, and put on my make-up—dark red lipstick included. As I looked in the mirror, I smiled at my reflection. Before I met Wyatt, I never wore lipstick. He was the one who suggested it, along with more grown-up clothing. I liked the change. He was older than me and more knowledgeable. He'd lived a fuller life, so any time he made a suggestion, I took it to heart.

Before Wyatt, I dressed however I wanted—short dresses, tight skirts, big heels, you name it. He slowly got me away from those things and into more, what he would call "adult clothes." Mia thought I was an idiot. She said that, because we were only twenty-one, we could (and should) show off our assets.

"Especially you, with your dancer's body," she'd say.

I still wore Chucks and Doc Martens, and I got my nose pierced once. I just no longer walked around showing off too much leg or too much cleavage, and there was nothing wrong with that. I'm thankful for Wyatt and everything he gave me, but I decided I wouldn't change who I was for anybody again—especially a man.

I stomp down the stairs and grab a water bottle, drinking it as I flitter around looking for a snack.

"You look nice," Vic says as he opens the fridge.

I turn around and smile. "Thanks."

"Going on a date this early?"

I look at the time, it's ten, and Oliver should be here any minute now. And suddenly I start getting nervous. The whole reality of it slowly begins to sink in—Oliver will be picking me up for a friend date at my brother's house—his best friend's house. Clearly, we hadn't thought this through as much as we should have. I'm twenty-five. I'm not a child anymore, but to Victor, this is the ultimate no-no. I know because I've heard it time and time again. I know it because as much as he loves Oliver, and even goes as far as introducing him as his brother whenever they're together, he wouldn't like the idea of him dating me.

"Not really a date," I say. "I'm going out with Bean for a little while."

Victor frowns as he searches my face but nods slowly. "You guys seem to be bonding over the hospital thing?" He poses it as a question. A very curious question. Too curious coming from my attorney brother. I give him a tight smile and nod in response. The doorbell rings before he gets a chance to say anything else, and I practically sprint toward it.

"See you later," I call out over my shoulder as I grab my purse and open the door. I step outside without even looking up at Oliver, who's standing so close, the smell of his cologne hits me like a wall. I need to lock the door before I acknowledge him though. We need to get far away from here before Victor comes out and says something that would make us forget about this friend thing, forever.

"In a rush?" Oliver says with a chuckle as I sort through the million keys on my ring. My eyes snap to his dark jeans and trail up slowly to his narrow waist and to the burgundy polo clinging to his lean body. I glance at his face, flitting across the scruff that sort of hides his dimples, and the way his long hair brushes his high cheekbones. Those amazing green eyes are lit up in amusement. Fuck. He looks too good for a friend date. His eyes stay glued to my lips when I part them to respond, and he opens his mouth to say something at the same time, but before either of us can speak, the door opens and Victor peeks out.

"Huh. I thought you were kidding," he says, looking at Oliver.

"About?" I ask.

"What's up, man?" Oliver says at the same time, bumping his fist with Vic's.

"She said she was going out with you, but she was acting like she was hiding something from me, so I assumed she was lying."

My heart threatens to jump out of my chest, so I look away, focusing on the mountains in the distance.

"I'm not a child, Victor," I snap, as Oliver makes his own response.

"Why would she be hiding something?" Oliver says, his voice full of confusion. "Are you hiding something from us, Elle?"

My head jerks up to glare at him. "Are we going somewhere, or are you guys going to start grilling me? This is beyond ridiculous." I turn my glare to Vic, who laughs, shakes his head, and steps back inside the house.

"Have fun with Miss Grouchy Pants," he shoots over his shoulder.

I flash him my middle finger, which makes him laugh harder, and I stomp down the steps and head to Oliver's black Cadillac. I pull on the handle when I hear his footsteps approach, but the door remains locked. He stops beside me, and I see the keys in his hand, a thumb hovering over the unlock button.

"I'm not really into starting dates—friend or otherwise—on a bad foot," he says, beckoning me to look at his handsome, serious face.

"I'm not really into starting friend dates by getting grilled by both my brother and the dater."

His lips twitch. "The dater?"

"You know what I mean," I mutter.

Oliver smiles, a full-on devastating event. "I don't. I'd rather you clarify, so I don't get any funny ideas."

"Oliver."

"Estelle."

"You know the rules—no kissing, no touching, no funny business."

"And you know mine. No short dresses, no lipstick . . . yet here you are wearing red lipstick. *Red.* Total date color, by the way."

I bite the inside of my cheek to keep from laughing, but fail. "Red is a date color?"

"On those lips it is."

He holds my eyes for a moment—a really electrifying moment, where a current zips along my pulse—before he unlocks the car and reaches to open my door. I slip inside and wait for him to go around.

"Nice car," I say when he gets in and revs it up.

"Thanks. It was a med school graduation present from my dad."

I nod. "How is he?"

I only met his dad once, in passing, but have heard enough about him to know he's still feeling the effects of the strokes he'd had.

"He's . . . fine. Remarried. He seems happy, and his wife is nice, too. She stays on top of his health, so that's good."

"How are your mom and Sophie?"

He flashes me a quick smile before turning his attention to the road ahead. "They're doing really well. Sophie's pregnant again, and Sander is getting bigger by the minute. Mom's good too, she's so over the moon with them, that she cut back on work and stays home to help Soph."

"Wow. I'm impressed. I guess people do change."

"You'd be surprised at how much," he says in a low voice that resonates deliciously through me.

"So," I say, slapping my hands over my thighs. "Where are we going?"

"First, breakfast. Then a vineyard."

I turn my face to look at him. "You're trying to get me drunk on a friend date?"

I can tell he's trying really hard not to smile, or laugh. "You wore red lipstick on this friend date."

I laugh, sigh, and groan all in a matter of three seconds. "You're impossible."

"You make me this way."

"Let's talk about something else," I say, looking out the window. "Does this car have Bluetooth?"

Oliver chuckles. "Yes, Princess Estelle, is it up to par with your inspection?"

I stop moving my hand over the dash and set it back on my lap, feeling a blush creep into my face.

"I liked your old car better," I say.

Oliver's eyebrows hike up and he turns to gape at me. "You like my beat-up Maxima better than this?"

I shrug. "It was more cozy. This reminds me of the Batmobile, and there's nothing wrong with the Batmobile, but I like cozy."

He shakes his head and mutters something under his breath, but starts to look for my phone to hook up to Bluetooth. He already knows it's because I want to play my own music—I don't even have to explain. I used to bring my own CD whenever I was in the car with him. Oliver listens to two things: heavy rock and rap, and while I'm okay with both, I prefer the classics. The Steve Miller Band hasn't even gotten to the hook before they're interrupted by a call from Mia.

Oliver looks at me with a question in his eyes.

"If you don't mind," I say. He presses the button, and before I say hello, Mia's frantic voice comes through.

"What underwear are you wearing?" she asks.

My face goes hot for the second time this morning. From the corner of my eye, I see Oliver bite down on his lip.

"What?" I ask. "Mia, you're on speaker phone!"

"I don't care. This is an emergency. Do you not hear the shrill tone in my voice? What are you wearing under your clothes?"

My eyes snap to the side of Oliver's face, then out the front window, and finally, I pull my shirt slightly and look down, because I completely forgot what underwear I have on.

"Can you disconnect the phone?" I say to Oliver, who shakes his head in refusal. "Please. This is like . . . monumentally embarrassing."

"Just answer," he whispers.

"Who's that?" Mia asks.

"Oliver. We're in his car, and you're on the fucking Bluetooth."

She laughs. "Oh my God! I am so sorry, Bean!"

"What?" I shout. "He's not the one being harassed!"

"Oh, but now he is. So tell me—underwear?"

"White lace bra and matching boy shorts," I say, almost through my teeth, not missing the way Oliver's eyes snap to me with an approving look. I want to slap him for it, but I know nothing good would come of that, so I just cross my arms over my chest like a petulant child.

"Well, you know that favor you owe me," she begins. "The male model can only come at noon. Will you be available at that time?"

I look back at Oliver, who shakes his head. "Can we do it later? Like at. . . . six?" I say, asking him more than her.

"Elle! This is huge. I'll have to make more calls, and nobody can do quick shoots because they're all in LA for some sort of fashion thing!"

I huff out a breath and close my eyes, leaning on the headrest. "Let me call you back."

"Please let me know within the hour. Please."

"I will."

Oliver disconnects the call as we park in front of a little shack by the water.

"What was that about?" he asks, turning the car off and turning to face me.

"She has this photo shoot that has gone wrong in every way imaginable, and she asked me to do it for her, but apparently can't find a guy to shoot with me on such short notice."

"Do you want to do it? I mean, we can eat and go there instead . . ."

I sigh, looking out the window. "I know this isn't what you had planned for our friend date."

"But you want to be there for your friend. I get it, Elle. We can go over there after."

I turn back to him with a smile. "Thank you."

He shrugs like it's no big deal. "Are you hungry?"

"Starving."

We head inside and sit down in the balcony, where we're steps away from the water. There is a group of surfers out there tending their boards, while others are in the water waiting for better waves.

"This okay?" Oliver asks, nodding to the surfers.

I smile. "It's perfect."

"Okay. I wasn't sure." Realization dawns on me when his eyes move back toward the beach full of surfers.

"We can talk about it, you know? I'm really okay."

He smiles softly. "I don't want to make you uncomfortable."

"I'm fine."

He nods. "Have you gone back after it happened?"

"To the beach?" I ask, frowning. "Of course. I was there recently . . . a couple of days after the anniversary."

Surprise flashes in his green eyes. "I wanted to reach out to you after it happened. I'm sorry I didn't. I kept tabs through Vic, but I should have been there. Every time I thought about showing up at the gallery or seeking you out, I . . ." He sighs and turns his face away, his gaze back on the water. "I kind of panicked."

When the waitress comes, and we order our drinks and some food, I know I can just drop what he said. It's an out for both of us to go back to treading on more comfortable ground, but his words keep playing in my head.

"Panicked why?" I ask quietly, breaking a piece of bread and lathering it with strawberry jam, as he does. I feel his eyes on me and I look up to see him shrug.

"Because of the last time I saw you."

"At my parents' house," I say, nodding in understanding.

When the waiter comes back with our drinks, we drop the subject, because that one is too much for a friends-only date.

"So, Doctor Hart, how are you doing in your residency so far? Do you get quizzed? How does that work?" I ask, smiling. Oliver chuckles, as his eyes light up and those dimples flash in amusement.

"I'm proud to say all of my quizzes are behind me, but they do stay on my ass enough to know if I mess up . . . which I don't," he adds with a wink.

I grin. "Of course you don't, Mr. Perfect."

"*Doctor* Perfect," he corrects, raising an eyebrow. We share a laugh over that, but it dies down quickly when his gaze turns serious again. "Can I ask you something?"

"Of course," I respond, just as the waiter sets down our food. He ordered egg whites and bacon scramble, and I'm having Eggs Benedict over avocado. We push our plates toward the middle of the table so we can share, like we used to. Everything feels so . . . natural.

I smile, watching as he takes a bite of the avocado and eggs. He groans, making a face of pure bliss, and then smiles and cuts a piece to feed me. I place my hands on the edge of the table and lean into the fork, my eyes on his as I do. As soon as the explosion of flavors hits my tongue, I match his moan and close my eyes.

"That is so good," I say once I finish chewing. I smile when I notice Oliver's eyes are still on my mouth. "You had a question for me," I prompt. He swallows and nods.

"Was he really controlling over you?" he asks. I guess my face shows how taken aback by his question I am, because he adds a quick "If you don't mind me asking" to his statement.

"I wouldn't say he was controlling . . . not in a bad way, anyway . . . I'm sure Vic has painted a terrible picture of our relationship for you—this guy goes out of town constantly and leaves her alone without calling her for days and days and then comes back and tells her she can't dress the way she normally dresses and has to give up dance classes," I say, mimicking my brother's angry voice. "But he didn't make me do any of those things. I did those things because I wanted to."

Oliver's face twists into something I've never seen before. It's like grief or something, I don't know—but the sight of it makes my heart drop to my stomach.

After a moment, I whisper, "What are you thinking?"

He looks away from me, into the ocean, and when his green eyes find mine again, that look hasn't gone away. "I'm thinking . . ." He stops himself, as if he's having this tug of war in his mind over whether or not to tell me. I nod, encouraging him. "I'm thinking that I don't think I could go days and days without hearing your voice."

His answer is so not what I expected. The way it makes me feel, is so not what I was expecting. And the fact that I like both things makes me feel conflicted.

"What are you thinking?" he asks after a moment.

"That this is nothing like the last date I went on."

Oliver chuckles. "With that Derek guy?"

"Why must you have such a good memory?" I ask, smiling and shaking my head.

"Did you ever go out with him again?"

"Nope. Definitely not my type."

"What is your type?" he asks, his eyes dropping to my lips, which I lick because they're suddenly dry.

"I don't really have one. I just know he's not it," I say, shrugging.

"I think you do have one."

"Really?" I say. "Enlighten me, oh, wise one. What is my type?"

Oliver smiles, that lazy smile, and leans back in his seat, pushing his cup of water away slightly. "You like guys with long hair."

"You're only saying that because Wyatt had long hair," I say. He gives me a pointed look. "And you had long hair."

"Have," he corrects.

"It used to be longer."

"You want me to grow it back?"

I shrug, ignoring the butterflies circulating inside my stomach. "Doesn't matter to me. What does Jen like?"

Oliver smiles wider, scratching the scruff on his chin. "I never really thought to ask for her opinion."

The fact that he's not denying that there was something going on with her makes me want to chuck my silverware at him. His deep chuckle snaps me out of my murderous thoughts.

"What?" I ask, sounding snappier than I intend.

"You're so cute when you're jealous."

My mouth pops open. "I am not jealous. I don't get jealous—ever. I couldn't care less what you do in your free time."

He keeps smiling at me, both eyebrows raised now. I close my eyes when I feel my face heat, because I can't stand to look at the laughter in his eyes.

"Elle," he says. I jolt and open my eyes when I feel his large hands covering mine on the table. "I already told you I'm not sleeping with anybody. Now tell me—what do you like?"

"It doesn't matter what I like. Ask one of the nurses," I throw out and regret it immediately, because I realize that I do sound jealous.

Oliver laughs again. "Their opinions don't matter either."

"Yet mine does." I raise an eyebrow.

"Yours does," he responds, his smoldering look beginning to affect me in a way I can't handle well.

"What else is my type?" I ask, taking my hands from under his and putting them on my lap.

"You like older men."

"Again, you're just saying that because Wyatt was older."

"Too much older," he counters.

"No such thing."

His jaw tightens and he throws a curve ball my way. "Do you know how shocked I was when I found out you were engaged to him?"

My stomach flips. I know the answer to this. I could never forget it, but I somehow manage to shake my head slowly, suddenly wishing the wind would take me far away from here before I get lost in the look he's giving me. "How shocked?"

"Very."

"Why?"

Oliver closes his eyes and breathes out harshly. Just as he opens them again, the waitress comes back with the bill. He pays, and we thank her as we leave out the side door, closest to the beach.

"I always thought you were mine," he says. His words are so quiet they almost get lost in the gust of wind that attacks our faces, but I hear them as if he was screaming them to me. What do I say to that? How in the world could I possibly respond after all this time?

I'm thankful when Mia's phone call interrupts us. I close my eyes. "I forgot to call her back," I say, to him . . . to the beach . . . to no one in particular, before I answer.

"Elle, twelve is all I got. Nobody else can come at that time."

I look up at Oliver, who's staring down at me, and mute the phone. "Are you sure you're okay with me cutting this short? Do you want to go with me?"

"And watch you pose with another guy?" he says with a smile and a shrug. "Fuck it. Why not?"

I beam at him and un-mute the call. "I'll be there at twelve, but Oliver is coming with."

Mia laughs loudly. "This should be fun."

Chapter 17

FUN IS WAKING up on Christmas morning, or taking a ride in a brand new car, or having drinks with friends . . . or even that first cup of coffee in the morning that gives you the sometimes-false feeling that maybe the day will be awesome. Fun is a lot of things. Taking off your clothes and knowing that you agreed for an ex-fling, or whatever he was, to watch you in your underwear in bed with another man, also in his underwear? That is the polar opposite of fun.

"Elle, you can come out now!" Mia says, pounding on the door for the second time. I open it a little, just enough for me to poke my head out and take in the room. The bed is covered in fluffy white sheets, the window behind it is open to let in the natural light, and in the middle of it all, Oliver is talking to the half-naked model guy. He keeps nodding his head at whatever the model guy is saying.

"Is the guy gay?" I ask Mia in a low whisper.

"Marlon?" she asks with a laugh. "Most definitely not, according to the females he's worked with before."

My eyes widen. I'm already picturing his unwanted boner poking me in the ass. "What does that mean?"

"Relax. He's a total professional. I mean, he's fucked some of them, after the fact. Not on my bed . . . on theirs."

"Oh." I pull my robe shut and follow her out to the room. Both Marlon and Oliver turn their heads to look at me. Oliver is serious, while Marlon flashes me a huge, model face Colgate smile as he walks over to me.

"I'm Marlon," he says, extending his hand out to me.

"Estelle," I respond, shaking it.

"I know you don't usually do this, but relax, I'll take care of you," he says, pulling me toward the bed. I flash a look at Oliver, who raises his eyebrows and shakes his head at the whole thing.

"How long is this going to take?" I ask Mia.

"About an hour, so get comfortable, Bean."

"I'm not sure comfort is a possibility right now."

Mia looks over at him with a smirk. "Would you be more comfortable if you took over for Marlon?"

As Oliver seems to consider it, Mia tells me to take my robe off, so I do. It slides off and pools at my naked feet. Marlon is already sitting in the middle of the bed adjusting his boxers.

"Can I?" Oliver says suddenly. I look over my shoulder, wide-eyed.

"Are you serious?" Mia asks, gaping at him.

"If Elle is okay with it. I'm not here to dictate your shoot."

Mia doesn't think twice before ordering him around. "Take off your shirt. I need to make sure you're still in good shape before I kick Marlon out."

I'm about to put in my two cents, when Oliver pulls his polo over his head and my words, along with my sight, get lost somewhere between his sternum and the dips of his narrow waist.

"Yeah, still hot," Mia says. "Marlon, off the bed. You're not needed."

"What?" he says in disbelief. "What do you mean I'm not needed?"

"Sorry. You and Elle have zero chemistry, and I need major chemistry on this shoot."

"We only just met," he argues, as he gets out of bed.

"And I already know the chemistry isn't there," Mia says. "I'll call you next week when Miranda is back and schedule something then."

"Okay," he says with a shrug. "Have fun," he says to me.

When he leaves to get dressed, Mia turns to me and says, "Just to be clear, I wouldn't kick him out of bed under normal circumstances, if you know what I mean."

I laugh. "Neither would I."

Oliver clears his throat behind me, and I look at him with a smile and a shrug.

"All right, Ollie boy, strip and get on the bed. Elle, make yourself comfortable on it. You want music? I'll play music anyway, so just nod."

"You're such a pain." I laugh, as she taps her iPod and *Just Breathe* by Pearl Jam stars playing. I stop laughing and glare at her. "This is the kind of music you're going to play?"

She shrugs. "My shoot, my rules."

Oliver walks over to me on the bed, wearing a pair of black boxer briefs and nothing else. It takes every ounce of everything inside me not to devour his body with my eyes. He's not even really muscular like Marlon, but he's perfect, in that lean, California surfer–dude-and-former-baseball-pitcher kind of way. He gets on the bed and practically crawls to me like a fucking lion, and I'm starting to feel like a cat in heat, so I look away.

"You okay?" he asks, low enough for only me to hear.

I nod, still not looking at him.

"You don't feel like I completely took over the shoot, right? Or like I'm being controlling or anything, right?" he asks.

I meet his gaze with a frown, and realize I don't feel that way at all, despite the fact that he sort of did and he is sort of being a little controlling . . . sort of . . . right? I mean, he's a goddamn doctor, not a model. This isn't even his world!

"I'm not mad or anything, if that's what you're asking."

"That's not what I'm asking."

He settles himself so that his legs are around my body, not touching me, but just . . . around, and my legs are together and bent. I bring them closer to me and place my chin on my knees.

"You're different people, you know," I whisper.

A smile tugs on his lips. "So you agree that it was a good call for me to let the model with a thing for fucking the women he shoots with leave?"

"I didn't say that," I respond, hiding my smile behind my leg.

"But you agree. I know you," he says, running his hand up my leg ever so softly until he reaches the hand I have resting on my knee. He holds on to the tip of my ring finger, and I'm reminded of the last time he touched it.

"You have an obsession with my ring finger. Have you noticed?"

He drops my hand suddenly. "Do I?"

I nod, not breaking eye contact. "You always touch it."

He doesn't say anything, but something in his eyes makes my insides stir and his words from earlier—the ones he doesn't think I heard—come back to whisper at me.

I always thought you were mine.

I wish I had the balls to ask him about that, but I don't, and Mia's clicking camera interrupts us anyway.

"Okay, here's the deal, I'm going to sort of guide you through this, but I want this to be as natural as possible. We'll do a couple where you guys are looking at each other first, and then we'll see where it goes."

"I'm kind of worried about your 'we'll see where it goes,'" I mutter under my breath, earning a laugh from Oliver.

"All right, darlings, let all that pent-up sexual tension come out and play," she says, stepping away.

Oliver and I stare at each other, wide-eyed, wondering what we've gotten ourselves into. Or at least I thought we were both wondering that, until his shock dissolves and his face darkens, and I'm left with a thrashing sense of holy shit as Mia walks away to open the blinds. Suddenly it hits me that I'm in my underwear with Oliver—who is also in his underwear—and we're surrounded by needy music. I gulp in a deep breath.

"You okay?" he asks, his voice too low, too husky, as his fingers run over my calves.

I shiver, close my eyes, and nod.

The bed shifts, and I feel him move closer. When I open my eyes again, his nose is almost touching mine.

"Perfect!" Mia says. "Hold that pose!"

The look in his eyes holds me there. I can't really think of even blinking anyway.

"Elle, do you mind taking off your bra?" Mia asks, lost behind the lens, and Oliver inhales sharply, his eyes widening at the request. "You're not showing your boobs in the pictures, I promise."

"Ummm . . . okay." I have zero qualms about nudity, though I have to admit that this entire thing is making me nervous as hell.

"You need help taking it off?" Oliver asks.

"No."

"Actually, that would make for good pictures," Mia chimes in, and I turn to glare at her. She shrugs. "What? Bean, you've seen your fair share of tits before, right? You don't mind?"

"This is definitely the most awkward form of punishment I have ever received. I think I'll take the spanking next time," I say to Mia, making her smile and Oliver laugh.

I drop my head as he wraps his arms around me and finds the clasp of my bra.

"You need to look at him," Mia says. I take a breath, and with what I find in his gaze, it takes everything in my willpower not to look away or close my eyes again.

His fingers unclasp my bra, and as soon as it loosens, he brings his hands up to my shoulders and ever so slowly, drags the straps down my arms, never breaking eye contact with me. My stomach flips, my heart is in my throat, and I feel like I may or may not vomit because of the amount of nerves circulating inside of me right now. I just pray really hard the last one does not happen.

"Okay?" he whispers, his breath on my mouth.

"Perfect," I whisper back.

Our noses touch.

"Elle, put your right hand over your boobs like you're shielding them. Bean, keep looking at her like that and fix her hair on the side facing me," Mia says.

I bring my arm over myself as one of Oliver's fingers thread into my hair and the other cups the side of my face. I'm completely lost in his eyes. I'm mesmerized by the way he's handling me, looking at me. I can't seem to do anything else but breathe and stare back.

"You are so beautiful," he says. His guttural voice mixed with the lust in his eyes make my stomach dip and my lips part. Oliver takes it as his cue to inch his face closer and brush his mouth against mine.

"Perfect," Mia says, reminding me that we have an audience. "Shit. I'll be right back. I need my back-up battery, and I left it in the fucking car."

I pull back, not taking my eyes from his, and drop my hand from my chest. I can tell he's having a really hard time not looking down. I smile at him, wondering how long it'll take for his eyes to drop, but they don't. He continues to look into my eyes, search my face, touch my hair, my cheeks . . . He scoots forward and pulls my legs apart so that they're overlapping his in a scissor on either side, and our naked chests are almost touching.

"How much longer do you think we'll have to do this?" I whisper, my eyes flickering between his mouth and his eyes.

"I don't know. I'm kind of hoping it takes all day."

"It definitely makes for an interesting friend date," I say with a smile.

He flashes his charming half-smile. "You still think this is a friend date?"

The door opens and shuts, and we turn our heads at Mia's return. She stops dead in her tracks when she sees us. "Holy shit. That pose! If I can get a couple of shots with that pose, I think we're done!"

Oliver and I face each other again as she sets up the camera.

"Why'd you do it anyway? Take over Marlon's spot. I mean, other than the overprotective, big brother thing."

He gives me a confused look, which almost looks comical with the way his mouth drops. "You think this is a big brother thing?"

I shrug. "You tell me."

"Elle, I'm sitting in a bed practically naked with you, doing everything in my power to keep myself from getting hard because we have an audience, and as you can see, nothing is working." I look down, of course, and gape at the large condition inside his boxers. "Yeah. So obviously, I don't see you as a little sister. I can't believe you would even . . ." He trails off with a huff.

"Okay. Look at each other again," Mia says. "Same pose and hold it."

His hand goes back to my hair, mine goes back over my boobs, and we look into each other's eyes again.

"I want to kiss you so bad right now," he whispers against my lips.

"Don't," I say in a breath. "That's a rule."

"I don't like rules."

"Oliver, please don't."

"I love it when you call me Oliver," he says, his bottom lip settling between both of mine. He doesn't move though, just stakes out there until I have to close my mouth over his lips. Then he groans and moves his mouth against mine, and before I know what's happening, I'm on my back, and he's on top of me deepening the kiss that wasn't supposed to happen. But when his tongue touches mine, and his fingers thread into my hair, I can't help but reciprocate, and we end up in a tangled mess of sheets and tongues and rough hands down my sides, and mine down his toned back. It isn't until we hear a loud cough that we snap and tear away from each other.

"Well . . . that was . . ." Mia says, fanning her face with her hand. "I can honestly say that I've seen a lot of shit happen in shoots, and that was by far the hottest. Okay, lovelies, we're all done here. Go get dressed. Elle, we need to talk."

Oliver pushes himself off me and brings me up with him. We're both still catching our breaths from the kiss, but now that the lights are on again and the moment is broken, I feel the weight of what just went down, and I can't bring myself to look at him. Instead, I look around, trying to locate my robe, which I wrap around myself as I stand up. Heading to the bathroom, I refuse to turn and look at him. This is what we do, anyway. We have our moments and then nothing. And this wasn't even supposed to be a moment, so I have nobody to blame but myself for the way my heart feels like it's going to break at any moment.

In the bathroom, I look in the mirror and bring my hand to my lips. Why does he make me feel this way every time? I close my eyes, think of Wyatt and his lips . . . his touch . . . and I feel guilty for having this moment with a man he would never approve of. Not that Wyatt knew Oliver, but he knew of him. He got an earful from me about Oliver when we first met, and after that, he just never liked him. He was furious when he found out I extended an invitation to the grand opening of the gallery to him, because he said Oliver didn't deserve to breathe the same air as me. He said that I was too good for somebody like him. At the time, I believed it. I believed it because when we want to believe something, that's what we do. Wyatt loved me despite my brokenness. I loved him because of his. But now I'm back at square one, and I can't figure out if there's anything really left of me to love.

Chapter 18

I WALK OUT of the bathroom and find Mia and Oliver engrossed in a quiet conversation. From the look on her face, I know she's telling him to stay away from me, as if I'm some damsel in distress who can't fend for herself. When they hear me approach, they stop talking and turn their attention back to the camera in her hand.

"The pictures look incredible," she gushes, turning it so I can see the little screen.

"Wow. I can't even believe it's us. We look so . . ." My eyes snap up to Oliver, who's staring at me with a look I want to get lost in forever. I look away quickly, back down at the rest of the pictures.

"Won't this be bad for you?" I ask, looking at him again. "I mean, for work. For your residency or future work."

He shrugs and looks at the pictures. "I want copies."

"For what?" I ask a little too defensively.

"Your faces aren't going to show all that much," Mia says, interrupting us. "Trust me, when I'm done editing these, you're both going to want to frame them."

"What magazine did you say this was for?" I ask.

"V!"

"Holy shit," I breathe, looking at Oliver, who looks impressed.

"I know. I'm so excited!"

"Yeah. Exciting. I feel like I might throw up," I say quietly.

"Why? They're beautiful pictures."

"Yeah, but I'm posing half naked with Victor's best friend!"

"And?" she says.

I look at her like she's crazy and turn my attention to Oliver, who's looking the other way now. Of course, he hadn't thought of that.

"When does this come out?" I ask.

"In . . . a month? Right before Thanksgiving."

I nod. I guess if I tell my parents and Victor about this before they have a chance to see it, it won't be so bad. Victor will definitely need time to process it.

"Okay. What else do you need?"

Mia looks at Oliver. "I need to talk to Elle. I can take her home if you want."

He looks at me, scratching the back of his neck. I shrug, he shrugs back and then says, "Sure," before giving us each a kiss on the cheek and leaving.

That's when I start to feel murderous. How can he just leave?

"Can you believe this shit?" I say after he's out of earshot. "We just did all of that." I signal to the bed. "And he still leaves in the middle of what was supposed to be our date, right after my brother and these pictures being viewed by the public is brought up. I don't even know why I bother."

Mia rolls her eyes. "You know exactly why you bother. He's like your drug. No matter how far you go or what crazy measures you take to stay away from him, you always end up back where you started."

"Not this time," I say with finality. "Nothing has really happened this time."

Mia laughs. "Elle, what I just saw, I mean, what I just captured, says otherwise," she says waving her camera around. "You can't make this shit up."

"It doesn't matter."

"You said you needed to move on."

"Yeah, but not with him. You said so yourself, it's a bad idea."

"Maybe I was wrong. Maybe it's not a bad idea."

"Oh, really?" I roll my eyes. "You got all that from a few pictures?"

"No. I got all that from talking to him. I think he's grown up."

I wave frantically in the direction of the door. "He just left! Again!"

Mia shrugs. "Yeah, because I asked him to. Do you feel guilty for entertaining the idea of hooking up with someone?"

"I don't think so. I think it's just him I'm afraid of."

Mia leans forward and gives me a hug. "Love is supposed to be scary."

"Love is supposed to be comfortable," I reply.

"Do you really believe that?"

"Wyatt was comfortable."

"Wyatt didn't make you go on tantrums and break your brand new Isaac Mizrahi Target plates because he didn't call, or go into seclusion for weeks on end when you heard he was going to be living four hours away."

I drop my arms and stare at her, feeling like she just said the most significant thing in the world.

"Do you think it's possible to have different kinds of love?"

"You mean like head over heels in love and then just in love?" she asks.

I shrug, following her out the door. "Yeah, like soul mate love as opposed to just regular love."

"Soul mate love?" she asks, laughing. "As far as I'm concerned, the only soul mate I have is you. And maybe Robert, since he's my twin, and you know how we twins are."

"I don't think . . . I mean, I don't want to think that I didn't love Wyatt with everything I had. That makes me feel so bad, you know? He died so young, and to think I wasn't the love of his life makes me sad."

"Oh, honey," Mia says, pulling me to her as we walk side-by-side to her car. "You loved him so much, though. You gave up so much for him, Elle. Dance, your friends, time you used to spend with your family . . ."

"Yeah, but he gave me a lot too. The studio . . . he taught me how to hone my craft . . . and he left me his house."

"I'm not saying he wasn't a good guy for you, but was he your forever guy? You know I can't agree to that."

We drive in silence, only singing along to her Taylor Swift CD when a song we both like comes on. When we get to my brother's house, I'm a little sad that Oliver's car isn't there. He really ran off. Again. Unbelievable.

It isn't until after I shower and climb in bed, that I decide that I can't leave it alone. Not this time. I send him a text message and look at my phone until he responds.

I can't believe you left.

Mia said you needed to talk. I would have stayed if you wanted me to.

I wanted you to.

Why?

I stare at the phone as if it's going to explain why men are so stupid, and when it doesn't, I decide that I can't give him an answer either. I toss it on the nightstand and pull the covers over my head. The sun is just going down, so it's still early, but I feel drained. I sleep until something wakes me . . . a whisper on my face . . . the caress of a hand on my head. My eyes pop open, and I push myself to sit quickly.

"It's just me."

I gasp and look at Oliver beside me.

"What are you doing here?" I whisper, looking from him to my slightly open door. "Where's Vic?"

He shrugs a shoulder and puts a finger over my lips to silence me. "He passed out already. Can I stay?"

I frown. "What's wrong with your bed?"

"You're not in it."

I push aside the way my heart is thundering inside me. "I've never even seen your bed."

"Would you like to?" he asks, dropping his voice.

"Stop looking at me like that."

"Like what, lovely Elle?" he asks, trying to smother a smile.

"Like you want to swallow me whole."

"Has it ever occurred to you, that maybe I do?" He moves closer, and I hold my breath. "But no funny business tonight. I promise. Scout's honor."

"You were never a Boy Scout."

He grins. "Okay, but I promise I won't try anything. I just want to be with you tonight."

"The last time you said that—"

"I was an idiot."

I close my eyes. "What about my brother?"

"What about him?"

"What if he comes up here and catches you?"

Oliver's hand grabs my waist, and he pulls me to him so that we're nose to nose. "What would you want me to do if he does?"

"I don't know," I whisper, my breath catching at the dark look in his eyes.

"Do you want me to tell him that you're all I think about?" he asks, matching my whisper.

I shake my head, and our noses kiss. I'm not ready for Victor to know about whatever this is yet.

"Tell me why you wanted me to stay."

"Because we weren't done with our friend date."

Oliver chuckles. "That friend date had me going home and taking the longest shower of my life."

"I took one too," I say in a whisper, my cheeks burning as I look at him through my lashes. His face turns completely serious, and he groans.

"God, Elle, why'd you have to say that to me?"

I laugh. "Say what? That I touched myself thinking about you?"

His eyes hood a little. "If you want me to keep my word, you need to stop talking about that."

"Okay." I grin and turn around so that my back is on his chest. He snuggles me close, creating a nook for my body. "Tell me a story," I say, yawning.

"About what?" he murmurs, dropping a kiss on my head.

"Anything. Like the ones you used to tell me when we were young."

"Okay." He pauses and holds me tighter. "Once upon a time, there was this little girl named Cassia. She used to walk around talking to herself."

I nudge him. "To the plants, not herself."

He laughs. "Oh, that's right. She used to talk to the plants. One day this little boy named Jeter asked her—"

"Jeter?" I ask, looking at him over my shoulder. "Like the baseball player?"

Oliver laughs and shakes his head, snuggling into me. "I forgot how many interruptions these stories lead to," he says against my neck.

"Well, you're always talking about how weird I am, but listen to your stories."

His sigh sends a shiver down my body. "Okay, let's move on to joke time then."

I groan. "I hate your jokes."

"You're not supposed to tell me that!" he scoffs as his hands trail down my body. "What are you wearing anyway?"

My eyes snap open, and I'm glad we're cloaked in darkness. "It's one of Wyatt's shirts," I whisper.

Oliver's hands stop moving over my stomach. "Did you keep a lot of his things?"

I turn around in his arms and prop my elbow up on the pillow. He does the same. "Only his shirts. I gave his parents back his pictures and a couple of other things I didn't want. But I can't seem to get rid of the shirts."

"Is it because you miss him?" he asks.

"Is it bad that I was wondering the same thing the other day? That all these questions are suddenly popping up in my head?"

Oliver brushes my face with the back of his hand. "Like what?"

"You really want to know?"

"Of course. I want to know everything you want to tell me."

I stay silent a moment longer, and once again wonder why he really took Marlon's spot in the photo shoot. Maybe he was just protecting me from a creeper, and it wasn't really his way of marking his territory. This is Oliver, after all. He doesn't really mark territory; he just goes over it on a bulldozer and leaves before he can even notice the damage.

"Okay. Well, when he first died, I felt like I couldn't breathe—especially at night when I was alone—but as time went on, it got better . . ."

"And now?"

"And now sometimes I don't miss him at all," I whisper. I feel ungrateful . . . un-loyal. Like it's a disgrace for thinking it, let alone voicing it aloud, especially to Oliver. I turn back around and settle into Oliver's warmth again.

"It's okay for you to find happiness after him. You know that, right?" he says, his voice on my neck again.

I swallow. "I guess so. Sometimes I feel guilty about it though. We lived together. We were engaged. It was a big commitment."

Oliver stays quiet for a long time before speaking up. "For a long time, I couldn't imagine myself ever getting married. It's no secret that I've always had an aversion to commitment," he says quietly. "Unless you count school and work—those things I can commit to—but women . . . growing up, I never found one I wanted to commit to." He whispers the last part, and my heart lodges in my throat before he continues. "Except this one girl. She always looked at me like I was somebody, even though I wasn't. And of course, my luck would have it that the one person I feel like I can actually commit to is the one person I can't have. I tried so hard to stay away from her." He drops a kiss on my shoulder. "I kept reminding myself what would happen if my best friend were to find out about my feelings. I kept them to myself for so long, even after the girl asked me to kiss her. And after I asked the girl to let me kiss her. And after she let me touch her in the bathroom of a party. And after she touched me in a stranger's bedroom."

"Why didn't you ever tell her how you felt?" I whisper. He tucks his face into my neck, and I close my eyes when I feel his breath on me.

"Because I was an idiot."

"Hey, Oliver?"

"Yeah?"

"Do you think I can sleep with your shirt tonight?" I whisper.

If possible, he squeezes me tighter and buries his head further into me. I'm about to take the words back and say I was just kidding or something, when he pulls his arms away and sits up. I follow his movement and watch through the darkness as he pulls his shirt over his head. I do the same, slowly pulling mine over my head and tossing it to the furthest corner of the room, by the closet.

"Hey, Oliver," I whisper again.

"Yes, Elle?" he whispers back. I can make out the way his chest rises and falls, but not much else, so I inch closer.

"I want you to touch me." I screw my eyes shut. Not because I'm shy by any means, but because I haven't had this in so long. So, so long. And I'm scared at what his reaction will be. Worse, I'm scared of what mine will be if he gives in.

He throws his head back and exhales. Just when I think he's going to tell me he can't, or that my brother will wake up at any moment, or that he needs to go, his hands reach out and graze my arms.

"Only if you want to," I add when his hands stop moving.

His deep chuckle vibrates the bed. "Only if I want to," he repeats, leaning closer, his hands splaying over my ribcage on either side. "God, Estelle, you don't know how bad I want to."

Pushing my body forward, I brace myself on his shoulders. His thumbs brush just under my breasts, so I lean in a little more, hoping he gets the hint. His laugh lets me know he totally gets the hint and is purposely ignoring it.

"Bean, please," I whisper-pant as my hands grip him tighter.

"Bean isn't in right now," he whispers, dipping his head and plucking tender kisses from my neck to my clavicle, over my shoulder and back in.

"Oliver, please," I say, throwing my head back when his lips reach the hollow of my throat.

"Tell me what you want, baby. Tell me where you want me to touch you," he murmurs against me in a voice that sets me on fire.

"Everywhere. Just . . . anywhere."

His hands finally move up so that his thumbs brush over my nipples slowly, causing a shiver of pleasure to rock through me.

"More," I say, pulling him down on the bed so I can straddle his legs. I rock against him as I bring my lips to his. He groans against my mouth, plunging his tongue into it and exploring like a starved man looking for his next meal. The pressure on his hands doesn't increase though. He just continues to softly explore my body as if I'm made of glass. His fingers feather up and down my sides, over my breasts, along my neck, down my stomach, and stop right above the elastic of my panties.

"Please keep going," I say in a voice that's not mine. My legs are quivering, and he hasn't even really touched me where I need him to. Oliver moves his head back and pulls my face into the moonlight coming through the window. He searches my face, and I nod frantically as he smiles.

"If I do this, are we still on a friends date?" he asks. The fact that he can make jokes when I feel like I'm falling apart is a little infuriating, so instead of answering, I grab his hands and push them down so that he gets the hint. Oliver shakes his head. "Is this still a friends date?"

"I don't know," I whisper, rather loudly, my impatience beginning to get the best of me. "I don't care. Just touch me!"

He grins and moves a hand into my panties, his moan matching mine when he finds how wet I am already. "You're hazardous to my health. You know that?"

"It's a good thing you're a doctor then," I whimper when he plunges his finger inside me. He does a little hook with it that makes my eyes roll back.

"You like that?" he asks against my neck. He increases his tempo when I nod against him.

My hands move from his shoulders down his chest and into his boxers. Before he has a chance to say anything, I close my hand over his length and squeeze.

"Jesus fucking Christ, Estelle," he groans, shifting his weight to give me better access.

"You're so hard," I whisper, leaning forward to kiss him again.

"You're so wet," he says against my lips.

"You're so big," I say. I had forgotten how he looked, how he felt. He chuckles breathlessly, as I continue to move my hand to match the rhythm he's making with his.

"You're so tight," he groans, his thumb circling over my clit as he moves his other fingers inside me.

"I'm going to . . . I'm going to . . ." I pant just before my vision becomes bright lights. I keep moving my hand over him until he's grunting, and I feel hot liquid over my hand.

We sit there for a moment, wordlessly, only the sounds of our heavy breaths audible in the room. Finally, he drops a kiss on my forehead and gets up to go clean himself. I don't know if he expects me to follow, but as I look at his broad shoulders walking out of the room, I can't help but wonder if that was a mistake. He brings back a wet towel and wipes my hands thoroughly, and when he comes back again, he takes the place he had before.

Neither of us says a word as we settle down again, his arms around me as I lay in the little cocoon that might as well have been carved out and made for my body to fit in.

"I like you in my arms," he says, finally, his breath against my ear.

My eyes close. "I do too." Too much. Way too much.

"We broke a lot of your rules today."

"We did. Too many of them," I say, smiling into the darkness.

"When do we go on our next friends date?"

"You're sleeping in my bed tonight," I remind him.

"You wore red lipstick."

I laugh. "You and the stupid lipstick."

"I'm just saying—a woman only wears that color on dates when she wants to get laid."

I shake my head, laughing, and he laughs along, holding me tighter. We're quiet for a while, and I think maybe he's fallen asleep. I feel myself relax, and sleep begins to drag me under again. When I wake up the next day, to the sun blasting in my face, I realize I'm alone in bed. A sense of sadness threatens to wash over me, but I push it aside. This was my own doing. I asked for it. I pushed him for it. Those thoughts don't alleviate the pain I feel though. I close my eyes again and exhale. When I open them back up, I spot Wyatt's discarded shirt, thrown in a corner like some washed up memory, and suddenly I get even sadder. He may not have been the perfect man, and we may have had a lot of differences, but Wyatt never made me feel like I wasn't special to him. He never walked out after sex without giving me a kiss or telling me how lovely I was. He would have never, ever just left me alone in bed without acknowledging that we shared something special.

Tears brim in my eyes as I stagger to the closet and pick up the shirt. I hug it to me, asking it for forgiveness, because that was a total dick move on my part. Then I start crying because I'm talking to a shirt while wearing another man's shirt. A man I let touch me, a man that once again left me without a goodbye. The door opens suddenly, and I look up just in time to see Oliver walk in. The smile on his face instantly drops when he takes me in—the crying face . . . me clutching my dead fiancé's shirt for dear life . . .

"I thought you left," I say in a hoarse whisper.

He doesn't move, doesn't speak . . . just stares for a moment longer. Finally, he walks over to me and wraps his arms around my head, pulling me into his hard chest.

"I wasn't going to leave without saying goodbye," he says against my hair. I think of all the times he did . . . all the times *we* did . . . and wonder if this time it'll be different. "I had a great night."

"I did too," I whisper against him.

He drops a kiss on my head. "I don't want to mess this up, Elle. So I'm going to give you some space, okay? Not because I don't want you . . . not because I don't think last night was incredible . . . but because I don't want to push you." He tilts my face to look at him, and my heart lodges in my throat as I wait for those green eyes to spear through me. "I want this to happen."

"Okay" is all I get to whisper before he drops his hand and walks out the door. I'm not sure what to do with any of that. I don't know what "that" is. All I know is that I'm scared to want him as much as I do. I'm terrified that I'll get burned again.

A couple of days later, I wake up and throw on the navy scrubs Nurse Gemma gave me on a day that painting got extra messy. When I show up at the hospital, I see her at the nurses' station, and she laughs.

"You here to offer back up?" she asks.

"Not unless you want the malpractice lawsuits to start pouring in."

"Never give Estelle anything with a needle. Noted."

I laugh, shaking my head. "I'll be quick today. I just want to make sure it looks perfect."

"Last day," she says, smiling. "I won't lie; I'm going to miss having that Micah guy around."

"Well, there's always the maternity wing."

"Nooooo! Don't send him over there! I have to stake my claim over him first!"

After talking a little longer, I finally make it to the room we've been working on, and pull the blinds open to check on the progress of the drying paint. I smile at the beauty of what we created and select a small brush to touch up the clouds that are missing some color.

"I heard you were in here," Oliver says behind me, almost making me paint outside of the lines.

"Never sneak up on a person holding a paint brush."

He chuckles. "Sorry. You want help?"

I stop moving the brush and shoot him a frown over my shoulder, which makes him shrug.

"I can fill in."

"Grab a brush. The clouds need another coat."

He does as I ask and stands beside me. I look over at the cloud he's painting and move on to the next one, which is a couple of steps further away.

"You look great in scrubs, by the way."

I try not to smile and fail. "Thanks."

"You would make a good nurse," he adds.

I stop painting and turn to him with a raised eyebrow. "But not a good doctor?"

"Entertaining that question would mean that I'm saying doctors are more important than nurses, and they're not. If anything it's the other way around . . . either way, I'm not going there. I will say, though, that you would be good at any profession where you deal with people."

"I'll keep that in mind if this painting thing doesn't work out," I say with a smile.

"Meaning never?" he responds with a chuckle as he moves to the next cloud, on the opposite side of the room. "What do you think you would be if art didn't exist?"

"Dead."

Oliver lowers his paintbrush and looks at me. "Don't ever say that."

Somehow, with one look, he makes me feel the intensity in his words.

"Okay, fine, probably a teacher or a school counselor."

He nods and goes back to painting. "For the record, I think what you do for a living is perfect. This whole project is really incredible."

"Just doing what I can." I shrug.

"Why are you doing it?" he asks, walking toward me. "I know how much you love working with kids, so I knew coming here and painting with them would be something you would like . . . but this? This is a lot, Elle."

I turn away from his gaze—back to the cloud in front of me—and look at the wall as I answer. "It sucks to be having a bad day and have to get up in the morning and go about your business because it's expected. Imagine having an illness and having no choice but to come here and be stuck looking at the same four ugly walls, every single day. It makes all of my bad days seem so stupid when I hear these kids talk about what they're dealing with, and they don't even complain about any of it," I say, letting out a breath as I drop my hand and turn to face him. My heart skips a beat at what I find in his eyes. I walk to him and brush my fingers under his left eye. "You look so tired."

"This is what twenty hours straight looks like, but it's like you said, they don't complain, and that gives me no reason to complain either," he says.

I drop my hand and rock back in my heels, still looking at him. "You're a good man, Oliver Hart."

His lips curve into a smile, and I watch his hand come up. I brace myself for his touch, but he drops his hand before it reaches my face. "You're a great woman, Estelle Reuben."

"Art is pretty selfish. I create things for myself and hope others like it, but it's not like I'm thinking about the greater good when I make anything. What you do, on the other hand, is completely selfless."

His green eyes twinkle. "That's where you're wrong. This job may seem selfless, but helping those kids makes me feel like I'm leaving my footprint. When I help them leave in a healthier state than when they got here, that's . . ." He sighs, looking away for a moment. When his eyes meet mine again, he looks completely happy. "It's everything. It makes me feel like I matter."

"You do matter," I say with a smile.

"So do you. You think art is selfish, but I think it's pretty giving. I can't do this." He waves his hands around the room. "I spend sleepless nights and endless days in here making sure these kids are getting better, but aside from the days that I announce that they can go home, I won't put a smile on their face like this will."

His words make my heart soar. I turn back to the wall and finish the cloud I'm working on before walking back to the supplies and dropping my brush there. Oliver has a way of making even the smallest things you do, seem like they're making a worldly difference. It's part of his charm, I guess.

We say goodbye, teetering on unchartered territory. I've never gotten one hundred percent of Oliver. As far as I know, only his job gets that. In the past, we've been friends . . . and then more than friends . . . but this feels like something else. I'm scared to let go and get more than what I bargained for. I'm also scared that I won't.

Chapter 19

Past

Oliver

I COULDN'T REMEMBER the last time I'd cried, if ever, but when I went to visit my dad in the hospital and saw the way half of his body was slouched, that's exactly what I felt like doing. He may not have been an ideal father to us, but he was always larger than life. Between seeing him all crumpled up, trying to ace all of my finals, and my job as an undergrad student helper—which consisted of everything from tutoring to helping them pick their classes—I was stressed.

This particular morning, I'd settled myself into a corner table in the coffee shop by my mom's house, and was working on a Quantum Physics paper and trying to keep my mind off my dad's condition, when Estelle sat down in front of me. I looked up in time to see her cross her legs and smile at me as she closed her mouth over the straw of the cup she'd been holding.

"What are you doing in this neck of the woods?" she asked.

I let out a deep breath and put my pen down. I hadn't seen her in a couple of weeks. The last time we'd hung out was in a crowded Chili's. I'd gone with Victor and took a girl with me because I had no idea Estelle would be there. She hadn't acted like she cared. She'd been talking to Mia and Jensen most of the time, but it had felt awkward to me, having her there after we'd kissed so many times . . . after I wanted more all of those times . . . and there I was with someone else. I felt relieved seeing her now, and having her talk to me as if everything was totally okay, which was something I'd feared wouldn't happen after that night.

"You cut your hair," I said after a beat.

"Only the front, and I'm already regretting that decision." She brushed the long bangs out of her face.

"It looks good on you."

"Are you meeting someone here?" she asked, looking around. She looked hesitant suddenly. I smiled, wondering if she meant the girl from Chili's.

"Would it bother you if I was?"

Her eyes widened before her face settled into a small, thoughtful frown. "Not really."

"Are you meeting someone here?" I asked, hoping she wasn't. Why? I didn't know. She was free to date whomever she wanted, but that didn't mean I wanted to witness any of it. Her mouth turned up slowly as if she could read my thoughts. I was starting to think she could.

"Nope. I just left a terrible date."

"Why was it terrible?" I asked, leaning in a little closer, both of my elbows on the table, as hers were.

"He talked about himself the entire time. Total jock move. All the girls want him, all the guys want to be him," she said, mimicking a guy's voice as she rolled her eyes. I laughed.

"That sounds pretty terrible. Why would you even give a jock the time of day?" I asked, raising an eyebrow.

"I can think of one jock I like . . . but he's sooo nerdy," she said, her eyes dancing in so much amusement that I had to chuckle.

"Tell me more about this nerdy jock."

"Well," she started, dropping her gaze. She started using the condensation from her iced coffee to draw circles on the table as she spoke. "He's really good looking, if you like tanned surfer dudes with long hair . . . and ridiculous dimples . . ." She looked up at me and smiled shyly in a way that made my heart stop. "He's a really good guy, but rumor has it he's not much into relationships."

"It doesn't sound like he's good for you. You can't base a relationship on hard abs and dimples."

She grinned. "I didn't say anything about hard abs."

I shrugged. "I put two and two together. What else do you like about this nerdy jock?"

"I like how smart he is. I like the way he makes me feel when he talks to me . . . when he looks at me . . ." A blush spread over her cheeks. "When he kisses me."

I tried to ignore the hammering in my chest. "You think pretty highly of a guy who's not into relationships . . ."

"We all have our downfalls, and that just happens to be his," she said, shrugging as she looked away.

"What if he was into relationships?" I don't even know why I asked. It didn't matter. Not only was I not into relationships, I was totally against them.

Her gaze cut to mine again. "I have it on good authority that he's not."

I nodded sharply and exhaled, looking away.

"Did I upset you?" she asked, her words bringing my eyes back to hers.

"No. Why?"

"You look . . . I don't know . . . you're acting weird."

"I'm . . ." I ran my hands over my face. I wasn't planning on telling her or anybody about this, but the way she looked at me with those beautiful, nurturing eyes made me want to lay it all out there for her. "My dad's in the hospital."

She gasped and reached for my hands. I let her take them. Hers were small and cold, but her touch warmed through me. "Again? Is he going to be okay?"

I let out a short laugh. "He had another stroke. He should be fine if he takes care of himself this time. He's so stubborn though. He won't quit smoking. He won't diet or exercise. It makes me crazy." Estelle squeezed my hands and gave me a small smile.

"He's going to be fine. I have faith that he'll change."

Her words made me smile. She'd only met him once. She had no idea what he was like.

"Do you think people can change?"

Her eyes flickered between mine. She moved forward until half of her torso was over the table, closer to me. I wanted to take my hands out of hers and pull her face to mine. I wanted to kiss her and get lost in the feel of it, the way I always did. Her face stopped centimeters from mine.

"I know they can. They just have to want to," she whispered in a breath against me.

"You have a lot of faith in people."

She backed away, leaning back into her seat. She smiled, wide and confident, as she picked up her cup and put her lips around the straw again. "I sure do."

You make me want to change, I didn't say. *You make me believe that I can.*

The next day, at the same time, we ran into each other there again, and the following day one more time. We sat down, talked, made each other laugh, and went our separate ways after. She made me smile on days that laughter seemed impossible. She made me see hope in things I didn't know existed. That was when she truly became my Estelle. She just didn't know it. Hell, neither did I.

Chapter 20

Present

Estelle

A WEEK LATER, my painting team is done with the rooms and the hallway. We've turned an ocean into a field filled with flowers and kids playing. Everyone has been working around the clock to make sure we meet the deadline, so needless to say, when we're finally done, we all cheer loudly about it. We walk out of there, with our arms linked to one another's, fighting the urge to close our eyes in exhaustion.

"I am so ready for sleep," Micah says, leaning his head on mine.

"Me too," I say with a yawn.

I nearly trip over my own feet when we round the corner, and I see Oliver talking to a nurse I haven't seen before. He's standing against the wall, and she's leaning into him like he's her next meal. I catch his eye and he straightens a bit, but I look away and lean into Micah, walking out of the hospital before he can approach me—not that I expect him to. It kills me to admit to myself that I feel anything when I see something like that happen. It kills me, because I'm really not the kind of girl who gets jealous over anything, yet when it comes to Oliver, I feel possessive.

I go home and sleep like the dead. I don't hear my phone calls or text messages or shouts from my brother downstairs telling me I need to eat. I don't even care about any of it, until I realize I have a missed call from my realtor, and I call her back frantically, hoping for good news.

"Hello?"

"I don't want you to get your hopes up, but we have a possible buyer."

"Oh, thank God! Finally!"

She goes on to tell me how much they offered and lets me know she'll get back to me as soon as she needs me again. I stretch and go downstairs, half expecting not to see my brother there, but unfortunately come face to face with not only him, but his friend Bobby from work, as well. And I look like shit.

"Hey, Elle, good to see you again," Bobby says, smiling as his eyes run up and down my body.

"Hey. Sorry you had to see me in this condition, but I've been sleeping for like . . ."

"Eighteen hours," Vic interrupts.

"No shit."

"Yes, shit."

"Wow. I guess I was really tired."

"Yeah, I guess. Bean called asking for you."

I frown and pop my head out of the fridge. "And?"

"And I thought that was odd," Vic says with a shrug. "You've been hanging out a lot, right?"

"Not really." I go back into the fridge, looking for nothing in particular.

"He says he tried calling you and couldn't get through."

"I'll call him back later. I think he's working tonight anyway."

"Yeah, isn't tonight Grace's night?" Bobby asks with a laugh over a mouthful of muffin.

Vic doesn't respond, just looks at me for a reaction I don't give him. Inside I'm screaming "Who the fuck is Grace?" but I can't let that show. If anything, this cements the reason my brother shouldn't know anything about Oliver and me. It just bugs me that they seem to know his every move. It makes me realize that I don't.

"Mom called too."

"Okay, Vic. What are you, the freaking operator? I'll call everybody back when I feel like it." I turn around and head back up to my room.

"Damn. Maybe she needs more sleep."

Vic scoffs. "She was born bitchy."

Chapter 21

WHEN ALL ELSE fails, run home to your mother. At least those were my thoughts when I woke up this morning. I didn't consider that, once I pulled into her driveway, I would be accosted by her and asked a gazillion questions I didn't want to deal with. *Have you been eating well? How has it been staying with your brother? Is he eating well? How did it go with Derek? I'm setting you up on another date, you'll like this guy, I promise. How's the studio? I heard you did a great job with the hospital.* And lastly . . . *Come in, let me feed you!*

Which of course, I did. I sat in the dining table overlooking the mountains and the ocean behind them. Vic and I were water babies, but my parents preferred the Santa Barbara Mountain View. They owned a house in Malibu that we used to drive to on weekends. Sometimes we were with them, but mostly we were with friends.

"Vic says you've been hanging out with Oliver a lot," my mom comments, using her nonchalant voice, as if curiosity isn't coloring the undertones of her voice.

I groan. "Vic is so annoying. We see each other a lot in the hospital. We hung out once outside of work. Big deal!" Her laugh makes my eyes snap to her. "What?"

She shrugs. "Your brother didn't think anything of it until I mentioned it was odd that you were hanging out. You used to hate him, didn't you?"

"No I didn't." I frown. Where the hell would she get that idea?

"I thought you did. You were always talking about what a player he was."

"Because he was," I say, giving her a "no shit" look.

"And now?"

I stare at her for a while, my hands playing with the napkin on the table. People say I'm a carbon copy of her, and that if they cloned me I wouldn't have looked more like her than I do. The thought makes me smile, because my mother is really a beautiful person, inside and out. Even with her demanding career as a professor, she's always managed to put her family first. Like today, when she saw my car pulling into the driveway, she immediately called out sick. I'm used to telling her everything, but for some reason, I can't talk to her about Oliver. I just can't. He's like a third child of this house. It's not like Wyatt, where I could come and complain about him or say beautiful things about him, and it wouldn't matter either way because he was an outsider to everybody. Oliver practically lived here growing up. And even though absolutely nothing is going on, as usual, I would hate to paint him in a bad light.

"I don't know, Mom," I say, finally. "I honestly don't know. I'm sure Vic can tell you better than I can."

"But you see him at work."

"Yeah, and?"

"Does he have a girlfriend? Or girlfriends?" she asks, rolling her hazel eyes.

I shrug. "You know him. He flirts with anything that walks, so I guess."

"Do you think he sleeps with all of them?"

My eyes widen. "Okay, this is getting awkward, and again, I don't know."

"Sometimes guys like him get a bad rap, don't you think? I mean, he's always been such a good boy."

I make a noncommittal wave of my hands. "I don't care. Why are we talking about this?"

Then she smiles, really wide, and I sink back in my seat. I'm half expecting her to tell me she's setting me up with him on a date.

"Because, this guy, Zach, sort of has that reputation with the ladies, but I hear he's not a player at all," she starts.

"Mom."

"And he is so cute, Estelle!"

"Mom."

"He owns a gallery in Malibu."

"Zach Edwin?" I practically shout.

My mom smiles, nodding and raising her eyebrows as if she just tasted all the cookies in the jar and didn't get caught.

"How the hell do you know him?" I ask a little too enthusiastically for my own good.

"Well, it's a funny story, Bettina and I were doing some shopping a couple of weeks ago and happened to step in his shop. He has gorgeous things in there, by the way, but the piece that caught our eye was a heart—one of your hearts. We stepped in, pretending we didn't know anything about anything, and asked him how much the heart was." She pauses for dramatic effect. "Four thousand dollars."

My mouth drops.

"He says he sold the last one for three thousand, and this is the only one he has left, but the person he bought them from didn't leave a card so he can't get in touch with who made it. Elle, are you all right?"

I shake my head, my mouth still hanging open.

My mom laughs and taps my hand with hers. "Can you believe that? I'm assuming he bought them from Wyatt."

I swallow, recollecting myself. "Yeah, Wyatt mentioned selling him a few pieces years back but . . . wow . . . four thousand dollars?"

"So you haven't gotten a cut from that?" my mom asks, frowning.

"It wasn't on consignment. He sold it to get rid of them, because I had made too many for a show we were attending, and Wyatt thought selling to Zach would be good for me later on. Obviously I never followed up, and Wyatt probably forgot his cards, as usual, but oh my God."

"I know!" my mom squeals.

"Okay, so how did the date thing come about?"

"Oh. Well, I told him my daughter was the one who made it, and he was very impressed."

"Uh-huh?"

"And then I got on my phone and showed him the website to your studio. He saw your photo, and I just saw his eyes light up."

"Oh my God, Mom," I say, burying my face in my hands.

"So I told him the short version about Wyatt and that you're dating now. I asked him if he would be interested, and he jumped on the chance."

"Oh my God, Mom!" I say again, still talking into my hands.

"Have you seen him, Elle?" she asks. I peer at her through my fingers and nod. "He's good looking!"

"He's freaking hot, but I can't go out with him! This isn't the fifteen hundreds. You can't just go around trying to court me to people!"

"Why the hell not?" she says, frowning. "Haven't you seen those shows on television where people are actually paying to be set up with others? Millionaire Matchmaker or something?"

I stare blankly. "No, I haven't had the pleasure of watching that. Just . . . I don't know, I mean, I would love to sell him some of my work, but I can't date him!"

"Is it because he's a player?"

"What? No!"

Zach does have that whole player reputation, with good reason. He doesn't usually date people in the industry, but the one girl he dated, he married, cheated on, and divorced within a year. After that, he'd been known to sleep with models, actresses, and whoever else walked into his shop on two slender legs and a short skirt.

"Are you sure?"

"I'm positive! I'm not looking for anything serious, so why would I care about his reputation?"

"I don't think his reputation is who he is. I'm telling you, he's a charmer, but I don't think he sleeps around as much as we're led to believe."

"Are we done? I'd really like to eat my pancakes in peace now," I mumble.

"Of course, dear. More coffee?"

"Sure. Where's Dad?"

"He left at sun up. Long day today. Three celebrity clients."

"Fun."

"Yeah, I'm sure we'll hear all about it when he gets back. Are you staying here tonight?"

I sigh and pour syrup on my pancakes. "Yeah, I think I will."

"You're sure you don't want to meet Zach? He lives a couple of blocks away."

My gaze cuts to hers. "You're kidding."

"What if he just comes over for dinner? That way it won't be a date, but a way for you to talk about your art."

"Since when are you interested in art? You hated when Wyatt used to come over and talk about art."

She gasps, placing a hand over her heart. "I never hated when he came over! I just didn't like how he spoke to you sometimes."

"Really? How's that?" I say, stabbing a piece of pancake. I don't mean for her to answer, but she does anyway.

"Like you were a child."

My chewing slows. I was a child. He was eleven years older than I was and had the experience of an eighty-year-old.

"He didn't speak to me like I was a child," I say.

"You were his muse . . . his light, I guess. I see that now, but at the time, it was unnerving, the way he wanted you stuck to his side every time your father's friends were around. As if he thought they would take you away from him. You never got that vibe?"

I shoot her a look. "Of course I did. Men are like that."

She tilts her head, seemingly weighing out my words. "I suppose they are. Anyhow, he obviously loved you in his own way and helped you a lot. But, just think, Zach Edwin!"

The rest of the day is spent shopping with my mom and Bettina (Mia's mom), talking about Zach and how he's coming over for dinner. Mia called threatening to kill me if I don't call her as soon as he leaves. At one point, between trying on shoes at Neiman Marcus and having drinks at Chili's, my brother gets wind of the whole thing and calls me to tell me he'll kill me if I hook up with Zach because he heard he hooks up with everybody, including a client's ex-wife. I turn off my phone after that. I have enough chatter to listen to from Bettina and my mom as they go on and on talking about all the guys Mia and I could have married by now. I don't know if they forget that I was engaged, or they just choose to ignore it because I wasn't engaged to somebody of their liking.

At night, I wear one of the dresses I bought earlier, a short—but not too short—flowery dress that hugs my torso but opens up and flows past my waist. My mom insists I wear a pair of red heels with it because it'll make my legs look miraculous (her words). When the door swings open at seven o'clock, I practically jump on my father before he has a chance to put his briefcase down. He laughs, his big Santa Claus-like laugh comes straight from his core, and he hugs me tightly.

"Someone missed me," he says, smiling when he lets me go. His once sandy brown hair is now covered in salt, and the lines of his face are marked with every time he's laughed—and there have been a lot of those. His brown eyes shine when he looks at me, and it makes me feel like a kid again.

"You're the only other normal person in this house," I whisper-shout dramatically as he continues to chuckle and shake his head.

"Nobody told you to stay alone with you mother," he whispers back conspiratorially.

"And Bettina!"

His eyes widen. "Oh Jesus, you need a drink."

"Or twenty."

He laughs again, putting his hand over my shoulder.

"Thomas! You're home!" my mom says, smiling widely as she saunters over to us, wearing a knee-length black dress.

"Are you trying to give a man a heart attack, Hannah? What are you wearing?" he asks, dropping his arm from my shoulder and reaching for my mom.

Watching them is like watching Gone with the Wind. You know, that last part, where Rhett Butler holds Scarlett O'Hara's face in his hands? That sums up my parents. Every. Single. Day.

"Oh, stop it, Tom, you know Elle hates public displays of affection," my mom coos as she throws her arms around his neck.

I laugh, shaking my head. "I do not, but I'll be outside if you need me."

"Why do you insist on setting her up on these stupid dates?" I hear my dad whisper to her as I walk away.

"Because, she needs to move on!"

"She'll move on when she's ready, honey. Your meddling isn't helping. And now I have Victor calling to say he's coming over to intervene," he says. I freeze with my hand over the doorknob. I have a moment of clarity, where I think maybe I'll call it a night and go home, but then remember where home is right now and decide to walk outside and sit in my parents' yard.

Growing up, I had two types of friends: the ones who had overbearing parents and the ones who had parents who didn't care what their kids were doing. I always wanted to have the second type of parents. Mine weren't strict, unless I got bad grades, and they only meddled when . . . well, they always meddled. When Wyatt died, I was grateful for that because I would have probably gone weeks without eating had it not been for them practically spoon-feeding me. Needless to say, I'm not surprised Vic decided to follow me home after he learned about the Zach thing, especially after he made the comment about his client. This is more than his normal big brother overprotection; it's about work.

My dad joins me outside after he's showered and hands me a glass of white wine.

"Figured you'd need it," he says, toasting me with his own.

"Thanks," I respond, taking a sip and leaning back into the cushions of the seat.

"I heard you did a great job at the hospital."

I glance at him and smile. "I think we did."

"I'm proud of you, Elle. I know I always said art was a waste of time and you should have stuck with something else, but then you go and do things like this, and I can't help but to be proud of you."

"Thank you," I say, leaning over and giving him a kiss on the cheek.

"Your mom isn't going to give up until you find a new boyfriend, you know? I think you should just pretend you're in love so she can let this go already."

"Mom isn't going to stop until I have kids."

"I thought you didn't want kids," he says, taking a sip of wine. He doesn't look at me when he says it. His eyes are far off into the distance. He doesn't see the crumbled look on my face. Wyatt didn't want kids. I turn my body away and mimic his pose, staring at the mountains—at the spot where I know the ocean is, but it's too dark to see right now.

"I haven't decided yet," I say finally.

"Sometimes we give up a lot of ourselves for the people we love," my dad says. "It's hard knowing when to stop doing that, because you feel like if you love someone, you should be okay giving things up for them." I nod and sip on my wine. "When I married Erika," he says, recalling his deceased wife—the woman he lost years before he met my mother. "I gave up everything I loved. I gave up school and got a job because I felt I needed to provide for her. That's what men do, you know, we provide for our woman—for our family. Then I lost her to a drunk driver and thought—what is my life now? I have nothing. And the thing is, I didn't feel that way because I lost her, I felt that way because of the things I'd given up for her."

I gulp a big sip of wine, knowing exactly how he feels. "And with Mom? And us?"

"Well, by the time I met your mother, I was back on track. She was younger, so I waited for her to graduate, I didn't want her making the same mistake I made with Erika. I never wanted to be the reason she looked back on her life and regretted the things she didn't do."

"Do you think all men are like that? Waiting for the right time to do things?" I ask, thinking of Oliver.

"No, not all of them. I think your brother does. I think he's waiting for his career to blossom before he settles down with somebody, and if he had met someone already, I would tell him he's an idiot for doing that at his age, but he hasn't met anybody that makes him reconsider, so I guess he's on the right track."

"Yeah, I guess."

"My point is, Elle, you probably gave up more than you think when you were with Wyatt, and that's not a bad thing. It's the way of life. I just don't want you to jump into a new relationship with that mentality. No matter how good looking your mom says the guy is." He flashes a smile that I return.

"Well, we both know Mom's taste is often a little screwed up," I say, making him laugh.

"Ain't that the truth."

Chapter 22

Past

Oliver

I'VE ALWAYS CONSIDERED myself lucky to have Victor for a friend. He's been selfless, ruthless, and above all, loyal. When I didn't have any place to go after I graduated and my lease was up, Vic didn't hesitate for a moment.

"You're living with me," he'd said.

"Okay, let me know how much I owe you. I only need a place to stay for a couple of weeks," I'd said, and he'd looked at me like I was crazy.

"You're my brother. You don't owe me shit!"

And that was how I ended up sleeping in the small cottage beside the house he'd been renting for the summer. Summer break—*the last hurrah*, he was calling it. The last hurrah before I left for medical school, and he settled down in law school at UCLA. Life was good during those weeks—wake up, catch some waves, eat something, drink, party, and hook up with the girls that hung around. We were treating grad school like some men would treat their last weekend as bachelors, which was funny because we'd been self-pro-claimed lifers. "Who needs one woman when we can have ten?" those were Vic's words, followed by Jensen's, "Bros before hoes." Junior was the only one who couldn't participate in our crazy summer, since he'd been tied down to the same girl since the first semester of school. As much as we made fun of him, I think we were all slightly jealous that he'd found a girl he actually wanted to be with every day.

I dressed that night, much like I did every other night, but I was ex-hausted from being in the sun all day, and I needed to get up early the next morning to start hauling my stuff upstate. One drink . . . maybe two . . . then sleep, I promised myself as I walked over to the main house, where the party had already started.

One drink, maybe two, then sleep, I repeated, the mantra becoming like second lyrics to the song bumping off the speakers. One drink, maybe two, I was about to tell myself again when I spotted Estelle walking into the house. I felt a slow smile creep up on my face as I watched her finger comb her hair, wild from the wind outside. Her lips were pressed into a sexy pout as her eyes wandered over the room. She shrugged off the jacket she was wearing, which revealed a low cut black shirt that pressed her tits up, and a short sequined skirt that showed off every curve of her legs.

I guess she felt me staring, because her eyes caught mine a beat later, and she smiled that wide smile of hers. It told me she was up to no good tonight and that she wondered if I was fair game. One drink, maybe two, then sleep, I said to myself again, this time kicking the frontal lobe of my brain, in the hopes I'd knock some sense into myself before I reached her. My treacherous feet walked toward her, as they always did, and she stood there waiting for me, as she usually did.

"I haven't seen you in a while," I said, my eyes taking in those marbled orbs of hers, as she slowly looked me over from head to toe. "What's the verdict?" I asked when her eyes finally stopped at mine. She blushed slightly and looked away, laughing.

"You look good," she said, turning her gaze to mine again.

"You look great," I said, and she smiled. "How have you been?"

It had been maybe two months since we'd last seen each other. Two months since our tongues did the song and dance they usually did whenever we were at one of these parties . . . or at the movies . . . or anywhere that afforded our sneaking around. We'd never gone too far, usually kissing and touching over clothes before we were interrupted by one thing or another. Our hiatus wasn't a coincidence. I'd been going to Cal parties instead of Vic's because the guilt of everything I felt whenever Estelle was around was starting to weigh down on me. Like the time I saw her at the mall a couple of months ago and cornered her in a long hallway that led to the bathroom. I only wanted to talk to her about stopping this madness between us, but then she pulled my face to hers and kissed me so deeply, I forgot my fucking name right then. She was dangerous for me. What I felt when I was around her wasn't right. I had my life planned out, and the things she made me want didn't fit into them. Not yet.

"I've been pretty good," she said. We started walking to the kitchen and grabbed red cups with beer when we reached the table. "How about you? I heard you're leaving for Berkeley soon. I knew you would get in."

I smiled. The last time I saw her, I was still waiting for my application. "It almost seems surreal."

She tilted her head and looked at me for a long moment before her lips turned into a small, warm smile. "I'm proud of you, Oliver."

My heart thumped a little at that. I smiled and drank some beer.

"You still all about having fun?" I asked. I didn't necessarily want to hear about her love life, but I wanted to know everything she was up to. Everything I'd missed.

Elle laughed as we reached a bench outside and sat down. "I guess you can say that."

"Still haven't met *the one?*" I asked, hoping my voice sounded light—unlike everything I felt squeezing inside me.

"Maybe I have, maybe I haven't. How would I know if he's the one?" she said with a smirk and a shrug.

I looked away, out into the distance where I knew the beach was just steps away. "I'd like to think we know when we meet that special person."

"Have you met her? The one?" she asked.

I swallowed, closed my eyes, drank more beer, and let out a breath.

"I decided a long time ago to avoid meeting her until the time was right," I said in a low voice, as if I was confessing a crime to a priest.

Estelle scooted closer to me, until our arms were touching, then she rested her head on my shoulder. "Is there ever a right time?"

"I don't know," I whispered, turning my face to smell her hair.

"I met a guy," she said suddenly, quietly, and my heart dropped.

"Yeah?" I said, drinking the rest of my beer.

"He's . . . different. He's nice. Older."

"How much older?"

She lifted her head to look at me, and the movement had us sitting nose to nose. A jolt ran through me, and I inched closer. Because I'm a bastard. Because I'm selfish. Because I wanted those lips to be mine, and those eyes to be mine, and that voice to only be heard by me—even if it was only for one night.

"Older than me," she whispered, her nose brushing against mine. "Older than you." I reared back, taking a quick moment to glance around, as adrenaline at the possibility of getting caught coursed through me. I berated myself for a moment—a quick, fleeting moment—that got lost as soon as I looked back into her eyes.

"Do you like older guys?" I whispered, my lips feathering over hers.

Her eyes flashed. "I like some."

"Yeah?" I asked, plucking at her bottom lip with my teeth.

"Yeah," she said breathily.

"Do you think he's the one?" I asked in a whisper, planting a kiss on the edge of her lips.

"No," she said, repeating my movement and dropping a kiss on the edge of mine.

"Have you ever been in love, Estelle?" I asked quietly, backing away slightly to search her wide eyes.

"Have you?" she whispered, staring at me, waiting.

"I . . ." I didn't know what to say, and before I could say anything at all, boisterous voices came from behind us, and we inched away quickly. We turned to see some guys cheering on another as he chugged his beer. The crowd cheered and hollered, but died down quickly, and we looked at each other again.

"I really want you to kiss me," she said, bringing her eyes to mine.

If possible, my heart spiked harder against my chest. I dipped my head until we were nose to nose. "I really want to kiss you again."

"I want you to do more than kiss me this time."

I held my breath. "Estelle . . ."

"Please."

I closed my eyes at her plea. I took that moment to tune out the loud party and focus on why this couldn't happen. *Victor is your best friend, and you promised you'd take care of her, not hurt her. He will kill you. He's your brother. How would you feel if he did this to Sophie?*

But then I felt Estelle get even closer to me. I felt her soft breath over my ear, and as her hand reached down between us and settled right over my dick, I couldn't breathe, let alone think.

"I want you, Oliver," she whispered. My eyes popped open in a flash and when I looked at her, I knew I couldn't deny her even if I wanted to. Even if I should.

She stood, grabbing my hand and started to walk toward the cottage. I looked over my shoulder to make sure nobody saw us. My eyes scanned the party and looked for Vic specifically, but I never found him. Then I felt like an asshole for doing that. I was about to disappear into a room with his little sister, and I was making sure he didn't see us. I was supposed to protect her from the big bad wolf, yet here I was, feeling like a wolf myself. But I couldn't help it. I didn't see red lights when it came to Elle, I only saw green and go, and felt things that made me want to be a better man for her, even though I knew I couldn't.

The door opened and closed behind us. As soon as we faced the other, she jumped on me, wrapping her legs around my waist and throwing her arms around my neck as she smashed her lips to mine. I held her, grabbing her ass as I plunged my tongue inside her mouth. I couldn't help but moan when she bit it lightly, sucking it in and out of her mouth. I set her on her feet only to let her take my shirt off. Her eyes blazed as she looked at me, from my face down to my torso. Her small fingers touched every line I had, leaving a trail of fire behind every spot she touched.

"You're ticklish," she said, looking up at me in wonder.

I wasn't, not really, but when she touched me like that, my muscles contracted, so I shrugged and let her think I was. I didn't want to rush her, so I let her undress me completely. I let her take the lead and decide what came next.

"You're beautiful," she breathed, as I stood naked in front of her. Her hand reached out and grasped my cock, and it jumped. I groaned, biting my lip and throwing my head back, asking all the gods to please give me enough control not to come in her hands as she stroked me. Finally, my control broke, and I stepped forward, reaching for the hem of her shirt. I waited, watching as she nodded for me to take it off. I did, then stayed fixated on her bare chest. I'd pictured what she looked like a million times, and none of those did the reality justice. She was just . . . perfect. I unzipped her skirt and let it pool at her feet around the strappy heels she wore. Then I dipped my head and kissed her—a slow, leisurely kiss that deepened as my hands trailed down her body. My lips left hers and made their way down to her neck, her collarbone, the valley between her breasts . . . then I pulled each nipple into my mouth. She grabbed onto my hair with a deep moan of encouragement, so I continued plucking kisses down her body, and over her panties, which I pulled down with my teeth. I pushed them down her calves and then her feet, where I unstrapped each shoe and helped her step out.

I was still on my knees, making my way back up when a surge of desire hit me like a ten-foot wave. I stopped and looked into her eyes when I reached the inside of her thighs to push them apart. She watched me in rapt attention, as if I was some sort of beautiful puzzle she had to figure out.

"Bed?" I asked as my hands stroked her thighs softly. She nodded, lips parted, those multi-colored eyes glazed over. I stood and carried her to the bed like a bride. Neither of us spoke as I moved down her body again, my mouth kissing her, teasing her, communicating how much I wanted her. Her body thrashed against the bed . . . against my wet lips . . . and she pulled my hair as she said my name over, and over. *Oliver, oh, Oliver.* I'd never heard such a beautiful melody.

My fingers replaced my mouth as I moved back to her breasts, tweaking her nipples, and squeezing them lightly.

"So good," she whimpered in a pant, and I smiled. I wanted to make her feel good. I positioned myself between her legs and paused. I never paused. I always looked for a condom, put it on and continued. I never paused and wondered if I could possibly get away with no condom. I never paused and wished that there would be no barrier between us. But this was Elle. *My Elle.*

Her hands moved down my chest and to my cock, where she squeezed again. "I'm on the pill," she said quietly.

"Do you do this often? No condom?" I asked, matching her tone. My heart was tripping over itself in anticipation. Why had I asked that question? Did it matter? Since when did I care what my lovers did with other partners?

She shook her head. "Never."

I let out a sigh of relief. Never. I felt high. I could give her something she'd never had. I wasn't the one who took her virginity. I wasn't the one who'd had the pleasure of her first kiss—but this, I could give her. I bent lower and teased her folds with my cock.

"Please, Oliver," she said, doing a shimmy below me. "Please."

I dipped my head and kissed her again, letting her taste herself on my lips, moaning when she pulled my hair to bring me closer. "We'll go slow," I whispered against her.

"No. I don't want slow," she said, her eyes wide. She moved her hips up. I grinned.

"I want slow," I said, pushing myself inside her with one deep thrust. Her body bowed off the bed with a yelp. I pulled back, and she sighed, I pushed back in, she yelped again. "You still want it fast?" I asked, groaning when she clenched around me.

"I still want fast," she panted, meeting my thrusts. I pulled out completely, then pushed back in slowly, and smiled when she growled at me. My thrusts were long and hard. I relished the way she felt around me. I tried to absorb her heat, her wetness—everything I could—so I took my time. I took my time until she trailed her hand down her flat stomach to the spot where our bodies were joined and began to rub, and then I lost it. I lifted her leg and started to move—really move. She screamed my name, I groaned out hers. She clawed at me, and it made me move faster. Then she started whimpering *Oliver, Oliver, I can't, I can't,* as her head swayed side to side and her eyes rolled back. I pulled out of her, and she gasped, and looked like she was going to kill me, so I scooted back and sat down, picking her up and positioning her over my hips. We never lost eye contact, and when she took me in and started to move, I was a goner.

The way her eyes searched mine said, *do you feel this? Can you feel it too? Am I making this up?* The words were never verbalized. They were spoken with our tongues against the other's. *Are you still searching? Do you still believe someone else is better for you?* My hands framed her face as hers did mine, and we held each other there as she reached the brink of her orgasm. I fell right behind her. It was slow at first, then all consuming and powerful. We looked at each other as we caught our breaths, still searching . . . questioning . . . wondering things we didn't dare ask.

Chapter 23

Present

Estelle

"IS THAT A new dress?" Vic asks as I take a seat across from him at the table.

"I got it with Mom yesterday. Mom and Bettina."

Vic groans. "God, what a pair. And they managed to pick up a douche for you to date while you were shopping."

I laugh, because he's not completely wrong. Zach coming over last night solidified my belief that the dating pool available right now is less than spectacular. He's good looking, charming, and talks about himself ninety-percent of the time. He used the other ten percent to tell me how much he could profit from my kaleidoscope hearts. By the time Victor got there, I was ready to go to sleep, but I stuck around because he was so flustered. On his way to our parents' house, he'd gotten a flat tire and had Oliver pick him up because he'd already been riding on his spare. That led to a confused Oliver standing in the dining room, looking between Zach and me with a weird look on his face. I wasn't sure if he was jealous or if he was just put off by how much Zach talked. At any rate, he excused himself pretty early, and as soon as he left, I went upstairs.

"All he did was talk about himself," I say, shaking my head.

"Like a true artist," Victor says, and grins when I slap his shoulder. "You have great luck with dates, huh?"

"You dated him longer than I did. I went to sleep," I say, raising an eyebrow.

"Whatever. You're not dating him. He's a womanizer and a cheat, and I'm pretty sure he's involved in some weird shit."

"You say that about everybody. 'I'm pretty sure he's involved in some weird shit,'" I mimic, rolling my eyes.

He shrugs. "I'm usually right."

"You're worse than Dad. You're never going to approve of anybody I date."

"That's not true," he says, his brows furrowing. He looks up at the sound of the door closing behind me, and before I turn around, his eyes lock with mine. "As long as he's a good guy, not a player, and isn't involved in weird shit, I approve."

"Approve of what?" asks Oliver, whose voice makes me shiver. I stand up and head to the kitchen, glancing back and greeting him with a smile.

"Vic is telling me who I can and can't date. Don't worry, so far, you are not on the list of contenders."

Vic spurts out a laugh and mumbles something about, "That'll be the day." While Oliver just stares at me like he can't believe I just said that, it takes everything in me not to flash him my middle finger. Instead, I turn my attention back to the pantry and sort through the cereal. I don't know what I'm so mad about, but it seems like every time my heart involves itself in Oliver, everything inside me goes haywire. My already loose screws rattle. My already questionable judgment vanishes. And lastly, the possessive chip I never knew I had, surfaces. The only thing I remember is Bobby mentioning "Grace night," and that's enough to make me want to throw something at the man who's not even mine.

"Mom only has healthy grain cereals in here," I call out. "What the hell!" I say when the pantry slams shut in front of me, and I find Oliver glaring at me. I frown. "What?"

"Who's on the list?" he asks, and it takes me a couple of seconds to realize what list he's referring to. I laugh.

"What does it matter?"

"It matters," he presses.

I raise an eyebrow. "How was 'Grace night?'"

Oliver's eyes widen in shock. "What?"

I open the pantry again, effectively making him move out of my way.

"There is no Grace night," he whispers loudly. I feel his eyes burning the side of my face as he glares at me over the pantry door. "There is only Mae night, Danny night, Patrick night, Justin night . . . do you want me to continue? Because I spend most of my nights doing rounds in a hospital, unless I get really lucky, and then it's Estelle night." His words make my heart quicken, but I refuse to look at him. "Now tell me, who's on the list of contenders?"

"You really want to know?" I ask in a quiet voice, closing the pantry.

He crosses his arms over his chest. He's not wearing his scrubs today, but instead, a navy t-shirt that hugs his frame, and jeans that cling to his hips as if they were tailored. His hair is wet and brushed back, and his stubble looks cleaned up. He looks like a goddamn model, and I hate it. Stupid boy. Stupid cute boy.

"I'm asking."

"Go ask my brother," I say, nodding in that direction.

"I'm asking you."

I cross my arms over my chest and stand in front of him. "And I'm telling you to go ask him, because I don't know who is on the approved list. Is there a reason for you shutting the pantry in my face, or are you just here to annoy, Bean?"

He opens his mouth and closes it, then opens it again. "I want your list. I don't care about Victor's list. I know I'll never make it on his. I want your approved list."

I can't come up with a comeback for that, so I'm glad when my dad walks in clearing his throat, and I have to drag my eyes away from the intensity in Oliver's. Dad's brown eyes bounce between us, and his brows raise in question.

"Interrupting something?"

"No," Oliver and I say at the same time.

"I heard this is your last week at the hospital," my dad says, using his enthusiastic voice, as he rounds the corner and opens his arms to hug Oliver. "Congratulations, my boy. I knew you had it in you, despite those late nights out."

I groan and fake gag. Can the people in this house not stop talking about this guy's past? Jesus.

"Thank you," Oliver says, laughing. "Now it's time for the real world."

"Do you know where you'll be working?" my dad asks as he opens the fridge. Oliver turns his body to face me as he answers.

"I've gotten some calls, but I'm holding off for the right one," he says. I scoff like a bratty schoolgirl and turn around.

"Dad, what's up with the Lucky Charms?"

"Your mom won't buy them anymore."

"What? Why?" I ask, opening the freezer. "You guys have nothing to eat!"

My mom's laugh rings throughout the house. "We have nothing you like to eat, but we have plenty to eat. Sit down, I'll make you some eggs."

"I hate eggs," I mutter under my breath. As I stand with my back against the counter, Oliver's fingers brush mine, and I feel a jolt that makes my eyes snap to his.

"You like eggs," he says.

I shake my head. "I really don't."

"With goat cheese?" he asks, his fingers now intertwining with mine.

"I like them a little bit if they have goat cheese," I whisper, trying to untangle my hand from his, but he makes it an impossible feat. "What are you doing?"

"I want to be on that list," he says quietly so only I can hear, but my eyes automatically pop around the room, making sure nobody is paying attention.

"Then get on it."

"Your list or his?" he asks, throwing a nod in the general direction of where Victor is.

"Whichever one matters most to you."

I reach up to push his hair out of his face, threading my fingers through it so that it stays back. His eyes close at the movement, and my heart spikes at the intimacy of it all. My dad clears his throat again, and I push away from Oliver, giving us enough distance to look like nothing is going on. Because nothing is going on. *At all.*

"Do you want coffee, Oliver?" my dad asks.

"Yes, please."

As I walk past, Dad twists his lips into a smile. "Your brother would kill him. You know that, right?"

I grab on to the edge of the counter. "He has no reason to."

He laughs. "You sure about that?"

And with that, I scurry over to the table and sit in front of my brother, as usual. Oliver sits beside me, as usual, and my mom and dad sit in their seats as she places the food in the middle of the table—scrambled eggs, sunny side up eggs, poached eggs, toast, jelly, and butter. I go for the toast. Oliver takes it upon himself to serve me some scrambled eggs, because they have goat cheese and bacon. I thank him and eat with one hand while I fidget with the napkin on my lap with the other. My dad is looking at us like we're about to announce my pregnancy, and the entire breakfast feels awkward.

"I like that dress on you," Oliver whispers, and my face flames.

"Oliver, Tom says you'll be finished with your residency soon. Will you stick to pediatrics?" my mom asks.

"Definitely. I love working with kids, so I'm trying to find a small practice to join."

"You must see so much in the hospital though," my mom says sadly.

"It's not easy," Oliver says, his hand reaching for mine under the table. "It really makes you realize what you have and how lucky we are to be healthy."

"I bet. I'm sure it sheds a different light on your life," my dad comments.

"It does," Oliver responds, squeezing my hand. I feel like he's squeezing my heart. "It's made me see a lot of things clearly."

"I think this year has opened our eyes to a lot of things," my mom starts, until Victor interrupts.

"Did I miss the memo about this being a Thanksgiving breakfast?"

I bite my lip, trying not to laugh, and glance up at Oliver, who's apparently doing the same. Our hands squeeze tighter together.

"It doesn't have to be Thanksgiving for you to be grateful," my mom says.

"Vic is just upset because that girl he's been seeing hasn't come around in a couple of days," I say, sticking my tongue out at him when he makes a face.

"Whatever. At least my mom doesn't have to play matchmaker for me."

"She doesn't have to for me either!" I say, shooting a glare at my mom.

"Prove it," Vic says. "Prove it. Go out tonight and get yourself a date the old fashioned way."

I laugh. "By go out, I'm assuming you mean to a club, and that is the last place I want to get a date. Besides, since when do you want me to date?"

"Since you started pointing out my dating life when you have none."

I roll my eyes. "I'm happily single, thank you very much."

"I'm just saying—I have no issues finding women who want to date me."

"I have no issues finding guys who want to date me either."

He raises an eyebrow, but makes no further comment.

"I'm serious, Victor."

He raises his hands up. "I'm dropping it, Elle. Are we still going out to celebrate me closing this case?"

"I guess we are, right?" I say with a shrug.

"Maybe you'll find a date there."

"You are so infuriating."

"You never know. Maybe you'll find love in a hopeless place," he says and laughs.

"Mom, you're not going to say anything to your idiot son?"

"Estelle!"

"Estelle, what? He's being a moron!"

"I think your brother just wants you to move on with your life," my dad chimes in. "He just has a weird way of showing his feelings. Besides, who's to say she isn't moving on with someone right under our noses?"

Victor scoffs. "One, we would have noticed. Two, we don't know anybody she would date."

"This is not happening," I say, muffled into my hands, while Oliver laughs beside me.

Victor calls Jensen, who seems to be in town every weekend, to join us. His invitees end up being: Mia, Jensen, Victor, Oliver, Bobby and me. Oh, and whoever Oliver and Jensen decide to bring along, because God knows they don't travel without a date unless they're going to find one there.

"Why the hell would he want to go to a club?" Mia asks, as we sort through her closet.

"Because obviously Victor has no life outside of his workplace, which, may I remind you, consists of divorcees trying to screw each other over."

"Ugh. Why is Jensen even here again? It's getting annoying. I like it better when he stays on the east coast," she says, and suddenly stops looking through clothes, to sit on her bed. I face her and take in the sad look that invades her face any time Jensen is mentioned.

"You don't have to go," I say. "Just sit this one out."

Mia brings her gaze to me. "Are you sure you'll be okay?"

"I'll be fine. I'll have three body guards, and I can't blame you for not wanting to see Jensen."

She sighs. "I'm just not ready."

I take a seat beside her and hold her hands in mine. "I know." I don't mention how Jensen seems upset every time Mia's name is brought up, because there's no point. "I hate that he makes you so sad."

Mia smiles. "Me too, but that's life."

The conversation shifts to my outfit and hair as I start getting ready, and for a while, we both let go of the ghosts of our pasts.

Chapter 24

WHEN I GET to the club, I'm escorted to the VIP area, where Victor, Bobby, Jensen and Oliver are talking to some women at the table beside them. I watch for a couple of beats, but the loud house music and dim lights make it impossible for me to understand what they're saying. The fact that none of them feel my eyes on them enough to look up is telling though—they're all completely lost in conversation. Oliver throws his head back in laughter, and I swear I can feel it rumble from his chest to mine. Or maybe it's the speaker I'm leaning against. Either way, it's enough for me to finally shuffle my feet in the opposite direction and head to the bar. I'll go back over there after I've supplied my body with the liquid courage it needs to sit next to them . . . next to *him.*

As soon as my ass touches the stool, I ask for a drink and start looking around, watching the bodies move and the women strut across the dance floor in search of their next victim. Two drinks later, I get up and walk back to the VIP area, giving a wave to the girl who walked me in before. She smiles and escorts me back to where Vic is, and I stand directly in front of them so they'll hear me over the music.

"Hey."

Victor looks away from the woman practically sitting on his lap, but then, it seems like all of the women are sitting on the men's laps right now. I try to avoid getting in a twist by not letting my eyes drift to Oliver.

"Finally! You made it," my brother says, looking genuinely happy as he stands to pull me into a hug. "This is my sister Estelle. She can vouch for us and tell you that we're all single."

I must be making a face, because the one clinging on to him laughs loudly. "Hi, Estelle. I'm Marie." Then all four women introduce themselves to me.

"So they are single," a brunette says. She looks a little drunk, with her way too-wide smile and her grubby hands on Oliver's lap. Still, I smile, though it feels tight on my face.

"Sure. Some come with more baggage than others do. Take your pick." I shoot Jensen a pointed look, and he shakes his head at me in disbelief. I guess it was a bitchy thing to say. I groan. "I'm just kidding. I'll see you guys later." I give them a small wave and one last smile before heading to the same bar I was at earlier. I feel somebody take a seat beside me, but don't acknowledge him. I keep sipping on my drink and tapping the counter with my fingernails as I debate whether I should stay a little longer, or leave and call Mia so we can go somewhere.

"What's a beautiful woman like you doing here alone?" he asks, and my eyes practically jump out of their sockets, because he has the sexiest British accent I've ever heard. Not that I've heard many, movies aside. I pivot in the seat and find a good looking, older man. He looks like a businessman, which has more to do with the suit he's wearing than anything else.

"Not alone. I just needed a little space from the people I'm supposed to be here with."

His lips twitch. "That bad?"

My eyes trail over his features, and notice thin lips, dark eyes, short, light curls on his head, and the lack of hair on his face. I wonder if it feels as smooth as it looks. His smile broadens, as mine does.

"I'm here with my brother and his friends. Celebrating some big work thing. It's pretty bad."

"In that case, would you like another?" he asks, looking at my now almost-empty glass of vodka tonic.

"Sure," I say, smiling. "Are you here alone?"

"With a couple of blokes from work." He points over to a table close to where Vic and the guys are sitting.

"You're sitting in VIP and came all the way out here to refill your drink?"

He leans forward so that his mouth is beside my face. "I saw you and thought I should come introduce myself before someone else got a chance to."

I smile and focus my attention on the drink the bartender places in front of me.

"Miles," he says, offering his hand.

"Estelle."

"Beautiful name. What do you do for fun, Estelle? Other than avoid boring celebrations with your brother."

My eyes find his, and I flash him a smile. "I dance."

He raises an eyebrow. "Show me."

I stand, gulping down the drink in a less-than-ladylike manner, and grab his hand, pulling him to the dance floor with me. I glance over my shoulder to where the guys are, and see they're still talking, save for Victor, who's now dancing with one of the girls. The only one who takes notice of me is Oliver, and the look he's giving me is enough to set my insides on fire. Miles grabs my hips, and we begin to sway to the music. Finally, I close my eyes and ignore Oliver's gaze, along with everything else. I let the music travel through me, and I let my body take over to the point of forgetting where I am and who I'm with.

"You're really good at this," Miles says into my ear. "What else are you good at?"

I can't keep the smile off my face, but I keep dancing and ignore his question. We stay on the dance floor and, as the songs get more provocative, so do my moves and Miles' hands on my body. Where they were once on my waist, they've gravitated down to my ass. I turn around in his hold and pull his hands higher so they're at my waist, and as I do, I spot a tall figure walking toward us. Normally it wouldn't be weird, since we're in the middle of a crowded club, but I'd know that strut anywhere. My heart picks up a little as my gaze finds Oliver's. I look past him and notice Vic and Bobby are both wrapped up in the ladies beside them. If they notice Oliver is gone, they don't show it. He doesn't stop until he reaches me.

"I need to speak to you," he says, leaning his face between my dance partner and me.

"We're dancing," Miles says, frowning, but he stops moving so the three of us are standing.

"And now you're not," Oliver says in a voice that makes the hairs on the back of my neck stand up.

Miles takes it as a challenge and cocks his eyebrow at me, saying *can you believe this guy?* And honestly, no, I cannot believe this guy.

"Oliver, what do you want?" I ask. He doesn't even look at me. He continues to glare at Miles.

"I'd like to leave my days of fighting back in middle school, so if you could just do me a favor and take your hands off of her ass and step away, we'll be okay," Oliver says.

Anger simmers in the pit of my stomach as I watch the exchange. The only thing I can think about is "Grace's night." The words repeat themselves inside my head. "Grace's night" followed by Bobby's amused chuckle, and suddenly I'm livid, just like that.

I take a step back and shoot him a murderous glare. "What is your problem?"

"I take it you know each other," Miles says, shaking his head. He looks at me one last time. "When you're finished playing whatever game it is he wants you to play, you're welcome to join us at our table." Then he turns around and disappears into the crowd, leaving me gaping at the empty spot where he was standing.

"Elle," Oliver says, but I put my hand up to stop him and turn around, walking to the back of the club.

The line for the women's bathroom is insane, as usual, so I look both ways and figure out my next plan. When I see a figure coming up behind me, I bolt to the nearest exit, shivering at the wall of cold air that hits me.

"Estelle!" he shouts as the door closes behind him, the noise of the club fading along with it.

"What do you want?" I say. What could he possibly want? I'm holding my arms together as the residual alcohol travels through my system, warming me against the outside air. Suddenly I am so upset with everything—with everyone. This was supposed to be a night out. Maybe even a night where I could show Vic that I can get a guy by myself, without Mom's help, without school, without art, just me. And it's stupid. It's stupid because I'm at a dance club trying to prove things I didn't realize I needed to. What was I going to do, anyway? Have a one night stand with some random guy? Find a real chance of starting over at a place where conversation is completely optional, and dry sex is the norm? A laugh escapes my lips at my stupid, idiotic thoughts. And another one follows when I remember who's behind me—the only guy I want, but shouldn't. The one I don't *want* to want. The one I'm *terrified* to want.

When Oliver doesn't respond, I turn around and face him. He has his eyes closed as he runs a hand through his hair, brushing it back as if he's doing outtakes for a Pantene commercial. He looks exhausted, like a man who had an eighty-hour workweek and still managed to come out tonight to help his best friend celebrate a win. But when he opens his eyes and looks at me, it's as if he gets a second wind.

"I know I'm fucked up, Elle. Or at least I have been in the past," he says with a short laugh. He strides over and I stay still. I don't want to interrupt anything he's going to tell me in that voice, while he's looking at me with those eyes. "You have no reason to open yourself up to me. I know I can't have you, Elle. I know I shouldn't have you. The job offers I'm getting are in San Fran, which means I'll probably leave soon . . . again. Your brother would never approve of this . . . of us . . . of me being with you," he says, sighing. He runs his hands through his hair again as he stands in front of me. He's so close that the only thing between us is my crossed arms. He drops his forehead to the top of my head and lets out a long breath that fans over my face. "So why do I want you so bad?"

"How many times are we going to go through this?" I whisper. *How many times am I going to let you break my heart?*

"Just give me one date," he says just as low, moving his face so that our noses brush.

"Just one date, and then what? You leave the next day?" I say, stepping away.

"Give me time to figure that part out," he says, his eyes pleading with mine. I shake my head.

"I can't."

"Why not?"

"Because last time we did this, you left me!" I say a little louder than I intend. He flinches. "We had that night, and you freaking left me! I woke up the next day and you were gone. All of your shit was gone! You didn't even leave a note, just a 'Bean left to Berkeley today, he says he'll catch you next time' from Victor who thought we hadn't even seen each other at the party. Do you know how bad that hurt?"

He looks away. "I thought we established that I'm fucked up."

"Yeah, well, stop fucking us all up along with you!"

His eyes flash to mine. "You got engaged a year later!"

"Oh, was I supposed to wait for you? Did I miss the memo where you told me you would come back, and we could actually have a chance at something? I'm so sorry, King Oliver. I must have missed that one, along with the apology for leaving me and then making me miserable at my own—"

His lips smash into mine before I can finish the sentence, and I back him into the wall behind him. He moans when I press my body flush against his and dip my tongue into his mouth. My head clouds with his scent, his taste, and the hint of iron in our mouths that our nipping teeth have made. We kiss like we're hungry . . . starving . . . for each other. Through the haze inside my head, I hear our names being called out, but I don't process it until I hear the voice getting louder, closer, and our phones start to vibrate (his in his pocket, mine in the wristlet I have on).

"Elle?"

"Bean?"

Jensen's voice cuts through us, and Oliver gasps against my mouth and pulls away, or pushes me away. It feels about the same. The vibrating of our phones grows frantic. I look down, taking it out, and see Vic's name on the screen. My eyes flicker to Oliver, who says Jensen is calling him. We nod at each other and answer our phones at the same time.

"Yeah, she's with me. We're outside," Oliver says into his phone.

"I'm outside," I say to Vic.

"Oh. Is Jensen there with you? He went out for a smoke."

"No. I haven't seen him."

"Are you coming back with us? I didn't get to hang out with you inside."

"You were a little occupied inside," I say and open my mouth to agree, when he cuts me off.

"Okay, well we'll see each other at home. Tell Bean the girls we were talking to are coming over," Victor says, and my stomach turns.

"Sure. I'll tell him," I say, looking at Oliver, who's watching me intently.

As soon as I hang up and put my phone back in my purse, Oliver reaches for me, but I put my hands up to stop him.

"Don't bother. Victor says you have company tonight. He wants you to know the girls are coming over," I say, sauntering out of the alley and to the front of club. I catch Jensen standing, gaping at us with his mouth hanging open and everything. I don't even care that he saw us right now. Tomorrow I'm sure I'll give it more thought, but right now, I feel like I need to get out of here.

"I'm taking a cab," I say as I reach him and open the door to the first one I see. I glance over my shoulder and catch the torn look on Oliver's face before I slide into the car and close the door—then I head to the only place I've been able to call home for the past two years. Thankfully, I still have a key.

Chapter 25

Past

Oliver

THE DOWNFALL OF ambition is sometimes letting life pass you by and only realizing it did so after the fact. Like the seasons, people change—their lives change—and suddenly you're stuck between fall and winter, not knowing whether you should step forward or back. I didn't go home on my breaks during my first two years of school, because my mom and Sophie came to see me at Berkeley. Then the guys came up for Spring Break one year, and the next we went to Vegas. Being back home felt weird at first, as if everything stayed the same except for me. That's what I thought until I met up with a stressed-out Victor at Starbucks one morning.

"If you don't stop bouncing your leg, I'm going to stab it," I said, looking up from the textbook I had in my hand.

We were supposed to be studying—him for the LSAT, me preparing for a Genetics final.

"I'm just . . . sorry. I'm just dealing with a lot of shit right now."

I put the book down and leaned back in my seat. "Talk."

He closed his eyes and breathed out through his nose, long and heavy. I didn't know what to expect him to say. Maybe he'd failed a class. Maybe he'd gotten a girl pregnant. Maybe he got himself a hamster. With Vic, there was no telling.

"She's engaged," he said finally.

"Okay?" I drew out slowly, waiting for him to elaborate.

"Estelle," he said, his brows bunching up. "She got engaged."

A couple of things happened at once: my mouth dropped, the air left my body, and the barista dropped the coffee she was making, causing a stir in the coffee house.

"She's what?" I said.

He nodded, raising his eyebrows like we were on the same wavelength. Little did he know, while his wavelength was down where the familiar territory lay, mine was leaping into the mountains where warning bells rang. I felt like huge claws were squeezing around my neck. Estelle was engaged. My Estelle.

"To who? I didn't even know she had a serious boyfriend," I said, trying to keep my voice even, trying not to get upset, because then my ears would get red and he'd know something was up. Where the fuck have I been? Where the fuck has . . . why hasn't anybody told me anything?

"She's been dating that painter, Wyatt, on and off for a while now."

"Yeah, more off than on though, right?" Was I crazy? I'd heard it wasn't serious. Or maybe I just assumed that.

Vic shrugged. "Well, it's fucking serious now. They're moving in together, engaged . . . it's just . . . she's my little sister, you know? One thing is for Junior to go and get engaged, but when Elle does it, it's like . . . I don't know. I feel like I'm going through a midlife crisis."

I couldn't even laugh or joke about what he'd said. I was too hung up on *Estelle is engaged.* Estelle is moving in with somebody—somebody that's not me. Somebody that obviously has his head on his shoulders and was smart enough to not let somebody that perfect pass through his life without locking her down.

"Aren't they always breaking up?" I said again.

"I guess he wants to make it so they don't," he said, biting on the tip of the pencil in his hand. "He's such a pompous dick, too. He thinks he's better than everybody."

"Really? And Estelle is moving in with him?" I looked down at the discolored wood between us on the table.

"She says she loves him."

My chest squeezed, but I nodded and made a sound to show I was listening.

"She says she's happy with him and that he's taught her so much. I think she's just comfortable with him. I mean, he's older, he has all this success, and they're opening that gallery together."

"They're opening a gallery together?" I asked. This couldn't be going any worse.

"Dude. I haven't shown you the pictures?" Vic asked, taking out his phone and scrolling through photos. The one he landed on happened to be the picture they used to announce their engagement. Estelle had her hand over the guy's chest, and they were both smiling widely for the camera. He had long blonde hair, like mine . . . a beard, like mine . . . and a girl that should have been mine. Estelle had her dark hair down in loose curls that winded down the front of her thin frame. Her hazel eyes were as wide and smiling as her beautiful mouth. I looked at the rock on her finger and quickly looked away. It felt like a boulder on my collarbone. I couldn't breathe. I put the phone down and looked the other way.

"So I guess she's happy," I commented, picking my book back up. I could feel Vic staring at me from across the table. I half expected him to call me out on why I was acting weird. I prepared myself a little speech where I would tell him that I was in love with his sister and that I knew he didn't approve, but I didn't care. I said I would do it. Call me out, I begged, but he didn't. He sighed and leaned back in his seat.

"I feel like an old man. My sister getting married—"

"Engaged," I corrected. "A lot of people get engaged and don't get married."

Was I a dick for wanting that? Was I terrible for hoping the engagement would fall through? Why did it bother me so much anyway? I hadn't been there. I left. I left. I had nobody to blame but myself.

"You wanna come to the engagement party tonight?"

He might as well have asked me if I wanted to wear a pink leotard to a football game.

"What? You might as well keep me company," he said, laughing at the look on my face.

Because I needed to see her despite the circumstances, I agreed. Of course, I agreed. I would go and ask her not to marry that stupid painter. Or maybe I just needed to see her to make sure that she was truly happy. To make sure that the spark between us no longer existed. Maybe whatever we had in the past was gone now that she had something real. Maybe I waited too long. Of course, I waited too long. Every second it took to get ready to go to Vic's house became the countdown to doom. I changed my clothes five times. *Five.* I felt like Sophie. On that note, I called my sister. I'd never told her about Elle because I knew she wouldn't approve, but I needed to tell somebody, anybody. I needed to lay it out there for the universe to hear me, and maybe telling Sophie would make it real. Maybe telling her would stop the engagement . . . stop the wedding—I don't know.

"If you're not calling to tell me you're coming over to feed Sander, your voice is not welcome right now," she said, sounding completely wiped out.

"Soph, I fucked up."

She stayed quiet for a long moment. "Did you . . . okay, I can't think of how you would fuck up, so enlighten me, oh perfect one, what did you do?"

"You remember Estelle, right?"

"Uh-huh."

"Well, we kind of hooked up in the past. A few times . . . more than a few times," I admitted quietly.

"Ohmygod don't tell me you got her pregnant."

"No! God. No," I said, my voice slightly defeated. Would that be the worst news ever? For me to have gotten her pregnant? Normally I would have said yes, but today, I wasn't so sure.

"Okay, so? Victor caught you and gave you a black eye?" she guessed again.

"No!" I said, groaning. "She's engaged!"

More silence. The only tell I had that she was still on the line was Sander's cooing.

"And you're upset about it because you can't hook up anymore?" she asked.

"I'm upset about it because I think I'm in love with her," I said, my voice quiet. I hadn't even admitted that to myself. "I mean, I don't know for sure, but I think," I added.

Sophie laughed. "Well, this is . . ." she sighed. "This is something . . ."

"Sophie!"

"Bean, you call me in the middle of feeding to tell me that you're possibly—but don't know for sure—in love with the little sister of your best friend from third grade and that she's engaged to be married to somebody else. I mean . . . I have no words. When did this start? When did you figure this out?"

"It started years ago, but it's never been anything real, you know?"

"Only real enough for you to freak out when you hear she's engaged?"

My eyes screwed shut.

"How can you not be sure you're in love with her? Do you guys keep in touch?"

"No. No. We haven't spoken since . . . in a while. Since I came home last time . . . and even then, it was quick hi and bye—awkward because I was leaving a restaurant with a date, and she was getting there to meet hers."

"And now?"

"And now . . . she's engaged to some prick."

Sophie laughed again. "And you're Prince Charming."

"I don't know what to do. I'm going to her engagement party, and I don't know what to do."

"You're going to her engagement party?" she said. "Are you crazy? What do you think she'll say?"

"I don't know. I'm hoping she'll take her ring off and throw it in the guy's face."

"Ollie . . ."

I groaned. My sister only called me that when she was about to cajole me and say something I didn't want to hear.

"Maybe you should let her go. Maybe she wasn't the one."

"She was! She is!" I said, pacing my room.

"If you feel that way, why didn't you try anything sooner?" she asked with a sigh.

"Do you remember what it was like when Dad left?"

"Dad didn't leave. They got a divorce. There's a difference."

"Whatever. Do you remember when that happened? What he would say? How he felt like he was unaccomplished and couldn't provide Mom with anything?"

"Oh my God. You actually listened to the crock of shit Dad fed us when he was probably drunk?"

"Of course I did! I was a kid! He was my dad! And all my friends were so . . . I don't know. I just had this vision of what I wanted to be when I grew up. I wanted to be successful so that my wife didn't have to work unless she wanted to."

"So you planned out this entire 1950's reality for you and your future wife without taking into account that life actually moves on with or without you?" she said after a long pause.

I let out a harsh breath. "Fuck. Fuck. Fuck. Fuck." I spewed, kicking the wall beside my closet.

"Well, that's my cue," she said when Sander started crying. "Good luck tonight. And Bean?"

"Yeah?"

"Sometimes we let the first ones get away, but it teaches us to cherish the second ones that much more."

I mumbled a yeah, thanks, and promised her I'd visit tomorrow. I couldn't deal with the idea of letting Elle get away. Was it so bad that I wanted to keep her? I finally stuck with what I was already wearing and left my house. Instead of taking my car, I walked to Vic's. I needed to think about what I was going to do once I got there. Thinking didn't help. If anything, the rustling wind in my ear confused my thoughts that much more. When I finally got there, I didn't know what to do. Normally I went in through the back door, but today I wasn't here as Victor's friend, I was here as Estelle's . . . something . . . so I used the front.

Thomas, Victor's dad, wore a shocked expression on his face when he opened the door for me.

"I don't think you've ever used this door," he said with a frown.

"I figured I should, since it's been a while."

"You're still our boy, no matter how old you get or how many lives you save, Doctor." He laughed the same laugh Victor had, with his shoulders quaking and his perfect, straight teeth shining.

"So, big day," I said.

"Big day . . ." he agreed, looking around. There were only a handful of people there, but I figured this was only the beginning. "Vic is in the game room with Mia's brother, and Estelle is in the kitchen. Her fiancé is . . . around."

I had no intention of meeting him, but as soon as the words left his mouth, the fiancé from the photo appeared in front of us. I sized him up quickly. He was definitely older than me, skinnier than me, a bit shorter than me, but he had a smile that demanded attention. I knew that smile, because I saw it on my own face when I looked in the mirror. So evidently, Elle had a type. If he hadn't given her the ring on her finger, I would have smiled, too.

"Wyatt! This right here is Oliver, one of Victor's oldest friends," Thomas said, swiveling around and signaling at me.

Wyatt looked at me with the most serious brown eyes. At first, he frowned, then, as if something dawned on him, he smiled. "Of course. Oliver! I've heard a lot about you. Good to finally put a face to the name," he said, offering me his hand, which I took and squeezed a little tighter than I normally would have.

"Interesting. I just heard about you today, and I guess on that note, I must say you're a lucky bastard," I replied, earning a raised eyebrow from him. I should have probably toned down the mirth in my voice, especially being that Elle's dad was standing right there, but the filter over my mouth was nonexistent.

"You know what they say about the early bird," he said, and with a wink, walked away. I wanted to clobber him.

"What does she see in that guy?" I muttered under my breath, low enough that I thought Thomas couldn't hear me, but his healthy chuckle rang out. He clapped a hand on my back and walked me toward the game room.

For what seemed like an eternity, I watched Robert and Victor play some stupid video game where they shot up everything that walked by. Such pointless garbage.

"I'm going to grab a beer. Want something?" I said, getting up.

"You sure you don't want to play?" Vic asked, even though he knew I would only play Madden. When I didn't respond, he shouted for me to bring him a beer.

I walked to the kitchen and greeted the people I knew. Mia, who was having an argument on the phone, managed to roll her eyes and signal at me in a way I understood was code for *can you believe this shit?* I saw her mom and Elle's, hugged them quickly, and talked to them about Berkeley. I spotted Wyatt through the window. He was outside on his cell phone, smoking a cigarette. I paused. Elle was marrying a smoker?

Every hint I caught from this life of hers seemed the opposite of what I would have guessed it would be. I pictured her painting, making her beautiful sculptures, eating those granola things she liked to eat, and drinking lattes. I didn't picture her with . . . this guy. Maybe there was nothing wrong with him. Maybe I was just looking for an excuse to hate him, but I didn't like the way he'd greeted me as if he knew me. Like he'd heard every stupid mistake I'd made when it came to Elle, and he'd righted all my wrongs.

When I rounded the corner to the kitchen, I finally saw her and paused at the doorway. She was definitely one of those women who got better with time—like a good scotch. She was wearing an ivory dress that reached her knees, and it hugged her body like a glove. Her shoes were gold with spikes on the heel. Her hair was down her back in natural waves, but the front was cut shorter, and every time she bent over, she had to blow it out of her eyes. I waited for her to stand upright before I barged in, because when it came to us, that's what we did. We didn't knock, and we didn't ask for permission. We just invaded.

"Hey," I said to her back. She gasped and stiffened, taking a moment before turning around to look at me.

For what seemed like an eternity, she just stared at me, eyes wide, clearly questioning what the hell I was doing there.

"Hi," she said finally, her voice a croak before she cleared it.

"I heard you're . . ." I couldn't even say the words. My eyes fell on her finger. The ring was glaring at me. Yelling.

"Yeah," she said.

Our eyes met again. I didn't know what to say. I couldn't congratulate her on something I wasn't happy about.

"Are you happy?" I asked, inching closer to her. She took a step back, hitting the counter behind her with a gasp.

"Don't," she said, putting her hands up defensively. "I . . . yes. I am."

"So he's the one?" I asked, my voice steady, my heart coiling, my eyes begging.

She tore her gaze away from mine. "He makes me happy, if that's what you're getting at."

I moved closer. "Is that what it takes to be the one?"

Her eyes flashed back to mine, and I swear, in that moment, I lost whatever doubt I had left. Right there, in those eyes, in the turbulent sea she created with just one look.

"What it takes is showing up. What it takes is not walking away every time something possibly meaningful happens. What it takes is . . . Jesus, Oliver, I don't even know what you want me to tell you!" she whisper-shouted at me.

"Tell me he's the one. Tell me he makes you feel the way you feel when you're with me," I urged, getting closer to her face.

She let out a short laugh. "I haven't seen you in what? Over a year? And you come in here looking at me like that and talking about how I feel when I'm with you. What am I supposed to do with that, Oliver?"

I grabbed her elbows and held her there so that we were breathing on each other's faces. The smell of cookie dough and wine infiltrated my nose, and I could only close my eyes and picture what it would taste like on my tongue.

"Let go of me," she said, in a low voice. "You are not going to kiss me. You do not get to kiss me. Not today."

"This may be the last chance I get to kiss you," I said softly, my lips falling over her cheek. "This may be the last time I get to hold you."

"Oliver, please," she said between a whisper and a plea.

"Does he make your heart race like I do?" I whispered beside the corner of her mouth. "Does he make you feel like you can't breathe sometimes?"

"I like breathing, thank you very much," she whispered, but sagged against my touch.

"How often do you think about me, Elle?"

"I'm not answering that," she said, closing her eyes as my lips brushed against hers.

"You're not stopping me from kissing you," I said, in warning.

"I should. If he comes in here, he's going to be upset."

"He shouldn't have left your side to begin with."

She pressed against me, pushing me back slightly. The sound of heels clinking against the floor startled me, and I dropped my hands from her elbows, taking a step back.

"Are the cookies ready, honey? I have nothing else to give people," her mom said, appearing beside us.

"Yeah, here. I'm making one more batch of pigs in a blanket and then I'll be done," she responded.

Hannah stopped beside me with the tray in one hand and held my chin. "Doesn't he get more handsome every time he comes home?" she said, pinching my cheek as she walked away.

Estelle glared at her mother's back as I smiled slightly.

"He seems to know a lot about me," I said when we were alone again.

Her face clouded. "He knows enough."

"Enough to know he should worry about me and you being alone together?"

"Enough to know you're trouble. Deadly. Hazardous to my health."

I sighed, running a hand through my hair. This wasn't going as planned.

"So you're doing it? You're going to marry him?" I said, finally realizing this was a losing battle.

"We're engaged, Oliver. We're living together. We're opening a gallery together. That alone is like having a child," she said, her words making me flinch. A child with him.

"This is so hard for me," I whispered, stepping in front of her again.

"What we had . . . it passed," she said, her eyes on the floor beside us.

"Do you really believe that?" I asked, cupping her chin so that she could look at me.

"You need to stop," she whispered, her eyes shining with unshed tears. I hated to be the cause of them. I wondered how many I'd been responsible for throughout the years. That was when it really hit me: I messed up royally. This wasn't an easy fix. This wasn't a *let me come over tomorrow and fix the training wheel I accidently broke.* Or *let me replace the canvas I threw a football in the middle of.* This is life. This is what happens when you stop living in the moment. People grow up. They change, they move on, and you find yourself wishing you had looked up in time to walk with them.

"You're right," I said, stepping back and dropping my hand. "You're right. I'm sorry. If you're happy, I'm happy for you, my beautiful Elle."

I leaned in, gave her a kiss on the cheek, taking one last moment to smell her, and walked away.

Chapter 26

Present

Estelle

MY PHONE RAN out of battery a couple of minutes after I made it through the door last night, and I was actually grateful for the quiet. I'd slept on the couch the realtor insisted I leave in the living room, which was the only room in the house that was somewhat decorated. When I woke up this morning, I went upstairs and sat in the middle of my unfurnished bedroom, thinking about the last time I'd done that. It was when Wyatt had insisted on getting a new bed since I was moving in. He'd bought the house with an ex-girlfriend, way before we met. It didn't bother me until I realized I would sleep in the bed they'd bought together. That was when he threw out the old mattress and told me to go to West Elm to pick out a new bed, which I did. The room is so dull now though—so vacant without the bed sitting in the middle. The bed, I gave to his mother. I couldn't bear to sleep in it anymore. I slept in it for an entire year after he died, and I was done with it. Moving on meant giving up even the smallest sense of comfort I'd shared with him.

Yet here I was, back where I started. It's not that I don't have an identity without Wyatt or our life together, but I liked the simple act of coming home and knowing what I would find here. For some reason, knowing that this place would no longer be mine soon made me feel a little lost. Where do I go now? Sure, I would buy a new place. Sure, I would decorate it to my liking, but would it feel like home to me? I gather myself up and walk downstairs again, peeking into all of the rooms as I go. And when I open the front door to leave, I drop everything in my hands, because Oliver is sitting outside on the steps with his back facing me.

"What are you doing here?" I ask.

He sighs but doesn't turn to face me. His hand runs through his hair. It's getting long again. I'm surprised he doesn't have it up in a small bun already.

"I had this whole speech planned out, and now that you finally came out, I can't even think," he says.

"How long have you been out here?" I ask, sitting beside him on the step.

He shrugs, still not looking at me. "It doesn't matter."

"What was this speech you had planned?"

He dips his head between his legs, resting it in his hands. "That's the problem, Elle. Everything I had planned to say makes me sound like a complete asshole when I repeat it in my head. All my life I've been all about preparing for things and planning things out, and when it comes to you . . . I'm completely lost when it comes to you," he says, tilting his face to look at me.

"I'm not that confusing. I'm simple," I say quietly, tucking my hands behind my knees to resist the urge to touch his hair . . . the scruff on his face . . . his full lips.

"Your simplicity is maddening. Everything about you drives me crazy. The way you smile at me, the way you look at me, the way you talk to those kids at the hospital as if they're adults—as if they matter . . . Not a lot of people do that, you know. Even me sometimes. When I'm working insane hours, I go into their rooms and only address their parents. I saw you teaching them to paint—teaching them to do something with their hands, with their time—and the way you looked at them . . ." he pauses, sighs, and looks at me with those evergreen eyes of his shining like I'm his world. "You know what it made me think? I want to have kids with that girl, because every child deserves to be looked at that way. Everybody deserves to feel that important."

My heart squeezes at his admission. I open my mouth to speak, but words fail me, so instead, I scoot closer and lean my head on his shoulder. He kisses the top of my head and wraps his arm around me.

"Do you think I'm crazy?" he asks after a beat.

"Absolutely," I say, smiling, as I pull back to look at him. "Your complications are completely maddening. Everything about you drives me crazy."

He chuckles, shaking his head. "It sounded better in my head."

I lean into him and brush my nose against his scruffy, cold cheek. "I thought it sounded pretty good."

"You're not mad that I came here?" he asks, running his hand down my side.

"How did you even find me?"

"I called Mia. I mean . . . after a while, I had a feeling you weren't coming back to Vic's house, and then I called Mia. When she said you weren't there, I asked her for this address."

"That girl . . ."

"I owe her a week's worth of coffee."

I laugh. "You're going to be able to afford her addiction on your residency paycheck?"

He smiles. "Maybe she won't notice if I brew it myself."

"Doubtful," I say. We both laugh and look at each other again, my breath catching in my throat at the emotion in his eyes. He brushes his hand over my cheek softly.

"One date, beautiful Elle," he says in a whisper that makes my stomach coil. I take a deep breath, and I let go of my reservations along with my exhale. I want this. I believe in this.

"One date," I agree, smiling at his wide grin.

I look over my shoulder, at the house I shared with the man I loved, and I sigh. I don't feel as bad as I thought I would, agreeing to this date. Maybe for once the stars will align for us.

Chapter 27

I CHOOSE NOT to tell my brother about my date with Oliver because, well, I don't have the guts to. I know he'd try to stop it before it happens. I don't need him to verbalize that he thinks Oliver is a huge player and isn't worthy of me. Besides, it's just one date. Chances are it'll be a lot less tame than our friends date anyway. In the back of my mind, I'm screaming *don't get attached just yet!* But the thing is, it's Bean. I will forever be attached to him, no matter what happens. I drive to Mia's place and park my car in the visitor's spot, where it'll stay until we get back, then I go upstairs and wait.

"I heard you have a date with Oliver, and from the looks of it, you definitely do. You're sweating like a whore in church!" Rob says as soon as he sees me. I punch him in the shoulder.

"No I'm not! Oh God, am I?" I head toward the bathroom and look at myself, realizing that he was exaggerating. But, damn. I am nervous. "Why am I so nervous about this? And where is Meep?"

"She's in the shower, and you're nervous because this is your first date together. I mean, real date. Shenanigans don't count." He raises a blonde eyebrow and laughs when I glare at him.

"I need a drink," I announce, heading to the kitchen.

"No, you don't. You need to sit and relax and be still. You're going to give me a heart attack!"

"Stop being a pest," I mutter, plopping down on the couch.

"Okay, but on your date, do not sit like that. Nothing is more gross than a careless sitter in a dress."

My eyes widen, and I cross my legs, sitting upright. "Damn you. Maybe I should have worn jeans."

Robert laughs, throwing his head back. He looks so much like Mia when he does that. "I was joking! Geez, you really are nervous."

"Who's nervous?" Mia asks, walking over to us.

"Jitterbug over here is acting like a virgin going to prom," Rob says, earning a laugh from me, and a look from Mia.

"Way to lay it all out there," I say.

"She looks fine," Mia says walking over to me. "It's just Bean."

"Exactly. It's just Bean . . . do I look okay?"

Mia gives me a onceover and nods. "You look beautiful, like you do every other day, when you wear make-up and brush your hair and dress up."

"Meaning not like every other day?"

"Well, you have to save beauty for special occasions, Chicken."

"Bitch," I say, laughing until the knock on the door swallows my smile.

"Ohh here he comes," Rob starts singing like he was singing *Man Eater*, and I want to crawl into a hole and die. Mia swings the door open and whistles loudly.

"Looks like somebody wants to get laid tonight," she announces.

And this time, for real, I want to crawl into a hole and die. I can feel my face burning as I walk to the door and tell Mia and Robert to shut up. Oliver is wearing dark jeans, black shoes, a gray button-down, and a fedora on his head. It's simple and hot, and it matches the gray dress I'm wearing, so I have to laugh.

"It's like they're meant to be!" Rob states loudly. "They match! This is too fucking cute! Mia! Get the camera!"

"I hate you." I say, looking at him. "I hate you." I say, turning to Mia's face, red from laughing. "I don't hate you . . . yet." I say, turning to Oliver, who gives me a slow, cocky half grin that makes me melt a little.

"Please have her home by midnight, and make sure she lays off the vodka," As Mia starts rattling off her list, she stops to look at my blushing face and bursts out laughing. "Awww . . . I'm sorry, Elle, this is so cute though. You haven't been this nervous since you lost your virginity to Hunter Grayson." She stops laughing and turns to Oliver with a serious face. "All jokes aside, if you hurt her again, I will fucking murder you, and I'm not talking about a nice quiet murder, I'm talking dick cut off, internal organs everywhere kind of murder. So please, be mindful of that."

"Okay, time to go," I say, pulling Oliver's arm out the door. "Some people have officially lost their marbles."

Oliver is doubled over in laughter as we walk down the stairs, so he has to stop every so often to catch his breath. I can't even turn to look at him because I'm so embarrassed. And I shouldn't even be embarrassed! We ALL grew up together! This is absolutely ridiculous. When we get to his car, he wipes a tear from his eye as he opens the door for me. I don't even look at him when he gets in. I just stare straight ahead. But then he gets quiet, and his hand reaches for mine on my lap. He squeezes it gently, to get my attention.

"Hey," he says quietly, his eyes smiling.

"I'm glad you enjoyed the show. We'll be here all week," I mumble, making him chuckle. He brings my hand to his lips and brushes against it. I shiver at the feel of his scruff prickling over it.

"They mean well," he says, kissing my hand. "You look beautiful. I'm so happy I finally agreed to go on this date with you."

That makes me laugh. "Really? Were you being hounded relentlessly?"

"Like you wouldn't believe," he says, raising his eyebrows. "It's been exhausting having to dodge your advances."

I finally sigh and get comfortable in my seat. Oliver has a way of making me feel at ease in one moment. His fingers brush my knee and I jolt. *And completely electrified the next.*

"So, where are you taking me?" I ask, turning my face to look at him. He smiles, looking straight ahead.

"If I tell you, it would ruin the surprise aspect of the date."

"We're not going to dinner and a movie, are we?" I say, biting back a laugh when he shoots me a look.

"Do I look that dull to you?"

I shrug. "I don't know. Where do you normally take your dates?"

His gaze cuts to mine again. "To eat."

"And . . . that's it?" I ask, a little unimpressed.

"Well, that's not it, but I don't think you want to talk about that any more than I want to talk about Hunter Grayson."

I look away, smiling. "Fair enough."

"Unless, of course, you want to talk about Hunter Grayson," he says, as he parks the car in the marina.

"I'd rather not," I say, feeling my cheeks flush. Hunter is still a friend of mine, and we each did a pretty good job at burying the memories of the night we had together.

Oliver turns his body to face me and runs the back of his hand down my cheek to my neck, his eyes on mine the entire time. "I'm really glad we're doing this."

I smile softly, suddenly feeling shy under his gaze. "Me too."

He drops his hand, gets out of the car and, while I gather my purse, he comes around to open the door for me. We walk a couple of steps before his hand closes over mine, and he threads our fingers together. It's such a small gesture, but it sets my pulse on fire.

"We're going on a boat?" I ask when we walk past the restaurant there and head toward the vessels.

"Not quite," he says. "Maybe next time." He tilts his head to look down at me, and I feel the warmth of his smile curl through me.

We walk up to the edge of a dock, where there's a table set up. The floor around it is scattered in candles and it's completely desolate, except for the server standing beside it with a champagne bottle in his hands and a smile on his face.

"Mario, good to see you again," Oliver says, dropping my hand and offering it to the server.

"Pleasure is all mine, Dr. Hart," he says with a hint of a Spanish accent, smiling and nodding as he takes the hand he's being offered and shakes it.

"This is Estelle," Oliver says. "Elle, this is Mario."

"Pleased to meet you," I say, offering him my hand as well. Once we're settled in our seats, Mario pours us some champagne, hands us a menu, and tells us he'll be back. My eyes scan everything again—the candles, the table, the boats, the sun that's still setting over the ocean in the distance—and finally, I look up at Oliver's handsome face.

"You know you could have taken me to In-N-Out Burger and I would have been just as happy, right?"

His eyes flick to mine, and he gives me a slow, half-smile. "The night's still young."

I smile and reach for my glass of champagne. "How did you set this up, anyway?" I ask, when I see Mario walking toward us with a tray in his hands. He places it between us, bows and walks away. "Where did you find that guy?" I ask when he's out of earshot. Oliver chuckles, his shoulders shaking. I love that his dimples—although covered by the scruff on his face—are in full sight.

"Are we playing twenty questions?" he asks after a beat, his eyes sparkling with amusement under the brim of his hat.

"We might as well," I retort, smiling back.

"I met him when he brought his kid into the ER. I was on my way out, he and his wife were frantic because David, their son, wiped out and hit his head. So I helped them."

"And you stayed in touch?" I ask, frowning.

"Well, I had to make house calls," he says, looking away.

"You make house calls?"

He sighs and looks at me again. "Not usually." I raise an eyebrow and signal for him to elaborate. Finally, he sighs again, runs a hand through his hair and speaks. "They didn't have medical insurance, so I had to kind of do what I did off the books."

My heart squeezes in my chest and I smile, reaching my hand out and placing it over his on the table. He turns his over and holds it there. We don't say anything. I don't tell him what an amazing man he is for doing that, and he doesn't elaborate further. From experience, I know that Oliver is the kind of guy who would throw himself in front of a bus for you and then deny that he saved your life. He'll chalk it up to *anybody would have done the same*. He doesn't realize that people aren't that nice. People don't push aside their own agenda for the sake of the greater good. He looks into my eyes with this longing—this need—as he draws circles over my hand. For a moment, I can't remember what we were talking about, what we're doing, where we are, or what day it is.

"Shall we eat?" he says, flashing an easy smile that makes my heart stutter. I nod and take my hand back, putting it over my lap and folding it into the other while I wait for him to uncover the plate of oysters between us.

"Did you already work your last day at the hospital?" I ask, slipping a forkful into my mouth.

"Well, I'm done with my residency, so yes, but I've been picking up shifts here and there while I decide what to do next."

"I have to go back on Tuesday for a class. Mae wants me to teach the class how to make sculptures out of shattered glass."

Oliver picks up his gaze from the plate and looks at me, but doesn't say anything, so I continue.

"I wish the *powers that be* would let the kids come to the studio instead. Jen is asking Mr. Frederick about it to see if he'll let me set up a field trip there, just so they can get out. I mean, if it's possible. I'm sure it would be difficult to cover the doctors and nurses and stuff . . . I wish this house would sell already," I say, sighing.

"What are you going to do once it does?"

"Originally I was planning on giving all of the money to Wyatt's parents. Set up an account and be done with it. But then I thought, I mean . . . it was my house too. Maybe I should take some of it and give the rest to them. I don't know. It's confusing. They don't want it, and I don't need it, so I go back and forth on it."

Oliver nods and takes a sip of champagne. "Do you miss your life there?"

My eyes search his. I know what he's asking. I don't know if I want to answer. Finally, I take a breath and look away for a beat. Before I answer, he speaks again.

"Let's do something," he says, his hand reaching out for mine again. "For the remainder of this date, we ask and answer every question imaginable. It doesn't matter how dumb or how hard it is. I want to know everything. Nothing left unsaid, okay?"

"That's a lot for one date," I breathe. He squeezes my hand.

"Sometimes one date is all we have." His response makes me feel like crying, and I guess he sees that, because he brings my hand up to his and kisses it. "I want a lot of dates like this, Elle. A lot. But in the past, we've done things, and we haven't communicated and, well . . . I don't want that to happen again."

I take another breath. "I don't miss it. I mean, I miss the comfort of going there and knowing I was home. I miss Wyatt sometimes," I say, my voice catching. I swallow down the tears I feel coming. "I miss his enthusiasm about art and life and the stories he would tell me about his travels. Is this weird?" I whisper, looking up at him and wiping under my eyes.

He looks like he's being lashed at, but he shakes his head nonetheless. "It's . . . it's fine. I want to hear this. I don't want you to think you have to erase your past because of me, or forget about him or your life together. I just . . . I've never felt like I've had to compete with anybody for someone's affection, and now I feel like I'm competing with a ghost, and sometimes memories are better than realities."

I stare at him for a moment before I stand and walk around the table. Oliver leans back, wordlessly making room for me on his lap. I sit there and wrap my arms around his neck, placing my head on his chest. His arms automatically go around me, holding me there so perfectly, it's as if my body is a puzzle piece snapping in place. So many years I've dreamt of doing this with him and when we finally do, we have the shadow of my past over us. That's how life is—I know that—but it still breaks my heart for him . . . for us.

"Would it help if I told you that the whole time I was with Wyatt he was competing with *your* ghost?" I whisper against his neck, breathing in his calming, clean scent.

His chuckle vibrates through me. "Not really. That would just mean I should have tried harder before. Maybe if I had, you wouldn't have had to experience such a terrible loss."

I inch back from him, to look at his face. "How is it that you haven't found a woman yet? All those women you work with—that you went to school with—all, smart and beautiful. How could perfect Oliver not have found someone?"

He chuckles again, his eyes sparkling as he reaches up and combs the hair out of my face. I do the same for him, but leave my hand on the back of his neck. He closes his eyes for a moment and swallows. "I'm not perfect, Elle. Not even close."

"You are to me," I whisper.

His eyes darken when he looks at me. "Maybe that's your answer."

Chapter 28

"ON A SCALE from *happy* to *I can't stop smiling excited,* how thrilled would you be if I told you Mia packed an overnight bag for you?" Oliver asks, placing his fedora on the dashboard.

After dinner, we sat and talked about Wyatt and the house, mostly, and now that we're back in the car driving, I've been kind of anxious. I really, really don't want the date to end. We've been driving for quite a while, listening to music, talking about movies . . . so it isn't until he asks me this question, that I realize that the only thing we haven't talked about are what my plans are for tomorrow.

"Well . . ." I start, pausing to laugh. "I guess you've only given me choices I have to smile about so . . . *really happy?*"

He grins and looks my way. "Good, because it's in the trunk, and I'm kidnapping you for the night. Maybe for the rest of the weekend."

"You realize that you're setting yourself up for failure on any future date, right?"

"Never doubt an overachiever," he says, smiling as he pushes hair out of his eyes.

I laugh and resist the urge to lean in and run my hands through his hair. "Your hair grows so fast," I say instead.

"Yeah, that's the upside. Too bad I need to cut it short again soon. And shave."

"For job interviews?" I guess.

"Yeah, I let them hire me before I let my hair grow again. Nobody wants to hire a doctor with a man bun."

"It's not even long enough for one yet, but I happen to know somebody who thinks doctors with man buns are hot."

"Do you, now?" he says, flashing a grin my way.

"I'm sure I do."

"Does her name start with an E?"

"Possibly."

"Is she afraid of the dark?"

"No," I grumble, and look away, making him laugh.

"Does she happen to hate my jokes?"

My lips tip up, but I keep looking out the window. "I can't imagine any-body would like your jokes."

"Oh, but they do."

"Oliver," I say, turning to him with a long-suffering sigh. "I'm sorry to break it to you, but they're just pretending."

He scoffs, giving me a bewildered look. "Pretending? Okay, I get it. You just haven't heard my latest."

I groan and laugh at the same time. "Let's hear it."

He waits until we're stopped at a red light to lean in so that his chin is almost on my shoulder. For a moment, I forget how to breathe. Then he starts talking and drops his voice so low that everything inside of me zaps, and I can't help but hold my breath. "If I were an enzyme," he says, his lips, a soft tickle over my ear. "I'd be DNA helicase," he continues, as he trails his lips over my neck. My eyes flutter shut, and I grip on to my knees. "So I could unzip your genes."

I open my eyes as he pulls back, and my heart drops into the pit of my stomach at the hungry look in his eyes. When his gaze moves to my mouth, I can't take any more. I lose all pretenses. I pull him to me and kiss him, fran-tically at first, then slowly, so that the kiss teases . . . tastes . . . our tongues barely touching. He pulls away and marvels at me for a moment before the sound of honking snaps us of out of the moment and he continues through the intersection.

"Not bad, huh?" he says after a beat. I'm still trying to regain my breath. I lick my lips and close my eyes at the taste of him.

"That wasn't a joke. That was nerdy seduction," I say in a breath. I can't help but smile when he starts laughing.

"Nerdy seduction," he says, still chuckling.

"Next question, are you still dating or hooking up or doing whatever you're doing with Grace . . . or anybody else in the hospital . . . or elsewhere?"

I watch the side of his face as he frowns. When he stops behind a car, he shoots me a look. "I told you I wasn't, Elle. Do you think I would insist on a date if I was seeing someone else?"

"I don't know," I shrug. "I'm not sure how you work in that department."

He raises an eyebrow. "You know exactly how I work in that department."

"So you're not seeing anyone else right now?" I ask, ignoring his comment.

"Are you insinuating that we're seeing each other?" he says.

"No. Why would you . . ."

"You said anyone else, which would mean that we're seeing each other."

"Well that's not what I meant."

He rounds the corner to a nice hotel on the water and pulls up in front of the valet. Oliver's fingers paint over mine. "It's what I want it to mean."

My heart crashes in my chest as the valet guy opens the door for me. I make my feet move and step out of the car, just barely containing my composure. Oliver comes around with two bags in his hands, and I follow him inside. I look around, inhaling the aromas coming from the spa, and read that we're in the Sonoma Coast. I can't believe the car ride seemed so short—not that I'd ever been up here, but I've passed it plenty of times. This is the point where Vic and I usually start bickering, because the road trip is taking so long. I step aside as he goes up to the counter. I watch as he speaks to the lady, making her laugh at something he says, and then meet his eyes as he walks back to me. Oliver has always had this thing about him—this easiness that comes with him. He fits in with any group of people, because he embraces everybody with the way he is.

He carries himself with such confidence that you would think he owns the world. He's the kind of guy who can participate in a conversation amongst important businessmen and doctors alike, and they would never question who he is. They would never suspect he was the guy who arrived in a beat-up car and worked two jobs so he could get it. He has a smile that'll charm the pants off anybody if they're not careful enough, and pairs that with a heart of gold. As he approaches and flashes that very smile at me, I feel myself melt.

"Ready?" he asks. I tuck my arm in his and nod, following him to the elevator. I realize that I haven't asked him why he brought me to a hotel or what his plans are. Something happens to me when I'm around Oliver. It's like the world vanishes around me. Everything can be falling apart, but in his arms, I'm whole.

When we reach the room, he puts our bags down beside the door and waits for me to explore. It's a really big room, with a king-size bed, a bench by the window, and oversized, plush couches and a fireplace off to the side to make a living room. I walk over to the window and sit down on the cush-

ioned bench, touching the cold glass with my hand. Oliver hasn't said anything since we entered the room, and when I turn around, I find him propped
up against the wall on the other side of the bed, with his legs crossed and his
hands in the front pockets of his jeans. His fedora is slightly tilted down, and
his hair is seeping out of it. What I can make out of his green eyes makes my
stomach toss uncontrollably.

"Why are you standing all the way over there?" I ask with a nervous
laugh.

"I'm kind of worried of what will happen if I step any closer," he says. I
inhale sharply.

"Maybe I want you to step closer."

He shakes his head and bites back a smile. "I should have said this sooner, but I didn't bring you here to take this further than, well, sleep." I open my
mouth to say something, but stop and wait for him to continue. "This is still
part of our date. Tomorrow, the vineyards. We didn't get to do that last time."

I stand and walk over to him, stopping when we're toe-to-toe, and tilt
my head to look at him. I reach up, take the hat off his head, and toss it to the
floor by the fireplace. "What if I want to take this further than just sleep?"

His face darkens. A slow smile appears over his face as he reaches for me
and caresses my cheek softly. "I want to get it right this time, Elle. I don't want
to push you. I don't want you to wake up tomorrow and regret something we
do tonight."

"I won't," I whisper, leaning into his touch.

"Last time we slept together, I found you crying over a shirt," he says, his
voice soft and slightly pained.

"That was different."

"How?" he asks, pushing off the wall and cupping the back of my neck.
"Tell me how it was different, because if something happens tonight, it'll be
so much more than just touching. You know that, right? And I mean more
than just physically. Even if we only touch or kiss, it'll be more, and I don't
want you to wake up and feel like you're cheating or being unfair to his memory."

I close my eyes, needing to look away from his understanding gaze,
away from the love I see in it. He's right. I know this, and I know he doesn't
deserve to be a regret for me, but the thing is, Oliver has never been a regret.
Even when it hurt . . . even when he left. Even when he came back and sliced
me open again, he wasn't a regret because I loved him. Wyatt may not have
been the most understanding man—and maybe his ways of making me move

past things weren't perfect—but he did make me understand love for what it was. That's the little tagline I send off my shattered hearts with. Wyatt was the one who opened my eyes to it, but Oliver was the reason for the hearts and the taglines. He was the one I loved first. He was the one who broke my heart first, and here he is again. For how long this time, I wonder? Does it matter? My heart bleeds.

When I open my eyes again, Oliver is looking at me like I might bolt. I wrap my arms around his neck and lean up, kissing his stubbly chin, his strong jaw, and then move up to the shell of his ear.

"What we have isn't aligned with that part of my life. We live in a galaxy of our own," I whisper, kissing his earlobe. I smile when his breath quickens. "Where the storms pass, and the light fades, and everything ceases to exist except for us."

His hands squeeze my waist, and gently push me back. "I planned out this night where I would keep my hands to myself and sleep on the sofa if I had to, and then you say things like that and scatter every part of my brain—like only you can." He dips his face and kisses my neck once, twice, three times . . . soft wet kisses . . . before he leans back and pins his gaze on me again. "You make me get lost in you, Elle. The way you look at me, the way you touch me . . ." He doesn't finish his sentence, but instead, brings his lips down to meet mine in a long, slow kiss. As our hearts beat against each other's chest, and our tongues dance a slow sensual mambo, everything else fades away.

Oliver's hands make their way down my body until they reach the hem of my dress. He pulls it off me without breaking our kiss, while I unbutton his shirt and help him shrug out of it. Even though it hasn't been *that* long since we hooked up that last time, I feel like I haven't seen his body in ages. My eyes drop from his face to his chest. My hands trace every muscle, every contour, and every line etched on the beautiful man in front of me. My fingers reach the top of his jeans, and I begin to unbuckle his belt, and as I bring my gaze back up to his, I watch him as he watches me. A look of ecstasy clouds his face as I dip my hand into his boxers and test the weight of him, my hand squeezing as he sucks in a breath between his teeth.

"Elle," he says, his voice a hoarse whisper, as I kneel down in front of him. He kicks his shoes aside, and I help him step out of his jeans, his boxers, his socks . . . and align my face with his length. I lean forward, placing soft, wet kisses along his abdomen, smiling against him as his muscles spasm. I work my way down, licking each side of the "V" indented on his sides, until I reach what's beckoning me. My tongue slides under his shaft and he groans, his hand threading into my hair. I repeat the motion on either side as my hand holds his balls. He groans again, louder, when I take what I can of him into my mouth.

"Elle," Oliver says again, his voice low and guttural. I look up, meeting his hooded gaze, and a thrill runs through me when his hands brush my hair back, away from my face, as he looks down at me. He grabs my shoulders and pushes me back until he's completely out of my mouth with a pop, then he pulls me up so that we're chest to chest, his nose resting on my forehead.

"What you do to me, Elle," he whispers against me as I breathe into his chest. "It's inexplicable." He drops a kiss on my forehead and walks me backward until I'm forced to sit on the bed. He takes his time undoing the clasp of my bra and then pulls it over my shoulders. He does the same with my panties, sliding them down my thighs until they're off and on the floor with the rest of our clothes. Taking a step back, he looks at me—really looks at me. His gaze leaves a trail of heat with every inch it passes over, then he lets out a laugh. "For maybe the second time in my life, I don't know where to start," he murmurs, kneeling down in front of me and spreading my legs apart. Kissing my knee first, he makes his way up my thigh until he reaches my pelvis, grazing the patch of hair there, then he kisses his way up my stomach. When he reaches my right breast, he pauses and looks at me over the peak of my nipple.

"I can't tell you how many times I've dreamt of doing this again," he says, gliding the slick underside of his tongue over it. I gasp. My hands shoot out to grip his shoulders when he does it again. He blows softly over my little bud, the sensation of hot and cold making me shiver. He drags his face to my other breast and I shiver again, this time, at the feel of his chin scraping against my skin. His mouth closes over my nipple, sucking it into his mouth. As he pulls away and blows softly, his hand tweaks the other. My body feels like it's on fire, at the brink of combustion, and he hasn't even left my breasts yet.

As if hearing my thoughts, Oliver looks at me and flashes a smug smile before continuing to explore south of the border. Reaching the inside of my thighs, he nudges them to the sides and holds them apart with his hands, squeezing, as he dips his face into my center. His tongue peeks out and tastes me—just tastes—and he groans, his mouth vibrating against me. My already shaky hands find his hair, and I pull lightly, pivoting my hips against his face. He stills me with his grip on my knees, and raises his gaze to find mine. The intensity in them is so raw, so pure, that I feel my stomach begin to churn.

In his eyes, I find our past and our questionable future. It holds the sadness of lost years, the torturous longing of a million what-ifs, and the possibility of what could be. I try to look away . . . try to close my eyes and shut out the fervor his green eyes spear me with, because I don't want to admit that I'm scared. I don't want to open myself up and admit that he still has the ability to shatter me—to annihilate me completely.

His tongue lashes against me once more and I lose all thought . . . all reason . . . and come undone under his tongue. I finally shut my eyes and moan out his name as my back bows off the bed and an orgasm rocks through me. Oliver's kisses whisper over me as he makes his way back up my body. I open my eyes and he holds himself above me, arms on either side of me, and for the longest time, just looks at me, his eyes searching mine. My hand moves between us. His body shudders when I close my hand around his cock and grasp it, slowly sliding my hand up and down, up and down, until he's breathing heavily.

"We should probably get a condom," he says, his eyes bouncing between mine. I shake my head, bringing my other hand to clasp the back of his neck and pull his face to mine.

"No condom," I whisper against his lips. He stills, and for a moment, I wonder if he would rather use one. Maybe he regrets not doing so all those years ago.

"Elle," he says, letting out a breath. I'm sure he's about to climb off me and reach for a condom, but instead, he wraps an arm around my back and pulls me closer, settling himself between my folds. Slowly, carefully, he pushes in, giving my body time to adjust to his girth. I gasp when I feel him pulsate inside me. He stops to take a breath and chuckles into my neck.

"My beautiful little Elle," he says against my neck. The smile in his voice makes me smile. "You feel so fucking good around me, you have no idea." I arch my back, urging him to continue, because I do have an idea. I have a very good idea. He moves again, not stopping this time, instead, giving me long, deep strokes. "You just . . . swallow me up," he growls, moving faster now, his strokes becoming harder, as if he's staking his claim inside me.

"Do you ever think about this?" he asks, his voice somewhere between a grunt and a growl as he readjusts our position so that my leg is over his shoulder and he can get even deeper inside of me. I cry out, nodding. "Tell me," he says. Oliver pulls back to look first at the spot where we're joined and then to my face, where I'm sure he can see my desire for him.

"I touch myself thinking about you," I admit quietly, my eyes refusing to waver from his. He groans and stops moving, closing his eyes as if he's concentrating. "I picture you taking me like this, on top of me," I continue, pushing onto him. "And sometimes from behind."

Oliver's eyes snap open, and I whimper when he slowly slides out of me, then thrusts in hard and fast. My toes curl, and my eyes start rolling back as I grip on to his ass and encourage him to move faster. It's all I can do to keep myself from crying out at the level of emotion zip-lining through me.

"Please . . ." I'm actually begging. "Please, please, please keep moving faster."

He grins, slow and wide, and does what I say for all of four strokes.

I screw my eyes shut. "Please, please, please. Just . . . faster . . . harder . . ."

But Oliver has other plans. He leans down, stretching my legs further apart and kisses the calf I have resting on his chest. He rubs his face over the soft skin there, as his lips drag up and down, matching his hips in soft, slow, long, hard strokes.

"I want this to last forever," he says, biting the inside of my leg. "I want to make a little house inside your pussy," he says, and if it weren't for his hand tweaking my nipple and his cock pounding harder against me, I would make a joke. But the sensation of an orgasm begins to steamboat inside me, and I can't think anymore. He drops my leg and climbs over me again, his chest just over mine, so that his face is the only thing I can see. I don't know what he wants to find in my eyes, but I feel like he's boring into my soul, as if rummaging through a lost-and-found. Just when I open my mouth to say something, an orgasm slams through me, and I shriek his name instead. As if on cue, he grunts out my name and his eyes close in exhaustion. Oliver lets out a long breath, and when he opens his eyes again, he's wearing the goofy, lopsided smile I've always loved, and it makes me feel like whatever he was searching for has been found.

We lay in bed, naked, facing each other, his hand lazily drawing over my waist and mine over his chest. I've always been a go-with-the-flow kind of girl. I've never wondered where a relationship would take me—I never really bothered to care. But lying here beside Oliver makes me think about the future. It makes me *hope* for the future. And even though I told myself that this was just one date, I can't help the bubble of possibility that pops up in my head.

"What are you thinking about?" I whisper. He pulls my face to his chest, and then kisses the top of my head.

"I'm thinking that this is the best date I've ever been on."

I smile. "Really?"

"Yes, really."

"You realize you completely cheated, right? One date means one date, and you planned this out to be two dates."

He chuckles below me. "I told you I'm not good with rules."

"Thank God for that," I say, yawning against him.

I fall asleep in his arms, and even though I'm looking forward to the rest of our date tomorrow, a part of me is terrified of leaving this room and facing reality.

Chapter 29

I WAKE UP feeling overly warm, as if a heating blanket set on high was covering me. When I open my eyes, I realize that the blanket is Oliver. Our bodies are intertwined around the other's in such a way that I'm sure if there was a painting of this moment, the viewer would have a difficult time deciphering whose limbs were whose. My gaze ascends from his chest to his messy hair, enjoying all the parts in-between, and I sigh contently. Oliver's lids flutter open, and when his sleepy green eyes find mine, I am graced with a breathtaking smile that makes magical creatures ignite deep within my belly.

"Hey," he whispers in a sexy rasp that ratchets up my desire.

I smile, suddenly feeling a little shy. "Hey."

He lifts his hand from my waist and threads his fingers through my hair, pushing long bangs out of my face. He leans in slowly and brushes his soft lips against mine. Tender little bites have my eyelids fluttering shut. A moan resonates from me when his tongue scoops mine, twirling around it gently, and forming the beginning of a seductive dance that makes my breath quicken. Oliver breaks the kiss with the same gentle bites he started it with and drags his mouth down my neck, my chest, my abdomen . . .

My hands fly to his hair, clutching fistfuls, when he reaches my clit and begins to suck lightly. He runs his tongue over it sharply, last night's rendezvous becomes fresh in my mind. My grip tightens and, as my head falls to the side, I gasp simultaneously at the time on the clock, and at the feel of his fingers inside me.

"We're going to be late," I say, gasping again when his hands reach up and cup my breasts, tweaking my nipples.

"I'll make it worth it," he murmurs against me, sucking harder.

My eyes roll back.

"Oliver," I say, his name a guttural moan.

"Estelle," he answers, blowing over the wetness on my nipples as his fingers continue to move inside me.

"Oh God."

"Mmmm," he groans as he quickens the lash of his tongue.

My back arches at the wave of heat that courses through me. He makes his way back up my body with open, wet kisses, and positions the head of his cock at my entrance. I open my eyes to find him staring down at me, his eyes hooded with desire. He licks his bottom lip slowly and bites down on it as he begins to push inside me with a measured thrust.

"This is how all of our mornings should start," he grunts when he's all the way inside me. My eyes roll back at the way he fills me up. And then he begins to move, and I feel myself fall with every thrust, with every moment his green eyes stay on mine, and with every crease that forms between his eyebrows as he makes me feel like the most beautiful woman in the world. Yes, this is how all of our mornings should start, I think to myself. This is how they could have been before, but I don't think I could have survived them when he left.

"How did he propose?" Oliver asks later, after we've shared enough samples of wine to fill two bottles. We've been asking each other questions all day. It started as a game—so that the person who didn't want to answer would have to down a glass—but then we kept on hounding until we answered anyway, so we dropped the game and kept the questions.

I take a large gulp of wine. He doesn't laugh this time, because this particular question is as uncomfortable for him to hear as it is for me to answer. "It was the day we got the space for the gallery. We were home celebrating with a couple of our friends. Dallas and Micah were there," I say, pausing. When he nods in recognition of the names, I continue. "So we were home, drinking . . . the guys telling jokes, the girls laughing along . . . and suddenly, he gets down on one knee in front of me and just proposes." I shrug, recalling the memory and smiling sadly. I remember feeling so excited over it. I didn't cry of happiness. I wasn't overwhelmed, but I was so, so happy.

Oliver takes my empty glass and deposits it beside his, picking up our small tray of grapes and cheese as we continue walking along the vineyard. "Was it everything you hoped it would be?" he asks. I glance up to search his face. He doesn't seem angry or jealous, just curious.

"I had never really thought about it before that night," I say with a shrug. "Our relationship was kind of . . . I don't know. I just never really thought we would get engaged or married. We were living together and everything, so you would think it would be the next step, but I never really . . ." I never expected it. I never needed it. I never wanted it until the day he asked, and then suddenly I wanted it all. I don't say that because I don't want to go there.

"Are you happy you did? That you got engaged and moved in together?"

This time we stop walking. I tilt my head so I can see him, even as he keeps his eyes out into the distance. Every time I look at him, even now, it feels like my heart is getting tazed. I have to remind myself that this man—the one I've always wanted—is really here with me.

"I am," I say, because it's true. I loved him and don't regret a single moment I spent with Wyatt.

Oliver nods and throws a grape into his mouth. When he doesn't look at me, I reach out for him, tucking my hand under his bicep, needing to touch him and make sure we're still okay. His gaze cuts to mine, and the side of his mouth turns up in a somewhat regretful smile.

"I'm sorry. I don't want to be a mood killer. That was just a little harder to take in than I thought it would be."

I reach up and run a hand through his thick hair. He closes his eyes and leans into my touch, his nostrils flaring slightly as he takes a deep breath.

"Why didn't you get married? It was a long engagement," he says, keeping his eyes shut. My hand freezes in his hair. I drop it and step back. He opens his eyes when I do, and we look at each other for what seems like forever, before I answer.

"We never talked about it," I say, my voice a whisper. I look away from his intent gaze. I have to. The only other person I've spoken to about this is Mia, and although she held my hand and kissed my head, I could see the judgment and the sympathy she held in her eyes. I know she was thinking the same thing I was, but we were both afraid to voice it. The thing is, we were happy, Wyatt and I. We argued like any other couple, but we were happy for the most part. Things were comfortable with him, and I never really wanted to question the bigger things, out of fear that it would mean the end of our relationship. I figured that when we really got to those points in our life together, we would face any issues in real time.

"Ever?" Oliver asks, and I can hear the frown in his voice.

I shake my head.

"Tell me something else," he says, and the way he says it makes me want to tell him everything, because his voice holds understanding and a sadness that can only be formed through true comprehension.

"He didn't want kids," I say, still whispering, as if it's a great big secret I'm keeping from the universe, and I guess I was, for a while. "Or at least he didn't want kids with me. I can't really be sure."

Oliver's hand finds mine, and I finally turn to meet his gaze. As soon as I do, I regret it, because the look on his face makes me want to cry. "Not wanting kids with you is insane. He probably just didn't want any. Some people don't." When I stay silent, he squeezes my hand. "You're going to make an incredible mother one day, Elle." He leans down and kisses my lips softly. It's not a long, lingering kiss, but it's enough to warm me all over.

"Anyway," I say in a breath, as I reach into the little tub of cheese and pop a square into my mouth. "Your turn . . . How long are you usually with a woman before you go your separate ways?"

His mouth twitches, and I can tell he's trying not to laugh. "It depends."

"On the woman?"

"Yeah, and the situation."

"What's the longest you've stayed? I'm not sure if I should say *what's the longest relationship you've had* because I know you don't call them that," I say, looking away when I feel myself blush. This is more awkward than when he asked me about Wyatt.

Oliver chuckles. "The longest I've stayed . . ." My eyes cut to his when he sighs loudly. "Probably two months, give or take."

"That's it?"

He smiles, running his thumb over my eyebrows to clear my frown. "I had a romantic affair with my school work. You know that's always been my top priority."

I sigh and wrap my arms around his torso, burying my face in his hard chest. "Thank you. This date has been everything. I mean it." Against my face, I feel his abdomen constrict and hear him take a deep breath.

"Thank you for letting me kidnap you."

I smile, tilting my head back to prop my chin on his chest as he looks down at me. "You're welcome to kidnap me any time you want."

His entire face lights up as he smiles at me, his dimples wink, and his eyes twinkle. It feels like my birthday and Christmas all wrapped up in one beautiful face.

"I just might," he says, with promise in his deep voice.

Chapter 30

I WIPE MY hands on a kitchen towel and pick up my phone to read the incoming text message from Oliver.

Come outside.

I frown and glance over my shoulder at the open back door where my brother stands. I can't tell what he's doing, but I'm pretty sure his surfboard is involved. I walk to the front of the house, and look through the peephole, smiling at the sight of Oliver on the other side with his hands tucked into the front pockets of his jeans. He's wearing a gray-checkered button- down and a matching beanie pulled down so low, that his sandy hair brushes against the collar of his shirt. I open the door and lean against it, holding the knob as he gives me a slow onceover. As always, his eyes leave a trail of heat behind as they travel the length of my body.

"You look cute," I say, and laugh when he raises an eyebrow.

"Cute?"

"Cute is a compliment."

"For a four-year-old, maybe," he says, stepping in to share the space of the threshold with me.

I smile. "Nope. The word holds weight for life. You can be cute even if you're eighty."

The side of his mouth turns up slowly as he leans into me, stretching his arms above me so that he's clutching the top of the doorframe and his chest is flush against mine. I catch a glimpse of tanned stomach peeking out from under his shirt and reach out to touch it. He tucks his face into my neck, kissing me there and hissing when I grip tighter.

"I'll show you cute," he says, his voice low and husky. I smile, and throw my head back. "Where's your brother?" he asks, as his lips move from my throat to my shoulder.

"Out back," I whisper, closing my eyes as I push myself up against him.

"Let's go somewhere."

I bite down on my lip to stifle a moan, as his tongue runs over my clavicle. "Where?"

"Anywhere. The beach, pier, sushi . . . wherever you want." He kisses his way along my jaw and up my cheek.

"You hate sushi," I say, opening my eyes to meet his. He drops his hands from the door and straightens, brushing my face with the back of his hand.

"I can get tempura."

"Okay. Let me tell Vic I'm leaving."

Oliver steps away and signals for me to lead the way.

"What's he doing anyway?" he asks as we reach the back door.

"I'm not sure. I think cleaning his surfboards."

"Waxing," Victor corrects, startling me. "Why are you so jumpy lately?"

"I'm not jumpy," I say, swallowing to contain my rapid heartbeat.

"You are." He raises an eyebrow and runs a hand through his hair. "What's up, man?" he says to Oliver.

"Not much. Day off."

"I'm surprised you're not sleeping," Victor says, going back to his surfboard.

"Nah. I wanted to take advantage of the day. Estelle and I are going to go get sushi. Want to come?"

Victor's hands come to a stop on the board, and he looks up, his eyes narrowing as they look from me to Oliver and back again. "No, thanks," he says, looking at the board once more and then back at us. I'm pretty sure he can hear the hammering in my chest from where he's sitting. I brace myself for the inevitable question when he opens his mouth. "You're never going to get back on the dating bandwagon if you keep hanging out with Oliver. You realize that, right?"

"How many times are you going to wax over the same spot?" I ask, turning my back to him and walking back into the house to hide my irritation.

"This is a different board," he calls out.

"No, it's not. I've never seen anybody wax the same board as many times as you do," I call back.

I hear Oliver say his goodbyes before he walks back inside, and I feel him behind me shortly after. "Some people just don't know how to wax boards," he murmurs, his breath tickling the back of my neck.

"Do you?" I ask, flashing a smile over my shoulder.

He leans in and kisses me—a quick, hard peck on my lips. "How 'bout I show you?" he says in my ear.

"What do you have in mind?" I ask, as we step out and walk toward his car.

"Let's pick up the sushi and have a beach picnic."

"I like that plan."

"I love that plan," he says, depositing a kiss on my cheek before he drops his arms and opens the door for me.

He orders food for us, stopping and glancing my way for approval every time he names a roll he thinks I might like. Once he hangs up the phone, we're silent for a long moment until he speaks up again.

"I think we should tell him," he says, threading his fingers through mine. My heart threatens to leap out of my chest at his suggestion.

"What would we tell him?" I ask quietly, facing forward.

"That we're together."

"We're together?" I ask quietly, smiling at the thought.

Oliver chuckles and drops my hand, bringing it up to cup my chin. "Aren't we?"

My smile grows wider. "I don't know, Doctor. Are we?"

His hand makes its way to the nape of my neck. He pulls my face closer to his until the tips of our noses touch. "I think it's safe to say we are."

"What do you think he'll say if we tell him?" I ask in a breath against his lips.

"He'll be pissed." He pauses to search my eyes. "At me, not you."

"Aren't you worried it'll ruin your friendship?" I whisper.

The breath he releases blows over my lips. It smells like peppermint, the residue of the mints he constantly pops in his mouth. "Why do you think it's taken me so long to come around, Elle?" he says in a low voice, dropping a kiss on one side of my mouth and then the other.

I close my eyes, relishing the feel of his soft lips on me. "I think we should just wait a little longer," I say finally.

Oliver backs away and looks at me, waiting for an explanation. After a couple of beats, I finally open my mouth to voice my opinion, but shut it again when his phone vibrates. He answers, telling the restaurant he'll be right in for the food.

"Hold that thought," he says, tapping the tip of my nose before getting out.

I sag against the seat behind me, and let out a deep breath. How do I explain everything I'm feeling? I'm not sure I can put it into words. I can only remember what everybody said when Wyatt and I started dating. Their whispered disapproval becomes a shout in my head as I sit there, wondering if Oliver and I hold the same fate. Wyatt was just some random to everybody. Oliver is family to us. I have no doubt in my mind that Victor would see our relationship as incestuous, even though we have no ties aside from him. I watch Oliver walk back to the car with a bag in one hand and his phone in the other. He has a worried look on his face that instantly puts me on edge.

"Everything okay?" I ask when he gets in and closes the door.

"Yeah, I had to call the hospital and check on a patient," he responds, his lips pursed.

"Anyone I know?" I ask, waiting on bated breath when he doesn't respond right away. I don't know what I would do if something happens to one of the kids I've grown to love so much.

"No. It's one of my toddlers."

"I don't know how you do it," I whisper.

"Sometimes I don't either," he says quietly, letting out a sigh. He claps his hands together loudly, making me jump in my seat and look at him. He chuckles at the look on my face. "You really are easily startled lately."

I try to hide my smile by looking away as he starts driving.

"You never answered why you want to wait," he says once we're back on PCH.

I sigh. "I just want to keep this to myself for a while."

"You want me to be your dirty little secret," he says with a wolfish grin.

"I didn't say that."

He shrugs. "I'm not against it. I like being a dirty little secret."

Every time he says *dirty little secret,* something inside me stirs. Somehow, Oliver manages to make everything sound sexy.

"I'm not saying I don't want anybody knowing because I'm ashamed or anything," I say, feeling the need to make that clear.

He pulls into the parking lot of the 1,000 Steps Beach and smiles as he gets out of the car to open the door for me. Once I'm out, he pops the trunk and grabs a couple of beach towels.

"Do you have impromptu picnics often?" I ask, raising an eyebrow as I hold out my hand to take the towels.

Oliver laughs, shakes his head, and pulls me into an embrace. "Only with women named Estelle."

"I can think of a couple of Estelle's," I say, pushing him away from me lightly, as I feign anger.

He cocks his head, still smiling. "So can I, but I can only think of one I would resort to eating Japanese food with and take to the beach without demanding she dress down to a bikini."

I purse my lips and walk toward the stairs. "Does that mean you don't like to see me in a bikini?"

We step to the side so that some people leaving the beach can walk by us, and Oliver leans down to whisper in my ear. "You look great in a bikini, but you look better naked, on my bed, with your legs spread open for me."

I stop suddenly, holding on to the rocks of the wall beside me. Oliver's arm goes around my waist to keep us from toppling down the nine hundred steps we have left to navigate. I turn around in his arm and crane my head to look at him.

"You need to keep those comments to yourself when we're in public," I say.

He bites down on his bottom lip, trying, and failing, to hold back a smile. "Why? Because it gets you all hot and bothered?" he asks, dipping his face to meet mine when I nod. He runs the tip of his nose from my jaw to my ear in a slow caress, breathing me in as he does so. "What if I told you I want you that way?"

"Why would you want to do that to me when we're about to eat on a public beach?" I ask in a whisper against his neck.

He chuckles. "Maybe I like knowing that I get to you."

"You know you get to me," I say, leaning away so that I can take a good look at his face.

His green eyes twinkle. "Maybe I want you begging me to take you back to my place," he says, his voice low as he runs his hand under the filmy shirt I'm wearing. I suck in a breath, my eyes widening as I look around at the people walking past us, up and down the stairs.

"Oliver," I say in warning.

"Estelle," he says, mimicking my voice as his hand moves up to the side of my rib cage and stops there, right below my left breast.

"Do you want to just go back to your place?" I ask breathily.

His lips slightly part as he shakes his head slowly. When he looks at me the way he's looking at me now, like it's the first time he's seeing me—like I'm the most fascinating woman he's ever laid eyes on—I'll melt in his arms.

"I want to do what I promised and take my girl on a picnic," he says quietly, before leaning in closer and letting his lips fall over mine. His mouth molds against mine, moving slowly, as he takes his time to feel me. His tongue dances with mine in a slow seduction—the complete opposite of the rapid fire coursing inside of me. At the sound of a catcall by one of the bystanders, we break away and look into each other's eyes with a short laugh. He runs the tips of his fingers over my bottom lip and smiles.

"Let's go eat before this sushi goes bad and we end up in the ER," he says, turning me around to keep walking.

After we eat, we sit on the beach with our legs outstretched and braided around the other's. We people-watch, as the beach is full of runners, surfers, sunbathers and tourists.

"I think I've only been here a handful of times," he says after a while.

"Yeah?"

"My parents used to bring us here when we were kids. Every time we came, Sophie would bury me in the sand, until one day she put so much sand on me I almost drowned in it," he says, chuckling at the memory. "My dad was so mad at her at first because he had to unbury me in a hurry, but then I was fine, and we all laughed until we had tears in our eyes." He pauses and flashes me a sad smile. "I think that was the only time my parents cried out of happiness. That I saw, anyway."

I scoot closer to him and lean my head on his shoulder. He puts his head against mine and reaches out to hold my hand.

"It's a good memory," I comment.

"This one's better," he responds, squeezing my hand.

For the next week, Oliver and I meet up like that. Not at the beach, but in quick segments that turn into long installments. We talk, we laugh, we kiss, we make love, and we joke around. I don't want to say that I feel complete when I'm with him—because I'm complete without him—but when I'm with him I feel like a better version of myself. And I think that's what has always drawn me to Oliver. He makes me feel good about who I am, and I don't feel like I need to change or pretend when I'm around him. I'm just me, and being me has never felt better.

Chapter 31

THE FOLLOWING SUNDAY night, I opt out of dinner at Wyatt's parents' house. I don't even bother hiding the reason from Felicia.

"I went on a date last week," I tell her, to which she gasps. I don't mention that a date turned into a weeklong event of non-stop dates. Even when we don't see each other, we talk on the phone or text message back and forth.

"And? How did it go?"

"It went well," I say, holding a breath. "I . . . it went really well."

"Good. I'm glad. We're happy for you, Elle. You know that, right? We're happy if you move on. You're young, you're beautiful . . . you deserve it. Wyatt would want that."

I don't tell her that I kind of doubt that, because I can't imagine him wanting me to move on, but obviously I'm doing it anyway. The worst part is, that I don't even feel guilty about it when I'm in the moment. It isn't until late at night when I'm alone and think about how happy Oliver makes me, that it kind of seeps in. It's like my heart has already decided what to do with itself, but my mind keeps tripping over the box of guilt. When I hang up with her, I head downstairs to make myself a sandwich because I'm starving. It seems that unless I set the Crock-pot before I leave for the day, nobody eats around here.

"Elle, can you order pizza?" Victor yells from the living room, followed by a slew of curse words aimed at the television. My best guess is that the Forty-Niners are losing.

"Yes!" I shout back. I order it, make my sandwich, and take a bite as I walk over to where he is. "What the hell did you do when I wasn't living here?" I ask, opening my mouth to take another bite and stop when I see he's not alone. Oliver holds his beer up to me, as does Jensen, who shoots a weird look between Oliver and me. I know it has everything to do with what he saw—or thought he saw—outside of the club a couple of weeks ago. Victor just watches the game and waves his hand.

"Obviously I survived," he says.

Normally Oliver would pat the seat beside him, but he doesn't today. I take a seat beside Victor and prop my foot on his coffee table, as I take another bite of my sandwich.

"What does that have in it?" Jensen asks, looking at my sandwich like he's going to bite it out of my hand.

"Turkey and Swiss," I respond, and hold it out for him to take, because it's either that, make him his own, or tell him to go fuck himself—which will result in an argument I don't want to start—especially with his big mouth.

"Thanks," he says, taking it from me with a wide grin. He winks at me and makes a satisfied sound as he bites into it. I roll my eyes and lean back into the couch. I sort of watch the game until the pizza gets there, and then end up falling asleep leaning against Jensen's muscled arm. I only wake up because I hear Vic screaming again, and it startles me. That's when I realize I am completely wrapped in Jensen's arm. He hugs me closer when I jolt and try to pull away. My eyes flicker to Oliver, who's relaxed and watching the game, but I keep staring until his gaze finds mine. I catch the discomfort in his eyes as they jump from me to Jensen. He grumbles, exhales and looks away. I don't know what I expect him to do, but the fact that he does nothing at all makes me want to scream. It's not like I want him to be jealous over this—it would be ridiculous for him to be threatened over Jensen—but still. I berate myself, since I was the one who insisted we keep whatever is going on between us a secret. *Give me time,* I said, but I kind of wish he would just tell Victor despite what I said. I wish he wouldn't listen to me for once. I sigh and pinch the inside of Jensen's arm hard. He yelps and lets go of me.

"You had that coming," Victor says with a chuckle.

"Are you regretting moving to the big apple?" I ask Jensen, as I fold my legs underneath me.

"Nope. Most of the time I like it, but I miss home . . . and I have stuff I need to take care of here."

I sink back into the couch and think about this scenario, wondering if this is what it would be like if Oliver and I were really dating. Would we hang out with my brother and their friends? Would it be awkward? Would we sit across the room from each other because he's too scared of his best friend and what he would have to say about our relationship? My shoulders slump at the thought. I look up when I feel Oliver's eyes on me, and smile when he taps the spot beside him on the couch. Finally, against my better judgment, or maybe because of it, I stand and sit beside him, snatching the huge Forty-Niners throw draped over the couch to bring with me.

"I missed you today," he whispers as soon as my ass touches the couch. I try to hide my smile with the throw I'm adjusting, but fail when he speaks up again, louder this time. "Are we sharing that? It's cold as hell in here."

"Sure."

"It's not cold," Jensen says, raising his eyebrows at us.

"We're sitting right under the air vent," Oliver says, nodding up. I bring my knees up so that they're touching the side of his leg, and he scoots closer to me, pulling my knees so they're completely on his lap. He leaves his hand there, running his palm over my thighs, making me visibly shiver with the movement. Our eyes meet at the same time and my stomach dips because I know that look. I know in an instant that his gaze will drop from my eyes to my lips, and then he'll lick his slowly, while my heart begins to thunder in my ears. The moment drowns out the game, and Victor and Jensen's shouts at whatever play Frank Gore made or missed. It doesn't matter to me either way, because the only game I want to play involves the long fingers that are inching up my thigh, and the lips that part as I near them.

A loud cough snaps us into reality, and we practically jump away from each other to look at Jensen, who's shooting us a *what the fuck are you doing* look.

"You all right?" Victor asks, tearing his eyes from the TV to look at him.

"Yeah, sure. Beer went down the wrong pipe."

Vic shakes his head and pops open another can. "Hey, Bean, you heard anything from those practices?"

"I go for an interview at the end of the week," he replies.

"San Fran?" Jensen asks.

"Yeah."

"Damn. Won't you miss being home again?"

I really try not to look at him when he answers. I try not to focus my peripheral vision on the way he shrugs his shoulders, or the way his hands move in a motion that says he's fine either way. I try not to let that pierce a hole in my heart, but it happens anyway. All of it does. We've talked about his job and the fact that there aren't too many openings here in his field right now. It doesn't lessen the blow that he's been looking at places that are far away from here when our relationship is finally on the right foot for once. That is, until his job is mentioned and his natural ambition takes over, squashing it all. As usual.

"Home is where you make it," he says.

I close my eyes and stand up, dropping the throw and going around the couch to leave the room. "I'm going to . . ." My voice trails off, and I just keep walking when I can't think of an excuse. I stop by the kitchen to grab a bottle of water, and as I'm closing the refrigerator, Oliver steps in.

"You're mad," he whispers.

I sigh. "Yes, I'm mad, genius!"

He's looking at me as if the answer may be written somewhere on my face, and that's when I realize that he really doesn't get it. He really doesn't understand how the possibility of a job in San Francisco would affect me.

"Why didn't you tell me about the interviews?" I whisper-shout. When he doesn't respond, I shake my head. "I can't do this right now. I promised my mom I would go help her with some things. I have to go."

"You can't leave in the middle of this," he says, turning me to face him and ducking his head to look me in the eyes. "I haven't even interviewed yet, Elle. It's not like I got a job over there."

"But you will."

"I may not, babe," he says, his voice a rasp against my ear.

"You will," I say, feeling tears prick my eyes. "You will, because you're smart and you're a hard worker, and you graduated with a damn near perfect GPA, and any practice would be lucky to have you. You told me you couldn't compete with a ghost. Well, I can't compete with your job." I pull away from him.

"You're not," Oliver says, just as Victor walks into the kitchen and bumps into me.

"What's wrong?" he asks. "What's going on?"

"Nothing," I say.

"Just talking about life," Oliver chimes in.

"I'm going out. I won't be back tonight," I respond, as I head toward the door.

Victor whistles. "Damn, three nights in a row? Do I get to meet the bastard any time soon? Did you tell him your brother is a lawyer, has a gun, and knows a lot of people in law enforcement?"

"I'm going to Mom's house, doofus," I say, shaking my head. I look behind him when he moves toward the refrigerator, and catch Oliver's eyes.

"We need to talk," he mouths. I nod in agreement and signal him to call me before I turn to leave.

An hour and 100 holiday cards folded and put in envelopes later, I go upstairs to check my phone. Seeing a missed call from Oliver, I call him back.

"Where are you?" he asks after the phone rings once.

"My parents."

"I'm on my way."

"What? No," I say, looking around at the mess I managed to make in less than ten minutes of being in my old room.

"Leave your window unlocked."

"Oliver! We're not teenagers. How are you going to climb a tree?"

"Are you calling me old?" he asks, and I can hear the smile in his voice.

"If the shoe fits."

"It doesn't," he says in a little growl that makes me laugh, despite myself.

"Are you saying you have small feet?"

"Are you telling me you need me to remind you that I don't?"

Somehow, I manage a laugh over my stuttering heart. "Fine. I'll leave the window unlocked."

What feels like hours later, Oliver climbs into my window and settles in beside me in bed, pulling me so that my back is to his chest.

"You took forever," I whisper.

"I took ten minutes."

"It seemed like forever."

"It always does when I'm not with you," he murmurs, pulling me into him.

"You said you couldn't compete against my job," he says against my neck. "And I agree. Is that the only part you can't do?"

I breathe out loudly. "That and the part where we have an amazing weekend together, and then you leave me. I don't have it in me to let you in completely and then lose you. But I did, Oliver. I let you in completely this time, despite my reservations," I respond, closing my eyes.

It seems like we've done this song and dance a million times before. Yet, here we are, and I realize that I'd rather let history repeat itself because the other option—the one where I live life without the way he makes me feel when I'm with him—seems like it's missing everything I need. If this is love . . . real love . . . like I've always thought, it's nothing more than a vicious game of Russian roulette. The gun clicks when it comes to you, and you cringe in anticipation that this may just be the last breath you take, but then it continues on, until the next round . . . and the next. Then there's that one time when it clicks and hits you, and you just can't walk away.

"And I'm thankful for that, Estelle. I really am." He exhales. "I wish I had all the answers. I wish I knew what tomorrow would bring, so that this wouldn't be so difficult."

"I don't care what it will bring, Oliver."

"You do, Elle. You can lie to yourself and say you don't, and that you just want to have fun and take what you can when you can, but you do care."

I pause. "You date women and never get involved in anything serious. All my brother talks about is how easy it is for you to walk away, and how little you care when they do, so why do you care when it comes to me?"

He drops a kiss on my shoulder and settles his face into my neck. "If I get offered a job I want, I'll tell you, and we can figure out what to do together, okay? I don't climb into windows, Elle. I don't do chasing. I don't go out of my way to explain my decisions to women I date. If they don't like something about me, they're free to go, as am I. I think the fact that I'm here right now says a lot."

"I know it does," I whisper.

"So you believe me when I tell you that I care?" he murmurs against the back of my shoulder.

"I do believe you, and I don't want you worried about me when you go up there next week." I doubt he would be worried about me. When he gets his game face on, he does a good job at tuning everything else out, but I figure I should say the words out loud anyway. I feel myself begin to pull back, gathering the scattered notions of hope I've been putting into this thing between us.

He lets out a heavy sigh and wraps his legs over mine, his face in my neck, and his arms around my middle . . . and that's how we spend the night. But even though I'm wrapped up in my favorite little nook, I get little sleep. The only thing I can think about is how I'm in too deep, as usual, and I know I won't make it out unscathed.

Days later, when I walk into the hospital, I spot Oliver from afar talking to one of the doctors—a man I've seen, but don't know. I don't catch his eye before I slip into the art room, and I prefer it that way. I told myself I wouldn't lose my head over this man, even if I never got it back from him to begin with. Still, with the talk of his interviews, I need to keep taking this one day at a time. The last time we were together, when he left my parents' house at the break of dawn, I told him we needed to slow down. I've dodged the calls he's made my way, although there haven't been many of them. I heard through the grapevine (or really, Mae), that he's been working non-stop these past couple of days, so I know he hasn't had much down time.

In the art room, I lay newspaper over the long table and place transparent, empty boxes by each setting. In the boxes, I place different glass pieces, all colorful and pretty, and then put a mallet beside each box. When the kids come in with their nurse for the day (today it's Tara), I welcome each of them and signal to the seats. Oliver walks in shortly after, shooting a lingering smile and a wink my way. He approaches Danny and checks the chart that hangs from his oxygen pump.

"Don't tell me we're going to break these things," Mae says.

"Holy shit, we're going to break things!" Mike shouts, doing a fist pump in the air.

Tara, Oliver and I laugh and shake our heads at his excitement.

"You may want to put the mallet down for now, Thor," I say, raising an eyebrow at Mike, who smiles widely.

"Thor, huh?" he says. I roll my eyes.

"Remember the rules."

"I don't really like rules," he says, and I laugh, looking at Oliver. I expect to find him laughing, but instead, he is glaring at Mike, which makes the entire thing even more comical.

"Anyway, to answer your question, yes, we are going to break things today."

"But . . . a dolphin?" Mae says, bringing up the glass dolphin in her box. "And a surfboard?"

I smile and nod. "They're just things."

"Pretty things."

"Well, we're going to make something even prettier with them. Besides, if you notice, they're all a little broken," I say, pointing at the dolphin missing a tail and the chip in the surfboard.

I don't notice when Oliver steps out of the room, but when I glance up at the sound of the door closing behind him, we're already well underway with the project. We're able to make very small versions of the heart, although all of them look more like a ball, but the kids are excited about them nonetheless.

"Now I have to take them home to bake them," I say.

"Bake them?" Danny asks.

"Yeah, they have to bake, then dry, and then they'll be done. Do you want to make them into key chains or just leave them as is?"

"Key chains!" Mae says.

Mike furrows his eyebrows at her. "We don't even drive."

She smiles. "Speak for yourself. I'll be driving soon."

"Fine. I'll take a key chain," Mike mumbles.

They start heading out, and while I'm cleaning up, the door re-opens and Jen walks in with a guy in a suit.

"Hey! I'm so glad I caught you," she says, smiling. "This is Chris. He's the head of my department, and the reason your project got the green light."

I step back, a little stunned, because Chris looks like he's about my age, so I'm surprised he's in a position above Jen's.

"It's so nice to meet you," I say, wiping my hands over the now dirty apron I have on. "Sorry, I'm kind of . . . dirty right now." I let out a small, nervous laugh.

Jen smiles. "Hey, at least nobody can say you weren't working . . ." She looks around and gasps when she sees what we were making. "You guys made these today? They're beautiful."

"They're not set yet, so I have to take them home," I say, hoping she catches the caution in my voice and doesn't try to pick them up. Thankfully, she just looks at them in amazement, which makes me smile brighter.

"I love what you've done with the place, Estelle. Everybody does, actually. The rooms, the hallways . . . it doesn't feel like a hospital anymore," Chris says, turning his attention to me.

Jen looks down at her watch. "I'm so sorry to step out, but I have a meeting with a vendor." She looks at Chris, who smiles and nods her away. When she leaves and the door closes, I start feeling a little awkward just standing there with this guy in a suit, and I don't know what else to say. He's looking around though, so I don't feel weird for too long. I wash my hands and take off my apron, kind of bouncing from one foot to the other, before heading toward the door. He opens it for me, and we walk out together.

"How long were you thinking of continuing the program?" he asks.

"Honestly? I hadn't thought about it. I figured Jen would tell me to stop when I wasn't wanted anymore," I say with a smile.

"Well, that's why I wanted to meet you, actually," he says, stopping when we get to the nurses' station, which has been moved back over since this part of the hospital is open again.

"Because you want me to stop coming?" I ask slowly. I wouldn't take it personally if he said no, because I knew this was temporary to begin with, but I definitely need to see this project through. I gear myself up to tell him that while I wait for his response.

Chris frowns and looks behind him at nurses chattering and turns to me again. "Do you think we can go somewhere and talk?"

"Sure. Your office?"

"Actually," he says, cringing a little and looking sheepish. "Would you mind if we go down to the food court? I kind of missed lunch . . . again."

I laugh. "Not at all."

On our way down, Chris tells me that although he started working in the hospital while he was in college, he moved up to a higher position when he graduated, and even higher once he got his Masters.

"What do you do when you're not here?" he asks, when he gets a tray of food and meets me at the table.

"Make art," I say, and smile when he nods, as if making art is a hobby. "I also have an after school program for kids who have no place to go."

"Wow. You must really like kids," he says, wiping his mouth.

"I guess I do."

"Do you have a lot of siblings?"

"Just one. Older brother, but we had a house full of boys growing up, so I guess I might as well say that I'm the youngest of four," I say with a laugh. I look away as he eats and spot Oliver sitting in a table on the opposite side of the room. He's with the same doctor guy I saw him talking to earlier. I don't know how I hadn't spotted him, but from the way he's looking at me, it seems as if he saw me a while ago. I tuck my hands into my purse to fish out my phone, and notice I have one missed call and two text messages.

"I know what that's like, sort of. I have two younger brothers," Chris says. I make a sound letting him know I heard him as I sort through my messages.

Did you leave?

Never mind. Just saw you.

I frown.

"Everything okay?" Chris asks.

I bring my eyes to him. "Yeah, sure. So what did you want to tell me about the program?" I ask, as I type a message.

Just saw you too.

"I was wondering if you could keep coming. The program was kind of dull when the last lady was running it. I think maybe the kids couldn't relate with her since she was older and more strict, and quite frankly, her art wasn't as nice," he says, smiling.

"Was she responsible for the fish on the wall?" I ask.

"You have no idea how bad I wanted to cover those walls up myself."

I laugh at the horrified look on his face. "And here I thought nobody in the hospital had good taste."

"My taste is perfect. Anyway, so maybe once a week? Would that work for you? We'd love to keep you here twice a week, but I'm not sure the board would be willing to pay for that."

The mention of pay surprises me. "I didn't really sign up for this to get compensated."

"I know, but everybody needs something," he says with a shrug, checking his own phone.

"Not me." I match his shrug, and look down at mine.

I miss you.

My stomach flutters. I look up and see that he's still sitting at the same table, by himself now, still looking at me.

Is that why you're staring at me like you're mad at the world?

"Those hearts that you had the kids make," Chris says suddenly. "Is that what you do?"

I nod.

"You sell them?"

I nod again. "Yeah."

"How much are they?"

"Well, it depends on the size, I guess."

"Do you custom-make them, or do you have some already made?"

I frown slightly as I smile. "I have some made, but I also accept custom jobs."

Chris breathes out harshly and rubs his forehead. "I kind of have to get my fiancée a gift for our anniversary, and I have no clue what to get her. You would think after eight years of being together I'd know, right?" He laughs. "She would love one of those hearts, though."

"Well, I can bring some by on Thursday when I come back with the ones for the kids."

He smiles. "That would be awesome. Do you know where my office is? It's on the opposite side of Jen's, same wing as you."

"I'm sure I'll find it."

We get up at the same time and awkwardly looking at one another, back to our phones, and then to the other. Finally, he holds out his hand, and I shake it. "I'll see you Thursday."

I say goodbye and walk over to Oliver's table, but he stands before I get there, and signals me to the hallway. I follow him into a room beside the food court. He closes the door behind us and pins me to the wall, kissing me before I can get a word out. I tug on his hair, he pulls on mine, and our hands hold the other's face as our tongues collide. I pull apart on a breath.

"You really did miss me," I pant. "Do you normally accost women in random hospital rooms?"

Oliver puts his forehead against mine and breathes out heavily. "Definitely not. I'm usually never this desperate."

He groans when I drag my nails down his chest. "Tell me more about this desperation, Dr. Hart," I murmur, leaning in and licking the seam of his lips. He pushes his hips against me, and I moan at how hard he feels.

"I need another date," he whispers against my lips, his hands going under my shirt.

"Are you trying to take advantage of me in the middle of the workday?" I ask, arching my back when he tucks his hands under my bra.

"I clocked out over an hour ago," he says, brushing my nipples with his thumb.

"And you stayed?"

"I wanted to wait for you."

"Really?" I ask, gasping when his mouth dips and he takes in my nipple.

"Hmmm," he responds against my skin.

"And then you sat there staring at me from across the room?"

"He's not your type," he says, licking my other nipple.

"What?" I grab his head to stop his movements, and he looks up at me.

"That guy you had your little lunch with. He's not your type."

I can't help but smile. "You think I was on a date with a guy in the lunch room of the hospital you work at?"

He lets out a long breath, still cupping my breasts. "What would you call it?"

I laugh, shaking my head and cup his chin so that he looks at me again. "Calling it a date would be ridiculous. Would it bother you if it was?"

It takes everything in me not to laugh at the way he shrugs and looks away.

"Are you telling me you brought me in here because you got jealous?"

His eyes flicker to mine. "I'm not jealous."

"So if I tell you that the guy you saw me with asked me out on a date—a real one—outside of the hospital, you wouldn't mind?"

"Did he?" he growls.

"Would it matter?"

"Yes."

"Because?" I ask, running both of my hands through his hair. He closes his eyes at the motion.

"Because." He leans into my touch. "Because . . ."

"Uh-huh?"

His eyes pop open. "Because I want it to be me. I want to be that guy who takes you out all the time."

"So be that guy," I respond.

"I will be," he says, leaning in to kiss me. "I will be."

"Okay," I respond, folding into his arms, wishing I could stay in them forever.

The reality that this may not be something I can do every day makes me ache.

As if uneasiness is seeping from me, he pulls away and touches my cheek with the back of his hands.

"It's just an interview, Elle," he whispers, looking at me.

I take a long, deep breath and close my eyes. It's not really just an interview, though. It's a life-changer. Life is short, I remind myself. Look at what happened to Wyatt. I'm not going to make Oliver feel bad for doing something he loves. I can't be that girl—the one who demands someone give up their dreams in exchange for my happiness. When I feel calm again, I reopen my eyes. "I know. Go kick ass on your interview, Bean. Do what you need to do."

I reach up and kiss him on the cheek. He grabs for me again, but I stop him.

"Call me when you get back."

Somehow, I turn away from his big green eyes, from those large, warm hands, and from the sense of comfort he brings me. I walk out of the room and the hospital without looking back.

Chapter 32

SITTING OUTSIDE on one of my parent's lawn chairs, I reach over for a bigger piece of glass and prick myself with it. I start swearing and alternating between flicking my wrist and sucking the tiny cut on the tip of my finger. That hasn't happened to me in . . . a while.

"Today is supposed to be a celebration," my mom says, coming up behind me with two glasses of lemonade in her hands.

"It is," I say, reaching out for the one she hands me.

"Are you happy you finally sold the house?"

I sigh, moving the box on my lap aside and propping my legs up on the chair. "Happy, relieved, a tiny bit excited."

"Not sad," she says in a statement. I look over to her and catch her smiling at me.

"Not sad," I reply, and am relieved that it's true. Maybe it has to do with the fact that I've been living with Victor for what now feels like forever. Maybe I've come to accept that, while a part of me will always be sad when I think of losing Wyatt the way I did, I survived it and have found a way to move on.

"And you sold that painting of Wyatt's you love so much. You're taking a lot of big steps. I'm proud of you," she says with a smile.

"Thanks. I am too," I respond with a small laugh.

"But you will keep the gallery?" my mom asks, again in what's more of a statement than a question.

I frown at her words. "Of course."

"You know if you need help opening up a new one and getting a fresh start, we'll gladly do that for you, right?"

I stay silent for a moment. The gallery has as many memories as the house does, but somehow I've managed to compartmentalize them differently. When we were in there together, I was off in my studio, and Wyatt was off in his. We didn't share the space the way we shared our bedroom.

"Thanks, but I'm fine for now. I'll reconsider when my lease is up."

"When is that?"

"End of the month," I snort. My mother shakes her head.

"You embody procrastination so well," she responds with a small laugh. "That's a lot of glass. How many hearts have been broken this time?"

My parents have a running joke about my hearts. They don't even know how they came to be, but they think they're pretty and are in support of me making them. The first people who bought the hearts were a group of pissed off older women with no Valentine dates. They made them the center of their "Who needs a man anyway? Party." The next year, all three of them were married. That last part is usually ignored in the broken hearts conversation though, because everybody prefers to recount the sadder part, which was that they were divorcées who were sick of going on bad dates.

I smile. "I am pleased to report that these hearts are for a bridal party."

"Really?"

"Really. The guy that runs the department in charge of the art program at the hospital bought one for his fiancée, and she decided she wanted one for each of her maids."

"That's nice. She must have a lot of money to dish out," she comments. We both turn around at the sound of my father shouting that people are starting to arrive for the barbeque.

"I'm going to put this away," I say, standing and stretching.

"I'm here," Mia calls out, stepping into the yard. For the first time in a couple of days, I feel something other than stress.

"Help me with this, please," I call out as I pick up one of the boxes. She saunters over to me and picks up the other box.

"They're so pretty," she says, as we walk toward the house. We set them aside in the sitting area by the front door and end up staying there as her mom arrives. Conversation continues about the hearts, Mia's pictures, and boys. It's the same thing every time my parents have a barbeque. Same conversations . . . same people . . . yet it never gets old. I skipped out on a ton of these when I was with Wyatt because, well, he didn't really like coming. He said everybody made him feel like an outsider, and it hurt me that he thought that, so I didn't come either. I don't regret it, even though I did miss it at the time. My family understood it. They knew that if they were in my shoes, they would have done the same.

Victor gets there shortly after, with some girl I've never seen before, in tow, followed by a friend of hers.

"This is Madelyn and her friend Emma," he says by way of introduction. "Madelyn is Bobby's sister."

Mia and I share a look, and then share it with Victor before we greet Madelyn and Emma, who look like they could be *my* little sisters. My first thought is—I wonder what Oliver thinks about this whole thing. We haven't spoken much since he left for his interview last week. There have been a couple of text messages and a phone call one night when he called "wanting to hear my voice," but nothing about where we stand has been established. Thankfully, I've been busy enough that I'm only left to wonder about those things at night or in times like these, when the reality of everything closes in on me.

"Jensen's on his way," Vic says after the girls walk off. He likes to give Mia a heads-up on his friend's status. At least he's not clueless enough to let him trample in here and catch her off guard.

"I thought he was away on a job," Mia says, her voice quieter than it was just moments earlier.

"Got rescheduled." Vic says, as he turns away.

"How did you end up bringing Bobby's sister anyway?" I ask, nodding at the women who are now talking to my mom and Bettina.

"She stayed the night."

I gape at him. "You hooked up with your friend's sister? How old is she?"

"Relax," he says, laughing at the look on my face. "She's old enough, and we're consenting adults. Staying over just seemed like the gentleman thing to do since they were over so late, and Emma was sick from drinking all day."

I feel my ears get hot at his easy confession, but I try not to let my bubbling anger seep through enough to show. He's right about the consenting adults part, but he's such a hypocrite for hooking up with his friend's little sister, when all he's ever done is warn his friends away from me.

"Where was her brother?"

"Working on a case."

"I can't believe you hooked up with her," I say, glaring at him.

"It's not like she's seventeen," he says back, as if he's offended or something.

From my peripheral vision, I see Mia cross her arms. I do the same and glare at him harder, mentally shooting daggers through his brain. Vic laughs under his breath, then looks down at the floor.

"I like her, okay?" he says, walking away. I turn to Mia and wordlessly tell her I hate him, to which she nods sharply in agreement. After our mutual hate for my brother is established, we head back outside and pour ourselves extra large glasses of her mom's Sangria.

"You okay?" I ask Mia, who looks like she's swallowed a frog.

When she nods without saying a word, my gaze follows her to Jensen and Oliver who are laughing and talking as they walk in, looking like they just got out of a goddamn Abercrombie photo shoot. As if they're not responsible for our discomfort and restlessness. The sight of them makes my insides churn.

"You want to leave? We can just skip out," I suggest, hoping she agrees, but she doesn't. She puts a smile on her face and turns to me with suddenly clear eyes.

"Nope. Your parents are really happy you're here this year," she says, placing her hand in mine. "I'll survive."

"We always do, don't we?" I say, smiling sadly, as I watch Oliver and Jensen walk over to Vic and the girls. They both greet the guys with overly excited hugs that make my stomach dip. I squeeze Mia's hand tighter as I watch Emma practically drape herself over Oliver, who's smiling down at her.

"I'm calling Nathan," she says suddenly, which makes my mouth drop open.

"You're not," I say, smiling despite myself. Neither of us normally plays head games or tries to make anybody jealous. I guess I never needed to make Wyatt jealous because he was born with an overly jealous bone, but Mia has never been like that either. My brother's friends are all similar in one thing: They're sure of themselves. So confident, that they believe every woman is a sure thing when it comes to them. Jensen always treated Mia like she would never go anywhere—not that he was mean, but he clearly took her for granted. As outlandish as Mia is now, she was the opposite with Jensen—always serving him, always quiet when he was around, because he was the boisterous one. When things went wrong, she climbed out of her shell like a mummy ready for rebirth. I know she uses her loud comments as a shield more than anything, because she's never been the same after Jensen. Not out in public anyway. The only time I get the real Mia is in times like these, where she's quietly vulnerable. I look over at them, talking and laughing with those girls. I decide that . . . fuck it . . . we can have fun too.

"Tell him to bring some friends," I say, glaring at the back of Oliver's now short hair. He must have cut it before his interview. Of course, it's still gorgeous, brushed back so that it curls over the collar of his polo. He shaved down his beard too, so it looks lighter, barely there.

"Let's go," Mia says, typing furiously into her phone. "We'll be back." I follow her out the side door and laugh when she lets out a grumbled "motherfuckers" under her breath. I love her.

We go upstairs to my room, and she helps me sort out the hearts I was working on, until Nathan calls to let us know they're outside. We practically trot downstairs and bolt outside to meet Nathan, Hunter (yes, my "first" Hunter), and Steven. They're guys we hung out with through high school and college. They're just downright fun, nice people.

"I haven't seen you in ages," Hunter says to me after he gives us each a huge hug.

"I know. Whatever happened to that girl you were dating? Emily?"

"We're kind of on a break. Long distance relationships are tough," he says with a shrug. "I do think we have something though."

I smile at that. We talk for a while, and I completely forget about the party in the backyard and the guys we were going to try to make jealous. I'm pretty sure Mia does too. It feels like high school all over again, and sometimes acting juvenile is all you need. We're laughing and joking about Nathan's wrestling days, and after a stupid demonstration of one of the moves—where I was used as a sparring partner—I land knee-first on the ground. Even though I laugh, it hurts.

"You okay?" Nathan asks, inspecting it like the concerned EMT he is.

"I'm fine. Obviously too old to be playing this crap, but I'll live," I say, making us all laugh.

"Come on, I'll piggyback you inside for old time's sake," Hunter says with a wink.

Hunter, for some weird reason, runs into the yard shouting something about a zombie apocalypse. I'm pretty sure he's trying to imitate somebody from The Walking Dead, but the voice he's using is way off. I hang on for dear life, laughing hysterically, my hair swinging back and forth, as Mia, Nathan, and Steven follow behind. We are all laughing so hard, the crowd in the backyard turns as a unit to face us.

"Great, there goes the neighborhood," Vic says, smiling when Hunter stops to greet him, still holding me over his shoulder. Vic and his friends have always been fond of these guys. They used to surf together, and I'm pretty sure they still play football together on Thanksgiving.

"Long time no see, man," Hunter says, walking around and greeting everyone with me still hanging on his back. I complain about my knee and am about to hop off, when he swings me and catches me in a cradle like we're on the cheerleading squad, my head hanging upside down, and hair dragging on the grass.

"Are you going to put her down? You know it's not safe for her circulation to be in that position for too long," says Oliver the doctor, as if anybody asked him.

Everybody snorts at that.

"Dude, please, leave work in the workplace," Jensen says.

"Will you put me down?" I say, laughing as I push the hair out of my face.

Hunter laughs, looking down at me and shakes his head. When he leans into me, my eyes widen. I don't think he's going to kiss me or anything, but still, I inwardly freak out. He leans into my ear and whispers, loudly, so that everyone can hear him. "The zombies are still out there, but sure, if your knee feels fine, I can put you down."

I laugh when he pulls back and slap him on the chest, then shimmy so he drops me on my feet. I hold on to his arms, steadying myself.

"If you wanted to cop a feel, all you had to do was ask," he says, flirting.

"I told you we were too old for that stuff. Now I'm dizzy," I say.

"*You're* too old for that stuff. I feel fine. If you want another go at it later, you know where to find me."

"Elle, can I talk to you for a second?" Oliver says suddenly. Both Hunter and I dart our eyes to him, as does Vic and Jensen.

"I guess?" I squeak. When my eyes meet his glaring green eyes, my heart plummets to somewhere between my liver and my gallbladder. I look at Hunter and smile. "I'll be right back."

He smiles and shrugs. "We'll be here. Come here, Meep, you're next," he says, lunging at Mia, who laughs and backs away.

"This just got interesting," Jensen mumbles under his breath.

"You can't afford another black eye," Vic says, as I follow Oliver out of earshot.

He leads me under the huge tree on the other side of the yard. I walk until I'm standing directly in front of him, where the trunk of the tree mostly blocks us from my brother and the rest of the people.

"What's up," I say, keeping my gaze on the grass between our feet.

"What's up?" he says. "What's up? That's what you're going to say?"

I sigh and look up at him tiredly. I hate that his face makes my heart pound the way it does. I hate that his eyes and the way he looks at me makes everything else seem so . . . small.

"How'd your interview go?" I ask.

He closes his eyes for a moment and runs his hand over his hair.

"I like your hair like that," I offer. "And your trimmed beard."

Oliver opens his eyes again and smiles—a small one—but I'll take it. "Thank you, and the interview went great. The interviews . . . there were two . . ." He looks away, over my shoulder when he says that, so I wait. When he doesn't make further comment, I smile uneasily.

"Good. I knew they would."

We look at each other for a long, silent moment, and I wish so much he would put his soft lips on mine and kiss this hesitation away.

"So . . . Hunter . . ." he says, finally.

I let out a short laugh. "We're not dating or anything, if that's where you're going with this," I say, recalling our hospital run in.

"I wasn't . . ." He stops talking, sighs, and presses his back against the tree trunk, tilting his head up so that his throat is exposed. I want nothing more but to lean in and kiss the knot of his Adam's apple.

"This is so hard for me, Elle. I don't think you understand how hard."

"What is?" I ask, my heart lurching into my throat as I wait for him to drop the bomb that he's leaving on me.

He looks at me again. "I really thought I was going to hit him earlier. Hunter, I mean."

My heart lurches at his admission, and I feel sick for his jealousy having that impact on me. I hated Wyatt's jealousy; it annoyed me, and it made me angry, but Oliver saying these things makes my body feel like it's going to break out in song.

"Why?" I ask, stepping closer.

"He came in here carrying you without a care in the world. It's so easy for him. Vic didn't even bat an eyelash when he saw you guys."

"Because we're friends," I whisper, moving a little closer to him.

"I know that, but still. I pictured what would happen if I did the same thing, and the outcome didn't turn out so nice in my head."

"Are you saying we should put a stop to this?" I ask, looking between our feet.

"No. I would never say that." The sternness in his voices brings my eyes back to his.

"Why?"

"We already went over this," he says quietly, his hand reaching out to take mine. "I want you."

"So take me," I respond, and his face darkens. He threads his fingers through mine and pulls me a little closer. "We're going to get caught," I whisper.

"I want you so bad right now," he says, his voice a growl against my cheek.

I pull away from him and drop his hand, looking up at him through my lashes. "Maybe you should go to the bathroom on the side of the house in a couple of minutes," I whisper in a conspiracy. I want this . . . whatever this is. For as long as I can have it, I want it.

He bites his bottom lip. "Five minutes."

"Five minutes," I say, smiling as I walk away from him and head over to Mia.

"What did he want?" she whispers.

"He said he wanted to kill Hunter when he saw us walk in."

She laughs. "That was quite a show. Jensen has been glaring at me since we got here, too."

"Well, we knew that would happen."

"He's such an asshole. Such a good-looking, too responsible, asshole," she says in a breath, referring to Jensen as she shakes her head. "Did Bean say if he took the job?"

I purse my lips. "He had interviews. I doubt they offered anything on the spot." The idea of him taking a job so far away any time soon, makes my heart hurt. I decided to use these final weeks, or month together to be just that—together. I'll worry about the rest later. I'll deal with the pain when it comes, and I admit that I'm secretly hoping it doesn't.

"Guys! The steaks are ready!" my mom calls out. The crowd seems to shift her way as a group.

"You're not coming?" Mia asks when she notices I stay behind.

"I'll be right there. I have to go get something inside," I say, walking the opposite way when she darts ahead to catch up to Steven, Nathan, and the rest of the crew.

Once I'm in the bathroom, I blow out a breath in anticipation. At the sound of footsteps, my heart skips a beat, and then stops beating altogether when Oliver steps inside the bathroom with me, his presence commanding every bit of my attention. My eyes travel the length of a body I don't think I'll ever tire of seeing. It feels like he's been getting this reaction out of me for as long as I can remember. His arm reaches back to turn the lock on the door and he smiles that slow, sensual smile that always makes me turn into a softer version of myself. In another breath, his hands are around my waist, pulling me forward, as his lips capture mine in a slow kiss. It's a sweet, tender kiss that wraps my insides in knots.

My hands reach for his face, frantic to touch everything at once—his neck, his arms, his shirt . . . and even though we're in a bathroom, and this is supposed to be quick, the look he gives me says otherwise. He unzips his jeans and pulls them down along with his boxers. His eyes tear down every bit of resolve I had built up, as he watches me do the same. I slip out of my flip-flops, my jeans, my thong, and turn around, bracing myself on the sink, and my eyes meet his in the mirror. When I lean over, his gaze leaves mine momentarily to look at what I'm baring for him. When his eyes return to mine, the hunger in them makes me hold on tighter. My eyes linger on the length of him, and I lick my lips in anticipation of feeling him inside of me again.

Oliver moves between my legs, and for a long moment, simply palms my ass in both of his hands, eyes closed, his chest expanding heavily. I step back and urge him to push inside me, but he continues to feel my cheeks and run his fingers up and down my wet folds.

"I'm ready for you," I whisper, shivering at his touch.

"I know." He leans in and drops a kiss between my shoulder blades. "You've always been ready for me." He sinks into me slowly, fully, and I bite down on my lip to keep from crying out. "You are so ready for me," he says, groaning as he picks up the pace. One of his arms goes to my shoulder, and the other moves to my waist as his thrusts get harder. I try not to make a sound, but I can't help it. I feel so full, so good.

"Shhh," he murmurs under my ear, licking there. "You're so perfect, Elle. So perfect for me."

His words, and the look of adoration I see in the mirror, make my heart quicken further. I push into him as his teeth clamp down on my shoulder.

"Oliver," I moan, biting my lip, when his hand moves to rub my clit. His strokes quicken, the wet sound of his pelvis slapping over my ass becoming louder and faster.

"Elle," he groans against me, followed by a slew of *come, please come, baby. I can't take it when you clench around me like that.* A spark blazes through me, starting from the tips of my toes to the top of my head, and spreads like rapid fire as my core tightens and my insides coil. An orgasm rocks through me as he unloads inside of me, his cock jerking in spurts.

Oliver tucks his face into my neck and breathes hard as my head falls forward, and I try to catch my breath. Footsteps ring out outside and our heads snap up to look at each other in alarm. I flinch when he pulls out of me quickly, handing me tissues, and I start redressing as he buttons himself up. We're not even close to being presentable—my hair is a mess, our faces are glistening with the aftermath of our quick sexcapade—but I signal for him to go outside anyway. He closes the door behind him, but I hear loud voices as soon as he steps out, followed by the doorknob turning.

"Who the fuck is in there?"

My breath catches in my throat in a panicked gasp, when I realize it's my brother's accusing voice outside the door.

"I swear to God, Oliver, I love you. You're my brother, but if who I think is in there is . . ." he says, letting that thought hang and marinate a while. He slams his hand against the door. "Open the door!" he shouts, making me jump back a step.

But I can't, because I am completely frozen. Completely and utterly frozen, just staring at the door, as a new wave of anticipation rocks through me—a very different one than the one I had coming into this bathroom. Finally, feeling tears prick my eyes, I go to unlock the door, but stop when I hear him speak again.

"Estelle is missing from the table . . . Estelle and you are the only ones missing. She's not in her room; Mia has no idea where she is . . . Hunter doesn't know where she is . . . and I am really trying to assume she wasn't in there with you," Victor says, his voice low and menacing.

"I'm in love with her, okay?" Oliver says suddenly. My knees go weak, and tears brim in my eyes. I turn the lock on the door and open it. My brother's mouth goes completely slack, and as soon as he composes himself, his glare turns murderous.

"My sister?" he says. "You're fucking my sister?" he shouts as if he needs confirmation beyond seeing me right there.

Oliver shoots me a look that makes my chest squeeze tighter. "I'm in love with her."

"In love?" Victor screams, pushing him back. I scurry toward them and grip on to Victor's arm.

"Vic, stop!"

"You're in love with her? How can you be in love with her if you're leaving? You just accepted a job four hours north of here, you fuck," he yells.

"They offered you a job there, and you took it?" I ask quietly, my voice shaky as I drop my hand from Victor's arm. He uses the moment to tread forward and swing at Oliver, clocking him in the face.

Oliver flinches and grabs his face, but his eyes stay on mine. "I was going to talk to you about that."

"You didn't even tell her?" Victor yells, punching him again. "You're fucking my sister, and you didn't even have the decency to tell her you're leaving? How long has this been going on?"

"That's between me and her," Oliver says, spitting out blood, his hands bunched at his sides as if it's taking everything in him not to hit back.

"You and her? There is no you and her!" Victor yells, panting a breath and turning to me. "Elle, there is no you and Oliver."

He says the words, and I don't know what my face must look like, but if it's as crumbled as my insides, I guess he sees it. It ignites another round of anger within him.

"You motherfucker," he says, stepping toward Oliver again, and that's when I snap and react, grabbing on to Victor's arm for dear life and dragging him back. As much as I'm hurting, I don't want him to keep throwing unsheltered punches at Oliver, who's just taking the beating as if he deserves it.

"Stop, Victor. Just stop," I cry.

"Do you know how much she's been through? Do you fucking know how much she's been through in the past year? She doesn't need a guy like you to tear her up all over again!" Victor continues, yelling.

Finally, a crowd runs to us, everybody appearing out of nowhere all at once. Jensen drops his plate on the floor and runs full speed at us, pushing Victor back.

"This bastard is . . ." he takes a ragged breath. "Screwing around with Estelle!"

"I'm not screwing around with her!" Oliver growls. Victor rears forward again, but Jensen holds him back.

"I trusted you. When did this start? I fucking trusted you! You're like my brother! How could you fucking do that?" Victor shouts.

It isn't until Mia runs over to me and wraps her arms around me that I realize how bad I'm shaking. She walks me backwards, away from the commotion, but I don't budge until my dad stomps over to us.

"Victor, my office. Now," he says in a tone that doesn't leave room for discussion. "Oliver. My office. Now."

Victor shoots him a look. "Can you believe—"

"Shut up and go to my office, and don't touch him again."

Silence falls over us, and Oliver tries to walk past them and over to me, but I shake my head slowly, not wanting things to get worse. Either way, I need to think. I need to get away from these people and think. I swallow my broken emotions and walk to Mia's car in silence. My mom and hers stop us to hug me and say how sorry they are, amidst a million different questions. *When did this happen? Are you in love with him? Why did you keep it from us?* But I don't respond. I don't say that it happened so long ago, I can't remember a time when it wasn't happening. I don't yell that I kept it from them because I wanted to avoid exactly what happened, or that I didn't know what there was to report in the first place. And lastly, I definitely don't talk about the way my heart feels like it's been split open so completely that it didn't even shatter, it exploded in a big, bloody mess.

I get in the car, and the guys, Nathan, Steven and Hunter come with us. Steven and Nathan find a way to squeeze in the back, as I'm forced to sit on Hunter's lap in the front. As soon as my face touches his chest, I lose it and sob into him. He just holds me, wordlessly, until we get to Nathan's house, and they get out of the car.

"I'm so sorry, Elle," the three of them say, giving me a quick hug. They know what I've been through. They were present at the funeral, and after. They've held my hand through the years when my heart was only a bit chipped, and later, only a bit broken, so it's only right they'd be present to see the complete demise of it all.

When I get back in the car, we drive quietly to the beach, where we usually go when we're having extra good days and pitifully bad ones. We walk to the black rocks that have become our third wheel—our extra best friend—a stepping stool for our successes, and a mule to our problems. Once we take a seat beside the other, she offers me her hand . . . her shoulder . . . her ear . . . and I cry until my tears compete with the waves in a sad, broken symphony.

Chapter 33

I CONSIDER MYSELF lucky to have been in love twice. Some people don't have the luxury of finding one person they connect with on a deeper level. I found two. I loved both the same, yet differently. One was my mentor, my friend, my lover. He opened my eyes to the greatness I was capable of. He believed in me when others thought I would fail. When I lost him, I cried every day for weeks, grieved for months. I grieved for the loss of a young life, a loved artist, a beacon of light in our community and my life. I still miss his smile and the smell of his hands, even after he'd smoked ten cigarettes. I miss listening to him tell me about the villages he saw and the people he met in them. I even miss his temper tantrums and the way he would throw paint everywhere when the outside light was fading into the moonlight. The day Wyatt taught me to channel my pain in my art was the day I fell in love with him. Shatter it all, he said, helping me break plates and glasses. Hate the world, he shouted, taking a mallet to wooden serving spoons. He watched me break down, and when I was finished, he scooped me up along with the shattered pieces of glass around me. One by one, we glued it all together, and when we were finished, we'd made the most beautiful broken heart I'd ever seen.

The first boy I fell in love with used to regale me with stories about kings and queens and war and peace, and how he hoped to one day be somebody's knight in shining armor. I lived vicariously through his late night adventures, watching the way he swung his hands animatedly as he told his stories and loving the way his green eyes twinkled when I laughed at his jokes.

He taught me what it feels like to be touched and thoroughly kissed. Later, he taught me the level of pain one feels at the loss of someone you've grown attached to. The one thing he forgot to teach me was how to deal with the pain that squeezed my chest after he broke the ghost of what heart I had left. I'd always wondered if it had been a missed lesson. Now, I wonder if maybe he'd been trying to figure it out for himself, or if he just never felt anything at all. I'd wondered, when he left that night, if he would come back. When things got serious with Wyatt, I found myself lying awake at night thinking, *what if Oliver came through that door right now and asked me to be with him? Would I leave?* I never found my answer, because he never came. I like to think I didn't base my engagement on anything but my love for Wyatt, but still, that "what if" always remained.

Unlike Wyatt's loss, I never stopped mourning Oliver. I never stopped, because my heart didn't have time to mend before he came back in and surged through it again. Oliver taught me heartache and longing. He taught me to greet pain with a smile, because as beautiful as life is, sometimes it comes to us in forms we don't recognize. He taught me to understand that the thing about love—real, over the top, makes you feel crazy, overpowering, strips you bare kind of love—is that when you're soaring, you're higher than you dreamed possible. But when you fall, you land inside the deepest darkest crevices, and are left alone to pull yourself out.

The hearts I make are shattered, but whole. They're kaleidoscopes that beam under the sun. They signify hope in love when you've lost it because, like love, you can look at a kaleidoscope a thousand different ways and find something new every time. Shattered or not, if you look carefully enough, you'll find something beautiful in them, and all beautiful things are a little broken.

Chapter 34

WHY COULDN'T I just ship the painting? I sigh for what seems like the millionth time, and Mia finally switches off the music.

"Okay, talk. I know you're miserable, and I know how annoying you get when you mope internally, so let it out. What are you thinking?"

I sigh again.

"And stop fucking sighing!" she says in a tone that makes me laugh.

"Sorry. I'm just . . . I feel like an idiot. I knew," I stop to take a breath and hold back fresh tears. I am so sick of crying over this guy. "I know him . . ."

"You know what bothers me about him?" Mia says suddenly, reaching for my hand to squeeze. "How can someone so smart be so fucking stupid?"

I wipe my face with a laugh. "I wonder that all the time."

"Just goes to show you. Men. No matter how strong, how smart, how successful . . . they're just missing that chip that separates them from the better gender."

When our laughter dies down, I turn and face her. "You know what bothers me about him? That I truly believe that he loves me. I see it when he looks at me. I feel it when he touches me. For the longest time, I wondered what this was to him and the fact that I still can't get him to actually stay, is pretty telling, isn't it?"

I lean back in my seat and shake my head, a short laugh escaping me. "Funny thing, all of you think I'm in love with a ghost, and I do love Wyatt, but I've been in love with Oliver for as long as I can remember. And everything I love about him is a memory. Good memories, bad memories . . . and it hurts more since Oliver is a ghost I can touch, and feel, and one that beckons to me and brings me under his spell every time he's around." I sigh. "Life's a bitch."

I check in the painting and board the plane just in time and, as I'm about to switch the phone off, it vibrates with a call from Oliver. I stare at it until it goes to voicemail before I put it in airplane mode. During the flight, I watch a movie that makes me cry, because I'm an idiot and chose to watch one that was nominated for a ton of Golden Globes. By the time I get to New York, I'm ready for a shower and my bed and, after a lengthy conversation with my realtor on the cab ride, I feel like I need a drink to add to all of that. After a long shower, I settle in bed and listen to my voice message from Oliver. My phone is about to die, so I just want to get through this one before I call it a night. As soon as I hear his voice, I close my eyes and wrap my arms around . . . *myself.*

"I'm so sorry, Elle," he says, his voice a low rasp. "I know you're in New York, but we need to talk. Call me, please. I understand if you're busy, but I'll be here, so please . . ."

My battery dies before he finishes his sentence. I put it down with a trembling hand and close my eyes. I have other things I need to focus on right now, and even though it may not seem like a huge deal to everybody else, it is to me. Selling Wyatt's painting was one thing, but physically letting go of it will be a different task.

The next morning, after pushing the snooze button a million times, I rush to make it to the buyer's apartment on time. Just as I'm reaching her floor, my phone buzzes again. I tear my eyes away from the painting, sitting on the bellman's cart, to rummage through my purse. When I find it, I see the picture I took of Oliver one night at the hospital. His flirty grin, the twinkle in his green eyes, his dimples, they all beam at me as I hold my ringing phone. When I can't bear to look at him anymore, I answer the call.

"Elle, I'm sorry," he says instantly, as if I'm going to hang up the phone before he gets the words out. His words do nothing to alleviate the pain I feel inside.

If anything, it feels like his voice is breaking me open once again. I take a breath once the elevator doors open, and I'm standing in a foyer. Priscilla Woods, the buyer, owns the penthouse.

"Hey," I respond.

"How was your flight?" he asks, and when I don't respond, continues, "Elle? Are you there?"

"Yeah, yeah, I'm here," I reply, staring at the dark, paneled door as if it's going to give me the strength I need to get through this conversation and the meeting inside.

"You busy?"

I clear my throat when the door opens for us, and the bellman greets the coiffed socialite inside. "Yeah. I'll call you when I get back home."

He pauses for a long time, and I can hear the argument going on in his head. *Do I force the issue, or do I give her space?* When he finally speaks again, he sounds defeated. "Please do. We need to talk."

I press the end button without saying goodbye, and glance up as Priscilla ushers the bellman inside.

"Estelle," she says, smiling as she turns her attention to me. "Great to see you again."

"Likewise, Mrs. Woods." I walk over and extend my hand to her, which she takes.

"Please, call me Priscilla."

I trail behind her, our heels clicking against the marble floor of her lavish apartment.

"Connor, just settle it down there, please," she says to the bellman. He does as she asks and bows upon leaving. "I'm thrilled to finally have my painting," she says, looking at me again. "I was surprised to hear from you as soon as I did. What made you decide to let go of it?"

I stare at the canvas, still covered in layers of wrapping, and shrug. "I realized that sometimes in order to move forward you have to let go of the past, even if it hurts. Especially if it hurts," I correct, smiling sadly.

Priscilla nods. Her pristine hands reach for two glasses of champagne waiting on the table. I hadn't noticed them there. She hands one to me and takes a sip of her own. "I lost my first husband when we were pretty young. We were so in love." Her gaze wanders to the side as she smiles at the memory. "He got killed in a car accident. Drunk driver. We had only been together for a couple of months. We got married after a week of knowing each other. It was a whirlwind romance," she says, laughing lightly before taking another sip. "When I lost him, I thought I would die, but I didn't . . . and I found love again in Matthew. We've been together for twenty years now. It's been twenty-three since I lost Eric, and still there's not a day that goes by when I don't think of him."

I take a gulp of champagne hoping to push down the knot in my throat, and realize that the knot is not there because of Wyatt. "You've made a beautiful life with him," I say, pointing at the photo frames on the mantle that hold pictures of her with a smiling man. Others hold photos of graduates and small children.

"We do have a beautiful life," she says, smiling as her eyes follow mine. When our eyes meet again, hers are full of compassion. "Okay, let's see my new painting."

Her painting. I take a breath and realize that I'm okay with that this time. I unwrap the canvas, and as I tear the layers off, the image becomes visible. My fingertips graze the outer part of the eye and the memory of watching him paint it resurfaces. This is my goodbye, I say to myself.

Priscilla clutches the pearls of her necklace as she admires it. "It's even more beautiful than I remember," she whispers.

"It is," I agree, twisting the paper in my hands, as I stare at the eye that's been watching over me for the past couple of years—the one I felt more potently after Wyatt's death.

We talk a little longer and when my kaleidoscope hearts catch her attention, she promises to give me a call soon so that she can look at the rest of my catalog. When we say our goodbyes, I look over my shoulder one last time, and I burn the image of the way it looks on her wall into my memory bank. I go back to the hotel and let myself cry a little for my losses, and when I'm finished crying, I put a smile on my face. I'm okay despite these things, and maybe even better than I was before them. When twilight rolls around, and I realize I have one more night in the city with nothing to do, I decide to take a page out of the book of Wyatt and go explore on my own.

Chapter 35

Oliver

Present

I CAN COUNT on one hand the amount of times I've felt anxious in my life, and I'm not proud to say that this is one of them, and furthermore, that I have nobody to blame but myself. I don't allow myself to entertain the idea that maybe this time I lost her, because I refuse to accept that possibility. I pick up my phone and dial the number I've been calling every day since she left.

"What's up?" Victor says after two rings.

"Has she called yet?" I ask.

"Dude, you need to chill. Maybe you should take an extra shift or something," he offers.

I laugh. "I just worked fourteen hours. The last thing I need is an extra shift."

"I don't know what else to tell you, man."

I sigh. *Tell me I still have a chance. Tell me she's mentioned me, that she's thinking about me, and that she hasn't given up on us.* I don't say any of those things, only because I know I'll never hear the end of it.

"Have you talked to her?" I ask finally. She's been back for two days, and I haven't heard a word from her.

"For like two seconds. Other than the fact that she's pissed off at me, she's been busy. She's . . ." he pauses, letting out a breath. "She's moving her stuff out of my house. Apparently her realtor got her a place on the beach that she's in love with," he adds in a lower voice.

That she's in love with. His words simmer in my head for a beat. I want to be the object of that love. I'm not worthy of it, but I want it.

"When is she moving?" I ask.

"I'm supposed to help her this weekend. She's been busy with the gallery too, though, I don't think she's purposely avoiding you, I just think it's bad timing."

"Fuck bad timing," I say, hitting my steering wheel. I let out a long breath.

"I'll . . ." he pauses. "Bean, you're my brother, you know that. You've been there for me more times than I can count, but she's my little sister."

"I love her more than you can ever imagine," I say, not caring whether that makes me sound like a pussy, because it's true.

"I know. That's why I'm going to talk to her, but I really think she'll come around and call you."

"Just tell her, please. If you talk to her before I do, make sure you tell her."

"I will," he promises. "All right, I gotta go. My client just got here."

Chapter 36

A WHIRLWIND OF emotions runs through me as I leave my realtor's office with the keys to my new place. When I left, she promised she would call me soon with some possible gallery locations. The lease is up where I am now, and after discussing it with Wyatt's mom, I decided I want to move the gallery closer to me. It's currently positioned conveniently close to our old house and his parents', which is far from my new place and my parents'. Felicia, once again, gave me her blessing and told me to do whatever I needed to do with it. She did ask for one of Wyatt's paintings, but that was it.

I park outside the gallery, where Dallas has been a permanent fixture for a couple of weeks now, and I'm grateful for it. He's standing right by the front door, giving me a grand smile when I walk in, and he greets me like a game show host.

"Oh God, I hope this isn't how you greet people, because at this rate, my three customers will turn into none," I say, and laugh when he waggles his eyebrows.

"This right here," he says signaling at himself. "Sold a painting today!"

My mouth drops in surprise for a moment before I beam at him. "What? You're serious? Which one?"

"One of Wyatt's," he says with a shrug, walking toward the one with a sold sticker on the sign beside it. It's one he drew of a naked woman . . . well, her silhouette. He never told me who she was, but I assumed it was his ex.

"My God," I breathe. "You really should keep working here."

Dallas laughs. "I do what I can. I put the paperwork in your studio. By the way, Oliver has come by a couple of times."

I stop walking and turn around. "And?"

"Just letting you know. He has a busted lip. He still looks good though," he says with a wink. I roll my eyes and smile. I step into my studio, picking up the paperwork as I sit in my chair. I leaf through it, making sure Dallas filled it out properly, and look up when I notice something in front of me. There's a large white canvas sitting on the easel that faces my desk. Oliver's handwriting covers it. *This is our canvas. Let's paint it how we want it. I love you, always, Oliver.*

Happiness blooms inside of me as I stare at it. It's so simple . . . so him . . . and I love it. I know I have to call him, but every time I think about it, my heart sinks at the thought of him leaving. I finish signing the papers and leave them in the same spot. When I step out of the room and start making my way back to the door, I see Dallas on his phone.

"When did he do that?" I ask, nodding toward my studio.

"Last night."

"Does he know I haven't been in since I got back?"

"I told him you hadn't," he says.

"If he comes back, tell him I saw it. I left the contract on the table. Thank you so much, Dal," I say, kissing him on the cheek.

"Anything for you, dahling," he responds. "I'm taking lunch in two minutes, wanna grab something?"

"Not today. I have to go have an actual conversation with my brother and convince him to help me move this weekend."

"You let me know if you need anything," Dallas calls out as I shut the door behind me.

On my way to Victor's, I call Mia and tell her about the canvas.

"That's so sweet," she says. "Are you going to call him before or after you move?"

I groan as I park my car outside of Victor's law firm. "I haven't had time, and I don't think what needs to be said can be said over the phone."

"I don't think he's left to San Fran yet," she says.

"I don't know what I'm more scared of—calling him and him being over there or calling him and him being here. If he's over there, I know he left for good. If he's here, I'll get my hopes up that maybe he's staying . . . but it's Oliver. He's not going to back out of a job once he got it," I say with a sigh as I turn off my car and walk toward the building.

"He might surprise you, Elle," she says reassuringly.

"I don't know if I want him to. I don't want him not to take the job and hate me for it."

"You'll figure it out."

Upon hanging up with Mia, I greet Victor's secretary and sit and wait until he's done with his meeting. She calls to tell him somebody outside of his schedule is there to see him. He growls for her to let whomever it is in, and I can already picture him rubbing his forehead as if he has a ton of bricks on it.

"I would never hire you if I was a new client," I say, walking in. His head snaps up from his hands, and his eyes widen. He stands quickly, but stays behind his desk.

"I wasn't expecting you."

"I noticed." I take a seat in one of the chairs across from him. "Don't worry, I'll only be ten minutes."

"I can cancel my next meeting."

I put my hand up. "Not necessary."

His lips twitch into a smile. "You ready to talk to me without chopping my head off?"

"I can't promise that last part, but yeah," I say with a smile.

"Sit," he says, taking a seat across from me.

I take a breath and let it out, trying to figure out where to begin. "You tried to kill Oliver," I say, pausing when he rolls his eyes and shakes his head. "The guy who beat up those guys who were making fun of you and kicking you into the ground in sixth grade. The one who was there for you when you didn't make the varsity baseball team in school and decided to quit, even though he would have been starting pitcher. The guy who left his house, numerous times, in the middle of the night to pick you up at parties because you were too drunk to drive. The one who would take you home and make sure you made it all the way into your room."

"How did you know about that?" he asks quietly.

"Because he told me. Because every time he did those things for you, he would come up to the roof to talk to me, because I was up."

Victor looks away, his eyes settling somewhere between the big globe bar in the corner of his office and the bookshelf beside it. "I was pissed off. We already hashed it out, Elle. It was just a tough thing to come to terms with like that . . . and it's Bean, you know? I freaked out."

"He's a good guy," I say quietly.

"He's a great guy, but you're my baby sister. Nobody's good enough for you," he says, flashing a smile my way. I return it and lean forward, resting my elbows on his desk.

"I don't know if it'll work out," I whisper, dropping my eyes to the stack of papers on his desk.

"Why not? Because of the job?"

I nod, looking at him again. "Yeah. He lied to me. Or omitted the truth, I guess."

Victor shrugs. "That doesn't hold up in court, you know?"

I frown. "What?"

"Omitting the truth . . . it's not really the same as lying. If you were getting a divorce . . ."

I put my hands up before he can finish his sentence. "Victor. For five minutes can you please not talk about work or divorce or court?"

He makes an apologetic face. "Sorry. Anyway, I think you should just talk to him, Elle. Hear him out."

I nod slowly, tearing my eyes away from his.

"How did you know?" he asks. "That you were in love with him, I mean."

I shrug, smiling. "One night, he dropped you off after a party, and I was crying over my blown knee. It was the day I found out I wouldn't be able to dance. He came up and talked to me. I asked him to come back, and he did. It was innocent. We were just talking, but you know how Oliver is when he tells a story. He gets all animated, and his eyes light up, and well . . . I fell in love with him. I fell in love with the way he was, with his caring heart and his loyalty to you guys. I guess I've been in love with him since," I end in a whisper.

"You were engaged to another man. Obviously it was puppy love, and you grew out of it," he points out. "Just playing Devil's Advocate," he adds with a shrug.

"Sometimes I wish it had been. You don't know the amount of times I've wished so badly that what we had was just a stupid fling. I tried to lie to myself and say it was about the hook ups. I tried to bury any remnants of my feelings for him countless times. Nothing works, Vic. The heart wants what it wants, and mine is clearly a sucker for pain."

He rubs his temple. "I was so mad at him. At first, because he went behind my back, and then the more I thought about it, the angrier I became. He's a serial dater, you know? If you can even call it that. He likes women. He likes older women. I think in all these years, he's only dated one girl our age, and that was in middle school, so when I found out about you I was just . . . at a loss, I guess."

"I know. I get it. You see Bean, the player . . . the guy who has a different girl every month . . . so I get it. I grew up with him too, but I truly believe he loves me. Despite the fact that I'm younger than his usual," I add with a laugh.

There's a slight smile on his face as he shakes his head. "I think he loves you too."

"But it doesn't matter," I add. "His profession comes first, and honestly, I don't blame him. I get that, too."

He closes his eyes for a moment and takes a deep breath. "He's always been the planner . . . the perfectionist . . . the one who needs to have all his ducks in a row before he attacks. I don't know anybody else who sets up a spreadsheet for a fantasy football draft." He raises his eyebrows. "And I know a lot of nerdy guys."

His secretary buzzing in the next client interrupts our laughter, so I stand. Victor goes around his desk and wraps his arms around me.

"I love you, and I'm with you, okay? If you want to be with him, I'm okay with it. I'm sorry I freaked out like that, because you're right—if it weren't for Bean, none of us would be where we are today. I wish you weren't moving though."

I kiss his chest and rear back to look at his face. "You just want me to stick around so I can cook for you."

He laughs against my face. "Yeah, that's part of it, but I like having you around."

"I'm not moving far, Vic."

"I know, I know. So this weekend?" he asks.

"This weekend," I respond with a smile as I back away. "And for the record, I am really pissed off that it happened the day you admitted to hooking up with your friend's little sister."

Victor lets out a loud laugh. "Bean said the same thing."

"I'm sure he did," I reply, shaking my head as I leave. I bump into an older man in a suit and excuse myself.

"Did hell freeze over, or did I just hear you laughing?" the man says as I walk.

Vic's secretary thanks me for putting him in a good mood, and I make a mental note to send these people a box of donuts or something for putting up with my jerk of a brother every day. Then I smile, because I know how lucky I am to have him.

Chapter 37

I DON'T GO on the lunch date my mother sends me on because I want to. I go because she proposes it as a business opportunity. Really, it's more of a delivery than a date, but Derek said we may as well eat while we're there, so I accept. When I get to the place, I feel terribly underdressed, even if it is a Friday afternoon, and we are eating in a restaurant inside the mall. Everybody else seems to be wearing nicer clothes, and I'm in ripped jeans, boots, and an off-the-shoulder sweater. I set down the box with the heart his mother bought from me, take a seat, and look at the menu, while keeping an eye out for Derek. When my phone buzzes in my purse, I start flipping through the million items I have in it while my guest finally arrives and sits across from me.

"For a moment I didn't think you were coming," I say, without looking up.

"For a moment I didn't think you would bite," a voice says, and my heart just stops. I look up to find Oliver sitting in the chair reserved for Derek, and for a multitude of reasons, I'm confused by his presence. I don't gasp because he's there, though, I gasp because his mouth is still swollen, and he has a couple of stitches on his jaw. His green eyes scan my face, and his lips slightly part with the longing I see on his face.

"What are you doing here?"

"Picking up a heart," he says, folding his hands on the table. I let out a sarcastic laugh. "I'm serious," he adds.

"Okay. Well, it's in the box," I say, nodding toward it.

He leans down and lifts the box beside my feet, bringing it up to the table. When the waiter finally comes back, we both ask for more time and send him on his way. Oliver opens the lid and looks inside it, taking out the heart and the tag it comes with before he puts the box back under the table. I watch as he looks at the heart, turning it over and over, the light from outside bouncing off it with each twist of his hand.

"I took that job because I was thinking like my old self—like Oliver, the guy who tries to set up everything in his life because he needs it to be perfect," he says, his eyes shifting from the heart to meet mine. "I'm sorry that I didn't think to ask what you thought about all of it."

"I wasn't angry because you took the job, I was angry because you didn't tell me that you did."

He opens his mouth to say something, but closes it quickly before turning his gaze back to the heart in his hands.

"Is this your definition of love?" he asks, reading the little tag.

I swallow and nod.

"Love is beautiful, shattering, moving, haunting. Love is everything," he reads. His eyes flicker to mine. "Who defines love?"

"People who have it. People who had it and lost it."

"Which are you?"

"Both." I pause and look around. "Is Derek really not coming?"

He picks up the heart and puts it back in the box, sliding the tag in and closing it. He looks at me again, folding his hands on the table, and smiles slowly. "He's really not."

"But I spoke to him."

"And he lied, like he was asked to."

I shake my head. "The people in my life know no bounds."

"Go out with me tonight."

My gaze cuts to his. "Why would I do that?"

"Because I'm asking you to," he says quietly, reaching for my hands, which I quickly hide under the table. If he touches me, I'll agree. I'll probably agree anyway, but if he touches me, I'll agree too soon.

The waiter comes by and asks us if we'd like to order something, and we both look at each other like, *are we staying? Are we leaving? Can you really eat in a time like this?*" We each ask for water to buy time.

"So I go out with you and then . . . ?"

He sighs. "Give me one date, Elle."

I mimic his sigh and look away. "I feel like we've been here before."

Oliver gets up suddenly and comes around the table, moving his chair with him until he's sitting next to me. He turns my chair so that our knees our touching, and when he takes both of my hands in his, my heart starts to sledgehammer inside my chest.

"What are you doing?" I whisper loudly, looking around at the occupied tables with curious patrons who are now interested in this beautiful, crazy man playing musical chairs inside the quiet restaurant.

One side of his lip turns up, and for a split second, I get lost in the little dimple I see, finally not hidden by facial hair. "Relax. I'm not asking you to marry me . . . yet," he says. All of my thoughts go haywire for a second . . . *Yet?*

"What are you doing then?"

Oliver leans into me, his face inching closer to mine, and I hold my breath. My eyes flutter closed as his breath whispers over my face, slowly moving over my cheeks, my nose . . . my mouth. His air is everywhere. His lips touch the tip of my nose, my cheek, then the corners of my mouth, and when I no longer feel his breath on me, I open my eyes and seek him out.

"I know you've been patient enough with me in the past, and I'm asking you to be patient with me one more time." I don't move away when his hands close over mine.

"I can't keep doing this, Oliver. I can deal with being second place to your job sometimes, because I know how demanding it is and how much worse it will probably get, but I can't be continually thrown for a loop every time you decide to do something to better your career," I say, searching his face for a sign of understanding.

He opens his mouth, then closes it, pausing for a moment as he lets his eyes wash over every single one of my features as if he'd forgotten them in the weeks we've been apart. "Taking the job was a knee-jerk reaction. I was thinking like the single, ambitious Oliver, and I screwed up. I do that a lot. I didn't tell you about it, because when I saw you at that barbeque, I knew I wouldn't go through with the job. I don't want to move four hours away from you." He pauses to search my face.

"You will never come in second place in any aspect of my life, Estelle. Yes, sometimes things will be difficult. Yes, some days I may have more work than others, but you will never come in second. I promise you that. What we have is so special. It's so real. I don't want to lose this ever again." His fingers thread through mine as he speaks. "This is what people spend their lives dreaming about. I'm asking you to go out with me tonight," he says, bringing my hands to his mouth and setting them there. "I'm *begging* you to go out with me tonight."

He has a look I've seen on his face a million times before, when he's changing a flat tire or when he's reading a patient's chart at the hospital. I realize it's his determined look. His *I'm not going to stop until you say yes to me* look. And then he smiles, this sweet, charming, boy next door, *let's pretend*

I'm not a wolf in sheep's clothing kind of smile, and I know I'm not going to turn him down.

"This is the last time I'm agreeing to this," I say after a long pause.

"This is the last time I'm asking," he replies, winking as he stands and brings me up with him. We gather our things and leave after I give him the address of my new place. Later, when I'm home, I wonder if part of his grand plan is to ask me to move to San Francisco with him. I honestly don't know if I would do it, but I also don't know how I wouldn't. I feel like I've waited for this for . . . ever.

I shower and dress casually, as he asked me to. I wear jeans and boots and throw a scarf over my simple t-shirt. After I close the windows around the house, I sit outside on the porch to enjoy the view while I wait. The cottage is small, and the front door is really the back door, since the porch faces the beach, and where you park your car faces PCH. I'm not surprised when I hear the sound of his footsteps on the pavement on the side of the house, though. Oliver has never been one to use the front door.

He appears at the foot of the porch steps, but he hasn't spotted me, and if he has, he gives nothing away. I see his eyes close as he faces the water, and I smile. His hands are tucked into the pockets of his jeans, his face is tilted back slightly, and the look on it is the embodiment of relaxation. He runs a hand through his light brown hair when a gust of wind flitters through it. After a moment of standing like that, he straightens and turns to face me, his green eyes flashing in surprise when he sees me sitting there.

"I got a little distracted," he says with a chuckle.

"It's hard not to," I respond, standing up. Victor helped me bring the most important things over here, because once I got the keys, I didn't want to wait until the weekend to move.

Oliver takes the two steps it takes to get to me and sighs when he looks down at me. "Ready?"

"You look like you're regretting the date," I say with a laugh.

He looks over his shoulder, and my eyes follow. The waves are slowly tumbling into the sand, dying down as the sun begins to dwindle. His gaze finds mine again, and he smiles.

"If I would have seen this place before, I would have moved the date here."

I smile and take his hand, stopping when he starts to lead me down the steps. "Car's that way," I say, laughing when he gives the beach a final, forlorn look. "We can come back," I whisper loudly, as if it were some kind of big secret.

His face is serious when he turns to face me again, walking me back a step until my back hits the closed door. Suddenly, as if he's warring with himself, he rears back with a breath.

"Let's go. Lead the way."

I'm a little stunned. A part of me wishes he'd just kissed me and gotten it over with. Another part is glad he hasn't, but that part is so tiny I can barely hear it. Turning, I open the door, lock it behind us, and walk through the cottage slowly so that he can look around as we pass through.

"You like it?" I ask.

"I think love is a better word," he says, eyes on me. My stomach dips a little, and I smile.

We drive a very familiar route, and he ignores the questioning glances I shoot his way, but the ghost of the smile on his face lets me know he feels them. Although I want to ask, I am quiet, waiting for him to speak first. He doesn't though; he stays silent until we get to a house on the hills. The car stops in front of a gate, and he clicks a button that opens it gracefully. He drives in slowly and parks the car in the circular driveway.

"I have to drop something off for Sander," he says. "We'll only be a minute."

"Okay." I'm not sure whether to get out of the car. I haven't seen his sister in years. The last time I saw her, she was carrying baby Sander in a sling over her stomach, and from what Oliver has told me, he's almost four now.

He pushes the button to switch off the ignition and shoots me a smile. "One minute."

I smile and get out of the car, walking toward the trunk when he does.

"You have to be the neatest person I know," I comment, looking at his nearly empty trunk. What he does have in there—a white doctor's coat and a pair of sneakers—are neatly stacked to one side. He smiles, putting the bag in his hands on the ground, as he pulls the black knit sweater he's wearing over his head. It tugs the gray V-neck t-shirt he's wearing beneath it up his stomach, and my eyes stay glued there until he chuckles and pulls it back down. My eyes snap up to his, and his hand taps my chin up as he ducks his face to mine.

"You, my little Elle, are trouble," he says, his green eyes twinkling. He drops his hand, picks up the bag, and starts walking toward the house. I follow closely behind him and watch the door as we wait for somebody to answer.

A little flash of curly brown hair runs to the door, and Sander's little face appears on the other side of the glass. His big green eyes widen into saucers when he sees Oliver.

"It's Uncle Bean!" he shouts. "Mommy, Uncle Bean is here!"

"I heard you. I'm coming," she shouts, walking down the hall and smiling widely when she sees me. Oliver crouches down, and as soon as she unlocks and opens the door, Sander throws himself on top of him, wrapping his arms around his neck and squealing as Oliver makes raspberries on his neck. The sight of him with this adorable little boy is almost too much for me to handle.

"Long time no see, Elle," Sophie says, reaching out for a hug.

"It seems like every time I see you, you have exciting news to share," I say, smiling as my hands rub over her very pregnant belly.

She makes a face, smiling and shaking her head. "This news was not planned." She gestures for us to go inside, and we follow her to the kitchen.

"Sander, this is Estelle. I think you met her once, but you were a baby, so you probably don't remember her," Oliver says, flipping him so that he's looking at me upside down.

"Hi, Estelle. You have pretty hair," he says, making me laugh.

"Hi, Sander, you have pretty eyes."

Oliver grins at me, and I feel like he's reaching into my ovaries and squeezing to make sure I'm paying attention.

"Your house is beautiful," I comment, looking around.

"Thank you. Dan will be happy to hear that," Sophie says, smiling. "How's the art business?"

"It's going pretty well." I smile and think about the painting Dallas sold, and the amount of kaleidoscope hearts I've been selling lately.

"I'm in love with the hearts you make," she says.

"On that note," Oliver says, as he deposits Sander on the countertop and reaches into the bag for the box I gave him this morning. He hands it to his sister and reaches back into the bag again, lifting out a superhero toy for Sander.

"Whoa! Cool! Thanks, Uncle Bean," Sander says, trying to rip the toy out of the package.

"This is so beautiful," Sophie says, holding the heart in her hands. "Thank you."

I smile, blushing a little and look at my feet. Oliver's chuckle makes my face heat further. I love what I make. I'm proud of my art, but it makes me feel weird when someone like Sophie, who I guess I kind of seek approval from, examines it.

"Stop being so fucking cute," Oliver growls into my ear. I smile and nudge him away with my shoulder.

"Have you been making a lot of these?" Sophie asks.

"Yes, actually, but I'm going to stop for a while."

"Really?" she asks, looking surprised. I can feel Oliver's eyes on me as well. I haven't really told anybody yet.

"I feel like if I make too many, they lose their uniqueness. Not that they're so special, but you know what I mean." I blush again. I can't remember the last time I felt like I was under a microscope.

"I know exactly what you mean," Sophie says, nodding. "That's how I feel about my stories. I love writing and illustrating them, but sometimes I feel like if I put too many out there at once, it'll be 'just another Sophie Hart story.' I get it."

"Yeah, so I'll probably take a little break. I mean, I'll still be painting and making them—it's not like I can switch myself off—but I probably won't sell them for a while."

"All right, guys, we need to get going. I just wanted to bring this by before I get busy," Oliver says, kissing Sander on the forehead and helping him hop off the counter. He rounds the counter and gives his sister a hug, laughing at whatever she whispers in his ear.

I say goodbye to Sander and Sophie. "Do you know what you're having?" I ask after I give her a quick hug.

"We want it to be a surprise. At this point, it doesn't matter, it's coming anyway," she says with a laugh that makes me smile.

"That's kind of cool."

"It's completely nuts is what it is," Oliver says, shaking his head.

"Don't start, Oliver."

"I'm just saying." He shrugs.

Sophie rolls her eyes and looks at me, pointing at him. "That is why it's taken him so long to get you, you know that, right?"

"Sophie," Oliver groans.

"I'm just saying," she responds, mimicking him.

He wraps his arms around my shoulders from behind as we walk to the car, tucking his face into my neck. "You think that's funny?"

"The fact that everybody says you have the ultimate anal retentive personality? Yes."

He nips my earlobe and opens the door for me. "Speaking of anal . . ."

"Ohmygod," I say, groaning and laughing as I sink into the seat.

"I'm just saying," he says, grinning as he starts the car.

After a couple of minutes of arguing about whose music we're going to play—his hip hop or my folk—we end up playing none, because his phone rings and my brother's voice seeps through the speakers of the car.

"You're with my sister?" he asks from the get-go.

"Yeah, and you're on Bluetooth," Oliver responds.

"Hey, Elle," Victor says.

"Hey, Vic," I respond.

"What are you guys up to? Jensen's in town again and wants to meet up for drinks at the usual bar, want to come?" he asks.

Oliver glances at me from the corner of his eye.

"Is this code for 'bring her to the bar for a group date so she'll know you're not serious about her?'" I ask, raising an eyebrow at Oliver. His mouth drops, a surprised laugh leaving his lips. Victor stays silent for a beat before he joins in on Oliver's laughter.

"Hell no," Victor says.

Oliver finds my hand and squeezes it. "Just so we're clear, this is going to be the complete opposite of that. This will be me saying, 'I am so serious about this girl. I want to take her everywhere with me, any chance I get,'" he says, looking at me when we reach a red light.

"This is going to be interesting," Victor mutters. "I'll save you two seats."

We laugh once the line is disconnected.

"I want it to be like this, Elle. Always," he says as he parks in front of the bar. When we get out, he wraps his arm around me and pulls me into his side. "I want to bring you here, and if you decide you don't want to come, I want to get texts from you that say you miss me."

I turn to face him when we reach the door. "I want that too," I respond with a smile.

We walk in with our fingers intertwined, and are greeted with a catcall from Jensen and claps from Victor. We sit down beside each other, talking and laughing the way we always have, but this time freely, and everything feels like it's finally falling into place.

Chapter 38

"YOU'RE SO GOOD with kids. Do you want any?" I ask, as Oliver winds down the road after we leave a charity event at the hospital.

His hand finds mine on my lap, and I sneak a look at his serious face. "Are we starting twenty-one questions?"

"Maybe," I say, a smile tugging my lips.

"Can we start in about . . . three minutes?" he says. "How many dates do you think we've been on now?"

I frown, trying to figure it out in my head. "I don't know . . . wow, I really don't know," I say quietly. "Definitely more than I bargained for."

Oliver chuckles. "Nice, Elle. Real nice," he says, as he turns onto my parents' street.

"What in the world?" I say in a breath, more to myself than to him. He squeezes my hand and doesn't respond, only winks as he parks the car in my parents' driveway. "You know they're out of town this weekend, right?"

Oliver doesn't say anything, just gets out of the car and rounds it quickly to open my door. He grabs my hand and looks at me before sighing and placing a kiss on the top of my head. I follow him as he opens the side gate and walks to the back of the house, passing the bathroom where we were last together. He stops when he reaches the back door.

"Go to the kitchen. I left something there," he says.

I stare at him. "Are you going to climb the tree?"

He chuckles. "Would you stop asking questions until it's time?"

"Okay," I say, sounding unconvinced. I unlock the door and open it, heading to the kitchen. I pick up a note card that reads:

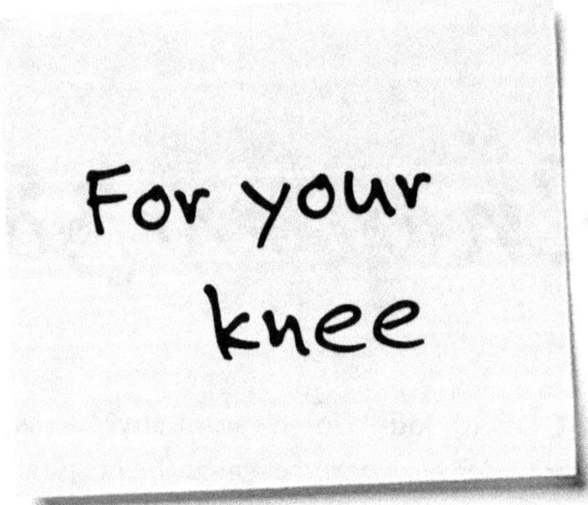

I frown at it until I notice a piece of broken, black glass under it. I fight the overwhelming emotions that start building in my chest as I pick it up. I leave the kitchen, and make for the stairs. I lift my foot to take a step, but stop with a gasp when I notice there's a note card on every step, all beside a piece of broken, black glass.

For dance.

For that time I locked you in a dark room.

For the time I broke your canvas.

For the time I called you a Chicken
(and meant it).

For every time I pretended not to see you.

For every kiss I didn't give you.

For every laugh I missed.

For every accomplishment we didn't get to
share.

For every time I left.

For every tear I made you shed.

By the time I reach my room, I'm holding eleven broken pieces of black glass with as many note cards, and the tears are falling freely down my face. I push the door open with my foot and find Oliver sitting on the roof outside my window, holding a little white box in his hands. I walk over, placing the glass pieces on my desk and duck my head as I make my way to him. He frames my face with his hands and wipes my tears with his thumbs, but the motion makes me cry harder, until I'm laughing and crying at the same time.

"I'm sorry. I think the tears are stopping now," I say, wiping my nose with my hand as I kneel in front of him the way he's facing me. He opens the box as he looks in my eyes, and mine leave his only to see what's in the box. It contains more broken glass pieces, but these are colorful and vibrant.

"For every smile," he says, taking out the first piece and putting it beside us.

"For every happy tear," he sets down another.

"For every laugh."

"For every time your eyes light up."

"For every piece of good news."

"For every piece of bad news."

"For every fight."

"For every kiss."

"For every hug."

"For every morning."

"For every night."

"For every wrong I'll try to make right."

When he's finished setting down every piece, he looks at me. "I want an October 21st," he says, and continues when I just stare. "I want to travel back in time and go back to the beginning. I want to tell my father he was wrong about life. I want to tell him that it doesn't wait for anybody, and that you can't put love on hold for trivial things like money. I want to climb back on this roof and shout on the day I fell in love with you. Because I do love you, Elle. And despite my stupidities and my running away, I never stopped being in love with you. I want to go back to that party and make myself stay in bed with you so I could have dealt with this." He points at his chin. "And we could have figured out the consequences together. But most of all, I want to go back to all the times I dodged your questions about love and tell you that I did find the one. I found her crying on this roof one night. I found her in a coffee shop when I needed her. I found her dancing with another guy and planting edible trees. I found her caring for strangers and kids who needed someone to listen to them."

"And how do you know she's the one?" I whisper, wiping the tears spilling down my face.

He brings a hand up to my cheek and caresses over it with his thumb. "I know because, when she's not with me, I feel like I lack oxygen, and even when I am with her, I feel like I can't breathe enough. You asked me if I want kids, and the answer is, that I want anything—everything—you want to give me. I want your mornings and your nights. I want your bickering and your eye rolls. I want your nudges when I'm hugging you too tight at night. I want your groans when I tell you a joke, and your moans when I'm making you feel good."

"And what do I get?" I ask, my voice a hoarse whisper.

"You get everything," he says, looking at me like I'm insane for even asking. "My career is just starting, and I have a million student loans. I don't have a million dollars, and I can't buy you a gallery yet." He pauses to flash me a smile. "Or take you on a hundred trips. And it might take me some time to find a job here with more stable hours than the hospital has to offer, but if you're with me, Elle, I don't care. My body is yours." He puts my hands on his chest. "My mind is yours. My hands are yours. My heart is yours. Everything I have is yours. Everything I am is yours."

I lean up on my knees and take my hands from his, wrapping them around his neck. "For every time you made me feel smart," I say, dropping a kiss on his temple. "For looking at me like I'm the only girl in the world." I kiss the edge of his eye.

"You're my favorite girl in the world," he murmurs, closing his eyes and breathing deeply as if he's claiming my scent as his.

"For treating me like I'm important." I kiss his cheek.

"You're the most important person in my life," he says, opening his eyes to meet my gaze.

"For giving me space so I could grow." I kiss the side of his mouth. "For loving me." I kiss his jaw, over his stitches. He watches me in awe when I back away and smile.

"Marry me," he says with a determination in his voice that makes my heart shake uncontrollably. "I don't mean get engaged for a year and just live together. I don't want to put a ring on your finger to claim you so the world can know you're mine. *I* want to know you're mine. I want you to know I'm yours, and that this isn't some relationship we can easily get out of. I want your forever, and I want it to start now." He takes a breath, his eyes flickering between mine to make sure I'm still with him. "Let's go get married tomorrow. If you want the big wedding, we can do that after."

When I pause for too long, because I'm in complete shock, he chuckles. "Or not. If you just want to move in together, let's do that instead, but I don't want to do this thing where we go our separate ways after our dates. I don't want the one drawer in each house. I want the whole closet full of both of our clothes," he says, grabbing both sides of my face. "I want the bumping into each other when we're trying to get dressed in the morning. I want it all, Elle. I don't—"

I lean in and kiss him, swallowing his pending words and hopefully whatever thoughts are running through his head. The picture he paints is too beautiful for me not to want it. I want all of his mornings and his nights. I feel like I've been waiting to hear those words from him for ten years, and even though I had the engagement and the living with somebody else for a while, I never got the *what if it had been Oliver* out of my head. We kiss for a long moment, our tongues intertwined, my fingers buried into his hair, his hands on my face, and our heart beating against each other. When we break the kiss, I nod furiously, and he sighs the longest, relieved breath, and looks like he just won some kind of silent auction.

"I want that too. I want everything," I whisper, earning a huge grin from him. "I can move, you know . . . my lease on the gallery is almost up." I pause to take a deep breath. "I can move with you, anywhere," I say, smiling up at him when we climb back into my room.

"Move? Are you kidding? I'm thinking about putting down whatever I have in my savings account to buy that cottage you've been living in."

I laugh. "I'm just saying that—if you want to go—you have my full support."

"This is home, Elle. I want to stay." He stops when he reaches the bottom step and brings his hand to my face, brushing over my lips. "Besides, I'm simple. I just need you."

And that's the promise we made to each other. No matter how crazy life gets, we'll always stick by the other. We'll share our dreams, our failures, our smiles and our frowns. Day after day, we'll drive each other a little crazy and remind the other how head over heels in love we are. Because that's the kind of love we have—the kind that doesn't come in a bottle, but can fill thousands of them, because we have that much of it to spare.

Epilogue

Oliver

WHEN WE WERE kids, my sister always wished upon stars. She swore that all of her wishes came true because she did that. Being that she was older and wiser, I believed her, and I too started doing the same. When I was five, I wished for toy dinosaurs. When I was seven, I wished my dad would come back home. When I was eight, I wished my mom would work fewer hours. When I was nine, I realized wishing upon stars was a waste of time because none of my wishes came true.

Still, when I was nineteen, I sat on the roof of a pretty girl's house and wished for things to be different. When I was twenty-one, I realized that circumstances were everything, and I wished we met under different ones. At twenty-six, I wished things had turned out differently, and that I hadn't lost her. At twenty-eight, when life brought us together again, I stopped wishing and started doing.

And here I am, at twenty-nine, watching as she walks over to me in a long white dress, in front of a crowd of our loved ones, wishing I could freeze frame this moment in time. I want to remember the one where her expressive, hazel eyes find mine, and she's visibly taken aback by the emotion she sees on my face. I know, without a shadow of a doubt, that I will never tire of watching her walk toward me. I hear the clicking of the camera beside me, and smile as a gust of wind hits us. It awakens the waves behind us, and makes Estelle's long, dark hair splash across her face. She takes a moment to gather it in one hand and push it aside, as I give her father a huge hug.

"I don't need to welcome you to the family that you've been a part of all along, but I'm proud to call you my son. Officially. Again," Thomas says with a hearty chuckle and a squeeze.

I don't respond, opting to smile instead. I'm not a crier, but his words make a surge of emotions rise inside of me. I turn to the woman who has been my wife for the past four months and grin, feeling like the luckiest motherfucker in the world, because I am. We married the day after I proposed, just as I told her we would. As soon as her parents' flight landed, we picked them up from the airport, called Vic and Mia and had them drive to the courthouse. Even Dallas showed up to help us celebrate, which was an added bonus, since I associate him with her Wyatt-era, or used to.

I moved my stuff into her cottage on the beach and worked in the hospital while I found a permanent job, which took a couple of months, but it happened. The best part about my job, aside from the fact that I work with a great team of doctors in a good environment, is that we stayed in Santa Barbara. When Estelle's lease was up, we bought a space together, close to our little beach cottage. It's still a work in progress, and although I help her as much as I can with it, ultimately it's her space. It's her dream that she brings to life every time she walks in there. I'm just happy she lets me be a part of it all.

At the feel of Estelle's hand sliding into mine, I smile and lead her to the officiate to be married again, in front of all of our friends and family.

"You're supposed to look at him," she whispers.

"I'm here to marry you, not him."

She laughs, her eyes flittering up to mine. "I promise you can stare at me for the rest of your life. But not all the time, because that would be totally creepy."

I lean down and kiss the tip of her nose. "Kind of how you were staring—"

"Okay, you guys need to seriously shut up," Victor interrupts from beside me with a groan.

"Yeah, nobody wants to know where that conversation was going," Mia adds.

"Keep it PG," Jensen chimes in.

"I'm about to kick everybody out of here," I say in response to the officiate clearing his throat and raising his eyebrows with impatience.

The ceremony continues without interruptions. We say our vows, which are short and generic, and we both smile at the memory of our longer vows, the ones we recited to each other in bed the night after we got our marriage license. We slide the rings on each other's fingers and hold hands again, and, as soon as we're pronounced Mr. and Mrs. Hart, we turn to one another. It's as if everybody around us disappears. Our eyes lock, my hands comb into her hair, hers cup my jaw, and we move almost as if in slow motion, our eyes scanning every inch of the other's face, completely immersed in this moment.

At the sound of the waves crashing in the distance, Estelle's eyes start to brim with tears, but she's smiling, the elation in her eyes matching what I feel inside. Suddenly, the moment right before our lips touch, droplets of rain start to fall over us. We pull back slightly and turn our heads up to the sky. Our guests start chanting for us to kiss. A slew of "Hurry up already! What are you waiting for?" surround us, but Elle and I remain unmoved. We smile, we laugh, and finally I pull her face to mine and my lips close over hers, taking, giving, offering, asking, pleading, promising. I kiss her with all that I am, imperfect but willing, hopeful and full of potential. Take me, I say with my tongue. Let me prove myself to you. I'll be worthy, I promise. And she kisses me back with the same ardor, sealing our vow.

Acknowledgements

Corinne Michaels & CD Reiss (for giving me great and useful feedback!), Christine Estevez, and my Crazies.

MIA ASHER (if it weren't for you, this would not have gotten written), BARBIE MESSNER (for your expertise LOL). RACHEL KEENAN (for EVERYTHING, as usual), BRIDGET PEOPLES, CALIA READ, JENNIFER WOLFEL, MILASY, HAPPY DRIGGS, TRISH MINT, JESSICA SOTELO, ROXIE MADAR, TARYN CELLUCCI, SANDRA CORTEZ, YAYA CITRON, CRYSTI PERRY, TRISHA RAI, LISA CHAMBERLIN, MJ ABRAHAM, STEPHANIE SSB BROWN, AMY COSSE

My agent, Rebecca, for being a badass.

My editor, Tracey, who worked tirelessly on this during the holidays!

My cover designer, Sarah (Okay Creations), for creating something beyond what I had envisioned.

Stacey at Champagne Formats for always taking the time to fit me into your schedule!

My PR girls, Melissa and Sharon at Sassy and Savvy . . . I would be lost without you. Literally.

Perrywinkle Photography, for taking the most amazing photos ever.

Jenn Watson for your incredible graphics.

Rockstars of Romance- for handling my promo and dealing with my crazy freakouts.

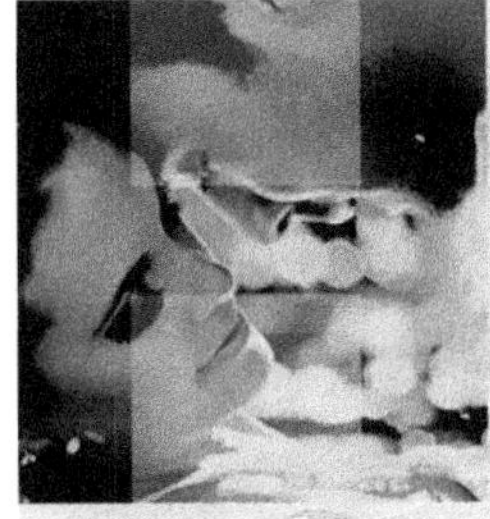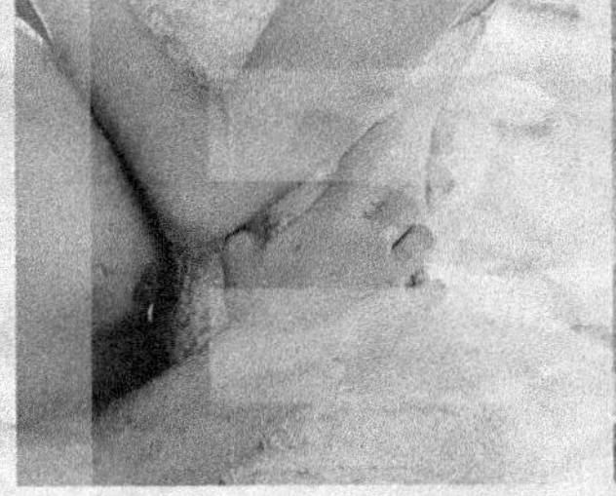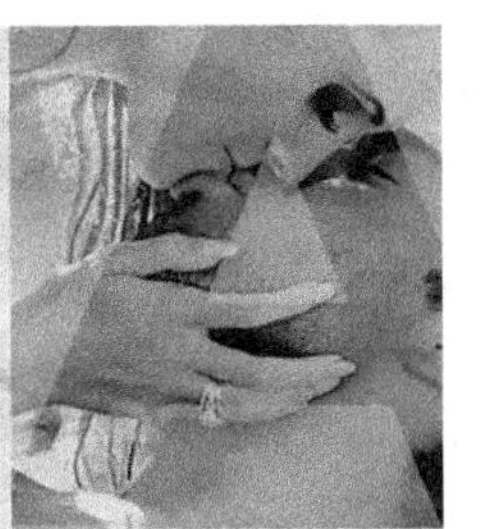

A love like this
is worth fighting for.

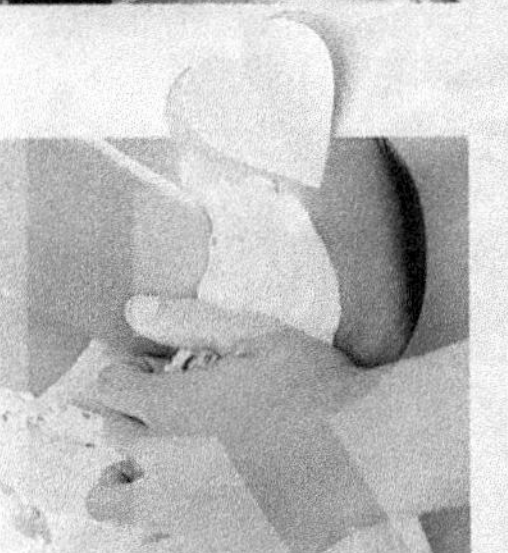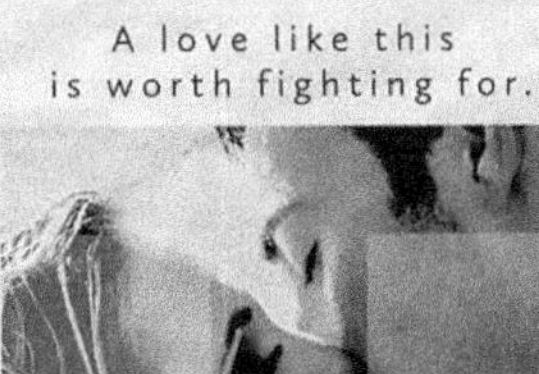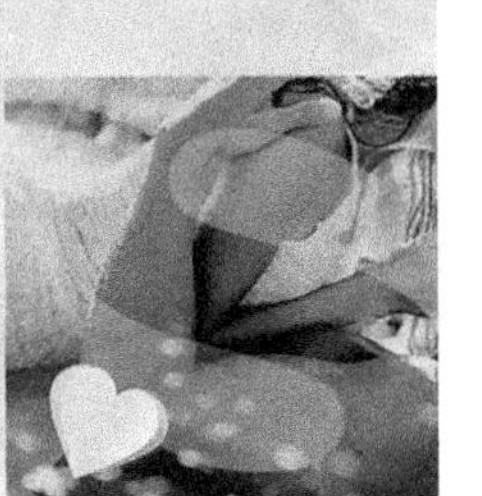

PAPER HEARTS

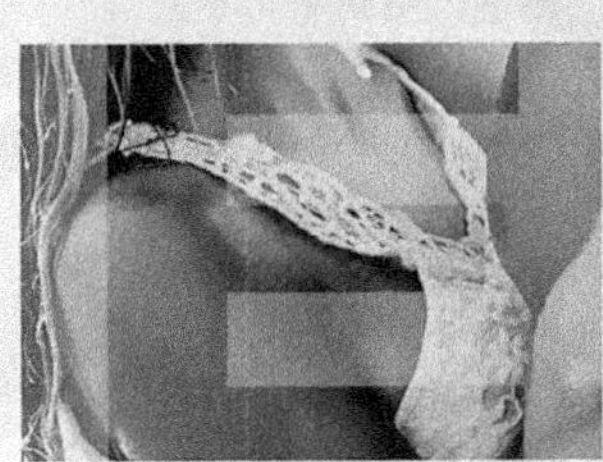

New York Times & *USA Today* bestseller
claire contreras

Torn Hearts

A Novella

Claire Contreras

Chapter One

"A date?" my mother asked as I stepped into the kitchen.

"Yes, a date." I picked up my long, damp hair and wrapped it into a bun as I weaved my way toward the fruit.

"Hm," she said, earning my attention with her non-committal statement. She was leaning back in one of the wooden chairs in our breakfast nook, a newspaper in hand, looking at me like I was wearing a bikini, not skinny jeans and a floral top.

"What?"

"Nothing. You look beautiful," she replied, going back to her paper.

She looked like a sexy schoolteacher. That was what all the kids I grew up with said about her—that she was a MILF, in a sexy schoolteacher kind of way, with her long, wavy blonde hair and her librarian glasses.

"Spit it out, Bettina, you know you want to," I said, turning to get myself a bottle of water. I smiled when she groaned. She hated when I called her by her first name. I turned around when I heard the newspaper crinkle and took a seat across from her. I had fifteen minutes to kill anyway.

"I haven't seen you date anybody, or even heard you mention any guys, for that matter, since Jensen left," she said, cutting straight to the chase. My mother was no-bullshit like that.

My gaze fell to the paper on the table, away from her questioning blue eyes. The headline story was about the Clark Estate … again.

"Maybe I hadn't met anyone worth mentioning until now," I said, bringing my eyes to hers again.

She raised her eyebrows. "Really? So who is this guy worth mentioning?"

I bristled, feeling like she caught me in a lie. I'd dated guys since he left. The last one was definitely more serious than this one, not that it made a difference to her or anybody else. "What does it matter anyway? You guys hated Jensen and me together."

"Nobody ever said we didn't like you guys together," she said.

"You didn't have to. It was pretty clear. Dad didn't like him because he's broke, and you didn't like him because you knew he'd never be a doctor or lawyer or whatever other fantasy man you envisioned me marrying."

"Mia, that is simply not true!"

"Really? Because I clearly recall you saying, 'He's not good for you Mia. You can do better than that,'" I countered.

She looked at me for a long moment, releasing a long breath. "He used to pick you up on a motorcycle, looking like he rode straight out of a Sin City movie. What was I supposed to say? Besides, I know his reputation; I hear the way he and Victor talk when I'm over at Hannah's house."

My nose scrunched up. I looked away, not wanting to hear what was said in those conversations. I knew Jensen's reputation. I'd known him my entire life. I didn't fault him for the man he was or the past he had. He was a good person and had a good heart, despite his asshole tendencies and the bad boy appeal.

"He's a good guy," I said, feeling the need to defend him, as usual.

"I agree. He is a good guy, and I will admit I pegged him wrong before. But if he's such a good guy, why did you break up with him?" she asked. I felt myself heat beneath her stare.

"Because, Mom, he went off to school in New York, and I hate long distance relationships."

"Do you hate long distance relationships, or do you dislike the idea of him being surrounded by women and you not having control over what happens?" she asked as I stood to grab my purse.

"I..." I stopped short. She'd hit the nail on the head, and it made me fume. "I don't need you to psychoanalyze me, thank you very much. If you're that bored with being a housewife, maybe you should go back to work," I said as I walked away from her. "Thanks for the pep talk," I threw over my shoulder before I walked out of the house.

It wasn't until I got in my car and drove a couple of blocks out that her words hit me and I felt the need to slam my hand on the steering wheel and scream. By the time I got to the movies, I was calm. I'd sent Adam a text and asked him to meet me there to avoid the awkward pick up at my parents' house. I really needed to speak to Rob and convince him to let me move in with him. I didn't think I could deal with another one of those pep talks, though they didn't happen often. If it were up to my mom, I would get my degree, meet a rich man, and become a housewife, dedicating my life to having babies for her to dote on.

Things with Jensen were complicated. We spoke a lot in one form or another: text, email, or phone call. We agreed that we would see other people while he was away, but I didn't feel like I needed to date somebody else. And he never mentioned anybody else to me, but I wasn't an idiot. I knew he was seeing someone. Maybe even plural. He'd occasionally throw in the "So, met anyone lately?" probably to lessen the blow of his telling me he had if I ever asked him, which I wouldn't. I didn't want to know.

I was sitting in a dark movie theatre, about to watch *Inception*, when I got a text from him saying he was in town and needed to see me. My insides flipped. I tried to focus on the movie, but my mind was elsewhere, which was a pity because I loved Leonardo DiCaprio. When the movie was over, I had no idea what I'd just watched. Adam, on the other hand, was "mind blown" by it. He kept saying, "Oh my god. Mind blown!"

"Want to grab dinner?" he asked when we got outside. I automatically clutched my phone tighter. I hadn't put it away since I got Jensen's text, just in case.

"Maybe another time. I have to do a couple of things," I said.

"Mia, you know I like you, right?" Adam asked in a soft voice.

"I like you too," I said, looking up at his bright blue eyes.

"But," he said, chuckling as he ran his hand through his blond wavy hair. "It's just…"

"You're still into Jensen." Adam and I hung in the same crowds— the artsy types—as did Jensen.

"I'm…" I took a deep breath and smiled at him. "Can we still be friends?"

He nodded, smiling, then shook his head. "I can't believe you friend-zoned me on our third date."

"I'm sorry."

"Don't be. I've always known it would be hard to get you to stop think-ing about him. I mean, he's all you talk about when we're together anyway," he said with a shrug that made me frown.

"That's not true."

"Hey, I'm cool with it. I get it. He has the motorcycle, the cigarettes, and the aviator shades."

That wasn't why I liked Jensen, though the appeal wasn't lost on me, but that wasn't why I fell in love with him. I gave Adam a long hug and made him promise me we'd still hang out, because I truly did like spending time with him. Then I got in my car and headed toward Jensen.

As I drove to Patty's house, where I knew he'd be, I thought about all of the things I loved about him: the way he looked at me; the way he spoke to me; the way he listened; his brokenness; his hands; the way he made me feel when he touched me; the way he made me laugh; the way his hands were always stained from the charcoal he used to draw. The more things I cataloged, the bigger my smile. Our story wasn't always pretty. Some would argue it was quite the opposite, but it was beautiful to me.

Winding down that road brought back memories of my first glimpse of the teenager who made girls' heads turn—myself included. Growing up, I saw him around a lot, and he intrigued me like crazy, but Jensen wasn't a chaser, and I wasn't up to doing the chasing. I parked my car in front of the house and closed my eyes for a moment, remembering the stupid game, during spring break my freshman year of college, that changed everything.

Chapter Two

2 years prior

"Did you pack your bathing suit?" Estelle called from the bathroom stall beside me.

"Yeah, didn't you?" I replied and groaned, looking beside me. "Do you have any toilet paper in your stall?"

She handed me the paper under the partition as she flushed. "I did. I just wanted to make sure I wasn't the only idiot thinking we were actually going to use the hot tub."

I laughed as I opened the door and stood beside her to wash my hands. "I doubt it. Corinne said she got ten confirmations—four guys, six girls—and that's only people who are actually staying over."

Estelle's eyes widened, her smile matching it soon after. "This is going to be insane."

"Spring break, baby," I said.

We originally planned to go to Cancun, but Estelle's dad ended up in the hospital, and she didn't want to be too far from him, just in case. Everything turned out fine, and he went home with a high cholesterol warning, but by then it was too late to book Cancun, so we opted to go to Malibu for the weekend. Our friend, Corinne's, family had a huge empty house there, and it was a hop away, so it was perfect.

That night, after we got the house and helped set everything up—towels in every room, more alcohol than a sports bar, and enough chips and salsa to supply a Mexican restaurant—I decided to take a short nap.

"Who's coming?" I asked Corinne, stretching my hands over my head as I woke up and saw her doing her make-up in the Jack-and-Jill bathroom.

"Well, Fern, obviously," she said with a huge smile.

"Obviously," I said, smiling back at the mention of her new boyfriend, who she'd crushed on all through high school, despite the fact that he always had a girlfriend.

"I think Carlos, Logan, and Jensen, too, and as far as the girls go, you, me, Elle, Pamela, and Danica."

I blinked a couple of times. "Jensen Reynolds?"

Corinne stopped applying her liner mid-lip as her eyes snapped to meet mine in the mirror. "Yeah, why? Oh my God, you don't hate him or anything, do you?"

"Hate him? No!" I said, frowning. "I'm just surprised. I mean, I've seen him hanging around Carlos sometimes, but I didn't realize they were that close. I know his best friends," I explained. "Estelle's brother and their whole clique—that's who he usually hangs out with."

"Oh," she said, back to applying her make up. "I think Estelle mentioned her brother coming by later, so I guess that explains it."

I nodded and waited for her to leave before getting ready. I'd been seeing Jensen more and more around campus, and every time he looked over and smiled at me, my insides flipped. I couldn't understand why I was having this sudden reaction to him, but I was, and I wasn't thrilled about it. I'd had three cups of beer from the keg one of the guys brought before Jensen finally arrived, and when he did, Estelle kicked me—very obviously—under the *glass* table.

I glared at her, which made her laugh (she was already drunk).

"What?" she said, shrugging and hiding a laugh behind her hands, which were small, but she had a ring on every single finger, and that managed to actually hide her face.

"You're an idiot," I muttered. "Oh, look, there's Oliver!" I said brightly and laughed when her face morphed from amusement to complete composure in less than two seconds. She turned around slowly, as nonchalantly as possible, and shot me a murderous glare when she realized I was kidding.

I shrugged. "What?"

"Not funny," she said, trying to contain her lips from smiling.

I looked over her shoulder and saw the back door open, and laughed again when Oliver really did step in. "Okay, this is awkward, but Oliver really is here," I said.

Estelle rolled her eyes. "Sure."

"I'm serious," I said, still laughing.

"I'm sure you are, Meep. I'm sure you are."

"Man bun, check. White Nirvana shirt, check. Damn, he makes those cargo shorts look so fucking good," I said. I could tell she was straining not to look over her shoulder, so I kept going. "Huh. He's wearing flip-flops. I don't think I've ever seen him wear flip-flops…"

"For the record, fuck you," Estelle muttered before she finally conceded and looked over her shoulder.

"I told you!"

She smiled when she looked back. "So you did. You want to move in that general direction?"

I laughed. "Nope. I'm going to sit right here and drink my next beer."

"You're going to get a beer belly," she said, making a face at my red cup.

"Well, what the hell are you drinking, Almighty One?" I asked.

"Vodka, obviously," she said, raising her cup as she stood. "Want some?"

"Sure," I said with a shrug and let my eyes drift over the party once more. Oliver was talking to Victor, who'd just walked in, and some girl who looked like she was ready to take her clothes off for him. I glared at her extra hard, hoping to catch her eye. Better me than Estelle—not that she cared much about the girls who flirted with them. I guess it was better that way since I seemed to feel enough rage for the both of us. I finally spotted Jensen walking outside, and stood, grabbing the cup from Estelle's hand and pulling her along with me.

"I thought we were staying in place?" she asked. I heard the smirk in her voice but chose to ignore it.

We said hi to the guys and stood around listening to Victor talk; it seemed like he was always droning on about something. I walked toward the back door before I could give it much thought.

"Hey Jangles," I said as I stepped outside.

He grinned, looking up from his phone as he flicked his cigarette. "What's up, Road Runner?"

I smiled a little too widely. "Funny how you gave me the nickname and couldn't seem to stick with it."

Jensen shrugged. "I swim against the current."

"Is that from one of your poems?" I asked.

"It's not," he said. "But…" he let the words hang as he put out the ciga-rette, reached in his back pocket for the torn up little black Mead notebook he carried around, and wrote something down.

"Do you buy your notebooks like that?" I asked.

"Like what?"

"All ripped up. I've seen you with a million different little notebooks, and they always look like they're on the brink of falling apart," I said, nodding at the one in his hand.

He chuckled. "They're kind of like baseball gloves. The more beat up, the better."

I nodded and gave him a once-over. He was wearing dark jeans, boots, and a white shirt that read, "I am." You couldn't see the tattoos I knew he had because of the quarter sleeves of his shirt, and I was dying to pull them up to see if he'd added any new ones. His face was closely shaved, and his hair was mussed, from the wind or his motorcycle helmet, there was no telling. What mattered was that he looked good—better than good—and I was ogling. I needed to stop ogling.

"Hey Jensen," a group of girls said as they walked by. His eyes left my face for a second, just to acknowledge them with a nod, but he looked right back at me.

"You want to come drink with us? We're going to play a game," one of them said.

He was still looking at me, and my heart felt like it was having a seizure. "I'd rather stay right here," he said, finally, not taking his dark grey eyes away from me.

"You can go," I whispered when the girls were out of earshot. "I don't mind."

"And lose track of my muse? I don't think so Road Runner," he said, smiling, as he flapped his notebook in the air.

"Afraid you can't keep up with me?" I asked.

His chuckle warmed me all over, and when his expression turned serious as he searched my face, I felt a shiver spike through me. "I am, actually."

Chapter Three

Present

The loud knock on my car window snapped me out of my reverie. I gasped and sat up straight, looking out to find Jensen standing there with a confused look on his face. From the look in his eyes, I knew something was wrong. I stepped out of the car, closing the door behind me.

"What's wrong?" I asked. He didn't respond—just pulled me into his arms and held me in a tight hug.

"I'm not going to slither out of your arms, you know?" I said jokingly against his chest. He breathed heavily against my head and held me tighter before finally letting go.

"Yes, you are," he said, his words muffled.

His words made my stomach dip. "What's wrong?" I asked again, this time pushing away from his chest.

He blinked a couple of times as he looked down at me, as if he'd forgotten what I looked like. It occurred to me that maybe in the five months he'd been away, I'd forgotten what he looked like as well. I raised my hand and flattened it against the stubble on his cheek. I ran my eyes over his face, stopping at the faded scar on his left cheek, and continuing on until I reached his full lips.

"I won't be here long," he said, finally breaking his silence. My eyes snapped back up to meet his.

"When do you leave?"

"Sunday night."

I nodded, tearing my eyes away from his to look over his shoulder, at the slightly open door of the house behind him. I hated the fact that he only came to visit for one or two days at a time, but I understood. His life was in New York. Had it not been for his foster mother, Patty, I wasn't sure how often he would come, or if he'd even come at all.

"Is Patty home?" I asked, raising my chin in the direction of the house.

Jensen shook his head, letting out a harsh breath that tickled my cheek. "She left a few minutes ago." He put a hand on my waist then, the feel of his long fingers curling to grip me igniting a fire deep within my belly. I wanted nothing more than to push him back into the house and rip his clothes off. Something told me that he wanted me to do that. That he preferred for me to do that instead of making him talk about whatever it was that was clouding his head. So I decided I wouldn't. I couldn't push him to talk to me; I knew that from experience, but I also knew that using sex to try to ease his pain was something Jensen fell into when he was young, and I liked to think I could do more for him than just that. I liked to think I would be the one who would ultimately tame the bad boy in him. I already was, in a sense. I'd been his longest relationship thus far.

"Will you go somewhere with me?" he asked, making me blink in surprise.

"Somewhere like…" I prompted, confused.

"Away. Let's get a hotel somewhere, just for tonight. I need to…" he breathed out again. "I need to be with you," he said, bringing his other hand to my other hip and holding me there before trailing them both along my sides until he reached my face. "I want to be alone with you. Only you and me."

He could have asked me to kill the Pope, and I would have in that moment. When Jensen looked at me like that, with those soulful gray eyes that begged for somebody to just understand him, I couldn't say no. I placed my hands over his on my face, and then brought them in front of my mouth. He closed his eyes as I kissed his calloused palms.

"I would go anywhere with you," I said in a whisper. My words seemed to rock something inside of him, because when he opened his eyes he looked torn, broken. That's how Jensen was, though, and with the baggage he carried, I couldn't blame him.

He didn't say another word—just nodded once and pulled me into the house. I walked around his room as he packed his overnight bag. I busied myself by picking up and putting down random things he had scattered on his nightstands, his desk, the floor. His room looked the way it always had, as if he still lived here and not thousands of miles away.

"How was your flight?" I asked, breaking the silence as he opened and closed drawers.

"It was okay."

I looked over at him. His brows were pulled together as he rummaged through his duffel bag.

"Did you lose something?" I asked.

His hands stopped moving, and the edge of his mouth moved into half of a smile. "Found it."

I smiled back, searching his face for clues as to what was wrong with him. I wanted to ask if he'd spoken to his mother, or if he'd gotten fired from his job, or if maybe the children's book he was shopping to agents got turned down, but I didn't want to push him, and I didn't want him to close himself off again, so I stayed quiet.

His smile wavered as he looked at me; the longer he stared, the harder I found it to stay rooted in place.

"Come here," he said, the need in his voice carrying me to him. "You know you mean the world to me, right?"

Normally those words would have made me melt right in his hands, but the way he looked at me when he said them made my heart hurt.

"What in the world happened?" I asked. "You're really starting to worry me."

He breathed out heavily, crushing my body against his again. "God, Mia, I don't even know where to start. Can we pause the conversation and have it later though?"

I reared back and looked at him, nodding. "But you'll tell me," I said. I didn't want this to be one of the situations where I hated that I had to practically extract the information from him. I wanted to think we were in a place where we could tell each other everything and anything and not worry about the other judging.

"I'll tell you everything, baby. Everything," he said in a whisper as he ran his thumb over my bottom lip. "God, I missed you," he said, pulling my lips to his. We definitely needed to talk, but I was willing to wait a couple of hours if this was his way of temporarily shutting me up.

Chapter Four

Past

"Our waiter keeps staring at you," Jensen said, glaring at the man standing a few feet away from us.

"He does not," I said, shaking my head with a smile. The waiter *was* staring at me, but he always did when we ate there. More than a handful of times I'd caught him looking at my boobs as he refilled our water, and that alone was pretty funny considering I didn't have much to look at. I didn't want Jensen getting mad though. Especially not when we were celebrating our two-year anniversary. As it was, he'd gone from zero to ballistic earlier today when my friend, Nathan, sent me a text to wish me a happy belated birthday.

"He is, and I don't like it."

"Hey," I said, placing my hand over his to beckon his attention. "What's with you tonight?"

His eyes flicked to mine. "I just … nothing."

I raised an eyebrow and opened my mouth to press him further, but our food arrived. "Saved by the food."

Jensen grinned. We talked about our classes as we ate, debating which class was better and what teacher taught it better. He was graduating soon and had been accepted into the Graduate English program at NYU; he hadn't planned on going for it, but I pushed him. His argument had been that he wanted to be a writer, and he didn't need one. In the end, after we visited the school together, he decided he wanted to do it. It didn't hit me right away that he would be leaving soon, and I was staying behind. We would be worlds apart, but I loved him enough to let him go and support him while he was there. We'd decided to take our relationship a step at a time while he was away, and that was something that made my stomach coil with unease.

We stood up and held hands, and, just as we walked out, he stepped up to our waiter and said something to him. I couldn't hear what it was, but from the look on the guy's face, I knew it wasn't anything nice.

"What'd you tell him?" I asked as he opened my car door.

"I told him that if I catch him checking you out the next time we come here, I would rip his eyes out and stomp on them." He closed the door and left me gaping at him as he rounded the car to get into the driver's seat.

"You did not," I said as soon as his ass hit the seat.

He glanced at me. "Did you not see the look on his face?"

I nodded slowly. "Yeah, but he's bigger than you." Jensen was athletic, but he wasn't a gym rat. That guy looked like he could bench two football players.

"I'm bigger where it counts," he said with a shrug.

A small laugh escaped before I could stop it. "You are just … too much."

He reached for my hand and kissed the back of it. "Are you having fun?"

"I always have fun when I'm with you."

"Good, because I have an entire weekend of fun planned."

"Does it involve you and me naked on a bed?"

His nostrils flared as he pulled out of the parking lot. He brought my hand up to his mouth and grazed his teeth along the tips of my fingers. "And the kitchen table. And the floor. And the shower. And the beach. The possibilities are endless, really."

My insides tightened.

"You want that?" he asked, his voice low.

"I want that," I replied in a whisper.

"I want to peel that dress off you slowly, kissing every inch of bare skin as it falls." He smiled when he saw my face flush. "Then I'm going to lay you down on the kitchen counter and lick my way down your body until your legs are trembling with need." He paused to lick my wrist. "Then," he said, as he parked the car in front of his place, his voice a raspy whisper against my ear. "I'm going to lick your pussy from one side to the other and bite your lips the way you like."

"Jensen," I said, pulling away from him. I was on fire. "Let's go inside."

He put his hand on my thigh and moved it slowly until he reached my already damp thong. "I'm going to take my time with you, baby," he whispered, bringing his mouth up to mine as he hooked a finger inside my underwear to stroke me. "I'm going to make you beg for me to fuck you."

"I'm willing to beg," I said against his lips. "I'll beg right now."

I felt him smile. "I'm crazy about you, Mia Bennett."

"Likewise, Jensen Reynolds." I kissed his lips lightly. "Now can we please go inside so you can make good on your promise?"

He chuckled. "So impatient."

Once we were inside, Jensen asked me to wait for him in the kitchen so he could get my present. We'd said no presents. We shared a birthday so presents were exchanged the other day, but I couldn't help buying him something for the occasion, and evidently he felt the same. I ran my fingers over the bracelet he gave me, and smiled as I examined each charm—the number 31, for our birthdate; the camera; the feather pen; the anchor; the sailboat; the heart that read, "I'm yours."

I dropped my hand onto my lap when I noticed him walk out of the room with a large box in his hands. He smiled as he set it down on the counter and stood behind me, wrapping his arms around me.

"Open it," he said.

I picked up the top of the box to reveal a smaller box. I frowned as I took that one out. It was wrapped in a brown paper filled with words. Normally I would have torn it right open, but something about it made me stall. My breath caught when I realized it was his handwriting. I turned slightly to look at him over my shoulder.

"It's just wrapping paper, Mia," he said with a tender smile.

I looked at the box again and examined it, trying to read what it said. "Are these your words?"

Jensen rubbed the back of his neck and smiled as he looked at the floor. He was so sure of himself most of the time, so he looked adorable on the rare occasions that he got shy. He peered up at me.

"They're just words," he said.

I pulled him between my legs, but he was too tall for me to kiss, so I hopped off the stool. He was still too tall. Jensen chuckled, understanding what I was trying to do, and lifted me on to the counter, standing between my swinging legs.

"They're your words," I whispered against his lips.

"Open the box, please," he said, pressing his lips against mine before giving me space again.

I brought it in front of me again. I couldn't figure out what it was. I tried to think about everything I'd said I wanted and came up short.

"Stop trying to guess what it is and open it."

"The wrapping paper in itself is a gift," I whispered, taking my time to remove it so that it wouldn't tear. "Oh my God," I breathed when the camera lens I'd been saving up for came into view. "Oh my God."

Jensen was grinning when I looked up at him.

"This is … this is too much," I said finally, putting the box down beside me. There was a reason I hadn't gotten it for myself yet. Though this explained why he'd picked up so many hours at the coffee shop where he worked.

"Nothing is too much for you," he replied, bringing a hand up to caress my face.

"Jens—"

His mouth landed on mine before I could finish saying his name. My eyes slammed shut as his lips teased mine until they parted, his tongue snuck into my mouth, stroking against mine as his hands framed my face. My fingers threaded through his hair, and I scooted forward, rocking into him. We were panting when we broke our kiss.

"You deserve everything, Mia," he murmured as he looked at me. Those gray eyes of his would be my undoing, of that I had no doubt.

"I only want you," I whispered as I unbuttoned his shirt and tucked my hands inside of it, feeling his warm, hard chest under my small, cold hands.

"You have me, baby. You'll always have me." He shrugged his shirt off and wrapped his arms around me to unzip my dress.

"And you'll always have me." I hopped off the counter and let the dress pool at me feet, watching the way Jensen's eyes darkened as they left my face and raked my body slowly—so slowly—leaving tiny trails of heat in their wake. He made an animalistic sound in the back of his throat as he charged me, lifting me back up on the counter and spreading my legs.

"You know what my greatest fear is?" he asked, his mouth below my ear as he placed a kiss there. I shivered at the sensation his breath left as he kissed his way down to my chest.

"What?" I asked in a pant as he reached my breast.

"Losing you," he said, looking up at my face. "Losing this." His lips closed around me, his tongue flicking my nipple. His hands worked their way between my legs as he gave attention to my other breast. "You're everything I've ever wanted," he said, whispering kisses down my stomach. "You're everything I need." My head hit the counter with a thump when I felt his tongue on me.

"Oh God," I said.

"I would die if you left me, you know that, right?" he said against me.

"I would never leave you."

"You might. Maybe you'll find someone better than me when I'm away," he said, flicking his tongue against me.

"Shit."

"A successful guy," he continued.

"I only want you," I responded, my fingers pulling his hair as I writhed against the hard counter.

"Maybe someone with less baggage," he said.

"I love your baggage," I said.

That earned a chuckle from him. He blew on me, his fingers toying.

"Jensen, please."

"Keep going?" he asked.

"Keep going," I chanted. "Keep going."

He did. He didn't stop until I saw fireworks beneath my eyelids. When I opened my eyes again he was lifting me up. I wrapped my arms around his neck and sighed against his chest.

"Why do you always do that?" I asked quietly.

"Do what?"

"Talk about that kind of stuff when you're … you know." I looked up at his face. His steps faltered. He stopped just as we reached the threshold of his room and looked at me. He opened his mouth to say something, but closed it, shaking his head.

"Tell me." I ran a hand through his hair.

"Ever since we got together, I've had this terrible feeling that I'm on borrowed time with you," he said in a whisper, his eyes sad. "Nothing in my life lasts. Nothing good." He shook off his words and walked over to the bed, dropping me on it as he kicked off his boots. I stood on the bed so that I could be at his level when he looked at me and grabbed his wrists as he took off his belt, pulling him toward me.

"You've been saying this for two years, yet here we are," I said.

He nodded slowly, still looking unconvinced.

"You are a beautiful human being. You know that, right?" I asked, searching his face. "You're funny, you're kind, you're talented as hell, so attractive it hurts to look at you sometimes," I said, making him laugh and roll his eyes. I smiled.

"You're so much more, Mia. So much more," he said, threading his fingers through mine.

"When I'm with you, I am."

"I'm leaving soon," he said, looking at our joint hands.

"Temporarily," I reminded him.

"It's still a long time apart."

"Do you love me, Jensen?" I asked.

His eyes snapped up to mine again. "More than anything."

"Then we'll take a break and meet at the end of the road."

Before he could delve deeper into his nagging fears, I pushed him away, jumped off the bed, and started working on removing his belt. That weekend was still one of my favorite memories with him.

Chapter Five

Present

I snapped back to the present as he parked the bike and held out his hands for me to pass him the helmet.

"I was just thinking about the day you gave this to me," I said, smiling.

His lips twitched. "Before or after I made you cry with my dick?"

I slapped his chest. "You didn't make me cry with your dick," I muttered. "It was an emotional night."

Something in his gaze shifted, but he pulled my hand and walked me across the street to check in at the hotel before I could acknowledge it. As soon as the door to our room closed behind us, I stripped off my shirt and bra to change into my bathing suit. I was tying it when I felt Jensen's large hands on my back and shivered uncontrollably. He finished tying it for me and dropped a kiss on my bare shoulder, turning and going into the bathroom before I could thank him properly.

On the beach, we sat in silence—I took pictures of the water, the sun, some surfers in the distance, while Jensen used a charcoal to sketch beside me. I turned my body to snap a picture of him, and pressed the button on my camera to examine the picture. I would never tell him, but he was my favorite subject to photograph. His Dodgers cap was on backwards, keeping his hair tucked away from his eyes. He was squinting and biting the side of his lip in concentration as he drew. My heart sped up, just looking at the picture. I jumped in surprise when his arm wrapped around my shoulder and lowered my camera to look at him. There was a sea of turmoil in his eyes. I was sure that no matter how many things I went through, the look in his eyes had the most power to sadden me.

"Are you going to tell me what's wrong?" I asked in a whisper, closing my eyes as his breath fanned over my face. He smelled of the mint gum he'd been chewing on.

"You remember how I ended up living with Patty, right?" he asked quietly.

My eyes popped open again, and I nodded. I would never forget a drunken Jensen spilling his disgust for his father and the way he impregnated his mother and paid her off to keep quiet, or the way his mother abandoned him when she got into a relationship with a man who hated children. He looked away, worrying his lip. My eyes followed his and landed on the sun disappearing into the ocean. I snuggled my body into his, and he tightened his hold on me, his chin resting on top of my head as we watched it go.

"What about her?" I asked when we could only see the very tip of the sun.

"I never want to be like my mom. Or him. I won't let myself be that selfish. I don't want to be a liar, a cheat," he said. I frowned, pulling away from him.

"Okay?"

Jensen breathed out. "This is so fucked," he said, looking at the sand between our bodies. The look on his face when he brought his eyes to mine again nearly ripped me apart. "I…" He took a deep breath. "I was seeing somebody while we were apart," he said, the slap of his words leaving a sting behind them. "It wasn't serious at all, which is why I never told you about her."

"That's fine," I said, waving him off. "Don't. I don't want to hear about her."

"Mia," he said, his Adam's apple bobbing as he swallowed. "She's pregnant."

Chapter 6

Present

Jensen

I never knew my father. I knew of him, but never knew him, not even by name. It wasn't until the eve of my thirteenth birthday that I discovered his first name. That night, when any of the other mothers I knew would have been packing up their kid's gift into a bag, she was packing up her suitcase. I walked into her room because I heard a noise and thought maybe she'd fallen. She was a heavy drinker, and while most of the kids in my class wore bags under their eyes because they'd stayed up late playing video games, I had them because I was usually holding her auburn hair out of her face while she threw up. Teachers called me irresponsible for forgetting my homework most days, and I didn't have the heart to tell them that I did it on the bathroom floor most nights, and my mother's puke often ended up smeared all over it.

I wasn't a bright kid like Oliver, or well-to-do like Victor. I didn't excel in sports like Junior, but I had heart, and that can go a long way. Often times I woke up after two hours of sleep and studied, just to prove to my mom that I, too, could get good grades. I joined the baseball team and mowed the lawn for our neighbors, thinking those things would earn her respect. But that night, when I caught her packing her bags, and she turned to look at me, her gray eyes going wide when she saw me standing by the door, I realized none of those things mattered to her. They never would.

"Why aren't you sleeping, Jens?" she asked, her words slightly slurred.

"What are you doing?" I asked quietly as I watched her hands stop in her bag.

"I can't do this anymore," she replied in a cry. "I can't stay here and pretend I know how to mother when we both know I don't. I can't … you look too much like him. The older you get, the more you look like him. I don't want to…" she

paused, sniffling. "I don't want to hate you."

"You're leaving?" My voice cracked. The doorknob was rattling in my shaky grip.

"Only for a little while. I just need time to clear my head," she said. "Archer set us up. I'm splitting the account two ways—that way you get what you're owed too."

"Archer?" I whispered, trying to focus on blinking the tears filling my eyes. "Your ... father."

"You mean my donor," I said. "That's what you call him. My donor."

"Well, he isn't here, is he?" she spat, narrowing her eyes. "He promised me the world, impregnated me, and threw money at me to quiet us. Well ... I can't do it anymore. I can't do it anymore." She was wailing now, burying her face into her hands as her hair curtained her face. I stared at her, at the bag on the bed, at her room, at the floor.

"Why are you leaving?" I asked. "Why?"

She sniffed. "I'll be back when I get my shit together."

"Please don't leave, Mom. I'll try to be better," I pleaded.

"Patty will be here soon," she said, zipping up the bag and wiping her face. She walked over to me and cupped my chin with one hand. We were already the same height. She always made jokes about that when I had to help her into bed. "I love you, Jensen. I do, but I'm not well. You have to know that."

She kissed my cheek and walked out. I stayed rooted in place until I heard the door close behind her. I kept replaying over her words: 'I love you, Jensen. I do, but I'm not well. You have to know that.'

I thought back to that memory often. Probably more often than I should, and I always came to the same conclusion—she loved me, but not enough to stay. Not enough to put me first. I only told three people that story: Oliver, Mia, and now you. I didn't tell it to gain pity. I chose my own destiny, and whether it was good or bad, I had to accept the consequences of my actions. I told it because I believed history was something we should learn from. We studied it to not repeat the mistakes of the past.

I wouldn't say I had a rough childhood. I knew people who had worse. I was never molested or beaten. I was never told I was a piece of shit nor was I undermined. I just wasn't cared for. I was never nurtured. I never felt love from my biological parents, but I felt it elsewhere. Love was in friends who became brothers. It was in their parents, and Patty, my foster mother, the woman who taught me what a mother was supposed to be like. And it was in a girl—a bite-sized, sassy blonde named Mia.

Mia was love. She was everything. She loved me, she pushed me, and she inspired me. Leaving her for New York was one of the hardest choices I'd ever made. Being in a huge city by myself wasn't exciting for me the way it was for the people I met in school. I liked my life back home. I loved my city, I loved my girl, but I saw the way she got wrapped up in me. I saw the way her parents didn't approve of our relationship, and so I ended things when I left. I figured a break would be good for both of us. I didn't set out to date anybody, or even have sex with anybody else, really, but somehow it happened. I couldn't fault the girl for our mistake. It was irresponsible, unforgivable, but it happened. That was life. I couldn't expect Mia to understand. I didn't expect her to understand, but as I watched her pack her bag, the way I watched the first woman I loved pack hers all those years ago, I couldn't help but wonder what I could have done differently.

Not have sex with that girl from poetry class. I knew that much. Obviously. But even before then, I wished I had held on to this one a little tighter. I wished I had talked to her more. I wished I had begged her to go with me. I wished I could wipe the tears from her face, but she wouldn't let me go near her.

"God, you are such an asshole," she said, sniffling. "I fucking trusted you."

And that hurt more than anything, because she was right. I could have stood there and pointed out the semantics of it all: we were on a break, and I knew for a fact she was dating some dude named Seth, until this Adam guy came along. I knew for a fact they went out every weekend, and that he sometimes drove her home and stayed over. I knew all of it. I could have called her out, but I didn't, because we were on a break, and we could have done anything we wanted, but at the end of the day, we were supposed to be together and I fucked that up.

"I'm sorry," I said, taking a step toward her. Her head snapped up.

"Don't. Don't even try to touch me right now," she said, her chest heaving in sobs. I'd seen her cry, but never like this. Not even when her family dog died did she cry like this, and it fucking killed me. Her blue eyes were filled with pain that I'd caused. She raised her finger and pointed at me. "It should have been me. That's all I can think about right now."

I closed my eyes to try to contain my sorrow, but it was no use. I bit down on the inside of my mouth to keep from crying, which was all I wanted to do, but I wouldn't do it in front of her. So I bit until I tasted blood.

"You're my best friend, Mia," I said, opening my eyes again. She had her bag slung over her shoulder. "Please don't go."

She shook her head furiously, her wavy hair sticking to the wetness of her face. "Don't ask me to stay," she said hoarsely.

"Please," I whispered anyway.

"Jensen, I can't!" she said in a loud sob. "I can't even look at you right now!"

"So look away, but please stay. Just for tonight."

She closed her eyes and took a deep breath, wiping the tears from her face. "I really hate you right now," she said once she opened them again. "I really, really hate you."

"I know, baby," I said, stepping toward her and pulling her into my chest. I knew she would push me away, and maybe claw at me, but I needed to feel her. I needed to hold her.

"Don't call me that," she said, wailing into my shirt. "Oh my God. I feel like I can't breathe."

I held her tighter. I didn't want to let her go. Ever. When she pulled back, she looked up at me. "What will you do now? Move to New York for good?"

I bit my tongue hard and nodded.

"And then?" she prompted.

"Mia," I started, taking a deep breath. "I have to marry her."

If I could erase one thing from my memory for the rest of my life, it wouldn't be my mom on the floor, or the way she looked at me when she left, or the way Patty looked when she told me that my mother was never coming back. It would be the look on Mia's face the moment I dropped that bomb.

"Wh-what?"

"She got kicked out of her house. She's young; she has nowhere to go. Her father—"

Mia's hands went up before I could finish my statement. "I don't want to fucking hear it. I don't want to hear it."

"Please let me explain."

"Don't." She was holding on to her stomach as if she was going to heave at any moment. "I have to go. I just. I'm sorry, but I have to go." She walked to the door and looked back at me one last time, her eyes trailing all over my face and down my body, and I just knew this was goodbye. I don't know why I expected anything more.

"I'm sorry," she said as she walked out. "I'm … I can't."

I stared at the back of the door for a beat, waiting for the anger to seep in, but it never did. I thought I loved that girl my entire life, and I knew I would for the remainder of it. It didn't matter that I had to go back to New York and marry somebody who was a virtual stranger to me, or that her father held my future in his hands, or that the baby she carried was mine. Nothing mattered more than the fact that I'd lost the most important thing in my life. I knew I would never get her back. Regardless of what the future held for us, for me, I knew I wouldn't get her back. I didn't deserve her.

I sat on the floor in front of the door until the sun came up, just in case she decided to walk back through that door.

She never did.

I called, and I showed up at her house. I emailed. I texted. But nothing ever seemed to get through to her. So I started writing.

We were dared to kiss, and from the moment her lips met mine, I was a goner…

My Best Friend's Wedding

5 YEARS LATER

Mia

I was convinced that major life events existed for us to measure how fast or slow we were progressing according to society. Weddings were one of them. When all of my friends started getting married, and I was sitting in the corner like, "Don't mind me. Party for one over here," I knew that everyone in my life was moving along a little faster than I was willing. From an outside perspective, depending on when you met me, you could say one of two things about me: "Poor girl, she's been through so much. I wouldn't be surprised if she ends up buying ten cats and living alone for the rest of her life." Or, "One of these days she's got to settle down with one of the men she … fools around with."

I'd actually heard my mother state the latter of those options to her friends during book club. She used book club as a way of whoring me out to her friends' eligible sons. It was annoying. The latest book club meeting was held a couple of weeks ago, and the big discussion was whom I would take to my best friend's wedding. Thankfully, that night I'd agreed to go over there with my brother so we could watch the Clippers game with our dad, and I was able to intervene in the conversation as they handed around an iPhone opened up to the Facebook page of one of their son's.

I'd never understood why people associated weddings with dates. Was it because they didn't want to seem lame for not being in a steady relationship as they watched somebody they loved get married? I was secure enough on my own. I didn't need a man's presence to show me my worth, thank you very much. But as I handed my car keys over to the valet of the hotel where my best friend and most of my loved ones would be getting ready for her big day, a wisp of longing hit me, and I kind of wished I did have somebody to share this important event with.

"You did it!" Estelle said as soon as she saw me walk into the bridal suite. She stood quickly, practically sprinting toward me, long, loose strands of waves bouncing against the white robe she was wrapped in. I stood still as she touched the tips of my now short hair, waiting for her to tell me the truth: she hated it.

"I feel like I pulled a Britney," I said with a groan, tugging on the ends as if the movement would make it grow back. I'd had long hair, Rapunzel-length hair, since I was a kid, and this drastic change was way out of character for me.

Estelle laughed, her big, bluish eyes shooting up to mine. "You've been talking about cutting your hair for months, and it's not *that* short," she said, while I tilted my head with raised eyebrows. "Okay, fine, it is that short, but you look great!"

"Thanks," I said with a smile. "But enough about me. Are you ready to get married … again?"

She married our longtime friend, Oliver, the guy who'd owned her heart ever since I could remember, a few months back, but today they were having their formal celebration.

"I am!" she said, smiling. I was glad for the infectious giddiness that radiated off her. I knew the event would be a difficult one for me to get through, not because I wasn't over the moon excited for my friends, but because all of our mutual friends would be there, and the one I'd been avoiding like the plague for the past five years was one of the groomsmen, and, in turn, walking with me.

Oliver's sister, Sophie, joined us as we dressed and sipped on mimosas, laughing at our drunken bachelorette party adventure from a few weeks earlier. I slipped into the soft pink maid of honor dress and scrunched my dirty blonde hair before working on my mascara. From the corner of my eye, I caught movement and dropped the tube of nude lipstick I had in my hand with a gasp, turning to give Estelle my full attention as she walked out of the in-suite bathroom wearing her wedding dress. I'd seen it on her when we went wedding shopping, but seeing her in it now, with her hair and make up done, made it real.

"My best friend is getting married," I whispered, smiling as tears pricked my eyes. Estelle laughed lightly, fanning her face with her hands.

"Don't. You're going to make me cry! I've been married for four months!" she said, but continued fighting tears nonetheless.

I gave her another once over and admired the way her dress hugged her body perfectly all the way down to her knees, where it fanned out.

"You picked out the most perfect dress. I could never pull that off," I said, referring to the feathers that adorned the bottom half of her dress.

She smiled at me and walked up to the mirror, holding her veil in her hand. "My mom is supposed to put this on me," she said.

"I'm sure they'll be here soon. Sophie went to check on Sander and the baby," I said. "You look incredible, Elle, and I'm not just saying that because it's you. You really look unbelievable."

She took a deep breath, smiling even brighter as her eyes met mine in the mirror. "Thank you. Thank you for everything," she said, pausing to swallow and blink back tears. "Thank you for my beautiful pictures and just … everything. If it weren't for you, I wouldn't be here right now."

"You would be. This was inevitable," I said, leaning in to wrap my arms around her, placing my chin on her shoulder. "But I am so fucking glad I get to share this day with you." I squeezed her a little. "I think Bean is going to come in his pants when he sees you walking down the aisle," I said, dropping my hands.

"I sent his gift with Vic, so maybe he already did," Estelle said with a laugh. His gift was a custom photo album that included super sexy pictures of her in his doctor's coat and other things from her boudoir shoot with me.

"Umm yeah, I think that probably did the trick," I said, turning toward the door when we heard it unlock. Estelle's mom and my mom walked in with Sophie trailing behind, all three of them gaping at Estelle in her wedding dress. I stepped away so that they could appreciate it and felt a ball form in my throat when her mom started crying.

"You look so beautiful," she kept saying.

"Mom, please stop, you're going to make me cry and ruin my make up," Elle said.

"Ohmygod, my brother is going to die," Sophie added.

"Our little girls are growing up," my mom said.

"You guys are impossible to be around!" I said, dabbing the edges of my eyes, trying not to cry again.

Estelle stayed behind while the rest of us went downstairs and out back to the beach, where the wedding was happening. Anxiety crashed through me like a wave when I saw the groomsmen standing around talking animatedly as they looked out at the beach. *I'm ready*, I told myself. *I'm fine.* But when he turned around, and I caught a glimpse of his profile, my legs stopped working.

"Uh oh. I can already see where this is going." My head turned back when I heard my brother's voice. "Deep breath and step, sis. Deep breath and step."

"I know how to walk, Rob, but thanks for the tip," I said.

He shrugged, smiling as he stared ahead at the group of guys. "I walked before you, so I figured you might need a little help."

I rolled my eyes with a laugh. "Actually, I walked before you, thank you very much."

"Yeah right," he said with a scoff. He put his arm around my shoulder and pulled me into him. "You're in charge of your sail," he said against my hair. "Say it."

"I'm in charge of my sail," I said, taking a deep breath. "What am I going to do without you when I move?"

"Easy," he said, dropping his arm and leaning away to look at me. "Don't go."

"Ha ha," I said, smiling at him. "You know I'm not going to pass up this job."

Rob let out a long breath. "I'm just saying—if you're with me, you're twinning, and if you leave, well, you won't be."

I laughed, pushing him off me. "You're so stupid. We're always twinning."

We started walking toward the group; Rob's presence gave me the strength I needed to keep my head held high. There was a time in my life that I hated being a twin. Even though I didn't have a girl twin, with matching clothes and all the competition that came from that, I still felt overwhelmed by it sometimes. More often than not, it was a fleeting feeling, because at the end of the day nobody understood me the way my brother did, and I wasn't sure if it had anything to do with the twin thing or if it was just a sibling thing in general, but I was glad to have him. That was why when I got this incredible opportunity to take photos for a magazine in New York, I actually gave it a lot of thought. Two years ago I would have jumped on that opportunity, but I felt like the older I got, the more important family was becoming to me, and the thought of leaving them behind was something that wasn't as appealing as it once was.

"Hey, Meep, you look beautiful," Oliver said once we reached them.

"Thanks. You look fucking hot, but what else is new?" I said, making all of them laugh. All of them except one. The one who made my heart hurt every time I laid eyes on him, so I tried not to look directly at him.

"Ready to get married?" Rob asked Oliver, who flashed him the biggest smile I'd ever seen.

"I'm already married, but yeah, I'm ready to marry her again, and again, and again," he said, earning a groan from Victor.

"Please stop there. I'm afraid what your next comment will be, and I really don't want this day to be ruined for all of us."

"Did you get the present?" I asked, ignoring Victor's plea and adding fuel to the fire as Oliver started chuckling loudly.

"Oh yeah. Thank you for taking those. I'm going to make her reprise the roles in some of them," he said.

"What roles? What are you talking about?" Victor asked, because his nosiness knew no bounds.

"The boudoir shoot I did for Elle," I replied. Rob started coughing beside me, Jensen added an "Okay, that's enough of that," but Victor just looked at me, his eyebrows drawn in confusion.

"Boudoir shoot," I said. "You know … sexy pictures?"

"Of my sister?" he practically yelled. "Okay. I'm sorry I asked. I'll see you guys at the altar!"

We all laughed as we watched him retreat from the conversation. He stopped only to say hi to Sophie and offer her his arm, then shot us an impatient look.

"That's my cue," Oliver said. "I have to walk in first. Where's my mom?" he asked, looking at me.

"I have no clue," I replied, looking around.

"There she is!" Rob said, pointing at Oliver's mom, who walked in with an unfamiliar looking man and another woman.

"Now there's a picture I never thought I'd see," Oliver said as he walked over to them. Jensen chuckled as he looked over at them, and I swear I felt my insides shake in its wake.

"That's his dad?" Rob asked Jensen.

"Yeah, and his stepmom," Jensen answered, still looking at the trio.

"They seem friendly," Rob said.

"Yeah, they do," Jensen replied.

"Demi and Bruce Willis are friendly, and they've both been married to other people. It happens," I said with a shrug. It wasn't until Jensen's eyes flashed over to mine that I realized what I'd said. The intensity behind his stare made me step back.

"Some people know how to act like grown ups," he said, his words dropping tiny matches onto the gasoline that ran through my veins.

"Oh, you hang out with grown ups?" I said, tilting my head. His eyes narrowed on mine.

"I think the ceremony is about to start," Rob said, squeezing my arm to call my attention. I knew what he wanted to say to me before I even looked up at him, so I took a deep breath and nodded as I regrouped myself.

"Let's get on with it, Reynolds, and because this is the only chance you have of touching me, I suggest you revel in it," I said, stepping closer to him and grabbing his arm. I tried not to think about the way my arm felt thin against his muscular one. I ignored the way his chuckle sounded and the way it made me feel. I ignored the way being near him made the endorphins in my brain haywire.

We took our place behind Victor and Sophie and waited as the wedding song started to play, which was an acoustic version of "Thinking Out Loud" by Ed Sheeran. He moved his hand and entwined his fingers with mine, making my eyes widen in shock as I looked up at him.

"You told me to revel in this," he said, the sound of his voice making my heart beat in overdrive.

"Please don't," I whispered.

"What's the matter? You lost your bravado?" he asked as we walked, smiling for Finley, the photographer I'd appointed the job to.

"I didn't lose anything," I said, practically yanking my hand away from him and walking to my assigned spot when we reached the pastor.

It wasn't until I saw my beautiful best friend walking toward us that thoughts of Jensen vanished. I'd seen Oliver and Estelle together so many times before, but today, as the sun set, and they declared their love for each other, what they had finally hit me. They had what we all wanted, that thing we craved. As we stood there, soft droplets of rain began to fall.

"A sun shower," Sophie said beside me. "They say it's good luck."

"Yeah well, I hope they kiss before that good luck starts ruining our make up," I whispered back, unable to hold back my smile as I watched the bride and groom kiss. The entire thing was magical, despite the guys and small crowd rising from their seats and telling them to hurry up before the skies opened up above us. I didn't have to walk back to the hotel with Jensen, because everybody was running by the time they finished kissing.

At the party, as they swayed slowly to their first dance, I drank. And drank some more.

"Rough night?" Rob said as he took the seat beside mine.

I met his concerned blue eyes and smiled. "Beautiful night."

He gave me a look, his eyes flickering from mine to the flute in my hand.

"It's time to wine," I said.

"It's champagne."

"Yeah, well, tonight we shall whine over champagne," I said.

"Yeah, well, you better hope your whining doesn't turn into puking, because your girl just got married, and I highly doubt she's going to hold your hair up tonight," he responded.

"Well, duh, I know that. Why do you think you're here?"

Rob laughed, shaking his head as he picked up his flute. "To eat." He smiled when my eyes narrowed. "And shake my ass, of course," he added, to which I rolled my eyes. "Fine. I'll hold your hair. Actually, it's pretty short now, so I think it'll hold itself," he said, frowning as he looked at my hair.

"We almost look like twins," I said, laughing when he poked me in the ribs.

"I'll have you know that I am much more good looking than you," he said, standing as the song came to an end and the next one started. He held his hand out to me, and I took it, following him to the dance floor.

I laughed as he swung me exaggeratedly, and squeezed his arms when he dipped me. "You better stop before you end up wearing my champagne," I said when he pulled me back up.

"Meep, you sure know how to kill a mood," Rob said with a groan. "I think I'm going to look for another dance partner."

"Knock yourself out. I have to use the restroom anyway," I said as we walked off the dance floor.

I heard my mom's laughter ring out as soon as I stepped outside and followed the sound until I saw who she was talking to, but by then, she'd spotted me and was calling me over.

"Mia, come here! Did you tell Jensen about the job in New York?" she asked.

"Uh… no," I said, not daring to look at him.

"Did you know he still lived there?"

If looks could kill… my poor mother. I wanted to drag her out of the party and yell, "Of course I know that!"

I knew his address by heart, too. Not because I was a stalker, but because I visited with Patty and she made me mail him boxes of all kinds of things.

I could have just not sent the things, and she would have never blamed me, but it was the only way I could help, and now that she was dealing with health issues, she needed all the help she could get. I'd sent everything from boxer briefs to blankets for his daughter. I didn't know what hurt me more—knowing I would never see the boxers on him or giving something to the little girl that should have been ours, but wasn't.

"Oh, well, why don't you tell him about your move?" my mom asked. My eyes snapped to hers. Was she crazy? What was she playing at?

"What move?" Jensen asked, probably more to be cordial than because he actually cared. I looked over at him to make sure I could still read him, but he was looking at my mom.

"Mia's moving to New York soon!" my mom said, her smile wide as she looked at me. "She got a great job over there as a photographer—"

"Mom," I said, stopping her before she carried on. "I'm sure Dad is looking for you, and I doubt Jensen cares about my whereabouts or my career, so you should probably go find Dad, or maybe Hannah needs you for something."

Leave it to Bettina to wave me off as if I was some pestering child. "Mia, we're having a conversation here. I'm sure Jensen would love to know what you're doing in New York. You are in the same line of business and all. Actually maybe you know where she'll be working—"

My mouth popped open.

"Yeah, Mia, I would love to know what you'll be doing in New York," Jensen said. I turned to glare at him. I hated him. Absolutely and completely hated him, in his stupid white shirt that covered his perfect frame and the navy blue bow tie and slacks to match. *Fuck you*, I wanted to say, but didn't. *Fuck you for being so fucking irresistible to me, even now. Go back to your snotty little girl and perfect wife, you asshole.* That was what I wanted to say. That would make me happy. I didn't say it, though, because even I have my boundaries.

"Well, have fun, cool kids. I'm going to go pee, and then go back to the party," I said instead.

"Mia!" my mom said with a shocked gasp.

"Oh, excuse me," I said, bringing my hand to cover my mouth as I looked at Jensen, who was clearly trying to hold in his laughter. "I mean the restroom. Ladies don't pee."

As I walked away I heard him laugh under my mom's apology, and when I walked into the bathroom, I looked in the mirror and caught myself smiling. I narrowed my eyes and repeated the mantra I'd been telling myself since

Jensen stepped out of my life: *He has a family. He doesn't need you anymore.* Besides, he had enough reasons of his own to never want to see me again. I couldn't believe he was being as cordial as he had been.

I went back to the party, ate, and drank with no further interruptions other than Estelle, when she sat beside me for all of two seconds to rest her tired feet.

"So, New York." I was standing by the bar, getting myself another drink, when I heard the question behind me. I turned around and met his grey eyes.

"Yep," I replied, swallowing, hoping to wash out the sudden pain in my chest.

"You wouldn't have told me at all?" he asked, tilting his head, his eyes unreadable. "You would have moved over there, maybe lived right beside me, probably worked with colleagues of mine, and not have told me at all?"

My heart thundered inside its cage, like an animal trying to get out. Eventually, when Jensen and I were together, that feeling of butterflies every time I saw him went away. After seeing him every day, kissing him every day, waking up in his arms, the excitement of newlywed bliss faded. I didn't love him any less, didn't want him any less, but this feeling I feel right now? The one where I feel like my heart is literally in his fist? I had stopped feeling it, and I wasn't sure I liked it being back.

"I … I'm sure you would have found out. I mean, I'm sure Patty would have told you," I said, turning back around to face the bartender when he said my drink was ready.

"Patty, but not you," Jensen said, moving closer to me, the heat from his body rolling through mine. When I felt his breath over my neck, I closed my eyes and pictured his breath over my bare breasts, teasing me the way he used to, and then over my stomach, and lower…

I stopped, opening my eyes once more. I got a funny look from the bartender and pushed off of the bar, colliding with Jensen's hard chest.

"Sorry," I said, turning around and taking a step back to give myself space from him, away from his air, even though I still craved it. "I honestly, I mean, we don't talk Jensen." I stopped talking and craned my head to look up at him. "So no, I didn't have any intention of sending out a carrier pigeon or anything."

His eyebrows rose. His lips twitched in amusement, and I fought the urge to wrap my arms around his neck and pull his mouth to mine. His face darkened suddenly, and I was sure he could read my thoughts. I cleared my throat and took a sip of the screwdriver in my hand.

"Don't write that in one of your stories," I said, and held my breath as soon as the words left my mouth.

"You read my stories?" he asked, his voice low as he took a step forward. We were being quiet, off in a dark corner where the bar was located, but I felt every pair of eyes staring at us in that moment. I felt like we were screaming over the electric dance song that people were happily participating in. I took a step back.

"No," I said. "But once a writer, always a writer, right?" I said lamely. My statement made him grin—that stupid, wolfish grin of his that made me cave to him to begin with. I'd convinced myself that I hated that grin, until this moment, when I saw it in front of me and not in one of my twisted fantasies, in which reality never kicked in.

"Did you ever read—" he started to ask when my brother interrupted.

"Meep, I have to head out. Are you coming or do you need a ride?" Rob asked, his eyes not leaving mine.

"Is everybody leaving? Where's Elle?" I asked.

"They're about to leave," Rob said. "But Bean said they were just going to slip out, no big charade with bubbles or rice or whatever."

"Well, technically we can't do the rice thing. It wasn't permitted in the last wedding I shot," I said.

"I'm pretty sure that only applies in Catholic churches," Jensen said.

My eyes snapped to his, and suddenly all of the anger I thought had washed away came crawling back. "You would know, wouldn't you?" I said, pulling Rob's arm and stepping away.

"It was good to see you, man," Rob said over his shoulder.

"Yeah, it was great," I muttered under my breath, earning a laugh from Rob and a jaw twitch from Jensen.

"You seemed like you were actually getting along," he said once we were out of earshot.

"Yeah, smoke and mirrors and all that jazz," I replied, waving my hand.

"I take it Mom told him about the move."

"She sure did," I said with a sigh as we reached the front of the hotel, where Oliver and Estelle stood, talking, their arms wrapped around each other. "They have to be the most beautiful couple in the universe," I commented. Rob nodded in agreement.

"That's what love looks like," he said.

"It is, isn't it?" I said, smiling. I smiled brighter when Estelle's happy eyes caught my gaze and she squealed, walking toward us with Oliver in tow.

"Thank you so much for everything," she said as she wrapped her arms around me, pulling me away from Rob. She backed away to hold me at arms' length, her eyes searching my face as if she was cataloging it. I knew I was going to cry before I felt the tears pricking my eyes. They were leaving on their honeymoon to Italy tonight, and I was leaving for New York in a couple of days. This was our last day together, and I swear if it weren't her wedding I would beg Oliver to let me be a third wheel tonight.

"I'm going to miss you so much," I managed to choke out as I threw my arms around her again. "I'm so fucking happy for you, Elle. After everything you've been through these past years, you married Prince Charming."

"I love you so much bee-eff … so, so much," she said, crying with me.

"Stop being so melodramatic," Rob said, making us laugh. "You act like you're not going to take the next flight to New York when you're back from your honeymoon."

Estelle laughed, and Oliver joined in quickly. "I totally am," she said, backing away and wiping her tears away.

"You better," I said, also wiping my tears. "You can come, too, Bean," I added, looking at Oliver, who chuckled, shaking his head.

"I wouldn't miss it for the world," he said. "You're going to kick ass, Meep."

"I know," I said, making the three of them laugh.

We finished saying our goodbyes and let them walk to their car when the valet drove it up.

"I can't wait to show you how charming I can be," Oliver said as he opened the door for Estelle.

"TMI!" I screamed. "TMI!"

Oliver barked out a laugh and shot a wink my way. "You know you love hearing about our sex life."

"Not from you!" I responded with a laugh.

He shrugged. "It doesn't matter who the source is, the news is always the same. I rock her world. End of."

We all laughed one last time before they drove off.

"You going to be okay?" Rob asked as we stood there, waiting for our car to arrive.

"Yeah," I said, drawing in a breath. "I'm excited. I mean, despite the whole missing my family and friends thing, I'm excited."

"You should be. I don't think you've wanted anything more than this," he said. As he spoke, I looked over my shoulder and caught a glimpse of Victor and Jensen talking inside the lobby, with drinks in their hands, and nodded.

"I can think of one other thing," I said quietly.

PAPER HEARTS

DEDICATION

To Cam,

Who never tried to alter my language, but instead learned to translate the meaning behind my silence.

And to you, because you look like you need a lighthearted second chance romance in your life.

"Her heart was a little bruised up
His had not yet learned to forget
When they hugged, there were fragile parts."

—MJ ABRAHAM

Prologue

Jensen

I don't take ownership in a lot of things. I rent an apartment, lease a car, and go to a no-contract gym. I have a wandering heart—an incessant mind. It's hard for me to look at something and see forever; though I had a forever once.

I let her go, not because I loved her too much to ask her to stay, but because I couldn't bear to hear her tell me she wouldn't. Still, every once in a while I wonder.

And nothing is more haunting than regret.

Mia

I used to wonder what I would do if I had the chance to go back in time and right something. Would I take it? Would I look at it as a second opportunity, or would I just let it go, knowing the experiences I went through and learned from?

Discomfort spread through me as I walked into the building of my new, albeit temporary, job. The feeling stayed there, stuck to the lining inside of my uneasy stomach, echoing its way into my mind until I reached the twentieth floor of the building. As I exited the elevator and stepped into the lobby of the magazine, a smiling brunette, who was sorting through a colorful cup of pens, greeted me. Something about her—maybe her fidgetiness, the Lisa Loeb look she had going, or the welcoming smile on her face—made me breathe a little easier.

"How can I help you?" she asked in a singsong voice as she swiveled slightly in her chair.

"I'm here to see Mrs.—I mean, Dr. Zamora."

"Fran," she said. "She likes to be called Fran. Are you Mia?"

"Yes."

The girl smiled and gave me a quick onceover. "Cool. I'm Katie. Let me make sure she's in. Take a seat."

I let out a breath as I placed my bag on the floor and sat across from her in a sleek white chair, taking in the vast space filled with photographs shot by people whose work I admired. In an effort to calm my nerves, I picked up one of the magazines beside me and leafed through it, and even went as far as to try to channel my inner zen, remembering what an incredible yoga session I'd had earlier that morning. But nothing worked. That sticky feeling of *what did I get myself into?* could not be soothed.

It felt like the time I let my twin brother talk me into letting him cut my hair so that we could "really be twins," and I ended up looking like Peter Pan for two months while my mother cried into her pillow every night. I fished out my phone and contemplated sending him a text. Rob had always been the brave twin, with words of wisdom to get me through these times. But, I'd dug my grave, and now I had to lie in it.

When I ran into my favorite college professor months ago, a local magazine had just published some of my pictures for a special they were circulating. The accomplishment I felt at telling her this dwindled when she asked the dreaded words: *what next?* But then she offered me the opportunity of a lifetime: to take pictures for a huge magazine, one I probably wouldn't have had an opportunity to work for had my professor's sister not been the person in charge of the project. The catch, of course, unbeknownst to my professor or her sister, was that my ex-boyfriend, The Dream Crusher, wrote for the same magazine. But I'd have been an idiot to turn it down. Regardless of where I worked after this, to have this experience on my resume would be incredible.

"She just got here," Katie said, jerking me out of my thoughts. I stood quickly, hitching my bag on my shoulder as the glass door to my right opened and a tall woman with an uncanny resemblance to my professor—wild red hair and bright green eyes—walked through it.

"Mia," she said, smiling wide. "I'm Fran."

"Great to finally meet you," I replied, shaking the hand she offered me.

"In person, you mean. Janna speaks very highly of you, and we've become quite the duo on Twitter."

I laughed when she winked at me. After she hired me for this job, we started following each other on any social media that allowed for stalking.

"It's like we've been friends forever."

"Social media will do that," she responded with a laugh as she turned on her heels. "Let me show you around."

If Fran were a car, she'd be in fourth gear at all times. By the time she finished showing me around the place and we got back to her office, my legs felt like they were on fire. I wasn't sure if it was because of the heels I was wearing, or because I had to take four strides to her two. Being short could be a bit of a curse.

"We already got the clearance from *W Magazine* and are keeping the title 'What Would You Do With Your Second Chance?' I'm sure they told you already," she said as we each took a seat.

They hadn't told me anything. Not that it mattered. I'd taken pictures for an article with a similar name, but it was for a small, local magazine, nothing of this stature.

"I hope your friends don't mind that we're stealing their limelight," Fran added with a smile. She'd become completely fascinated by the fact that the couple on the cover of the magazine, my best friend and her now-husband, were a second chance love story.

"They definitely don't mind," I replied with a laugh. "They wanted to kill me when they saw the magazine in our grocery stores, so replacing it will be a good thing."

She laughed. "Were they uneasy because they weren't an official couple yet?"

"Basically. Her brother wanted to kill Oliver … the guy," I paused to clarify before continuing, "when he found out about the whole thing."

"But it's so romantic," Fran said, letting out a deep sigh.

"I guess it is."

"Oh, don't tell me you're one of those girls!"

"One of what girls?"

"The ones who are all 'I don't need a man' and 'I hate romance.'" She rolled her eyes, but I could tell she was biting back a smile as she said it.

I shrugged. "I'm not any kind of girl. I don't need a man, but I don't hate romance. I think I'm kind of obsessed with romance, really, which is probably why I'm still single."

Fran laughed loudly. "Funny how that works, right? I'll tell you what, had it not been for Match, I would have never met mine. I'm sure you don't need any help finding a guy, though." She waved the length of my torso as if she was presenting me to someone as some kind of trophy.

"Finding a guy isn't a problem. Keeping a guy is a problem, and finding *the* guy is a complete catastrophe."

Fran nodded in sympathy. "Yep. I've been there. But alas, you'll find *the* one. You're young, adorable, funny, talented, and smart. Hell of a combination."

I smiled and looked away. "One day."

"Anywho, enough about boys. Let's talk about work. As I stated in the email, you'll be taking your headshots today. You don't need to come into the office every day, but feel free to use our facility for anything you need. I sent you the contact information for the couples you'll be shooting so that you can schedule their test shots first, and after that, we'll let you know who we narrowed it down to. We only want to select four couples to feature: two young, and two older. They all have different stories, anyway, so that'll be fine."

She paused for a breath as I nodded, taking mental notes.

"And … oh yeah, here are the names of the writers working on the special. Carlos and Deborah are regular staff; the other two are freelance, but work with us often. I wrote down their emails and will send them yours now so they can contact you. Sometimes they like to go along for the shoots and do their interviews there."

My eyes scrolled down the list as I nodded. I stalled when I saw his name. Just words on a page, but they made my heart flip once, twice, and finally nestle its way into the pit of my stomach. I was prepared for this.

"You should meet us for drinks on Wednesday," Fran said, pulling me out of my thoughts. I was so not prepared for this.

"So I only see them on days that I shoot?" I asked, waving the paper slightly.

"Well, that only happens if they want to interview the people in their element. Otherwise, we only see each other during meetings, and we don't have many. We'll be having one this Wednesday over drinks, though, and then again to lay out the final plans."

I swallowed loudly and nodded. "Okay."

"It would be great for you to come on Wednesday and meet them," she said again. I felt like I was on a downward spiral, moving here, knowing this job would mean I would be insanely close to him, secretly hoping that I was, while reminding myself of the reasons I'd avoided him in the first place. I took a breath and braced myself for the inevitable fall.

"Sure. Drinks sound great."

Jensen Talks

I was talking to a friend of mine about this column the other day. He kept making fun of me, saying it sounded like an episode of *Sex and the City*. I gave him a hard time for even knowing what was on that show, but then I asked my date the other night about it, and she laughed endlessly. Apparently, if I was a woman, and the show was real, I would be Carrie. Jeff (editor), I'm cursing you.

I've found that dating now, opposed to when I was younger, is more difficult. People have certain expectations. As a man, you constantly feel like you're getting felt up (Not in the literal sense. FYI: I welcome the literal sense.). By the time you're done with your first drink, you might as well be a puppy wagging your tail, waiting for approval from them. Adult dating is exhausting. Take me back to college!

Restaurant: Glasserie

The verdict: Jensen Approved.

Question of the week from: @Margie17: "Where in your life do you feel most accomplished?"

My answer: As a father. That's probably the greatest thing I'll ever do. Cheesy, cliché, but true.

Mia

If nothing else, I was grateful to have amazing people in my life. When I decided to embark on this journey, I received nothing but support from everyone. My friend, Millie, who roomed with me in college at UCLA, offered me a place to live. She also made sure I was constantly entertained—taking me out to dinner and happy hours while her fiancé was away on business. When I got to the apartment, she was there, waiting for the technician to fix a leak in the air conditioner.

"I mean, seriously, why does the tenant have to be missing in action when things like this happen?" she said as she paced around the small living room.

"You don't have to stay here until he comes, you know? I'm perfectly capable of watching him fix it. It's not like we can supervise something we know nothing about anyway."

She stopped pacing suddenly and turned to me with a small frown. "I guess you're right."

"I usually am," I said with a sigh, which made her laugh and roll her eyes at me.

" What are we doing for your birthday?"

"Nothing."

"Nothing? Shut up. We do something almost every day of the week, and you want to do nothing on your birthday?"

My birthday was in two days. I'd never had anything against turning a year older; in fact, I'd always celebrated it like it was the last one I'd live to see. But celebrating without Rob didn't feel right. For the first time in twenty-five years, we'd have to settle for a long distance celebration. He was fine with it, of course, since he had Juan Pablo to keep him company. But everybody I knew was back home. Out here, I was alone, except for whenever Millie was actually in town.

"Well, I have to get drinks with the people from work that night, so maybe we can meet up afterward?" I said once I realized that her brown eyes were glued to my face as she waited for an answer.

"Oh my God. Does that mean you-know-who will be there?"

"I don't know if you-know-who will be there. It's his birthday, too, re-member?"

"You know that you-know-who knows you're working there, right? Do you really think he won't be there knowing you probably will?"

I sighed. I didn't know anything about you-know-who anymore. I couldn't read his thoughts or try to make out his steps before he took them. I'd lost that instinct the same night I lost him, and I was totally fine with that. He moved on, as did I.

"I don't know, Mill, but I'm not here to reacquaint myself with him. I'm here to take these pictures, try to get my pictures displayed in as many places as I can, and then I'm out."

She plopped down on the couch opposite me, draping her legs over the armrest as she turned and rested her chin on her hand to look at me. "Are you still dead set on the LA job?"

I nodded. Ultimately, having my prints displayed in museums was just a dream of mine. It wasn't something I depended on happening, and, even if it did, I wasn't depending on that for my number one source of income. I loved what I did. Loved taking pictures and living behind my camera lens. It wasn't something I would give up for anything. Right after I took the temporary job with *Newsweek,* I also signed on to work for a fashion magazine based out of LA. It'd been my dream job all through college, so when I finally got it, I was beyond excited.

"Well, you already know how I feel about that. I don't think fashion is your calling, but if it makes you happy, I'm rooting for you," Millie said as she stood.

There was a knock on the door as soon as she righted herself. We spent the next half hour watching the repair guy fix the leak. After Millie left, I went to my room and sorted out my clothes for the dreaded happy hour. At least drinks would be involved, and, who knew, maybe he wouldn't show up after all. Millie's words rung in my head again, and with them I felt my nerves tighten in my core. Jensen did know I was working there, and I had a feeling he would show up at happy hour just to spite me; because that's the type of shit he liked to do.

After a couple of minutes of moping about things that couldn't be undone or fixed, I grabbed my camera and headed out. I wasn't in love with New York. The hustle and bustle of it wasn't my style, but there was no denying the enigmatic qualities it had. Every time I stepped out of the apartment I felt the city's heartbeat—frantic and full of possibilities. With each turn of a corner came a different story—a single mother trying to make ends meet, a workaholic father, a student trying to pass the semester, an implant from Idaho trying to land a modeling gig. There was so much beauty in the struggle of trying to find your place in the world.

I let myself get lost in the fantasies I created when I was looking at the world through my lens. Life was easier to ignore when I was busy pretending for other people. It was easier when I didn't have to be Mia, the girl who was lost, not just wandering, and I didn't have to think of my own struggle to find my place in the world.

That was what I found most comforting about it all: we were all confused together, and ultimately, all lost together, despite our ages, races, genders, and anything else that set us apart.

I treated myself to not one, but three mimosas for breakfast on my birthday. Sadly, I was drinking alone, and drinking alone led to overthinking, and overthinking led to disappointment, and disappointment led to regret. And that led to another mimosa to wash it down, because fuck if I needed any more of that in my life. My best friend, Estelle, had sent me a care package, as if I was overseas and not in a city that had absolutely everything you could think of getting, and in the package was everything from a funny birthday card to a dildo. She obviously thought she was the funniest person ever.

Before I got to my fifth mimosa, I pulled out my phone and FaceTimed Rob. It was six in the morning in Santa Barbara, and it was a weekday, so he had to be up for work anyway. He answered on the fourth ring, and I smiled at his wide smile, with the dimple on his left cheek showing. His dark hair was rumpled from sleep, and his deep blue eyes still hazy.

"Happy birthday, Meep."

"Happy birthday, Robbie." My eyes watered as the words left my mouth.

"Oh God. You've been drinking champagne," he said.

"How do you know?" I asked, laughing. My eyes fell over the champagne flute that he couldn't see from the way the camera was positioned.

"You always get emotional when you drink champagne. And your face is red as hell."

"Oh." I placed the back of my cold hand over my face. "What are you doing today? Aside from missing me so much you could cry."

He chuckled and shook his head. "After I get that good cry out of the way I'll try to see if I can make it through work without dying of sadness, and then head to Mom's for dinner with Juan Pablo. You?"

I groaned. "I hate you. What's Mom making?"

"My favorite meal, obviously."

"You mean *our* favorite meal. And I hate you. Officially."

He laughed. "Shut up. You're in New York freakin' City!"

"I know, but I miss home."

"You've been there for two weeks, Mia."

"Yeah. Two months to go."

He shook his head. "Well, you started off the day with a bang. Mimosas?"

"Yeah, by myself!"

"Where's Millie?"

I shrugged. "I told her I'd meet her later tonight, after the happy hour I have to go to for work."

Rob frowned. "Will Jensen be there?"

My shoulders slumped. "Why is everyone making such a big deal about that?" He shot me a look that made me quickly glance away. "I don't know. He might be, but I doubt it. It's his birthday, too."

"Yeah, I know. I'll be expecting his yearly shout-out in the paper."

I closed my eyes. "Rob."

"I know, I know, don't talk about him, but you knew there was a strong chance that you'd see him if you took that job, so…"

I rolled my eyes. "I'm a photographer, he's a writer. It's not like we're going to be working in close quarters."

"True."

He looked like he wanted to add more, but didn't. I already knew what he wanted to say anyway: *just be careful.* I didn't need a warning from anyone. I had enough alarms ringing in my head without need for more. We talked for a couple more minutes as he filled me in on happenings back home, which wasn't much. I'd have to get the gossip from Estelle when I spoke to her, but until then, I was going to take advantage and go shopping.

In the subway I made sure not to make eye contact with anyone. I'd made that mistake my first time and was met with a lot of crazy eyes, so I was trying to avoid that now. I busied myself by rubbing antibacterial gel on my hands for the tenth time. I was looking up at the advertisements when the train came to a stop. When I heard the last announcement for Rockefeller, I bolted out of my seat, knowing that I only had a few seconds to get to the door, if that.

"My stop. My stop," I said frantically, trying to squeeze through the crowd. I was hopping over a bag on the floor when my leg bumped something out of a little girl's hands. Sighing heavily, I resigned to missing the stop and bent over to pick up the aqua-colored book. My eyes fell over the picture first. A girl with rosy cheeks was drawn on it, her long, dirty blonde hair winding over the cover in waves as she smiled at the baby turtle in her hands.

Mia Goes to the Beach by J. Reynolds.

Unbidden emotion spread through me. I reached my hand back, in search for something to hold on to, and found the pole just as the train started to move again. I felt my heart everywhere. Throbbing in my ears like a warning bell, nestling into my throat, spiking through my veins. The little girl, in an apparent effort to make me snap out of it, kicked me out of my reverie, the tip of her tiny pink Doc Martens hitting me on the knee in one quick movement. My eyes cut to hers. She had hair and eyes that matched mine, and the Mia on the cover. I managed a small and shaky smile and turned the book over once more to look at the back.

"Sorry. Is it any good?"

She nodded fervently as her mother answered, "She made me pre-order the rest of the collection. It's our favorite bedtime story."

"Wow," I breathed. *A collection.* Clearly I hadn't followed Jensen's career as closely as I thought. I knew that somewhere between having a baby and getting a columnist job at the newspaper he'd landed a publishing deal, but this was…

"May I keep it?" I asked before I could stop myself. "I'll pay you for it, of course."

The tiny kicker frowned at me, then at her mom. "Maybe tell your mommy to buy you one."

I sighed. My mother would so not buy one for me, and hers was now giving me a concerned look, as if she thought I was going to run off with their precious bedtime story.

"We got this copy signed yesterday," she said finally.

I nodded slowly, processing the fact that Jensen, *my* Jensen, was popular enough to sign books for people. Unable to stop myself, I opened the book and looked at the inscription. *Be brave*, it read.

"Be brave," I whispered aloud, snapping the book shut before I could look through it. I wasn't sure I could bear to do that in public. "The signing was in the city?" I asked.

"A little bookshop in Brooklyn. I'm pretty sure he has another one in the same shop sometime this week."

I tried to picture him holding a baby in his arms as he strolled the few streets that I'd been able to explore when I went out for drinks with Millie. I could see him holding a stack of his books as he walked into those small bookstores. I wondered if he read them aloud to the kids in attendance or if he just signed them. Even though I'd seen him a month ago at our friends' wedding, time had blurred his face from my memory. Sometimes, if I was alone, and something reminded me of him, like a song we both used to like, or a movie we used to watch, I would close my eyes and try to remember what he looked like on those nights when we were alone. I only did it when I didn't mind falling into a pit of depression, which was less often these days.

Those nights, I tried to remember the lump that rested on his throat, the outline of his jaw, the fullness of his lips, the hollows of his cheeks, the lines of laughter that framed his gray eyes, and the long lashes that covered them. Some nights I thought I remembered better than others. I realized two things long ago, during one of my mental sketches. It wasn't his physical self that I missed most. It wasn't his strong arms or the way having them wrapped around me made me feel safe. Safety was an illusion. I realized the day he left. What I missed was the way we could look at each other and know what the other wanted to say. I missed having somebody who understood me and made me feel cared for. Most of all, I missed all the fun we had together.

All of those things also made me bitter, for his mistakes and mine. And seeing this book that he wrote with my name on it was a little too much for me to bear. Maybe if I'd seen it back home, it would have been different. Maybe if I'd heard about it from Estelle, I would have had a different reaction. But out of the blue like this? During a week when my nerves were already all over the place at the mere thought of possibly having to see him in a city that was more his than mine and threw off the balance I'd created in my own mind when it came to us … it was too much.

I scrambled off the train as soon as it stopped again and sprinted to the other side of the platform to take the one going the opposite way. As I boarded the next train, I tried and failed to shake the book. I wanted to call Estelle or Rob, but couldn't form enough words during my mental freak out to bring myself to dial either. I glanced at my watch and calculated that I had exactly eight hours to process and freak out before I saw him. A knot curled up in the pit of my stomach, and I placed my hand there to control its throbbing. I wasn't sure I could see him now, not after seeing the book. I took a deep breath. Eight hours. I had eight hours to sort myself out before I had to meet with Fran and the rest of the people from work.

Jensen Talks

I get a lot of tweets asking what places to visit with kids while in New York. Aside from the obvious (Statue of Liberty, Empire State, etc.), I recommend The Bronx Zoo. This past week I took my daughter, and she loved it (as did I). Then, the night after, I was telling my date about it, and she said she'd never been. It didn't surprise me, since, as people, we are always on the go and rarely take time off to go sightseeing, especially in our own cities. It's something that has been on my mind since I moved here, and a friend of mine, a Brooklyn native, told me he'd never been to Ellis Island. At first I was shocked, but once I'd been living here for a month, I got it. We have no time. Actually, I take that back, we *make* no time to do these things. And I get it. You get a day off, and you're doing house chores, and when you're not doing that, you go and do something that helps you relax. It doesn't really occur to you to visit a landmark. Well, New York, I don't want you to die without visiting these landmarks, because while you're in a frantic fog of hustle and bustle, these beautiful things are staring you right in the face. Look up once in a while!

Moral of today's talk: Look up!

Question of the day: From @AmandaLovs2Read: "Do you enjoy art or photography? If so, do you follow the work of any artist, photographer, or have a favorite?"

Answer: I love art and photography. I dated a girl once who took the best photographs I've ever seen. I enjoy Patrick Zaphyr. His photos remind me to take a moment and enjoy nature. I

also like M.C. Escher's
work.

Eight hours wasn't enough time to do anything, not even calm nerves over hypothetical situations like him maybe showing up … but maybe not. What was worse was that I didn't know whether or not I wanted him to. If he did, I'd get it over with. Rip the Band-Aid, as they say. If he didn't, I could continue living in a world where he didn't exist to me. I dressed the way you were supposed to when there was a high chance of running into an ex, wearing my best jeans, a cute flowy top I'd gotten during my failed shopping trip, and killer boots that added at least four inches to my barely five-foot-three height. It took me all of twenty steps to the corner before I started berating myself for my clothing choices. On the one hand, I knew I looked hot. On the other hand, I wanted to kill myself for not breaking in the boots before I put them on.

When I finally reached the small bar where Fran told me to meet them, I stood outside, trying to look in through the fogged glass. After a couple of beats, I took a deep breath, then another, and pulled open the door. The energy coursing through my body was surely enough to light up Brooklyn. Fran spotted me and waved as I was shrugging off the jacket I'd thrown on. I smiled to acknowledge the wave and folded the jacket over my forearm as I made my way over to her table. Four people sat with her, and, as I neared, I felt my heart start to quake in its cage. His back faced me, and even though he wore a beanie over his head, and a quarter-sleeved navy blue gingham shirt that covered most of his tattoos, I'd know him anywhere. His right hand held a beer—Stella, his favorite. I could make out the skull tattoo on his pointer, and the unfinished infinity symbol between his thumb and pointer, the one he'd gotten when we were together, when he promised me a forever and said that he wouldn't finish the tattoo until I gave it to him.

I grit my teeth together, controlling my eye roll. *Forever.* Yeah, right. Somehow, my feet and my brain got on the same wavelength and continued pushing me forward until I reached the table. Fran stood, and three heads turned my way, though I didn't acknowledge them, opting to keep my eyes on Fran.

"Mia!" she said, pulling me toward her. "Everyone, this is Mia. Mia, this is Anabelle, Ross, and Jensen."

My eyes left hers and met Anabelle's brown eyes first. She was thin, with beautiful dark hair, exotic features, and a warm welcoming smile. I returned her smile and said hello before shifting my gaze to Ross, a red-haired guy with a full beard that matched. Finally, I readied myself for the last victim and looked over at Jensen. He was watching me with a curious expression on his face, scanning each one of my features as if I was a puzzle. As if he didn't damn well know what I looked like. After two long beats, his mouth moved into a slow smile.

"It's Jensen's birthday today, so I just ordered a round of celebratory shots in his name," Fran said as we sat down, me beside her, across from Jensen.

My gaze got momentarily caught in his. Would he tell her we knew each other? I sure as hell wouldn't. As far as I was concerned, we didn't know each other at all. Nothing about the way his eyes traveled from mine, down to my lips, past my chest, and back up in a slow motion that heated me from the inside was out of the ordinary. She must know he knew me. Someone must know. You didn't look at people you didn't know that way in public unless you wanted to screw them. Goddamn him for even trying that. Goddamn him for everything. He raised an eyebrow at me, and I snapped out of my glaring and turned my attention back to Fran.

"Well then, I guess I should drink up." I lifted the small glass to my lips as they did, and we all threw it back together. Jensen's chuckle brought my attention back to him.

"Maybe we should have another. I'm sure somebody else is celebrating a birthday today."

My eyes widened. Maybe he would tell them after all.

"Hey, I don't need an excuse to get drunk," Ross said with a laugh as he signaled the bartender for another round.

"Neither do I," I said with a smile.

After our next shot, we all ordered our own drinks, and Fran went into telling me stories about Anabelle, Ross, and Jensen. Anabelle and Ross were employed full-time. Jensen was freelance, as was another guy who couldn't make it. In addition to journalism, Ross also wrote science fiction novels.

"But you won't find them in stock anywhere because they don't sell … like, at all," he added behind that.

"I guess we can't all be like Jensen," Anabelle added, laughing when he rolled his eyes.

"He writes children's books. He also has a Sunday column in the newspaper," Fran said to me.

I nodded.

"Impressive," I said.

Jensen's mouth twitched. "It's only impressive if all of it is good, which I'm not sure it is."

"Always fishing for compliments," Ross said. Suddenly, he paused and looked at me for what seemed like a stretch too long. "You'd like the books, though! The girl's name is Mia."

I felt all the color drain from my face, but smiled and laughed lightly, hoping it came out less forced than it sounded to me. After taking another sip of my cranberry-vodka I decided I'd been there long enough to excuse myself and go to the bathroom. I was standing outside of the door, in a dimly lit hallway, when he appeared beside me. The clean and spicy smell of him enveloped my senses. My hands clenched together, my jaw tightened. I felt like a caged fighter ready to pounce.

"How's New York treating you so far?" he asked, his voice a deep rumble.

I took a breath, two, and counted to ten before acknowledging him. "It's been fine."

"Where are you staying?"

I turned my attention back to the door, willing it to open. "Millie's old place."

"In the city?"

I nodded, crossing my arms in effort to contain the goose bumps spreading over my flesh. His voice was too close to me. He was too close to me. I wasn't made of metal; I knew I'd react to him. I wasn't wired smart enough not to.

"Chelsea, right?"

Another nod.

"That's nice. I'm surprised you didn't move to Brooklyn. It's closer to where she lives now."

My gaze snapped up to meet his. *And closer to where you live as well.* I wondered if he could read my mind, the way he used to. From his exhale and the way he ran a hand through his hair, I wasn't sure. Apparently we'd both lost our touch.

"Yeah, well, I can't afford Brooklyn."

He raised an eyebrow, and I restrained the growl that threatened to escape. I knew what he was thinking. *Your rich parents couldn't help you pay for rent?* When we were together, that was always a rift between us. He thought my parents hated him because he had no money and came from the wrong side of the tracks. In reality, they hated him because he had a bad reputation and drove a Harley. Jensen was insecure, though. He thought if he'd had money, they would have accepted him. It annoyed me to no end.

"Are you going to ignore me the entire time we work together?" Jensen asked. The frustration in his voice made it nearly impossible to leash my own.

"We don't have to work together! I email you the pictures, you write a story. Isn't that what Fran just said?"

"What if I want to interview them while you take pictures?"

I took a step back. "That … that's a terrible idea."

"Why?" he asked. The way his eyes roamed over me, leaving tingles in their wake, that was the exact reason why. Because every time he looked at me that way, like I was special, like I was some sort of medal he wanted to win, I felt like melting. And also because I really wanted nothing more than to go back to hating him and being around him for more than fifteen minutes made that an impossible task.

"You know why!"

"I don't," he said, licking his lips. My gaze caught on them, on the pout of the bottom one. On the memory of how they felt on me, all over me. I stifled a shiver.

I swallowed and signaled between us and then toward the general direction of the bar. "You just pretended you didn't even know me."

"You did the same thing." He paused, his eyes narrowing on mine slightly, his tongue running along the seem of his lips as he seemingly weighed something out. "You knew I worked with the magazine."

"What's your point?" I said, trying not to bristle.

"You were probably expecting to see me."

"A lot of people write for them." I glanced away, unable to hold his stare.

"Either way, you pretended you didn't know who I was either."

My gaze cut to his. "I was going along with what you were doing!"

"You got here after I did. You could have said, 'Hey, Jensen. Nice to see you again.'"

"But it wasn't nice to see you again!"

He let out a heavy sigh and ran a hand through his hair. "You know what? That's fine. You've been ignoring me and pretending you don't know me for five fucking years. I do it once and you flip the hell out?"

I closed my eyes and shook my head, letting out a frustrated growl.

"You have to be the most frustrating person I have ever met."

"The feeling is completely mutual."

"All right then. Get lost and let me pee in peace," I said, walking into the bathroom as a girl walked out of it.

Jensen wasn't there when I was done, and I felt a little lighter for the full ten seconds it took me to get from the bathroom to the main room, because once I rounded the corner, his head snapped up. In the long seconds in which we held each other's attention, I felt him reaching into me, his long arms working like tentacles, grasping my attention and holding it in his clutches. My feet might as well have been gliding toward the table, because I couldn't tell you how I got to my chair. I couldn't tell you what I was asked, or what response I gave, because my attention was on him.

"So you surf?" Ross asked. "Mia. You surf?"

I blinked in an effort to snap to and looked at him, his green eyes expectant on mine. I nodded.

"But actually surf? Not paddle or whatever?"

I laughed. "Yes, actually surf, like with a surfboard, where I paddle out with my arms and stand on the board and catch a wave."

"Holy shit," he said in a breath that held an impressed whistle.

I shrugged. "It's what we do in sunny California."

"Do you miss it?"

"God, yes."

"You haven't been here long enough to miss it." The words came from Jensen, and they made my stomach do a little dip. Our gazes caught, mine challenging, his brewing.

"Home is home."

He took a swig of beer, eyes still on me. "Home is where you make it."

I tore my gaze away from his, hoping to get rid of the heavy tension between us. I wondered if everybody else could feel the electric field we seemed to carry around us. Before we officially got together, our friends said they could feel the sexual tension radiating off us. This was anything but that, though. This was real, cut throat, I hate you and want to choke you, tension. And I knew the feeling was mutual. At least tonight. Later, we talked about coffee, and Jensen and Ross got into a debate about which Brooklyn coffee shop was better. I took mental notes, but didn't get involved in the conversation as they went back and forth.

We had one more drink before we called it a night. Everyone had someplace they needed to be. Ross had his girlfriend waiting at home, Anabelle had her husband and kids, Fran had a friend she had to meet, and Jensen never said what his plans were, but nobody asked.

"Mia, your first shoot is next Tuesday, right?" Fran asked as we walked outside.

"I think so."

She nodded once. "I won't be here, so you should exchange phone numbers with everyone, in case anyone wants to tag along and do their first interviews there."

"Sure!" I was happy to give my number to Anabelle and Ross before they said their goodbyes and walked off. As Jensen took my phone from my hand, his fingers grazed mine. I felt my heart rattle. His touch everywhere.

"I'll probably tag along on Friday," he said, our hands still touching as he gave me a long, hard look that made me swallow heavily to calm my nerves.

"Okay," I said, my voice a little hushed, my bravado from earlier a little chipped.

"I'll be calling you soon," he said. The husk in his voice traveling through my body as his fingers let go of mine. My hand dropped against my leg, clutching on to the phone with a vice grip. I turned to walk away before he could see how much he still affected me.

I nodded and turned to walk away.

"And Mia?"

I glanced over my shoulder. He was standing with his hands tucked into the pockets of his jacket, his hair moving with the gusts of wind, his eyes on mine.

"Happy Birthday."

I felt the beginning of a smile blossom on my lips. "Happy Birthday, Jensen."

I turned away for good. I needed to get out of there before I brought up the book I saw, knowing that if I stayed there I would. I needed time to process that before I brought it up, if I ever decided to. It wouldn't end well if I did. Of that I was certain. Shaking my head, I called Millie and headed to the bar where she was drinking with her fiancé. For the rest of the night I would relax.

if I did. Of that I was certain. Shaking my head, I called Millie and headed to the bar where she was drinking with her fiancé. For the rest of the night I would relax.

My birthday was this past week, and in order to celebrate, my daughter brought me an octopus cake. I have it on good authority that her mother tried to convince her to get me a plain blue cake, and she insisted on the octopus. Obviously that means I had the best birthday yet.

If I had to title this article, it would be a toss up between "WTF" and "IRONY," because after I spent time with my daughter, and went for drinks with my editor, Jeff, I ended up meeting up with some friends of mine at a little bar called Reunion. As I was sitting there, arguing with my friend Ross about Yelp reviews, in walks in my life sweetheart. I know people say "college flame" or "high school sweetheart," but to me, she was basically my life sweetheart, even though technically we didn't start dating until her freshman year of college.

So the WTF was seeing her stroll through those doors and join *my* friends for drinks. The IRONY was that the bar was called Reunion, and it happens to be a surfer bar, which is a sport we both enjoyed back home.

She also shares a birthday with me. If you've been following my blog, etc., you already knew that since I always give her and her twin brother, Rob, a birthday shout-out every year. Yes, THAT GIRL. And I can report that the feeling in the pit of my stomach every time she looks at me is still there. More on this later—maybe when I get her to be cordial and not want to slap me every time I open my mouth to say something to her.

Reunion: Jensen Approved.

If you're looking for a hip version of Margaritaville, this one's for you!

Question of the week from: @FrogsLive: "Do you believe in soul mates?"

Answer: Yes.

Photography is a lone art. That was one of the things that drew me to it. *Newsweek* apparently hadn't gotten the memo. Evidently, Jensen hadn't either. I got the much-dreaded call from him Monday afternoon. I'd just stepped out of yoga when my phone started vibrating in my hand, alerting me of an unsaved number with an 805 area code. I examined each digit as if there was a possibility they would change before my eyes. It was a phone number that haunted me on drunken nights and moments of uncertainty. One I swore I'd never use again. It wiggled in my hand four times before I answered it.

"Hey," he said, returning my greeting.

My heart skipped at the sound of his voice. It seemed like an eternity since the last time I'd heard it on the other end of the line.

"I'm taking the pictures in Central Park tomorrow," I said after a moment of silence.

"At what time? And where?"

"Eight-thirty, and I just told you, Central Park."

His rich chuckle permeated through the line. "Have you ever been to Central Park?"

I paused, frowning. "Of course I have." When I was five, not that he needed to know that.

"Okay, so you know how big it is."

"Obviously." It was a park. How big could it actually be? I'd seen it on TV a gazillion times, and everybody always ran through it pretty damn quickly.

"Well, okay, so let me know when you figure out where in Central Park you want me to meet you."

"Okay. I'll go over there today and scope out some areas."

He cleared his throat. "All right. Good luck. Talk to you soon."

It was all so awkward, so informal, the way he spoke to me like I was an associate of his and not somebody he'd once made love to. I reminded myself that I wanted it that way. I needed it to be that way. Later that day, after I'd gotten a good location in the park, I took the train to Brooklyn. As I walked around, I saw a monkey coffee shop and decided to stop in there. I was waiting for the barista to hand me my drink when I saw Jensen sitting in the back corner. His back was to me, and I had to do a double take to make sure it was him because of the angle he was positioned. My stomach tightened as my eyes fell over his left arm and the tattoo of the octopus that wrapped around it. I turned around quickly, like a kid caught doing something wrong.

It wasn't like he owned Brooklyn, or this coffee shop. I could go wherever the hell I wanted. The barista held a cup in his hand and frowned as he turned it, looking for the name.

"Mia!" he shouted.

My eyes widened. Reaching out, I grabbed the cup from his hand, whispered a thank you, and got out of dodge. I didn't breathe easily, or take a sip of coffee, until I was back on the train. As soon as my butt hit that seat I let out the longest, most relieved breath and held the cup up to my mouth with both hands, savoring every sip until it ran out. I couldn't believe I saw him. I just couldn't believe it. I wondered if he went there every day. The coffee definitely made it worth going every day. Maybe I'd go again … just for one more cup.

"You are the most confusing woman on earth," Estelle said later when I recounted my little trip to Brooklyn.

"How so?" I asked, sorting through my underwear drawer.

"You went all the way to Brooklyn to get coffee from a place he spoke about during drinks the other night."

"It's not like it's *his* coffee shop! It's a public place. It's not my fault he's decided to call it his own personal office space. God, he's annoying."

Estelle laughed. "You stalked him. Again!"

"I did not!"

"Mia."

I felt myself coil between my dresser and closet, holding the phone a little tighter to my ear. "I was just curious. Weren't you ever curious as to what Oliver was doing when you weren't together?"

"Yeah, it's called go on Facebook and scroll through all his pictures."

I groaned. "Jensen doesn't have Facebook anymore."

"That's right … he went on a whole rant about Facebook recently."

My ears perked up. I didn't question her though. If I questioned her, she would know that I legit stalked the shit out of him, and that was something that I would take to my grave. Estelle was like a sister to me; we told each other things I didn't even talk to Rob about, but when it came to Jensen, I always liked to keep a bit of mystery. Hell, Jensen himself was a bit of a mystery to all of us. A mystery I wanted to solve so badly. I groaned again. I needed to stop. That kind of thinking was what got me in trouble and that was the last thing I needed.

I got this question the other day. It seems to be a reoccurring question amongst my twitter followers, so I figured I would dedicate a column to it. The question is: "What is your ideal first date?"

Brace yourselves for the letdown, ladies. This will be the column that will make you fall out of lust with my weekly columns, but please come back and let me try to redeem myself.

Truthfully, I'm not good with dates. I normally ask the woman what she likes to do, but I find that often they respond based on what they think I like to do. "Go to baseball games." "Go bowling." "Watch a movie."

And the thing is, while I do enjoy doing all of those things, I'm not sure any of them, aside from bowling, is good first date material. I've tried it all out, I should know. Movies lead to little talking. Baseball games are great for conversation, but when you go with a man to a game, you have to leave room for yelling (obscenities cannot be judged upon here. This is our safe zone.), not paying too much attention to talk about your dog or cat or anything else for that matter if a good play is happening, and well, then there's the messy peanuts and hot dogs and beer.

For these reasons I stick to dinner. Dinner is always a good first date. It can be dinner at a fun place like Dave & Busters. It can be dinner and then a walk on the beach (cheesy? Yes, but effective for both parties … if you're into each other by the time said walk is set to take place).

Lastly, everybody puts so much emphasis on

the first date. It used to drive me crazy because it made me feel like I was going in for a job interview and my nerves didn't leave room for easy conversation until well into the date. My advice? Remember that the person you're on the date with is just, if not more, nervous than you are. Break the ice early on. And if somebody asks you what you like to do, be honest. Just because you're looking for the one, doesn't mean that you have to subject yourself to every single lousy date you're set on.

Dave & Busters in the city: Jensen Approved.

I'd sorted out the park situation with Jensen and my subjects and was there at seven forty-five making sure the lighting would work in that particular section. It wasn't long before I spotted Jensen walking over to me with a notepad in his hand. He wore jeans that looked like they were made for him, and a black hoodie that had the Dharma Initiative logo on the front. His hair was swaying with each gust of wind that hit. When he reached me, he stood in front of me and tucked his notepad, his *Spiderman* notepad, under his arm. I craned my neck to meet his gaze, my heart thumping wildly.

"You picked a good location," he said, voice low, eyes searing through me.

I nodded, trying to contain the pull between us. I wasn't sure whose game of tug of war was stronger, his or my feelings. And the way his eyes searched my face, and how his jaw was working, I could tell the feeling was mutual. Our greetings were so grandiose when we were together, when I would jump on him and mold my body to his, and he'd kiss every inch of my face. Our goodbyes held the same intensity, maybe more of it since neither one of us wanted to untangle from the other. While we were apart unsupervised greetings were unnecessary since I'd run the other way the moment I heard he was in town. On the occasions that I did see him, we'd always been around our friends and were able to ignore each other.

"Maybe we can be cordial today?" he said, his voice still low.

The look in his eyes was making my insides flip. He stepped forward half an inch, still far enough to give me personal space, but close enough that the smell of him wrapped around me.

"Maybe," I whispered.

He lifted his head and looked away momentarily. My eyes trailed down his cheek, his jaw, his neck, and snapped back to his gaze when he looked at me again.

"I'm not good at holding grudges, Mia. You know that. I don't know how to hate you. I've tried. I was so angry at you for so long, for shutting me out when I needed you most, for not being there, but I don't know how to hate you." He paused, letting out a sigh. "Maybe we can try being friends."

"Maybe."

"Maybe you can start answering with yes or no, preferably the first option."

I smiled at his low chuckle and the twinkle in his eyes. "Maybe I'll try."

Silence fell over us, and I felt as if every inch of me was wired, dependent on what would come next. I swallowed and took a step back, clutching to the camera around my neck.

"I like your sweater," I said.

He gave me a lazy smile and opened his mouth to say something, but shut it quickly and shook his head, looking away from me. For a split second I could hear his thoughts: *We need to go back to the island.* It would have been a totally normal thing to say to anybody, had we not used that line in reference to our sex life once upon a time.

"Is that them?" he asked.

I followed his gaze and spotted an older couple holding hands walking toward us. They were both tall, with gazelle-like features—long legs and long arms. The woman, Katelynn, I assumed, had short brown hair that matched her husband, Jon's.

"Yeah, I'm pretty sure. She said she'd be wearing red pants," I said, giving them a small wave that Katelynn returned.

"Hi! Oh my God, you're so adorable," she said as she reached me and gave me a hug like we'd known each other forever.

Adorable was the word people used to describe petite girls. My entire life I'd been "adorable." In college, sometimes I was "hot." With Jensen, I'd been "beautiful."

I laughed. "It's great to meet you."

She let go of me and turned her attention to Jensen, introducing herself as I shook Jon's hand. We went over what we were going to do: I would take pictures of them first, and Jensen would do his interview while I packed up.

They sat on the blanket I'd put down, and I took some there. Her short brown hair kept getting in her eyes, so I took more pictures than usual. I shot until I got enough pictures, so the magazine would have options.

"After this shoot, how long do you think it'll take for them to let us know if we'll be featured?" Katelynn asked.

"I'm not sure, honestly." I looked over my shoulder for an answer, at Jensen who was sitting nearby, watching us.

"I have no idea. I'm just here to ask questions." He tapped his notepad two times.

"You can do that already," I said, waving my camera. "I have enough pictures."

"May I see them?"

"Of course, but keep in mind that they're unedited."

He nodded and stood to walk over. He took a seat beside me, facing them, and opened his notepad. To my surprise, he had no questions written down. I started packing up the different lenses I'd used while he started.

"How old were you when you first met?"

"Twelve." That was Katelynn.

"Fourteen." That was Jon.

"He was fourteen, I was twelve," she said with a laugh.

Jensen chuckled and wrote it down.

"When did you start dating?"

"High school," she said. "Our families were friends. I always thought he was cute, but I never thought he'd like me."

Jon laughed. "I liked you all along."

"Yeah, well," she said with a shrug. "So I started dating his friend in high school, and suddenly he was all over me about it. He made it impossible for us to go on dates, and finally I broke up with his friend and started dating him."

Jensen didn't have to do much prompting. Katelynn recounted their story pretty well on her own. I could tell she'd told it millions of times. They broke up when Jon left for college because Katelynn wanted him to stay local and he wanted to go away. She started dating somebody else, as he did, they married other people, and reconnected at a family party years later when they were both divorced and single again.

"And the rest is history," she said.

"You mentioned you have a son from your first marriage. How did he handle it?" Jensen asked.

I held my breath and wished I could leave. Instead, I started rearranging the lenses inside my camera bag to busy myself.

"Dan was eight when he met Jon, and he took a liking to him right away."

"As soon as I met him, it was like he was my own. I was always respectful of his father, though. I didn't want him to feel like I was trying to take over his dad's role," Jon added.

Jensen jotted something down. "How long have you been married?"

"Fifteen years."

Jensen nodded. I was still struggling to breathe properly. Finally, we all stood, and Jensen spoke to them as I finished packing up the blanket. I promised Katelynn I'd email her a few of the pictures once I edited them, and we all walked toward the exit together. They said their goodbyes and walked to the left.

"You want to grab brunch?"

I clutched the strap of my bag and looked at Jensen. He chuckled at the look on my face.

"Just brunch, Meep."

I groaned at his use of my nickname. "No. Definitely not."

He shrugged. "All right."

"Okay. I'll see you around or something." I started walking in the direction of the subway. He was still walking beside me. I couldn't think when he was walking beside me. I could barely breathe. Finally, I looked over at him. "Why are you following me?"

He raised an eyebrow as his lips moved into a smile and then a full-out grin as he tried to contain his amusement. "You think I'm following you? Jesus, you're presumptuous."

"You came over here to interview my people, started talking about how you can't hate me, invited me to brunch, and now you're walking beside me … yeah … I think I have valid reasons to think you're following me."

He made a face as he shook his head and tore his gaze from mine.

"You were the one who got this job, knowing there would be a possibility I'd be working on this project."

"Yeah, thanks for reminding me. I'm starting to regret that."

His eyes met mine again, and my breath caught. I clutched the strap of my camera bag so tight, I knew my hand would be marked.

"Do you want me to tell them I know you?" he asked. "The people from work. Do you want me to tell them I know you?"

I exhaled and rolled my eyes. He thought this was about that? Not about his stupid book or the way he used my name? Not about our past or the way he decided he absolutely needed to interview these people while I shot their pictures, but about the people from work not knowing we knew each other?

"I don't care."

"You obviously care."

"I couldn't care less what you tell people about us, Jensen."

His hand closed over my forearm then. He pulled me so that we weren't in the middle of the sidewalk with people trying to dodge us.

"What's wrong?" he asked as we faced each other.

His voice too calm, too quiet. Too comforting. His eyes scanned my features. Every inch they fell over felt like a soft kiss. I closed mine momentarily, trying to catch the temper I felt floating away from me.

"I saw the book. *Mia Goes to the Beach.*"

"What'd you think?" he asked after a stretch of silence.

"I don't know what to think," I said in a whisper.

"Why?"

He moved closer, until our faces were mere inches apart. Until I felt like I couldn't breathe if he didn't put his lips against mine. *Breathe*, I told myself. *Just breathe.* But I could feel the heat coming from his body.

"You used my name, Jensen." I paused, searching his face.

There was no trace of remorse there, not an inkling of confusion as to why it would bother me. He looked at me like he owned the name. Like he had every right to use it.

"You had to know I'd have a problem with that. I haven't even spoken to you since you left. You just said it. Every time I see you I run the other way."

"You didn't at Oliver's wedding."

"That was different, and you know it."

"It's been five years, Mia." He stepped closer. I flattened myself against the wall. "Five."

"I know exactly how long it's been, Father Time." He smiled, but got serious quickly.

"I can't not use your name," he said quietly.

"Why?"

"Because you're a big part of why I'm successful." He paused, and let out a curse under his breath before adding, "Because I never let you go."

My jaw unhinged. "Are you freaking kidding me?" When he didn't answer, I soldiered on, placing my hand flat on his chest and tapping with each statement. "You got married! You had a kid! You have no right—" I paused, letting out a frustrated breath, and taking another to calm down. I channeled Frank Costanza. *Serenity now. Serenity now*, and took another breath. Just as I felt ready to unleash the rest of my frustration, he placed his hand over mine on his chest.

"I'm not married anymore. I made a mistake five years ago, for which I've apologized a thousand times." He paused to exhale and run his other hand over his head. "God. Did you even read my letters?"

I blinked and took my hand from under his. "Fuck your letters," I said, but my anger was no longer laced with its original poison.

He blinked away the longing that had taken place in his eyes, fiery anger taking over.

"Yeah, fuck my letters," he said, raising his voice with each word he spit out. "Fuck my letters, fuck me, fuck my existence. You've made it perfectly clear that you hate me, and I'm sorry for that, because despite all the shit you did to hurt me, I haven't fucking stopped thinking about you for one second!"

His words slammed into my so hard, I physically reared back for a second before I slapped his face. Hot, angry tears filled my eyes as his hand covered the area I'd smacked. I made a fist with my hand, hoping it would soothe the sting.

"You got another woman pregnant and married her. You fucking left me. You. Left. Me. Next time I run through your mind make sure that thought follows closely behind." I brushed past him, but he caught up with me quickly. He didn't grab me this time, but he might as well have because his presence beside me was huge.

"One of these days you're going to wake up and ask yourself if all the anger you feel toward me is worth your energy."

I shoved my hands in the pockets of my sweater as we reached the end of the block. When I looked up to see if he was still there, I caught a glimpse of his back as he walked away. Watching him walk and eventually disappear into a sea of people without looking back made me realize how much I still cared. Even if I didn't want to. Even if I told myself I didn't, I obviously still cared, and that bothered me more than the fact that he walked away in the first place.

When I got home, I put my stuff down and noticed I had a text message from him. I opened it quickly, expecting an apology. Instead, it read: Send me the information for your next shoot. My stomach flipped at the thought.

Jensen Talks

I love technology. I'm the tech guy who constantly upgrades his software and switches out his laptop when a new model comes out. This past weekend I was invited to attend the grand opening of a small tech shop in Chelsea, and I have to say, I was like a kid in a candy store. Basically, it was a mini Apple store nestled into my second favorite neighborhood in New York (the first being Brooklyn, of course).

Most of us were there to write a story about the place, so as you walked into the store you saw people trying out the computers, looking at accessories, or typing into their phones.

The experience really got me thinking about how much we depend on technology to reach loved ones and potential loved ones alike. Whenever I'm out of town, I FaceTime my daughter so I can see her pretty face. Normally, I'm not huge on texting, as easy as it may be, but recently I reconnected with somebody and I'm torn between calling, texting, or emailing. Texting seems like the "normal" thing to do. Calling seems like the "adult" thing to do. Emailing seems like the best way to say, "I want to stay in touch, but not seem desperate to stay in touch." Obviously this also depends on your relationship with the person. A business relationship is different from one between you and an ex-lover, which is the case for me. Alas, I went with texting … for now. I'll keep you posted since I know you're nosey and love to know.

Mike's Tech Shop in Chelsea—for products, data recovery, little-to-no wait time on services, etc.: Jensen Approved!

Question of the day from: @atipyam: When & how would you introduce your kid/s to the person you're seeing?

Answer: Depends on the situation. I think when the person is 100% serious about me and vice versa.

As much as I tried to fight myself on it, I looked up Jensen's readings and found one in Brooklyn. I blamed my loneliness on all of this. I blamed not having my friends and family around to tell me to stop being a fucking girl and go out with somebody else. But I had nobody else to go out with. I was a single girl living in New York who was scared of fucking ÜBER, let alone Match.com. The idea of that shit gave me the creeps. Millie had met her fiancé, Seth, on there. When she looked at it she saw opportunities and love stories. I saw serial killers. My curiosity was greater than my will to stay away from him, so I took a train to Brooklyn and went to the small bookstore. By the time I got there, there was a crowd of people with their kids. A large crowd of people—so large that I had to squeeze through them in order to get inside—and when I finally got in I was forced to stand against a shelf completely hidden from where he would be sitting. Maybe that was a good thing. Maybe it was best I didn't see him. I definitely didn't want him to see me.

I knew he finally showed because of the cheers and phones taken out to snap pictures of him. For some reason, the idea of all these women, who were clearly checking him out, having pictures of him on their phones, bothered me. I glared at all of them as they smiled, laughed, and nudged the moms beside them with knowing looks on their faces. I hated all of them. Officially. Jealousy stuck to me like unwanted glitter from a party bag.

"Are you ready for story time?" Jensen asked. The air in my lungs constricted at the sound of his voice. The kids clapped and their floozy moms cheered along. "I like to read the dedication first."

Finally, I got sick of not seeing what they were seeing, so I moved and plucked a book from a shelf, squinting through the space to catch a glimpse of him. He was wearing jeans, a charcoal gray T-shirt that matched his eyes, and a charming smile. His hair was in its usual state of disarray, and a shadow of a beard coated his face. It was his aura that mesmerized me, though. Everything about him screamed bad boy, and everything inside of me begged to be closer to him.

"For Olivia," he read, clearing his throat before he continued, "who taught me the importance of bravery." I felt myself smile at that. "And for Mia, who believed in me when nobody else would."

I blinked a couple of times and braced myself on the edge of the shelf. I felt the air leave my lungs the way a balloon deflates—slowly at first and then in a quick, winding zip. All of these things happened, yet I stood with my mouth hanging open, staring at him. I tried to regain my composure as he started reading, but my head was swimming with the words in his dedication. I registered the kids laughing and the mothers snapping pictures, but I could no longer concentrate on any of it.

Finally, when I came off the state of shock I'd been in, I started listening, but even that gave me a nervous buzz. A part of me didn't want to accept that pieces of me lay on the pages he held in his hands. Pages he wrote and illustrated and dreamed up on sleepless nights. As he continued, the familiarity of the actual story tidaled over me like a wave.

Mia was an adventurous little girl.

Mia's golden locks glittered in the sun.

Because of Mia's kindness, Hester the Turtle got back to his family.

The room erupted in claps and cheers as he finished reading, and I could only stand there reeling.

I *thought* I wanted to see him.

I *thought* maybe I would even talk to him.

But I couldn't trust myself to do it now. I started weaving my way out of the room, only stopping to let the kids cross my path. I looked over my shoulder once, just as his head snapped up from a book he was signing. At first he frowned, as if he wasn't sure what he was seeing was correct. Once realization seemed to hit him, he smiled, lazy yet charming, and excused himself from the crowd of people he was talking to. I turned back around and picked up the pace, practically barreling through the front door, into the freezing cold streets of Brooklyn.

"Mia!"

I cringed, wrapping my arms around myself. Not even the sweater I wore was a match for this weather.

"You're just going to leave?"

I turned to face him, squeezing myself tighter. "I have to go."

"Were you here for the whole thing?"

I shivered. "Yep."

"Why?" he asked, tilting his head, examining my features.

I shook my head. "I don't know."

"Come inside, you're obviously cold."

"No, no. I'm leaving. Just … go be with your people; they're here to see you."

"And you're not?"

A frustrated growl left my lips. "I'm trying really hard not to go off on you right now." I let out a heavy sigh. "Go back inside. I'll talk to you another day."

He continued to stare at me, his turbulent eyes scanning my face, dipping down to my body, back to my face, finally locking on my eyes once again.

"I'll go back inside in a minute. Right now I'm interested in knowing how you're feeling."

"I … I'm really…" I paused, waiting for my teeth to stop clattering. "I'm really fucking cold. And mad."

"Because I used your name," he said.

"And because you included me in the dedication. And you talked about Hester the freaking Turtle! How do you even remember that?" I sighed, letting out a cold breath. "I came to see you for…" The chattering of my teeth didn't let me continue talking, and he took it as a sign to jump in.

"For what?"

I shrugged, a shivered shrug that shook my shoulders. His gaze dropped momentarily.

"Let's go inside. You're shivering."

I shook my head. "No."

"What did you come for? To get upset and yell at me?"

I shook my head again, though I couldn't figure out why the hell I went. "Closure?"

"Ma … ma … Maybe."

"You came here for closure?"

I threw my arms up. "No! Yes! I don't know! What else would I come for?"

A smile bloomed on his lips.

"You need to st … st … stop looking at me like that. Do you think this is funny?"

He chuckled. "No, I don't. I think this is crazy, but so are you, so I guess this is our normal."

"I am not crazy!" I jabbed a finger into his chest.

He looked down at my hand. The amusement on his face made my blood boil. "No?"

"I hate you," I said loudly. "Officially."

"Officially."

I growled again, louder this time, and retreated. "I'm going to go. I shouldn't have come, and I'm not about to make a scene in front of all of Brooklyn!"

He grinned broadly, folding his arms in front of his chest. "What's this called?"

I paused, fuming on the edge of the sidewalk, and turned to glare at him. "It's called … it's called theatre!"

I'd reached the corner when he caught up to me, his arm wrapping around my middle as he pulled me against his hard chest and brought his lips to my ear.

"Hate is a strong word," he said, his voice making my stomach drop.

I shimmied until he dropped his arm. "Super strong word."

"You know what else is a super strong word?" he asked, his gaze on my lips, my cheek, my hair, my eyes.

My insides tumbled. I knew what he was thinking, but I wouldn't give him the satisfaction. I didn't want to feel any of that. I didn't want to feel anything at all. Yet there I was, feeling.

"Let me go," I said, my gaze dropping to his hand, holding the hem of my jacket. He closed his eyes briefly.

"I don't know how," he whispered.

The ache in my heart returned then. I swallowed. With one look he'd managed to stumble into my life, the way a drunk undressed in the dark. With one look he'd managed to bring my guard back down. If I stayed any longer, I would let him break down all the stones I'd built in the aftermath of his love, and I couldn't bear it. I couldn't bear to let one night break me open like that. So I did what any smart woman would do in my shoes. I forced his hand off my jacket and walked away.

On my way home I sulked, until I showered and snuggled into bed. Then I replayed everything over. I'd stalked the guy, yelled at him, and tried to stomp away from his flippin' book signing. The more I thought about it, the funnier it became, and it wasn't long before I began to laugh. It died down as I remembered everything I said to him.

Did I tell him I wanted closure?

Fuck. Of course I did. I was an idiot. Officially.

Jensen Talks

I had a book reading/ signing this past weekend. To those of you who came out to support, thank you. Being in WORD is always a pleasure. I wrote that book, *Mia Goes to the Beach*, about a girl I love. A girl who brought me an equal amount of love and pain. But, beyond everything, brought me hope. She showed up when nobody else did, and sometimes that's all you need … for somebody to show up. She showed up again this past weekend, at the reading, and once I realized she was there, I had a pretty surreal experience. I never thought she'd ever hear the words of the story coming from my lips, yet there she stood, listening, like she did countless times many years ago.

And I have to wonder if she'll show up again. It's been said we're only given one chance at things in life. I'd love to prove that wrong.

Question of the day from: @LilouBlue: "Do you think we should always follow our hearts no matter what? Do we even have the choice not to?"

Answer: Sometimes the consequences of it are worse in reality than they are in our mind.

"So you guys are talking now?"

That was the first thing my brother, Rob, asked when I told him about my encounter with Jensen and the very few text messages and conversation that followed. They'd been direct, about work, and once about food. That hardly counted as reconnecting.

"No."

"You just said—"

"Texting doesn't count as talking."

Rob laughed. "Is there really any difference nowadays?"

"Obviously."

"You know most people carry on entire relationships via text message?"

"Yeah, they're called teenagers."

"Adults do it too."

"Robert, you and everybody else are crushing my dream that maybe I still have a chance at what apparently is an old school relationship. I'm not twinning with you anymore."

He laughed louder. "Sorry. That's one thing you can't escape."

"Mom should have waited a few more minutes to push me out."

"You would be dead if she had," he reminded me. I was born at eleven fifty-eight, three minutes after Rob, so I like to joke that if she waited a little longer, we technically wouldn't be twins. *Technically, we were still being carried at the same time,* Rob liked to say, because the guy loved being my twin. I couldn't blame him.

"My point is, this means nothing, Jon Snow."

"Your obsession with that show and that character is driving me crazy."

"You mean *your* obsession with that character. I'm a Tyrion kind of girl."

He made a disgusted sound. "Moving along. What does Elle say about all of this?"

"She doesn't watch that."

"About Jensen! Focus, Mia!"

"Oh. Nothing. I don't know. What's she supposed to say?"

Rob stayed quiet for a beat. I could picture his blond eyebrows pulling toward his hairline. "No wonder you're telling me about it."

"It's not like I need advice or anything," I mumbled.

"But you want it anyway."

I groaned. "No. I don't know. I mean, it's not like we're having full conversations or anything. It's mainly 'When is your next shoot?' followed by 'I don't know, Jensen. I told you I'd let you know as soon as I find out.' That's pretty much it, unless he texts me pictures of food, which I really don't respond to. Anyway, how's your hot, Brazilian lover?"

Rob laughed. "He's good. Great!"

Juan Pablo had moved to Santa Barbara for school and stayed for Rob.

"Are his parents on board with him staying?"

He paused. "Well … he's going to visit them in a couple of weeks while I'm visiting you, so I guess we'll know then."

Rob filled me in on the happenings back home: Mom now had eight orchids in her garden, three of which she hadn't yet managed to kill. He was helping Dad design a house for one of the San Francisco Giants' baseball players, and our friend Victor started his job at a new law firm where it looked like he could make partner faster. I told him about the pictures I'd been taking and what I wanted to do with them someday.

Finally, after a couple of minutes of him reassuring me that somebody would give me a chance to display my prints in their gallery, and me reassuring him that Juan Pablo would come back to him regardless of what his family said, we hung up. I hung around my apartment for a couple of hours, binge watching yet another show I didn't need in my life, before grabbing my camera bag and heading out. I spent the rest of my day exploring a different part of Central Park and taking pictures of everything from fallen leaves to laughing mothers swinging their toddlers in their arms. When the sun started to disappear behind the skyscrapers, I decided to call it a day and go home and get ready for happy hour with Millie. I could no longer trust myself to stay home and not be distracted by thoughts of Jensen, and I needed to do everything in my power to not think about him. Happy hour meant drinks and talking crap, two of the things I loved most in life.

After discussing her wedding and how she was really considering eloping instead of making a huge deal about getting married, she returned to her favorite thing to poke fun of me for.

"I just don't understand why you insist on trying, and failing, to hail cabs anymore when there's ÜBER," she said.

"I took the train here."

"Because you gave up trying to hail a cab!"

"Maybe I just wanted to walk a little."

She shot me a look, her brown eyes narrowing in disbelief. "Please. Yesterday you were complaining about the 'cold ass weather.'"

"Because it's cold as hell here! I can't believe people live here willingly." I paused when she shot me another look. "What? I'm only here temporarily, then I go back to sunny California." I sighed dramatically as the words left my mouth, and she laughed.

"You're cray. But seriously, just download the stupid app."

"This is New York, Mil. Besides, you take the train every day!"

"Yes, but I don't get lost! You get off at wrong stops and take wrong trains. You're a hot mess!"

I tried not to laugh, but Millie was an animated talker. She swung her hands and tossed the ringlets of curls that framed her face.

"I am a mess, but I'm a contained mess. There are places in the world for us. You should know." I winked.

"Girl, nothing about the two of us is contained, and you know it."

"And I like it that way."

"Me too." She smiled, her hugely perfect toothpaste commercial smile. I took a sip of my gin and tonic to brace myself for what she was going to say next. "Anyway, you know how I take pictures of events…"

"Nope. Not doing it," I said before she could finish the thought. She'd mentioned wanting me to take pictures of an event she couldn't do, but I'd decided not to do it before I could even find out what it was.

"Mia!"

"Absolutely not. I didn't move a million miles away from my friends and family to get stuck in the same box I was already in back home."

"What box is that?"

"You know, the 'lifestyle photographer' box." I sighed. "I'm not saying I didn't love doing that, or that I won't do it again in the future, but I want to explore other things. I need to go back to the dream I had in college, the reason I got into this to begin with. I want to have my prints in museums and publish a coffee table book that paints every day life in a beautiful light, or an ugly light that people can't look away from. I want—"

"You want to be Diane Arbus."

I sighed. "I want to be Mia Bennett, with a Diane Arbus flair."

"It won't happen overnight, you know."

"I'm completely aware of that, but the thing is, I know it won't happen at all if I keep shooting events or families."

Millie took a sip of her mojito and looked at me for a long moment. Finally, she tossed her dark, curly hair back from her shoulders and smiled. "It's only one job. I promise."

"Mill," I groaned.

"You're the only one who can do this for me, Meep. I leave on Friday, and I can't risk some asshole going there and ruining this for me. Besides, it'll be published in a magazine, so you technically won't be veering too far from your goal." She paused for a moment, then sighed. "Do this for me, and when I get back from my trip I'll talk to one of my connections at a couple of places to see if they're looking to display new photographers."

That held my full attention. I weighed my options: the pictures of the event would be in a magazine. Millie wasn't just some random wannabe photographer. She'd made a name for herself in the industry, and also had gotten me my current job, which afforded me the opportunity to move here and explore my options, and my pictures at a New York art gallery…

"I'll do it."

Her smile was wide and cheerful.

"But you're paying for these drinks," I added.

She laughed. "Anything you want."

"Tell me about this event. Do I have to wear a long dress?"

We stayed in the bar for hours, talking about the event, wardrobe, my potential coffee table book, and the art gallery idea, which we concluded could also include local artists. Later, while we were waiting for Millie's ÜBER, while I was spewing my hatred for the company and how creepy it was, I saw him again. There were enough people walking by us that I could have missed him. I didn't know if it was the cold, or his presence, but the hairs on the back of my neck stood up. I felt like I had to turn my face, and when I did, he was there, walking toward us in a pair of jeans that would only look good on him—or a mannequin—boots, and a black leather jacket over a white Breaking Bad T-shirt.

His head was bent as he spoke to another guy, so he hadn't spotted me. Maybe he wouldn't have, had it not been for the weight of my stare. I could tell he was mid-sentence when his head snapped up and his eyes met mine, and I felt like the earth literally shook beneath me. So much so that I grabbed Millie's arm, my eyes still on Jensen's. He was looking at me as if in awe, the way he did when he finally saw me all those years ago. As if he'd just discovered a fairy amongst monsters.

I was reminded of a time when we'd just started dating and I showed up at a family picnic Patty, his foster mom, had dragged him to. It was at a nice park up in the hills, overlooking the water. Not knowing what else to take, I showed up with two bags of chips and liter of Coke. I was trying to juggle the chips, the liter and the purse in my hand when our eyes met. He was leaning against a picnic table talking to a cousin of his, but when he saw me his lips froze and parted slightly. He straightened and said something that made his cousin's head turn toward me. For a long moment we just stared—Jensen and me—at each other. His cousin was between the both of us, probably wondering why we were rooted to the spot. And the thing was, I couldn't move, and I could tell he was having a similar problem.

When he looked at me like that, like I was the only thing he saw, it was hard for me to function. The chips fell out of my grasp. The Coke bottle shook in my right hand. My purse slid from my shoulder to my elbow. My heart pounded as he finally made his way over to me, cupping my face with both hands as he stood in front of me.

"You came," he said, his voice a whisper.

"I told you I would."

"But still … you actually did it."

I'd known family gatherings were hard for him. I could only imagine what he must have felt like, being that his mom left him and dropped him off with his aunt when he was a kid. I put myself in his shoes, but the pain of being an unwanted child would be too much for me to bear. I smiled up at him while he ran his thumbs along my cheekbones.

"Thank you for coming."

"I go where you go. Always," I'd said.

I tried to break eye contact when my stomach flip-flopped, but my body turned toward his instead, as if somehow the wires in my brain decided to crosswire and do the opposite of what they were supposed to. A nudge on my arm snapped me back into reality, reminding me that that was then and this was now. He'd gone without me, and I'd stayed heartbroken in the wake of his absence.

"Holy shit, is that—" Millie started, her words fading into the backdrop as he reached us.

"Interesting running into you here," he said, only looking at me, like he only had eyes for me.

"Hey."

We stared at each other for what felt like an endless minute before he started speaking again and snapped us out of our haze. "I got an email from your mom today."

"What the hell? About what?"

He grinned. "About you, the city, things to do, stuff like that."

I blinked rapidly. How did she even get his email? My parents hated Jensen when I'd been with him. It wasn't until after we split up that my mom started liking him, and it was only because she'd run into him and Olivia one day, and seeing him with a little girl made her suddenly forgive everything. I shook my head. I couldn't believe she was such a traitor. My own mother! Maybe I should have told her about the stupid book and the signing and all the shit that happened there.

"What about the city?" I asked, but Millie jumped in and interrupted us.

"Jensen Reynolds. I haven't seen you in, what, a year?" He turned his eyes away from me, to her, and smiled.

"Hey! I didn't realize it was you," he said, pulling her into a quick hug. She laughed.

"You didn't see me at all."

"That happens to me sometimes," he said, meeting my gaze with something hot, and I tightened my sweater over my body.

"Hi, I'm Mia," I said, turning to the guy beside Jensen. He gave me a long, curious, yet knowing, look that made my face heat up.

"I'm Jeff," he said, offering his hand, and then turning over to Millie to do the same.

"You still with that guy…" Jensen asked, his brows pulling in as he thought long and hard.

"Seth. We're engaged now. We live in Park Slope."

"No shit! I live in Dumbo."

Millie made an impressed face. "Look at you! Little Jensen from the block movin' on up!"

Jensen chuckled. "For the record, I was never referred to as 'Little' Jensen," he said, shooting me a look that made my heart trip over its beats.

"Well, there's my ÜBER! We'll have to catch up another time. I leave for India on Friday, but let's see if we can link up when I get back. Maybe you guys can come over for dinner," she said, her eyes bouncing from mine to Jensen's. Mine widened. I couldn't even respond to that. Thankfully she leaned in and gave me a huge hug. "I love you. Thank you so much for doing this for me. You're the bestest ever. I'll email you the rest of the information, and we'll sort it all out."

"Go take kick ass pictures," I said, dropping my arms from our embrace.

"Get the ÜBER app!" she yelled as she climbed into the back of a black car.

I flashed her my middle finger and a smile. She laughed.

"You're not walking, right?" he asked, concern clear in his voice.

I shook my head. "Subway."

"By yourself?"

Because I felt like being an asshole, I looked around as if I was looking for my invisible friends. "Clearly."

He pulled his bottom lip into his mouth, and I could tell he was mulling something over. He had that look on his face he got when he was worried about my reaction to something he was about to say or do. It was the last look I saw on his face when we broke up five years ago, and one I didn't want to reacquaint myself with.

"Do you want to join us for a drink?" Jeff asked suddenly.

Jensen's lip popped right out of his mouth, and my stupid, idiot self wanted to suck it into mine.

"You should," he added.

"I'll take a rain check on that, but thank you for asking."

"Just one drink, Meep," Jensen said.

"I'm fine," I insisted, turning my head toward the street to hide the flush that took over my face.

"Okay. Well, let me get a cab for you," he said, turning to the street.

"Good luck with that."

His shirt rode up as he did his crazy cab-hailing dance, and my eyes fell to that spot. I was hoping he'd developed a gut over the years. One I hadn't been able to make out from the shirts he'd worn when I'd bumped into him. He hadn't, of course. I lifted my eyes before my imagination got the best of me. *He's an asshole, remember? That makes you crazy and irrational.*

To my surprise, a yellow car pulled up shortly after. Jensen held the door open for me as I said goodbye to Jeff. Just as I was about to slide into the car, I stopped to thank him, but the words got lost somewhere between my brain and my mouth. I could only stare at his face, which looked so different with a beard.

"I like your beard," I whispered.

"Thanks," he said, not taking his eyes off mine, and clearly taken aback by my compliment.

My heart was picking up its pace and treading into the danger zone. We were so close. I could practically feel the heat from his body against mine. I could easily close my eyes and lean forward so that he could press his lips to mine and slip his tongue into my mouth.

"Text me when you get home," he said.

I nodded. "Thanks for getting me a cab."

"The fare is paid."

"You don't even know how much it is from here to my place."

Jensen shrugged one shoulder. "I guesstimated."

I looked at him for a long beat. "Well, it was good seeing you."

That earned a chuckle from him, deep and velvety. "Liar."

I tried to fight a smile, but it appeared on my face nonetheless. "Hey, you hailed a cab and paid the fare for me."

"Always the opportunist," he said with a wink.

"Always the charmer," I replied, winking back as I slid into the back of the cab. "But really, thank you."

He gave me a single nod. "I'll see you at that shoot."

I gave him a small wave and watched as he watched me retreat into the cab. My heart felt like it wanted to leap out and settle inside of his. Not again, I told myself. I knew if it did, I'd never get it back.

Jensen Talks

They say it takes twenty-one days to break a habit. It's been approximately one thousand eight hundred and twenty six since I last held her hand in mine and I'm still waiting for the remnants of her to break off of me.

It poses the question, are habits worth breaking? Sometimes the answer isn't a simple yes or no. Sometimes we're forced to try to break a habit because life is complicated and you know that if you kept at it, things would end in heartache. And even though you're the reason for the pain, you can't bear the thought of that person going through it again. So you pretend. You pretend you broke the habit. You pretend you kicked the addiction.

And you get so good at pretending that you manage to convince yourself that you succeeded, until you're tempted again and then all bets are off because your mind remembers. Your senses remember. Your heart remembers.

Some habits are definitely worth breaking, though, like buying Krispy Kreme donuts every Sunday, which I'm about to break this week. They're tempting, they're mouth-watering, but I need to cut them out of my life! I found some vegan donuts in Brooklyn that I may need to replace them with. Maybe I'm just bad at breaking habits.

Dun-Well Doughnuts: Jensen Approved.

Question of the day: @ SidekickA7x "What's your favorite book?"

My answer: The Little Prince

I was standing on the corner of Canal and Bowery, like the song says, taking a picture to send to Estelle and Rob as proof while I waited for Jensen. We were set to meet the couple in a small Chinese restaurant they owned—"one where they hang ducks," according to Jensen. I shivered at the thought, and the cold breeze that hit.

"I belong with you, you belong with me, you're my sweetheart," Jensen sang as he approached.

My heart dipped into my stomach at the sound of his voice, and thumped wildly as I turned to face him. He gave me a full once over before pointing up to the Canal and Bowery sign as explanation of his singing, as if I needed one.

"I sent a picture to Rob and Elle."

"I'm not sure your brother will get it. He was never good with song lyrics."

I lifted my scarf to my mouth to hide my smile, completely giddy over the fact that he remembered that about him. We'd been in the car so many times together, the three of us, arguing about shows on our way to dinner, singing loudly on the way to concerts. He'd been such a staple in my life, in all of our lives at one point. I sighed, pushing the memories back once more and returning the once over he'd given me. He looked casual in his jeans, black jacket and black Timberland boots.

"Are we waiting for their call?" he asked, rubbing his hands together and blowing into them.

I looked at him but quickly averted my eyes. Why, oh, why did he have to be so fucking good looking? Why, oh, why did my heart have to act like a moron every time he was near? *Ugh.*

"Yeah."

"You okay?"

"Yeah."

"You sure?" he asked, stepping closer, until he was right beside me and the smell of the city evaporated until my senses were infiltrated by him. I breathed in deeply, just once, before stepping away.

"I'm positive."

"Cold?" he asked in a voice that promised he'd warm me up. I shivered and shook my head, looking away quickly.

"Maybe I should start interviewing you while we wait."

My gaze snapped to his. "What?"

"Yeah, I told you I wanted to interview you."

"Are you going to let me take pictures of you?"

His mouth pulled up into a half-smile. The way his eyes twinkled gave me enough time to brace myself for whatever it was he was going to say.

"Why do you want pictures of me when you can have the real thing?"

"Ohmygod." I looked away, covering my mouth again, this time to keep from laughing, but then he laughed, and I couldn't hold it.

"That was one of my best lines right there."

"So corny."

He grinned. "Now I know not to use it on a stranger. I mean, if I were to meet a photographer or caught someone taking my picture."

"I'm sure you're already on *Hot Dudes Reading*," I said, trying to ignore the way my stomach turned at the idea of someone taking his picture. I really needed to get over that. People were bound to take his picture!

He chuckled. "Is that something I should know about?"

"Only if you enjoy looking at hot dudes reading."

He made a face and I started to laugh, but it faded when our gazes locked. Suddenly I couldn't remember what had been so funny. He was looking at me like I'd just said the most incredible thing.

"I miss the sound of your laughter," he said, his admission so quiet I wasn't sure he'd meant to voice it or for me to hear it, but I had, and it rattled me. My phone rang then, interrupting the moment. I answered the call and we started walking to our destination.

"And your smile. I miss that, too," Jensen whispered behind me, his chest on my back, his mouth near my ear.

I shivered against him. I probably would have had more of a reaction if I wasn't suddenly feeling queasy at the amount of dead animals they had hanging inside the butcher shop we were about to go into.

"Is that a rabbit?" I asked. He nodded. I blinked. "I can't go in there," I whisper-shouted.

"It's not like you're going to eat a meal in there, Mia."

"Jensen!" I whispered.

He looked at me with a look I hadn't seen in a while. The tenderness in his gaze made my breath hitch. He placed his hand on my shoulder. "I'll be right there. If it's too much for you, you let me know and we leave."

My stomach sank. It wasn't like I was a vegetarian, but seeing the animals hung like that made me want to become one. They were completely skinned, but I could see them. I could picture them hopping around, alive and well. When my stomach turned a second time, my hand shot out to grab Jensen's forearm. He placed his other hand over mine and squeezed once. I didn't look at him, but in that moment I needed a familiar touch, one that made me feel like everything would be okay, and I found that in him. He moved so that his fingers threaded through mine, and I felt my heart jump. I looked up at him, he looked down at me, and something passed between us. There was an ocean of possibilities swimming in his eyes but with it came a wave of realization and I was quickly reeled back from its current.

"This doesn't mean anything," I said quietly, taking my hand from his.

"This means everything," he said as I pushed open the door.

I was too annoyed with myself to even care about the dead carcasses. I heard him laughing behind me but refused to turn around. I took pictures of Sue and Tom, and Jensen interviewed them. We were in and out in less than an hour, which I was thankful for since most of my pictures included things in the background that I would have to crop out, and I really wasn't sure how much longer I could stand to be in there, with the dead rabbit behind them staring me down.

As we stepped out, he said, "That wasn't terrible."

"I guess. Thanks for asking quick questions."

"Are you kidding? I felt like Bugs Bunny was glaring at me."

"Oh my God! Me too!"

We laughed as we reached the stoplight.

"So, where to now?"

"Home. I need to edit these and some others."

"I need to go pick up Scout." He smiled when I made a face. "Olivia."

"You call her Scout?"

"Sometimes."

I smiled. "I take it you're excited about the prequel, or whatever?"

"Fuck no."

"No?"

He shook his head, letting out a harsh, foggy breath. "I just ranted to Jeff about that for like three hours. I don't think I can do it again."

I laughed. "Jeff, your editor with the beard?"

"With the beard." He laughed. "Yeah."

I shrugged. "It was the first thing that came to mind."

"Yeah, you and Olivia use the beard to describe him."

"It's a very well-pronounced beard."

He laughed again, his gray eyes filled with amusement as he looked down at me. "I'm not sure I like how much you paid attention to his features."

"I can pay attention to as many features as I want," I said with an eye roll.

His eyes darkened, but he didn't add anything to that. The look in his eyes was enough to let me know how he felt about my statement. We walked together two more blocks, until we got to the train I needed to take and he had to go down the block to the other.

"I guess I'll see you in a couple of days?" I said, putting my hands in the pockets of my jacket.

His mouth twitched as he nodded, as if the very thought was the greatest thing in the world. He took a step until he stood in front of me, completely blocking everything else from view. His hand came down to the strap of my camera bag, tucking his fingers under it, against my shoulder. Even with the two layers of clothing I had on, I felt his touch deep in my bones. My breath hitched as I took a step back, swallowing down the nerves that bubbled up inside me. He adjusted the bag so it sat higher on my shoulder and leaned down, tiny prickly hairs on his face brushing against the side of mine.

"I look forward to it," he whispered, placing a kiss on my cheek as he backed away again.

He gave me a wide grin when he stood at his full height, and I stood there, frozen to his touch, to his lips against my face, to the words he'd whispered. I managed to say goodbye as I rounded the corner and disappeared into the stairwell, but I could feel his gaze on my back the entire way down.

Jensen Talks

Have you ever stopped to really consider how many people we share the universe with? I mean, really. I did the other day, and it made me feel smaller than an ant. It's a great exercise to do when you feel overwhelmed, though. When you think you're having a bad day because you missed the train, stop to remember that some people don't have trains to take. Some people have to walk miles to get to where they need to go. Some people have more mouths to feed than you do. Others don't have mouths at all because they live in oppressive countries where they don't get a say in anything.

We live in a good country, America. Despite the problems we have. We live in a good country. The fact that I can write that we have problems, and if I wanted to, I could go on a rant about the problems I think the government needs to fix, without fear, proves that we live in a good country. All that I got from paying a cab fare for someone. Because, as I sat there, worrying about whether or not she made it home, I realized that she must have (I double checked anyway, out of habit). How lucky are we in New York to have such a great system of transportation? I know we complain about it sometimes (often), but really, we are lucky. Our cabbies may be a little crazy, but they're only a reflection of their passengers, right?

I kid.

America: Jensen Approved.

Question of the day from: @The_Review_Loft: "How would you describe the #feeling of #love in 140 or less characters?"

Answer: Like somebody is gripping your heart,

but you don't want them
to let go because the
ache would worsen with-
out them.

"I think you're totally going to fall for him again," Estelle said when I filled her in on everything going on with Jensen.

"What? No! Why would you even say that?"

"Because I know you."

"Whatever. Nobody is falling for anybody. We just have to survive the next couple of months, and then everything will go back to the way it used to be."

"With you hating him and him trying to get you back?"

I paused, putting down the glass of water I'd picked up. "He wasn't trying to get me back."

Her scoff filled the phone line. "Are you being serious right now?"

I paused again. He hadn't been trying to get me back. Had he reached out to me after he left for New York? Absolutely. Had I ignored the crap out of him? Definitely. But he wasn't trying to get me back.

"He only wanted to talk to me because he wanted me to forgive him," I said.

"How would you know? You never let him explain himself."

I sighed. "Because I know. I know him. Knew him. I knew him. I have no idea who the hell he is now."

Estelle laughed. "People don't change that much."

"They don't, but I know he has. He talks a lot now. Remember how quiet he used to be?"

She laughed again. "He was never quiet, unless you mean he likes to discuss his feelings now?"

"I guess you can say that."

"Maybe since he writes so much about his life in his column he figures he might as well just talk about things?"

"He writes about his feelings?"

"Not particularly," she said. I could practically hear her frown. "But he does write about his dating life."

The last thing I wanted to read about was his dating life. That was why I'd stopped reading it in the first place, though I was definitely going to pick it back up soon. I just hoped it wasn't on a day when he'd write about another woman. My stomach churned at the very thought.

"Well, whatever. It's not like that. We just have to pretend to get along while we're in front of the couples we're working with."

"Uh-huh," she said.

"I'm serious."

"Mia, you took a subway to Brooklyn and then to further prove my point, you went to his book signing."

I gasped. "He wrote a book with my name on it! About a girl who looks like me!"

She laughed. "I'm not saying you were wrong to do it. I would have probably done the same. I just think you're going to totally fall for him again."

We spoke about that for a while, but when we hung up, her words kept replaying: *I think you're going to fall for him again.* Some might argue I never fell out of him, but I didn't think love was about falling in or out; it was about staying in. And we didn't. I kept repeating that to myself as I sat on the subway, and then as I sat on the park bench that gave me the perfect view of the city. For a while, I watched people go by, mothers with their kids, fathers with their kids, families walking together, people jogging with a partner. The minute you started thinking about the things you were lacking, the universe found a way to smother them in your face. Suddenly, every single child in New York had two arms to swing from, and every couple was in love. I sighed, sitting back, and adjusted the settings while I watched the homeless man two benches over rustling out of his sleep.

My gaze cut from his, to the other side of the street, where I noticed mobs of people overtaking the sidewalks. The echo of their hurried footsteps vibrated the street beneath me. I hadn't been out during lunch hour, not this far from my place, anyway, not with this amount of distance to analyze the way we looked when we were in a rush. It saddened me more than it excited me. The amount of sorrow each of them carried around. The homeless people in the parks, in the subways, had become my preferred subjects, and I'd completely ignored everybody else that had that look. I'd never stopped to think about it—about my face and the way I probably carried my pain. Even the successful-looking businessmen looked sad and tired. As a whole, we looked sick. Sick of being sick. Sick of being tired. Sick of being homeless and helpless. It didn't take not having anything to feel that way. It didn't take much to make us feel sad and unappreciated. I blew out a breath then and let myself live in the moment, and I knew that I needed to show the world what had been in front of me all along.

On Tuesday morning I headed over to Cassie and Logan's house. They lived in Brooklyn. DUMBO, Brooklyn, which was where Jensen said he lived. On my ride there I was half expecting to find a sculpture of the elephant, but lost the thread of hope when the dream-crushing cab driver told me what DUMBO stood for. It was the first thing I told Jensen when I spotted him standing outside of their building. He looked up from his Spiderman journal and smiled as he pushed off the wall. I tried really hard not to feel anything, tried really hard to smother any sense of attraction I felt at seeing his bearded face and how toned his body looked in the long-sleeved cotton shirt he wore.

"I thought you hated that movie?" he said on our way up the stairs.

"I do, but still."

He chuckled, shaking his head.

"You know what else I don't like?" I asked, tilting my head to peer up at him when we reached the platform of the second floor. He gave me a questioning look.

"Spiderman." My eyes flickered from his to the journal in his hand. He laughed.

"I'll have you know that my daughter gave me this journal for my birthday, and I'm very proud to be using it for such a great cause."

"I never pegged you for a romance writer."

He pinned me with an ardent stare. "Some say that's all I write."

I felt my face heat, because he made me feel like he was talking about me, but I knew better. "Because you write about your dates in the paper?"

"If you think my articles are about my dates, you're definitely reading them wrong."

I let out a relieved breath when we reached Cassie's floor, and I was able to busy myself by knocking on the door.

"Do you like interviewing people?" I asked in a hushed whisper while we waited.

He nodded.

"You'd be surprised at what you learn when you ask the right questions."

Inside, I felt something stir uncontrollably. I cleared my throat, willing Cassie to hurry the hell up. "That's nice."

"You know what I'd really like?" he said, the deep husky tone he used making my insides flip, but drawing my eyes to his serious gaze nonetheless.

"What?" I whispered.

"To interview you."

My mouth dropped just as the door swung open. A tall, blue-eyed, blonde woman, wearing jeans and a nice yellow blouse stood on the other side of it, smiling.

"Hi, I'm Cassie," she said, holding the door open while offering me her free hand. It felt thin and fragile as I shook it. She did the same to Jensen and let us in, closing the door with the swivel of her hips.

"Logan! They're here!" she called out.

Cassie moved gracefully, like a ballerina. When we fully entered, my eyes roamed over the large space. It was then that I realized it was a penthouse, with a kitchen that took up nearly half the floor plan, and a large living room that looked like it had never been touched. Everything was decorated in hues of blues and whites. White couches, blue walls. Blue chairs, white walls.

"Would you like something to drink? Coffee? Juice? Water?" she asked as she rounded the kitchen island and walked toward the coffee maker. It was one of those brushed chrome espresso machines that looked like it could supply a small coffee shop.

"Coffee, please," I said, my eyes glued to the machine. She smiled.

"Logan got it for me for my birthday last month. I don't know how I've survived this long without one."

"I think that's going on my Christmas list," I said.

Jensen made a sound like something between a cough and a laugh. I shot him a look that made him straighten out and try harder to hide his amusement. I took a seat on one of the barstools as Cassie waited for our coffee to brew (of course, Jensen agreed to some as well).

"So you're only here from Santa Barbara for a couple of months?" Cassie asked once we started talking about New York and how cold I thought it was here.

"I was hired as a freelance photographer for the special they're doing, partly because I did a similar special for a magazine back home. On a much smaller scale."

She nodded and shifted her eyes to Jensen. "And you? You're also temporary?"

I shifted in my seat to look at him over my cup of coffee.

"Nope. New York is home. I write for them whenever they call. One of my mentors is the Editor-in-Chief there, so when she calls I usually go, unless I have too much on my plate."

"He also writes children's books," I said, knowing he wouldn't. He'd never been one to toot his own horn.

"Wow," Cassie said, making an impressed face.

"And a column in the Sunday edition of *The Times*," I added, smiling at her.

She looked at Jensen again with a deeper appreciation. "That's impressive."

I was still smiling when I looked at him again, but was taken aback. The look in his eyes made my heart fumble. I couldn't be sure if he was angry at me for bringing attention to those things, angry at me for sounding impressed about them, or if he was just in awe of the fact that I was showing him off. Whatever the case was, the smile wiped right off my face. I went back to my coffee.

"Why go home, Mia? Can't you just get a full-time job with the magazine?"

I shrugged. "Maybe."

Cassie smiled. "Is there a boyfriend back home?"

I laughed. "No boyfriend, but I have a job waiting for me."

"No boyfriend? Really?" she asked, eyeing me curiously.

As if a light bulb switched on in her head, she smiled widely.

"I have a son who can take you out," she said.

Out of habit, I glanced at Jensen. From the way his jaw was working, I knew he was not amused by her suggestion. A small laugh flittered out of me when I looked at Cassie's serious face.

"I'm serious! He's a great guy; he just works too much. But I think you'd make a good match."

I laughed again, because I didn't know what else to do, and she didn't know enough about me to make that assumption. Suddenly she looked from me to Jensen and back to me.

"Unless you guys are … oh my gosh, I'm so sorry," she said, and laughed.

I looked at Jensen, then at Cassie, and, as it dawned on me, I began to shake my head. "Oh! No! We're not together at all!" I paused and laughed again. "It's just … I'm not looking for a boyfriend or anything."

"Oh. Well, you don't have to date him. He can just take you out while you're here. He's thirty-one, works as a financial advisor, and he lives in the city. You said you were coming from the city, right?"

I nodded. "Chelsea."

She clapped her hands together once. "Let me get a picture of him and see if Logan is finished with his conference call while I'm at it!"

She walked off, looking giddy, and I sat there completely dumbfounded at everything that had just happened. After a long, silent moment, I shook my head and laughed.

"That poor guy. I wonder how many people she tries to hook him up with."

"Does that happen a lot?" Jensen asked.

The biting tone in his voice surprised me, and I cut my gaze to his.

"What?"

"People trying to hook you up with their kids?"

I frowned, scanning his serious face. His jaw was still working and from the way his forearms flexed as he squeezed the ceramic cup in his hands, I knew he was fuming and trying to contain it.

"Sometimes," I said with a shrug.

He shook his head and looked away as he stood up to take his cup over to the sink. I was holding mine in my hands, looking at the bottom portion of the coffee I'd left, wondering what the hell was taking Logan so damn long. I just wanted this shoot over with already. I felt Jensen's breath on the back of my neck and jumped.

"What are you doing?" I asked, my voice a near whisper. I held my cup firmer, trying to contain the shakiness.

He leaned in, his hand caressing the side of my arm from my shoulder to my hand until he reached it and closed his hand over mine.

"Taking your cup," he said, his voice low and deep, near my ear.

I swallowed. "Maybe I'm not finished yet."

"Maybe you'll never be finished," he said right by my earlobe, so close I felt his lips against me.

I closed my eyes and tried to regain my breath. I swallowed again.

"What are you doing, Jensen?" I whispered.

"What do you want me to do, Mia?" he whispered back.

"I don't want you to do anything."

"Then I'm not doing anything," he said just as low.

I let go of the mug and slid my hand out of his grasp. He took the cup and backed away from me until I could no longer feel the heat of him against my back or his breath over my neck. Until I felt like I could breathe just enough, because even though he'd given me the space I thought I wanted, I would have conceded to limiting my air supply if it meant feeling all the things I felt in those two seconds.

Cassie came back, scrolling through her phone, and showing me pictures of her son, Carson. He was cute, and I could totally picture him in finance, but suddenly I wasn't as interested in the idea of him taking me anywhere.

"Just give him a call," Cassie said, sliding me his card. "I'll talk to him about you, but trust me, he'd love to take you out. You are completely his type."

I looked down at his card, all white with nothing but black letters explaining his role in the company he worked for. It was so boring, so not … I glanced up and looked at Jensen, who was watching me throughout the whole exchange.

He didn't say anything to me the rest of the time we were there. He asked his questions once Logan finally showed, and I took their pictures. We left with one last reminder about Carson.

"He's not your type," he said on our walk down.

I looked at him. "How do you know?"

"Because I know your type."

"And you think you're my type."

"I know I'm your type."

I rolled my eyes as I rounded the corner of the stairs and continued on down. "Because we dated?"

"No. Because I'm everybody's type." He grinned.

I slapped his arm.

"Your humility is astounding. And remember, you and I are just friends."

He chuckled and held the door open for me.

Once we were outside, I zipped up my jacket and shivered. Snowflakes were trickling over us. I'd never seen it fall. It had snowed over the weekend, but by the time I'd woken up, I'd found the white coating the streets already. Seeing the tiny specks of white come down from the sky made me smile. I tilted my head as I brought my hand out to catch a few.

Even though I didn't love the cold weather, I had to admit that experiencing the snowfall was a magical experience. I closed my eyes, still smiling, as some of it fell on my face. When I opened them again and straightened, I let out a breath, still smiling. Jensen was looking at me with a slight grin on his face, the way he often looked at me when he thought I wasn't watching.

"Do you do this every time?" he asked, his voice filled with a softness that surprised me.

I shook my head.

"It's my first time."

He repositioned his journal under his arm and took a couple of strides until he was directly in front of me, and I had to crane my head to look at him. For a couple of beats, we just looked at each other. I couldn't feel my lips, but I was pretty sure his would be on them soon enough. My heart thumped. And thumped. And I waited. He brought his hand down and grabbed the front of my scarf.

"Let's go have lunch, *friend*," he said, enunciating the word.

"Let's go," I said, and returned the smile he gave me.

Just lunch. Just friends. I could do that.

We walked a couple of blocks and passed by a group of people letting go of balloons. I stopped and took some pictures of them.

"They do this every weekend. They fill the balloons with things they want to let go of."

"Like what people do with lanterns?"

Jensen nodded and patted over the pocket of his jeans. He fished out a vapor cigarette and switched it on, taking a hit.

"Huh. I thought you quit."

His gaze flicked to mine. "I did. I rarely even do this. I only have it for desperate measures."

"Like?"

"Like when my anxiety starts to eat at me at the amount of shit I have to get done, and when it's cold."

I looked back toward the people. One kid in particular caught my eye. He was probably about fifteen and looked like he needed a hug. I stepped closer to him and snapped a picture, then another, before finally putting away the camera. I continued to watch him from afar, wishing I had the balls to offer him a hug.

"You always get caught up in the broken people," Jensen said. He had one hand inside the pocket of his leather jacket and the other holding the vapor.

"You would know."

He didn't look at me, but I saw the twitch of his mouth.

"I want to do that one day," I said, looking at the floating balloons one last time before we started walking again.

"You don't think you've let go of enough?" he asked.

I let out a laugh. How weird was it that we were talking about this in such a natural manner, as if it hadn't altered our entire lives?

"There's always something to let go of," I said.

"And there's always something to pick up."

At that, we fell into comfortable silence until we reached the little restaurant. As we took a seat at a tiny table near the kitchen, he opened the journal back up and jotted down something.

"Do you usually do this on dates?" I asked. His head snapped up. His eyes searched mine for a moment before he smiled, so I added, "I'm not saying this is a date. I'm just saying when you go on dates and write about whatever it is you write about, do you take a journal?"

He chuckled. "Not really."

"What are you writing?"

"Something hit me just now, and I needed to write it down, that's all."

"What hit you?"

He smiled. "Why are you so curious?"

I scanned his face, his lips, his chin, his jaw, his cheekbones, the way his eyes were full of mischief. "You're right. Sorry I asked, friend," I said, articulating the word.

Jensen chuckled. "Ah, so I guess I need to answer after all."

I shrugged and picked up the menu as the waiter filled our water glasses. I picked mine up and continued scanning the page.

"I'm working on a story I'm not sure will ever be published."

"Why's that?"

"Because it's different for me, and publishers don't necessarily like different when they know you can sell one thing for certain."

"Hmm. What is it?"

"A romance. Sort of," he said, then laughed at the shocked expression on my face.

"Well, you were always good at poems, so…." I shrugged.

"I haven't written a poem in… " He paused, looked away for a beat and looked at me again, his eyes turbulent as they fell over my features. "Years."

How many years? I wanted to ask, but didn't. He probably wanted me to. Bastard. I tore my gaze away from his.

"A love story is different for you," I said finally.

He chuckled. "You're worse than my agent."

"What'd he say when you told him?"

"She," he corrected, "said it was a stupid idea."

"Yet you continued to write it."

"Yet I continued to write it," he said with a grin.

"What happens in this love story? Does the couple end up together?"

"Maybe." He shrugged. "Maybe not. I guess time will tell."

"Time in the story or time in your head?"

He looked at me in a way that made my skin prickle. "Is there a difference between the two?"

"You're the author. You tell me."

"Well, technically the story is inside my head, so time is irrelevant. Unless I die before it's finished."

"What happens then?"

"It never gets published."

I smiled. "Unless someone finds your file and decides to publish it anyway."

"In which case they better find a damn good ghost writer to finish it," he said, glaring at the very idea of that. I smiled because he looked adorable when his face got all cloudy like that. "What's so funny?"

"Nothing. I hope you don't die, and finish your story so that I can read it."

He stayed quiet for a beat. Two. Three. "I can read it to you."

"Umm … no. Thanks. Definitely not."

Our meals got there in sync with the silence that stretched between us. We talked about our friends, home, New York, everything that kept us in the safe zone. A few years I would have bet my life savings that this scenario would be the most awkward thing in the world, but sitting here felt good. It made me realize that we came into contact with a lot of people in our lives, but there was always that handful of special ones, the ones we didn't have to talk to every second or see all the time, but when we did it was like we hadn't spent time apart at all. The ones who made us feel normal and understood in this crazy, cruel world. I guessed that was what Jensen was to me. I realized then that he'd always be that, despite everything we'd been through or how badly I wanted things to be different. Maybe we really could do the friends thing.

"Are you free Saturday night?" he asked, snapping me out of my thoughts.

"Why?"

"I want to take you somewhere."

The way he looked at me, that was why being friends was doubtful. He made me want to say yes. Everything about him made me want to say yes. I sighed and took a sip of wine.

"I'm actually busy. I have to take pictures of some event for Millie."

"What kind of event?"

"A gala or something? I'm honestly not sure. I have to read the email. It's at the library."

"No shit," Jensen said, raising his brows. "On Saturday?"

"Yeah."

He made another non-committal sound before going back to his steak. I kept eyeing his journal throughout the meal, and he noticed, because at one point he laughed and shook his head.

"What are the characters' names?" I asked, because I couldn't help my-self.

His mouth twitched. "Mia and Jensen."

He shocked me into a silence I didn't know I was capable of. Then I realized his shoulders were shaking in silent laughter, and I shook my head, pursing my lips to hide my own smile.

"Asshole."

"What if I'm serious?" He was smiling that stupid lopsided smile that did annoying things to me.

"Well, then, for starters, I think I'll have to start charging you a fee for using my name. And secondly, I'll save you the headache of plotting and tell you right now the way that story ends."

The smile dropped from his face. He pushed his plate away slightly and leaned into the table, placing his elbows on either side of it, only backing away to let the server take the plates from us before moving back, closer to me.

"Enlighten me then, almighty one. How does this story end?"

His legs brushed against mine under the table and I stiffened, inhaling sharply. I swallowed, trying to regain my composure.

"Okay. I'll tell you the way I think it ends, if you tell me the way you think it ends."

After a moment of his eyes bouncing between mine and narrowing in thought, he conceded with a nod.

"I think it ends in heartache."

"For which character?"

"Hers." I paused when he continued to stare and corrected. "Both."

"What kind of heartache? Does one of them die? Does one of them leave?"

"One of them leaves."

"I wrote that part already. I'm at the part where one of them comes back and they meet again." I couldn't say anything, and he knew it, so he continued, "He left, married another woman, divorced that woman, and tried to go back to the first one…"

"But she didn't take him back," I said.

"She didn't." He paused. "Not right away, anyway."

"And when she finally did, she had to leave, because she lives in a far-away land."

Jensen chuckled. "This isn't a fantasy novel, Mia. There is no 'faraway land.'"

I nodded. "Okay. Just … a faraway state."

"And he fights to keep her."

"But she doesn't listen. She leaves anyway."

He gave me a sad smile and drummed his fingers over the journal. I looked at his hand, at the skull on his finger, the words in between: I, leave, my, pain. My gaze flickered to the other hand, on the table near mine, and I read the rest: on, the, page.

"So what's your ending?" I asked, my gaze finding his again.

His eyes raked over me, stopping for an extra long moment in specific areas: my throat, my lips, my eyes. Finally, his lips spread into a slow, wide smile that would've made me feel like I was melting in front of him, had it not been for the reality of our story. He baited me with that smile, and I took it, leaning forward in my seat as I waited. When he had me where he wanted me, he leaned even closer, until his mouth was right beside my ear, and then he whispered the words.

"Real love stories never end."

Real love stories never end.

The words became another ingredient in the stew bubbling inside me. I wouldn't let it get to me, though. I refused to let it get to me. I also refused to let him tell me who was and wasn't my type. He couldn't play mind games with me. He wasn't going to try to brainwash me into thinking he was the only type I had. Fuck him. I had no type. I'd dated guys from all different backgrounds with a million different jobs after he and I split up. Not successfully, obviously. If successfully meant taking things to a level that ended in a forever. Not that I needed a forever with anybody. Those were the thoughts that floated around in my mind and eventually led to me calling Carson. I only called because Millie told me to take a date to the event on Saturday, and I had nobody to take, but clearly I loved putting myself in awkward situations, so I called and asked him. He said yes and agreed to pick me up at seven o'clock sharp.

The only thing left to do now was go shopping. I called Estelle on my way to the store and went over the latest happenings, while she laughed and laughed about my calling Carson and asking him to go with me to a gala.

"I can't fucking believe you called a stranger and asked him to go with you."

"Yeah, well, he said yes," I responded with a laugh of my own. "And he's cute."

"So you say."

"I'm serious! Go search him on LinkedIn!"

She laughed again; the sound of her hysteria was like she was wheezing. "You're going on a date with someone who's on LinkedIn?"

"You're married to a guy who's on there, so stop making fun!" I paused. "God, Elle, our hipster days are over."

She stayed quiet on the end of the line, and finally said, "You think?"

"I think. They were probably over the day you decided to marry a freaking doctor."

"Hot doctor, but he surfs … and he had a manbun!"

I laughed. "Yeah, maybe he's exempt."

That was one of my goals for the exhibit, if I was ever able to set it up. I wanted to show that we were all the same, regardless of what label we put on each other. Nobody really labeled themselves, unless they wanted to escape someone else doing it for them. I said as much to her, and she agreed that it was a great idea. After arguing over what store I needed to go to for a dress, I ended up at Neiman Marcus. I tried on ten gowns and sent Estelle pictures of all of them and shoes that matched. I left there with a mermaid gown that cost more than my car payment. It was also something I felt beautiful wearing, and that alone was worth the price.

"Do you think it's too formal?" I asked Millie over a Skype call later that night.

She shook her head as she eyed it again. "No. It's perfection. I usually wear a long black gown. Last year I wore a yellow one with no back. Everybody goes all out for this one, which is funny considering the crowd. Some of the men wear sneakers sometimes."

I gaped at her. "Sneakers? I just bought a dress with a crystal bodice and some people wear sneakers?" I paused and looked back at the dress. "Maybe I should exchange it?"

Millie laughed. "Don't you dare! You're supposed to be representing me, remember? Trust me, I go decked out. I still can't believe you asked the Carson guy to go with you."

"I spoke to him briefly last night. He's really nice. Besides, who else would I have asked?"

Her eyes widened. "Jensen? Duh."

"Jensen? What the hell are they feeding you in India?"

"I ate curry lamb last night," she said, rubbing her stomach.

The sound of that made mine growl.

"I hate you. Officially." I groaned. "Now I need to go find a good Indian spot."

"Maybe Carson will take you," Millie said, looking completely amused by this suggestion.

"You're an idiot. I can't wait 'til you get back so I can slap you."

She stuck her tongue out. "Have fun. Remember, pictures of all of the people with their awards and cocktails. The magazine is big on the cocktail portion. If you can get some of them speaking amongst themselves, you're golden." She paused and turned her face away from the camera to listen to somebody—Seth, I assumed—and looked back at me. "'Kay, I gotta go. Love you! I gotta go eat some more yummy food."

"Love you too. I hope you gain ten pounds!"

We laughed as we signed off, and I went on Google to search for restaurants in the area. When I looked down at my phone, I saw I'd received a text from Jensen: *What are you up to?* I stared at my screen for a moment, waiting for his words to disappear.

Real love stories never end. The words came back to me unbidden. Fuck real love. Real love didn't hurt you the way ours had. Wasn't staying together through thick and thin a requirement for *real love*? I picked up my phone, because an hour later the message was still in the back of my mind, and I finally responded: *Getting Sherlocked.* Because I was. I didn't expect him to respond, but when he did, I smiled.

Are you a Moriarty fan? I picture you as one.

The fact that those words made me feel giddy was a testament to how ridiculous I was, but I was cheesing big time at the fact that he knew the show. Like, *knew* the show. Then I reminded myself it was Jensen, not Carson, I was talking to, and I shouldn't be giddy over anything he said to me. I needed to cling to my anger. One more text though. One more and I was done.

I am. I totally am.

I put down the phone and went to take a shower, hoping to find my anger in there. I didn't, though. Even after I replayed our breakup in my head. Even after I reminded myself that he'd been with another woman for the past few years. Even after I repeated over and over that he had a daughter, one who wasn't mine. I found that I wasn't angry. Not tonight, anyway. It wasn't until I got dressed and was back tucked in my bed that I picked up my phone and read the next message he'd sent.

I know you well.

Those words felt like a Taser to my emotions, zapping logic back into them. He didn't know me at all. Not anymore. Still, as I went to sleep I wondered if we'd given each other such a big part of one another that we lost ourselves when he left? Why was I losing sleep over it, though? Why was I losing sleep over him?

The doorman called when Carson arrived, and I agreed to go downstairs to meet him. The last thing I needed was somebody coming up here on laundry day. I grabbed my camera bag and put my extra makeup in there. I took one look in the full-length mirror, just as I was about to step out, and smiled at my reflection. I looked hot. My dirty blonde hair was done in waves that reached my shoulders and my makeup was subtle, with light gold eye shadow and a hint of bronze over my cheeks. My lips were what popped, a bright pink that matched the bottom of my mermaid gown. I wore nothing on my chest, as the front of the dress was a halter, crystal-beaded bodice that went up and rounded over my neck. On my ears I wore round crystals that matched. I pivoted to look at the back, which was what sold me on the dress. It left my back completely bare, save for the line where it clipped over the small of my back.

I took one last breath before heading out and taking the elevator downstairs to meet Carson. As soon as I stepped out of the hotel, I spotted the back of his blond head. He wore a tuxedo, and when he turned around to face me, we looked at each other for a long, appraising moment, our eyes traveling the length of one another. He was tall, really tall, and thin, with his hands tucked into the pocket of his pants. He took the strides needed to reach me. The way he moved reminded me of his mother—fluid and graceful. He offered me his hand, and I placed mine in it.

"Nice to meet you in person," he said, bringing the back of my hand to his lips.

Even with the height of my heels, I was eye level with his shoulders. He reminded me of one of those Precious Moments ceramics, with doe-eyed crystal blue eyes and a small pout on his lips. He looked like a man who'd lived an easy life. He didn't have the rough edges Jensen had. Didn't have the pained eyes or that aura about him that made you wonder who'd wronged him and what you could do to make it all better.

Carson dropped my hand and offered me his arm to loop my hand through, which I did as we walked out.

"I called an ÜBER," he said, smiling down at me. "Didn't think you'd want to walk in your heels all the way there."

I stiffened, but smiled nonetheless. "That's fine."

If we got a serial killer, he'd probably kill Carson first anyway, and maybe I'd have time to make a run for it. As we stepped out, I threw the shawl I'd brought over my shoulders and shivered.

"My mom said you're from Santa Barbara; have you gotten used to this weather?"

"Hell no," I said. "Does one get used to this? I can't imagine."

He laughed as he looked at his phone. "Okay, he should be…" he looked up and scanned the street, "right here."

I followed him a couple of steps until we reached a black town car. Carson held the door open and helped me with the bottom of my gown so I wouldn't step on it as I slid in.

"I should have probably considered the whole sitting down and climbing into the back of cars thing when I was buying this dress," I said once we were settled in, with a portion of my gown resting on Carson's long legs.

He chuckled. "For what it's worth, I think that's the perfect gown for you."

I smiled.

"So tell me about the pictures you take," he said as he fished his vibrating phone out of his pocket.

I glanced at him, at the phone, and finally started talking despite his typing.

"Well, tonight I'm photographing this event for a friend. I'm in New York temporarily, taking pictures for a magazine … *Time*," I added. He glanced up from his phone momentarily to shoot me an impressed look before going back to it. "I want to get my prints up on museum walls someday, though; that's my dream."

"That's a big dream," he said, still looking at his phone. "What kind of prints?"

I looked out the window, wondering if he'd notice if I told him I took pictures of cheetahs and hyenas having sex. Instead, I sighed. "Just people. Life. Homeless people, business people, common everyday kind of stuff."

His face scrunched up. He looked at me again. "Who wants to see pictures of homeless people?"

"I don't know if people would want to see them, I just think they need to see them."

He raised an eyebrow, shrugged, and looked at his phone again. "I don't understand."

Of course he didn't understand. He lived on his goddamn phone. He was the perfect person for the damn exhibit.

I held in my rant, because if I let it out, I would have no date tonight. When we got to the New York Public Library, Carson helped me out of the car, and we walked arm in arm. He put the phone in his pocket long enough to pick up champagne glasses for us while I went off in search of Beatrice, the woman Millie asked me to look for. I found her quickly, as she was directing the servers on where to go. She was a tall, dark, big-bosomed woman with jet-black hair and a wide friendly smile.

"Hi! Oh, that dress is lovely on you," she said, eyeing me.

I laughed lightly because she'd never seen me before, so she wouldn't know what looked good and what didn't, but I went with it anyway.

"You look lovely as well," I said.

"Oh, I know, honey. After the amount of money I spent to get dolled up, I better look lovely."

We laughed and she handed me a pamphlet. "This is the basis of it. I'm sure you searched for this on Google and didn't find much. We like to keep this within the community."

I looked down at the Literary Awards pamphlet and smiled. As I flipped the pages with my free hand, my smile widened.

"Oh my God. All of these people are here?"

Beatrice laughed. "I get just as excited about it and I've been planning it for the past ten years."

My eyes widened as I looked up at her. I felt my heart beating heavy and fast. I couldn't believe I'd be in the presence of some of my favorite authors. I'd be seeing the people whose words I got lost in time and time again … in person!

"I'm going to do my best to take great pictures, but if I see Neil Gaiman, I may lose it, and I can't be held responsible for what'll happen."

Beatrice shot me a look that teetered between amusement and wariness. "Just be sure you get those pictures before you do anything crazy."

I laughed. "Definitely. I'm too afraid of Millie to have an actual fan girl moment."

She shook her head and laughed again. We spoke for a couple of minutes about my photography and what she did as event coordinator, and in the conversation she mentioned museums, and I told her what I wanted to do with my prints eventually, which held her interest. When people started sweeping in, she said a quick goodbye and promised she'd look for me later. I went over to find Carson, who was still on his phone, and stood beside him for a couple of beats.

"Champagne's good," he commented, sliding his phone back into the inside pocket of his jacket.

"It is." I looked back down at the pamphlet. "Did you get one of these?"

He nodded. "Impressive attendance."

I raised my eyebrows, taking a slight step back. "You've read some of them?"

He grinned. When he grinned like that he looked like Edward Nygma before he became The Riddler. I wasn't sure if it was creepy or cute. I went with cute.

"Of course. Junot Diaz is a favorite of mine."

I smiled. My heart stirred a bit. Junot was a favorite of Jensen's as well. I wasn't going to bring up an ex on a date, so I just nodded and said I liked him as well. The main doors opened for the cocktail hour, and we walked in, as did the majority of the people who'd been waiting for them to open. Once inside, it seemed like the event size doubled, with people coming in from every angle.

"I guess I'll have to start working now," I said, taking the last sip of champagne and setting it down as a waiter came by with a tray.

"I'll be around—eating, drinking, mingling with my favorite authors. You know, enjoying all the things you won't be able to do."

"Ha, ha," I said with a smile. "I'll be back."

I went off and started snapping pictures of everybody. Every time I snapped one, I felt myself smiling. It felt good to take pictures of people having fun again. I felt their laughter in the images on the screen on my camera. It was infectious. I snapped, and snapped, and stopped to talk to them when they asked me how they were looking. We joked about the camera weight and how the magic of Photoshop existed for a reason. I was talking to one of the women, an editor at some publishing house, when I caught a familiar face at the table a couple of steps away. Had I not been already sort of expecting to see him, since it was a writers' event, after all, I would have stumbled.

As it was, my heart dropped into the pit of my stomach with such a force, that I gasped. I swallowed, clutching on to my camera, and continued my walk. I knew I had to take pictures of his table because of the other people standing around him. I took a breath, hoping to rid myself of my nervousness. My camera went over my face as I reached them, and I snapped. They laughed, I snapped. Jensen's arms waved wildly as he told a story. Click. He placed his hand over the shoulder of the woman beside him. Click. Click. Click. Finally, one of the men in the group signaled his flute toward me in a toast, and all heads turned toward me. Click. Jensen's jaw went slack as he spotted me. Click. His eyes traveled down the length of me. Click. The intensity in his gaze when they reached my lens again. Click. I swallowed again, my hands shaky because I couldn't not react when he looked at me the way he was doing, as if the room was a pit of darkness, and I was light. My heart thumped, thumped, my breathing was wild and erratic, but I managed to take another one.

I gave them a smile and a wave, thanking them for cooperating as I lowered my camera. My legs felt shaky when my gaze met Jensen's again. I'd never seen him wearing a tuxedo. Even for Estelle's wedding, he'd worn slacks and a nice button down, like all the other groomsmen. To see him, this tattooed, hot, smart guy with the mysterious aura and the charming appeal all dressed up was more than I could handle. I walked away and decided to take a break, stopping at the next empty tall table and setting the lens part of my camera on it so that I could scroll through the ones I had so far.

"Anything good?" Jensen asked, his breath warming the back of my neck. I shivered.

"You knew I was coming," I said, not taking my eyes off the screen. I didn't sound upset. I didn't sound like anything.

"I had an inkling." His voice was still just a murmur against me.

I wished he'd back away so that I couldn't smell him or feel him so close to me. Instead of giving me space, he placed his hand on the small of my back, his fingers below the clip of the bodice of my dress.

"You look incredible," he said.

I closed my eyes.

"I brought a date," I said, and heard him take a sharp breath. His hand left my back, and I felt my breath come back to me for a split second, until he touched my elbow and turned my body toward him.

"Did you know I'd be here?" he asked, his eyes darkening as they searched mine. I shook my head. His hand squeezed a little over my elbow and he pulled me an inch closer to him, his eyes narrowed on mine. "It didn't occur to you that maybe I'd be at a literary awards gala?"

"I didn't know it was a literary award thing. I thought it was for the library," I said, my voice low.

He stepped even closer. With my heels, I was eye level with his mouth, his plump lips. He'd trimmed his beard, some, but not enough for me not to want to run my fingers over it just to feel the prickliness of it against the pads of my fingers.

"Who did you bring?"

"You don't know him," I said, but he caught the widening of my eyes as soon as I said the words and realized that he knew of him. He waited. "Carson," I added.

Jensen's mouth dropped. He let go of my elbow and ran a hand through his hair, which was brushed and gelled. "You brought..." he let out a breath. "You brought a numbers guy to a room full of writers?" he asked in a shouted whisper.

I couldn't help it, I laughed. And when I didn't stop laughing, his expression changed from incredulous to amused.

"It's not funny, Mia."

"It's a little funny."

He got serious again, his hand on my wrist now, over my semicolon tattoo. He rubbed it with his thumb. I swallowed, trying to calm the butterflies his touch ignited.

"The thought of you here, with my colleagues, while you're with another guy, is going to drive me crazy for the rest of the night," he said, his voice deep. His eyes scanned over my face as if he was savoring every single one of my features.

"I'm sure you brought one of your brunch dates," I said in a quiet whisper. Jensen smiled and shook his head. "I already told you, I had an inkling you'd be here."

His words were light, but the ardor in his eyes carried enough weight to make my heart flip twice.

"So you didn't bring anyone?"

He shook his head, still looking at me that way. I tore my gaze away from his and looked over his shoulder, taking a step back when I spotted Carson walking over to us. I had a split second to look between the two of them and actually see the contrast between them. It was almost laughable. Not that Carson wasn't good looking, but the fact was, he'd never be Jensen.

"Hey, they just opened up the other room," Carson said as he reached us.

He came over to stand beside me and wrapped an arm around me, holding my waist. My eyes widened as I watched Jensen, who hadn't even acknowledged Carson's presence. He was too busy shooting daggers at me.

"Umm…" I said and cleared my throat. "Guess we better go."

"You're the guy on the Sunday paper, right?" Carson said, holding his free hand out to him. Jensen tore his gaze from mine and acknowledged his hand with a shake. "I'm a huge fan. I like the ones about your dating life. They're freaking hilarious. I think every single man in the city, with or without child can relate."

Jensen gave a small nod. The edge of the left side of his lip raised slightly in a sign I knew was gratefulness, but another may have mistaken for cockiness. He looked at me again, down at Carson's arm around me, and back at my face. He walked away without saying a word. Carson looked down at me as I gathered my camera and followed him into the room. I watched Jensen's back as he walked into the double doors. He walked like a man on a mission. Like he had no time for bullshit.

"Not much of a talker, huh?" Carson said, signaling at the doors that Jensen had walked into.

"Not really."

"You guys seemed to be talking for a little while, though. Did you have to interview him?"

I frowned. "Oh. No. I'm only here for pictures, no interviews. I, uh…" I paused. "Went to school with him."

"Nice. He's pretty popular with the ladies in my office. They're always drooling over him."

I bit the inside of my mouth and shook my head. Carson laughed.

"I take it you're not a fan?" he said as he held the door open for me.

I shrugged.

We found our table easily. It was right by the front of the stage, where everybody had to walk by in order to receive his or her award. They served the food first. I looked for Jensen but couldn't find his table, so I went back to my conversation with Carson and finally met the other photographer, Daniel, whom I'd only waved at from afar earlier.

While we were finishing up dinner, the host got on the microphone and started making a toast to the people who put the event together. Then he asked a presenter to go up to the stage. Everybody clapped for the known author, and I took the opportunity to snap a picture. More of those went on. After they presented the tenth award I started to wonder if they had a prize for anyone who could string a sentence together. When the eleventh person went up to present an award, though, my hands started to shake a bit. I brought the camera up to my face and snapped a picture.

"Is he your favorite?" Carson whispered near my ear. I jumped, but nodded. "You look like you got it bad for him," he whispered. I felt my lips tug into a smile.

"Neil Gaiman is king," I whispered, snapping another picture.

I looked over at Carson momentarily, in time to catch the shake of his head and the amusement his blond brows showed as they bounced up.

"Jensen Reynolds." The words came from the stage. I gasped and looked back over.

Jensen Reynolds?

Holy shit.

At the sight of Jensen walking toward us, I fumbled my camera. He looked over at me for a split second as everybody continued to clap, and walked on the stage, taking the award and standing behind the podium. Seeing him up there, holding that gold award in a room full of prestigious people made me tear up. A wave of emotion assaulted my senses. A rush of blood pounded in my ears as I watched him. He carried himself with the sureness of a god, summoning our attention, and in that moment, we were all his servants. Pride trickled through me as his eyes fell over the award before he scanned the crowd. It reminded me of his college graduation, when he reached the stage and held his degree in his hands and looked out into the crowd, his gaze searching until he'd found mine. My heart felt both heavy and filled with joy that day. Heavy because while the rest of the people in his graduating class were up there smiling at their parents, Patty and I had been the only ones there to support him. Joy because he'd worked his ass off to get up there.

"I guess I'm supposed to form coherent words now, huh?" Jensen said with a chuckle.

The crowd laughed along. I tried not to let any tears slip out of my eyes.

"This is my first award, and the man who handed it to me is one of my idols, so he could have handed me a handkerchief, and I would have probably cried into it and called it a night."

More laughter.

"And the fact that it's for breakout author of the year, that's…" Jensen shook his head, his words disappearing into the ambience. "Wow. It's just … I'm honored. I am really taken aback by this, so thank you. I want to take a moment to say something to that table over there." He lifted a finger and pointed at a table in the middle of the room. "They're young writers. Young, incredible minds who have found an escape in a craft most of us in here are fortunate enough to call our careers. I've spoken to a lot of you, and I know you're probably looking around this room, at these guys in tuxedos and these women in extravagant dresses, thinking, 'I'm from the Bronx, I don't fit in.' Well, I'm from the rough side of Long Beach, and spent a lot of my teenage years in Santa Barbara around kids who had a lot more than I did." He paused for a moment, and I felt new tears inside my eyes.

"The only thing I had was a journal, a pen, and a dream. I didn't even have somebody who believed in me until my foster mother, who happens to be my aunt, took me in, but even then I felt like I had nobody. Then I met this girl. This sweet, crazy, innocent girl named Mia, and everything changed. I shouldn't say I met her. I'd known her for a long time, but I hadn't seen her until that one night."

His eyes moved around the room until he found me. "And that one night, when we finally opened our eyes to each other, I went home and wrote ten poems about her. I turned those poems into a couple of stories, and that one story, written about that one girl, changed my life forever. So, I say to you, young writers: You only need one person to believe in you, even if that person is yourself. And I say to you, old writers, and there's a hell of a lot of you in here," he said, cuing more laughter.

"Thank you for accepting me into your tight circle. And I say to you, Mia Bennett—my photographer, my eyes, the girl of my dreams, the villain in my nightmares—that everything I owe, I owe to the night you let me look into your eyes and see the possibilities the world had to offer." He held my eyes as he said the words, and I could no longer keep my tears from spilling. I put my camera down on my lap and let him see them, let him see me, and even as I cried, I smiled. He said one more thank you before stepping off the stage.

"Holy shit," Carson breathed out. I wiped my face and turned back around when I felt like I'd regained my composure. "I guess you did more than just go to school with him."

Instead of answering, I took a sip of wine. When I looked out into the crowd again, my eyes found Jensen, still talking to the group of men. He lifted his award up to me in a toast. I did the same with the glass of wine.

"Congratulations," I mouthed.

"Thank you," he mouthed back. Just as I was about to turn back to Carson, who'd tapped me on the shoulder, Jensen said, "Wait for me."

I blinked rapidly. Wait for him where? *Here?* My head snapped to Carson.

"I'm pretty sure this is over," he said, dragging his hand across the ivory table linen until he reached my hand. "Shall we go?"

My mouth opened and closed like a puppet's. I nodded and exchanged information with Dan, who said he was going to stay and speak to Beatrice. Then I excused myself to go to the bathroom, trying to buy time. And finally, when I realized Jensen wouldn't be out of there anytime soon, I let Carson lead me out to yet another ÜBER of doom. In the car, he held my hand.

"Thanks for coming with me," I said.

He smiled. "Of course. Thank you for bringing me. Now you'll have to let me take you out to eat somewhere." He paused, tilting his head. "Maybe Friday?"

"Uh…" I let my response hang as the car slowed down and stopped in front of my building, Carson helped me exit. We stood, looking at each other. I wondered if he'd try to kiss me. This hardly constituted as a date, with him being on his phone the whole time and me crying over another man's words. Not that a kiss has to happen on a date, first or otherwise. Lord knew I'd kissed men in much more informal settings, but still. I hoped he wouldn't try to kiss me. When he leaned down, his lips brushing against my cheek, I didn't back away. Maybe I should let him kiss me. Maybe that was exactly what I needed after a night as emotionally draining as this had been. His lips touched the edge of mine for half a second, before he backed away slowly and gave me his best Riddler grin.

"Kissing is for real first dates," he said.

I chuckled awkwardly, because what else could I do? What kind of a man did that kind of shit? I sighed as I watched his ÜBER take off. Clearly a man that was not my type did that kind of shit.

Jensen Talks

I went to a gala at the New York Public Library this weekend, and it was phenomenal. From the attendance, to the speeches, and finally the awards. I was honored to get one. I don't know how I did it, but I gave the longest speech of my life up there, and was fortunate enough to have one of the people I thanked sitting in the audience to witness it. I'm not a big crier; people seem to think I am because they think writers are in touch with their feelings. While that may be true, I'm not a crier, but if I ever had broken down in public, it would have been while I was up there accepting that award.

I said all of these things to this woman, my life sweetheart, and she disappeared after that. When we were together I used to call her Road Runner, partly because she was the fastest girl on the Cross Country team, but mainly because whenever she got mad at something, or didn't know how to handle a situation, she would get out of it. That's basically what's happening, and there's nothing worse than deafening silence. Especially this kind. The kind that happens when you desperately need a job, or when you're house hunting, or you're waiting for acceptance letters from colleges. It seems like every time we need something, life finds a way to tell us to sit and wait. Basically, that's what I'm doing right now.

New York Public Library: Thumbs Up.

Question of the day: @chrisalbano422 "Do you believe that you never love anyone completely after you lose your first love?"

My answer: Although

this hasn't been the case
for me, I believe other
people might.

Of all the things I could have misplaced, my phone was the worst one. The next morning I had to be in the conference room for a meeting to discuss what couples we agreed on and which ones we didn't think should be in the main part of the special. Since I was a couple of minutes early, I was able to catch up with Katie before heading to the meeting room. My stomach was turning at the thought of seeing Jensen after the speech he'd given. I hadn't waited and now I didn't even know if he'd called. I hadn't seen my phone since before the event, which was starting to worry me. I blamed it on ÜBER.

Fran gave me a huge hug as soon as I reached her outside of the conference room.

"Did you get my tweet about the Public Library?"

I nodded. "Did mine not go through? My reception was crap in there, and to top it off, I can't find my phone, though I'm sure it's somewhere in the pile of laundry I have to get done."

"Oh no! Hopefully you find it soon."

"Hopefully," I said, following her into the room. I waved at Ross and Anabelle who were already in there.

"I saw the picture you posted on Twitter! You looked stunning in that dress. I'm so sad I missed it." Fran said, pausing to look toward the door. "And here comes the man of the hour! Jen, did you see Mia at the gala? Didn't she look stunning?"

I looked down at my feet, hoping to hide the way my face heated at the mention of his name.

"She looked exceptional," he said. I brought my gaze up to his and smiled. He returned it.

"Did you take a date?" Fran asked.

Jensen's demeanor changed instantly, darkening and getting serious.

"I did."

Fran gasped and clapped once. "You did! You met someone … or was it a friend?"

"I sort of met someone."

Her mouth hung open. "Did you end up going online?"

I laughed. "No. I didn't think it was safe to jump in the same waters you swam in."

"Nonsense," she said with a laugh. "So, tell me, was he cute?"

"Yeah," I said, feeling hyperaware of the weight of Jensen's stare.

"Did you kiss him?" I felt my entire body heat up at the question. When I didn't answer, she soldiered on. "Oh my God! You totally did. So there's potential there!"

I brought my gaze back up to where Jensen stood. He was staring at me in a way that made me feel guilty so I looked away quickly. As much as I liked making him jealous, disappointment was not a look I liked to see on his face. The meeting started fine. Ross said he'd contacted some of the people I was set to take pictures of this week, Anabelle said the same, and Jensen stayed quiet, brewing, the entire time. It shouldn't have bothered me, really. I owed him nothing. Yet I felt like I owed him at least the decency to not talk about my dating life in font of him, especially after all of the things he'd said in that speech.

After the meeting was over, I stayed behind, looking at the prints of the couples they thought they'd keep. It meant that I would have to take new pictures, probably tell them to dress up more and meet me in a different location. Because of the snow as of late, I wasn't sure where I would take them. When I heard the door slam, my head snapped up. The room had cleared out, save for Jensen, who was leaning against the door looking like a schoolteacher monitoring Saturday detention. He wasn't even looking at me. The short-sleeved Sherlock Holmes shirt he wore rode up as his hands tucked into the back pocket of his jeans. Finally, after a moment, as if he'd figured out what he was going to say to me, he looked up.

Our eyes met like two freight trains that had just noticed they were on the same track, on full alert and full of caution. We looked at each other for one beat, two, before he strode over to me. I flattened against the seat I was in and clutched the armrests when he reached me and swiveled the chair to face him.

"You fucking kissed him?" he asked, sitting in the seat beside mine and moving until our knees were touching.

I swallowed.

"I would hardly call it a kiss," I whispered.

The ghost of a smile tugging at his lips was the last thing I saw before his mouth was on mine. I forgot to breathe. People said that was impossible, but I completely forgot to breathe, and when my mouth opened it was to take some of his breath, or maybe some of what I'd left behind inside of him when he left me. My hands reached out and grabbed his hair, tugging as his tongue met mine. He eased away from me slowly, placing chaste kisses on my lips and the corners of my mouth as he did. Finally, he looked at me. I took a breath, let it out, and looked at him like he was crazy.

"What would you call that?" he asked.

I tried not to smile. Looking in his eyes, I reminded myself of the storm they so often held. Told myself how difficult it would be for me to trust him again. But as he sat there, smiling at me like he knew he'd kissed me into submission, I could only smile back.

"A decent kiss."

He grinned. "Only decent?"

I shrugged.

"Want another go?"

"Definitely not! We're at work!" I pushed his chest.

He shrugged. "You're at work, I'm just here to work."

"You make no sense."

"I'm offering you my services since you're in need of a good kiss."

"I didn't say it was a bad kiss; I just said I wouldn't even consider it one."

His eyes narrowed, as if the thought sunk in again. "I can't believe you fucking kissed that loser."

"Now he's a loser?"

"He was always a loser. Now he's a bigger loser."

I laughed. "You're an idiot."

"But not a loser. There's a difference," he said. A smile tugged at his lips as he looked at me. "Go out with me tonight."

I stopped smiling and wheeled my chair back slightly. "Where?"

"A concert."

"A concert?" I frowned, trying to think of what concerts I'd heard of. The problem is I hadn't heard of any. The only gossip I got was from a homeless dude on the subway on my way to yoga in the mornings, so if Dave didn't know, I didn't either.

"Yes. A concert. Tonight. I'll pick you up at five, we'll eat, have a much needed conversation, go to the concert, and have fun."

"I haven't even agreed to this and you have it all planned out?"

"I don't have time to waste, Mia. Say yes and get it over with."

My mouth dropped. "For your information, the only reason I'm not concerned about whose concert you want to drag me to is because we have the same taste in music, but dinner?"

"Yes, dinner. Consider it a perk since you clearly need better people to hang out with while you're here … and the concert is Mumford, so you're welcome."

I gasped. "No fucking way."

"Yes fucking way."

I bolted out of my seat and into his with a force that kicked us both off the chair and onto the floor in a series of "fuck," "shit," "fuck that hurt," "what the hell did you do that for?" and ending in a fit of laughter as we lay on the floor looking at each other. When our laughter died down, he stood and offered his hand to help me up, which I took.

"I'll pick you up at five," he said, his voice deep and quiet.

"Okay, but no more kissing," I whispered.

It wasn't until I was on my way home to look for my phone that it dawned on me that he had no idea where I lived. How the hell was he going to pick me up?

I found my phone exactly where I thought it would be, inside the basket of dirty laundry. I was rushing out, brushing my wet hair and trying to towel it dry so that streaks of water would stop pouring down my shoulders when I heard a loud knock on the door. Because I didn't have my phone on me earlier, I wasn't sure if it was the air conditioning guy again or someone knocking on the wrong door—again—since that had happened three times in the past week. I tied the towel around myself and walked over. Looking through the peephole, I gasped and took a step back. Jensen was standing on the other side of the door, wearing jeans, a short-sleeved black V-neck shirt, and holding a jacket in his left hand. I swung the door open.

"How the hell do you know where I live?"

He stiffened as his gaze washed over me, traveling from my face down to my bare feet and back in a slow sweep. He didn't say a word for a moment, and I finally backed up to let him step in.

"Hello?" I said, closing the door behind us.

He turned to face me, stepping closer to me, and suddenly I was very aware of how naked I was below my towel. When he reached me, he closed his eyes and took a deep breath.

"Go get dressed. I can't fucking think right now!" He waved his arms once as if he were annoyed at the mere fact that I was in front of him to begin with, and it pissed me off because I hadn't even invited him over!

"There's not much to think about! How did you know I was staying here?"

"You said you lived in Millie's old place. This is Millie's old place. I came over once when Seth made steak. There. Go get dressed," he said in a huff.

I let out a frustrated growl and rolled my eyes. As I brushed past him, I purposely pressed the front part of my body against his arm. He groaned.

"Mia."

"I'm going to get dressed!"

"I'm trying not to accidentally rip that off you, and you're rubbing yourself all over me!" he said in a low growl that sent a shiver down my spine.

I disappeared into the bedroom and dressed quickly. As much as I loved how much I affected him, I knew I had to keep myself in check. It would be easy to go down that road again with him. It was easy the first time, and it ended badly. It would be the same this time around.

"Isn't it freezing outside?" I asked once I stepped out of the room.

He gave me a full onceover. I was wearing black Converse, like him, jeans, like him, a black shirt, like him, and had a jean jacket over it. He chuckled. "This is interesting. And no, it's not, the bipolar weather decided to grace is with warmer weather today."

I disappeared into my room again. I wasn't going to change just because we looked like we'd planned our damn outfits to match. Fuck that. But I did want to wear a hat.

"Cute," he said upon my return. "I'm sure the temperature will drop later though."

"This place really does have the most bipolar weather."

"Only as of late," he said, waiting for me to lock the door. "It's almost as if California spit out all of its crazies and they landed in New York."

I bumped him with my shoulder as I put my keys away in my purse. "You're hilarious."

"I try."

"Where are we going?" I asked, as we walked past the cabbie sitting in the front of the building. "Subway's the other way."

Jensen ignored my question, but reached out for my hand and held it as he continued walking around the corner, into a parking lot. There, on the side, before you got past the cashiers, was a familiar matte black bike. I tightened my grip in his hand.

"You still have your bike?"

He chuckled. "Evidently."

"I thought you would have gotten rid of it."

"Why would I get rid of my Harley?" he asked, frowning.

"Because you have a daughter! Oh my God. Don't tell me you make her ride this thing." I paused. "Kids aren't allowed to ride motorcycles, are they?"

He shrugged nonchalantly. "It's not like she doesn't wear a helmet."

I gaped at him and covered my mouth with my hands, but narrowed my eyes when I caught the twinkle in his eyes before his lips spread into a grin. I charged toward him, and he laughed, catching my hands over the lapels of his jacket before I could fully shove him.

"You're such a bastard."

"You're cute when you get worked up," he said, bringing his mouth down to my ear. My grip tightened over his jacket when he dragged his tongue along the shell of it. "Even more so when it has to do with Olivia." My heart spiked. "Are you still scared of bikes?" he asked. I was surprised I could hear him over the roaring in my ears. I nodded in response to his question. His lips made their way down to my cheek, and then the corner of my mouth. "Do you trust me?" he asked.

My eyes slammed shut at his whispered words and the memory of the last time I'd heard them. My then-teenage self so eager to climb on whatever it was he was offering. Our breaths mingled in anticipation for my answer, and when I opened my eyes and our gazes met, I found it in the sincerity his eyes held, and the countless feelings that shone behind them. I nodded.

"I do."

He breathed out heavily, his large hands framing and covering the sides of my face as he pulled me in for one last kiss before we got on the bike.

The bike roared down the streets in an effortless weave, folding into the darkness. I gripped my arms around his waist and lay my face on his back, closing my eyes to the unchartered territories in my thoughts. What if this ended up being more than I could handle? What scared me most was that I wanted this to be a date. I wanted to treat it like a date. I wanted him to kiss me and touch me and fold me into the side of his body while we stood at the concert. I squeezed my eyes shut tighter. *Remember what he did. Remember why he left. Remember why you avoided him all these years.* And I did. I did remember all of those things. I'd been so busy reminding myself of his past mistakes, that I'd forgotten what it felt like to live in the moment. Fuck it. I owed this to myself. I needed closure, and I was going to get it while I was here. I opened my eyes once more and smiled as we zoomed by the sidewalks of people, most in business attire, some holding shopping bags.

The bike came to a stop once he pulled in an alley between two old buildings. I took a couple of steps out onto the sidewalk and smiled at the gay pride flag that waved across the street.

"What is this place?" I asked, looking over my shoulder, then turning fully so I wouldn't miss Jensen's confident stride toward me. I missed seeing that. Damn it. He walked like a man who knew he was the sun and all the planets were in his orbit, not the other way around.

"Hell's Kitchen."

"Oh, where is it?" I asked, looking in both directions on the sidewalk.

Jensen chuckled as he grabbed my hand, lacing his fingers through mine. My heart spiked at his touch, and when he stroked my hand over with his thumb as he gave me a tender look, I felt something quake inside of me.

"All of this is Hell's Kitchen."

I was impressed. We went into a little hole in the wall that he'd heard had amazing chicken and waffles. Of course, I ended up getting that. Jensen ordered octopus. I shook my head.

"What? I heard it's good."

"What's the deal with you and octopus?" I asked, my eyes falling over his now-covered forearm.

He smiled. "I like them."

"They're kind of ugly and slimy," I said, my nose scrunching at the thought. "Not saying your tattoo is ugly. I like it."

He chuckled.

"But really, why an octopus?" I only asked because he was the kind of person who didn't just do anything. He didn't just go and get a tattoo because he liked some words. He got them because he felt the words. It took him a while to get the ones I knew were on his ribs. I tried not to think about it, and cleared my head when the waitress came and got our drink orders. We both got water. He was driving, and I wanted to watch the concert completely sober.

"They intrigue me. They have three hearts," he said, and paused when I coughed over my sip of water.

"Why the hell would you want three hearts? Most of the time I want to give up the one I already have."

Jensen only smiled. I could tell he wanted to say something, but he continued on, "They also die after they mate."

"You're not selling me on this creature thus far."

That made him laugh and shrug. "I'm not trying to."

"You're not telling me anything. I want to know why."

He gave me a look that zipped through my bones and seeped into my bloodline. I sat on my hands, suddenly feeling really cold.

"Obviously they have three hearts for a reason, and I'm not an octopus, but one of their hearts doesn't function when they're swimming. I saw it on a special once, and I thought, 'Shit, that's me.' My heart doesn't function when I'm doing ordinary things."

I was afraid to ask, so I cleared my throat. "And the dying thing?"

He gave me a small, sad smile. "I love Olivia. She's the thing I'm most proud of, and if I had to go back…" He paused for a moment to make sure I'd understand it. I nodded because I knew what was coming and I was okay with it. "I wouldn't change anything, but only because my mistakes brought me her." He took a sip of water. "But when that whole thing happened, a part of me died. A big part of me died."

I could only nod in response.

We small talked a little bit, about my family, my mom, my dad, Rob, and his boyfriend. Then we talked about his foster mom, Patty, Victor, Estelle, and Oliver. When we had exhausted that topic, he looked at me again, and I knew what was coming.

"We need to talk," he said.

"I thought we were doing that already."

He shot me a look. I sighed and made room for the server to put our plates in front of us.

"I'm sorry I took a date the other night. I really didn't know you would be there," I said first.

"It's fine. I'm over that. It obviously didn't go well, and selfishly that makes me happy. I want to discuss other things."

I laughed nervously. "Let me guess, you want to talk about things that happened when we broke up."

He bobbed his head side to side. "Sort of. I want to talk about my dating Krista and her getting pregnant."

Something lurched inside my stomach. I put my utensils down with a clink. "Over dinner? You want to discuss this over dinner?"

"We need to talk about it, Mia."

"Why?" I groaned, rubbing a hand over my forehead.

"Because we're never going to move forward if we don't revisit the past and discuss our problems."

"I don't want to move forward." I knew I was pouting like a baby, but I couldn't talk about that stuff. I couldn't bear to relive it.

His hand slid over the table and covered mine. He turned it over and placed his on my palm, waiting for me to look up. In that moment, his eyes were so soft and understanding that I wanted nothing more than to do what he asked of me, but I couldn't, not there.

"After," I whispered, feeling tears prick my eyes. Clearly I wasn't as healed as I once thought. He conceded with a nod and continued to eat.

"Where do you meet the women you take on dates?" I asked, taking a bite of my chicken when my appetite found me again.

Jensen chuckled. "You can't talk about Krista, but you can talk about current women I date?"

I groaned at the mention of her name, but pushed it away and shrugged. I didn't really want to picture him with any woman, if I was being honest, but it was easier for me to accept that he was a young, single male who dated.

"I'm weird," I said.

He shook his head in amusement. "Match, E-Harmony, shit like that."

I gaped at him. "You're on Match?"

His brows rose at my loudness. He looked around the restaurant and chuckled. "Yeah, I am. Why is that so hard to believe?"

I was still gaping. *Because you're hot? Because you're so successful? Because ... you're really freaking hot?* I didn't say any of it, but I knew he knew what I was thinking. I could tell from the sure smile on his face.

"There are a lot of good looking people on there, you know."

"Had I known, I would have joined a long ass time ago."

He smiled. "Maybe they would have matched us."

"Maybe." I paused, mulling that over. "That would have been awkward."

"Or perfect."

I sat on my hands again. "So have you found '*the one*'?"

He raised an eyebrow, shooting me a look as he tried to contain his smirk. "I sure have."

"You make it impossible to have a conversation with," I said, but I found that I was fighting a smile.

"You make it impossible to live life without," he said, looking straight into my eyes.

Despite my rattling heart and the way my blood fired through my veins, I managed to hit my forehead with the palm of my hand in an effort to defuse the moment, because I couldn't handle it. I couldn't handle the feels. Jensen smiled at my attempt, but the gleam stayed in his eyes. We left the restaurant smiling, just the way we arrived, and he promised to take me back to eat at other spots around there. As we walked back to the bike, I looked around in disbelief. I couldn't believe how many good looking gay men and women there were in one area.

"I mean, it's astounding," I said as we climbed on the bike.

Jensen chuckled. "It is. It's a cool neighborhood, right?"

I nodded, looking around one last time before we zipped off. We ended up parking the bike outside cute little houses in Brooklyn and riding the subway to Coney Island for the concert. While we were sitting on the train, I rested my legs over his in order to save space for the people beside us. He was rubbing over my thighs in a massaging motion that made my insides a puddle of mush.

"I want to take you home," he said in a soft murmur against my ear. My heart doubled in speed.

"Maybe I'll let you," I whispered. I only knew he'd heard me because he pulled me closer until my face was resting over his hard chest and he kissed my forehead.

When we got to our stop, it seemed like a million people got off the subway. Jensen held my hand tighter as we made our way through the crowd and onto the street.

"Holy shit. It's freezing here," I said.

His arm was around my shoulder, pulling me to his side before I could finish my sentence. I shivered as I moved further into him, trying to steal all of his warmth.

"It's because we're on the water."

As soon as we made it into the park and handed our tickets over, I pulled his hand and led him inside and to the front of the stage. I was smiling so wide when I turned around, and he was laughing at my excitement.

"Nobody's here yet, babe."

My smile slipped away slowly, and he noticed. He pulled my hand until I was pressed up against him, my head on his chest. We stood like that for a little while, his chin resting over my head and his arms around me while mine hung loose on either side of me. I was sure I couldn't do this. With anybody else? Hell yes. I'd had one-night stands before. I could be totally unattached to men. But this wasn't any man. This was *the* man, or who I thought was the man. I pushed my thoughts away when he led me to the merchandise tent. By the time we'd both pulled our matching hoodies over our heads, only because they only had one style, and got a beer each, we were back to laughing as we pointed out different people in the crowd.

When I looked around again, I was surprised to see how many people had gotten there while we'd been talking. Soon we were squished a little closer, but still had enough breathing room that we hopped around. The opening act started and the stadium became alive, jumping along and snapping pictures, but it wasn't until the main act came out that you could really feel the vibrant crowd. I'd been living in Manhattan long enough to know that the city had a heartbeat, fast and resilient, but Brooklyn was a different story. Brooklyn's heart beat. It actually beat. As I looked around, I felt like I was home. I felt it. Despite the cold, despite the fact that I was miles away from my family, I felt like I was where I belonged in that moment.

Jensen's hand closed over mine as "The Wolf" started. We smiled at each other as we jumped and sang along. We did that for three songs, back to back, and I couldn't stop laughing and smiling. I couldn't remember having that much fun since the last time I'd hung out with Estelle and Robbie. A couple of songs went by, but when I heard the beat to "After the Storm" start playing, it was like something poignant was being pumped directly into my heart, and spreading through me like a slow insulin. As if on cue, we both stopped moving. Our hands found each other's again, and our eyes quickly followed. Suddenly, Marcus wasn't singing to me, but to us, and I couldn't stop the tears from swimming in my eyes. We faced each other. Jensen's hands framed my face; mine held his wrists, closing over the scripted name of his daughter and the words *Let it Be*.

As if the song and the moment we were sharing weren't emotional enough, his lips started moving along with the lyrics. When he started singing about taking me by the hand and standing tall, and then about a time when love won't break my heart, I felt something inside of me shift. Some part of me made room for feelings I'd tried to bury. And once that happened, I felt everything. I felt him asking me to forgive him, to let go of the past and embrace this moment. It was then that the tears began to spill, and once they did I couldn't stop crying.

Soon my crying went from just crying to full on bawling, and Jensen's thumbs moved to wipe my tears. He brought his face down, his lips pressing against mine softly, his tongue seeking permission I quickly gave, and we stood there, in a crowd full of people, with our favorite band playing, and gave into something unstoppable. Because that was what we had. It was unstoppable, unyielding, and all-consuming. And it wasn't perfect. It never had been, because we weren't perfect. He was a mess of brokenness, a mess of emotions that had been fucked with long ago, and I was the glue that once tried to fix him. But I couldn't. I couldn't fix him because I wasn't his savior, as he wasn't mine. I was just as lost as he was, and maybe that was what attracted us to one another, our vulnerability and willingness to be with another lost soul.

When we pulled back from the kiss, his hands still on my face, I continued to cry. I didn't cry because I was sad. I didn't cry because I was letting go of my anger. I cried because I felt it. I felt everything. And I hadn't felt emotion like that in such a long time that I was sure a part of me had broken off when he left me. Maybe it did. Maybe he took the part of me with the ability to give herself fully to another human being. I wasn't sure I wanted it back. Not if he was the missing link.

I managed to collect myself when the band started a more upbeat song, and wiped my tears, took a breath, and after a long moment, we started jumping again. After that point we were always touching, always hyperaware of each other's presence. Even more so than we already had been.

When it was over, we waited until some of the crowd walked out and followed suit, but took a right, toward the water, instead of a left toward the subway.

"It's so quiet out here," I said.

"It is. I've never been out here before," Jensen said, pulling me into his side.

I looked up at him. "You're kidding."

"Nope."

We stopped walking when we got to the edge, right by the sand. I turned to face him then.

"Do you miss home?"

He tilted his head, seemingly mulling something over until he finally looked at me, his gaze serious.

"I miss you," he said, and paused to let that sink in. "I miss you," he repeated, louder, his gaze not moving away from my wide eyes as he caressed my cheek with the back of his hand. "I miss you, and I'm sick of treating this like a crystal vase I'm afraid to tamper with in case it breaks." He leaned down and placed his forehead against mine, letting out a cold and smoky breath that tickled over my nose.

"The vase is already broken," I whispered.

"If it's already broken, why are you so afraid of it?"

"Because I don't know if I want to walk on all that shattered glass again."

He cupped my face with his large hand, his thumb caressing my cheekbone. "I'd walk on glass if that meant getting to you. I'd swim an ocean, climb a mountain, I'd do anything."

I blinked my eyes away from him, back in the direction of the vast ocean just steps away from us, and shook my head. "Words are just words, Jensen."

"Words are my life."

"I know that, but saying things, writing things, those aren't things that are going to get me back. You have to see that. You have to see that you leaving and getting married was an action I'm not sure I can move past far enough to trust you again."

He sighed heavily and clasped his hands behind his head. He closed his eyes for a second before dropping his arms and looking at me again. "Tell me what to do. Tell me what I need to do to get you back."

I stood there, gaping at him for a moment. Waves crashed, people laughed in a far distance, yet the world stood still for us, for this moment. Once upon a time I'd dreamt of those words coming from his mouth. Once upon a time I craved them, I felt like I needed them, but that time passed. And as much as I loved to hear them even now, all these years later, I didn't know what to do with them.

"I don't know, Jensen. I honestly don't know," I said finally.

"Why did you tell me you wanted closure?"

Oh my God. I knew the closure thing would come back to bite me in the ass. I let out a laugh.

"Because I'm crazy, obviously." When he shot me a look, I got serious and conceded to tell the truth. "Because I want to stop comparing every asshole I date to you."

His chuckle was deep and rich. "No matter how much closure I give you, you're going to compare me to every single man you meet, Mia. It's the same for me. Nobody is ever funny enough, annoying enough, crazy enough, or beautiful enough to equate to you."

I looked away. "You can't say things like that."

"You want me to stand here and lie to you?" he asked. I shook my head and looked back at him. He had the most serious expression I'd ever seen on his face. Ever. His hands framed both sides of my face. "I'm sorry. I made a mistake. I've apologized a million times. I don't know what else you want me to say to you, but if there's something I can do, tell me."

I shook my head. "What's done is done."

He nodded. "Okay, so let's have that talk now. I'll start," he said, shooting me a pointed look as he dropped his hands. "I thought you were dating someone when Krista and I were…" He let the words hang, thank God, because I wasn't sure I could take it. "I heard it was serious, and I hadn't spoken to you in a couple of weeks, so…" He shrugged. "And then it happened, and I realized what a monumental thing it was because I couldn't have both. I couldn't have you and have the baby."

"Maybe you could have. You didn't even put that out there as an option for us."

"I couldn't, Mia. I couldn't." He let out a heavy sigh. "It was too much. Her family is too … they have money, and I was nobody. A poor little punk with a ride to a good college who got a rich girl pregnant." He paused again, reaching out for my hand as if he needed to make sure I wouldn't bail. "It was like my parents all over again."

I nodded in understanding. His parents, but backwards, because in his parents' case, his mom was the one without a dollar to her name.

"I get it, Jensen. I do. Honestly, I do. I've had five years to process this, but every time I see you—"

"Your world is thrown off its axis," he said.

"Basically."

"Do you think that'll happen to you again? Do you think that feeling of imbalance can be caused by just anything?"

I shook my head. I knew it couldn't. I'd dated enough guys to know few could do this.

"Don't you think it's worth the risk? Yes, you're leaving soon, but while you're here, don't you want to find out what this is?"

I tore my gaze away from his. "You should sell cars."

"I sell love. That's a lot harder to sell than cars."

My eyes fell to our joined hands, his unfinished infinity tattoo glaring at me, saying, *Remember me? Remember love? Don't do it.* On the other hand, when I threaded my fingers through his I focused on *Leave.* And then, I looked again, blinking my eyes to focus on the letter written by the fold of his ring finger. I squinted in the dim light, peeling the fingers. My eyes snapped up to his, heart hammering. I rubbed over the scripted *M* with my thumb. It had to come off, right?

"It's not temporary, Mia. You'll have to cut it off my skin."

"Jensen," I whispered, looking up at him again.

"Always," he said, cupping my face with his other hand. "You're always with me."

"When did you get it?" I asked, my voice a rasp.

"The last time I told you that I loved you."

This time when the tears pricked my eyes, it wasn't because of music or ambiance. I wrapped my arms around him and kissed him. It was soft, slow, and tender. It wasn't forgetful, or even forgiving, but one that held potential.

"Take me home," I said, a murmur against his lips.

"You're going to have to be more specific than that, babe," he said, tugging my bottom lip between his teeth.

"I want you to take me to your house," I said, tucking my hands into the back of his jacket. I slipped the tips of my fingers into the bottom of his shirt and ran them up his hard back. "Please," I added in a whisper as I scratched my way down his back. I could feel the heavy breathing in his chest against my own.

Hunger flashed in his eyes. His grip tightened over my hips. "Let's go, beautiful."

He weaved his bike around a two-story house and stopped in front of the garage as he waited for it to open.

"You may want to hold on to me again," he said.

My hands flew around him as he revved up the bike and moved it inside the garage. I looked around the two-car garage, which didn't have much aside from a black truck, a tool cabinet, and a pink Jeep suited for a little girl. My eyes stayed glued on that. I had a similar one as a kid. Our parents would take us out almost daily to ride around our neighborhood, me in my pink Jeep and Rob on his GI Joe bike as we tried to race to each stop sign. I wondered if Jensen got together with Krista to do things like that. I wondered if they got together often at all.

"Mia," Jensen said.

From the tone of his voice I knew I missed whatever he'd said before that. I blinked rapidly and looked at him.

"Yeah?"

He cocked his head, signaling the house. "Come on."

I followed him up two steps and into the house. The smell of wood hit me first. It wasn't the overpowering Abercrombie store type, more like new wood cabinets. As my eyes scanned the white walls, I wondered if he'd opted to keep them that way or if he just hadn't gotten around to painting them.

"How long have you lived here?"

He was standing beside me with his thumbs tucked into the front pockets of his jeans, his eyes on my face. "About two years?"

I breathed out heavily. Two years. "Did Olivia and her mom live here as well?"

"Just me. Olivia is here a lot, though, so technically she's been living here for just as long."

I walked forward, through an area with a long wooden table that looked like a park bench, until I reached the large kitchen.

"Oliver wasn't exaggerating," I said.

"About what?" Jensen asked, trailing closely behind me.

"He said your place was really nice." I looked around the kitchen and rounded the corner of the island in the center. "This is beautiful," I said, looking up to meet his gaze.

He stepped forward until he was on the other side of the island and placed his hands flat on the surface of it. The way he looked at me made me grip the counter on the side I was on.

"You haven't even seen the rest of it."

"This preview is enough for me to make a pretty accurate assessment that it is beautiful."

He grinned. "Maybe that's what I want everybody who comes here and stays on this floor to think."

"Maybe you're just trying to get me in your room."

That made him chuckle. He pushed back and shrugged off his leather jacket, laying it on the counter. My eyes made their way down his body and my heart picked up speed as images of what was underneath his clothes flashed in my mind.

"You want to see the rest?" he asked.

His voice was grating and deep, and made me want to lose all my inhibitions. My heart ricocheted wildly. One second stretched into two, then three, and all I could do was stand there, holding on to the edge of the counter as we gazed into each other's eyes. Neither of us wanted to make the next move first. The aftermath of our actions teetered on this moment, and we both knew it could either be tragic or beautiful. We didn't know how to have one without the other. I took a step away from the counter. He followed my lead. We moved until we reached a middle ground, and he held his hands out to mine.

We were spiked feelings and muted pleas, only daring to speak with our eyes. And as he led me up the stairs it occurred to me that I'd put so much emphasis on our love, on him being my other half, and how being near him and touched by him made me feel complete, that it wasn't until he left that I really became a whole person by myself. And that was what scared me about all of this. I was scared that I would lose myself so deeply in him again that when this was over, I wouldn't know where I ended and he began. I shook the thought away. I wasn't that girl anymore. I knew I was a whole person, and I'd survive without him just fine, but a part of me couldn't help but wonder.

The smell of him engulfed me as we walked into the first door we reached. He didn't drop my hand, but caressed my arm as I looked around his room, at the dark blue walls and low king-sized bed sitting in the middle. Everything, from the minimalistic décor to the scent screamed organized and embodied man.

"It's very … you."

Jensen chuckled. "I hope that's a compliment."

I dropped my hand from his as I looked at him, pulling my bag over my head as I did. "It is," I said, and looked at my bag momentarily.

"What's the smile for?" he asked.

"You should let me take pictures of you."

He raised an eyebrow. "What kind of pictures are we talking?"

I laughed, slapping his chest. My amusement died down when he held my hand there, on his hard pec, right over the thumping of his heart.

"Are you going to let me interview you?" he asked, still holding my hand. His heart matched the rhythm of mine.

I nodded, my response caught in my throat.

He turned our bodies to face each other and grabbed the strap of my bag with one long finger. With the other hand, he cupped my face, tilting it until our gazes were locked again.

"Come. Take your pictures," he said, moving me forward as he moved back, toward the bed. He sat at the foot of it, scooting back so that I could straddle him, then leaned back on his hands.

My hands shook as I opened my bag and got the camera out. I'd taken my smaller one, the one I carried with me most of the time. Taking the lens cap off, I snapped a picture. He frowned, because he wasn't ready for it, and I smiled and snapped one of his frown.

"Do you take pictures of every asshole you date?" he asked.

I smiled, looking at him through the lens.

"Is that your first interview question?"

"How many are you giving me?"

I shrugged. "Five?"

"So then yes."

"No."

He shot me a confused look. I snapped another picture.

"No, I don't take pictures of every asshole I date."

"Too personal?" he asked, his voice a soft murmur. He sat up and placed his hands on my thighs, moving them up my jeans and squeezing at the thickest part. My heart jumped.

"Way too personal," I whispered, looking into his eyes through the lens, the longing in them making me let out a shuddered breath.

"Maybe we should do this naked," he said, and smiled when he felt me stiffen. "To increase vulnerability."

I put the camera down beside us and pulled my hoodie over my head, tossing it aside, then lifted my head in a nod. He chuckled and pulled his shirt over his head, his muscles tensing with each movement. I let out a breath, pulling back slightly so that I could look at him. He'd always been lean, a swimmer's body, but he'd filled out in the past five years. The cut of his muscles more defined. I put my hand on his shoulder and dragged it down slowly. He sucked in a breath. I could feel his eyes on mine. The ink on his chest spread further than what I'd seen before, more art added. My breath hitched at the sight of the Road Runner tattoo on his inner bicep. My eyes flew to his. *When did you get this?*

He smiled. "It was a birthday gift I gave myself a few years back."

A few years back, when I'd been ignoring the hell out of him, probably dating some other guy. The thought stabbed at me. I swallowed, feeling ashamed as I looked back at it. I moved on to the poem written on the other side, taking up the length of his ribcage. How often had I dreamt of being that bluebird it spoke of? The things I would have given to tuck myself into the cage inside his heart…

His arms wrapped around me, the warm feel of them against me making a rush of blood flow through me. His hands unsnapped my bra, his eyes on mine the entire time, even as he dragged the straps down my arms. He leaned in then, tucking his face into my neck and kissing me there before his lips began to make a trail from the hollow of my throat down my sternum, leaving a warm blaze in their wake. I felt myself flush and pulled away slightly.

"More pictures?" he asked, his hands back on my ribcage, making their way to my breasts.

I rocked slightly, rubbing against the hardness in his jeans. He groaned, covering my breasts with his hands, kneading softly, his thumbs brushing against my nipples. I moaned.

"More pictures."

"Okay." He brought his mouth down to where his thumbs had been, and my hands flew to his hair as I rocked against him once more.

"Mia," he said, his voice a growl on my nipple.

"What?" I said in a gasp, tugging harder when I felt his teeth on me.

"You need to stop rocking like that if you want to finish this photo shoot."

"You need to stop moving your mouth like that if you want to finish this interview."

He pulled back, looking at me with a smile, and I took the opportunity to grab my camera as he switched our positions and shifted so that my back was on the bed and he was between my legs. I snapped a picture just as his face was coming down, and set it aside right before his lips met mine.

"Maybe those pictures will give you the proof you need," he said, unbuckling and tugging off my jeans, my panties going with them.

"Proof of what?" I asked, gasping loudly at the feel of his hands exploring my fully naked body, my neck, my breasts, my stomach, my thighs.

"Proof of how much I want you." His hands moved slowly, as if he was looking for something he'd lost inside my body. Maybe he was.

My hands were working on his jeans when he stopped me and stood, taking them off himself, slowly, as if he was doing a striptease for me. I sat up on my elbows to watch him.

"I don't think the proof is in the pictures," I said, my eyes dropping.

He grinned as he walked toward the bed, grabbing my feet and spreading my legs when he reached me.

"That's not the kind of want I was talking about," he said as he nestled between my legs again, dipping his head until his lips were pressed against mine, his tongue slipping into my mouth. . Our tongues moved in a synchronized motion of lifelong lovers. His body covered mine as he placed me back on the bed, and he broke the kiss, brushing the tip of his nose against mine.

"I want to touch you," I whispered, moving my hand between our bodies, along the squares of his abdomen. His cock twitched against my stomach, but he stopped my hand from reaching it.

"I want so much," he murmured, tugging on my bottom lip. "I want to get inside of you and fuck you endlessly." He dragged his mouth down to my neck. "Hard and fast." He pulled a nipple into his mouth and swirled his tongue around it. He paused, his eyes flashing to mine when he felt my hands in his hair, pushing him into me. "And then slowly, taking my time with you. You like that?"

I nodded. He did it again before he pulled back to rain kisses down the middle of my stomach, nipping every couple of movements, on my hips, by my belly button, right over my folds. I was running out of breath, and he hadn't even reached his destination. My lips parted, a moan escaping me. I arched off the bed when I finally felt his tongue between my legs. His hands held down my hips as he went back in and did it again, letting out a sated moan.

"But first, I need to taste you." His tongue flicked against my clit. "I need to erase any memory this has that doesn't involve me." My back arched as he licked again. "I need to make sure," he said, sucking my clit into his mouth and letting go with a pop. "That I get reacquainted with you properly before I can bury myself inside you." He licked again, and this time, brought his hands up to my chest and tweaked my nipples. I panted and writhed, as he continued to feast on me. I moved, my feet rubbing against his cock, and rubbing again when I felt just how hard he was. He made a growling sound in the back of his throat, breathing heavily. And then I couldn't move my feet anymore. My eyes closed, and I let myself get lost in feelings that were too powerful for me to deny.

The feel of his tongue, thick and hot against me. His large hands expertly making their way up and down my body. The nips of his teeth against me. I couldn't think as the tingling feeling started at the base of my spine and made its way through my body. I let out an unintelligible scream and begged him to fuck me as my orgasm rocked through me. He chuckled at my command, his wet lips making their way up my body again, slowly, in a torturous pace that nearly made me cry. And then he finally reached my face, gray eyes flickered between mine as his thumb caressed my jaw, then made its way into my mouth, dragging out slowly against the inside of my bottom lip.

"I need to get something," he said, his voice low, his breath ragged, his eyes raw as they looked into mine.

I felt the question at his pause: do I need to get something? I nodded.

He stilled momentarily before conceding, leaning over me, to the drawer of the nightstand, ripping it open and sliding it down his length. The tattoo on the inside of his other bicep caught my eye, the one that said *Olivia*. One last warning from the past looked back at me, but was quickly forgotten when he thrust inside of me. I took a loud, gasped breath and arched my hips to welcome him fully. He rocked out slowly, in a way that stifled my airwaves, and back in deeply, hard, but just as slowly. His forehead dropped to mine as he breathed out heavily.

"God. I missed this," he said, his voice strained. He pulled out again, nearly all the way, and pushed back in hard and fast. I yelped. "I missed you." His movements became more frantic, picking up speed and strength each time he entered fully.

I felt everything. There was desperation in our lovemaking. It was a defining moment for me, for us, one in which we looked directly into our pain and questioned its weight on us. *I missed you, too*, I answered with my mouth on his. *I missed you so much, I was sure it would kill me some days.*

I'm sorry, the backs of his hands said in their caress.

"Give me a chance," he murmured aloud. His thrusts deepened as beads of sweat formed over his pulled brows. "Let me show you how good it can be." His teeth grazed over my earlobe. "Let me show you how good *I* can be."

I didn't have an answer to that, so I closed my eyes and scratched down his back as he rode me harder, deeper, until everything around me burst and blended, like watercolors.

Jensen Talks

I took my lovely date to Eataly this past weekend. If you're ever in the city and want a one-stop shop where you can get wine, chocolate, and incredible food from different places, this is the place you need to visit. From pizza to pig ears. I hadn't been there, so my idea wasn't to impress her, but if you want to impress a woman, TAKE HER TO EATALY.

They have a Nutella Bar.

Nutella Bar, gentlemen. And in case I need to state the obvious, Nutella is a bigger aphrodisiac than oysters.

My date and I, we had a good weekend.

Eataly: A MUST if you're in the city.

Question of the day

from: @JugiandLiba

The perfect New York hot dog has…?

Answer: Mustard and relish.

"You weren't lying about the cold," were the first words out of Estelle's mouth when she hugged me. She and Oliver had arrived to visit for the weekend and were making a stop at my apartment before they went to their hotel.

"I never lie about dreadful things," I said, squeezing her tight.

"Stop fondling my wife," Oliver said behind us. I dropped my hands and turned around, smiling as he drew me into his arms.

"We all know I have first dibs on her, Bean, so shut up. You're lucky you're hotter than me, because let's be real, that's the only reason she married you," I said, making him laugh as he let me go.

"Yes, thank God for my hotness," he said, pulling Estelle closer to him as he rolled their suitcase into the lobby of my building.

"This place is nice," Estelle said.

"I know, right? Sometimes I wonder why Millie and Seth didn't move here instead, but then I visit their place, and it's pretty damn clear why."

Estelle laughed. "That nice?"

"Hell yeah."

"Did you ever look for places in Brooklyn?" That was Oliver.

"Nope."

"Really?" he asked as we all stepped into the elevator.

I took a breath and pushed down on my floor. "Really."

"Jensen's place is nice," he said.

I could feel him watching the side of my face.

I tried really hard to hide my smile, but it was impossible. Jensen and I had agreed we'd take things one day at a time. We'd also agreed not to tell Oliver and Estelle until they visited. Agreed, but then he decided to write about our visit to Eataly in the damn newspaper, and I knew because I'd decided to start reading his columns again the day he wrote that one.

"Really?" I said when I felt I could manage a straight, nonchalant face.

"Wait. Have you seen him again?" Estelle asked.

"Do you not read the paper when I tell you to, Elle?" he asked.

I glared at him. Motherfucker.

She frowned. "You told me to read the paper?"

Oliver chuckled, shaking his head as he pulled her closer. "I put it beside you when you were eating breakfast on Sunday."

"Oh. I thought you were just putting it there so I could use it to cover the table so I wouldn't dirty it with my crafts. I didn't realize you wanted me to actually read it."

Oliver and I laughed, but mine was cut short when he turned to me with questioning eyes.

"Dude. Stop it. He could have been talking about anybody in that stupid paper!"

He shrugged. "Maybe, but he said 'lovely date.' Vic and I have been making fun of him all week for that shit."

I laughed because I couldn't help it. "That's so mean, Bean."

"I knew it!" he said, as if he'd won a stupid gold medal. "I fucking knew it."

He fished out his phone, and I snatched it from him quickly.

"Don't you fucking dare," I said. "Seriously, first of all, it's nothing serious, and secondly, we wanted you to see for yourself how not serious it was when you got here."

"Not serious," Oliver scoffed, taking his phone from my hand. "Have you met him?"

I shot him a look. Estelle shot me a look. I shot her a different one, one that screamed, "We'll talk later!"

I showed them around the apartment, which didn't take long since it was one bedroom in Chelsea, and sent Jensen a text message that read: *I'm going to kill you for those stupid articles you write*! I nearly flung my phone across the room when he simply replied: *Whoa. You sent me a text*! He was impossible. Adorably impossible, but impossible nonetheless.

"I'm not saying I hate you right now; I'm just saying that if I had a knife in my hand, you would be bleeding," I said to Estelle as we walked toward the little restaurant where we were meeting Oliver and Jensen. She laughed.

"Oh, shut up. You've been seeing him behind my back, and you're the one who's mad?"

"That's different, and it's not that much of a new development!"

She stopped walking and pivoted toward me. "Are you kidding me? That's a very new development! Last I checked you were stalking from afar, only meeting up because you had to for work stuff, and then suddenly all of this!"

I hesitated for a beat. "Well, you were busy moving to a new gallery and stuff!"

"Oh, now you have an excuse," she said, rolling her eyes and grabbing my arm as she started walking again.

"I can't believe you guys dragged me here knowing he may have Olivia today."

"Shut your whore mouth. You're going to walk in there, and be okay with her maybe being there. She's probably not here anyway."

"Fine."

The structure of the place looked like a plastic, see-through bin. If Estelle hadn't dropped the bomb that we were meeting him for lunch, I would have guessed based on the way it looked alone. With the black fixtures and sleek décor, it screamed simplistically cool. We walked in and spotted them almost instantly. They were hard to miss—two hot guys accompanied by a little girl. The visual had Mommy Porn written all over it.

"He brought her," I whisper-shouted. "I am going to fucking kill you guys. Officially."

"I really thought he wouldn't bring her," Estelle whispered back. "But Oliver is her godfather, so…"

My head snapped toward her. I didn't know that. She shrugged.

"Bunch of traitors," I whispered as we reached them. Estelle laughed loudly.

"What's so funny?" Oliver asked, getting up to greet his wife and pull her into a huge hug.

"You act like you didn't see her a few hours ago," I said, rolling my eyes at the affection.

"Don't get jealous. You're next," he said, pulling me into his arms.

Once I managed to remove myself from the death grip he held me in, I looked at Jensen. I was trying not to look at the little girl beside him yet. I didn't even know how to broach this situation. How do you say hello to the man you're sleeping with in front of his daughter, whom you've never met? There definitely needed to be an idiot's guide for this. I took a breath and smiled at him.

"Hey," I said. Then I turned my attention to her.

Up until that point she was just a girl. A girl who'd single-handedly ru-ined my relationship with the love of my life. Not that she was to blame. I blamed him. And her mother. And distance and insecurities and a whole slew of things I realized had contributed to our demise. The girl was just an innocent bystander in the warfare we'd created around her.

Jensen stood, and I took a step back to look up at him. Damn the flats I wore for making me feel so small beside him.

"Mia, this is Olivia," he said, taking a second to glance at the girl and right back at me. "Scout, this is Mia."

I felt my heart rattle in my chest, and then stop all at once as I met her gaze. Big grayish-blue eyes looked up at me, thin cherry lips smiled, and tiny little teeth welcomed me. Just like that. I'd built five years of preconceived no-tions about that moment, about her, and she just smiled like it was no biggie.

"Like *Mia Goes to the Beach!*" Olivia said.

She flashed me a smile that looked just like her father's, and I felt myself smile back at this piece of the man I once loved.

"Just like that," Jensen said.

I could hear the smile in his voice, though I couldn't bear to look at him now. I felt like I was about to cry. We were in a restaurant, where other families and lovers were enjoying a peaceful lunch, but inside I felt like I was going through the most monumental transition I'd been through since … well, since the night of the concert.

"And this is Estelle," Jensen said as I took a seat across from Olivia. "You remember her?"

My eyes snapped up to Estelle's. She gave me an apologetic, yet not, shrug that I read as code for: "*You asked me to never talk about them, so I didn't.*"

"I remember," she said, smiling at her. "She married Uncle Bean."

"She did," Oliver said with a wide grin.

He wrapped his big arms around her and squeezed until she giggled, and I realized that I was an outsider here.

This full-fledged little girl had no idea what a huge part of my life her dad had been. Even if we sat her down and explained it to her, she would never be able to comprehend it because she had a mother who wasn't me, and a father who wasn't with me when she was growing up. She'd never know our love as more than just a story, one you told over dinner when you were sharing things about your past, if you ever told it at all. Some things people talked about freely. Others, like Jensen and me, were things people remained tight-lipped about. Even now, people who knew us when we were together asked me, "Whatever happened between you and Jensen? I thought that was the real deal." Or "I thought you guys would have been married by now." Ours was a story that would remain untold, because living it was painful enough.

"You okay?"

I blinked away from her face and nodded at Jensen before busying myself with the menu as Oliver, Estelle, and Jensen spoke to Olivia about kindergarten and her friends and what movies she loved. My eyes lifted once, and I saw Jensen kiss the top of Olivia's head with such ease, such love, a way that only a father did, and I decided that it was the hottest I'd ever seen him. I brought my eyes back to the menu and stared so hard at the blue cheese burger on the menu, that when a hand landed on mine, my entire body jumped in reaction.

"You sure you're okay? You're really quiet," Estelle said.

I nodded, lifting the menu higher so that it completely covered my face from protruding eyes, even though he could still see me. I couldn't very well put a paper bag over my head, but if it were an option, I would have. After another moment, I put down my menu and looked at Estelle.

"Can you order me the blue cheese burger and a cherry coke? I have to go use the restroom." I said the last part in a shouted whisper that made Olivia giggle.

Estelle shot me a look, but nodded as I stood and walked across the restaurant, disappearing behind the wall that I hoped led to the bathrooms. I half expected her to follow me, and breathed a sigh of relief when I got into the bathroom stall with no one in tow. I needed a moment to clear my head. I needed to go back out there and actually talk to the girl.

She was just a girl.

Except she wasn't.

She was Jensen's girl.

His sweet, beautiful little girl.

With another woman.

I pounded my fist on the door of the stall and groaned. I wish they'd warned me about this little meet-and-greet. Those bastards. At the sound of knocking on the door I took my last deep breath, washed my hands, and walked out. I was staring down at my pointy boots when I walked into him and hopped back.

"Holy shit—" I said.

He grumbled at the same time, "You should really watch where you're going—"

Jensen was rubbing his chin while I rubbed the top of my head.

"Sorry. You shouldn't sneak up on people, though."

"I'm standing outside of the bathroom. That hardly qualifies as sneaking up on anybody."

"It does when you have ulterior motives."

He rolled his eyes and shook his head. I smiled because I got the last word.

"I'm sorry we sprung her on you," he said after a beat.

"She's beautiful," I said.

"Thank you."

"She looks just like you."

"You think so?"

"Well, it's not like I've met her mom." Or stalked the crap out of her on social media…

"I like that you think she looks like me," he said, staring deep into my eyes.

I blinked away from him and cleared my throat.

"Well, we should probably go back," I said, turning to walk away.

He reached out and pulled my arm until my back crashed against the hard planes of his chest. I stopped breathing. I wanted to move, but I seriously stopped breathing. Being in his arms like that, in this moment, was almost too much to bear.

"What are you doing?" I whispered.

He dipped his head, the hair on his cheek prickling the side of my face, until we were cheek to cheek, and engulfed me until he was the only thing I could breathe. My thoughts became filled with him. He held me so that I didn't have a choice but to be consumed by him. I let my head hang and closed my eyes.

"Your daughter is waiting for you," I said.

"My daughter is spending time with her uncle. Trust me, I'm the last thing on her mind right now, and I need to know that you're okay. Really okay. Not bullshit okay. Not, 'I'm fine, Jensen.'" He mimicked my voice, and I fought to hide my smile. "Until you pull a disappearing act. I need to know you're not going to go all Road Runner on me right now."

My heart leaped at the murmured words.

"I'm fine," I whispered, finally moving to pivot in his hold.

He loosened his arm but didn't let go, just snaked it along my side until it wrapped around my back.

"Look at me."

I took a breath and craned my neck until my eyes found his. He was looking at me with an intensity that rattled the cage around my heart.

"I'm looking."

He grinned, running his free hand through my hair. "You're so beautiful."

My entire body felt unsteady. "Jensen. Not here."

His mouth twitched. "Would you slap me if I kissed you right now?"

"Really hard."

He bit his lip and made a groaning sound that made me feel like I was coming undone in his arms, then he dipped his face closer to mine, brushing the tip of his nose to mine.

"I'll take my chances," he murmured, his lips inching in on mine.

He placed a kiss on one side of my mouth, then the other. I shuddered and brought my hands up to either side of his narrow waist, closing my eyes to all of the reasons I shouldn't want this as badly as I did, especially in that moment. I let go of my trepidation and accepted the bursts of energy that jolted through me when his lips fell over mine. He kissed me with creative imagery. As if he'd been picturing it his entire life. As if he'd written poems about the fullness of my bottom lip when he pulled it into his mouth. As if my tongue was a stanza he'd savored but hadn't had a chance to perfect.

I broke the kiss, in desperate need for air, but held on to him, unwilling to let go out of fear of what would happen once I did. His nose brushed against mine again, and he let out a breath that mingled with mine.

"That was…" he didn't finish his quiet words.

I looked at him and nodded slowly, in agreement that it was … something. Everything.

And then he let go. And I let go. And we stood farther apart than where we'd started. And once again I was unsure of it, not because I didn't want it, but because I wanted it that bad. We all ate our lunches just fine, and when we were finished, Oliver suggested we walk across the street to Central Park since he hadn't been in a while.

"Isn't it insane how big it is?" I said.

They all looked at me like I was crazy.

"My soccer park is big, too," Olivia said.

I looked down and smiled. "Is it? Do you like soccer?"

She nodded and smiled. "I scored a goal last week."

"Awesome! I always wanted to play soccer."

"I can teach you," she said, letting go of Jensen's hand and suddenly grabbing mine. It was so unexpected, that I jumped and nearly dropped my camera bag.

I looked down, at our joined hands, hers small and pudgy, mine thin, nearly doubling hers, and I felt a quick wave of emotion wash through me as my heart thundered.

"I would love that," I said quietly.

In the vast park, we found a playground and sat on the grass across from it, watching Olivia play. Oliver joined her for a little while, then Estelle, then Jensen, and after she'd been in there for a moment, socializing with other kids, she looked over at us and waved.

"Mia! Come play!"

I stiffened and looked at Jensen beside me. He'd been talking to Oliver about football as Estelle told me about her gallery. Aside from the kiss we shared earlier, we'd both kept our distance. Me out of respect for Olivia. Him? I had no idea. What I did know was that the looks of longing that passed between us were few and far between, and that made my anxiety rise. Did he not want me here? Was he okay with this? With the way his daughter took to me? I tried to push the thoughts away. I tried to sate my quickened pulse by reminding myself that this was Jensen. This was the boy I'd run away with long ago, for weekends at a time. And she was his daughter. I told myself that if the tables were turned, I would be completely okay with him getting to know my child. But she wasn't my child, and I wasn't the one who'd been cast aside by somebody I loved and thought of as my best friend when I had this child.

I stood and walked over to Olivia, because I couldn't bear the way she was looking at me, like maybe she'd read me wrong and I didn't want to be her friend after all. She had eyes that looked sad by trait, not because they carried any, and I couldn't imagine anybody denying her such a simple request. She got on the swing, and I pushed her. She giggled, kicking her legs high. Once she'd gotten the hang of it, I sat in the empty one beside her and swung with her. We looked at each other and laughed, and I was struck by how easy she was with me, how a simple gesture could make her look so happy. Jensen joined us moments later, and stood behind us, pushing us both simultaneously as Olivia and I tried to figure out who could go higher. Later on, as we headed out of the park, I let her wear my camera around her neck and take pictures. Her favorite subjects were dogs, and a few squirrels. She seemed fascinated by my camera, and I felt happy to have something to share with her, aside from her father, who was still acting strange.

It occurred to me later, while I replayed the day in my head, that he never once spoke to her about me in terms in which he'd have to define what we were. Not that I expected him to. I wasn't his girlfriend. I wasn't even sure I was his friend. For a person who hated labels and didn't want to be defined by anything, I was sure having a hard time letting this be. I took out my camera and scrolled through the photos I'd taken, and my heart caught when I saw one of Jensen, Olivia and me by the swings. My lips blossomed into a smile as I looked at her, with her messy dark hair and wide smile as she looked at her father. His smile matched hers, and my own as I watched on, allowing myself to be a part of that frame in his life, even if it was just for a moment.

Jensen Talks

What a weekend I had! I've mentioned before that dating is a little (meaning: very) different when you have a child. And I know some of you single moms are rolling your eyes, thinking, "What do men know about that, anyway?" Well, some of us know a lot. When my ex and I divorced I wanted to make sure I got to see my daughter whenever I wanted. I didn't want to be the "every other weekend" parent, so I see her almost every day. The days I don't see her, we talk.

This past weekend my best friend and his wife were in town. Being that he's my daughter's godfather, and the person I named her after, he always plans his trips to New York around her schedule. And the woman I'm currently dating met my daughter. You're probably sitting there thinking, "What's so crazy about that, Reynolds?

Well, I'll tell you what: EVERYTHING.

She happens to be "the one who got away."

Remember how many times I've written about her?

This is huge.

But now that she met my daughter, we had a great day, and we had a moment that made her cry—now she's gone AWOL. Completely dark.

My daughter is the cutest though. She keeps asking me if she's going to see Mia again.

My answer: I hope so, Scout. I hope so.

At least we had a good brunch and hung out in Central Park before she completely vanished … right?

Question of the day from: @Twihardmomof3: "Name three things you want in your life."

Answer: Health, love, happiness.

I had an early morning shoot for the magazine, and after they told me their own second chance romance story—he was her father's employee when they had their forbidden love the first time around, and they reconnected years later—I spent the rest of my morning taking pictures of people who looked like they were grieving something. Then I headed out to meet Estelle for lunch.

I spotted her as soon as I walked through the doors of the little café where we agreed to meet. She was picking at her nail polish and staring at a painting on the wall beside her. I wondered what she saw when she looked at paintings. Did she see them objectively or appreciate them? I wondered what Jensen saw when he met people. Did he analyze them as deeply as I did, or did he accept their flaws and try to write them as beautifully as I tried to capture them?

"What do you see? A heart or an apple?" Estelle asked as I sat across from her.

I looked at the painting. "It looks like a red blob."

"Seriously?" she asked with a laugh.

I looked at the painting again and nodded. "Yeah … or like a heart drawn by a fourth grader."

"Hey, don't knock the fourth graders. They actually make some pretty kick ass art."

"I'm sure." I paused. "Where'd Romeo go?"

"Out with Jensen, which could mean anything from a strip club to a coffee shop."

I laughed. "I'm sure they wouldn't take Olivia to a strip club."

"I'm glad one of us has faith in them. So what's up with the pictures? Has Millie heard back from her friend? Are you sticking to the theme you'd told me about?"

I sighed and put down the menu as we ordered our food, then clasped my hands together and explained my idea.

"Are we going to talk about you meeting Olivia?" she asked suddenly.

I paused. "Okay. Random. What's there to talk about?"

"Maybe the fact that Jensen told Oliver that he hasn't been able to reach you after the fact."

I gaped at her. "I played with the girl the entire time at the park. I even let her use my camera, and then Jensen goes and tells the whole fucking nation that I went AWOL and makes me look like an asshole! It's only been two days!"

"Oh God. I need to start reading his column," she said with a laugh. "What'd you think of her though? You did look like you were freaking out."

"That's because I was freaking out! I wasn't expecting to see her."

"And?"

"And she's adorable." I shrugged. "I don't know what you want me to tell you."

"Well, that's a start considering just last week you were convinced children were the devil's spawn."

"That's not true. I like kids. I just don't necessarily want to spend copious amounts of time with them. There's nothing wrong with that."

"What about when I have kids?" she asked.

I leaned back in my chair and gave her a onceover.

"Are you pregnant?"

"Not yet."

"You know I'm going to love whatever comes out of your vagina."

"Mia!" she said, coughing as she laughed.

"What?"

"Filter!"

"I get sick of using filters. I'm too old for that shit." I paused to take a bite of the sandwich on my plate. "Did you deliver the painting to your number one fan?"

"Oh God, yeah, and she was practically drooling on Oliver the entire time. It was so funny." She took a bite of her food, not taking her eyes off me.

"So what do you think will happen with Jensen now?"

I shrugged as I finished chewing. "Considering he acted totally weird the other day, I have no idea."

"It must have been weird for him."

I shot her a look. "It was weird for me too, Elle."

"I can't believe after everything, all the ignoring and the avoiding and all the shit you tried, you still ended up falling for him again."

"I did not fall for him," I said, trying not to choke on my water.

She smiled. "You sort of did, and it's my fault since I wasn't here to shield you from his moony eyes."

"Moony eyes?"

"How would you describe them?"

"Grayish-blue, I guess."

She tossed her napkin at me and laughed. "You're a moron."

"A realistic, non-cheesy moron."

"Whatever. I think you're still crazy about him."

I bit my tongue. *Maybe.* "And I think you are crazy—period."

"I'm serious, Meep."

"I know. And I thought we were doing okay, talking and hanging out and stuff, until Saturday, and then when I got home I saw the pictures you'd taken of us at the park and…" I stopped talking, remembering the pictures I'd found on my camera when I went to look for the dog pictures to send to Jensen. Estelle had taken pictures of Olivia, Jensen, and me. We looked like the American Dream. We were only missing one more kid and a dog, but that picture encompassed everything people wish for. It might as well have been pinned with #familygoals.

"And you saw what could be."

"I guess, but he was still acting weird. Really weird."

She searched my face for a beat. "Just be careful, Meep. I love Jensen, but nowadays he comes in a package deal. Him, Olivia, Krista and her family and whoever she's with, etcetera."

My heart sank at the reminder, but I shrugged nonetheless. "I'm sure I'll never meet her anyway. My time here is limited, remember?"

"Thank God for that! It's too cold here for you."

"And you, apparently," I said with a laugh.

22

Once Estelle and Oliver left, I felt a bubble of emptiness fill me again. The reminder of home and all the things I missed nudged at it, making it impossible to breathe without feeling like I was missing something. I left my house the next morning seeking magic, which I found in the form of a homeless guy on the subway who was spewing headlines as I was on my way to Brooklyn. I marveled at the fact that I really didn't need the entertainment channel or gossip magazines to keep me in the know. Today he was bellowing about a new lesbian in Hollywood.

"Bruce Jenner is a lesbian!" he said loudly, pushing into a sitting position so that his back was against huge black trash bags he carried with him, which I assumed were filled with clothes.

Even the guy who sat across from me reading the newspaper had to pause at that. Usually I looked at the floor and listened, but I had to look at Headlines Guy when he explained this turn of events.

"Bruce Jenner is now a woman. He's a woman, who likes women. He's a lesbian!"

I looked at the guy across from me, and he looked back, wide-eyed, as we tried to smother our laughter—him behind his newspaper, me behind my bottle of water. When I got out of the subway, I found more people to photograph. In New York I learned something that hadn't struck me back home—inspiration was everywhere. Later that day, while I was reading the paper at a Starbucks near my place I found one right outside.

At first glance, I thought nothing of her. She was just a woman, dressed normally, in jeans and a nice long jacket, with a pudgy baby resting on her hips. When I looked outside again, I noticed she had bags in her other hand. When I looked a third time, I realized she was crying. I watched her for a couple of beats, crying and burying her face in the crook of the baby's neck, as if he was the only thing holding her up, despite her being the one physically carrying him. My camera went up to my face and my finger clicked before I could stop myself. I shot another, and another. Finally, when I couldn't bear to see her just standing there, crying the way she was and watching people pass her by like she was invisible, I grabbed my stuff and went outside to speak to her.

As it turned out, Theresa was having a bad day, nothing major, but by the end of our conversation, she was smiling and telling me about places she thought I could display my prints. We talked for a little while longer, until the baby got fussy and we went our separate ways. The fervent beat of the city led me to a small gallery in Brooklyn. There, I spoke to the owner, a young artist with similar ideas to mine. His pictures, a lot like the ones I'd been taking, were used to showcase the wrongs of the world in hopes people would open their eyes to them. Rodrigo had marched beside people taking a stand for things and sold his pictures to major networks and magazines.

"The best thing, though, is being there, in the middle of it all," he said, with a gleam in his brown eyes that made me wish I'd been there. He pointed at the one behind him, one with a little girl holding a gay rights sign as she stood in front of a man holding up a religious one that said something about not being saved. It was such a powerful image; I had to take a step back when I took it in.

After he saw mine in my camera, he looked up and said, "You need to showcase these somewhere."

"That's why I'm here."

He nodded. "Okay. Let's figure this out. You got time?"

I nodded. Time was all I had.

On my way home, I saw that I had a missed call from Jensen.

"Hey. I've been on a crazy deadline … but call me back. I miss you," he said in the message. He sounded tired.

When I called back, he didn't answer.

An uneasy feeling settled in my stomach every time I thought about it. His words meant very little, especially after the way he acted after the whole Olivia thing. I couldn't read him. Not the way I used to. And that bothered me more than anything else, because reading him, and having him read me was one of the best things about our relationship, even before we got togeth-er. There was a comfort that came with knowing you were understood on a deeper level, one that went beyond words. I wasn't sure we'd ever get back there again, and the thought bothered me more than I cared to admit to myself.

After visiting Rodrigo's gallery again to look at where he'd set up the prints I'd given him to display, I headed toward the coffee shop I knew Jensen frequented, not because I was planning on meeting him there or even bumping into him, but because I'd been really craving their coffee for a week and it was my first chance to get some. As I neared the place, anxious butterflies started to ignite in my core. What if I did see him? I'd spoken to him briefly the night before, about nothing, and he had to hang up quickly because Olivia was demanding his attention. I didn't even know why he'd called, but I was glad to hear his voice on the other end of the line for the two seconds I had. Even after reading his article, I felt like the whole thing on Saturday was awkward, and the more I thought of it the more I realized that it wasn't me and it wasn't Olivia; it was him who made it so.

I sighed. Whatever. We had an incredible night, and another after. I didn't have to do the girl thing and start planning nuptials that would eventually be broken anyway. Pulling open the door, I saw no sign of him and let out a relieved breath. I went up to the counter, ordered my drink, and rounded it while I waited. Then I pulled out my phone to call Rob since I wanted to make sure I was still staying at our place, or technically his and Juan Pablo's place now, when I went home for the weekend. As I dialed his phone, I saw more people come in from the corner of my eye. Jensen was holding the door open with one hand, his computer in the other. He wore all black today, from his beanie to his converse, and the person he held the door open for was a woman, with light brown hair. She had pale skin, like a porcelain doll, and a smile that seemed to evoke calmness, maybe even in me if I wasn't wired so tightly at the sight of this whole thing.

It wasn't that she was a woman, or that she was obviously with him. From past Facebook stalking, I knew it was Krista. As soon as the guy with the blue Mohawk placed the cup of coffee on the counter, I reached out and grabbed it so that he wouldn't call my name. His pierced eyebrow shot up. Mine arched in response. He chuckled lightly.

"All right, all right," he said.

I smiled and shrunk back into the corner of the counter, where the sugar was. He must have thought I was crazy, and maybe I was, but I didn't care. Through the cracks between the coffee machines, I was able to catch a glimpse of Jensen and Krista. Either she was a lot taller than me, or she was wearing huge heels. Her eyes reached his nose, at least. Jensen was laughing at something she was saying, and she started waving her hands wildly. That was when I caught a glimpse of the ring on her left hand. I swallowed, and looked at my phone. Putting down my coffee, I went on Facebook and searched for her. She had it set to private, and her fucking profile picture was of just herself, which told me nothing. I tried to think, looked at mutual friends. We had Oliver in common. That bastard. I clicked on pictures to see if they had any together, which they did, but they were all old, of her pregnant, sitting in the backyard of a house, smiling at something Oliver was saying while Jensen drank a beer in the background. It said nothing. Fuck my life. Of course it said nothing.

I tucked my phone into the back pocket of my jeans and grabbed my coffee again as I looked back up. They were walking toward me, so I pushed out through the side door beside me and stood outside, leaning my back against the wall as I tried to regain control of my rapidly beating heart. After a moment, when I felt like I could handle it, I looked back inside. He was looking forward, at the barista, and she was standing beside him on her phone. After she put it away, she looked up at him and smiled at something he said, then extended her arm and touched his face with her fingertips. My insides rocked, my heart dropping into the pit of my stomach. As if on cue, his head snapped up, his eyes met mine, all stormy gray with a hint of confusion. I bolted, because I really couldn't take it. I couldn't handle seeing how they looked together. I couldn't handle the idea of them being together at all.

I made it home faster than I ever thought I would. He hadn't followed. Hadn't called. And I was able to hold in my emotions until I closed my door behind me. It started with my shaky hands dropping my camera bag beside me. My bobbling knees followed, giving out on me so suddenly, I had to throw my hands out behind me to break my fall. The tears I thought were coming never did. Dry sobs racked through me, settling inside my lungs, making me feel like I couldn't breathe. I gasped for air, but couldn't fill myself with any. I felt like a volcano that just wouldn't erupt, all heaving breaths and rattling nerves with no real outlet.

I blinked when my phone started to vibrate against my butt, snapping me out of it. As if on autopilot, I reached behind me and wiggled it out. Seeing Estelle's name on the screen made tears prick my eyes, because it wasn't him. He'd seen me, and he still hadn't called. He'd seen me see what I saw, and he hadn't called.

"Robbie said I could pick you up on Friday," she said in a sing-song voice, then added with a laugh, "Actually, he said we both could."

"Awesome."

"What?" she said in a loud tone. "What's wrong?"

"Nothing. Everything. Probably nothing, though."

She laughed lightly. "That sounds catastrophic. What's going on?"

"I saw Jensen and Krista today."

"What! Where?"

"At the coffee shop he goes to."

"Oh my God, Mia. You were stalking him again?"

"No!" I shouted, then added a quieter, "No. It wasn't like that."

"What happened?"

"I went to get coffee. I really liked their coffee. And I figured I would take some pictures since the sky is actually cooperating today, but then they walked in together."

"And?"

"And she had a ring on her hand."

"Like a wedding ring?… Well, it's not like it's his ring she's wearing, Meep."

I nodded, even though she couldn't see me. I felt some of the tears that had been swimming begin to spill over. "Yeah, I get that. And either way, that's fine, right? It's just a ring, right? No biggie. But then she was touching him."

Estelle gasped loudly. "Touching him how?"

"Like touching him."

"What. The. Actual. Fuck?"

"I know," I said, my voice quiet as I wiped my tears. "And maybe it was nothing," I said, now sobbing. "Maybe it was nothing, but it felt like something, you know? And I fucking hate her."

"I know, honey, with good reason," Estelle said.

I felt the soothing in her voice everywhere, over my hair, my back. I sighed.

"I'm not being stupid, right? This isn't just me being a girl?"

"No. You're not being stupid. I get why you're upset, but I think that you're taking all of this way out of context. Has he called you?"

I let out a bitter laugh. "No. The fucking bastard saw me, he fucking saw me, and he didn't even come after me or fucking call me."

She stayed quiet for a moment, then whispered. "You're kidding me."

"I wish I was." I paused, wiping my tears.

"I don't know, Meep, that…" she paused, sighing into the line. "It just … it's not Jensen, you know? I'm going to call Oliver."

"Don't you dare! Girl code!"

"Fuck girl code! You're obviously upset and I'm positive you're making crazy scenarios up in your head. It's better that we get this sorted out so you don't drive yourself crazy about the ring, and the touching." she said louder, as if I needed a blaring reminder of what I'd seen.

I sighed, leaning my head back against the wall and closing my eyes. "I hate him. I hate him. I hate her. I hate New York. I hate love. I hate my heart for being a fucking living reminder of his love. I fucking hate everything."

"I'm so sorry," she said in a whisper. "I'm so, so sorry. I wish I was there."

"I want to come home," I said, crying openly now. "I just wanna come home."

"We're waiting for you. Always."

And that was the meaning of home to me. It was a place. It was the place where my family was, where my friends were waiting for me, where I always felt welcome, and, even despite the bad shit that happened, I was always loved. I didn't have to stay here and deal with Jensen and the bullshit that came with him. I closed my eyes, the memory of us at the beach when he told me he'd gotten her pregnant infiltrating my thoughts. Pain shot through me as if I'd just heard the words for the first time. It was something I'd never forget, his words, the pained look in his eyes as he said them, the way those three simple words made me feel like the earth was being pulled from beneath me.

I thought about the coffee shop. Him standing there laughing as Krista brought her hand to his face, and his face when he saw me standing on the other side of the glass. Why did it have to hurt so much to see that? And how could I have been stupid enough to let this happen again?

I fell asleep in a heap of blankets and towels I'd been trying to fold after I did laundry. It wasn't until I heard pounding on my door that I realized it. Once I hung up with Estelle, I'd showered and spent nearly an hour just sitting on the cold tiles, crying as the hot water hit my back. I didn't want to do anything. I didn't want to be. I wanted to go home and see my family, but most of all, I wanted to go home and hug my brother. I wanted to let him wrap his arms around me and cry into his chest until I no longer felt like my heart was ripping apart inside me.

"I'm coming!" I yelled as I padded my way over there.

I stretched one last time before looking into the peephole and stared for a beat. Jensen was standing on the other side of the door, his eyes staring right into mine with a somber look in them. I reared back, letting go of the doorknob as if it was burning. My heart spiked once more.

"Mia! Open the damn door. I know you're standing on the other side!"

I held my breath. How the hell did he know that? I looked down to the crack of the door at the bottom. You couldn't see anything. I backed away a little farther, my bare feet not making any noise against the carpet.

"Mia!" His fist met the door again. I stepped forward when I heard him say something else, and I noticed he was talking to the man who lived across from me, an older guy dressed in slacks and a long-sleeved white shirt who looked like he'd just gotten home from work.

"I don't care. Go back inside if you don't want to hear me," Jensen said to him. I couldn't hear what the guy said; I could only make out bits and pieces.

"Well, call the goddamn cops! They'll have to drag me out of here, though, and that'll cause a bigger scene than this!"

"Maybe she doesn't want to see you!" the guy said.

I placed my hands over my heart and smiled a little, feeling like maybe I wasn't completely alone after all. This stranger was sort of on my side.

"She doesn't know what the fuck she wants! Why don't you mind your own business?" That was Jensen again.

"I am minding my business! I'm in my apartment, and all I hear is your yelling!"

Another door opened, the one beside that guy, diagonal from mine, and a girl my age stepped out. Dana. I'd seen her a lot around here, on the elevator, walking to and from the subway. We'd bonded over *Game of Thrones* at one point when she wore a shirt with Tyrion's face on it that read, "Hold Me Closer Tiny Lannister," and I laughed until I cried.

"Maybe she's in there with her boyfriend," Dana said.

"I am her boyfriend!" Jensen roared.

She raised her eyebrows, crossing her arms in front of her. "Uh … I'm pretty sure you're not. I've never seen you around here. The only one I've seen is a blond, tall guy." She dragged her eyes up and down his body, as if to say, "Definitely not you."

Jensen's face had morphed from anger to murder. He was fuming red, taking off his beanie to run both hands through his hair and pull, then lifted the sleeves of his shirt to expose his forearms. Finally, after letting out a harsh breath, he turned to my door again and pounded on it three times, louder this time.

"Mia, I swear to fucking God, if I get arrested over this, you're going to have to explain it to Olivia."

My heart jumped again. Fuck. I looked at Dana and the guy who lived across the hall, and finally, with a trembling hand, I unlocked and opened the door. Stepping only slightly into view, not pulling it open completely, I looked first at Dana.

"Sorry," I said, then looked at the guy across the hall.

"I already called security," he said. "Do you need me to call the cops?"

I shook my head. "No, we're fine. I was … in the shower and didn't hear the commotion." My gaze met Jensen's narrowed stare, and my heart shot up to my ears and roared there.

"Let me in, Mia. Let me in, or you come out. Either way, we're doing this," he said. His voice, gratingly low, made a shiver run through me.

I held the door open wider, and he stormed inside.

"Sorry," I said again.

"Let me know if you need anything." That was Dana.

"I'm going to keep an ear out." That was the guy across from me.

"Thank you. It's not necessary, I swear. He's harmless." They both gave me dubious glances, and the need to defend him was bigger than my shame or my anger, so I added, "He would never, ever hurt anybody. He's just pissed off right now. I swear."

I closed the door behind me and locked it before turning to face Jensen. He was pacing my living room, running a hand through his hair, his beanie long gone. My eyes dropped to his left hand instantly, where his fingers were bare of metals. I wrung my hands together when his eyes finally shot up at me, and took a step back, into the kitchen counter, because the intensity I found there was too much for me to bear. His eyes were narrowed on mine.

"I can't believe you wouldn't open the door for me. I fucking know you were standing right there," he said, pointing at the door.

I let out a breath. "What are you doing here?"

"Why'd you run? Earlier, when I saw you, why'd you run?"

I shot forward. "Are you fucking kidding me? You have the balls to ask me that question? Why didn't you come after me? Why didn't you call? Probably for the same fucking reason I ran!"

He shook his head. "I don't know what you think you saw—"

"No. No. No! You are not going to do that right now. You are not going to stand here, trying to undermine me and shit. I know what I saw!"

"What'd you see, Mia?"

"I saw you with your ex-wife. I saw you looking real cozy with your ex-wife," I said, correcting myself.

He groaned, waving his hands and looking up at the ceiling as if waiting for something to come and help him. Had this been a comic, I would have probably been Magneto and used my powers to zap the shit out of him before flying away to Southern California, but unfortunately we didn't live in a book. We were just Mia and Jensen—flawed, crazy, and disastrously attracted to each other.

"That is not…" he sighed, his voice trailing off as he looked at me again, this time with more clarity in his eyes, a softness to his features. "Did you think…" His mouth hung open, as if something had just occurred to him. "What exactly did you see?"

I rolled my eyes, swallowing my reluctance. "Does it matter? Does it really matter? I want you out, Jensen. I want you out of my apartment and out of my life. Now. I'm not kidding!"

He took a step forward, closer to me, until he was just an arm's length away. "What did you see?"

I opened my mouth, closed it, and turned my face to look at the wall beside me. I swallowed to try to keep the shakiness from my tone, but it was moot. "She … she was touching you." I brought my gaze back to his, tears filling my eyes as I remembered the scene. "Like … lovingly and shit."

His eyes screwed shut. He let out a harsh breath as he brought his fingers up to the bridge of his nose. "Fuck."

"Yeah … fuck," I said, my words whispered as I swallowed past the knot forming in my throat. "Like I said, I want you out. Out."

His eyes popped open, scanning my face, looking between mine as he took another step closer. His hand reached out for my face, but I moved.

"Stop. I want you out," I said.

"I can't do that," he said, his voice a grave whisper. The pained look in eyes threatened to break me apart.

"I can't do this. I thought I could. I thought I could do it for fun, but I can't. I realize now that I really, really can't," I said, tears forming in my eyes again. I blinked rapidly, but they didn't go away; instead, they trickled down my cheeks.

"Mia, don't," he said, reaching out for me again. I took a step back, hitting the counter again.

"Please go."

"I swear to God, Mia. I swear to fucking God, there's nothing going on there." He paused, closing his eyes momentarily and letting out a breath. "I swear to God, Mia. I would never do that to you."

"You did once."

"No, I didn't! You know I didn't. Stop trying to bring that into this. We talked about it. Let it go already."

"I can't, okay? I can't let it go!"

"She's getting married, Mia. There was nothing going on there when we were married. We were roommates most of the time, but she's my friend." I scoffed, so he continued, "Friend, Mia. Maybe I had an eyelash on my face … who knows why the hell she touched me, but I can assure you it was friendly."

The pain stayed right where it was, unmoved. I wasn't sure anything could calm the throb at this point. "It doesn't matter. It doesn't matter what she was doing or what you were doing. Can't you see none of it matters?"

If nothing else, that was the one thing I realized when I saw them together; I couldn't let go. I couldn't just let go of something that cut me so deeply, because it hadn't just ripped a hole in my heart, it'd ripped me in half, and there were parts of me that were missing when time had tried to sew me back together.

"Mia, please," he said, his voice deep and pained. I shook my head, blinking away new tears. Somehow I found my voice, and surprisingly it was strong.

"No. Enough is enough."

He took another step closer, until his chest was flush against mine, and all I could feel was his heat, and all I could smell was his scent, and blinked and blinked, trying to escape the haze that threatened to pull me under.

"We're friends, Mia. We share a daughter. You have to accept that."

"I can't," I said, but my words were quiet, my voice held no resilience. And that was when he dipped his head and pressed his lips against mine. His tongue snuck into my mouth and washed over mine with a wave that wiped out my resistance and reawakened the electricity between us. I kissed him back with the same energy, with the same intensity. I kissed him like it was the last time, because I knew it was. When I felt myself escalating, and knew I couldn't go on with just a kiss. When I felt like what I needed was my hands under his shirt, sculpting over the muscles on his back, and his head between my legs as he caressed my thighs with his large hands, that was when I pulled back. That was when I shoved him off me with a force I wasn't aware I was capable.

"I can't do this. I thought I could, but I can't."

He nodded, but I could feel him brewing, and when he finally spoke again, my heart dropped. "What'd you do with those letters I sent you?"

I took a step back. "Why?"

"Did you read them?"

"No," I whispered.

At the sound of his huff, my eyes snapped back up. "What'd you do with them, Mia?"

I looked away again, wishing the entire conversation would disappear. I'd never regretted what I did with them until that moment; because his tone and the look in his eyes made me want to take it all back, even if it was for just a moment. He tipped my chin up to meet his gaze again.

"I burned most of them a while back," I whispered.

"What?" He dropped his hand and reared back as if the shock was too much to bear.

"I was heartbroken."

He shook his head and barked out a single laugh of disbelief.

"I was hurt, and you kept writing," I said.

"I … those pages know more about me than I know about myself most days." He paused and shook his head again. "I left hints of who I was on them hoping you would piece it all together and give me back to myself." His eyes met mine again, and a flash of pain passed through them. "Fragments of my soul were scattered on those pages … and you burned them."

I felt something inside of me crack, but not enough. I knew he could say anything to change my mind. I knew if he started to spew words of love right then and there, I would cave and let him back in. I would cave, not because I wasn't strong enough, but because I didn't want to be. I didn't know what to say to that, so I stayed quiet, bowing my head in shame, wishing I hadn't treated his words with such carelessness. Finally, he guided my face to look at him again.

"You can keep walking away from this, and I'm going to keep letting you, because even when you think you leave, your heart always stays, and it's something I carry with pride, and it's something I don't…" He paused, his gaze tearing away from mine for a second, his voice thick with emotion. "It's something I don't fuck with. Ever. So if you feel like you need a break, I'll give you a break, but don't think for a second I'm not coming after you again, Mia. And I swear to God, the next time I do, it's forever."

I shook my head, mouth agape as tears filled my eyes, but I couldn't form words. What could I say?

He walked until he reached the door of my apartment, standing by the door and clutching the handle for a moment. "That pain you felt at seeing me with her when you thought we were together? I've felt that for the past five years, because I was always looking at you, even when you were busy ignoring me. I was always there. I was there through Ben, and David, and Adam. I was there through Todd, and Scott, and Phillip."

He shook his head, still looking at the door, exhaling as he ran a hand through his hair. "Pain isn't just losing the person you love. Pain is losing the person you love, seeing them with somebody else, and not interfering because you know you can't give them the life they deserve."

He glanced over his shoulder, to where I was standing, and shot me a forlorn look that traveled all the way through me. "I've lived in pain since the moment I lost you. I've learned to live with it, but I haven't learned to accept it."

Then he walked out. And my knees hit the ground at his departure. That was when I started to sob because that was the moment it hit me. While I'd been busy ignoring this man, and burning his letters, he'd been watching me, waiting for the right time. *But he'd been married. He'd been married, and I'd been broken.*

Jensen Talks

One of the sports I enjoy most is boxing. Something about the way they're willing to go out there and get their faces bashed time and time again is pretty powerful. It's a draining sport, physically and otherwise, I'm sure, not that I've ever attempted it myself. I get enough boxing action in my own life, in my own mind and spirit, and I'm my own nemesis in there. The world is brutal, our lives are hard, and we are the biggest jerks we come into contact with.

My thought for today: be cautious with yourself.

Be cautious, because others beat you down enough. You shouldn't have to add to that pain. You will, though, because that's what you do. But you'll also get back up, because that's what you do. And you'll probably do it all over again, because you're a crazy, foolish idiot.

Why do we keep going back for more then? Knowing we're going to be knocked down time and time again? I think it's because, like boxers, we crave the intensity of it. Because we need to know that we're more powerful than our minds. We need to prove that we're stronger than our feelings, and, ultimately, we live with this hope that one day we won't be let down—by others or ourselves.

Question of the day from: @BookNerdCarmen: "Are you originally from New York? If not, where are you from and do you miss your hometown?"

Answer: Nope. Born in Long Beach, raised in Santa Barbara. My home is where my daughter is. The longer I've been here I realize that it's not California I miss, but rather the people I left behind.

25

Apparently I had hoarding issues, and photographs, books, shoes, and feelings were at the top of my list. I couldn't sleep after Jensen left. I couldn't eat, either, which was just as well since I was going home for the weekend and my mom would probably try to feed me enough food for five years. I kept replaying his words over and over, until it became a scratched record in my memory. His voice, his words, the broken look in his eyes when he looked back at me that last time before he walked out. It felt like a turning point, but it wasn't.

Our past was a photograph of memories frozen in time. And the most poignant ones hurt too much for me to dust off and look at. Still, I kept going through them. I kept replaying them in my mind. Whenever I closed my eyes, I kept seeing us at the beach together, running toward him when he got there with our friends, laughing as he caught me in mid-air, us fighting over my parents' disapproval of him. Trying to calm his nerves over things he had no control over and reassuring him that he was enough.

It was something that happened so often it became second nature to us. Trying to read his mind when he wouldn't tell me what was wrong and getting frustrated at the whole scenario. But then he would show up at my house past midnight, the rev of his bike alerting me of his arrival, and I would go outside, and he would just hold me for the longest time. And in our silence we would find our haven, one where nobody judged us or disturbed our peace. That was when we were Mia and Jensen, the couple people envied because we looked good together and we had that thing everybody dreamed of finding in their lifetime. That was when we found ourselves, through each other.

I thought of how horrible it must have been for him to see me with those guys, and how I would have felt if I'd been in his shoes. My younger self didn't care; she reminded me why it all went wrong, but the grown-up version shook her head in pity, for me, for him, for them since they could never give me what I'd yearned for … what I'd found in him. I wanted to call him. I wanted to apologize to him for the past, and the present, but I couldn't. I was too selfish. I was too stubborn.

So I didn't. I packed my bags up for my trip home, and I pretended we never were. That I'd torn and burned the chapters in the colossal history book we wrote together. And even as I pretended, I wept for him, for us, for the memory of what we once had together and what we could have had if I allowed myself to let go.

"You had sex with him?" That was the first thing that came out of Robert's mouth when he picked me up at the airport.

"Where's Elle?" I asked, glancing around.

"She couldn't come. Something about a leak in the gallery. She said to call her. And again, I can't believe you had sex with him!"

"You're not allowed to say anything to me. Did you forget why I came here?"

His blue eyes rolled. Twice. For good measure, I guess.

"I'm sorry, but I have too much work going on, and my boss told me I couldn't take my scheduled vacation."

"Your boss is our dad, you asshole."

"Well, maybe if you would have waited one more day, I would have been there. You were the one who decided to jump ship and run here the first chance you got." He paused and took the carryon I had in my hand and wrapped his other arm around my neck. "I can't believe you had sex with him."

I groaned. "I can't believe he wrote about it in a national newspaper," I yelled loudly, then quieted down, sadness eloping with the elation I'd felt for seeing my brother again. "I don't want to talk about him."

Rob dropped his arm and searched my face. "What happened?"

I shook my head. "I can't talk about it," I whispered.

"I'm going to fucking kill him. I swear to God, I'm going to fucking kill him this time," he said, grabbing my hand in his and my rolling suitcase in the other as he stomped toward the parking lot.

I told him everything that had happened while he drove to my parents' house, and he listened with unyielding attention, the kind he only gave to certain people. When I was finished, I shot him a look that said, "Well?" He shook his head, eyes wide.

"Dude. I don't even know what to tell you."

"That's a first," I grumbled, looking out the window.

"Meep, he didn't do anything."

"You know…" I sighed heavily. "I've been thinking about it all week. He really didn't. I believe him about Krista. I do, but fuck, when I think about it, when I remember what I saw … it hurts, Robbie," I said, swallowing back tears. You'd think I would have been all cried out by now. "It fucking hurts."

"I know," he said, sliding his hand from the gearshift to mine on my lap.

"I just, I don't know what to think anymore. I don't know what to do."

"Don't do anything. You're coming home in less than a month. You have a second interview scheduled with the museum here. Why do anything? Would he move here for you?"

My eyes snapped to his. "I would assume not. Olivia lives in New York."

"Would you move there for him?" he asked, his eyes widening at the stretch of silence that followed. "You'd move to New York, a place you claim to hate, for him?"

I shrugged. "I've never claimed to be sane."

Rob shook his head. "Thank God for that, because I'd have to laugh in your face."

After another long stretch of silence, I placed a foot on the dash, until Rob shot me a murderous look and I dropped it.

"Do you think Dad read the article?"

"From Sunday?"

I nodded.

"If he hasn't called you screaming, I would assume no."

"He only said my name once. Maybe dad missed that one."

Rob shot me a look. "Mia, please. Any idiot could figure out that he's talking about you."

"Why do people keep saying that?" I groaned.

"Because it's true!" he said, then laughed. "Wait 'til Dad reads that shit."

My head snapped to him, eyes wide and full of fear. "We better go over there and burn it before he gets to it!"

Rob laughed as if it was the funniest thing since Chris Farley in *Tom-*

my Boy. When we got there, I looked at him and communicated the obvious: newspapers first. He nodded. My mother's laughter floated through the house as we walked in, and I smiled at the warm feeling it brought.

"We're home," Rob said, shooting me a quick look before he disappeared to the kitchen.

My mom let out an excited shriek. I pictured her unfolding her legs and jumping from the couch as we made our way to each other. Sure enough, when I crossed the threshold of the living room, she was running toward me, her blonde hair in a messy bun, her reading glasses dangling from the neck of her loose white shirt, and her arms open wide for me.

"Welcome home, baby girl," she said as she wrapped her arms around me and squeezed.

"I'm only here to visit," I said, my words a muffle against her neck.

"Don't ruin it for us," my dad said as he walked over.

I let go of my mom and threw my arms around his neck, squeezing him tightly. He smelled of suntan lotion and salt water. Like home.

"Catch any waves?" I asked as I settled back on my feet.

He smiled wide and nodded. "It was a good morning."

"I'm so jealous."

"Don't be. He wiped out before he even got to carve any," my mom said, laughing and jolting away from his attempt to tickle her.

"I caught a couple of good ones."

My mom nodded in agreement until he looked away and then she shook her head at me. I couldn't stop smiling. I hadn't realized how much I'd missed being there until that moment.

"Well, we're going tomorrow morning," I said.

"Where's your brother?"

"Right here. Had to take a detour to the ladies' room," Rob said.

My dad shook his head. "I hope you didn't stink the place up again."

"Me? I never do that!"

Dad shot him a look. "Last time you used it I had to light one of those candles and leave it on all day. And we had people coming over for dinner that night."

"That was probably Mia," Rob said.

"What the fuck? I haven't been here in over a month!"

"Watch your mouth, Mia." That was Mom. I rolled my eyes.

"And your eye rolls if you want to keep them in your head." That was Dad.

"Twenty-six, not twelve," I said.

"Under our roof, not yours," Rob said, imitating my mom's singsong voice.

"Where you don't pay one goddamn bill," I added, imitating Dad.

Both of them looked at us in amusement for a couple of minutes as we kept this up, until Mom finally said, "Okay, I'm sick of this. Let's go eat."

We sat around the kitchen counter and ate until we couldn't eat anymore. I had no thoughts on New York, or pictures, or even Jensen. For hours I was surrounded with boisterous laughter from architectural horror stories that Dad and Rob were dealing with.

"When does Juan Pablo come back from Brazil?" Mom asked.

Rob smiled. "Next week."

"Has he told his parents yet?" Dad asked.

"No," Rob said, looking away.

That stung as if it were happening to me. I knew how much the whole thing was affecting my brother, and how my mom would have kept drilling, so I got up to clear the table.

"I went out with Jensen."

Rob's eyes were wide when they flashed to mine. "Oh my God," he mouthed and shook his head, his way of telling me I didn't need to do that. I shrugged.

"What Jensen? Not Jensen the punk who used to come here and pick you up on his bike," Dad said.

"He's not a punk," I said under my breath, then added louder, "Mom emailed him, asking him to reach out to me."

"Bettina, what the hell?" Dad said, looking between her and me like we'd each grown a set of horns.

She shrugged. "Millie was gone, and I didn't want Mia to be all alone out there."

Dad shook his head. "I would have flown there if she felt alone! She doesn't need that punk keeping her company!"

"Stop calling him that!" I said, slapping my hands over the table.

"That's what he is!" Dad shouted. "Last time he was in your life you were a mess when he left. How long have you been 'reconnecting'?" Dad hammered.

The way he had both his hands in fists that made his large biceps flex would have made me nervous, if he wasn't our dad. At least Jensen wasn't in Santa Barbara.

"Not long," I said finally.

"You knew about this, Robert?"

Rob nodded.

"And you didn't tell me? I see you every goddamn day! How could you not bring this up?" he paused and looked at me. "I expected better from you, Mia. You go to New York for new opportunities, and you end up digging through the past?" He shook his head.

"He's a good guy, Marc," Mom said.

"Oh, for fuck's sake!"

"Marc!"

Dad slapped his hand down on the counter. "Where's my paper?"

Rob and I looked at each other, wide-eyed. Shit. Fuck. Shit.

"You don't like him, yet you read his column?"

"I don't like him for my daughter, especially not after what he did. I can't help that the guy's an entertaining writer, and now that I know you've been out with him I have to read everything all over again!"

I bit back the laugh that Rob let out, loud and sudden.

"Well, I like him, and I believe in second chances," Mom said. "However, I don't like the fact that I didn't know how serious this was. Does Estelle know? What did she say about it?"

"It's not serious. It's not even anything." I paused. "I don't know what it is yet."

I filled them in on pretty much everything—minus the fight, and the sex. Dad rolled his eyes and made huffing sounds the entire time. Mom smiled, especially when I got to the part about Olivia. She laughed about the article he wrote about some of our dates, and my dad shook his head in disbelief because he'd read it and couldn't believe it was about me. In the end, they were both very impressed with the award he'd won and the speech he'd given.

"But that's not enough to erase years of heartache. I don't want you hanging around him anymore," my dad made sure to say when I was done.

I laughed, placing my hand over his. "We'll see; besides, it's not like he cheated on me. We weren't even together when it happened."

"You sure acted like he cheated on you," he said.

I had. I still did, because I didn't know how to accept him with other women. I thought about what he said to me the other night and how he'd seen me with all the guys I'd dated after him. I wouldn't be able to handle that.

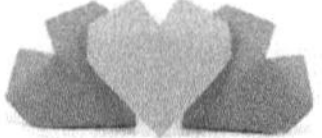

"I can't believe you told them about Jensen just to get me out of that," Rob said later, when we were sitting in front of the TV, in the apartment we used to share.

"It was nothing."

"It was something, Meep. I'm so sick of getting asked about Juan Pablo and whether or not he came out. I'm tired of hearing about it and thinking about it and wondering if it's because something is wrong with me, and he's ashamed of me." He paused to hold his hand up when I tried to interrupt. "I know it's not me. I've been there. I know how difficult it is to come out with it, even when you're positive your family already knows and accepts you for who you are. But still."

I reached out for his hand. "You are the most selfless person I know. I have faith that he'll do it, and you guys will be fine. Love always finds a way."

He stayed quiet but squeezed my hand back as we watched the season finale of *Game of Thrones*. When the credits finished rolling and the after show was starting, we looked at each other for a long wordless moment.

We spent the next hour talking about where the show could go next. It's not like we had the next book left to read, so we had to improvise and make up our own endings. When we were done talking and the only thing left to discuss was Jensen and Juan Pablo, we sat in silence and held hands, glancing at each other after long moments and speaking with our facial expressions.

It'll be okay, I said with a half smile.

I hope so, he said with his brows.

This is one of the many things I loved about hanging out with my brother, the familiarity of it all, the way words were optional between us. Maybe it was our cryptophasia. Maybe it was sibling solidarity. Whatever the reason, I was grateful for unspoken words, especially when it came to those subjects.

"I'm tired, so I'm going to crash," I said, finally, giving his hand one last squeeze as I stood and headed to the room I used to sleep in, which was now filled with boxes, even though the bed was still intact. I pivoted back around and looked at my brother, with his head thrown back over the couch, a hand buried in his dirty blond hair. Even with his eyes closed, I could see his anguish. It settled over his pulled in brows and worried lips. The feeling stirred inside of me, and all I could do was wish it away. "Robbie," I said, waiting for his eyes to snap open and look at me. "You're enough, and anybody who has your love should consider themselves the luckiest person on Earth." His mouth pulled into a smile. "And I'm not just saying that because you're my twin and we're the coolest people on Earth."

The sound of his laughter was the last thing I heard before I shut my door. Normally that was a typical day off for all of us, and those had been at the top of my list of how I preferred to spend my days, but for some reason, tonight it felt off. I felt like something was missing.

The sun was playing peekaboo behind a cluster of clouds most of the morning, but I felt my skin crisping beneath it nevertheless. I was staring at the tattoo of the artistic skull that took up most of my dad's back. It needed a serious touchup.

"You need more lotion." My head snapped up at the sound of Rob's voice, and I smiled at the sight of Juan Pablo walking up beside him. They both had their wet suits half-zipped and were holding surfboards under their arms.

"If I put on any more lotion, I'm going to feel like one of those salads you eat."

Juan Pablo laughed, dropping his black board beside mine and reaching for a hug. "She's right. Besides, she needs a tan. She's too pale."

I groaned. "Perks of moving to New York." I paused, squeezing Juan Pablo's torso as I hugged him back. "How was Brazil?"

"Good." He flashed me a wide grin and ran his hand through his long, wavy brown hair. "Really good."

I returned his smile as he sighed heavily and held my hands in his. "They took it well. Even my dad, surprising me."

"Surprisingly," Rob corrected, standing beside him.

"No. He really surprised me," Juan Pablo said.

We laughed. My brother couldn't stop smiling, which meant I couldn't either.

"So you're staying?" I asked.

My dad, who had been on the phone, finally ended the call and turned around. His eyes widened when he saw who was standing beside us.

"Juan Pablo. You're back…?" It was more of a question than a statement.

"I'm back. How are you?" he said, stepping toward him and shaking his hand.

"Ready to surf. Are you staying, or are we all going to have to get our passports renewed?"

Juan Pablo laughed, Rob's mouth dropped, and I slapped my forehead in disbelief. Unbeknownst to Juan Pablo, my brother had been toying with the idea of moving to Brazil, temporarily, if Juan Pablo felt like he needed to stay there.

"No rush to, but I would love to take you to my country. Good surfing over there, too."

Dad nodded and looked at Rob. "We should do that. Now let's go take advantage of the waves."

And we did. We spent the rest of the morning in the water, but I'd officially had the worst surfing day of my life. Dad kept saying I needed to concentrate. Robert said I needed to concentrate less. Juan Pablo summed it up by saying my heart wasn't in it. I didn't know where my heart was. It used to be full when I sat on this sand and stared at this beach. Now it was elsewhere.

I'd fused into Jensen, despite myself. I felt myself reaching for my phone constantly, and restraining myself from calling him every time. I found myself wishing he'd call me, and shuddered at the thought that maybe he never would. Maybe this time he'd let me go for good. He said he wouldn't, but he had in the past. Maybe he was sick of my shit and was the one who needed a break from me. The thought hit me like an unwarranted assault—quick, hard, and unforgiving, and I realized that I missed him a lot more than I cared to admit.

I missed his voice and his laughter, and just … everything.

Later, after I'd gone to my interview with Rob's friend at the museum, I agreed to meet my friends at one of my favorite sushi spots. Estelle and Oliver were already there when I walked in. I sat across from them, and ordered a drink. I was about to ask them who else would be joining us since we were at a big table, when Victor, Estelle's brother, and his friend and co-worker, Bobby, joined us.

"I thought we lost you to New York," Vic said as he leaned in to give me a hug.

"Never!"

He laughed as he took a seat beside me. Bobby sat across from us, beside

Oliver. "That bad?"

My eyes widened. "It's freezing there."

"Jensen seems to be okay with it," he said.

I rolled my eyes out of habit, because that was what I always did when Victor brought up his name, but inside I felt a pang of sadness. He laughed at my reaction.

"Well, all right then. I thought maybe he'd been writing about you as of late," he said.

I shot Estelle a bewildered look that said, "Tame your idiot brother!"

"Vic, shut up," she said, shaking her head.

"Hey, I was just making a comment."

I shook my head, and for once I was glad that Bobby jumped in with his overly flirtatious vibe.

"So, how long are you here for?"

"A couple of days."

"What are your plans for later?"

I laughed. Bobby was good looking, with the preppy, boy-next-door thing he had going. He wasn't totally *GQ* like Oliver, or Victor, and didn't have that unattainable charm that Jensen carried. In short, Bobby was not my type. He tried, though.

"I have no idea, but definitely not you, if that's what you're getting at."

He gasped, holding his hands to his heart. "Way to break a man's heart."

"I'm sure you'll live."

We continued our conversation throughout dinner, where Victor kept insisting we all go out.

"It's a new lounge. You guys will love it."

"Mia may love it. Some of us aren't about that life," Estelle said.

"Mia isn't about that life anymore either," I said, shooting her a pointed look.

"Since when?" Vic asked.

"Since … I don't know. Since it got old."

He frowned. "How could that get old?"

Oliver chuckled. "You'll see."

I laughed, and, when all eyes turned to me, I shrugged. "Fuck it. Let's go."

After dinner, I told Estelle I'd meet her at her place. I didn't go back to Rob's place right away. Instead, I went back to the beach and sat in the sand long after the dispersed surfers were gone, and it was only me and the impending sunset. I thought about my situation. About what I wanted and what I didn't, and the things I missed about home that I couldn't get in New York. I cataloged a list: my family, my friends, the beach, driving my own car places, the lifestyle, the weather. My list stopped there and looped back to the beginning: my family, my friends. Those things were irreplaceable to me.

When I got sick of sitting, sick of thinking, I pulled myself up, grabbed the camera I hadn't even taken out of the bag, and headed home. I ended up at Estelle's house on my way to Rob's, because suddenly I didn't feel like going out after all. She'd already started getting ready and was not keen on the idea of being the only girl at the lounge.

"No. You're not going to stay home and mope about this the one weekend you're here. You're going to get pretty and go out whether you like it or not."

"I'm already pretty," I said, groaning and burying my face in my hands.

She laughed and pulled them down. "You're so humble. I wonder why it is that you and Jensen get along so well."

My stomach dipped at the mention of his name. I started to smile, but it fell short quickly. "I miss him. So much. How is that even possible? God, I hate this. I'm not supposed to miss him!"

"I'm sure he misses you too. Have you spoken to him since the fight?"

I scoffed. "I would hardly call that a fight. It was a damn onslaught on his part. And nope, not a word."

"He's just giving you time."

I looked down at my lap. "I don't even know what I want anymore. All I know is that every time I think about him I want to be with him, and the entire time I was in my meeting with my new boss, I was wondering what he was doing. It's ridiculous."

She shrugged. "You'll figure it out. You don't need to have all the answers right now."

I let myself mull that over. I really didn't need all the answers right now. Maybe that was part of the problem. I was always trying to figure out what would happen next, making sure I didn't get hurt again.

"You're right."

"So you're coming out," she said. I smiled.

"I guess I am."

When I got back to Rob's place, he and Juan Pablo were in the kitchen cooking dinner. I ducked into the bathroom to get ready and told them I'd be out shortly.

"I feel like I'm finally getting my sister back," Rob said as he eyed my short little black dress, and my wavy hair, down to my shoulders now, and my ready-for-the-night makeup.

"Killer heels," Juan Pablo added.

"Yeah, so killer that I'm taking flats in my purse as backup."

They laughed and shook their heads.

"Where you going?"

"Some lounge. You know how Victor is when he plans an outing."

"That means you'll be drunk and hooking up with some attorney in no time," Rob said with a wink. He paused and frowned after mulling something over.

"Don't," I said before he could, but he went ahead and did anyway.

"Still no word from Jensen?"

I shook my head, sighing.

"I'm sure he is busy, Meep."

"Yeah, maybe."

"Go get drunk and have fun with random hot guys! Take one for the team!" he said.

"Hey!" Juan Pablo said, laughing behind us.

I smiled and gave him a small wave.

"Just don't hook up with his uncle again!" Rob called out as I headed down the hall.

My mouth dropped, and I stopped walking only to turn around and flash him both middle fingers. Fucker. I was never going to live that down. It didn't matter how many times I said that I didn't know the guy was related to him in any way. Or how many times I explained that we didn't even have sex.

The story would forever go down as, *'The time Mia was so drunk that she ended up in the corner of the club making out with Patrick Davis, who happened to be Jensen's birth father's younger brother.'* 'They don't even have the same last name!' I would yell in explanation. 'They don't even look alike!' And alas, the only reason people knew it happened was because Oliver was there and saw it happen and of course he told Victor, who told Jensen, who later came back and acted like I'd committed the biggest crime since Watergate.

The lounge was jam-packed. Victor had been texting a friend of his since we got inside, trying to figure out what our next move would be.

"You pay for bottle service someplace … the least they could do is save us a bigger space," he kept shouting over the music while he typed away on his cellphone.

Estelle and I shrugged and bumped shoulders as we shimmied along to the music. We didn't care where we partied, really. And when Oliver walked back toward us and leaned in to hand us our drinks, we were set.

"He's trying to see if we can rent out his friend's place in Malibu," Oliver explained upon sitting beside Estelle.

His friend's place in Malibu. Oh God. Suddenly the air started to dwindle out of my body. That house would forever be associated with Jensen. It was the reason I hadn't been back there since we broke up—not because the house itself brought up bad memories, but because I felt like if I saw him there when we weren't together it would have tainted all of the good memories we shared there. We weren't on bad terms anymore, though. Still, did I really want to go back to the house where we'd first kissed? The one we'd sneak to in the middle of parties to go make love near the ocean? For some reason, now, it made me miss him even more.

"Why does he always want to end up there?" I asked nobody in particular.

Oliver shrugged and took a swig of the beer in his hand. "It's more laid back."

"I'm surprised you're drinking."

Estelle laughed. "He'll drink one beer and then water the rest of the night."

"If I tell you the—"

"Effects alcohol has on your body you'd never drink it again," Estelle and I said in unison. She rolled her eyes while I shook my head.

"This is why I don't date nerds," I said.

Estelle laughed. Oliver let out a loud, hard laugh that made him slap his chest as he spurt out a cough.

"You don't think Jensen's a nerd?"

I took a sip of my vodka. "I'm not even sure I'm dating him, but for the sake of argument, no, I don't think he is."

Oliver chuckled. "Why? Because he drives a motorcycle?"

"And has hot tattoos," Estelle added.

Oliver rolled his eyes.

"He would never bring up the effects of alcohol while sitting in a fucking lounge. Only nerds do that kind of shit," I said.

"Really? What kind of people have key chains that say 'If found, please return to 221 Baker Street'?" Oliver asked.

I hid my smile behind my glass. "Really cool ones. Obviously."

Estelle laughed. "You just think that because you gave that to him."

"And because it's really freaking cool!"

"He writes for the newspaper," Oliver added, raising an eyebrow and the bottle of beer as if he'd just discovered a new elixir.

"It's not like he writes about the effects of global warming … but if he did, I still wouldn't think he's a nerd." I pursed my lips. "Well, maybe a little, but he would be a hot nerd."

Just as Oliver and Estelle's rambunctious laughter was dying down, Victor walked over and told us we were moving the party to the beach house.

"Just follow me," he said.

So I climbed in the backseat of Oliver's two-door coupe and scrolled through my Twitter feed as he drove. I stopped over Jensen's latest post and clicked it open.

"Jensen's in Santa Barbara?" I shouted, interrupting Oliver and Estelle's conversation.

Oliver's eyes flicked to me through the rearview. Estelle turned her body to face me.

"He is?" she asked. We both looked at Oliver, who resembled caged prey surrounded by lions. "Oliver?" she said, crossing her arms over her chest.

He stayed quiet, turning his car into the driveway of a white three-story house and parking it behind Victor's. When the engine was shut off, and the three of us took off our seatbelts, he glanced over at Estelle, then me, and shrugged.

"He comes home a lot, especially during football season." He paused when neither one of us said anything, just stared. "The Chargers play tomorrow."

"So? It's not like he's on the roster!" I replied. Oliver shook his head and got out of the car while Estelle laughed. "Does that mean he's coming?" I asked, shuffling after Oliver as soon as I got out of the car. He stopped walking and turned around, tilting his head to examine my face.

"Would it be a problem if he did?"

I frowned, looking down at my feet. "No."

"Did you invite anybody?"

My eyes snapped up to his. "What? No, I didn't invite anybody!" My stomach dipped. Oh God. "Is he bringing somebody?"

Oliver tried to smother a smile by scratching his nose. "I have no idea."

That feeling of my heart dropping into the pit of my stomach was unwelcome. I brushed past him and walked up the steps to go into the house. I could hear Estelle reprimanding him while he laughed, but I refused to turn around and acknowledge the stupid smirk I pictured on his face. After an hour of us sitting around the patio, drinking the vodka and wine Victor brought as the guys smoked their cigars, I felt myself completely relax. It was like college all over again—Victor, Oliver, and a few of their coworkers standing around talking crap while Estelle and I discussed my photography and what I would display if I ever got a bigger venue.

"You should go by your storage and see if you've taken any pictures like that," Estelle suggested.

I doubted I had. I'd mainly taken family portraits, aside from the more nature driven ones, and what I was trying to display was the dysfunction of our world.

"I guess I could very well put up pictures of families. We're all pretty dysfunctional," I said.

Estelle laughed.

"If you did, you'd have to display the beautiful *Game of Thrones* themed session you took of your own family." She paused, smiling. "Where you and Rob dressed as Cersei and Jaime. It's so sick. So sick."

I laughed. "You're never going to get over that."

"You know I won't. I'm going to get another drink. Want one?"

I nodded. "I'll be right back. I'm going to go out there to see if it still looks the same."

She laughed. "It's a beach, I doubt it's changed."

I shrugged, smiling as I walked over to the gate, pulling off my shoes as I got to the sand. I just stood there, by the gate, still within ear shot of the guys, who were talking and laughing, but closer to the ocean, where I could hear the waves crashing against the rocks at a nearby distance. Leaning my back against the wall beside the gate, I closed my eyes and wiggled my toes in the sand. With each splashing wave, the ocean lifted my worries and took them one by one, until all that was left was me, Mia, a girl who didn't feel as lost as she used to but couldn't have the things she wanted most. *Maybe you should allow yourself those things and stop second-guessing*, my thoughts yelled. *Maybe you should shut the eff up*, I replied back, and sighed.

I climbed back on the step and dusted the sand off my feet before stepping back into my heels. As I did, I heard the laughter get louder, and I stilled behind one of the bushes, because his laugh was among them. The sound made my nerves haywire, my heart flipped more times than I could count, until it settled in my sternum, holding my breath there with it. Even though I had warning that he would be, I felt shocked by his presence, and when I stepped forward and caught a glimpse of him, in his loose faded gray shirt and dark jeans, my heart picked up again. His hair rustled as a gust of wind hit. His shirt rode up slightly as he ran his fingers through it, and, as if feeling my eyes on him, he looked at me over Victor's shoulder.

For a beat, maybe two, we just stared at one another. Me on the other side of the pool, him in a crowd of friends, and it was like the first time we'd kissed, only backwards. He'd been the loner out by the pool, writing his little heart away, and I'd been the girl with the drink in her hand trying to flirt with him. The smile slid off his face, the charge inside of me building the longer we looked at each other. After what felt like an eternity, he walked over, his stride long and determined, until he reached me.

"Mia," he said, voice low and seductive.

"Jensen," I replied, hoping I didn't sound as breathless as I felt.

His eyes searched my face as if to ask, *Are you going to run? Are you going to stay?*

I swallowed, unsure.

Without preamble, he pushed his mouth against mine, prying my lips apart. My hands flew from my sides to his hair and tugged. I kissed him like I hadn't seen him in years, hadn't felt him in ages, and missed every second we'd been apart. We broke the kiss because of the hoots and hollers of those around us, but our foreheads stayed touching.

"I thought you were going to slap me for doing that in front of everyone," he said, breathing heavily against me.

"Did you want me to?"

He pulled away slightly and smiled. "No, but it would have been worth it."

"It was worth it without the slap," I said, and Jensen smiled.

"Okay, somebody needs to fill me in," Victor said in the background. "Last I heard she wanted to kill him."

Jensen shook his head. I laughed. He dropped his hand from mine as he stood farther away from me, letting his eyes roam the length of me, from my toes, to my thighs, to the tops of my breasts, and finally landed on mine. He swallowed, his eyes blazing with uncontained desire, and grabbed my hand.

"Was the purpose of you wearing that dress to give every man around you mental images of how you must look naked?"

"Are you asking because you're picturing me naked?"

He snaked his arm around me, still looking at me with the same heated expression, and spread his hand over my ass.

"You have no fucking idea what I'm picturing right now," he murmured, bringing his lips to mine again.

"Holy shit. Does this mean they're together, together?" Victor asked as we pulled away from each other.

"Why do you need to define everything?" I asked him as Jensen and I joined the crowd.

Victor shrugged. "I like knowing what to expect from things."

I groaned. "It must be so much fun to date you."

The guys laughed.

"I'd rock your world, Meep. You don't even know."

"Dude. I just got here, and you're already trying to start a fight?" Jensen said.

A wide smile spread over Victor and Oliver's face as Jensen stood there, scowling.

"Never thought I'd see the day," Victor said, then put a hand up. "Correction: never thought I'd see the day *again*."

"Get ready for all the calls he's going to start making once she moves back. 'Is she dating anyone? Are you sure? Who the fuck is the guy she took a picture with?'" Oliver said, laughing and stepping away as Jensen took a step toward him to grab the beer he had in his hand.

"Give me this. You've probably been nursing this shit all night," he said taking a huge swig of it.

My heart rocked at the mention of the guys I'd dated while he was gone, at the reminder of what he'd said before I asked him to leave, that he was always around, always watching. Jensen lowered the bottle from his mouth and looked at me, his brows furrowing at whatever face I must have been making.

"Walk with me."

My eyes flitted around the safe zone of the patio. If we left now, who knew when we'd come back.

"Let's just…"

"Walk with me, Mia." His voice was firmer this time.

I heard Victor say something about women coming over and glanced over at Estelle who was off to the side, talking to Oliver in hushed whispers. Everybody seemed to be doing their own thing anyway. I tugged on Jensen's hand and began to walk with him, stopping to take off my shoes when we got near the sand.

"God, you're short," he said once I was finished and took his hand again.

"I'm fun-sized."

"Fun you are," he said, lifting me up and carrying me like a baby.

"You're going to make me flash everybody!"

He repositioned me, and I tried to pull my dress down, to no avail. It was way too short and tight to fix.

"First of all, there's nobody around. Secondly, I already told you what I think about that dress."

I turned my face into his chest and hid my smile.

"Were those guys hitting on you? I know how they can be."

I chuckled against him. "Why do you care?"

He stomped on until he reached a spot beside an empty lifeguard station. He put me down so that we were blocked from view as he stood in front of me. It was dark and vacant out. The only sounds we could hear were our friends and others speaking at a distance and the water washing into the shore from the waves that died down steps from where we stood.

"You know why I care," he said, his dark gaze jumping from one of my eyes to the other.

"Because you're jealous?"

"I'm not jealous."

"You're a little jealous." I smiled and leaned in to run my fingers through his hair, tugging until he closed his eyes and let out a low groan.

"I'm not. I just don't like it."

"You don't want them telling me how I should give them a chance and let them fuck me the way I deserve to be fucked?" I said, biting back a smile as his eyes snapped open. "Or how they'd rock my world? Or how they want to feel my lips around their hard cock?"

Jensen stepped forward and walked me back until my back hit the wall behind me, then pulled us down. My back was against the cool sand as he hovered over me. He pulled my bottom lip into his mouth and lowered his body flush against mine.

"Is that what they said to you?" he asked as his lips explored my jaw, my neck, my shoulders. "Did they promise you'd be the only person they'd ever look at for the rest of their lives if you had them?" He brought his mouth up from my chest and to the side of mine. "Did they tell you they left an important meeting because the thought of you being here, so far away from them, was killing them?" His mouth fell over mine and captured my loud gasp. "Did they push back a deadline because they missed you, because they couldn't think without you," he murmured against my lips. "And the thought of this moment, just this, holding you like this, was enough for them to not give a damn about their publisher's threats to withhold their paycheck for three more months?"

"Jensen," I whispered, rearing back to search his face. "Why would you—"

His lips were on mine before I could finish my sentence. Our hands became desperate, tugging at our clothes until his jeans were pulled down, and my panties were ripped and thrown aside. He held the sides of my face as he pivoted his hips to guide himself inside of me, and when he did, he was there with one hard thrust that made me cry out and claw at his back.

"Because this is worth more than any of those things," he said, his voice a low purr. He pulled out slowly, letting me feel every ridge of his length, before pushing back in all the way and making me yelp again. He groaned.

"Because there's no price tag for what we have," he continued. His lips found my neck as he rocked against me in deeper strokes. "And even if there was one, I'd find a way to pay it four times over."

I whimpered as he increased his pace, and let my moans and screams get washed away in the waves before us.

"I wish we could spend the entire night wrapped around each other," he said regretfully. We were both full of sand, standing outside of my apartment.

"I would invite you in, but I'm not even sure this is my place anymore."

Jensen chuckled. On our way over there I'd told him about Rob and Juan Pablo and how I wasn't sure where I belonged anymore. *Move to New York permanently*, he'd suggested. *It's not that easy*, I'd responded. I couldn't just move. For a few months, sure, but forever? I couldn't.

"I would invite myself over, circumstances be damned, but Olivia's awaiting," he said smiling. I stiffened. He noticed and glanced over. "What?"

I shook my head. "Last time I saw her … when I saw her, you acted so weird around me. I guess I just want to know what I should expect."

He sighed. "I spoke to Krista about this the day you saw us, the day you ran," he corrected. "I don't know how to act around Olivia when I'm with you because I've never done it. She's never met anybody I've dated before. Not that I've dated many women."

"Maybe we can act like friends?" I said, my fingers scratching over his beard.

"I don't know if I know how to do that with you," he said. "I'm not sure I know how to pretend that I don't want to kiss you, that I don't want to touch you."

I smiled. "You can try. I'm fine with that. No handholding, no kissing, just friends, at least for now. We don't want to confuse her, especially if I'm coming back home soon for good."

His demeanor changed at the mention of that, but he didn't say anything about it, and I decided to change the subject to his foster mom. She was always a safe zone conversation.

"Do you bring her to visit Patty often?"

"When I can."

I swallowed. "You haven't heard from…"

He shook his head, knowing I was asking about his birth mother, the woman who'd left him and never turned back once she did. I would have thought she would have reached out when he started making a name for himself, but apparently I'd been wrong.

"I looked for her once, and found her, but I never contacted her. I always blamed myself for her leaving, until I realized it wasn't my fault."

"It wasn't. Did Olivia help you realize that?" I asked. He nodded.

"Children are so innocent. They try so hard to be good kids for us, and they are; they're the best things we could ask for, despite their tantrums and the hard moments. I don't have to prove that I'm a worthy son. I know I am, and if she was caught up in other things and couldn't see that, that's fine. I forgive her, but I don't want that kind of person, one who hasn't bothered to look for me after she left me, around my daughter." He shrugged.

I stayed quiet, not wanting to disrupt the unloading of his closeted skeletons.

"I thought about Olivia, and how if Krista just up and left, or if I did, she'd have to carry that burden for the rest of her life." He paused to swallow. His gaze found mine again. "I was lucky. Not everybody is as lucky as me. Not everybody has a Mia, or a Patty." I squeezed his hand when he finished speaking.

"But if that ever happened, she has you, and you're enough for ten people."

Jensen chuckled quietly. "I'm barely enough for one person, Mia, but for her, I try."

He raised his hand to wipe a tear that had escaped my eyes.

"I'm sorry," I whispered finally. "For not being there for you."

He kissed the tip of my nose. "I know, babe. So am I."

"I really was hurt by all of it. I didn't know how to cope."

He kissed the tip of my nose again before moving to the edge of my mouth. "I don't think I would have known how to either, Meep."

After a long silent moment, I leaned on my elbows and looked over again.

"My dad knows about us." I laughed at the horrified look on his face.

"Does he still have that Glock he used to have?"

I laughed again. "Yes, but that was a long time ago!"

Jensen stared at me for a long moment. "I really think he wants to kill me."

"Maybe so, but I'm here to protect you."

He scoffed. "We'll see about that."

Jensen and I had stayed up talking for hours; even after he dropped me off, he called me and we stayed on the phone. It was like we were teenagers all over again. As if being back there together brought all of the good times we spent together with it. In conversation he mentioned that Olivia was dying to go to the beach, and I knew he'd miss the day with the guys if he took her, so I volunteered to go with Patty.

I showed up at Patty's just as Jensen was leaving. Literally. I brought my hand up to knock on the white wooden door just as he was opening it. He grinned, running a hand through his hair, and if it hadn't been wet, the smell of his soap would have been enough for me to know he was freshly showered.

"Have I ever told you how awesome you are?" he said, still smiling, his eyes taking me in slowly. "What are you wearing under there?"

I laughed, taking a step back when he hooked his finger on the scarf I'd shifted into a sundress and tugged. "You're going to make it come undone."

His eyes flared as they locked on mine. He shook his head. "You say shit like that…"

"Like you making me come undone?"

"Like me making you come—period," he responded, wrapping an arm around my waist and pulling me flush against him. Every inch of him was hard. Every. Inch.

I inhaled sharply.

"You probably shouldn't do that … friend."

He growled, bringing his lips down to mine and kissing me with a passion that had me shivering despite the heat.

"I love your lips … friend," he said, a whisper against my mouth.

"I love yours too, friend."

"When is Mia coming?" That was Olivia's little voice, coming from inside the small house.

I dropped my arms from his neck and took a step back. He smiled at me.

"Somebody's excited."

"I'm excited too," I said.

He didn't respond to that, but the look of tenderness he gave me spoke more volumes than the Britannica. His lips pressed against mine one last time. A quick, soft peck.

"I'll see you later," he said, and walked off.

I waited for my heart to settle before knocking on the door. Patty, Olivia, and I headed off to start our day. Olivia kept saying she wanted to learn how to surf, so I started teaching her—on land, of course.

"But I want to do it in the water!" she said.

"But you can't yet, and your dad would put me in time-out if I let you," I said.

She laughed. "He can't put you in time-out. You're a grown-up!"

"Yeah, well, that doesn't mean I'm not scared of time-out."

She fell into a fit of laughter over that, and Patty smiled as she looked on.

"You're really good with her," she said when Olivia turned her attention to building a sand castle.

"When we both have adult supervision."

Patty laughed. "You're good with her, period. Do you know how many women in your shoes would never give that child the time of day?"

"Do you know how many women wouldn't have given her father the time of day?" I asked, smiling at her.

I'd always been thankful for Patty. I couldn't imagine what would have happened to Jensen had he not had her in his life. His life would have turned out so differently.

"That boy gave me more headaches than any person deserves."

"You and me both. But he's a good guy."

She raised an eyebrow. "He is. Does that mean you're back on?"

I shook my head, looking over at Olivia's castle. "It's more complicated than that."

"The best things always are."

"Can you help me build this?" Olivia said in a whine as she looked over at us. We both laughed and moved over to her.

We spent the day building castles that would eventually fall, with hope that they'd last long enough. I took pictures of them, of us, of the beach, of Jensen and the guys when we crashed their football viewing party at Victor's house.

"I didn't know we were letting people of all ages into our club," Victor said, smiling as he picked up Olivia and gave her a kiss on the cheek.

"You always say that, Uncle Vic."

"You're the only girl allowed here on Football Sunday," he whispered.

She frowned at him and pouted. "What about Mia?"

Victor chuckled as he looked from me to her. "She doesn't count."

"She does count." She grabbed my hand and walked over to the couch where Jensen was sitting. "Daddy, Mia's in my club. You're in Uncle Vic and Uncle Bean's club."

"What if I want to be in your club?" he asked, draping an arm around my waist and touching her face with his free hand as he rested his boot on the edge of Vic's coffee table. I shot him a look, trying to shimmy out of his hold, but he held me tighter.

"Well…" Olivia said, her eyes flicking to mine momentarily. "We'll have to see. Do you want him in our club?"

Jensen pinched my side. "Yeah, Mia, do you want me in your club?"

I laughed and tried to scoot away from him again, but he pulled me toward him and bit my other arm as I neared. "Shit, Jensen!" He chuckled. Olivia gasped. Victor and Oliver both looked over and shook their heads. "Sorry," I added in a mumble.

"Daddy, you can't bite her. She's not going to want to let you in the club if you do that. It's not nice."

"Yeah, Daddy, it's not nice," I said with a pout that made the look in his eyes heat up.

"I'm going to show you how nice I can be later," he whispered in my ear when Olivia stood up and sat beside Oliver.

"Yeah? You're not going to bite me anymore?"

"Maybe I will," he said, nipping my shoulder, and licking over the sting. "Maybe you'll like it."

I felt my entire body heat up at the promise in his gaze, his words, his touch.

"Friends, Jensen," I whispered.

He grinned and leaned in until his mouth was right by my ear. "I told you. I don't know how," he whispered.

Everything about being there, with our friends, in our hometown, was perfect. Often I wished I could rewind time, just to relive that day.

Jensen Talks

I don't claim to know everything, but I've lived enough to know that second chances don't happen often—if ever. This past weekend I was reminded of that. I went "home" for the weekend, and took my daughter with me, to visit my friends and foster mom. Being back there always takes me back to my childhood, which is both good and bad since my childhood wasn't full of the best experiences. Not all of it, anyway. Every time I'm there, I'm forced to relive those memories, and I never regret it. It seems like with each year that passes I appreciate those memories more and more. Some days I cling to the good ones. Other days I seek to remember the bad ones, so I can appreciate the good ones I make now.

I guess the reason this visit was different for me was because I was there with Olivia and Mia. Having them there together with our friends was definitely something I never thought would happen. I'd imagined it before, but that was all it ever was, a figment of my imagination. Having it come true was surreal.

Question of the day: @AnjeliMaed: "How to know that you've already moved on?"

Answer: Only you can answer that. I think when you're no longer comparing that person to everybody you meet.

I was back in New York when Millie called me and started apologizing profusely upon my answering the call, I braced myself for her to say she couldn't get any of her contacts to display my prints. But then she said the most magical words I'd ever heard, "I got you a spot in The MET! It's for this Saturday, and I know it's last minute, but they had two artists back out and now they're scrambling to find replacements."

"Oh my God. Oh my God. Oh my God!" I squealed over and over and over until my legs were tired from jumping and my eyes stopped producing tears. "My pictures are going to be on the walls of The Met! Oh my God. I die. I die. I die!"

Millie laughed. "You better not. I need you there Saturday!"

I squealed again. "I love you. I love you. I love you!"

My phone rang as soon as I hung up with her, and I answered without even looking.

"I need a huge favor." Those were the first words out of Jensen's mouth.

"Okay?" I asked as I tried to reel myself in from the high I was on.

"Is your day really hectic tomorrow?"

From the living room, I squinted to make out the time on the microwave. It was still early enough that I could go to the printer and tell them what photos I needed rush printed. Once that was settled, I didn't have much to do that couldn't wait until Thursday.

"No. What's up?"

"Do you think you can watch Olivia for a couple of hours?"

I dropped the phone. I picked it up just as quickly as I gathered my scattered thoughts. I'd hung out with her a few times, but a few times didn't make me an expert in little kids.

"Um … sure. Are you going to bring her over, or do you want me to come over?"

He stayed quiet for a beat. "Can you come over here?"

"Of course."

"You can come over tonight, if you want. I have this big empty space beside me with your name on it."

I laughed, but waved off the invitation. If I went over there I wouldn't get any work done. Upon hanging up, I started browsing through pictures I'd taken and transferring them to a USB drive. On my way to the printer Millie recommended, I crossed my fingers and said a prayer and a chant I learned in yoga that week to calm my nerves. The guy at the shop, who looked like he belonged in a motorcycle club, looked at me like I was crazy when I told him I needed them by Saturday morning.

"And that's kind of pushing it," I added, cringing when he shot me another one of his looks.

"I can have them back to you, but the size you want…" he paused to stroke on his beard, as I pleaded with my eyes. Finally, he sighed. "Give me a second."

He huffed as he stomped to the back of the store. I exhaled heavily and looked around at the beautiful artwork they had displayed.

"What kind of pictures did you say these were?" he asked when he walked back to his spot behind the counter.

"Mostly people," I said and could tell he was working hard not to roll his eyes at me. "Look at them," I added. "Please."

He raised a bushy eyebrow and let out a deep chuckle. "Okay, I'll look. But just so you know, even if I like them doesn't mean I can get them to you that quick."

I groaned and slid the USB drive closer to him on the counter. He laughed as he picked it up.

"Gum?"

"My brother's idea of a funny stocking stuffer."

The guy shook his head as he inserted it into the computer. I watched his face the entire time and smiled the moment the smile dropped from his face and his gaze turned serious as he scrolled.

"Fuck," he said.

I nodded, still smiling. When he finished he looked at me again and I felt like he had a different appreciation for me, maybe even respect.

"I really, really need to get these by Saturday morning. It's my only chance to display them at The MET. The MET!" I added with enthusiasm.

He nodded, stroked his beard again, and clicked on something in the computer. This time when he looked at me, he smiled.

"Come by Saturday at eleven. I'll have them ready." He laughed when I squealed and jumped up and down. Had it not been for the counter between us, I would have hugged him.

I woke up earlier than I needed and caught the seven-thirty Pilates class. My gossip homeless guy was missing from the L train, which threw me off since I counted on him for my current events. After showering, throwing on the warmest clothes I had washed, I grabbed my bag and headed to Jensen's. On my way there, I cataloged the pictures being displayed and tried to come up with names for each. WWhen the train reached the stop I needed to take, I got off, switching my phone as I started walking, and started scrolling through it. I still had a good five-minute walk ahead of me, after all.

"You should probably watch where you're going," Jensen called out as I neared his place.

"I would, but the homeless guy who keeps me up on current events wasn't on the train this morning."

"People.com is considered current events?" he asked, hopping off the steps when I reached him.

I scowled, pushing down on the button to hide my screen. "I wasn't on *People.*"

"Uh-huh." He wrapped his arms around me and squeezed, lifting me off the floor slightly as he buried his face in my neck. "Thank you for coming," he said as he set me down and grabbed my hand to lead me inside. "Olivia's still asleep. She's really sick."

"Poor thing. Is she running a fever?"

He nodded. "I'm alternating between Motrin and Tylenol every four hours. I just gave her some, so she should be good for a while."

"Will she eat when she wakes up?"

"Maybe. She didn't want to eat anything yesterday."

"Where's Krista?"

His eyes flickered to mine in surprise. I guess because I used her name and didn't attach a role like 'Olivia's mom' or 'your ex' to it.

"She's had meetings all week, so Olivia's been here."

I nodded and bit my tongue from saying anything else. Olivia wasn't my daughter, and I was sure this wasn't the first time Olivia had been sick. Maybe her mom was used to it. Maybe she was worried sick over the fact that she hadn't been able to take care of her. I wasn't here to judge. Well, I was *trying* not to judge.

"I have a meeting I can't miss today, and I'm on a ridiculous deadline that I don't think I'll meet because when she's with me it's nearly impossible for me to write."

"I can stay here a while." I paused. "I mean, a couple of days." I looked away from his stare. "I mean, if you need me to and need the help. I don't want to be in the way or anything. And I don't want her mom to get pissed off if she finds out I'm watching her daughter and she doesn't like me or something—"

"Mia."

"What?" I brought my gaze to his again.

"You can stay here as long as you want. Forever, even."

I felt my face heat up. "Stop."

His grin was wide as he walked over to me and tilted my chin up with his hand. "Thank you for doing this." He kissed my forehead. "And I would love it if you'd stay here for a couple of days, or forever, you pick."

My heart spiked. At his words, at the seriousness in his eyes, at the way his hand made me feel like I was the one running a fever.

"Don't you have to go?" I asked in a whisper.

He dipped his head closer and pressed his lips against mine. "I do."

"Okay."

"Call me if you need anything."

"I think I can handle it."

"I think you can handle anything," he said, dropping one last kiss on my lips as he shrugged on his jacket.

I watched his back as he walked down the hall and out and craned my head toward the upstairs of the house. Should I just let her sleep or go up there? Would she be scared if she woke up and he wasn't here? Did he warn her that I'd be here? Oh my God. What if her fever was really bad? What the fuck did I get myself into?

After a while, I decided to stay downstairs, at the foot of the stairs, to be specific and wait until I heard noise. At around eleven-thirty, I heard something loud drop onto the floor, and I rushed upstairs, taking them two at a time.

"Olivia?" I called out, my voice frantic.

When she didn't respond, I called out her name again, louder. I reached her door and found her standing in front of her bed, in a pair of pink *Frozen* pajamas. Her messy brown hair was covering most of her face as she looked down in front of her, whimpering.

"You okay?" I asked as I walked over. A foul smell annihilated my nostrils, and I realized she'd vomited on the floor in front of her. "Holy shit," I whispered. Her big gray eyes snapped up at that. "Sorry. Forget I said that. It's okay. It's going to be fine. Can you step over here?"

With one hand, I grabbed hers and led her around the vomit, and with the other I reached into the back pocket of my jeans and called her dad. He picked up on the first ring.

"Am I allowed to give her a bath? She kind of … had an accident," I said as I combed her hair out of her face with my fingers.

"Fuck. Maybe I should just cancel this meeting."

"No. No. She's fine. She doesn't seem to have a fever or anything, just this, but I don't want her to feel gross, and she got it on her pajamas and—"

"Mia," he said. "Yes, it's okay to give her a bath. Thank you."

"'Kay. I'll talk to you later. Go kick ass in your meeting." I shut my eyes. "Sorry. Go … do good!"

Jensen chuckled. "Thanks."

I hung up the phone and tossed it on the white nightstand as I crouched down to meet Olivia's gaze. "Did your daddy tell you I'd be here?"

She nodded.

"Is it okay if I help you take a bath?"

She stood frozen for a moment before nodding again.

"Can you help me pick out clothes for you?"

Another nod, and this time, a small smile.

I breathed out a heavy sigh of relief. I really hoped her mother wouldn't be upset about this. I thought if I was in her shoes, I'd be grateful. I sighed again. I hoped I would be grateful. After she was bathed and changed, I took her downstairs and gave her Gatorade, because that was what my mom would have given me.

"Do you think you can stay here and watch TV while I go clean up?"

"Yes," she whispered.

"Do you want me to make you something to eat before I do that?"

She looked at me, tilting her head the same way her dad did when he was trying to figure something out.

"I know how to cook," I added.

I couldn't believe I was convincing a little girl about my cooking skills. I couldn't believe she was even questioning them with one damn look.

"What do you know how to make?"

I smiled. "What do you feel like eating?"

"Ice cream."

I laughed. "Okay. I don't know if your dad will allow ice cream. What about soup?"

She pursed her lips.

"Really yummy soup. Like the one Princess Anna eats."

"She doesn't eat soup. She eats chocolate."

"And soup! Come on, it'll be good, and then we'll have something sweet."

"Like ice cream?"

"If your throat doesn't hurt, we'll reevaluate that after you drink your soup."

She let out a sigh and pulled her knees up to her chest. "That's what Daddy says when he means no."

"Hey, gimme some credit. I'm a little bit cooler than Daddy!"

She eyed me for a beat. "Can I take pictures with your camera again?"

I laughed. "After you drink your soup. And we can play dress up if you feel better in a little while."

She sat up straighter. "I feel better now."

"After your soup."

Finally, she nodded, and I went off to make her soup. The process of eating it went much smoother than talking about it. After she ate, I gave her my camera and let her use it while I went upstairs to clean up, and was unpleasantly surprised to discover that child vomit was just as bad as adult vomit. When I was finished, I grabbed my phone and headed downstairs again.

"I took a bunch," she said, handing me the camera to look through.

I laughed at what I found.

"You took a bunch of selfies."

"That's what Mom does."

"That's funny," I said, and snapped one of us together.

We moved on to dress up, and I made sure to continuously check her temperature, just in case. As she was applying purple glitter on strands of my hair, the phone rang, making us both freeze in place.

"Are we supposed to be using this for dress up?" I asked in a whisper.

She shrugged. "It was just there."

"Holy crap. Is this not child proof?"

The phone continued to ring, and I finally unfolded my legs and got up from the floor. I watched Olivia as I picked it up from the holster and answered it.

"Is this Mia?" said the voice of a woman on the other end. Her voice had a sweet melodic ring to it that tamed my nerves.

"Yes."

"This is Olivia's mom … Krista," she added after a pause.

"Oh. Hi."

"Is Olivia awake?"

"She is, do you want to speak to her?"

I let Olivia talk to her mom while I cleaned up the kitchen and read the back of the purple glitter bottle. When Olivia was finished with the phone, she called me over and handed me the phone.

"Thank you for watching her. If Jensen calls, will you let him know that I'm going to pass by around six-thirty?"

"Sure. That's fine."

"Okay, well, I guess I'll see you later if you're still hanging around."

"Sure."

I ended the call before things got any more awkward.

"Are you going to be like my mommy?"

My eyes flashed to Olivia, who was still sitting on the floor. It took me three tries to get the phone back on the base before I went to join her on the floor.

"Why do you ask?" I said finally, once we were side by side again.

She tilted her face to look at me. "I have two daddies."

I frowned. "You do?"

She nodded, looking at me with a serious expression on her face. "One lives here and one lives with my mommy. Are you going to live here if you become my mommy?"

This child was making my heart hurt with her questions and the way her eyes tried to focus on me despite their heaviness.

"Why don't we lie down for a little while?" I suggested.

"I'm not tired."

I pulled her onto my lap anyway and switched the TV to The Disney Channel. Soon she dozed off with her head on my chest and her arms dropped to either side of me. Somehow I managed to stand and set her down on the couch behind me, covering her with a San Diego Chargers blanket Jensen had draped over the sofa.

Her nap lasted all of fifteen minutes, and she woke up with the energy of a Jack Russell Terrier. It took me a while to convince her that we shouldn't use that purple thing on my hair anymore. As it was, I wasn't sure it would come off. It took ten minutes of going back and forth about ice cream before she let it go and let me give her Gatorade and grapes instead.

"Why'd you cut them?" she asked as I handed her a little plate. I glanced at her as I popped one in my mouth.

"Isn't that what people do for little kids?"

She made a face. "Not for me. I'm big. I'm almost five."

"I'm well aware."

"Do you know when my birthday is?"

"November eighth."

Her brows hiked up. "How did you know?"

I smiled. *Facebook, Olivia. Facebook.* "I think I heard Uncle Oliver talking about it once."

She beamed at the mention of Oliver. "You know Uncle Bean knows how to braid my hair."

"He does?" I asked, genuinely impressed.

She nodded furiously.

"Do you?"

"I think I still remember how to do a braid or two. Come here." I sat her between my legs, facing the television. I'd put on that stupid *Frozen* movie when she woke up and she hadn't even looked at the television. Gathering her hair, I split it into three parts. I stared at it for a couple of beats before I realized I only knew how to do a classic braid, so I took my phone out and watched some tutorials, which can make anybody a professional braider in less than twenty-minutes.

After the braid was done, I snapped a picture and sent it to Oliver, and laughed at the mad emoji face he used to reply. We ate soup together the second time around, and finally settled on reading some books she had. The TV was still on as the sun set, and I hadn't heard anything else from Jensen or Krista, aside from Jensen's texts, checking up on Olivia.

After talking about which movie is better: *Toy Story* or *Monsters, Inc.* *Toy Story*, we both agreed.

And who has prettier hair: Jasmine or Rapunzel.

She said Rapunzel, I said Jasmine.

We both ended up quieting down to watch *Frozen*. I was on a boat when I felt my body shake, but I was reaching the shore, extending a hand to Prince Hans, who looked like Kit Harrington, which was how I *knew* I was dreaming.

"I'm almost there," I said, battling as the rocking of the boat threatened to wake me. When I finally came to, I blinked a couple of times; slowly at first, then rapidly as Jensen's face came into my line of vision. Then it hit me—I was here to watch Olivia, and I fell asleep. I jolted quickly, but his hand steadied me so that I wouldn't get up, and I realized why: Olivia was sleeping peacefully, the side of her face on the top of my chest, one arm on one side of me, and the other hanging on the other side.

"Hey," I whispered, finally really looking at Jensen. He crouched down so that his face was beside mine and ran his fingers through my hair.

"Hey," he whispered back, his eyes washing over my features until they reached mine again. "How was she?"

I smiled. "Great."

"What were you dreaming about?"

I smiled brighter. "Kit Harrington."

Jensen chuckled, shaking his head as he stood. "I'm going to grab her and put her in her bed."

He did, and I sighed at the way she hugged his neck and snuggled into him as he walked. There was something to be said about a man holding a child in such a loving way. The only phrase that came to mind was: panty dropper. I realized then, as I watched and swooned, that if I spent any more days like this, in his house with him and his kid, I wouldn't want to leave. And I was not the mothering type. I really wasn't. I said like a hundred curse words in front of the poor girl and used some weird colored glitter glue on my head that was bound to stay there for life.

"You made this?" he asked, dipping a finger and sucking it into his mouth.

God. He even did that in a sexual way. I probably should've just gotten up and left right then. It wasn't until I spent the day with his daughter that I started feeling my ovaries kicking and my brain saying, "This could be you!" I never wanted that. Ever. But being there with him, with them, made me want to want it, and that was unacceptable for so many reasons. He picked up the pink bowl and cup that were sitting on the counter and put them in the sink and suddenly he looked even hotter. Was he always that hot? I blinked away from my thoughts because he was looking at me, probably waiting for an answer as he stirred the soup to heat it up and my daydream was bound to get X-rated quickly.

"Yeah. I know you said waffles, but I thought this was better for her since she's sick and soup always helps me when I'm—"

He was taking long strides over with a look on his face that rattled me enough to make me shut my mouth. He clasped the back of my neck with his hand and pulled my mouth to his, kissing me deeply, thoroughly. I could taste a hint of the chicken soup on his desperate tongue. And when he broke the kiss, I pushed against him for another. Finally, we broke apart, and his forehead touched mine.

"Thank you," he breathed.

The doorbell ringing interrupted us, and while he went to open it, I went to the bathroom. I wasn't sure I was ready to meet Krista in person just yet. I'd gage it according to whatever I heard while I was in there, but I didn't hear a woman at all. After washing my hands and fixing my hair, I went back to the kitchen and found him standing with his back resting on the counter as he typed something on his phone.

"That was Olivia's grandma."

"She picked her up?"

"Yeah, quick pick up. Something about the weather tonight. Olivia was sleeping, though, so you didn't miss anything," he said, setting his phone aside to look at me.

I wrapped my arms around his torso as he pushed the hair out of my face. "How was your meeting? Did you get any writing done?"

He ran his hands down my shoulders, my arms. "The meeting was fantastic. The writing … it took me a while to get into, but once I finally did, it went well."

"What was the meeting about?" I asked, leaning up to drop a kiss on his clavicle. He took a sharp intake of breath when I started unbuttoning his dress shirt, dropping a kiss on his bare chest, over the long black feather tattooed down his thorax between every button.

"Deadlines."

"Hmm." I made my way down, my tongue running over the contours of his lower abdomen.

"Mia," he said roughly as his hands went to my head.

"Hmm?" I unbuckled his belt and pulled down his jeans, craning my head to look at him.

The fervor in his eyes didn't match the tenderness in which he touched me. My heart pounded as I reached for his boxers and pulled them down to wrap my hand around him. He let out a shivered breath as I moved up and down slowly, and a groan when I pressed my lips against him, licking, tasting, sucking until his moans filled the space around us with low, altered *oh my god, Mia*, and *that feels so fucking good*. As I continued and increased the pace, his grip got tighter and his words became, *stay with me* and *I've missed you so fucking much*. And finally his words faded, and the only thing left was those low guttural grunts he let out as he pumped inside of my mouth until a shiver ricocheted through him and all that was left were the pieces of him I swallowed.

He adjusted his clothes, watching me as I stood up and wiped around my lips.

"You should probably just move in," he said.

I laughed and slapped him playfully. My heart tripped a little at the feel of his warm naked chest beneath my hand. I was in serious trouble if I was still feeling that way after going down on him.

"Are we still on for Saturday?" he asked, smiling as he buttoned his shirt.

I frowned until I remembered our deal about brunch on Saturdays. "Shit. I can't."

He looked at me, silently waiting for me to explain myself.

"Rob and my parents are coming in this weekend. Estelle too," I added.

"Oh. I thought you went home because Rob couldn't come?"

My eyes flitted around the kitchen, over the stove and the light blue backsplash over the counters. Finally, I looked back at him and couldn't contain my smile. "I … my pictures are going to be displayed somewhere this weekend."

"What! Where?"

I paused, biting down on my bottom lip to contain the squeal of excitement that derived from me saying the words aloud. "The MET!"

Jensen's jaw dropped. "No fucking way."

"Yes fucking way!" I said, letting out a laugh as I clapped my hands together.

"Why haven't you told me about this? First you don't tell me about the little gallery right around the corner and now this?"

"I…" I shrugged, looking away. "You've been busy."

"Mia," he said, tilting my face to look up at him. "I'm never too busy for you."

I shrugged again. He really had been busy. So busy that every time I did see him or speak to him I felt like making him go to bed and stay there until he got a good night's rest.

"Do you need help taking your things over there?"

My eyes scanned his handsome face, and I smiled as his lips formed a wide smile. "I'm sure Robbie will help."

"I want to help." He paused, stepping close enough that our noses were touching. "I want to help you, and I want to be by your side when you show the world your talent."

I swallowed past the knot his words managed to create in my throat. "It's not the world."

"I don't care if it's two people. I want to be there with you." He sighed and dropped a kiss on my forehead. "I've missed so much, Mia. Don't make me miss more. Let me go with you."

Because I felt like I was going to cry, I didn't speak. I just nodded and blinked away from the sincerity in his eyes. I wanted to shout, *"I'm leaving soon, remember?!"* but I contained myself.

"Is that okay with you?" he asked, flicking his nose against mine.

I nodded.

"Good, because I would have stalked the shit out of you and shown up anyway."

That garnered a laugh from me. He listened with ultimate interest as I went on and on about these pictures and how excited I was to finally have people see them, then he helped me title each one based on my descriptions for them since I refused to show him the pictures. I wanted him to get the full experience. We talked until dusk settled, and I decided I had to leave.

Even after all of my refusal he tried to bribe me with his skilled fingers and tongue, but slight insecurities nagged at me and I decided I needed to go home. He walked me down the steps and put his lips against mine in a kiss I felt all the way to my toes.

"You're not going to bribe me to stay, you know?" I whispered against his mouth.

He smiled. "Not today, but one day."

Davis, the long-bearded biker from the printing shop, ended up delivering the canvases for me. Rob and Jensen helped me set them up as I dictated and bitched when they put them up lopsided.

"Remember, we're not getting paid for this," my brother reminded me.

"I'll remember this moment when I'm getting paid to have my work displayed worldwide."

They both got a kick out of that. Once the canvases were set, Helen, one of the curators, and I went one by one and put the little description plaques beside them. Every once in a while you created something that made you proud to the point of tears when you looked at it. The photos displayed on that wall were it for me, and the reaction they got out of everybody, Helen included, drove that point home. Rob, Jensen, and I met up with my parents for lunch at a place Jensen said had the best Mexican food in the city. We were all way more interested in the margaritas, and those were delicious, so it worked. My dad's deep blue eyes were fixated on Jensen's arm around me as he sat across the table. I could tell that despite his excitement about Olivia when we visited him in Santa Barbara, he wasn't completely sold on this tattooed, motorcycle-driving writer swooping into my life again.

"How are things with your ex-wife?" Dad asked, his eyes narrowed at Jensen, the way a wild cat staked out its prey.

"Good. We have a pretty good schedule worked out, and we're friendly so it works."

"How friendly?"

The words made my insides flip. Jensen dropped his hand from my shoulder and onto my lap, where he squeezed my hand. I took a large sip of my margarita, hoping the tequila would kick in faster.

"We co-parent well. She's been living with a serious boyfriend." He paused and smiled as he remembered something. "Fiancé now, who also has a daughter from a previous marriage, and as far as exes and new fiancés go, I would say we're really friendly," he said, meeting my gaze with a smile.

I waited until the conversation veered off that topic to excuse myself and go to the bathroom, and when I came back and caught some of what they'd been talking about, I paused.

My dad's brows rose. "So if you get my daughter pregnant," he said, pausing to add, "which better not fucking happen … and she moved on with somebody else afterward, you'd be friendly with the guy?"

Jensen scoffed. "No chance in hell."

Rob barked out a laugh. My dad looked at Jensen with amused eyes as he folded his arms over his chest and rocked back in his chair. "Please, explain," he said, gesturing with his hand.

"Leave him alone, Marc," my mom said.

"Let the men talk, Bettina."

"Talk about something else, like sports."

"Sharing Mia like that isn't something I can handle." That was Jensen.

My heart lurched and got stuck somewhere in its cage. I felt my breath still.

"But you expect her to handle sharing you with another woman?" That, surprisingly, came from Robert.

And that was my cue to come out of hiding and get back in my chair. I shot Rob a look first. He shot me one back that said: *shut up!* Finally, I turned to my mom for backup, but she just shrugged, refusing to get in the middle of anything.

"She doesn't have to share me with anybody but Olivia. Krista is…"

"Somebody she'd deal with for the rest of her life if she stays with you," Rob finished.

After a moment, Jensen nodded slowly, conceding to agree. I let out a breath, surprised to realize that I no longer felt the heavy load that often came with that thought.

"Mia knows she has nothing to worry about there. I'll do whatever it takes to make her see that," Jensen said as his hand searched for mine beneath the table. "My concern is that Olivia gets attached to her, and then Mia leaves and isn't a part of her life anymore."

His words hit me, like the horn of a freight train announcing its arrival, loud, but too late. I brought my frown up to him. I'd never really considered what he thought about that. Or what she thought of that. Deciding that the subject was heading in a direction I didn't want to address in front of my overbearing family, I cleared my throat.

"Can we change the subject?"

There was a silent moment filled with unasked curiosities, until my dad finally asked, "What do you think about the trade the Chargers made?"

Jensen gave his animated response, and they kept the conversation going, but my mind was still on his previous words. I spent our meal filled with worries that hadn't plagued me until then.

My parents stayed at a hotel near The Met, and I stayed at Jensen's. I was rushing to get ready, dodging Olivia's scattered toys and trying not to trip over his sneakers every time I walked from the room to the bathroom.

"Jensen!" I shouted, letting out a breath. "Can you help me pick this stuff up?

His chuckle bounced off the walls as he walked up the stairs and into the room. "What stuff, princess?"

I shot him a glare. "Don't call me that."

"Sorry, I don't have a housekeeper to keep my stuff tidy," he said, grinning like an idiot, then laughing as he dodged the hairbrush I threw at him.

"I haven't had a housekeeper since I moved out of my parents' house. Learn to pick up your shit!"

He came over and wrapped his arms around me from behind, dropping a kiss on my neck as he looked at our reflection in the mirror. "Yes, ma'am. Is that what you're wearing?"

I sighed. "Yeah. Do I look okay?"

"You look beautiful." He ran his hands down my sides. "Am I supposed to keep my hands to myself tonight?"

I grabbed his hands as he cupped them over my breasts and pushed him off. "Yes."

His face fell. "But I'm your date."

"I never said you were my date," I responded, laughing as his eyes narrowed on mine.

"It's an unwritten rule."

"There are rules that apply to the people you're fucking?" I moved back to the bathroom to apply my lipstick and he followed me, his eyes watching my every move.

"I can't wait to lick that off your lips," he said with a groan, putting his arms around me again.

I slapped it off because he brought butterflies with him, and I felt my body warming at all of his promises.

"Stop touching me. You're distracting. And go get dressed before I leave without you."

"You can't do that."

"It's an unwritten rule."

He stared at me for a long moment, his eyes cataloging me in the mirror. "I'll be ready in five minutes."

As he got dressed, I picked up Olivia's toys. I was downstairs, drinking water out of a straw when I heard the sound of his footsteps, and nearly choked when he appeared in front of me wearing a dark suit over a white dress shirt and a dark bow tie to match.

"You clean up really nicely," I said in a croak.

He smiled, running a hand through his wet hair. "You ready?"

"I'm nervous."

"Why? Your pictures are spectacular." He walked over and grabbed my hand, lifting it to kiss the semicolon I had tattooed inside my wrist. "And I'm not just saying that."

I nodded and took a breath. "I'm still nervous."

He chuckled and led me out of the house. My parents and Rob were already at the gallery when we arrived, and Estelle, whose flight had been delayed, was running toward me.

"Oh my God. I made it," she said as she wrapped her arms around me. "Thanks for leaving your key with the doorman. I literally took a two minute shower and dressed as fast as I could."

"I can't believe you came."

"I can't believe you can't believe it."

We laughed as she let go and gave Jensen a hug. "Oliver sent something for Olivia. Remind me to give it to you."

I took one last deep breath and walked into the museum with everyone in tow. Millie caught up with us just as we reached the area where my pictures were being displayed.

"Oh my God. I just saw them, Meep. I cried. I seriously cried," she said, hugging me. "This is going to be so huge for you."

I talked to her for a moment, but stopped dead in my tracks when I walked into the room. The way they'd dimmed the room lights and set it up so that you could really see the photos around the room took my breath away. There were a lot of paintings showcased throughout by up-and-coming and renowned artists alike, and I made a mental note to go look at them all before the night was over. My feet led me toward my first one. I heard my mom gasp beside me, and my dad ask, "You took that?" as if it was the most unbelievable thing I'd ever done. It was called *Current Events As Told By Derek*, and showed a man in a torn up gray shirt with dreads holding his arms up animatedly as he spoke. I smiled.

"Did you tell him to pose for you?" Rob asked. I shook my head.

"I just took the pictures," I said, my eyes falling over the black trash bags filled with his stuff that contrasted the white of the train. "I gave him new clothes and gift cards for food as compensation."

Jensen's hand found mine. I knew it was his because of the size and the soft feel of his palms, and the way his long fingers threaded through mine. We moved on to the next one. It was called, *Baby Don't Cry, The World is Filled With Tears*.

"She's a single mom," I explained as they looked at the crying mother with her forehead against her baby's as they stood outside on a busy sidewalk waiting for the rain to subside.

I hadn't realized it until I turned around that I'd gained a small audience. I moved on to the next photograph and explained that one, then the next, until I reached the last one, my favorite. A larger than life canvas was displayed in the middle of the room. On it, a man in a suit, holding a briefcase in one hand and his cellphone in the other. Beside him was a man dressed in tattered clothes, holding a yellow plastic bag in one hand and a cup for change in the other. They were both walking away from the camera, at a distance the Empire State Building served as a clear divider between the two. I offered no words or explanation for that piece. It was the only one that stood unnamed. The powerful image spoke volumes that words couldn't reach. It showed hope and the loss of it. Power, and how out of reach it was for some. It spoke of differences among us in a city known for its opportunities and how not everybody is fortunate to be given any. And ultimately, I hoped it said, "You want something? Go and get it. You have the power to be something. It doesn't matter who you are or where you come from. You have power. So go, be!"

From the look in Jensen's eyes as he stared at the image, I knew he got it. I left there feeling more accomplished because I put that look on one person's face than I did about everything else I'd managed to take in there.

Jensen Talks

I've come to realize that my favorite thing about people is that even the ones you think you know best will occasionally surprise you. This past weekend served as proof of that. I went to The MET for a photography exhibit they have going on right now to support a person I admire to the point of (some say) insanity. Thinking that I knew what I was in for, since I've seen her work countless times, I offered to help set up and accompany her to the event. Basically I forced her to take me as her date, and I couldn't be happier I did. I've been writing about my dating life for a long time now, and I'm not sure whether or not you've picked up on it, but I've been dating the same person for a little while.

I know I said that nobody could entertain me as much as my four-year-old does, but if I had to pick one person for the job, I would pick this one. She's kind, beautiful, and is more talented than anybody else I know. If you're in the city this week, I urge you to go check out Mia Bennett's exhibit at The MET. It's called, "While You Weren't Looking" and it is stunning. I promise that after you see the photos, you will leave there and not look down at your phone for at least a few hours. I'm still thinking about them today.

My review of The MET: Must see.

My review of "While You Weren't Looking": Breathtaking.

Question of the week from: @Livlovesbooks : Would you compromise your dream 4 financial security / keep chasing it like Don Quixote no matter how old you are?

Answer: For my dream, in particular, I was able to find a balance. I wish that would be true for everybody else. There's always a way.

He gave me, quite possibly, the biggest shout out in the history of shout outs. I wanted to be mad at the fact that he broke the rules and used my name, but there was so much pride in that column that I couldn't bring myself to be a (complete) bitch about it. I bitched, and then I thanked him. He let me, and then laughed. I loved him. I realized then that I would quite possibly love him for this eternity, and maybe the next, but none of that changed the fact that when my new boss, Giselle, called me to ask me to go back to California so that I could start my job a week early, I agreed. I still hadn't told him about that. I couldn't bring myself to do it, even though I knew I had to. What made it harder was that it was a taboo subject in our relationship, one neither one of us had uttered a word about since we came back from Santa Barbara. It was as if the mere mention of it would pull us out of the blissful cloud we'd been floating on. I had to take the job, though. There was no way around it. It was either take it or live the rest of my life wondering what could have been and kicking myself for not agreeing to it. It was my dream job. I kept reminding of that. My dream job! But the more I reminded myself of it, the more I wondered if it was a dream I'd outgrown. Another thing I would never know unless I actually went through with it.

The guilty feeling lifted when I spoke to Rob and he told me the other applicants had more experience than me in that field, yet it had been given to me. The feeling of "am I making the right choice?" didn't come back until a few days later, when I was lying in Jensen's arms as he read some of his book to me.

"He was unsure of a lot of things, but never of them. She'd built a home in his heart, and he couldn't rid himself of any of the things she'd left behind. He wanted to go after her, beg her to stay with him, for him, but he was scared. He didn't let her go because he loved her too much to ask her to stay, but because he couldn't bear to hear her say that she wouldn't."

I waited until I was sure he was finished reading. Until I was sure my heart wouldn't combust the moment my eyes met his. Then, hesitantly, I looked at him. I expected to find some of the intensity that had taken owner-ship of his eyes as of late, but the grays were void of sureness and filled with as much trepidation as I felt. Did he know I was leaving for good? Had he read my thoughts the way he so often did? Did he expect me to tell him that he should have asked her to stay, knowing that she would have gone even if he had?

Instead of talking, I placed my hand over his and brought it up to my mouth. A wave of longing crashed through me as we looked at each other and I pressed my lips to the unfinished infinity tattoo on his wrist, then to the large feather that took up his inner forearm. I put his arm down gently when I heard his sharp intake of breath.

"I'm not sure which part sucks," I whispered as he leaned closer to me.

"Maybe I haven't gotten to the sucky part yet," he whispered just as soft-ly, his eyes washing over my features as his hands made their way down my torso and under the T-shirt I'd worn to bed.

"Will I be the first to read it once it's done?" I asked.

"Will you still be here?"

I tore my gaze away from his. "I don't want to talk about that."

"Neither do I," he said.

Then his mouth was on mine, and I couldn't conjure a single thought. We got lost in that kiss, the way secret lovers do, and when we broke apart, I asked him to read me some more. We stayed that way most of the night, our legs interlaced, our tongues tangled. I only left the bed and his place to run over to mine, and even on those nights somehow he ended up there, unwilling to let me go even for a second. I finished shooting for *Newsweek* on Wednesday, and wasn't expected back in New York until the following April, for the launch of the special. Fran promised me a job whenever I wanted one, and I thanked her. Like Millie, she didn't approve of my job with the maga-zine in LA.

"I just don't think that's where you belong," she said over lunch. We'd met with Millie in a tiny deli as a going away thing since everybody else had been busy.

"It's something I've wanted my whole life," I said. "I don't know how to not take the opportunity."

"Well, if you decide you want to come back, know that there's always room for you wherever I am," Fran said.

"And you know I can get you a job with a fashion magazine up here if that's what you want," Millie added.

I smiled, grateful to have awesome people in my corner.

On Saturday, while Jensen and I were eating, and I listened to him go on and on about his disapproval of the new Harper Lee book, I caught a familiar face over his shoulder. Jensen paused in the middle of his rant when he saw the sudden smile of surprise on my face.

"How are you? I thought you'd left without saying goodbye," Carson said as he stopped at our table.

"Nope. Still here. How are you?"

"I'm doing well. Trying out new spots in Brooklyn since a friend of mine just moved over here."

"That's nice."

He paused for a beat, shooting a look to Jensen who was watching us with a curious look on his face. "Hi again," he said to him. Jensen returned his greeting this time, and Carson looked back at me, "Well, enjoy your meal. Maybe we can do sushi sometime before you leave?"

Jensen cleared his throat, and I glanced over at him. He was shooting daggers at me as he waited for my response. I smiled and looked at Carson. "Maybe. Tell your parents I said hey!"

"I will. Bye, man," he said, addressing Jensen as he walked off.

"Sushi? Really?"

"He's being nice, Jensen."

"He looks like he's being more than nice."

I rolled my eyes, but smiled. "You act like you have something to be jealous about."

His eyes grazed over me slowly, tracing every inch of my face until he zoned in on my gaze again. "You're right."

"Look at you all grown up," I said, smiling.

He scoffed at that. "Yeah. Trying really hard not to rip that guy's head off is more grown up than actually walking over there and doing it."

I couldn't stop smiling at him, until I remembered that this was soon to be a rare occurrence. After we finished eating, he held my hand as he called his ex to ask about Olivia. His eyes kept flashing to mine during the length of the conversation, so I knew he was going to deliver news I didn't want to hear.

"We have to cut the date short," he said as he hung up. "Well, our alone time portion short since we have to go pick her up."

My brows rose. "From her mom's house?"

"From the soccer park."

"Where your ex will be."

"She has a name, Mia."

"I know she does, Jensen."

"Maybe you should practice saying it before you meet her."

"Maybe you should go fuck yourself."

His jaw dropped momentarily, but he laughed once he recovered. "We are divorced, Mia. Divorced! Not separated, not trying to see how we like being apart. We are one hundred percent divorced, should have never been married to begin with, and we're both happily involved with other people."

I stared at my hands on my lap for a second, remembering how it felt to see them together at the coffee shop that time, and let out a sigh. "I'm sorry. I just … I don't think I should go."

"Why not? You know Olivia will flip out when she sees you."

I closed my eyes. "I don't like her." My eyes snapped open. "Krista, not Olivia. I love Olivia."

His eyes softened. "You don't even know her, babe."

"I know enough. I know that for years I wanted to punch her, just for being alive."

"I'm sorry." He paused, running a hand through his hair as he let out a sigh. "I'm sorry you ever had to feel that way, but she's Olivia's mom."

I growled. "I know that! Don't you get it? That's the problem! She's Olivia's mom! You're forever bound to her. Not me." I paused. "There. I said it!" I let out a long, albeit relieved breath as I took my hand back from his hold. I leaned up and pressed my lips to his jaw. "I'll see you later."

I'd taken enough steps to reach the corner when he finally caught up to me and grabbed my arm.

"Will you stop walking away from me?"

"I have to," I said, shaking my head.

He registered the meaning behind my words, and brought me closer to him, until his breath was on the side of my face and I had to shut my eyes to contain the feeling coursing through me.

"No. You don't. Come pick up my daughter with me, meet her mother and her mother's fiancé, who happens to be a very cool guy, and come home with me so that I can give you multiple orgasms. It's a no brainer, really," he said, kissing his way up my jaw until he reached my ear.

"Fine," I said, my words whispered.

"Good. Now let's go before I have to put you in time-out for being a bad girl."

I let out a short laugh. "You should count your blessings if you make it through today without getting punched in the throat."

That made him laugh loudly, and heads turned toward us. He held me into the side of his body and squeezed, then let go of me and just held my hand as we reached the sidelines, where I assumed Olivia's team was playing. My eyes roamed the field, and I smiled wide when I saw her dribbling the ball toward the goal.

"Oh my God, she looks so damn cute in that jersey!" I said.

Jensen grinned as we came to a stop to watch her. "She does."

"Thank you so much for coming!" The voice was beside us before I could process it, and when I looked I saw Krista, dressed in jeans, Uggs, and a tight sweater. Her brown hair was picked up into a ponytail that she kept trying to fix with her left hand, where a ginormous ring sat. *Holy shit.* If I had seen it up close before now, I would have known Jensen hadn't given it to her.

"You must be Mia," she said, turning to me.

She was giving me a warm, genuine smile that gave me no reason to hate her, aside from the obvious. I didn't care that she was engaged to somebody else, because the thought of her sleeping beside Jensen for as long as she did was enough to make me want to grab a cone and hit her with it. I wouldn't, though.

"It seems like you're all Olivia talks about these days," she added, her tone light and comforting. I knew she was in the finance industry, but she really needed to become some kind of yoga instructor. "Thank you so much for watching her when she was sick. I felt terrible that I couldn't do it myself, but I was swamped at work and Barry couldn't take the day off." She paused and looked toward the field momentarily. "I'm glad she was able to be with someone she's comfortable with."

Finally, I exhaled a tiny bit of my rage over the sleeping with Jensen thing and felt myself let go of my discomfort. She'd obviously moved on. Jensen had given me no reason not to trust him. Olivia was the most awesome little gift anybody could ever want.

"It wasn't a big deal. She's a great girl."

Krista beamed at that. "She is, isn't she?"

We looked over to the field and watched as she ran the opposite way she was running before.

"When Jensen said soccer, I thought I was going to get here and see a bunch of kids standing around, but she really seems like she knows what she's doing out there," I said.

Krista laughed. "It was Barry's doing. He played professionally, and he thinks it's the greatest sport in the world."

My eyes wandered over the field. There were some pretty hot dads out there. Jensen included, of course, but aside from him there were some pretty hot guys. I found myself looking over at Krista's hand again. I guess the professional soccer bit explained that rock on her hand.

"Where is he?" Jensen asked.

I jumped slightly. I'd forgotten he was standing so close to me.

She frowned as she looked around. "He was right there…"

"Oh, saw him." Jensen lifted a finger and pointed at the field beside where Olivia was playing. There was a crowd of younger guys, college age I guessed, making a circle around a guy in a navy blue soccer jersey.

"He … coaches?" I asked.

"Yeah," Krista said, smiling wide as she looked on.

I nodded in appreciation and looked up when I felt Jensen's fingers thread through mine.

"Stop checking them out," he said, the low grumbled warning and look he gave me shooting a pool of warm desire shooting through me. He added an, "I'll be right back," before kissing and dropping my hand as he made his way over to them in a jog.

"Is this awkward for you?" Krista asked once he was far enough from us.

I turned to look at her, searching her brown eyes, and shrugged. "It could be worse."

She laughed. "Yeah, it could definitely be worse." She paused, her gaze turning serious. "I know it's not my place, and my word means nothing, but I've never seen him look at anybody like that. Myself included," she finished with a short snort of laughter I found hard not to laugh at.

I tore my gaze away from hers and looked over at him. He was talking to Barry now, laughing and shaking his head at something. Barry said something back, and they both turned toward us. Jensen pointed at me, or maybe at Krista, it was hard to tell, until Barry took a step back and gave him the most shocked look I've ever seen on a person, and I knew he'd been pointing at me. Krista laughed.

"If you haven't yet noticed, you're pretty popular around here."

I slapped a hand over my forehead. "What does he tell people?" I asked, more to myself than aloud, but Krista heard and laughed again.

"You do realize he has an entire book series about a character named Mia, right?"

I groaned and hid my face momentarily. She laughed.

"Aside from that, not much." She paused, tilting her head slightly. "Unless he's drunk, and then you're all he talks about."

"Oh God." I was afraid to ask.

"Yeah." She pursed her lips. "But whatever. That's in the past. We're all in a very good place, and I couldn't be happier that you're back in his life, and that you're so good with Olivia, which is really my only requirement."

I gave her a grateful smile and small nod before looking back at Jensen and Barry, who were walking toward us. Barry was shorter than Jensen, but not by much. I wished I had my camera with me because I was sure I could sell that picture to *GQ* for thousands. I sighed. Krista sighed. We looked at each other and let out a small, quiet laugh. When Jensen got closer, our eyes locked, and everybody else fell away, Barry included, because I could only see him. I was filled with him. I let out a deep breath as he reached me, his hand taking mine as he introduced me to Barry. The four of us spoke as we watched Olivia finish her game and when she did, she ran over to Jensen, throwing her arms around him first, then said hi to me and asked me if I saw her play.

I felt three pairs of eyes fall over us as I crouched down to tell her I did and recounted her awesome footwork. I knew nothing about footwork, aside from what I'd heard Juan Pablo talk about, but Barry gave me an appreciative nod, and I figured I'd said the right thing. I stood, carrying Olivia up with me and turned her so that she could say her goodbyes.

"Bye Mommy. Bye Barry," she said, giving them each a kiss, but not letting go of my neck.

Krista smiled at Olivia and me, Barry smiled at us, and Jensen looked at us like he was about to cry. As I walked off with Jensen's hand on my shoulder, and I carried his little girl in my arms, I felt my heart crack at the thought that I would be walking away from this in less than a week.

I got a call from one of the supervisors at The MET days after I left my prints on display. It started out with the usual pleasantries: thank you for participating; we loved your work, until she eventually asked me to meet with her. Jensen had stayed over at my place after we dropped off a begrudging Olivia at her mom's. She didn't understand why she couldn't have a sleepover with us, so I promised her one another day.

It was hard for me to untangle myself from Jensen's warm arms and get out of bed, but I did and managed to get ready and leave with five minutes to spare before my meeting. I used the extra time to walk around and look at all of the paintings on the wall near the offices. Knowing that my own work adorned the same walls as these paintings was enough to want to pinch myself. I didn't, obviously, but I wanted to so bad. I felt like I needed to wake up from this incredible daydream I'd been living for the past few months— taking pictures for the magazine, getting my personal collection displayed, spending time with Jensen and Olivia. It was all too good to be true, and I knew good things didn't last.

An older woman, with dusty gray hair and thin cherry red lips called me into her office. We made our formal introduction. She was Carol, assistant to the head curator. I was Mia, a girl with small hands and big dreams. We spoke about art and photography, and I told her about what I envisioned for my work. After a long talk, we agreed on things and I left feeling a lot surer of everything than I had in a long time.

The one thing that hadn't changed was that I needed to go home, and I still hadn't told Jensen. I kept giving myself a pep talk in front of every mirror I came to. I would just tell him that I enjoyed our time together, but my life was in California. My family was there, my new job was there, my future was there. It had never been anywhere else. He'd understand. But every time I saw him, I stalled.

"We need to talk," I said as soon as I got inside Jensen's place a couple of days later.

His head snapped up from where he was standing beside the stairs with the vacuum in his hand. He looked so comfortable in his gray sweatpants. Once he set the vacuum against the wall, he walked over and welcomed me with a huge hug, crushing my face to his chest, before letting go of me to give me a soaring kiss.

"Now we can talk," he said, once he managed to leave me breathless. He pulled me toward the living room and faced me.

"I have to leave soon," I said. Rip the Band-Aid. He gave me a blank look, waiting for me to continue. "My boss at *People* called me back to see if I would come early."

He gave nothing away, except for the twitch in his jaw. "When?"

"In a few days."

"When did you find out about this?"

I closed my eyes momentarily, let out a breath. "A couple of days ago."

"And you haven't told me anything?" he said, his voice a little louder.

I looked down at my feet, at the distance between us. "I didn't know how."

"When do you have to be there?"

"I start next week."

He let me see the storm brewing in his eyes before tearing his gaze from mine. "Okay. Well, we'll figure something out, right? I can go." He paused to let out a sigh. "I can see when I can get out there, and you can come back here."

"Jensen," I said, interrupting his calculations. I'd already done them a million times and kept coming up with the same conclusion—it would be impossible. "We can't. You know we can't. What are we supposed to do? Have a relationship based on Skype and once a month visits?"

He ground his teeth together, his jaw twitching. "So that's it? I let you back into my life, into Olivia's life, and you're going to walk away from me … from us, just like that?"

"Fuck," I breathed out as tears spilled onto my cheeks. "Don't do this. Don't bring her into this."

"I have to, Mia, because once you're gone, I'll be left to deal with the questions. You get to go home and do whatever it is you do there. I have to stay here, with your memory lingering around my house like a goddamn ghost."

I opened my mouth, but shut it when a sob escaped me. When I did speak, my words scraped against my dry throat and came out grated. "I don't want this either."

"So don't go. Don't go. What is it that you need? A job? I'll find you a job. Your family?" he asked, taking a step forward, his hand closing over my wrist. "I'll give you that. We can have a family here. I'll give you everything, Mia." His voice softened, my eyes watered.

"I … can't not go," I whispered.

His eyes hardened on mine, as if that was going to whip me into submission. As if the time we'd spent together was enough to erase a lifetime of bloodlines. I couldn't do it. I couldn't. Then he leaned in and kissed me, a fierce, unapologetic kiss that made me rock back against the couch. All the pent-up need I felt was poured into that kiss. I tugged his hair as he peeled my shirt over my head. We ripped each other's clothes off quickly, savagely, unwilling to wait another second without contact.

He turned me around suddenly, his chest at my back, his cock pressed up against my ass. Bringing his mouth to my ear as his hands made their way down between my legs to spread them wider apart. I moaned when he squeezed my breast and bit my shoulder.

"You can not go," he said, his voice a deep rasp as he spread my legs further with his palms and positioned his cock between my legs. "You can stay here," he added with a grunt as he thrust inside of me. I gasped.

"I can't."

"So we try," he said, his strokes long and slow. "You can't crucify me for something," he paused, breathing heavily as he pulled out and pushed back in harder. I yelped. "I did in the past." He paused. "When I've changed so fucking much."

He bit my shoulder again, and I felt everything inside of me begin to vibrate, from my core to the tips of my toes. He thrust inside, out, in, out, slowly, deeply, and I felt him everywhere. My eyes rolled to the back of my head, and I yelled out his name. He thrust inside me once more.

"I." Thrust. "Love." Thrust. "You." Thrust.

And I felt him explode inside of me.

When we'd regained our breath and he pulled out fully, my body rocked forward, onto the back of the sofa. I felt sated and spent. He cleaned between my legs, and turned the attention to himself. I faced him. We were both completely naked. Completely bare to one another. He walked over once more and leaned down for a kiss.

"I love you," he said in a breath against my lips.

I felt wild and out of breath, so I took a step back, dropping my hands from his narrow waist. Distance between us did nothing to calm my erratic heart, or the way my pulse was zip-lining through my blood stream. My eyes were wide. His were serious. He took a step forward until my lower back hit the sofa again.

"Jens—" was all I got out before his mouth was on mine again. His large hands traveled down my body until they reached my hips. There he held them still, just holding me as he backed away again, pulling my lower lip with him.

"I love you, Mia, and I'm not taking it back. I'm not going to pretend this thing between us was for closure or for fun when we both know it wasn't." He paused, letting out a heavy breath as he searched my eyes. "I love you, and there's no negotiating with what I feel in my heart. Trust me, I've tried. I've tried to use all the rational excuses my mind could conjure: it was young love, she was there when nobody else was, she made you feel like you were whole when all you were was shreds of two people's past mistakes." I blinked to hold back tears, but a sob racked through me as I wrapped my arms around his neck, and he pressed me into the hardness of his chest. "My life has changed. I've changed, but my love for you is constant. If anything, it's grown. You planted a seed inside of me, and it's spread like ivy over my heart. There's no room for anybody else."

"I love you," I said, sniffling as the words floated out of me. "I love you, and I never thought I'd say those words to you again." I put my hand up to brush away the hair that fell over his eyes. "But I don't trust myself to be okay with this once I'm on the other side of the country. I don't want to crucify you for anything. I don't, but I know myself, and I don't know if I can do this. We'll give it time. A week, two, and see how it goes, okay? I'm not saying no to forever. I'm not saying no at all. I'm saying I'll try, but I still need to go home."

"What about Olivia?" he asked, his voice wavering as he said her name.

I closed my eyes because I couldn't bear to carry the pain in his. My own load was too heavy.

"I'm only a phone call away," I said quietly. "And I'll be back."

He blinked rapidly and turned his body away so that his back was facing me. I wrapped my arms around him and put my face flat on his back.

"I'm sorry. I'm so, so, sorry. I didn't mean for this to happen," I said in a hoarse whisper as tears streamed down my face and down his back.

"Love happens," he said. "You can't apologize for that."

"I'm sorry for leaving."

"You have to do what you have to do," he said, holding my arms.

I dropped my arms and wiped my tears. I felt like I was stuck between two worlds that wanted the same part of me. When we picked up Olivia at Krista and Barry's house later that night, she was already sleeping. I held her in my arms when she woke up from the car ride to climb into bed.

"Do you have to leave?" she whispered, her voice filled with exhaustion.

"I have to," I said, combing my hand through her hair.

"Don't you like it here?"

"I do, but all of my stuff is there," I said.

"So bring it here," she argued. "You can put it in my closet."

And that was enough to make a huge ball knot up my throat. How was I going to let go of this little girl? Just when I'd convinced myself that I could live without her dad, she managed to weave her way into my heart and make her own little nook there.

"But I'm going to miss you," she said, opening her eyes long enough to let me see the sincerity in her words. "Will you come back the day after to-morrow?" I shook my head, my eyes filling with tears. "Will you come back on Saturday to see me play?" I shook my head and wiped my face. "Are you taking all your clothes?" she asked, finally. I nodded. "And your camera?" I didn't respond. If I had, I would have broken down right there. Instead I kissed her forehead and promised I would be back to see her soon.

As I was walking out of her room she called out for me once more. I turned around with my hand on the doorframe.

"Please don't go. I love you," she said.

The weight of my sadness crashed down on me in that moment, the knot in my throat throbbed, the tears in my eyes burned.

"I love you too," I said, and somehow garnered the strength to walk out of her room.

I found Jensen in the hallway, his chin resting against his chest, his eyes closed as he leaned on the other side of the hall.

I wondered if he'd blame me, the way he blamed his mother for walking away from him. No words were said after that. I left that night because I couldn't bear to look at our pain in the daylight. I went home. My body did. My mind did. But pieces of my heart stayed splattered on the wood floors of his kitchen.

Jensen Talks

My daughter has been playing soccer for almost a year now. The man her mother is engaged to is a former pro-soccer player, and I guess his enthusiasm for the sport mixed with her distaste in ballet pushed her to want to play. She loves it. Absolutely loves it, but this past weekend she decided, in the middle of a running game, that she was going to quit. Without preamble, she stopped running, kicked off her cleats, pulled her shin guards from her socks and threw it all. It looked a lot like that funny meme that goes around on Fridays with the guy throwing the papers up. I watched from a distance, my mouth hanging open, not knowing what to do. I let her soon-to-be stepfather coax her first since I figured it was some soccer-related incident. I mean, it had to be, right? My kid isn't a quitter! Then her mother tried to get her back out. Finally, they both turned to me like I was some sort of alchemist on the matter.

I'm not, and when I walked up to her and crouched down to her level to ask her what was wrong, she looked at me with tear-stricken eyes and said, "I just don't feel like soccer today."

And so, I took my girl in my arms and walked off the field with her on one arm and her shoes in the other. Because sometimes you don't want to soccer, and that's okay. I can understand not wanting to soccer. What I don't understand is fighting for somebody time and time again, and proving that you'll be there no matter what, and having them give up. Just like that.

I feel kind of numb today. Maybe it just hasn't hit me yet. Or maybe I'm trying to hold out hope that she just doesn't want to soccer right now, but will soon. The thing is, the next time she does want to, if the time ever comes, I need it to be forever. I need her to be willing to run non-stop during practice and games, because I no longer want tryouts with her. I want the World Cup. I want it all. And I'm not going to let her talk me into anything less.

For those of you who hate "vague blogging" (because you're nosey, because only nosey people hate vague blogging), I'll spell it out: Mia Bennett, I'm giving you time. Not because I need it or even because I think you do, but because the last time, I walked away and you let me go because you didn't have much of a choice. This time you have all the choices. You have all the moves. The ball is in your possession. Let me know when you feel like soccer again.

Question of the day from: @MJABRAHAM12

If you could go back in time, what advice would you give your 21 y/o self?

Answer: Think about your actions. They have consequences.

34

I thought living in Santa Barbara was it for me, until I stepped far away enough to see that it wasn't everything. Being home made me realize the blanketed comfort I'd created was just an illusion and that the clockwork habits I'd formed over the years were just that—habits. Habits I'd shed the minute I'd moved to New York and forced myself to step outside the box.

That stupid, annoying, cliché saying, "Home is where the heart is"?

I got it now.

I still thought it was stupid and annoying, but I got it.

The thing was that my heart was split in two: my family, and Jensen and Olivia, and I wasn't sure which way it would break first. The only thing I was sure of was that it was definitely breaking.

I'd only spoken to Jensen a handful of times since I'd arrived back home, and half of those times were because Olivia had asked about me and begged him to call. On the days that I didn't hear his voice, I felt restless. In the beginning I'd told myself it was closure, just closure. When had closure become more? Had it ever even been less than what it blossomed into?

"Who are you trying to convince? Me or yourself?" was what Maria asked when I told her that my job at *PEOPLE* was the right move for me. Maria was the friend of mine who took over my photography studio when I moved to New York. For a week I'd been waking up early to go shoot pictures of models and actresses who adorned the pages and some covers of the magazine. Most days when I got out of work, I drove toward the beach and followed the sound of the waves. That was what I'd said I missed most, right?

I sat there, staring at the empty ocean, for what felt like forever, until my grumbling stomach forced me to get up and walk away. Maria usually closed up around eight, and by then I'd stared at the blue oblivion for over an hour. Like clockwork, I walked into the coffee shop down the street, got us coffee, and walked through the doors of the gallery every evening.

"I'm not trying to convince anybody," I'd said in response to her question.

My eyes flitted around the gallery. She'd put up artwork from Italian painters, local sculptors, and somehow found a place for my photography. It warmed me to see that despite moving on to other ventures, I wasn't an afterthought.

Maria looked at me, sucking her teeth the way she did when she wasn't buying the Kool-Aid I was trying to sell. "You do realize you're in love with the guy."

"I do."

Her eyes widened. "Then?"

"Then nothing. Life is like that, you know? Unfair and shit."

"But it's not being unfair. You can go right back to New York. Nothing here is holding you back."

"Only the job. The one I've wanted my entire life."

"A job with a gossip magazine," she deadpanned. "You're on the wall of The freaking MET, and you want a job with a gossip magazine."

I sighed. "It's what I've always wanted. For my pictures to be seen, and on the cover? That's legit."

"Mia, legit is doing something that makes you happy. Legit is being on the wall of a prestigious art museum. I don't see how working for them fits your dream. What happened to the coffee table book?"

"Look at Annie Leibovitz."

Maria shot me a sideways look. "You're shitting me, right?"

I felt my mouth twitch. We both knew Annie-status was unlikely for anybody.

"I'm just saying," I said with a shrug, taking a sip of my latte.

I was shitting her. I knew I was, but whenever I thought about the consequences of moving, what I thought about was Estelle, Robert, my parents, the weather, the beach, the fact that I could use my car whenever the fuck I wanted, and the life I'd known. Those were things I loved about Santa Barbara and couldn't get in New York on a moment's notice.

But then I thought of Jensen and Olivia and the way they took me in like a stray cat and washed me down with their love and affection. I missed them. I missed them so much that every time I thought of them I felt my heart break into tiny pieces I knew were too small to put back together. And New York wasn't *that* bad. I mean, aside from the weather and overpopulation. I'd gotten used to the transportation, and I was okay with not driving a car around. I could just take the hit and tell Giselle that I didn't want the job anymore. It may look bad for the future, but I'd explain that it wasn't what I wanted to do and I'd tell her about my prints and where they hung and maybe she wouldn't be as upset.

When I went to Estelle's house for lunch, I told her as much, and she sat there staring at me. After a moment of not saying anything, she stared harder. I knew it was going to be a difficult thing for her to process. I'd had over a week to think about it and come to terms with moving there permanently, and it still made me sad to think about our kids not growing up together the way we did.

"I've made up my mind," I said.

"I can see that," she said as she poured us some wine. "Well, the good thing is that Jensen is here like every other weekend during football season, so I'll see enough of you."

I smiled, a sad smile that quickly led to tears. She came around and sat beside me, embracing me with one arm.

"It's going to be fine, Meep."

"I know! But our kids aren't going to grow up together the way we planned! They won't go to the same schools or gossip about guys." The more I talked, the harder I cried. "God, this is so stupid! I'm doing something that makes me incredibly happy, and I'm crying over potential best friends and potential gossip." Still, I cried harder as she held me. Then, when I was finished crying, I wiped my tears and saw she had her own.

"That does kind of suck," she said as she wiped under her eyes. "But … we can Skype all the time, and they'll always be in each other's lives."

I brought my gaze up to hers. "Do you think I'm doing the right thing?"

"Does it make you happy?"

I sighed, and nodded with a smile.

"Happier than your 'dream job'?" she asked, enunciating the words.

I laughed. "Definitely happier than that."

"Then do it," she said with a shrug. "Do what makes your soul smile."

I sniffed. "You're so lame."

"I thought you loved that one?" she asked, laughing at the distaste on my face.

"No. 'Do what sets your soul on fire' is the one I like. I don't like corny shit about smiling souls."

She laughed and rolled her eyes. "Whatever, dude."

"I guess I should call Carol at The MET and see if she has anything in mind for me."

"What about the prints you sold at the show? You must have some money stashed away from that."

I did. I'd made a killing from that exhibit, and much to my exhilaration, the museum offered to keep my favorite one up. Still, that concrete jungle would suck me dry before I could say, "latte."

"I do … but I still feel like I need income, and I can't just sit around. You know me."

The only thing left was to tell my parents and Rob, but my parents were out when I got back to their house for the night and Rob wasn't answering his phone. I spent the night moping around the empty house. I could have called Maria to see if she wanted to go hang out and do something, but what was the point when I knew I would be moping in public? It wasn't like I felt like I couldn't live without Jensen, but I was sad without him. I missed him. And there was absolutely nothing wrong with missing somebody. As I walked around the kitchen, trying to figure out what to eat next, I spotted a FedEx envelope and went over to it. My heart picked up a little at the sight of my name in Jensen's handwriting. *He'd sent me a letter via FedEx?* I was giddy with excitement as I ran up the stairs to my old room, closing the door behind me and tearing it open. I frowned when I put my hand in and didn't find a letter. Looking in, I noticed little pieces of papers. I turned the envelope upside down and let them flitter, like confetti, over my bed. As I lifted them I realized they were little paper hearts. A note fell out: *Are you reading my columns?* I took out my phone and sent him a text: Of course I am (reading your columns). I love the hearts. I kept glancing at my phone on the nightstand, waiting for his response, but it didn't come until the following morning. My heart sank when I read the simple, "This is killing me." It was killing me too, this time apart.

Jensen Talks

For those of you following me on Twitter, complaining that my column has been lacking heart lately, you're right.

I am lacking heart lately.

I'm lacking everything.

But as Jeff says, "The show must go on."

And so it does.

If you're going through a breakup, and are a single father, make sure you date a heartless girl. One who won't leave a scrapbook of pictures she took of you and your daughter while you weren't looking. One who won't go as far as to include pictures of your daughter and her mother, or your daughter and your ex.

If you're going through a breakup, and are a single father, make sure you date a girl who isn't selfless. One who won't leave her most prized possession behind for your daughter, with a note that says she'll be back for it. One who won't write your daughter a letter that tells her how special she is and how she can be anything she wants to be in this world.

If you're going through a breakup, and are a single father, make sure you date a girl you don't see as a good step-mother to your daughter, because once she leaves, you'll both be left wondering what you could have done differently to make her stay.

Question of the day from: @BristerRobin: Just shaved my 9 yr old's legs for the 1st time. Nair was easier last year. Makes me wonder what single dads do. @JRChronicles Any ideas?

Answer: I don't know anything about shaving legs! Stop scaring me! My girl is going to stay little forever.

35

Holy shit.
  I'm pregnant.

Jensen Talks

I got this question the other day, and it seems fitting. It was from @Wendylegrand58.

The question was, "If you could write the ending of your own life story, what would be included in your epilogue?"

My answer is simple: We're not meant to write the end of our own stories. If we did, most of us would cheat our way out of death because we're scared of the end. I know what would make me happy to have in the end. Nonetheless, I've learned that life isn't about the end, but about the chapters in between. The filling in that we do to get our stories told and how people react to it is what keeps us going.

The reality is that nobody looks forward to epilogues unless they're in fictional stories. I'm not an exception to that rule. I know my story will end, but I hope the legacy I leave behind is big enough that nobody remembers how or why it did. It'll just be another anecdote in the sequence of my very long and happy life (I hope).

Question of the day from: @FitchM: What authors do you enjoy reading?

Answer: Neil Gaiman & Stephen King.

"Holy shit. You're an idiot." That was Rob.

"Let's just wait until the lab results come back." That was Estelle.

"I don't like the predicament you're putting me in." That was Oliver.

"Oh my God. Isn't that part of the oath you swear? Besides, nobody told you to be here while I was peeing on sticks!"

He scoffed. "I'm not allowed in my own house? And I'm a pediatrician, so that I don't have to deal with stupid shit adults do. Like this! And I drew your blood and am running an analysis for you because you're too much of a chicken to face the facts and go to your fucking doctor!"

"So what? Do you want me to call my insurance so they can pay you for your services?"

"Hey! Enough!" That was Estelle, raising her arms between us as if she was the referee of a boxing match. She sighed and faced me. "When are you going to tell him?"

Tears pricked my eyes at the mere thought of that. "I can't."

"What! What do you mean you can't?" That was all three of them, in unison.

I sniffed and wiped my face. "I can't do it from here! I can't just call him and spring this on him. Oh my God. I can't even answer the phone when he calls. He'll know something is up." A whimper escaped me, followed by a choked sob.

Oliver made a sound that beckoned our attention. "So now you're going to ignore him? After you left him and Olivia, your plan is to ignore his calls and not inform him that he's expecting another child? A child with you."

"Bean, she doesn't need your bros over hoes bullshit right now," Rob said.

"He's right, Oliver."

Oliver sighed and dropped his head. "I'm sorry, Meep. I'm just … he's my best friend. How would you feel if this happened to Estelle behind her back?"

"Concerned," I said, chuckling at my own joke, then groaned when they all glared at me. "I'm freaking the fuck out, you guys. Officially."

Rob came over and wrapped his arms around me. "Let's wait for the results to come back before we do anything else, okay?" He paused, lifting his head to look at Bean. "Can you keep your mouth shut for a few days?"

He nodded. "All I ask is that you tell him as soon as you know for certain. Give the man that much. He didn't really enjoy Olivia's pregnancy, you know? He was too busy trying to get through to you to be present until she was born … and I know it's something he regrets now. Let him have his chance, Meep."

I nodded. "I just need to sort through this on my own until I see the doctor."

And I didn't want him to pull a Jensen and try to be a knight in shining armor and rush over here to marry me. Oh my God. What if he proposed? *Because of this.* I was so not okay with that.

I couldn't tell my parents I was pregnant. I didn't have the guts to. I did, however, manage to call a family meeting, which piqued their suspicion about everything. Every time we crossed paths in the kitchen that day, it was awkward. They looked at me funny and I could practically hear the things they used to discuss when Rob and I were teenagers and trying to "hide" his sexuality. *Do you think they're smoking pot? She's obviously having sex with that Jensen kid. He's trouble. He better not get her pregnant.* God. This was going to be harder than I thought, and I wasn't even a teenager!

Rob arrived to family dinner with two bottles of wine in his hand. He gave me a wide smile, as if he'd done the right thing, until I gave him an, "*I'm pregnant, remember, asshole?*" glare that wiped the smile off his face. He cringed and mouthed, "*Shit, I forgot! Sorry!*"

"Thank you, honey. Let's set them on the table. Your dad is already sitting down," Mom said, as she came by to greet Rob.

When I walked into the dining room, my eyes landed on the newspaper my dad had his hand over. I turned to Rob immediately.

"I haven't read it yet," Dad said.

Rob and I didn't lose eye contact. We both had the holy shit look on our faces we got when we were caught doing something wrong. I'd told him about my plans to move, and he immediately started trying to figure out how he could move too. *It may take me a little while, but I'll be there*, he'd said, and I believed him, because Rob would do anything to make me feel better.

"I'm going to read it aloud," Dad added.

My head snapped to him so quickly, I actually got whiplash.

"You can't do that!"

"Why not? Something is going on with you and if this paper is going to tell me what it is, I might as well read it during the family meeting." He paused and slid an envelope across the table. "By the way, he sent you something. It's in your old room."

I took my usual seat, directly across from dad, beside Rob.

"Do you want to open it now or in private?"

"In private, Dad! I'm not fifteen!"

"I didn't say you were." He sighed and opened up the paper.

"We're about to eat dinner," Mom said.

"Right after I read this." He didn't read it aloud, but I knew he was reading it because his eyes were moving across the page. When he was done, he shook his head as he folded it and put it down beside him. "Well, there's that."

"There's what? What did it say?" Rob said, and hissed when I kicked him under the table. "Sorry. I haven't read it today!"

"The usual. He's been a lovesick sap since Mia came back."

I groaned. "Can we eat and talk later? I'm losing my appetite."

They agreed. Not that I got any eating done with the way my nerves were bundled, but I appreciated the silence and getting off that particular topic for at least a little while before the next bomb dropped.

"Why'd you want to see all of us?" Mom asked, taking a sip of her wine.

I folded the napkin on my lap, then did it again. And again, and finally cleared my throat and brought my gaze to each one of them for a beat before landing on hers again.

"I'm moving to New York. Permanently." I thought saying the words aloud would bring some sort of relief, but all it did was twist the ache in my chest. My dad dropped his fork while my mom gaped at me.

"What do you mean 'permanently'?" she asked, not in disdain, just disbelief.

I blinked and blinked, but tears filled my eyes nonetheless. I hated this stupid hormonal rollercoaster I'd been experiencing.

"I feel like I can do more with my work up there. I can broaden my horizons—"

"You can do that here," my dad said, cutting me off. "Cut the bullshit, Mia. You want to move for that punk."

The tears did fall this time, but I wiped them away quickly. "He's almost thirty years old, dad. He's made an incredible life for himself, a far cry from what you thought he'd become, he's a great father and … yes, he's the main reason I'm moving, because I love him and I don't want to live without him if I can help it." I wiped more tears away. "Maybe you can stop calling him a punk one of these days, out of respect for me."

He sighed loudly, rubbing his tired eyes with his thumb and forefinger before dropping his hand to look at me again. "Old habits die hard. I know he's grown up and…" He let out another sigh and slapped the table once. "Dammit, he is a good father. I just don't want him taking my little girl with him!"

"He's not. You know that," I whispered, wishing the tears would stop coming.

My mom let out a quiet sob. "But you'll miss family Sundays. And who am I supposed to go shopping with?"

"Mom, you do that with Teresa," Rob said.

"And I'll come every other Sunday, if I can."

"Not if you can. You will," Dad said with finality. He was still looking like he might cry.

"What about the studio? Is Maria going to keep it?" she asked next.

I nodded. "She's doing really well there."

"What does the … Jensen say about this?" Dad asked, clearing his throat.

"He doesn't know."

They both stared at me for a beat, waiting for an explanation.

"She's going to surprise him," Rob said. "And I might move to New York too, so if you're going to kick and scream, get it out of your system right now."

"What the fuck?" That was Dad.

"Are you kidding me?" That was Mom's shriek.

From the corner of my eye, I saw Rob's shrug, and I had to laugh. Finally, as I mulled it all over for a couple of minutes, I realized that if I didn't tell them I was pregnant now, I didn't know when I would be able to do it in person, and it would kill them if I did it over the phone or even via Skype (if I could even get Dad to figure out how to use that). My hand searched for Rob's under the table. His head snapped to mine, eyes wide, his mouth dropped as he muttered a *holy shit* under his breath, and finally he squeezed my hand as I spoke.

"And I'm pregnant."

My parents, God bless them, just stared at me with their mouths hanging open.

"Tell me you're joking," Dad said, his voice low.

"Is this real?" Mom asked, looking at me, then at Dad. "Are we being *Punk'd*?"

Rob shook his head. I shook my head. "Mom, that show hasn't been on for over ten years, you need to stop saying that already," Rob said.

"You knew? Of course you knew," Dad said, shaking his head at Rob.

"Don't blame Robbie."

"'Don't blame Robbie,'" Dad mimicked. "I've been hearing that since the time he pushed you off the swings when you were three, and I had to spend the night in the emergency room. Maybe it's time I fucking blame Robbie!"

"It's not like I had unprotected sex and got pregnant," Rob said.

I let out a laugh. Dad's glare slid toward me. I stopped laughing.

"I'm twenty-six years old, I get paid for what I love to do, and I'm having a kid with a man I've been in love with my entire life," I said. "I think it's safe to say that this is not a fucking tragedy."

"But we won't see your belly grow, or spend enough time with the baby!" Mom said, and the water gates opened. She buried her face in her hands as Dad wrapped an arm around her and shot me a look that said, *"See?"*

"How are you going to move to the other side of the country with my grandkid?" Dad asked. "That's..."

"The same thing you did?" Rob said. Dad moved to California from Illinois when he met Mom in college.

"I guess you're right," Dad said in agreement. He searched my face for a couple of seconds, and, as if it suddenly hit him, tears started welling up in his eyes. He stood from where he sat across from me and rounded the corner of the long table. I stood as well, and threw my arms around his neck when he pulled me into a bear hug. "I can't believe my baby is having a baby," he said into my hair as he held me tighter. When he let go, he dried his eyes and looked down at me. "If it's a boy, you have to let him play baseball."

I laughed, drying my own tears. "We'll see."

Mom, who had followed my dad over, hugged me next. "And if it's a girl, we'll have tea parties, and we can have another shopping partner!"

"Oh God. Here we go," Rob said as he rested a hand on my shoulder. "Either way, the kid is going to be showered with love. Especially when I move over there."

My parents groaned, Rob and I laughed, and for the rest of the time I spent there, I felt so grateful to have people like that in my life. I thought of Jensen and how difficult it was for him when he found out about Krista's pregnancy. How hard it must have been to walk away and not be able to maintain a friendship with me, the person he shared his troubles with most.

"You guys have to be nice to Jensen when I bring him over. He doesn't have a mom or a dad to give news like this to, " I said shooting my dad a serious look.

He nodded. "I'll even add on a hug for shits and giggles."

"Dad." I groaned.

"Hey, you want me to treat him like a son, right? That's what Robbie puts up with."

"In the middle of fucking meetings," Rob added. "It's so embarrassing."

"That's probably why he wants to move away from us!" Mom chimed in.

"This house is a circus," I muttered. But hell, I was so glad to be part of it.

Jensen Talks

How do you know your heart is breaking?

It's a question I've heard women ask my best friend, who's a doctor, in a lame attempt to hit on him. Oliver, of course, goes into the whole scientific explanation—your heart is a muscle that can't physically break.

It's an answer I told myself repeatedly when I split from my long-time girlfriend to marry another woman. Your heart can't break. I clung on to that line as if it was a thread of hope I needed to keep the yarn of my life together. That thread snapped long ago, though.

Unlike Oliver, I do believe hearts break. I think my heart gets weaker with each day that passes without her touch. I think my lungs miss the air she provided, and that the gray hair I'm getting before my time is due to the worry she causes when she's not near. I think my appetite could use some help, yet I keep skipping my most important meal, since brunch doesn't seem appetizing without her to share my plate.

Question of the day from: @DMC_17

What would you say to a prof. who told you not to use certain words in your writing because they aren't commonly used?

My answer: A professor of mine once told me something that stuck: There are no rules in writing. If the words work for you, use them.

Estelle called me over for dinner, and as soon as I got to the house and saw her bouncing on her heels, I knew something was up.

"Jensen's on TV tonight! Did you know?" she asked as soon as I stepped inside.

I frowned. "No. Why would he be on TV?"

"Hello, he's doing a book tour and apparently that romance got picked up by movie people or something."

My mouth dropped. "You're fucking kidding."

"That's what Oliver said," she said with a shrug.

"No, that's not what Oliver said," Oliver said, stepping out of their bedroom.

He had on a pair of basketball shorts and was towel drying his hair. I assumed he'd just stepped out of the shower because he smelled like manly soap.

"You really need to put a fucking shirt on," I said. They both laughed. "And what are you talking about? Why's Jensen on TV?"

Oliver sighed, shaking his head as he walked over to the television, picking up the control and tuning it to a popular nightly news type show. He sat down first, Estelle followed, and I just stood there. They both looked up at me, but I was still in a state of shock, feeling like I was the one being *Punk'd*.

"Is this a joke? Are you guys going to make me sit down and then the doorbell is going to ring and it's not going to really be pizza, but Jensen standing on the other side of the door or something?"

Both their brows rose.

"Uh … no. That would have been good, though, considering you haven't been answering his phone calls," Oliver said.

"Yeah, that would have been pretty romantic," Estelle agreed.

I gave them both a confused look and sat on the other couch.

"So why are we watching this? I'm so confused right now. Is he going to be interviewed? Why'd everybody know except for me?"

The doorbell rang, and I jumped out of the seat, my heart pounding. "I swear to God, if that's him, both of you are dead. Like officially dead."

Oliver rolled his eyes and stood to open the door. It wasn't Jensen, or the pizza guy, but Victor.

"You've gotta be fucking kidding me," I groaned under my breath.

"What the hell? Nice to see you too," he said, strolling over and plopping down beside me. I rolled my eyes and scooted closer to him to give him a sideways hug.

"It's nothing personal, I just feel like I'm being *Punk'd*."

"Was that the show where people would get bombarded with things?" he asked.

"You pretty much just described every show on television for the past twenty years, Vic," Estelle said.

"But the funny one," he said.

"Again, all the shows," she replied.

"The one with the guy who's married to Demi Moore."

"They're divorced, but yeah, that's the one," I said.

"See? Why even get married?" he said, then added a quick, "No offense. I'm not talking about you guys. You guys will make it work."

Oliver shook his head. Estelle shook hers. I tried not to laugh.

"Mainly because I'll kill Bean if he breaks Elle's heart," Victor added, and then I did laugh. "So you're here to watch Jensen make an ass out of himself?"

"I just found out he was even going to be on TV."

He frowned. "I thought you guys were together."

"We were," I said, then paused. "We are."

"Were or are?"

"Are."

"Huh."

"Huh, what?"

"Huh, nothing."

"I'm going to stab you, Victor."

"You should never announce what you're going to do before you do it, Meep. They'll commit you for that."

I groaned. Estelle groaned. Oliver laughed. "Nobody wants to hear your attorney bullshit right now. She didn't know because he wanted her to be surprised."

The show finally started, and my heart began to race. Why the hell had his agent booked him to do an interview? Then I saw the title of the episode and relaxed a little. "Authors under Thirty-Five." Obviously they picked authors with upcoming book releases. Jensen was one of three. Apparently they'd all be interviewed one by one, because we were still watching the second author when the pizza arrived.

When they showed the clip for what would come after the commercial break, my heart took a seat in my stomach, and I had to put my half eaten slice of pizza down, suddenly feeling queasy.

"Oh my God, he's next," Estelle said in a near squeal.

"I don't know why I'm nervous, but I am," I said.

She laughed. "So am I."

Oliver and Victor shared a look.

"What?" I asked. "God. I can't even eat now." I put my plastic plate down on the table beside me.

The show came back on and the blonde woman introduced Jensen, who sat down across from her, wearing a white T-shirt, a black suit jacket, and dark jeans.

"He looks totally hot," Estelle said.

I couldn't take my eyes off the TV, but I heard her yelp and figured Oliver probably made his disapproval known.

"He does," I agreed with a sigh. His hair was brushed back, and his beard was nicely trimmed.

"He doesn't even look nervous," Victor said.

"I'd be nervous," Oliver replied.

"Shh!" I said.

They did. I scooted forward in my seat and leaned over the control to raise the volume.

The woman asked, "You're known for your children's books, and in New York, for your columns, what made you decide to write a romance novel?"

Jensen smiled and ran a hand through his hair. "I write what I feel like writing. What comes naturally, and right now it was this novel."

"Can you tell us a bit about it?" she asked.

"Sure. It's about a girl and a guy who are meant to be together, but life forces them apart for a while, until they reunite, and then they realize life has changed them a bit, and they have to figure out if the life they know now is worth changing just so they can be together."

She smiled. "Sounds romantic, and messy."

"Most romances are."

"Is it inspired by your life or anybody you know?"

"Yes. Definitely my life."

"So you wrote this for the one who got away?"

"I did."

"Can you tell us something about her, or about the story, or even maybe read some to us?"

He smiled again, looked straight into the camera, and winked. I felt the air rush out of me. My knee began to bounce in anticipation as I waited.

"Some say I loved her to the point of madness, bordering on obsession. She said I put her on a pedestal that her real self couldn't attain. Perhaps they're all right. Perhaps I am mad. And if that's the case, to be frank, I don't give a damn. What I know is that she sets me on fire, and if you were to perform an intradermal test on me, you'd know when she was in it because you'd see the trails of blaze she left behind. Because that's what I feel at the mere thought of her, and I'd rather live my life in flames than be numb without her." He paused, and I let out a breath, but then he said one last thing. "Come back to me, my little Road Runner, my world is cold and boring without you."

Both the reporter and the people in the room I was in were shocked to silence. She recovered with three blinks and said, "Wow. That was … I'll definitely be reading that. I hope the Road Runner comes back, but if she doesn't, I'm sure there will be a lot of ladies willing to fill her place."

Estelle and I shared a look that said, "*What a bitch.*"

He spoke more about the book and when it would be out, and I sat there, with my mouth hanging open. I looked around, at Estelle, Oliver, and Victor, who had the same looks on their faces.

"Well … I think it's safe to say you're still together," Victor finally said. "I mean, that was fucking… even I was moved. I still think he's obsessed with you, though."

A few days later, I sat at the center of my bed to open a box Jensen had sent me. A feeling of déjà vu crashed down on me as I sat there in the same place I'd received the letters he'd sent me once he moved away. The ones I'd burned, unopened. Many things were different this time around, my age, my experience, my life, but the feeling of anticipation that rocked around in my stomach was the same. And I realized it always would be. He could send me a post-it note, and I'd develop that feeling at the sight of his handwriting. I peeked into the box and smiled when I saw more paper hearts; this time with writing on them.

I read those first:

"Come home, my wildling. Winter isn't the same without you."

"I can't *Sherlock* without you."

"I hate brunch when you're not here."

"Missing: my muse. If found, please return."

I laughed as I read them, thinking about all the times Oliver had called Jensen a dork and how right he'd been. Lifting what was below it, I realized he'd sent me the manuscript for his book. I smiled at that. And lastly, a stack of papers. Setting the manuscript aside, I leafed through the stack first. The first page was blank, but the next held an explanation.

"Don't be mad, but I convinced Fran to let me include our story in the special. It didn't take much convincing though. Apparently she's a hopeless romantic. The only problem is that it's unfinished. I wanted to keep it that way, because there is no ending to our love, but Ross is on my ass about finishing it since he interviewed me. I did my part. The rest is up to you."

When I turned the page I was shocked to see pictures of us, of me, him, the ones of Olivia, him and me at the park. And then I turned to the next page and smiled when I realized he'd sent me the interview, and if I hadn't already decided that no dream job was better than waking up every day next to my dream man, I would have changed my mind right then.

Interview by: Ross Lindstrom for Newsweek

People talk about soul mates like they're the missing piece to the unsolved puzzle of our hearts. I'm not sure I'd agree with that notion, because I found the love of my life when we were both young. Too young to know love, some would argue, and I can't imagine how I could possibly complete her, since she's already whole. She always has been. Mia is one of those people who was undoubtedly brought into this world as a perfectly formed package, with her own thoughts and opinions, ones nobody could sway unless you're Arthur Conan Doyle or maybe George R. R. Martin.

We met when we were kids, but it wasn't until we'd finished forming our thoughts and opinions about people that we fell in love. Not to say we weren't lost. She would argue that we still are. She would argue that humans aren't meant to be found; she would say that our souls are left scattered all over the place in the people we love, in the lives we touch. I don't argue that because she's always been the brains in our relationship. We were away from each other longer than we were together, and often people brought that up in conversation with me. "With the amount of time you've been apart, you'd think you would have moved on from her." It's something I've had the opportunity to dwell on for a long time, and I agree, you would think I would have moved on, but I haven't.

We've both dated other people, and I'm going to speak on behalf of both of us when I say: it didn't work.

RL: Was there ever a time you didn't think you'd ever get back together?

JR: Every day. I take that back, every day it crossed my mind, and every day I thought, "Well, maybe. If the time is right, if the situation is good, if the stars aligned again."

RL: Some would argue that you're crazy for holding out hope for so long.

JR: They would be correct. I never claimed to be sane.

RL: Now that you're together again, do you think you'll jump right into marriage or wait it out?

JR: We waited long enough.

RL: How does your daughter feel about Mia?"

JR: She loves her.

RL: Are things rocky with your ex-wife now that you're serious about a woman?

JR: Definitely not. I think she's glad to see me happy.

RL: Anything you want to add?

JR: Maybe our souls really are scattered in the things we love, and we are all completely lost, but from the moment she looked at me, I felt like I'd been found.

Carol and I came to an agreement on the photograph she wanted me to leave up at The Met. She'd gotten a pretty hefty payment for my standards in exchange to keep it and possibly transfer it to other museums. She also said she'd talk to a friend of hers at *National Geographic* and put in a good word for me there. Once I left my job in LA, officially, I called Fran to tell her about it, and she offered me a job as a backup photographer for some shoots they were doing for the magazine, but it was a traveling job. I told her I'd let her know. I would have to talk it over with Jensen if he even let me talk to him at all.

I'd started reading his book, and got to the last page, thinking, "What the fuck?"

"He only sent me half of the book!" I told Oliver when I saw him during breakfast.

He laughed. "Damn, he's good."

"He's not. Did you read it?"

He frowned. "Does it look like I have time for romance books? The last book I read was on systematic desensitization."

"God, you're boring."

He shrugged.

"I'm so overwhelmed, Bean. I don't know what to think. This whole not talking to him is…"

"Crazy," he said.

I nodded. "Exactly."

He shrugged again. "I'm just glad he's on a book tour. As it is he's keeping tabs on you, and I'm getting pretty tired of lying on your behalf."

"Keeping tabs how?"

"Is she seeing someone? Is that why she's not answering my calls? Are you sure she watched the interview? I called her as soon as I got her text message about it, and she didn't answer. What the hell is going on over there? Maybe I should cancel my next signing and go there," Oliver said, imitating Jensen.

My shoulders slumped. I put my elbows on the table and rested my chin. "I can't talk to him, Bean. I'll tell him as soon as I hear his voice. I suck at lying to him."

He sighed, running a hand through his long hair. "I think it's shitty, but you're going soon, so…" He shrugged.

It didn't make me feel any better. I threw up the entire day after that.

A couple of days later, I asked my friends—my overbearing, imposing, adoring friends—to help me get Jensen back. Rob named it: Operation Get Jensen Back. It was a ridiculous name for an equally ridiculous task, so I went with it.

"I'll just show up at his doorstep," I'd said at first.

Oliver made a face.

"You're so annoying. Why are you here, anyway?" I asked, rolling my eyes.

He chuckled. "Because it's my house, dammit!"

Dammit was right. I'd gone over with Robert so that the three of us: him, Estelle, and me, could go over my plan, and Oliver happened to get home as soon as we got down to business. Shortly after, Victor rang the doorbell, and even though I begged them not to let him in, they did. Bastards. And then of course he sat down and gave his input.

"Can you imagine if you call him and tell him to meet you somewhere and he's on one of those dates he goes on?" Vic paused for good measure. "Awkward."

"You're such an ass," Estelle and I said simultaneously.

"An ass who thinks ahead."

"Seriously, can somebody get this guy a muzzle?" I groaned, burying my face in my hands.

The last thing I needed was to have more of that in the back of my mind. I knew Jensen enough to know he wasn't going on random dates right now. I knew he was busy. What I didn't know was how he felt, since he still wouldn't talk to me. We'd spoken one more time. Once, and it was because he wanted to know if I'd watched the interview. I said yes and didn't give much else away because I didn't know how to talk without saying, "Hey, I'm pregnant with your baby!" It was a short conversation, full of "yes" and "oh, okay" and "I guess I'll talk to you later." I'd been replaying it since the moment we hung up. It was awkward. Our conversations weren't usually awkward. Did he know something was up? Did he think I was going to stay?

"He thinks you're staying, you know that, right?" That was Oliver.

My eyes snapped up to meet his.

"Why would he think that? I haven't even spoken to him."

He shrugged, crossing his arms over his chest. "I think he was reading between the lines."

"What lines? There haven't been any lines!"

"The last time you spoke to him, I assume."

I let out a heavy sigh. I knew it.

"It doesn't matter," Estelle said. "It's fine. We have a plan."

"No, we don't. Maybe I should just do what I've been thinking of doing and go to his house and knock on his door and just … talk."

"Lame." That was Robert. I glared at him. He shrugged. "What? It is. He does an interview on national television and you show up at his house. It's lame."

I groaned. "What the hell else should I do?"

"What if I go with you?" Oliver suggested.

"I'm not twelve, Bean. I can do this myself."

"God, you're worse than Estelle. Shut up and listen. What if I call him up, tell him I have to go over there for a conference or something, have him meet me somewhere, and you take it from there?"

"And then what?" Victor asked. "She proclaims her love for him where exactly? In front of the big ass Christmas tree from *Home Alone*?"

I bit my lip to keep from laughing. Robert and Estelle laughed, and Oliver shook his head.

"No, you asshole. But that's actually not a terrible idea. Is it lit already?"

"I believe so," I said.

Victor and Rob got their phones out to check.

"Google says December third," Rob said.

"Yeah, December third," Victor added, as if Google was going to have two different answers.

"So you could do that," Estelle said.

"Or I could not. That's so corny."

"He's so corny," Vic said. "What? He is!"

"By the time I figure this out, I'll be eight months pregnant," I said, then cringed at Victor's face.

"No you're fucking not."

"Fuck," I said, slapping a hand on my forehead. "Don't you dare say anything!"

"Who am I going to tell?"

"Jensen, obviously."

"And ruin the surprise? Hell no. Who else is down to go to New York this weekend?" he asked, looking around the table. They all shared glances. "I know you want us to," he added.

"You know nothing, Jon Snow!"

"Who the fuck is that?" Vic asked.

I rolled my eyes. "Why would I want you to be there for this?"

"Maybe because we're all planning this with you?"

"You weren't even supposed to be here for this!"

"Hey! You get what you get and you don't get upset," he said.

I threw my pen at him.

"Now you're quoting Mom? You're such a loser," Estelle said, laughing. "We can go if you want, Meep. We won't even be in the way."

I threw my head back and closed my eyes, picturing how this would probably go down: all of them surrounding us, my parents would probably want to tag along. It was one of those things that seemed like a fairytale, but knowing my crew, would turn out to be a hot mess.

"I don't think that's a good idea," I said finally.

They stayed quiet for a beat.

"Okay, so we won't go," Oliver said. Estelle made a pouty face at him. He chuckled, wrapping an arm around her and kissing the top of her head. "Don't make that face at me. She's the one saying no."

"Come on, Meep. Please?"

"You guys are impossible."

"To say no to?" she replied.

I shook my head. I would have smiled, had I not been so anxious. Then something occurred to me, something Millie had mentioned in a conversation of ours.

"I think I know what I want to do," I said. Four sets of eyes looked over at me. "But it's really, really crazy, and I'm not sure I'll be able to pull it off."

After telling them my idea, they decided they were definitely going, whether I wanted them to or not.

A week and a half and a shit load of phone calls later, with the help of everybody I'd come into contact with during my time in New York, I made my way over to Times Square. There was still sufficient light that I could make out the faces of the people walking around. I sat down on one of the benches, smack in the middle of the chaos, and waited. Deep breaths weren't helping the anxiety. I should have just gone to his house. I should have just walked up his steps and knocked on the goddamn door like I'd originally planned. This was ludicrous. My nerves were haywire. I'd read online that people proposed like this all the time, renting out the space and writing the words on the screen, not that I was going to propose to him or anything.

I heard somebody in the crowd gasp, and I knew there was no turning back. My phone vibrated in my pocket. I didn't even fish it out; I just looked up, right at him. He was standing there, with his hands tucked inside the pockets of his leather jacket, his head moving to and fro as he looked at the images flashing behind me. I couldn't make out the look on his face. Couldn't tell whether he was happy surprised or mad surprised. With him there was no telling. I looked behind me just once, to see what picture was on when his head stopped moving and zoned into the center. It was us on my eighteenth birthday, his twenty-second. We'd spent the weekend in San Francisco—us, Rob, our friends. It was a great birthday, the last one we'd spent together. In the picture he was carrying me on his back, my long, wavy hair blowing in the wind as we laughed, his face turned to mine.

The thing I loved most about pictures was that with time, it froze our emotions. Even years after taking that picture, after all we'd been through— the heartache, the struggles—when I looked at it, I felt the happiness we'd shared that day. I made my way over from the benches to the middle, catching his eye along the way. He walked toward me, hands still in his pockets, until he reached me.

"I'm sorry I kind of sprung this on you," I said. "Well, not really. A lot of planning went into this, but now … I just…" I swallowed, managing not to look away from his steady stare. "I love you," I said. He blinked from me to the screens behind me, a smile tugging at his face at whatever was on there, and back at me with a serious gaze again. "And I'm sorry. I'm sorry for being selfish and shutting you out when Krista got pregnant and you tried to keep me as a friend, because I was your best friend, and I let you down." I blinked away the tears that threatened to fall. "I'm sorry for putting the blame on the most beautiful little girl I've ever … ever met," I paused, taking a breath.

"And I'm really, really sorry for walking away most recently." I paused again, wiping under my eyes. "I lied when I told myself this was just temporary. And I lied when I said I couldn't stay here." I sniffed and wiped my face, swallowing past the knot swelling in my throat before I continued.

"I'm sorry for taking what we have for granted and not telling you that I never fell out of love with you. I'm sorry I didn't tell you that the moment I agreed to go to brunch with you the first time I felt like we were kids again and had a new chance to start over." Tears started spilling down my face, so I stopped again and took a moment to compose myself.

"Most of all, I'm sorry if I ever made you feel like you didn't try hard enough to keep me when all you did was show me how every woman deserves to be treated. And for not telling you that you're enough, because you are; you are enough. You're more than enough." I wiped my face and exhaled a long breath, and when I knew I could speak again, without a quivering lip, I added, "And now I'm here after I messed up, and I don't even know if I took too long, or if you're pissed off, or if you still even want me."

His smile was warm as he closed the gap between us. He lifted one of my hands and took the glove off slowly, one finger at a time, as our gazes stayed locked, then he put my hand under his jacket, flat against his heart.

"Is this beating?"

I nodded slowly.

"Then I still want you."

His words fill my veins like a slow anesthetic. "Really?"

"Really." He brought his hand to cup my face. "This. What you did. Nobody has ever…" He took a breath, blinking away momentarily as he shook his head. "This is … thank you," he managed to say, his voice unsteady.

"What happened to your dream job?" he asked after clearing his throat.

"Dreams change."

"Yeah?" he asked, his voice low as his thumb moved in circles over my cheek, his eyes not wavering from mine. The look of awe and disbelief he was giving me was enough to set my heart on fire. "Some dreams don't."

"Some don't," I agreed, leaning into his touch. "I'm moving back. For good this time."

"To my place, I hope."

"Well, I stayed in a hotel last night, and I've been looking for places around here since I got back home, but everything is so damn expensive, and I wasn't sure how you—"

"Mia."

"What?"

"Shut up," he said, pressing his lips against mine. He kissed me the way he appeared into my life, intensely and impossible to forget. "You're going to move everything you own into that house. I don't care if I have to go to Santa Barbara and talk to your parents and Rob and whoever the fuck else you need me to get approval from."

I let out a nervous laugh, and dropped my arms from him.

"Don't tell me you didn't tell them you were coming here … or moving here? Mia, what the fuck?"

"No, they know."

"Okay…" he started, frowning as he examined me. "Then, what?"

"Well," I said, my stomach flipping. "Yes, I'll move in with you."

"But?"

"I'm … well, okay, but don't get mad…"

He crossed his arms over his chest and stared hard. So hard I had to take a step back as well. I was supposed to send a text for them to put up a picture, but my hands were trembling so much, I wasn't sure I could even reach for my phone. Finally, I took a breath and spit it out.

"I'm pregnant. I mean, we're pregnant. Well, technically I'm pregnant, but we're … having a baby?"

His mouth dropped. "What?"

"I didn't want to tell you over the phone, but then I didn't want to just come here and tell you without being for sure, and then Oliver ran blood work—"

"Oliver knows?" he bellowed. "Mia! What the fuck?"

"He was there when I was peeing on the fucking stick!"

Jensen shook his head, running his hand through his hair.

"Only him, Robbie, and Elle know, though, and my parents because I had to tell them in person. And Victor because he showed up when we were discussing this." I cringed when he shot me a look of disbelief. "Sorry, but I was freaking the fuck out! I mean, and I'm sorry that I got pregnant, and then I just kind of sprung all this on you, but I'm not really sorry that I got preg—"

His hand was on the back of my neck before I could continue my sentence, and he looked at me with soft eyes as he brought his lips to mine and kissed me tenderly.

"Babe," he said, a whisper against my lips. "I'm not upset that you're pregnant. I just wish…." He exhaled, his thumb circling over my wet cheek. "I want to be there when you're peeing on sticks." His lips touched the tip of my nose. "And freaking out." He kissed my forehead. "I want to be there for everything." He stood back a little so that he could look at me. "And I'm not saying this because I'm trying to do the right thing, Mia. I'm not a boy anymore. I'm not going to jump into marriage because I got a girl pregnant and I need to do right by her, because I don't need to do that in this case." He exhaled a shaky breath and smiled. "But damn, you'd make me the happiest motherfucker alive if you married me."

I flung my arms around his neck and laughed. "I'll think about it."

"Okay." He bent down and lifted me up, dropping a kiss on my lips. "Maybe I should take you home and fuck some sense into you."

"Maybe you should."

"Maybe I will."

He paused, looking down at me. "I can't believe this is really happening."

"I know." I kissed him again. "Before we continue this talk about sex and stuff … my parents are standing right over there."

The look on his face was so priceless, I was glad we were getting it all on camera.

"Holy fuck. Your dad is going to kill me."

"He is not," I said, laughing. "They're totally fine."

I waved a hand up and down as a signal, and suddenly they were all there—my parents, Rob, Juan Pablo, Victor, Estelle, Oliver, and Olivia holding his hand. She kept looking around, wide-eyed, with a smile on her face. I'd asked Oliver to tell her what was going on when he picked her up from Krista's house. Jensen somehow managed to carefully set me on my feet as he looked around in disbelief. Olivia shot toward me, her arms opened wide, and I kneeled to catch her in my hold.

"You came back," she said, her face tucked into my neck, her cold little nose brushing against me.

"I told you I would."

"I'm so happy you're here. I missed you."

"I missed you too. So much," I said as tears spilled down my face and onto the waves of her hair.

"Are you staying for sure?"

"I'm staying for sure, for sure," I said. "I'm never leaving again."

She pulled back to look at me with a smile. "We can take more pictures, and have more parties."

"Lots of them," I said, kissing her plump cheek as I set her down.

Oliver picked her up as soon as her feet hit the ground and smiled at me.

"It was a great show," he said.

"Thanks to all of you."

"I told you not to get my daughter pregnant," my dad boomed as he reached Jensen, who was standing behind me hugging my mom.

"Dad!"

"I did, but I have to say, I'm glad it was you and not one of the other punks she dated."

"Dad!"

Jensen chuckled, shaking his hand, and my dad brought him in for a full bear hug.

"Welcome to the family."

Jensen looked at me; it was a quick glance before he gave my mom a hug, but in those seconds I felt how much this meant to him, and I started crying again.

"Stupid hormones."

"Oh, yeah, blame it on that," Estelle said, crying, as she wrapped her arms around me. "I loved those pictures. Especially the one when we were twelve and had that food fight at Victor's party. How'd you get that one?"

"My mom got it from yours."

She smiled, wiping the tears from her eyes. "You totally need to show that at your wedding."

"Wedding? Oh my God, when are we having the wedding?" Mom asked.

My eyes felt like they were about to bulge out of their sockets. "We're not!"

"We are," Jensen said.

"We aren't engaged!"

"We will be soon."

I rolled my eyes. "I don't have to get married just because I'm pregnant."

Jensen walked over to me again and cupped my face with both of his hands. "You have to because if you don't marry me, Mia Bennett, I'll just keep using your name over and over until the world is sick of characters named Mia."

"The world is already sick of them!"

He chuckled. "So you better say yes, then."

I looked at him, then at my mom, my dad, Rob, Juan Pablo, Victor, Estelle, and Oliver, and back at Jensen. "I'll think about it."

"God, you're stubborn," Victor said.

Jensen kissed me. I wrapped my arms around him, and after going for cheesecake at Junior's and dropping Olivia back off at Krista and Barry's house, he took me home.

"Did you finish your book?" I asked him, later, when we were back at his place, standing at the foot of the stairs.

His smile widened. "I did."

"Why'd you only send me half of it?"

A deep chuckle rumbled from his chest and vibrated through me.

"How else would you have come home?"

I smiled at that. "Home."

"Home is where I am. Remember that next time you decide you need to run away."

I laughed. "Noted."

As he walked up the stairs, I started removing my sweater, my scarf, my shirt, and paused when he got to the top of the steps and kissed me again.

"Don't be mad," he said.

"Oh God. What'd you do?"

"I just remembered that I sent Jeff the dedication of my book so we could publish it in the paper on Sunday."

My mouth dropped. "Why would you do that?"

He grinned. "I had to pull out the big guns to try to get my girl back."

"The entire world doesn't need to know about that, Jensen!"

He chuckled as he threw me down on the bed. "Yeah, well, my girl is hard to get through to."

"She's an idiot."

"Sometimes." He started peeling my jeans off and placing kisses over my not-yet-round belly. His eyes snapped back up to meet mine. "I can't believe we're having a baby."

I smiled and ran a hand through his hair. "Believe it."

His lips continued to move over me in slow motion, first nipping, then kissing, and eventually sucking. "I can't believe you're going to marry me," he whispered against me.

"Of course you wait until your head is between my legs to bring that up again," I said in a pant.

"All you have to do is say the most simple word in the entire English language," he said, giving a long, tantalizing lick.

"No?" I said, my panting heavier as my hands tugged on his hair.

"What's the antonym of that?" he said with a chuckle against me.

"Oh my God, Jensen!"

"The other one," he said, licking again.

"Fuck."

"What goes after that?" he asked, adding his fingers to the mix until my hips were arched, and I felt a heap of blood rush through me and leave me all at once.

"Yes!"

His lips moved up my body as I regained my breath, and when his face reached mine, he thrust inside me in one quick, delicious motion that had me crying out another *yes*.

"And there you have it, folks, that was the day Mia Bennett finally agreed to marry me," he said, a murmur near my ear.

Later, he kept tracing his fingers over my stomach and bringing his gaze to mine with a smile.

"I can't believe this is real," he said.

"Me either," I replied, running my fingers over his face. "I can't believe you brought the hipster look back."

He chuckled. "You must really like the way this beard looks on me."

"A little." We were quiet for a couple of beats. "I thought about you every day. Every second, while I was gone; I just didn't want to ruin the surprise over the phone," I said in a whisper.

We faced each other, his hand caressing the side of my face, mine over his, combing over his beard.

"I never stop thinking about you. For years, my thoughts don't have any room that doesn't include you. You're everywhere."

I leaned in and kissed him softly. "That's why you went and wrote an entire book series about me."

He smiled. "Basically."

"How did your love story end?" I asked after a moment.

He smiled, a wide, slow grin right before he pressed his lips against mine. He backed away slowly and searched my face for a beat.

"Real love stories never end," he whispered.

I didn't think I would finish this story. For a while I was convinced that, even if I did, nobody would take interest in it. If you're used to my poetry and children's books, you know that this is not my usual, so thank you in advance for taking the chance to read it.

Paper Hearts
A Novel
By Jensen Reynolds

"For Mia, who never tried to alter my language, but instead learned to translate the meaning behind my silence."

Epilogue

Jensen

They say the world works in a balance. A yin and yang type shit some people heavily rely on. A life for every death; a new love for every loss. It's something I never really paid much attention to. Being the realist that I am, I chalked it up to another bullshitter making excuses for the unfairness of the world. But then came Mia, this selfless creature that taught me to see things differently. She taught me that we all deserve to be accepted, no matter who we are or where we come from.

And even though she left me and shut me out when I felt I needed her, I realize that my greatest lessons were learned in her absence. My biggest regrets became my biggest achievements, because I gained another selfless creature in the process. And I started to think that maybe those people hadn't been bullshitting after all. Maybe there is a +/- thing to it all. Maybe my losing the brightest star led to me learning how to view the world in a different light.

Then I got them both, and instead of being paranoid at the thought of losing one, I've started giving thanks to the universe, because maybe I'm Tatooine. Maybe life has garnered all of my losses and has decided I've had enough and finally gave me these gifts, ones I don't take for granted. If life taking things from me in the past has led to this point, and given me a wife, a daughter, and a son, then I say: take everything but them, because as long as I have them, happy and healthy, I'm whole.

Welcome to the world, Grayson Finch Reynolds. Know you will always be loved, and you will always be enough.

Epilogue

3 Years Later

I was rummaging through my purse, looking for my house key, when the door opened. My eyes, which were still glued to the inside of my messy purse, peeled away and landed on Jensen's bare feet. I frowned, my head snapping up.

"I thought you were working today?"

"I was."

My frown deepened as I took him in, all disheveled and unshaved, wearing nothing but gray sweatpants. "Are you becoming one of these parents who wear work out clothes all day and never make it to the gym?"

He chuckled, holding the door open for me as I crossed the threshold and put my purse down on the table beside the door. As soon as I pivoted back to face him, my breath caught. He was giving me that look, the one that made my knees go weak. My heart started thumping.

"Where are the kids?" I asked, my gaze dropping from his to his naked torso, my stomach dipping with each muscled ridge and tattoo I scanned.

"Rob and Juan Pablo took them to the park."

He bit his bottom lip as his eyes ran down my body and a slight shiver raked through me. I backed into the table behind me, rattling the candlesticks that adorned it with my movement. Jensen grinned as he stepped closer to me.

"How long will they be gone?" I asked, my voice breathy whisper as my heart rate picked up.

He placed his arms on either side of me and dipped his head to the side of my neck, his lips pressing there. I sighed and pushed against him, all of my trepidation of being caught in the act by our kids going out the window the moment his tongue flicked against my earlobe.

"Long enough," he murmured, his hands on my hips now, his erection pressing against me.

I threw my head back with a moan. "Good answer."

He ran his tongue alongside my neck, my jaw, working until he reached my lips. With small, teasing bites, he parted my mouth and molded his against it. He kissed me slowly like that, just our mouths getting acquainted as if they hadn't already met this morning, or last night, with unyielding passion. His hand cupped the side of my face then as his tongue joined mine in a slow tempo. When I was completely breathless, reaching for the strings of his pants, he backed away from me. I shot him a bewildered, confused look.

"Bedroom?" I asked a little out of breath.

He smiled, but shook his head.

"Kitchen." He reached for my hand then and walked me over there, and I followed, my eyes on his planes of his back.

Once there, he dropped my hand and walked around the counter. I was still looking at him, my head in a clouded lustful state. His deep chuckle made me blink and focus on his face, then around the room, but everything was just as I'd left it when I went to the museum this morning to examine a shipment of prints I had delivered there. Jensen leaned over the counter and pushed a stack of envelopes toward me, the smile still on his face as my confusion deepened.

I pushed my hair behind my ears. "Are you trying to seduce me so I can do the bills this month?"

"Will you look at it and stop trying to figure out what I'm trying to do?"

I hopped on the stool and put the envelopes in front of me. There were probably thirty of them in the stack. Grabbing the first, I looked at the one beneath, and the one under that and looked back up.

"Is there something I should know?" I asked, pausing. "Like, are you leaving me for this amount of days or something?"

He rolled his eyes, leaning forward on his elbows as he watched me.

"You're not going to say anything?"

"Open the first one, Mia."

I took a breath. "I'm afraid of finding out you did something crazy without consulting me, like wrote another story about me, in which I die this time because you're sick of me not wanting to clean the toilets or something."

He laughed. "That's a good one. Death due to discord. I'm going to have to write that down."

After a moment of trying to shoot him my best glare, I opened the first envelope. It was a letter. I frowned.

"You wrote me a letter?" I asked, then skimmed through it and opened the next. Another letter. And the next. Another letter. Finally, my gaze snapped back to his. "You want me to read all of these?"

"Look at the dates."

I did. They were all written on our birthday. I counted the envelopes. Twenty-seven. I frowned again. Finally, I read the first one.

Mia,

Happy Birthday. Officially. Because of you, I feel like the luckiest person alive, and because I'm writing this on the week of your twenty-ninth birthday, I can say that with certainty. The day you were born I felt a sense of accomplishment, and maybe it was the drugs, or the fact that I had to have an emergency C-section after hours of thinking we'd be able to do it the natural way, but the moment you were placed in my arms I felt like the very reason for my existence had landed on my chest. Through the years, you learned how to push my buttons, and taught me a patience I never knew I was capable of. I haven't always been on board with your decisions, but one thing has never and will never change, and that's the feeling of pride and accomplishment I feel when I think about you. I love you, my curious, bright-eyed little girl.

Love,

Mom

Ps. I want more grandbabies.

I wiped the tears that had trickled down my cheeks and looked up at Jensen again. He ran his hand across the marble counter and reached for me.

"You had my mom write letters for me?" I asked, sniffling.

"Not just your mom."

Letting go of his hand, I looked at the second letter I'd opened. It was from my dad. Then the third, from Rob. I opened a fourth, and fifth, from Estelle and Oliver. A sixth from Millie. Seventh, from Maria. The eighth one was from Tammy, the single mom I'd taken the picture of, who was now posing for a famous photographer in Italy. I kept opening envelopes and looking at the bottom of the page, my eyes filling when I saw one from Krista, and Olivia in her well-practiced third grade penmanship, and a funny scribble from Grayson, which I assumed Jensen did more than him, as he was only three. And finally, when I got to Jensen's, I smiled and flattened it against the counter.

M,

I met a girl once, who changed my world. Not just my world, but my life. I knew the moment we met that we were meant to be together, but then I left, and she let me. She let me think we were better off apart temporarily. Temporary stretched out until it became clear that apart would be something we'd have to accept. When I lost her, I didn't just lose the girl I loved, the one who had changed my life, but also my best friend, the one who acted like a rock, even when I pretended I was unmovable and didn't need one. I wrote letters every night and sent them to that girl, and later found out she'd burned each one.

The idea of her not reading my words, words I'd composed to keep myself sane, to keep us connected, saddened me. It's something I still think about, not because I think things would have been different had she read them, but because in those letters I let her know just how special she was, not only to me, but to everybody she came across. For the past couple of months I've asked people to write letters for this girl, because I think that for her birthday she deserves to know just how special she is. That it's not just me who feels this way.

I love you. Always,

Your husband.

Ps. I hid the matches in case you were ever inclined to burn these ;-).

Also, open the manila envelope.

I put the letter down and slowly moved my gaze up to his. He had a serious expression on his face as he watched me open up the envelope and slide papers out. I skimmed through them, seeing both our names on the contract. My heart pounded as I turned the pages until I got to the last one, a picture taken from a realtor website. It was an apartment in Santa Barbara. It was in a building I commented on during our last visit home. We were driving down to the beach when I saw the new construction and turned to him saying, *"I'd love to have a place there, on our beach. Wouldn't that be cool? To have a place of our own to stay in when we visit?"*

My eyes snapped to his. "You didn't."

"Will my confirmation get me slapped or fucked? Or maybe both?" he asked, his gaze heating as I hopped off the stool and rounded the counter.

I threw my arms around his neck and jumped on him, making him chuckle as he squeezed and lifted me up.

"I'm assuming it's going to get me the better option," he said with a chuckle as I rained kisses all over his face.

"I can't believe you did all of this."

"Happy Birthday, Mia," he said, pressing his lips to mine.

"Happy Birthday," I whispered, leaning in for another slow kiss. His hands tightened under my thighs as he pressed himself into me and sat me on top of the counter. When his mouth left mine and made its way down my neck, I gasped. "I can't believe you had all those people write me letters."

"I can't believe you're still questioning how far I would go to impress you," he said, his mouth stilling over my collarbone. His eyes snapped up to mine. "You are impressed, right?"

I smiled. "A little."

He peeled off my shirt and unsnapped my bra, dropping his mouth to my chest. "Well, then, let me see what I can do to change that."

"I haven't even gotten to give you your present," I moaned out as he worked his way down my body.

As far as I'm concerned, I'm about to devour my present," he said, breathing on me, making me squirm. My hand gripped his hair when I felt his tongue on me.

"Jensen," I gasped.

"Shh," he said, his eyes snapping up to mine as he gripped my inner thighs with both hands. "I'm trying to impress my wife."

Warmth spread through me, and it had more to do with the love that shone in his eyes as he said those words than with what he was about to do to me. Every time he called me his wife, which he did often, I was reminded of how lucky I was, we were to be given this opportunity. Every day he came home and doted on me like I was some kind of goddess. His mouth fell over my sensitive skin again and I threw my head back once more, all thought flittering away as his tongue continued to lash. I was definitely impressed.

Acknowledgements

Rachel Keenan, Jen Wolfel, Whitney Garcia, Corinne Michaels Katie Ross, Katie Miller, Milasy Mugnolo, Calia Read, Mia Asher, MJ Abraham, Barbie Bohrman, CD Reiss, Kristy Bromberg, Laurelin Paige, Lauren Blakely, Pepper Winters, Alessandra Torre, Bridget Peoples, Stephanie S. Brown, Diana D. Huet, Anabelle Martinez, Sandy Borrero, Sandra Cortez, Alison Phillips, Ciara Martinez, Christy Peckham, Mindi Lou, Leylah Attar, Tarryn Fisher, Karinna Baez, SL Jennings, Jessica Sotelo, Dianna Almanzar, Yaya, Tillie Cole, Lisa Chamberlin, Willow Aster - I don't know what I'd do without you. FYW, VIXENS, MY BOOK GROUP, BBFT, KINDLE BUDDIES, And everybody else who provides a happy place for me daily.

Rebecca Friedman. Melissa Saneholtz. Madison Seidler. TRSOR PROMO. OKAY CREATIONS. PERRYWINKLE PHOTOGRAPHY.

Flavia and Meire- your belief in me is the reason I continue to publish books.

Tiffany the Bibliophile, MT Reads- your excitement is contagious. I'm grateful for it.

Champagne Formats: You are the most patient human I know. Thank you for everything.

Twitter peeps: Thank you so much for asking Jensen questions that he could answer in his column!
The homeless guy on the subway who really does read headlines for everybody who climbs on board- thank you for the inspiration and for informing us that Bruce Jenner, is indeed, a lesbian.

Elastic Hearts

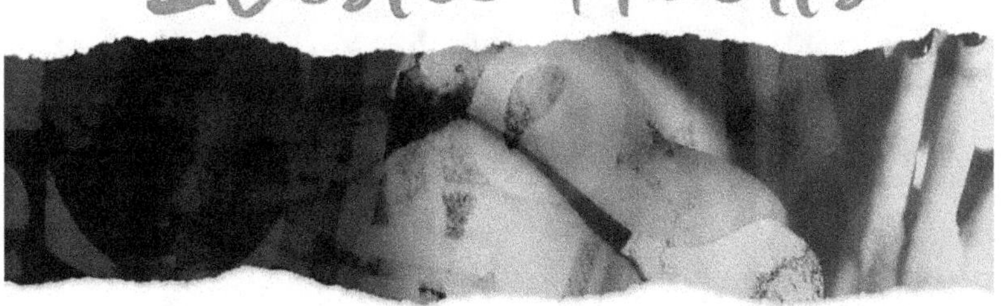

New York Times & *USA Today* bestseller
claire contreras

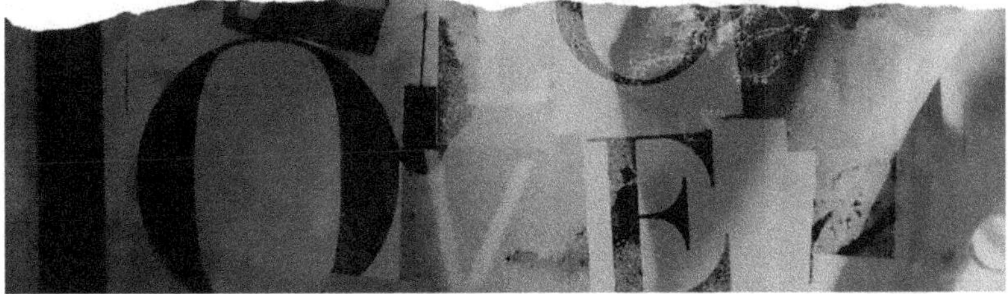

For anybody who thinks love only exists in fairy tales—

Love is limitless.

Believe.

"Give a little time to me or burn this out,
We'll play hide and seek to turn this around,
All I want is the taste that your lips allow . . ."

-Ed Sheeran

Prologue

"We can't do this anymore," he said.

Those were not the words I'd expected to come out of his mouth given the last time I'd been here, he'd growled my name against my throat, telling me to be quiet so nobody would hear us. I blinked, swallowed, and blinked again, trying to focus on his intense hazel eyes as they studied my face, as if to make sure I understood him.

"Okay," I whispered. I wanted to ask why, but held my tongue. I knew why. Or at least I felt like I knew why. Instead I gave myself a pep talk. We'd become friendly. We'd hooked up a couple times. It was no big deal for things to be over. No big deal at all. But if that were the case, why did I feel like he was ripping out my heart?

"It's not . . ." He paused, sighing and running a hand through his hair. The hair I'd run my hands through a couple weeks ago. "I was going to say it's not you, but that sounds lame. You know why we can't do this anymore."

"Because you're scared of what would happen if my dad found out," I said. He nodded. I figured as much. It wouldn't look right if the new add-on to the firm was caught hooking up with the boss's daughter, never mind the fact that we hadn't even met here.

"It's in bad form," he said. "If we hadn't met at the bar that night I would have never let it get this far."

"No, I get it," I said, not wanting to hear the predictable excuses he was sure to fire off.

"I need to focus on my career."

I swallowed. My eyes drifted over his features taking mental snapshots, which was all they'd become. In twenty-four hours they'd be grainy in my memory. In twenty-four days they'd be faded; I'd have to squint my eyes and rummage through boxes in order to remember how he looked, what he wore, where we'd been. The only things I'd remember would be his scent and how I felt when I was with him. Important, and sexy, and smart. Victor was only four or five years older than me, but those were things boys my age didn't have a clue about.

"You're just now finishing college. You have an entire life ahead of you," he said.

"I know." I paused. "You don't have to sit here and give me a pep talk. I totally get it."

He let out a long, relieved breath, closing his beautiful eyes, eyes I wouldn't look into again on the brink of passion. I wondered if he'd even considered asking me how *I* felt about telling my dad. Probably not. Vic was too driven. Too much of a rule follower, and deep down I knew he hadn't wanted more. I knew he'd just wanted to have fun with me. He didn't want to settle down until he'd built his empire over the lies he construed in order to win cases.

Just like my father.

I always swore I wouldn't fall for a guy like him. Like *them*. I always said I'd end up with a guy who fit my lifestyle. One who didn't over plan or over calculate. One who followed his dreams, regardless of how crazy they were. Guys like Victor weren't like that. They became consumed by work—real work—not creative, fun dreams like the ones I had. We'd never work. That's right. *We'd never work.* Maybe if I said that enough times I'd believe it.

"Well, it's been . . . nice." I stood up and walked toward the door. He stood as well, but stayed behind his desk, looking like he had no idea what to do. I let out a breath. "Remember to water your plants," I said, looking at the little bonsai on top of his desk that he never remembered to water.

"I will. Remember to try out those tennis lessons again just in case," he replied.

I smiled at the mention of that. I'd sprained my ankle a few months back when I went to play tennis with a friend of mine. He'd teased me relentlessly, not because I sprained my ankle playing tennis, but because I sprained it on a water break, when I stepped on the box for the water fountain. *Total* freak accident.

I closed the door and stood outside for a second, taking a deep breath to welcome air back into my lungs, wondering if I'd played it cool enough. When I felt settled, I left and drove to the set of a new sitcom where I'd been hired as a stand-in for a costume designer away on maternity leave.

By the time I got there, I'd replayed Victor and my short-lived history in my mind nothing short of forty times. I tried to think back and figure out at what point he knew things wouldn't work. Had it been when we went to the coffee shop downtown and ran into a friend of his? He'd introduced us as friends, which we were, but the tone in which he'd said it implied that it was all we could be. Was it because of my age? Or was it just him? We'd discussed marriage and relationships and our aversion to both. One of us had been dead serious; the other had made up lies along the way, because *I* wanted a relationship with real attachments and long-term goals.

I parked my car and waved at the lot attendee on my way in, and in those seconds where I was looking back as I walked in, I bumped into the person walking out.

"I am so sorry," he drawled, a slight southern accent I hadn't heard anywhere aside from movies. My eyes made their way up his body slowly until they landed on his face and caught on striking blue eyes. Holy wow. He was the definition of Hollywood.

"It's okay. I wasn't paying attention." We tried to sidestep each other three times, failed, and laughed. "Sorry," I said again, my cheeks blazing.

"The universe must really want to throw us together," he said, turning up his charming smile. "I'm Gabriel," he said, now blocking the door completely.

"Nicole," I responded, heart pitter-pattering.

"Are you an actress?" he asked. I shook my head.

"Costume design."

He nodded slowly, his eyes still on mine. "New?"

"First day."

"Nervous?"

"Very," I said, but smiled. He opened the door wider.

"I promise we don't bite," he said, his grin widening. "Well, some of us don't."

I laughed as I stepped inside. For the remainder of the day and week, Gabriel looked for ways to find me all around set, and just like that all thoughts of Victor began to vanish. As they should. Victor and Nicole were done. I needed to accept that, and Gabriel's charm was just enough to make me.

Chapter One

Victor

Nicole Alessi rarely visited the law firm these days. I could count on two hands the amount of times she'd come, and six of those were before she'd gotten engaged. One of the last few times was after the ring graced her finger. I saw her in passing and she made sure to steer clear of me. As if I was going to pull her into my office and have my way with her while that thing was glaring at me, reminding me she belonged to somebody else. It was fine by me. It wasn't like I felt hurt by the engagement, I was more caught off guard. One day we were talking about how crazy people were to want to get married, and the next she'd become one of those crazy people. She'd given me no inkling, no sign that she'd wanted more, out of me, out of life . . . out of anything.

Even though that ship had sailed five years ago, or more accurately had never taken off to begin with, the buzz of her name around the office put me on alert. Everybody from my secretary to the receptionist was whispering about the beautiful Nicole, wife to the handsome Gabriel Lane, coming for a visit as if she herself were Hollywood royalty. Maybe she was. I made it my job not to keep up with her whereabouts. What was the point, anyway? And because I knew she was coming in, I busied myself in researching Sam Weaver, a star running back I was representing in a high-profile divorce. I'd asked him more questions than the SAT, and the guy still hadn't been one hundred percent honest with me.

How people expected me to represent them in court without all the information I asked for and win was beyond my understanding. My focus was cut by the loud knock on my office door. It was pushed open before I gave permission, and I didn't have to look away from my screen to know it was

William. He was the only one with enough balls to do that. It also helped that he was my boss and owned the building.

"What can I do for you?" I asked as my eyes scanned the latest TMZ post about Sam and his encounter with not one, but two prostitutes. I looked away from the screen when I heard Will walk toward me without saying a word. He had *the* look on his face, the one that told me he was about to ask me to do something he knew I didn't want any part of. Like the time he asked me to take on the case of a porn-star divorce, which my sixteen-year-old self would have literally come all over, but the thirty-one-year-old me was too busy using disinfectant every time I went near any of my client's "work spaces."

"Fuck. Just spit it out."

Will chuckled, unbuttoning his suit with one hand as he took a seat across from me. The fact he didn't just come out with it and actually sat down to discuss it made me develop a little ringing noise in my ears. I gave him my full attention.

"You know you're the best damn attorney on my team," he said. I stayed quiet. I knew he wasn't going to fire me, but starting a conversation out like that could only mean . . . my heart skipped a beat at the mere suggestion in my thoughts. "Your worth ethic is enviable. You're driven, you're a cocky son of a bitch, but somehow you maintain a level of humanity with clients."

"Unless you're about to drop down on one knee and propose to me, I think you should just ask for what will clearly be a massive, Victor-please-don't-leave-my-firm-after-I-say-these-words favor," I said, mainly because I was starting to feel uncomfortable with the way his blue eyes leveled on mine. He smiled.

"I want to make you partner," he said.

My mouth dropped.

Those six words.

My reason for everything.

I reeled in my emotions before they let me get ahead of myself and sat back in my seat a little. "Just like that? What about Bobby?" Bobby, whose parents were old family friends of Will's, had been hired a year before I was. Even if I was a much better lawyer, I couldn't imagine him not giving Bobby the opportunity first.

"I've spoken to him about this at length. He knows where I'm coming from, and he agrees that you're better suited."

"Better suited . . . to make partner," I said, needing to clarify.

"To make partner, and for the job I need you to do in order to make partner." He delivered that with a wide grin. My heart sank. What the fuck was this man going to ask me to do?

"What is it this time? An actor needs representation because his wife slapped him with a divorce after he was caught cheating with their nanny?"

"Not quite, but good guess," he said, his smile turning somewhat serious. "I need you to represent Nicole in her divorce."

I blinked. *What? No.* I shook my head and swallowed loudly. It wasn't often I was at a loss for words, but this was just . . .

"She's getting a divorce?"

"Yes, and obviously I can't be her attorney, so I wanted her to get the next best thing."

Me. The next best thing. That in itself was high praise from William.

I closed my eyes momentarily, but the only thing I could visualize was the day she'd come in here and Will had introduced her as his daughter. Suddenly, I wanted the world to swallow me whole. It might as well have since I already felt like my career was beginning to sink as the memories of her and me in a bathroom stall at one of LA's most popular nightclubs choked me, and I barely got an audible nice to meet you out. She'd smiled, like it was no big deal, but the blush that crept over her face and neck had said differently. The way her eyes widened at the sight of me, as if her vision had to adjust to what I looked like in real life, outside of the dark club and dimly lit bathroom. And how that memory rushed through my body and to my cock when she came back the following week and started to flirt with me.

I'd promised myself I wouldn't get involved with her then, but from one second to another, Nicole's tanned legs were spread open in front of me on this very desk, and I became addicted to the way she threw her head back and said my name with that slight Spanish accent, regardless of what I did to her body. I swallowed, cleared my throat, and took a deep breath.

"I can't do it," I managed to say.

"Is this about the Sam Weaver case? If you want to take on less, you can give that one to Bobby. I want you for Nicole."

I want you for Nicole.

Nicole, who I knew the first time I laid eyes on her could be my downfall. Nicole, whose blue eyes held wicked promise every time she looked at me. Nicole, who had sworn she was completely against marriage, an oath I disputed when the tabloids dropped the bomb of her engagement. Nicole, who weaved some powerful shit with her wild streak and funny comments, rivaling anything that came out of my mouth. Nicole, whose fucking mouth was made by the gods for the gods and hadn't been anywhere near me for at least five years. I breathed out a heavy breath, trying to rid myself of all things Nicole. He had no idea what he was asking of me.

"Did she request me?"

"No. She doesn't know yet. She should be here shortly. I wanted to give you a heads-up first. But, Victor, you do this, you do right by her, and then I'll make you partner."

Fuck. My. Life. That *word* was too tantalizing to fuck around with. *Partner.* It was the sole reason I was billing so many damn hours.

"Okay."

"You'll do it?"

"Yes."

Now I just had to make sure I didn't do *her* and lose my goddamn license in the process.

Chapter Two

Nicole

"Divorce sucks," I said for what seemed like the millionth time since this whole ordeal started. Not that I needed to reiterate that for anybody. People didn't get married thinking they'd ever divorce. Being the product of a divorced household, and a father as a divorce attorney, I never saw myself getting a divorce. I always swore that if I got married it would be forever, but that was before the promise of forever became dreary and cold. It was before the word itself made me want to curl up into a ball whenever I thought of my estranged husband hitting the bottle or those pills he'd been partial to for the past two years. It was before shit went down the drain, basically. And that's how I found myself talking to the hot new security detail my soon-to-be ex-husband assigned me.

"Are you ready?" Marcus asked. Marcus. Even his name was fucking hot. The first time I saw him I wondered if Gabe's manager had picked him out on purpose, maybe to see if I'd cozy up to him and leave Gabe alone. Or cozy up to him and have something to hold over my head in this divorce.

"He's so full of himself, you know?" I said in response. Marcus's brown eyes flickered to mine in the rearview mirror, holding absolutely no amusement.

"Pardon?"

"Gabriel. He's full of himself. He thinks hiring a hot bodyguard is going to lessen the blow of the divorce. Let me tell you something, Marcus. I'm the one dealing with all this divorce crap. *Me.* I'm the one visiting lawyers and trying to sort things out quietly *for his sake.* You know why? Not because I'm a great human being, but because I still have feelings and he's a grade-A prick. Having a hot driver isn't going to make me forget that."

Marcus's light-blond eyebrows shot up in surprise momentarily. I wasn't sure if I was glad for his silence as he let me get that off my chest or pissed off that he had absolutely nothing to add to my rant. I hated when people didn't rant with me.

"I don't know him personally, and he's paying me, so I'm not sure what to say to that," he said. "Knock on the window when you're ready to get out." He opened his door and stepped into the swarm of paparazzi awaiting my arrival.

I was sure they were hoping they'd catch a glimpse of me crying. They would have to set up a tent outside my bedroom window in order to get that shot. I gathered my thoughts as I watched Marcus round the front of the car. As promised, he stood beside my door with his back toward me. I smoothed my hair and took a deep breath as I looked out into the crowd of photographers.

Of all the things Gabe had to endure on a daily basis, this was the one I'd never been able to fathom. When I was by myself they rarely followed me around, but if they caught wind that he was around it was no holds barred. They gunned for us, even if we were with my godchildren, who would cry because they hated the flash of the cameras and the nonstop questions.

A couple seconds passed before I knocked on the window three times. He held his hand out to help me exit the car and sidestepped a photographer who rushed toward me.

"*Nicole! How do you feel about the rumors that Gabriel is dating his new co-star, Lina?*"

"*Nicole! Over here! You look lovely today. Are you filing for divorce?*"

"*Are you going to press charges against Fey Winters for destruction of property?*"

"*Do you think Gabriel deserves a second chance?*"

"*Is it true he's screwing your best friend's nanny?*"

I never, ever showed emotion when being photographed under these circumstances, but that last question made me frown. *My best friend didn't even have a nanny.* I was sure they'd manipulate that frown to mean I looked like a mess when I went to visit a divorce lawyer, but who cares? Obviously Gabe's people, most likely his manager, called the paparazzi to tip them off about my whereabouts. Make me look like the bad guy, of course. Classic Hollywood tale, the less popular person was always at fault.

I was glad when Marcus opened the door of the building, and we were able to drown out their incessant questions, though the receptionist's voice replaced theirs immediately.

"My dad said you were coming by but I didn't believe him. Is what they're saying in the gossip blogs true? About Gabriel and you splitting up?" she asked.

I tried to swallow my pain and smile sadly, but my lips wouldn't tilt up, and the pain wouldn't stop grating against my throat. I nodded instead, a slow, small nod, and looked down. I'd always been sure of myself. Sure of my body, my career choice, my thoughts, my intelligence. Even after Gabe started going out more and not including me in his plans, and after he'd become so cold and distant, preferring to hit the bottle or stay on location longer than necessary, I was sure of myself. It wasn't until the rumors of infidelity began circulating that I began to feel the motions—my heart being chopped up. When the paparazzi started following me, putting their cameras in my face and their loud questions in my ears, I'd felt it going through the blender.

But that was then. Now I was back to my self-assured self. Or at least more than I had been last year. We'd kept it mum on the divorce filing, but when the papers were leaked, we were suddenly forced to confront the media, which was a nightmare in itself. I was coached weekly on what to say, or more accurately, what not to say. Gabe's publicist put out a statement saying we were working on our marriage. Gabe himself, whenever he was on camera, spoke highly of me and his commitment to our marriage. All the while I watched with a shocked expression on my face. At first, I believed it. I bought into it, because when it was all said and done, the guy was a hell of an actor. But that was before. And this was now. And I was tired of it.

"I'm sorry," Grace said, lowering her voice, her smile dropping. "You guys looked so happy together."

"Thanks," I said. It seemed like the wrong word for this, but I was used to girls like Grace, who were young with hearts in their eyes. I'd been that girl once. I was that girl five years ago. "Is my dad in the conference room?"

She looked startled for a moment before she began to move her feet in that direction. "Oh. Yes. Sorry. They moved it. Let me show you where it is."

Once the large wooden doors opened, I didn't have time to glance around and take in whatever décor my stepmother had most probably organized, because as soon as I stepped into the room my gaze froze on Victor Reuben. Victor, in a sharp navy suit that screamed sophistication. The way it fit him hinted at broad shoulders and hard planes I knew were beneath it. His expression was closed off, but the fact he was looking at me still made my heart hammer a little harder. I hadn't seen him in years, but my body remembered him well. His long hands and the way they'd gripped me. His deep chuckle and the way it had made my heart skip a beat the few times I'd heard it. The way he'd said my name, in a low, muttered, damnation that said he shouldn't be wanting, let alone doing what we'd done, but couldn't resist the temptation.

I swallowed to rid myself of the memories. I would've loved to say that having been married to one of the world's most sought-after celebrities had dimmed my lust for this man, but I'd be lying. I might have been the one who'd married, but to me, Victor would always be the one that got away. And even though I knew deep down we wouldn't have worked out, and it had been a long time since I'd seen him, the way his eyes caressed over me made me feel like I was slowly burning up. Like it was just this morning that he'd had me up against a wall. I shivered at the memory. His eyes heated in response.

"Nic. I didn't hear you come in," Dad said, standing from his seat beside Victor.

He came over and put his arms around me, and I reverted back to my seven-year-old self, leaning into his embrace. Dad wasn't much taller than I was, but he was tall enough that I could lay my head on his shoulder comfortably. I left my cheek there for a couple beats—inhaling the familiar smell of cigarettes and aftershave—my gaze on Victor's, his on mine, unmoving, unyielding, and completely unsettling.

"You remember Victor," he said, placing a kiss on my cheek as he moved slightly away from me. I almost laughed at that. Did I remember Victor? God. How could I forget? Victor stood, but didn't come around to greet me and I was glad for the space left between us. After the week, month, and year I'd had, I didn't think I could handle touching him even if it was just a handshake.

"Of course," I said, offering him a smile.

He was taller than I remembered, his shoulders wider, his hair a little longer, a little lighter, with scruff on his face I didn't remember him having. But those hazel eyes still hinted at wicked pleasures and wild sex, and the memory of all of the above made me flush and look away. I'd been with a Hollywood heartthrob for the last four and a half years, and I could still honestly say that I'd never met a man surer of himself than Victor Reuben.

"Nice to see you again," Victor said dutifully.

"Likewise," I replied, clearing my voice to rid myself of the scratch in it.

"Come, sit," Dad said, ushering me to the other side of the room.

He sat at the head of the table, Victor to his left, and I sank down in the seat across. I kept my face tilted to look at my dad, hoping to get out of this meeting without succumbing to the distraction of the man across from me. I didn't even question what he was doing in there. Dad liked to have people on hand to bounce opinions off during meetings with his clients, and I was just happy to be getting the best representation I could when it came to this divorce.

"We have more papers to fill out," Dad said.

I nodded, swallowing the small lump that threatened to form in my throat at the sound of the word. I hated so many things about this, but the failure I felt—as a wife, as a woman—was the worst.

"Have you spoken to Gabriel? After the papers were leaked to the media?"

I nodded again. "I spoke to him yesterday."

"And what did he say? Is he ready to proceed?" Dad asked. Gabe acted like my filing came as a shock to him. It wasn't a shock to anybody else, though, so I wasn't sure if he was really shocked or just wanted to treat it as an *out of sight, out of mind* kind of thing. Dad put his hand over mine when I dropped my gaze to the table. "Honey, it's okay. We need to talk about it."

I took a deep breath and wiped my eyes before I spoke. I was hyper aware of Victor's presence. I didn't want him to see me cry, hurt, or weak. I wasn't that girl. I'd never been that girl, but talking about this while my dad soothed me was more difficult than I could bear.

"He agreed on the motion and said he said he knew I would bail. That he knew when things got tough I'd leave him," I whispered. "That I couldn't deal with the reality of life."

I flinched when Dad slapped his free hand on the wooden table and stood suddenly.

"This is why I can't do it. I'll choke the bastard if I see him in court. I'd choke him if I'd see him right now."

I blinked, confused, looked at Victor, who was watching me closely and looked back at my dad. "What do you mean you can't do this?"

"Victor's taking this case. He's the best I got, love," Dad said. "It's like having me represent you. Promise."

Promise. I closed my eyes. He only said that when he was positive he wouldn't let me down. When I opened my eyes, I glanced at Victor, at his chiseled jaw and hypnotizing eyes, and that soft hair I'd loved running my fingers through. I tried so hard not to recall it, not to picture our back-and-forth banter before I'd locked the door of his office, and walked around his desk, possessed with lust—*with need*—with a hunger that wouldn't stop until I had him.

He must not have told my dad about us, because if he had he'd probably be looking for another firm, representing this divorce. Dad was weird about mixing work and personal life. Despite that, I knew Victor was a damn good attorney, the best, even. I had friends who'd hired him for their divorces and swore up and down by Victor Reuben. I didn't doubt his abilities in anything. I just doubted mine in being able to get through this without messing things up for the two of us, because when it came to *us*, things went up in flames. Or at least they used to. Perhaps he'd moved on, judging by his indifference.

"How long will it take to get this over with?" I asked Victor.

"The process has begun and it usually takes six months. So assuming he's on board and doesn't give us any trouble, and if he's not as . . . stubborn as you are, it shouldn't be too bad."

Dad chuckled at the mention of my stubbornness, and Victor's eyes flickered over there, smiling briefly before meeting mine again.

"Either way, I will do everything to make sure this is as painless for you as it can be. I'll be at your beck and call. Whatever you need, whenever you need it, I'm here," he said, his eyes dipping to my mouth briefly, to the low-cut dress I wore, and back to my eyes in a way that made goosebumps rake over my flesh.

What would it be like to have this man be *my* beck and call? I was sure he didn't do that often. He didn't seem like the type. Dad's cell phone rang, and he stood and excused himself. I looked over my shoulder to watch Dad walk out before turning back to Victor.

"What's your deal?"

"What do you mean?" he asked, pushing off the table slightly to cross his ankle over his knee. Totally casual, as if we were about to discuss sports.

"Why'd you agree to do this?"

"Why did I agree to do my job?" he asked, looking amused. "Let's see, there's the fact that I like it, and then there's the bit about those three years of law school I went through, and well, yeah, the most important part, it's what I get paid to do."

If I didn't know him, or know him as much as I thought I did, I would have been upset. Instead, I sighed. "Did you tell my dad about us?"

"Us?"

"Yeah, us. You know," I said, shooting him a look.

"There is no us, Nicole. There never was. We were friends, we had sex, but that was it. I thought that was clear."

There was no bite to his tone or the words he used. He said it soothingly, as if he were talking to a child or trying to calm down an ex-girlfriend after a breakup. Clearly I was in an overly emotional state. Had I not been, his words would have just rolled off me, but they didn't. They actually hurt a little. *I had gone off and gotten married.* It's not like I expected him to care. I looked at him momentarily. He didn't seem like he did, and at this point, what did it matter?

"You're right," I said once I collected my thoughts and looked at Victor again. "So, what do we do now?"

"The question of the hour is: did you sign a prenup?"

"Of course."

My father was a divorce attorney. Did Victor really think he'd let me marry with no prenuptial? Seemingly reading my mind correctly, Victor nodded.

"I'll have Corinne get it for me," he said, opening up the folder in front of him and jotting something down before picking it up and coming around the table.

"This will make it easier for me to explain," he said as he sat down beside me. The smell of his cologne enveloped me and I did my best to take it in small doses, taking small and quick shallow breaths as I focused on the papers in front of me.

"Nic?" he asked, his voice low and near my ear. My stomach did a flip-flop.

"Yeah?" I whispered.

"You're going to have to learn to breathe when you're near me. We'll be doing this a lot."

My head whipped toward him, and he reared back slightly to put a little distance between our faces.

"You're unbelievable," I said.

"So I've been told."

"Let's get on with this," I replied, trying my best not to roll my eyes.

And then Victor went over the process and explained each page. I didn't care to know all the details, and I knew he had my best interest and wouldn't screw me over, but I listened anyway. He leaned over me and pointed at the spots I needed to sign and I wondered how many women had felt the warmth of his chest against their shoulder. When we finished, he backed away and picked up the papers to go back to the spot he'd been sitting earlier.

"So now that part is over," he said, sitting across from me and taking a legal-sized notebook out, "let's go over things I should know about. How many houses do you own? By own I mean, how many is your name in the title for?"

"Two. One in Calabasas and an apartment in New York."

"And those are also owned by Gabriel?"

"Correct."

"Have either one of you moved out of your current residence?"

"No."

The tip of his pen stopped writing, and he glanced up at me. "Are either one of you planning on moving out any time soon?"

"I don't know."

He put the pen down and threaded his hands together as he looked at me.

"Have you discussed anything with Gabriel?"

I shook my head. "Nope."

"Why is that?"

"He's in Canada filming a movie, and I'm on set here working on one being filmed now."

"You're still doing costume design?"

I nodded, smiling that he remembered. It was the one thing keeping me sane these days. It had been for quite some time. Work and wine, maintaining sanity for unhappily married women everywhere.

"Okay. Let's go over a timeline." He slid the notebook and pen over to me. "I want you to write down your wedding date, and basically any date you remember that you think is of importance—good and bad."

I did as I was told, jotting down my wedding date and more or less the timeframe of when other things happened, though I didn't keep track of every major event of my life on my calendar. Now I kind of wished I had. When I was done, I slid the notebook and pen back to Victor.

"You were pregnant?" he asked, looking at me like I was a complete stranger. I nodded.

"Miscarried at nine weeks."

He gave a nod. "And you didn't try again?"

My heart squeezed in my chest. "It didn't work out," I whispered. We hadn't, even though I'd wanted to. Gabe then started getting major acting roles and got me a dog instead, saying we needed to wait to start a family. Wait until he could actually be there for his kids, and I couldn't argue that. I cleared my throat and spoke louder. "Why is that important?"

"Is it one of the reasons your marriage didn't work out?"

"No," I said, even though I'd often wondered if we'd had the baby, if things would have worked out between us. Would things with him have been different? I refused to put the blame of our downfall on that, though. We married each other, not the idea of having a child together.

"You sure? It took you a while to come to that conclusion."

I closed my eyes and huffed out a breath. "I'm positive. Can we move on now?"

Victor paused, his eyes searching my face. "I'm not trying to be a dick about this. I just need to know everything so I know what we're dealing with. I've had cases where the spouse came back and threw things like this in our faces in the middle of court and I wasn't prepared for it, so I try to cover all my bases. This is going to get personal. Are you okay with that?"

I took a deep breath and gave him a nod to continue.

"You put here that you got married in 2010 and you basically knew it was over by late 2013, early 2014. What happened at that point?"

I looked outside again, wishing so badly I was in that ocean and not sitting in this conference room talking about this.

"Being that I filed with the notion irreconcilable differences, can I just say he wasn't the same person I met and married?"

His eyes searched my face for so long, I was sure he was going to find the answers to all his questions written all over it. I shifted under his scrutiny before he finally cleared his throat and gave me a sharp nod, moving along to the next point I'd written.

"You want to keep the house?"

"Not really, but I want to kind of stick it to him and he loves that house."

Victor chuckled, the sound so sexy I had to contain the sigh that threatened to escape my lips. "People never cease to amaze me. You want to keep an eight-million-dollar house with six bedrooms to live in all by yourself just to 'stick it to him'?"

I shrugged. "What do you suggest I do?"

"Well, being that the eight-million-dollar house comes with an equally hefty insurance payment, I'd move the hell out of there, ask for more alimony, and buy a smaller house somewhere I'd love to live."

For the first time since I'd been there, I felt myself relax a little. I leaned back in my chair and set my elbows on the table.

"I like that idea. Let's do that."

His smile stayed intact as we went through the rest of the list. He even surprised me by laughing at the point about my dog.

"You want shared custody of the dog?"

"Yeah. Harlow Edwards just got a divorce and she has shared custody with her ex."

Victor closed his eyes and shook his head. "I should get a bonus for ridiculous requests."

"Yeah, well, I'm sure a bonus can be arranged," I said. *Shit.* I didn't mean for my voice to sound the way it did, raspy and needy, but that was the way the words came out.

His gaze heated and held. I could feel myself unraveling, could feel the pull between us in the suddenly too-hot-for-me office and wished so badly I could stand, hike my dress up, and ride him right there. I groaned at the thought.

I watched his Adam's apple bob as he swallowed. "We're going to have to end this meeting and pick up another day."

I blinked away from him and swallowed back the lurid and very dirty things I wanted to say. *What the hell was wrong with me?* I was there to organize my divorce. Never mind that we'd been living in separate quarters of the infamous eight-million-dollar house for a year and a half. Never mind that he'd been screwing half of Hollywood and acting like it was okay, while I stayed at home or enjoyed quiet nights with friends. *Me.* The one-time wild child staying quietly at home while *he*, the once good boy from a small town went out and screwed around. Regardless of the eighteen months of disappointment and hurt I had been through, lusting after Victor was still inappropriate.

He stood first, and I followed his lead, walking beside him to the door. I expected him to open it and get out of Dodge right away, but instead he held the knob in his hand and turned to look at me. I tilted my head to meet his gaze, which was serious, but not any less fiery than it had been before.

"This thing between us," he said, making the words slow so I understood each and every one of them, "is over. It never happened. You are my client. I am your attorney. There are laws against things happening between us, and I could lose my license if I break them. Do you understand that?"

I swallowed thickly and nodded, my eyes not wavering from his, my heart thumping loudly.

"Say 'yes, Victor, I understand that.'"

The man was completely serious. The problem was, being this close to him again, if I moved just a fraction, I could lean in and kiss him. His smell was intoxicating. His lips had always been so soft and fucking kissable. Damn him. I wasn't going to let him get away with making me feel this way, like I was the only one affected by our exchange. I let out a laugh.

"I understand, and I'm sorry to break it to you, but I'm not looking to hook up with you. Been there, done that, bought the shirt."

He scoffed. "That's a shirt I'd love to see."

"I'll show it to you sometime. It says, 'It wasn't a big deal.'"

His lips curled into a slow, full grin. "I'm sure the word big is definitely in there, but I highly doubt that's what the shirt says. Otherwise, why did you come back for seconds, thirds, fourths, and call me drunkenly on nights out with your girlfriends?"

My eyes widened. I took a step back. "I did not."

"Did too, and texted. I have those saved."

My mouth dropped. "Why would you . . . even if I did do that, which I'm pretty sure I didn't . . . why would you save them?"

"You're my boss's daughter. God forbid you decided on one of your rampages that you were going to bury me and say that, I don't know, I raped you or some crazy shit. I needed to have proof I was the one being pursued."

"You pursued me too in the past. Or do you think looking at me like you wanted to eat me for dinner didn't count?"

"Unless it's in print, it doesn't count."

I glared at him. "You are such a dick."

"I just want to be clear that nothing can happen here, so don't make those 'Victor, please fuck me' eyes at me anymore when we're talking about your divorce."

"I didn't do that, but okay. Now if you'll excuse me, I have someone in the lobby that I may actually be interested in."

He opened the door for me and followed me down the hall. I didn't bother looking for my father. I just wanted to get out of there. I knew I'd see him for dinner the following night anyway, so I kept walking until I reached the lobby where Marcus was waiting for me with his phone in hand. He put it away as soon as he saw me.

"Let's go, Marcus, I have a lot of pent-up tension I need to get rid of," I said. I looked over my shoulder to where Victor was standing. He looked at me, looked at Marcus, back at me, and if I didn't know him at all I wouldn't have noticed the way his eyes narrowed, or the way his jaw tightened. But I did know him.

"We'll be in touch. There are other things I'll need to ask you. I'll let you know when this is filed," he said, extending his hand for me to shake. I took it. "I look forward to working with you."

His grip tightened a little when he said that, making my heart gallop. I had instant flashbacks: arguing over insignificant topics, me walking around his desk and pushing his legs apart so I could stand between them, his fingers tantalizingly slow as they inched up my skirt, his hand gripping my ass as he thrust inside me, his mouth on my throat telling me to shut the fuck up so we wouldn't get caught.

God.

I'd be lying if I said there hadn't been times after I starting going out with Gabe that I didn't think about those moments, wondered *who* Victor was doing that to. I sighed as I walked out of the building and back into the commotion of the paparazzi. I knew Victor's warning was real. Five years ago, he'd been very clear. *I need to focus on my career.* Obviously, he'd done that. And done it well. Was I wrong to wonder if he would be tempted to dance along the line of attraction again? He'd turned me away then. He'd probably do the same now. Sadly, my body wasn't getting the memo. I couldn't help but wonder how far he would go without breaking the rules.

Chapter Three

Victor

One of the perks of having the beach in your backyard was being able to wake up, roll out of bed and catch waves. Unfortunately, today was not that day. I missed my alarm clock and showed up to breakfast at my parents' an hour late.

"You look like shit," my best friend, Oliver, said from across the table. I flashed him my middle finger. I didn't have enough energy to comment.

"What did you do last night?" my sister, Estelle, asked as she served herself orange juice for the third time.

"Nothing," I mumbled.

I'd stayed up until five "researching" Nicole and Gabriel. My associates often asked me if my extensive research was necessary and my answer was always a solid yes. Normally, I had my assistant Corinne do my research, but this thing with Nicole . . . it felt personal. I told myself it was because I'd seen how badly some of my high-profile clients treated their spouses in a divorce, and if what I'd heard about Gabriel had any truth to it, I was sure she wasn't doing well personally, but it was more. There was a sadness in her eyes and stance in those photos.

I hadn't seen Nicole since before she married, hadn't thought about her much after I found out she had, but seeing her again . . . it did something to me. I wasn't going to lie to myself about that. I just knew I had to keep it business. All business. The problem was that while my office was normally a second home to me, now it reminded me of her. I wasn't sure why after so many years it was happening, but it was. And after reading the abundance of damning gossip in the tabloids, about his affairs and his partying ways, I couldn't understand why she had married that guy. She said he'd changed. I had to take her word for it. Maybe she'd changed too. Maybe she wasn't the funny Nicole I used to know. The girl with the wicked smile and enough bite to make me want to settle down . . . just not enough to actually do it. Not then, anyway. Not now, either, for that matter. While all of my friends had married I'd stayed focused on my career. Truth of the matter was, I hadn't found a girl that sparked my interest enough to want to settle down.

"Let me get you more pancakes," my mom said, snapping me out of my thoughts as she reached for my plate. I stopped her before she could take it.

"Thanks, Ma. I can get it, though."

I needed a break from Oliver and my sister's questioning gazes. Ever since they'd married, they'd started acting like I was a little lost boy when they were around me for too long. I guess at one point they must have gotten sick of learning a new woman's name every time I brought somebody around, so they made it their mission to try and set me up with somebody they felt would gain my attention. That basically meant they were trying to set me up with every breathing female they came in close quarters with, which was what my mother had been trying to do since I graduated from law school, and having three fucking matchmakers breathing down my neck was something I could only handle in small doses. I was in the kitchen, smearing my pancakes with butter when Oliver walked in with his plate.

"What's the deal? I haven't seen you this tired in a while."

"Work. I stayed up late looking into a new client."

He frowned. "Doesn't your assistant do that stuff for you?"

I put the butter down and picked up the syrup.

"Your plate looks like a heart attack waiting to happen," he said. I looked at him as I poured the syrup.

"Oh, yeah? Did Dr. Oz teach you that?" I asked.

Much to his annoyance, I always joked and said his obsession with Dr. Oz rivaled my mom's with Oprah. He made a face of disapproval, but didn't bother to tell me he didn't care for Dr. Oz, the way he normally did. Instead he moved on to serve his measly oatmeal.

"Prisoners eat more food than you," I said, nodding at his plate.

He chuckled, pushing all that girly hair off his face before taking a spoonful into his mouth.

"I'm not even going to start a debate about prison food right now because I know how much you hate to lose. I'm just saying, you're not twenty-one anymore. You need to watch the shit you eat."

I sighed. "I'm tired and I only eat like this on weekends. You know this and you still give me this little speech every fucking week. I already told you, it's been proven that if you eat shitty food one day a week it speeds up your metabolism."

He scoffed. "Keep getting your information from those steroid-injecting wannabe nutritionists on Instagram and see where that gets you."

I smiled around a mouthful of pancake. I didn't even have an Instagram account. He knew this. My life wasn't exciting enough for me to document in photographs. We were eating in silence for a bit before he spoke up again.

"Do you want to go to a charity gold tournament next weekend?"

"Not particularly," I said. "I'll donate, though. What's the cause?"

"Childhood obesity."

"I'll donate."

"You sure you don't want to come? Lots of single women in those country clubs," he said in a voice that sounded like something he would use to tease a child.

Again with the trying to set me up with somebody. I resisted the urge to groan, but shot him an annoyed look nonetheless.

"Positive. You of all people should know I don't need help in that category."

"That's the problem. You only meet women who are looking for a good time. These women are looking to settle down."

"Which is the same thing I want," I scoffed. "Those country club women are looking for their next sugar daddy."

"No," he said, drawing out the word. "They're looking for men who have drive and know what they want. No shame in that."

"No," I said, mimicking him. "They're looking for money. Money and power."

As I'd looked at the pictures of Nicole and Gabriel that was the only thing I could come up with. Apparently that's what women wanted—money and power. It was unsettling though, because Nicole had both without him. Maybe she just liked that he was famous. Still, the Nicole I knew wouldn't have married a guy for any of those things. Or maybe the Nicole I *thought* I knew was a more accurate assessment. The Nicole I *thought* I knew didn't even want to get married. I wasn't sure what had changed, or where it did, but the thought that she had sex with me and accepted a proposal a few weeks later was just . . . mind-boggling.

"You listening to me?" Oliver asked. I blinked a few times and turned to set my empty plate in the sink.

"Sorry. I zoned out. What?"

"I asked if you want to talk about the case you're doing dirty work for."

I tore my gaze away from his and ran a hand through my hair. It wasn't that Nicole had been my dirty secret or anything, because in a moment of weakness I'd told Oliver and our other friend Jensen about her, but I didn't like talking about her. She was mine. *Mine.* That didn't seem accurate, though, since she wasn't mine and never had been. It still didn't help the sensation I got in the pit of my stomach when I thought about her. When I thought about the sex and the phone calls, and the way they'd all stopped after I broke things off. *All of it.* I was used to women lingering for a while after breaking things off with them. That didn't happen with Nicole. She didn't linger. She just moved on.

She just moved on.

"Vic?" Oliver said, snapping me out of my thoughts. *Again.*

"What?" My eyes snapped to his again. He was frowning, looking almost concerned.

"You wanna talk about it?"

"No, Dr. Phil, I don't."

He chuckled. "You're such a dick when you're stressed."

Stressed. I was used to feeling stressed. This was something else. This was the fear of the unknown—the unchartered—and I hated being faced with things I couldn't build a game plan for. I wasn't sure what it was, but I knew I needed to keep my head in the game and thoughts of being between Nicole's legs out of my head. Can't say that didn't cross my mind yesterday when she walked in looking like the queen she deserved to be. Stunning. Sexy. Yet, when I'd seen her sink into her father's arms, I knew she was hiding behind a well-preserved façade. I had told her she needed to keep her shit together around me, but it went both ways. I would not succumb to her provocative allure. *Could not.*

My sister opened the door and walked in with her hands on her hips before I could formulate a response to Oliver, and I was grateful for the interruption. These were people who could see right through me—read me like a book—and I couldn't deal with that right now. Not when I wasn't sure what language the words were even written in, and I needed to actually go see the person who had me feeling this way.

"This isn't Bean and Vic bonding time. You can do that tomorrow," Estelle said.

"You get more annoying with age. You know that, right?" I said, smiling at her when she stuck her tongue out at me.

"It was pointed out to me recently," she said, glaring at Oliver, who chuckled in response. "Anyway, I wanted to tell you that while you guys are cooped up in your living room all day tomorrow I'll be at an orphanage."

"Doing what?" I asked as we walked to the living room.

"Painting. I'm donating supplies and stuff."

"And her services," Oliver added with that love-struck smile he always had around my sister. How the hell I didn't realize they were together, or had been together, before I caught them was beyond my comprehension now I was exposed to their corny shit all the time.

"That's cool. And you're telling me this because?" I asked, plopping down on the loveseat.

"Because I haven't had a chance to make the stupid bean dip or anything else, so you're going to have to make your own or go grocery shopping."

"That's fine," I said, closing my eyes as I leaned back. I fell asleep to the sound of my sister and Oliver talking about groceries and my mom asking if she should make the dip for us. Despite the noise, I managed to sleep, and dreamed of Nicole Alessi and the sexy way she carried herself.

It was just sex. It was. Really good sex, but I could have really good sex with a lot of women. I hadn't planned on exchanging phone numbers with her after it was over, but then she adjusted her dress and laughed at the sight of her torn-up underwear and I wanted a repeat. I couldn't explain why. I just knew I did. I didn't expect to call her and end up staying on the phone when she turned down my invitation for the repeat. I didn't expect her to walk into the office two weeks after I'd gotten a job there, and I sure as hell didn't expect her last name to be Alessi.

So many wrong things.

So many illicit thoughts.

So many reasons why the repeat wouldn't happen.

But then she knocked on my door. Mouth ajar, blue eyes widened in shock.

"You're the new guy?" she asked.

In that moment, I didn't know whether to accept the shock I felt or call security because she was obviously stalking me. Even the rational part of my brain was on full alert.

"Yeah," I said, uncomfortably eyeing the door she closed behind her. "What are you doing here?"

Please don't say you work here. Please don't say you work here. Maybe she was just passing along a message for somebody. Maybe she was a florist making a delivery. Maybe she was also fucking one of my colleagues. At that I cringed. That would mean we definitely couldn't have another go.

"I'm . . . my dad . . ." She sighed, not waiting for an invitation before sitting down in one of the chairs across from me.

Under normal circumstances, that would have bothered me, but I was quickly realizing that things with "Nicole from the nightclub" weren't normal. She hadn't even called me back after turning me down. She'd sent me a few text messages, but that was it, and my text messaging skills were poor to say the least. I hated it. I hated the idea of her being able to show her friends what we talked about. I hated the idea of anybody knowing what our plans were. I didn't know why. There was no plausible explanation for me feeling that way. None. But now she was sitting across from me, I was starting to believe it was the right move.

"Your dad," I asked, "is getting a divorce?"

"Uh . . . no," she said, licking her full lips nervously. The same lips I'd kissed a couple weeks ago. The same lips I kept envisioning around my cock. "Will is my dad."

I blinked hard, away from her lips. "What?"

"He's . . . my dad," she said, her voice small, her eyes apologetic. Good. So she knew this couldn't happen anymore. But what the ever-loving fuck? This was definitely payback for me fucking my fraternity brother's girlfriend back in college. Definitely. Fuck my fucking life.

"Your dad," I said flatly. She nodded, tugging her bottom lip into her mouth with her teeth. The sight of it made something inside me ricochet.

"Yep," she said with a pop. She looked at me for a moment, just looked at me, her eyes scanning my face, dropping to my chest, and back up. "You look really good in a suit."

"Nicole," I said, a warning.

She smiled. "Yep."

"Stop looking at me like that."

"Okay." She shrugged, but kept smiling, taunting. "So, divorce law, huh?"

I kept my eyes on hers. "Yes."

"Are your parents divorced?"

"No."

She frowned a bit, looking pensive. "Interesting. Are they happy?"

"Yes," I said, feeling my lips tilt into a smile. "Are you a psychology major?"

"No," she said, eyes wide, drawing out the word as if that was a ridiculous

thought.

"What are you studying? Assuming you're in school," I added.

"Costume design. I graduate next week actually."

"Costume design," I repeated, letting my eyes drift down her body.

She was wearing a skintight dress with huge colorful flowers. It covered her entirely, with small sleeves and a neckline that didn't show much cleavage, but the way it fit her left little to the imagination. I could see the outline of her perfect tits—handful size—her tiny waist, and curvy hips. When I looked back at her face she was back to giving me a coquettish smile that I felt everywhere. And when she stood and gave me a perfect back view of her round ass and went to lock the door, I gulped and started to breathe a little heavier. And when she turned around and walked around my desk in long, slow strides I had to close my eyes.

I'd just gotten this job. My eyes snapped open. Surely she wasn't considering doing what I thought she was planning to do. Fuck. No.

"Nicole, I just got this job," I said, my words going from firm to low as she swiveled my chair and kneeled down in front of me.

"My dad left," she said, looking at me through her long, dark lashes.

I swallowed. "We shouldn't do this."

"We shouldn't do a lot of things."

"I . . . this can't . . ." I started, but she was already unbuckling my belt.

"Do you have a girlfriend?" she asked, her fingers stopping. "Shit. I should have asked that before. Do you?"

I frowned. "Fuck, no."

She leaned back on her heels, hands still on my pants, and looked up at me. "Is that a fuck no because you're opposed to having a girlfriend, or a fuck no because you would never do this to your girlfriend if you had one? I can't tell."

I put a hand over hers to stop her from moving because I was getting harder by the millisecond. "Both."

She raised an eyebrow. "Opposed to having a girlfriend, really? You're a player."

"Not," I said, my word strangled when she moved a hand to cup me over my pants. "Not a player."

"You just crush a lot?" she asked with a smirk.

"Fuck a lot. Yes."

"But you don't want to fuck me because I'm your boss's daughter," she said rather than asked. I swallowed again and nodded. "Doesn't that make it more exciting? We can be quiet."

I shook my head, but fuck, it did make it a little exciting. One more time and I was done. Definitely. After this I'd break it off, erase her phone number, and just . . . be done.

"It'll be the last time," she said. "You wanted to do it last week when you sent me that text. I've just been busy with final projects."

Our gazes met, both hot, both ready to pounce. My only response was to uncover my hand from hers and my fuck no turned into an instant fuck yes.

Chapter Four

Nicole

Living in close quarters with my estranged husband wasn't necessarily the smartest thing I'd done, especially when he suddenly came back from Canada where he'd been shooting, went out with his cast, brought the after-after party back to our place, and proceeded to invite me to join the fun when I woke up, looking for the source of the commotion. Being half-past drunk and fooling around with the husband I was in the process of divorcing, was an even dumber idea. Not for the first time since I woke up, I rubbed my eyes and groaned. It's not like Gabe and I hadn't hooked up since we decided to end things, but we'd steered far away from each other since making things official. I blamed my lapse of judgment on not getting laid in a year, the two bottles of wine I drank before he got there, and that one fleeting moment when he smiled at me when I thought that maybe, just maybe, this marriage could still work.

But that was before a woman barged into his bedroom, where were were almost naked, and asked him where he put the cocaine they'd just purchased. The words, their actions, the fact she knew where his room was *and* he didn't kick her out at first glance, kicked my senses into overdrive. I hopped out of bed, fixed my clothes, and went back to what we'd dubbed my side of the house.

I didn't acknowledge him when he asked me to come back. He never even got out of bed or came down the hall to stop me. Yet there I was, in our kitchen, picking up his mess as I'd done a million times before. I was half-tempted to call our housekeeper, Amelia, and have her come in on her day off, but I didn't want any more people suffering this divorce.

Our gate bell rang shortly after I was on my hands and knees, scrubbing off things I was sure you couldn't even find on floors of college frat houses to make my house presentable when Victor came over this afternoon. I pressed the open button on the gate without even checking to see who it was. I rarely did that, but I figured because of the time it had to be UPS or some other courier. Without giving it a second thought, I went back to scrubbing.

This was not how I envisioned this week panning out. Not at all. Not that I'd ever envisioned myself on my knees in this kitchen for any other reason than Gabriel standing in front of me. I sighed and pushed the thought away. That was over. Over. Never again, and I didn't want it again, especially after last night's rude reminder. I went back to cleaning whatever disgusting, sticky particle was on my floor at the moment. The loud knocks on my door snapped me out of what was becoming a pattern: scrub, cringe, scrub, cringe, repeat. I let go of the scrubber and stood with a sigh, taking off my yellow gloves and throwing them into the empty bucket. I washed my hands quickly before making my way to the front door.

To my complete surprise, Gabe was walking to the door at the same time. I would have sworn he'd sleep until this evening and only get up to eat and have a do-over of his drug-and-alcohol-infused night. I shivered at the thought. This man once made me shiver for completely different reasons. He still had that effect on women, with his toned body, striking features, and invented smile.

"You expecting company?" he asked, already looking through the peephole.

"Not until later today," I said slowly, looking around as if the white walls were going to tell me the time. A thought struck me as I picked up the pace and stood beside Gabe. "Oh, shit. What time is it?"

"Do you know this guy?" he asked as we reached the door.

I unlocked the door and opened it, ignoring his question. Victor stood on the other side of the threshold with a confused look on his face as his eyes bounced from Gabe to me, me to Gabe, and finally me again.

"Come in," I said, and moved toward Gabe so he had no choice but to take a step back and make room for Victor to enter.

I closed the door behind him and stood there as the two of them greeted each other.

"We'll be out back. Finish cleaning up your mess," I called out over my shoulder as I walked toward the living room, knowing Victor would follow.

I walked until I reached the back doors and opened them so we could sit out on the porch, where I found a single silver stiletto.

"Who the hell leaves one shoe behind at a party?" I muttered, picking it up by the strap and tossing it aside.

"Cinderella?" Victor said behind me as he closed the French doors.

I felt myself smile. He'd always been funny. Strange and intense and funny. He was the kind of guy that could have you pinned against the wall one second and kick you out of his office the next but not let you think he was kicking you out. He'd let you think you came up with the decision to leave on your own. I hadn't seen it then as manipulation, but now that I looked back on it . . . Either way, I always appreciated the short time we had together, especially the night I'd called him due to a flat tire and he'd bolted out of the bar he was in to come help me. I'd never forget the way he shook his head as he looked at me through angry eyes.

"You can't be going out at night dressed like that," he'd said, and I could tell he was trying not to look at me.

After he fixed my tire and followed me home, I'd wondered if he'd go inside with me, but he hadn't. A part of me knew he wouldn't, of course. I'd been living in my father's guest house. What would Dad have thought if he'd seen the new attorney he'd just hired walk into his daughter's quarters at midnight? A bigger part of me had wished we hadn't been in that situation at all. That I was just a girl, and he was just a hot guy who was okay with taking chances. But we hadn't been those people.

I pushed the memory aside and sat on one of the chairs, watching as he sat across from me. He was dressed down today, which apparently for Victor meant jeans, a checkered button-up, and Oxfords. His normally playful eyes looked tired and the rough scruff on his face suggested he hadn't shaved in days. He ran a hand through his hair and brushed it back in a way that made me try to fix my own and redo my ponytail.

"Rough night?" he asked, his eyes roaming over me.

"You can say that."

I fidgeted with my hair again, even though I knew there was no use. I suddenly felt completely aware of what I looked like in my black sports bra, matching yoga pants, and makeup-less face. He'd seen me in a form-fitting navy dress and sky-high heels a couple days ago. In fact, most of the times he'd seen me I had been dressed to impress, and even when we'd had sex, we'd both remained mostly dressed. I wondered what a naked Victor looked like. It was a fleeting thought, but it was one that made me flush. I swallowed when our gazes locked, feeling like I'd been caught in my sexual fantasy.

"Nicole," he said, a warning, but he kept that tempestuous gaze locked on mine and I knew he felt the same electric prickle I felt all over.

"Isn't it weird for you?" I asked, my voice a whisper.

Victor appraised me for a long moment, tilting his head as his inquisitive eyes scanned my face. I would have killed to know what he was thinking. I would have killed to ask. But I couldn't. I sat there, *wondering*, hoping he'd answer, waiting on bated breath for it. I leaned in a little, and he mimicked my movement, putting his elbows on his knees, letting his hands dangle between them.

"It's weirder than I thought it would be," he admitted, his gaze searing into mine. "I keep reminding myself that the Nicole I once knew isn't the same one sitting in front of me."

"What makes you say that?"

He leaned back in his chair and looked at the house, the pool, and back at me. "All this. The Nicole I knew didn't need the big house *or* the husband."

My heart skipped. The Nicole he knew was a damn liar. Another thing I wanted to say, but didn't. Instead I took a different approach.

"Maybe the Nicole you knew wanted you to ask her out on a real date."

"Maybe the Nicole I knew should have asked me on a date herself." His lip curled up into a sly smile. "She didn't have a problem asking for other things."

My cheeks blazed. "I didn't think you wanted to date."

His gaze softened, but his words still slapped me. "I didn't."

Yeah. That stung.

Thankfully, Gabe chose that moment to open the door beside us and we both whipped our heads toward it.

"So this is your attorney?" Gabe asked, raising his eyebrows when neither one of us answered. "Okay, then, I just wanted to let you know that I'm leaving, but the pool guy is coming today. He lost the key to the gate so he might ring. Thanks for helping me pick up." He tucked his head in, but then brought it back out as if he'd forgotten to say something. "And thanks for last night. It was really, *really* good."

What the fuck? Had he forgotten how that went down? Or rather how it didn't go down? *Perhaps the woman had stayed after I'd left. Bastard.* Nonetheless, there was no way to miss his innuendo, not with the way his voice dropped and he winked as he looked at my mouth. He shut the door and I watched as he walked off. Victor didn't comment, instead he opened up his briefcase to hand me some papers. I practically hid my face behind the papers.

"I need you to sign these," he said, going back to business mode. "There's an X on each page I need you to look at. It indicates you're moving forward with the motion and asking for alimony."

"What happens if I just poison him?" I asked quietly, still hiding my face as my eyes scanned the words on the page.

"Then I'd have to hook you up with a criminal attorney because I could no longer represent you."

I glanced up at him and found that his lips were curled into a smile, the sight of it doing things to me, and making me smile back. He had one leg folded on top of his knee at the ankle, athletic frame pressed back into the chair, sultry eyes on mine. *Just . . . wow.*

"Once this is over you can go on with your life . . . pretend this never happened," he said, signaling toward the house with his chin.

I looked inside. It was so big and empty. It always had been, I realized, but what once felt cozy and warm, now felt cold, the spaces wider, room for more problems. I couldn't afford to kick myself down over it anymore. Like my friends said, I'd kicked myself hard enough over things that weren't solely my fault while he'd continued to thrive and make a name for himself.

"I just feel like I failed, you know? I'm sure you get that a lot, but I just don't do well with failure."

"You didn't fail. Divorce doesn't have to mean failure, and it's certainly not one person's failure." He paused, scratching his chin as his eyes wandered over my shoulder, toward the pool. "How long ago did you decide it was over?"

"A year ago," I said. I'd already told him that the other day. Victor shook his head.

"I mean, you personally. When did you know it was over for you?"

I scooted back in my chair and lifted my legs, hugging them toward my chest. "A long time ago."

"Why did you wait so long?"

"Because I'm not a quitter," I whispered, tears filling my eyes as I said the words.

"Is that why you're still living here? With him?" There was bite to his words that matched the sudden anger in his eyes.

"I guess."

I wiped my eyes and went back to the papers in front of me. He continued to stare at me. The words kept blurring, so I didn't get very far into the document. I signed where it said I should and initialed the rest. I figured I couldn't be giving up any more than I already had, and my dad was Victor's boss, so he couldn't be screwing me. I looked up at him again. He could totally be screwing me. I shook my head, looking down at the paper again, and tried to bite back a laugh. Something was terribly wrong with me if the thoughts *screwing me over* were being misconstrued in my own mind. Massively, irrevocably wrong with me. I'd said the been there, done that thing to him the other day as an out because the longer I looked at him the less I believed myself.

"What's so funny?" he asked as I handed back the papers and pen he'd given me.

"Nothing. Thinking about a shirt I have."

His brows crinkled in confusion for a second before he got it and smiled.

"You must really like that shirt."

"You should see how it fits me," I said with a wink.

The way his eyes flared, I could tell my words evoked some kind of image in his mind. He didn't say anything like he would have in the past. That had been our thing all those years ago. I'd pull the string until he bit and caved to me. Not this Victor, though. He cleared his throat and stood up, offering me his hand to shake. I took it, and ignored the way my insides rocked when he touched me. We walked back through the house to the front door, and he commented on the electric fireplace and color of the dark wood floors. When I touched the door handle, he placed his hand over mine, covering it. My heart jumped at the sensation of his hand warming mine, his long fingers digging into my flesh just slightly, just enough. My eyes snapped to his.

"For the record, I would love to see how your shirt fits," he said in a low voice, lowering his face to mine so we were almost nose to nose, eye to eye. "Maybe once this is over, if the offer still stands, I'll take you up on it."

My breath hitched a little. I licked my lips. "That'll take months."

"It can take a year," he said. He was breathing a little louder now. I wondered what he would do if I leaned in and pressed my lips against his.

"We both know if I want it to happen, it'll happen," I whispered.

"It won't. It can't."

He straightened, turned my hand on the knob, then walked out to his black Jaguar without a backward glimpse. My heart was still rattling as his car purred to life. Our gazes caught momentarily as he waited for the gate to open behind him, and all I could do was stare. I was sure my gaze reflected my neediness. I hated the vulnerability I felt when I was near this man. I was living with last year's Sexiest Man of the Year, yet there I was, feeling things I hadn't felt in over a year. For Victor Reuben, of all people. I was so screwed.

Chapter Five

Nicole

"I don't know what's wrong with me," I said to my friend Talon as I continued to sew the eighteenth-century-style dress I was working on.

Talon had been the one who convinced me to work on this movie. Partially because she wanted to keep an eye on me with the separation and another because we always had fun when we worked on the same set, something we hadn't done in over a year. She was the makeup artist to the stars, while I was the costume designer. Completely different jobs with similar lunch breaks.

She sighed and pinned back the tight ringlets of dark brown curls falling into her face. "I don't know what to say, sweetie. You've been through a rough couple of years and now you're stuck with this guy you had a major crush on when you were younger. I just don't know what to say."

"I'm not stuck with him," I said, frowning. She shot me a look. "What? I'm not. I can hire another divorce lawyer. He just happens to be the best."

"At that and other things, if I remember correctly." A sly smile appeared on her face as she said it, and I couldn't help but laugh.

"This is a real problem. I'm around hot guys all the time. I mean, hello," I said, pointing at the poster for the movie we were working on. The poster had a partially naked Eric Austin dressed as Tarzan. "Yet for some reason I'm around this guy for two seconds and I become a fifteen-year-old girl at a One Direction concert."

Talon gasped. "I am thirty-two, thank you very much, and Harry is hot."

"So is Victor." Very, very hot.

"I know." She paused. "But you guys have history."

"We don't," I said, interrupting her. We didn't. We had a short-lived fling if you could even call it that. Late night phone calls, quick sex in an office, a bathroom . . . those things didn't constitute a fling. Right?

"Well, sexual history," she said. "And you clearly still want to jump into bed with him."

"I never jumped into bed with him," I said. True and pointless reminder.

"You know what I mean."

I shrugged.

"What happened with Gabriel? Was he weird after your almost hookup the other night?"

I groaned. "Weird? No. Annoying? Yes. He brought it up in front of Victor. I can't believe I almost did that . . ." I felt a little ill, not because I was disgusted, but because I was appalled at myself. If my dad found out about that he'd kill me. Anything that made this divorce more difficult would not be okay with him.

"That was the wine," Talon said. "We shouldn't have drunk so much, and I did push that second bottle on you, so it's technically my fault."

I laughed. "Thanks for that, but you're not going down for it, despite the fact it did almost cost me the embarrassment of a lifetime."

"Yeah, well, alcohol is normally served with a side of embarrassment. My point is, you didn't even want to touch Gabriel last year."

"That's because his nose was always powdered."

She rolled her eyes. "Save the saint story for someone who buys it. You've done your share of drugs. Don't act like cocaine isn't equivalent to a shot of tequila around here."

I slumped back in my chair. She was right. The difference was that when Gabriel did it, he became a different person. Aggressive and downright mean. I'd never told anybody, not even Talon, about the times I'd slept in the guest room out back because I knew if I went to a hotel I'd be photographed and rumors would start.

"Why is he here anyway?" Talon asked, snapping me out of my thoughts.

"Who?" I asked, looking around.

"Gabriel. I thought he was in Canada."

"Oh. Yeah. He said he was on a shooting break. I need to find out how long this break will last. I'm not sure I can actually stay there if he'll be doing that every night."

"Oh? So you actually might leave your humble abode?"

I sighed. "I didn't want to, but I don't think I can handle seeing him go to shit. That was what started this whole thing in the first place, and he's really not going to change. I see that now."

Talon took a seat in the chair beside me and took my hands in hers, her green eyes filled with concern. "You can stay with me. Mike won't mind at all. We have the room. The kids would love to have Auntie Nicky there."

I shook my head slowly. "Thank you. I can always stay at my dad's for a while. Or get my own place. I'll have to do that eventually anyway."

Her eyes widened. "So you're going to let him keep the house?"

"I don't know. Maybe. I'm tired of holding this grudge."

Talon nodded and gave my hands a squeeze before letting go and standing. "I have to get to work, but whatever you need, you know I'm here. And be careful with the hot lawyer."

"I don't have to be," I said, laughing. "He's already reminded me twice that we can't happen again."

"Well, he reminded you about that before and look how that turned out," she said with a wink before walking away.

Yeah, it turned out with him breaking it off just when I thought we were reaching a new level. A new, bullshit level that I conjured up in my head because that's all it was—bullshit. What bothered me most when he broke it off was that I didn't listen to him when he said he wasn't interested in a relationship. I didn't listen to him when he said we couldn't do what we were doing. I learned, though. I learned when people show you who they are, you should listen. And he showed me who he was the entire time. He never hid behind false promises or pretty words. He did what he said he would do, and I hadn't faulted him for that. I couldn't.

I didn't come to appreciate Victor's honesty until I realized the man I shared a life with had lied to me. *Continually.* And then I found out he'd lied *and* cheated. When I threatened divorce, he threw a hissy fit and started trash-talking me to anybody in the industry who would listen. In *my* industry. He'd been so conniving about it, too, only talking to people I didn't know but only hoped to work with. Shortly after a business friend of mine gave me a heads-up, the tabloids were talking about our divorce and how heartbroken he'd been. They stated his affairs began when *I* said I was leaving him. The sad part is that at first I thought the rumors were false. That there was no way he was already with another woman, but I quickly realized there was usually some truth to the stories printed.

If I were a different person, like Harlow Winters, I'd call in a favor and spread rumors about Gabe that made him look worse than Ben Affleck cheating on Jennifer. That wasn't me, though, and ultimately, underneath all of the shit that had smeared his character and our marriage, I still believed in the nice guy from the middle of nowhere that I'd fallen in love with.

Chapter Six

Nicole

I didn't hesitate in saying yes when my best friend, Chrissy, called me to meet her for dinner at a new hot spot. I called Marcus, who was more than a little surprised at my request for him to be ready at nine o'clock. It's not that I hadn't gone out since the separation, but I'd been very low-key about it, opting to go to friends' houses and get drunk there instead of out in public where anybody could take my picture and make a fool out of me. Not that I needed help making a fool out of myself when I was drunk. No, I did that all on my own, but I didn't need it all over the tabloids.

I'd agreed to meet Chrissy at nine thirty, and when Marcus knocked on my door a second time, telling me it was nine twenty and I was still trying to figure out what shoes I was going to wear, I knew I'd be late.

"Fashionably late," I said to him as we walked to the car.

"That's one way to put it," he responded. I smiled, feeling the excitement of my night out coursing through me. "Are we taking the Porsche?"

I nodded as he pressed the clicker to the garage. The white florescent lights flickered on and we walked toward the white Cayenne. I wasn't sure where Gabe stood on the cars situation and who would keep what, and I wasn't a big car person. Most days I drove my Prius, but if I had the chance to, I was totally keeping the Cayenne. We made it to the restaurant at the same time Chrissy did, both of us getting out of our cars at the same time. The few paparazzi standing outside ran toward her to get a picture. I started walking to the front of the restaurant, figuring I'd meet her inside to avoid the attention, but she squealed out my name and I had to turn around to acknowledge her.

"You look so good," she said as she ran over to hug me.

She smelled of flowers and Burberry perfume. The scent of our adolescence, when our only worries had been how late we could sleep and whether or not our parents would be home in the morning after we'd had a wild night out on the town.

"So do you," I said, bringing my hand up and touching the tips of her short, wavy blonde hair. "Love the new hair."

"I had it done today. Still getting used to it. The fam sends their love, by the way." She smiled big as she stepped aside for us to walk into the restaurant. I smiled at the mention of them. We used to be attached at the hip when we were kids and then in college. I don't think I had one memory that Chrissy wasn't in. I practically lived in her house during high school, probably because I didn't have any siblings and when I was there it was like I had three sisters. Some days, when life got shitty, I yearned for her and her sisters and this was definitely one of those times.

We were seated as promptly as you can expect to be seated when you're in the presence of a reality star. One of the reasons I hadn't seen her in a few months was because she was busy filming her show. Between her filming schedule and my work schedule, our free time rarely coincided.

"I see you still have all of your fingers," she said, taking a sip of her margarita. I smiled as I took a sip of mine.

"What makes you think I'm going to chop off my fingers? You need to get over that."

"I've seen how fast you work on those patterns. How's the set of the new movie? How's Austin?" she asked, her light brows rising provocatively. I laughed.

"If you're asking me if he's as hot as ever, the answer is yes. If you're asking me if anything has happened between us, the answer is never has and never will."

"Boring. Is it because of everything that went down with Gabe? Do you think you're swearing off actors from now on?"

"Are you swearing off athletes?" I asked, raising an eyebrow. Her past three boyfriends had been athletes, and all three had been cheating pigs.

"Touché."

We talked some more, ate some edamame, and clinked our glasses in a cheer before she dropped the, "Let's go to a club tonight!" and I was feeling tipsy enough to agree. We spent the rest of the time catching up and talking the way you can only talk to an old friend—loudly with obnoxious laughter and lots of pointing at each other whenever we remembered an old inside joke.

"That's your new security detail?" Chrissy asked when Marcus walked around the car and handed the valet a tip.

"That's him."

"Maybe I should ride with you," she said in a loud whisper. I laughed.

"Do it. Tell Frederick to follow us."

She turned around and told her bodyguard to follow us as he shielded us from the cameras snapping pictures of us climbing into the car.

"How's the filming going? Are you on break?" I asked.

"Yes. Thank God. My family is driving me absolutely crazy already," she groaned. I laughed. Only Chrissy could make a reality TV show that paid her hundreds of thousands of dollars an episode sound as grueling as hard labor.

"Poor you," I said, smirking.

"Seriously, Nicole. You look fucking awesome. Are you dieting?" she asked, giving me a once-over as we sat beside each other.

"It's called the divorce diet. You should try it. It works wonders, apparently."

She scoffed. "That would require me getting married."

"Although if he's on the table, I may reconsider," she said, nodding toward Marcus with a salacious grin on her face.

"Stop embarrassing him," I said, trying to keep the laughter out of my voice.

"Marcus, who have you worked for?" Chrissy asked, ignoring me.

"That's classified, ma'am," he said, eyes flickering to the rearview. I couldn't see his face, but I could tell he was smiling.

"Ex-military. Those are the only ones who always tell me their previous employers are classified, as if I can't just make a few calls and find out," Chrissy said, rolling her eyes. She tilted her head to look at me. "Those are always hot in bed, though. Marcus, we're going to Lure."

I laughed, feeling the alcohol swimming in my head. "You told him that."

"Oh. That's right. Have you been lately?"

"Nope. I've been staying out of the limelight, as per Dad's orders."

"We're going to have so much fun," she squealed.

By the time we got to Lure, there was a line circling the side of the building.

"Holy crap," I said, eyes wide. Truthfully, I hadn't been to a club in ages, so I'd forgotten about long lines and ID checks. That, and the last time I had gone was with Gabe and lines and ID checks didn't exist when you were with an A-list celebrity.

"Drive to the back," Chrissy instructed.

Marcus kept driving until we reached the corner, where he turned into the alley and slowed down when the mob of paparazzi perked up and spotted a newcomer. If we had any doubt as to where the back door was, we'd just found it.

"Oh God," I muttered.

Even in my tipsy state I knew it meant our outing would be all over tonight's TMZ, but then, any outing with Chrissy meant that, and I was okay with the dinner portion being in the tabloids. It was this part of the night that terrified me. I took a deep breath, perked my boobs up in my dress, and did a little mantra in my head to remind myself to suck in my stomach.

"You ready?" Chrissy asked when the car stopped in front of the mob of cameras, which had now turned toward us.

"I guess so."

Her security opened the door for us, assisting us in climbing out of the car without flashing anybody and instantly, the questions started.

"*Nicole, did you know Gabriel would be here tonight?*"

Holy shit. Thank God the club was huge.

"*Did you set up to meet him here?*"

Breathe. Suck in your stomach. Smile. No. Don't smile.

"*Are you guys getting back together?*"

Fuck. I smiled. Shit.

"*Is the divorce off?*"

Poker face.

"*How do you feel about him dating his co-star?*"

Poker face. Poker face. Poker face. If I said it enough I'd keep it, or become Lady Gaga. Either way was good with me.

Even though all I wanted was to scream all the answers, I kept my head down, because that's what you do when you're being bombarded with personal questions you have no answers to. The bouncer took one look at each of us and let us in without hesitation. That was another perk to having Chrissy in your squad. She had a face anybody from a tween to a geezer recognized. Because of the headlines, I was sure he recognized me as well, but I definitely wasn't the reason he let me in, especially not if Gabe was really in there. We walked down a dark hallway toward the loud house music playing, but before we reached the dance floor, we were met by a waitress, wearing what looked like a bikini top and boy shorts.

"Chrissy, nice to see you again. We didn't get a heads-up, so I don't have everything ready for you, but we can get that taken care of quickly. Do you want your usual spot?" she asked.

"Yes, please," Chrissy said, then shook her head, thinking better of it. "Actually, is Gabriel Lane up there?"

The woman's eyes jumped to me. "Yes, but not on that side. You will need to walk by his table, though. If that'll be a problem I can try to get you in through the employee stairwell."

Both of them looked at me. "I don't care. I don't need special attention. I just need a shot of Fireball and I'm good."

Chrissy laughed. "I love you."

We followed the busty blonde up the stairs to the VIP area, where people were dancing along to a new Fetty Wap song. The dance area was smaller and much emptier than the one downstairs, but just as lively. Even though it was dark, I tried to look for Gabe. Not because I needed to see him, but because I wanted to know what area to stay away from. I didn't see him, so I kept walking and figured I'd do the smart thing and not get out of my designated area unless I needed to break the seal, which I hoped wouldn't happen soon.

"Did you see him?" Chrissy asked as soon as we reached the cozy corner she apparently frequented.

"Nope. You?"

She shook her head and ran a hand through her hair. "Can we get some Fireball shots, please? And a bottle of champagne?"

The blonde nodded and scurried off.

"You don't have to stay," Chrissy said to her security guy, who was still in tow. "You can go hang out with Marcus, and I'll text you when I'm ready to go."

The way this pint-sized girl ordered such big males around was always amusing to me.

"I'm trying to see if my sister's here," Chrissy said, typing into her phone. Her sisters were as popular as she was, especially in these settings.

"She's right there," I said, looking across from us. Chrissy laughed.

"How did we not see her? Let's go say hi."

We joined their friends, catching up on whatever loud club music would allow us to talk about. Work, boyfriend, etcetera, until the inevitable subject came up. Gabe.

I shrugged. "Don't care. Honestly, I'd rather not talk about it. It's fine. I'm fine."

And surprisingly, I was. I always wondered what I would feel like if and when I actually saw him with another woman. I wondered if I'd be angry or jealous, but I felt neither. I felt nothing. It'd been so long, and I felt nothing. I started to laugh. It was a small laugh that became louder and then stopped altogether.

"I'm a little tipsy; I'm having a moment," I said. "And I need to pee."

Chrissy laughed and hooked her arm around mine. "Let's go."

We brushed past the crowd, and saw Gabe walking toward the exit with a blonde on his arm. Chrissy looked at me, her eyes wide and comforting.

"I'm sorry."

I blamed the alcohol running through me for the tears that burned my eyes. I wasn't a public crier and was definitely not going to cry over him. I was done with that. We weren't together anymore. We hadn't been for a long time, yet it felt weird to see him walk out with someone else. *Had he ever been faithful?* Between the woman walking into his room and the clear way in which he depicted that he'd moved on, I had to wonder. Had I been blind or had he been the man I thought he was? I sighed, and shook my head slowly. It was something only Gabe knew. And I wasn't hurting, just . . . taken aback by it.

"It's fine. I'm glad I saw it," I said, clearing my throat.

"I hope he gets herpes," she said. We laughed, holding on to the rails to keep from tumbling down the steps. "Oh crap. We're blocking," she said. "Sorry. We're blocking. Oh . . . wow."

I looked up and saw the *oh wow* in question. He was tall, and lean, with a pair of hazel eyes currently burning holes through me.

"Holy fuck," I breathed.

Chrissy got right into flirt mode. "Where are you going?"

"The question is, where are *you* going?" Victor asked, his attention fully on me, eyes roaming down my body slowly before making their way back to my face. I swallowed back the urge to launch myself at him and erase the past ten minutes from my mind. The shots had certainly done a number on me because I felt like I was totally ready and willing to do that.

"To pee."

Chrissy laughed. "She means to the ladies' room." She grabbed my arm and shot me a pointed look. "He's hot. Saying you have to pee is frowned upon."

I couldn't help but laugh. "*He's* my lawyer."

The look on her face was priceless as she looked between the two of us. Victor was two steps beneath us and at eyelevel to us.

"Well, then. I'm going to . . ." She pointed toward the door of the bath-room a few steps down. Before she walked away, she leaned into my ear and whispered, "He works for your dad?" I nodded. "He's the one you . . . you know . . ."

I tugged at my bottom lip, my eyes still on Victor, and nodded at Chrissy who let out a harsh breath on my shoulder before walking away. She glanced back to give me two thumbs up, and I found myself laughing again.

"Hey," I said once she'd walked away. My voice was drowned out when the music picked up again. Victor leaned forward, the scruff on his face brushing my right cheek as he reached up to speak into my ear.

"Hey," he said in a low voice that made me shiver.

"I see you still frequent night clubs," I said, pulling back a little to look at him.

His eyes heated, lips curled into a smile that told me he was remember-ing the same thing I was. *Us rushing to the bathroom of a crowded club, him tugging the birthday tiara out of my hair, ripping my panties off before putting on a condom and thrusting inside me with a force I'd never experienced.* Be-cause of where he was standing, I could feel his breath on my face, smell the hint of alcohol that lingered. The pull I felt was indescribable. It was as if in that small space everything vanished, including all rational thought.

Especially rational thought.

Because when he opened his mouth to say something, surely his next warning, I pressed my lips against his, and when he moved back slightly to steady himself, my body moved with his. He broke the kiss quickly, but not before sliding his tongue into my mouth once, curving in a deep full circle around mine, and *thankfully*, not before grabbing a fistful of my hair and groaning against my lips. Suddenly it wasn't the bass of the music thumping through my veins, but the feel of Victor pressed up against me, holding me, and then just like that, with the same quickness in which it had started, he pulled back.

"Nicole," he said, a warning. I opened my eyes and looked at him.

"Yeah?" I whispered.

"Follow me."

He turned around and walked down the stairs, and I trailed behind him, rounding the corner of the dimly lit hallway until we reached a door he pushed open. I blinked rapidly, looking around, at the desk, the glass walls beside us that overlooked the club, as my eyes adjusted to the red glow of the office.

"Who's office is this?" I asked.

"The owner."

"How do you know the owner?"

Victor tilted his head slightly, stepping closer to me so I had to crane my neck to look into his eyes. My heart lurched at what I saw in them.

"Is that really what you want to discuss?" he asked, his voice low.

"What do you want to discuss?" I whispered.

"You kissed me. In public, Nicole," he said sternly.

I blinked and blinked again to clear my head of some of the alcohol. "You kissed me back."

He closed his eyes, letting out a huffing breath. "That was a mistake. This whole thing was a mistake."

"You mean me? I was a mistake?" I asked, heart rocking a little.

I tried to gather my bearings, but it was a tough night. First I had to watch my soon-to-be ex-husband leave with another woman, and now I was going to have to stand here and listen to the reminder of why Victor and I hadn't worked out in the past. *A mistake.* My self-esteem was definitely taking a hit.

"Yes," he said.

Unable to stand there and listen to him berate me, and knowing that if I left the office and ran to the bathroom it would be to cry, I turned and walked toward the glass, placing my hand against it, feeling the vibrations of the muted house music on the other side, watching the colorful laser lights as they pointed in every which direction. I felt him, rather than heard him come up behind me. It was as if he couldn't just give me the space I needed. As if he got off on telling me to stay away but also needed to pull me closer. I closed my eyes.

"You weren't a mistake," he said, his voice dark and smooth. "Kissing in public was definitely a mistake."

"We were in a dark stairwell," I said. "And you know the owner, so even if we were caught on camera you can have the footage erased."

Victor chuckled behind me and my eyes popped open. I turned around, resting my back against the cold surface behind me, closing my eyes for a beat when I felt the massage of the bass.

"You'd make a decent criminal."

I smiled, meeting his gaze. "I know how to keep secrets."

"Nic."

"Hmm?" I asked, inching closer to him. *I wonder what if would feel like to fuck against this window.*

From the way he pulled away from me, I'd either said the words aloud, or he'd read them on my face. He started to pace around the office, running a hand through his hair as he muttered things I couldn't hear under his breath.

"This isn't going to work," he said finally, turning to face me as he stood behind the desk.

"What?"

"This. Us. Me on this case. It's not going to work."

"Because you want to fuck me against the window," I said.

He gripped the top of the chair tightly and dropped his head, but didn't comment on what I'd said. "Maybe we should just see each other when we have to . . . for the divorce," he said.

I let out a laugh. "I didn't plan to come here tonight, let alone run into you."

"You're right," he said, meeting my gaze. "You're right, but we should still stick to that plan."

"As my lawyer, I don't think you should let me make rash decisions when I'm drunk," I said. He looked down again, but I saw his smile before he tried to hide it.

"I'm serious, Nicole."

"That's fine, Victor. I get it. Is that it? I was talking to a really cute guy upstairs, and I still need to use the restroom. Maybe I'll take him with me." Even in my current state, I could see the way his eyes darkened at my suggestion.

"You just said you were drunk," he growled, gripping the chair harder.

"Not *that* drunk." I paused to search his face. "Would that upset you? If I hooked up with that guy in the bathroom? I kind of like bathroom hookups."

"Nicole," he said, his tone hard, his eyes searing into mine.

"You know, you're actually the only guy I've done that with," I admitted. "But it was so hot. You kept saying all these dirty things in my ear, remember?"

"I remember," he said, voice grating.

"You were doing that," I said, pointing at his fingers, which were digging into the top of the chair. "Gripping my ass. I had marks the next day, the soreness. So hot."

"Nicole," he growled.

"It's too bad you're all business, otherwise we could have had a little fun," I said, pivoting to face the door and walking toward it. "We done here?"

Before I could even turn the knob, Victor was at my back, his hand covering mine over the doorknob.

"Why are you making this so difficult?" he asked, his voice a deep murmur in my ear. I didn't know. I honestly didn't know. It was him. I blamed him for clouding my judgment every time he was around. I closed my eyes. I wanted to lean my head back, give him access to my neck for him to suck on. I wanted to get lost in the feel of him thrusting inside me. I really, really needed to get laid. *And my body really, really wanted Victor Reuben to satisfy that urge.*

"Why would you bring me into a dark office to talk to me about not kissing you in public? You could have told me that in the hall," I said, opening my eyes. His hand gripped mine so I couldn't move.

"I can't seem to think straight around you," he said, his breath on my neck.

He turned the doorknob and put his hand on the small of my back to lead me out of there and back to the VIP section. I shivered at the feel of his touch. I looked at him over my shoulder and locked eyes, wondering if he felt this pull too. His nostrils flared. When we reached the dark corner, where the hallway had three options: exit, bathrooms, or stairs to VIP, we stopped walking and I turned to face him. His hand ran from my lower back, to my side, and my abdomen before he dropped it.

"I guess we're sort of on the same page after all," I said.

"If that's the case, we need to get on different chapters fast," he responded, tearing his gaze away from mine and looking toward the exit.

"You're really leaving?"

He looked at me again. "It's best if I do."

"Because I'm tempting you," I said, my mouth dropping slightly open when he nodded.

"Nothing good happens after twelve," he said. "It would be wise for you to do the same."

"You just don't want me hooking up with anybody."

He smiled and reached behind me, grabbed a fistful of my hair and tugged it gently. It was something he used to do before and just like then, I felt the notion to the tips of my toes.

"You already said I was the only guy you'd done that with. I don't expect you to break the mold in one night." He winked at me as he let go of my hair.

"You know me, I like being spontaneous," I said. His jaw twitched as he tore his gaze away from mine momentarily.

"Be careful, Nicole. Please don't do anything stupid," he added, leaning in to brush his lips against my cheek before walking away and out the door.

It simply wasn't fair. The man was too sexy. Too enticing. Too desirable. *I wanted him. My body wanted him.* Although, after that encounter, I was fairly sure my heart wouldn't survive a repeat with Victor Reuben.

Chapter Seven

Nicole

I spent my morning off, nursing a hangover and dodging calls from both Gabe's manager and Victor's assistant. Around three o'clock, I got cozy on the sofa in my room, eating my cup of cereal and watching Peaky Blinders on Netflix. It was a perfect afternoon until the pounding on my door started. I closed my eyes, begging for Cillian Murphy to be the one on the other side of the door. Knowing I was about to be highly disappointed as soon as I stood to open it. I sighed, threw my blanket off, and unlocked the door. Gabe and his manager were standing on the opposite side. I closed my eyes and counted to three before opening them again. Darryl looked like someone's dad, with his salt and pepper hair, thick glasses, and round belly. Someone's dad or someone with an underage porn fetish. I was always crept out by him to the point that I may or may not have had him photoshopped from some of our wedding photos. But the guy could talk his way in and out of anything, and he was as ruthless as they came, which was a gift in this industry.

"I feel like I must have done something horribly wrong in my past life."

"Nice to see you again too, Nicole," Darryl said, flashing his megawatt fake-ass smile at me.

"What do you want?" I asked, looking at Gabe, who had his hands tucked into the front pockets of his jeans and his head down.

He looked like a sullen school boy, and the fact he looked that way and was standing beside his manager could only mean one thing. One really, *really* bad thing. My heart dropped.

"What?" I said, trying to ignore the way my heart spiked.

"We have a proposition for you. A very big one, one that will benefit you immensely if you agree to it," Darryl said. Despite the mistrust I felt for him, I knew he always had his client's interest at hand. My brows rose.

"Let's hear it."

We sat down at our long dining room table. The one we'd only used a handful of times to entertain guests on holidays or to talk about the laughable proposition, because that's what it ended up being. Absolutely ridiculous and laughable. They basically wanted me to pretend that maybe, just maybe I wasn't going to divorce Gabe after all.

"We haven't been seen out together in almost a year," I pointed out. "And in that time he has been seen with multiple women. All of whom weren't me."

"He's been traveling for work. You've been busy with your own career. He's back temporarily and is finally realizing how good he has it and he wants to save his marriage," Darryl said.

My heart sunk again. Did he not realize how much this hurt? Listening to this with my estranged husband, whom I had longed to patch things up with, sitting across from me? Yes, I was over him. Yes, I wanted to move on, but his manager pointing out that Gabe would never feel the way he just described, still hurt. I swallowed my emotions and tilted my chin up.

"What I'm hearing is 'Gabe wins again.' I still haven't heard the part where Nicole gets something out of this," I said.

Gabe cleared his throat, clasping his hands in front of him. "Maybe it's true. Maybe I want to try."

My jaw dropped. I blinked, blinked, blinked. "You can't be serious," I said, once I finally found my voice. The way he said he wanted to try made me think of the time he took me to my favorite sushi restaurant because he wanted to do something nice for me, but instead we ended up in the ER because he was allergic to the crab he'd ordered. It was sweet when I told him we could never go back there again and he looked at me, big puffy red eyes and said, *"Maybe I want to try again. For you."*

He shrugged those broad shoulders of his and I blinked out of my memory. "Why not?" he asked.

"What the . . ." I paused, trying to rein in my anger before it got the best of me. I took a deep breath in order to regroup. "Gabe. I just filed for divorce."

"Forget about that," Darryl said. "Let's leave emotions out of this. We don't need to complicate something simple. If you want to discuss your marriage, that's fine, even though I think we can all agree it's probably not working out for a reason." He raised his dark eyebrows over the frames of his glasses and shot Gabe and me a knowing look.

"Bastard," I said.

Gabe sighed.

Darryl shrugged. "The proposition is this. Go with him to the movie premiere this week, and give the media some comments about your relationship. Positive comments. Keep them guessing. Wear your wedding ring once in a while. Gabe will keep his on and just play the part."

"What's the point of that? The divorce has been filed. The papers were leaked. This whole thing will look stupid, and I still haven't heard the part where this benefits me." I looked at Gabe, who was watching me with a look I wanted to slap off his face. It was almost an admirable look, as if he was impressed with me.

"We talk to all of the production companies and tell them that I acted out of spite when I said I wouldn't work with them if they hired you as their costume designer," Gabe said. I clenched my jaw and stabbed him in my thoughts. Repeatedly. I put my hands under the table and sat on them when I felt them begin to shake.

"You guys think you're so fucking cute playing with my career. You think that just because you're Gabriel Lane, Hollywood's sweetheart, that I can't end you?" I asked. "You forget whose hometown this is, Gabriel Rogers. Or is your birth name something you've forgotten too? Maybe you should lay off the fucking drugs once in a while." My chair screeched against the marble floor as I stood up.

"I'll give you the condo in New York," Gabe said as I turned to walk back to my room. My heart lurched at the mention of my beloved condo. I stopped walking and turned around.

"Just like that?"

"I've fucked up, Nic. I know I have, but with all of my . . . partying and other things, my image is looking really bad right now and I have two movies coming out in the span of four months. I need to fix it," he said, blue eyes pleading as he stood and put his hands as if he was about to say a prayer. "Please. You're the only one who can help me. I swear I'll stop making things difficult for you."

I let that sink in for a moment as I looked into his apologetic blue eyes, eyes that could very well be lying to me. Eyes that had lied to me so many times in the past. He ran his hands down his newly shaven face and looked at me again. He was so damn handsome. Handsome, charming, great in bed, and he'd once been mine. Sadly, in this moment as I looked at him, trying to figure out whether or not he was just putting on an act, I couldn't even remember the good moments.

"I want this on paper," I said finally. "On paper and I want both of your signatures on it."

"I'll have Phil draw up a contract right now," Darryl said.

"Fuck Phil. I'll have my dad do it."

"Thank you, Nic. So much. I know I have no right—"

I put my hand up. "Shut up. If I'm doing this, you need to just shut up. I'll play along because for whatever stupid fucked-up reason I still care about you, but I can't promise anything more, and if during our mediation in a couple of weeks you say one negative thing, I'll do something crazy. Don't tempt me."

My dad was outraged. I knew he would be.

"What does Victor say about this?" he asked.

"I'm not telling him about this. I don't know. I wasn't thinking of telling him. I just need a simple paper stating my demands."

"These are things you need to discuss with your lawyer, Nicole. Why do you think I appointed you one?"

I could tell he was at his wit's end, and even though I was on the phone with him and I wasn't a six-year-old climbing kitchen cabinets, I felt the crack of the belt.

"Papi," I whispered. "Por favor."

He sighed loudly on the other end of the line, and I closed my eyes, letting out a breath.

"Fine, but you'll have to come to the Newport house to get it."

My mouth popped open. "Why? Just email it to me."

"No. We haven't seen you, you've been here a handful of times in the past year, and I'm having a barbeque. Tomorrow. Come early. Bring clothes," he said, his voice leaving no room for discussion. Leave it up to my dad to make a day at the beach house sound like punishment.

"Okay. I'll see you tomorrow."

Chapter Eight

Victor

When Will called me last night and invited me to his beach house, I'd been tempted to come up with an excuse as to why I wouldn't make it, but then I remembered the isolated private beach and the silence, and I agreed. I'd stayed in the seven-bedroom house in the past and had a good time, so why not now? I hadn't expected his first words over brunch to be, "We need to talk about Nicole." And I hadn't expected the way my heart launched into my throat at the sound of those words. Immediately, I thought of Friday night when I'd seen her at the nightclub. The kiss we shared, the way I asked to speak to her in private and spent the entire time trying not to lock the door, push her against the door and hike up her dress. I made an effort to keep my features as blank as I could.

"What about Nicole?" I asked, smiling as Meire, Will's wife, walked in with a tray and set cups of coffee on the table for us.

"Where's Maya?" Will asked her.

"I sent her to buy some groceries. We didn't have anything in the fridge, but I think I'll tell her to go home early if it's only going to be us," she replied as she walked off with the tray again.

"You're not going to join us?" Will called out.

"I want to make sure Maya prepared the room for Victor," she called out from the kitchen.

Will shook his head as he took a sip of coffee, and as much as I didn't mind delaying the Nicole conversation about whatever it was he wanted to discuss, I was on edge.

"So, Nicole?" I prompted.

"Right," he said, putting the cup down. "Let's start from the beginning," he said, and I groaned inwardly.

Will loved to make lengthy stories out of things he could have said in under two minutes. At least we weren't at the office and I didn't have a million files to get through. As long as my ass was sitting in his swanky twelve-seat dining room in his huge beach house, I had to suck up the story.

"When she told me she was getting married I was shocked," he said. *You and me both,* I wanted to say, but couldn't. "Not because I didn't think she wanted to get married. I think between her and her mother her wedding had been planned since she was six. They love that stuff." Definitely a surprise to me. "An aunt of hers gave her a Bride Barbie when she was small and two days later Nicole wanted a Barbie Dream House to go with it. Anyway, I was shocked because she'd known the guy for two seconds before she agreed to marriage."

I nodded, lifting the cup of coffee to my mouth and taking a sip.

"I tried to talk her out of it, but she wouldn't listen, and now she's getting a divorce and I can't help but feel responsible," he sighed. "My little girl deserves better."

"I agree," I said.

"She deserves somebody who gives her more than she gives," he added. I nodded in agreement again, not that I knew shit about what that meant. "She passed up jobs for Gabriel just so she could travel to where he was on set. Can you believe he turned her away one day when she showed up?"

I felt my mouth drop. Will nodded, eyebrows raised. "She flew to Canada to see him and he never made an effort to see her. His manager told her to leave."

"What an asshole," I said, feeling my blood start to boil. How could anybody do that to *her*? To his own wife?

"Complete asshole. And now he's trying to get her to—" Will stopped talking when the doorbell rang loudly, his eyes widened. "We'll talk about this later."

I wanted to press the matter, but then I heard Meire say hi to somebody and footsteps coming up behind me and saw the grin on Will's face. Before I saw her, I smelled her, the sweet floral scent I knew covered her entirely. When I looked over and she smiled at me, I felt the air squeeze out of me. She was wearing a long orange dress that fit her loosely, her dark hair was down and wet from a recent shower, her blue eyes vibrant as she looked at me. I smiled back and my eyes made their way down her body and zoned in on the overnight bag in her hand.

Oh no.

Oh shit.

Were we both staying here tonight?

"Hi, Victor," Nicole said, her voice soft, her cheeks pink as she dropped her gaze from mine.

I frowned. A shy Nicole was a first for me. Maybe it was because we were in front of her dad and stepmom. Maybe it was because she was remembering what happened between us the other night. I needed to keep reminding her not to do that. I needed to keep distancing myself *in that way.* She was too tempting. I had to keep thinking: forbidden fruit equals death. It would have helped if I would have actually paid attention during Bible study when I was a kid.

"Nicole," I said in greeting.

"Join us. We were just talking about you," Will said.

"I'll take your bag upstairs. I was going to put towels in there anyway," Meire said, taking the bag in Nicole's hand and excusing herself again.

"What were you talking about?" Nicole asked, taking a seat next to me.

Why next to me? It could've been because that was her regular seat, and as creatures of habit we were forced to always pick the same seat at the dinner table. It could've been because there was a setting on the table. It could've been because it was closest to the pancakes. It could've been many things, but the only one I wanted it to be was that she wanted to be near me. Beside me. And the thought that it mattered to me, because I wanted her to be as affected by me as I was by her, was fucked up. I'd ended things the first time and this time I couldn't afford to entertain the things circulating my thoughts half the time when she was around. I just couldn't. She was off limits. But then she was next to me, and her scent made me want to lean in closer, and I just didn't care. She infiltrated my thoughts in that moment, and I just didn't care. In that moment, if her father wasn't sitting across from us, I would have said something I wasn't supposed to.

"I was about to tell Victor about the contract you want me to draft."

I blinked, the pull of her presence replaced by curiosity. "What kind of contract?"

"It's simple," she said, keeping her voice quiet, in an almost whisper. "I agree to go with Gabe to some events, have some pictures taken, say good things about him and our marriage possibly working out to the media and he gives me the condo in New York. In addition, he will retract the lies he told the production companies I wanted to work with, stating he had been in a bad place."

I pivoted in my seat to look at her. She wasn't looking at me. Her face was cast down, her attention on her hands, but I knew she could feel my gaze. I knew because her cheeks were filling with a deep shade of pink, and I could tell I was making her uncomfortable. Making her feel that way wasn't my intention, but I was indescribably uncomfortable with that request. So uncomfortable that I wanted to yank her out of her chair and take her away from the attentive eyes of her father. I swallowed back my annoyance and the arguments that lay on the tip of my tongue.

"And you're okay with that?" I asked.

Finally, after what seemed like an eternity, her head turned and her eyes met mine. She nodded. "I am."

Our gazes stayed locked for a beat, or two, enough time for me to lose my train of thought as I looked into her deep-blue eyes. Enough time for me to recount the way her lips felt on mine, and the way she'd offered herself up to me. Will huffed from the other side of the table and both our heads whipped toward him. Spell broken.

"I don't think it's a good idea," Will said, looking at Nicole. "I think if you give in to these demands, you're going to find that spending time with him may make you re-think the divorce."

That thought alone made my heart squeeze in my chest. What the hell did I care? *Why* the hell did I care? I didn't have an answer to that, but it was clear I didn't want her going back and forth with a guy that treated her poorly.

"There's nothing to think about, Dad. I wouldn't have signed the papers if I even had an ounce of hope that this marriage would work," she said.

I stayed quiet until Will addressed me and told me to draft up the agreement for her, then I excused myself from the table, took my plate to the kitchen, and went upstairs to the room Meire had put me in. It was a damn big room, with a king-sized bed and a balcony that overlooked the pool and the ocean. I stood there, thinking about the wording I would use. I'd drafted agreements for celebrities left and right without second thought. This one was going to make me lose my mind. I was startled when I heard a sniffle beside me. My head turned in the direction of the sound, but I didn't see anybody. When I heard it again, I frowned, leaning forward in the balcony I was standing in and looking over to the one beside me. Nicole was sitting in one of the chairs with her legs propped up, her arms wrapped around her knees and her head tucked down. Was she *crying?*

I pushed off from where I was standing. I didn't want to intrude on her private moment. I didn't know how to handle her private moment. I could jump over and hug her, but that would be weird. I could knock on her door and ask her if she was okay . . . but that would be weird. I could just pretend I hadn't heard her, but something about that option made me feel like shit. I cracked my neck, shook my arms and measured how close the balconies were. They were made so close to each other that my body wouldn't fit in between them so I didn't have to worry about a fall. I just had to worry about where Will and Meire were and whether or not they would see me jumping over. Fuck. What a thought. It was almost enough to stop me from doing it. *Almost.*

Nicole shrieked when I landed beside her, her head snapping up, her hands wiping her bewildered, tear-stricken eyes.

"What the hell are you doing?"

I looked at her for a beat before stepping in front of her. "I'm telling you up front. I don't know how to deal with emotional women, and if you don't want me here, tell me, and I'll jump back over to my corner and pretend I never saw you."

She opened her mouth to say something, and closed it again, a slight frown on her face. "I don't."

Okay. Easy enough. I turned back around and just as I was about to climb on the balcony, she held my hand to stop me. I closed my eyes at the jolt. I felt her touch everywhere. What was up with that? Had it always been that way? It'd been so long, and I'd been so young and stupid, I couldn't even remember.

"Don't leave," she whispered. I opened my eyes and turned around, my hand still in hers as our eyes met.

"You said you didn't want me here," I whispered back, stepping closer. What I wanted was to scoop her up and put her on my lap. I wouldn't, though. *Couldn't.*

"Stay anyway," she said. "You could have broken your neck trying to get over here. I don't want your efforts to be in vain."

I chuckled, dropping my hand from hers as I walked to the chair beside her, taking a seat there. "You wanna talk about it?"

She sighed. "Not really. It's bad enough you saw me crying, and really, it's nothing. It's stupid."

I resisted the urge to reach over and cover her hand with mine in an attempt to comfort her. Instead, I scooted my chair closer to hers, so we were both facing the ocean.

"It's not stupid if you're emotional over it," I said, my eyes on the ocean, on the waves that splashed and disappeared out in the far distance, on the sailboats beyond them. I didn't do well with comforting emotional women, but having Estelle for a sister had taught me enough on how to deal with them, and I knew it wasn't wise to dismiss her current state.

"I don't want to talk to the media at all," she said after a few long beats. I looked over at her; she was looking out into the distance, so I had a chance to study her soft features, her small nose, and the apples of her cheeks.

"So don't."

She sighed. "It's not that simple. They ask. They always ask. This morning I got a call from a magazine that wants to run a story. I'm sure they got my number from Gabe's manager since he was the one who suggested it, but the thing is, there is no story here."

"They always find a story."

She shook her head, turning it to meet my gaze. "I would never give them a juicy one. I would never sell him out like that."

Her words shouldn't have made me feel anything, but I felt pride in her and annoyance in myself—in my old self—the one who'd thought she would have been responsible for us getting caught. The one who thought she'd throw me under the bus if the day ever came where she had to pick between the two of us, and my career would go out the window.

"You're a good person, Nic," I said. "And Gabriel is an idiot."

"Men usually are," she said, her lips curling into a small smile.

I looked at her mouth for a moment, desperate to lean into her. I'd had her lips on mine a few days ago, and I wanted them there again, but I couldn't do it, and I definitely wouldn't be the one making the move. Maybe it was unfair of me to want something this badly and not be willing to work for it. But I knew if I did work for it—if I did go after her—I'd go all the way, and I couldn't afford to do that.

"We are," I replied. "We're complete idiots. You should remember that."

"My eyes are wide open, Victor. I know you think they're not, but they always have been. This thing between us," she shook her head, exhaling, "it was good, and I know why you ended it when you did. I get it, but I don't think either one of us used the other. I think we were what we needed to be for each other at the time, and it's okay."

"Even if you did want it to be more, which I'm assuming you did," I said, hoping she understood I was referring to her marriage.

I didn't want to bring that up and tie it to me in any way, but I really wanted to fucking know why she jumped into such a serious relationship so quickly. I needed to know if I pushed her to it. She laughed.

"I guess we'll never know," she said, her eyes twinkling as she said the words. I scowled and she laughed again, but that was cut short by a loud knock on her door, and we both looked at each other, wide-eyed. "Stay here," she whispered.

I stood up and hid behind the French door, hoping whoever it was wouldn't walk inside. I felt sixteen again, my heart thumping in my chest as I listened to her talk with who I assumed was Meire. Instead of waiting around, I jumped back over to my balcony and sat in one of the chairs, my heart still pounding. Nicole walked back out onto her balcony shortly after, her head whipping over to me. She smiled.

"Got scared?"

"Fuck, yeah," I said honestly. She rolled her eyes, walking over to the part closest to me. I did the same, meeting her there. We both put our elbows on the balconies.

"You used to fuck me in your office, but you can't be caught in my room," she said, raising an eyebrow. My heart jumped at the mention of that. My dick was already halfway to hard at the mere mention of us fucking. I closed my eyes, tried not to picture it, but ended up with a mental image of Nicole's face between my legs, her eyes looking into mine as she sucked my cock. I groaned.

"Happy thoughts?" she said, her voice flirty. My eyes popped open.

"I was an idiot."

"So I've heard." She paused. "How long will it take you to draft up the contract?"

"About an hour, maybe less. Why?"

"You told me once that you tried to go surfing every day," she said. "You still do that?"

"Almost every morning," I said, smiling at the fact she remembered.

"I want you to teach me. Or try to. I can paddleboard, it shouldn't be that different, right?"

I chuckled. "Oh, Nicole, you have a lot to learn."

"Well, then, I'm glad I picked a capable teacher," she said with a wink as she turned around. "I'm going to put on my bathing suit. Meet you downstairs in an hour?"

"You're . . ." I shook my head. "Yeah, an hour."

I spent the next forty minutes drafting up a contract and trying not to picture her getting naked in the room beside mine. *Naked.* In the room beside mine. *Fuck.* How was I going to sleep there? Maybe I should head home early. Maybe I should just say fuck it and get out of there as soon as I prepared the contract. I was good at coming up with excuses. But then I remembered how emotional she'd been on that balcony, and I decided to stay. An hour later, I'd sent her the contract, put on my swimming trunks, and headed downstairs to meet her by the beach. I saw Will on my way over and updated him on everything. When I reached the end of their backyard, and my feet touched the warm sand, I saw her. She was wearing the smallest bikini I'd ever seen, and I was grateful when I saw the wetsuit in her hand that she was about to put on.

"Need help?" I asked as I walked over, when I saw her struggling to stay balanced on one foot. Her head snapped up, lips spread into a smile that promised the kind of trouble I enjoyed getting involved in.

"Considering I just fell on my ass," she said, pivoting a little to show a back covered in sand. "Yes."

I chuckled at the sight and gave *not* checking her out my best effort. When I reached her, she craned her head to look up at me as I extended my arm for her to hold on to as she pushed her foot into one leg of the suit. Our gazes held as she did it, and I was glad for the loud waves feet away from us. Otherwise, she would have heard my loud breathing, and I was sure I would have heard hers. As it was, the heated glances we were giving each other spoke volumes. I couldn't have her touch me and not think about my hands on hers, her lips on mine. When she finished putting on her suit and zipping it, I thought I'd be out of the woods, since her skin wouldn't be showing, but the way that thing fit her . . . fuck. I cleared my throat, looking out into the water.

"The waves aren't that good today," I said. "Paddleboarding may be the only option we have right now."

"That's fine," she said, following my gaze. "I think I like that option better anyway."

We walked over and picked up the boards set against the house and pulled them toward the shore. I jogged back and got the sticks, and on my way back all I could do was look at Nicole and notice the way she seemed contemplative today, not the spunky woman I was used to. We both settled on our boards, but instead of standing, we sat in the water, our legs on either side of each of our boards.

"Can I ask you something?" I asked, clearing my throat as we both faced the endless ocean, our backs toward the houses. She glanced at me momentarily and nodded. "You said the other day that I was the only one you'd ever . . ." I couldn't bring myself to finish the sentence.

"Had sex with in a bathroom?" she asked, smiling, her eyes assessing me. I nodded. "You are."

"I know you don't need a reason to do anything," I said. "You act on instinct more than anything, but I'm surprised."

"You think I'm a slut," she said, but her smile didn't falter. "It's a fair assessment. I'm not, but coming from you it's a fair assessment."

"I don't like labels," I responded. I didn't. Slut, whore, promiscuous. Those were all labels I'd never understood for men or women. As far as I was concerned, what you did with your body was nobody's business.

"I know you don't," she said, "Mr. I Don't Want a Girlfriend Ever."

"That's not the kind of label I was taking about. I don't have a problem having a girlfriend."

She raised an eyebrow and looked away from me, back to the ocean. "Maybe people do change, after all."

We were silent for a moment, the water moving us in small waves. We watched as a few families played in the shore with their kids, some joggers passed by, birds cawed.

"I've never just hooked up with a guy," she said finally, filling in the comfortable silence we had going. I looked at her. She was looking at me, but I could tell it was taking effort for her to keep her eyes on mine. "In college I used to make out with strangers, but that was as far as I got. Actually hooking up with strangers, though? Never."

"Why me then?" I asked, suddenly feeling a jolt of confidence. I felt like I needed to pat myself on the back for that achievement. She shrugged.

"If I told you, you'd think I'm crazy, or knowing the way you are, it will send you running the other way," she said, tearing her eyes away from mine again. My heart began pounding a little louder. Something about the way she said that. Fuck. Maybe I would want to run the other way, but I still wanted to know.

"The good news is, you're kind of stuck with me for a little while, so it doesn't really matter what you tell me. I won't run the other way," I said, smiling, trying to lighten the mood, but when she looked at me she wasn't smiling at all. The look on her face was a mixture of forlorn and uncertainty. "Just tell me," I said, my voice almost a whisper.

"I felt something when I looked at you. Something weird. Something

. . . not normal. I don't know how to explain it other than maybe my soul recognized something in you. And I know you didn't feel the same. I knew what we were," she said, giving me a pointed look. "Or what we weren't, since you said yourself we were nothing. But I felt it every time we were together."

Her words were claws that seeped into me and gripped the protective shell surrounding my heart. I couldn't explain it any other way. That's what it felt like when she said them. I swallowed past those unwanted feelings.

"Why didn't you say anything? Why didn't you tell me?"

She let out a single laugh. "What difference would it have made? If anything you would've ended things sooner." She paused, getting serious again. "I'm not saying I was in love with you, Victor. I'm just saying that a part of me felt like something bigger than what we actually had was there. At least the possibility was there." She shrugged. "Doesn't matter."

"You got engaged and married a few weeks later," I said, frowning.

Anger threatened to replace the feeling of confusion and wonderment I felt. I broke it off, but she got married. Who did that? A crazy person, obviously, but Nicole didn't seem like she was legitimately crazy, aside from her spontaneity.

"That should tell you what kind of state I was in. I guess I was a needy twenty-two-year-old," she said, shrugging. "I'm not saying I regret it, because I don't."

"Even now? With the divorce?"

She looked away, her words were low when she spoke again. "Even now. I loved him. In a sense, I still do. I don't want to be with him. I *can't* be with him, but I'm grateful for our time together."

The way her words made me feel bothered me, though I didn't let it show. Instead, I cut the conversation there and paddled to put a little distance between us. I wasn't sure I could handle any more revelations from her, whatever it was I was feeling, from this moment. I slept like shit that night, tossing and turning as her words replayed in my head, tossing and turning thinking about her sleeping in the room beside me, wondering what she wore to bed, wondering what she looked like completely naked. I needed to get a handle on myself before shit hit the fan.

Chapter Nine

Victor

Maybe I was being selfish, but I really didn't want her living in that house with Gabriel Lane. Especially not after the day we had on the beach, with her confessions and my fucked-up emotions. The worst revelation I got was the sight of what life could be like with her, away from the press and the confinement of my office. I actually felt . . . something. Which meant trouble. Big fucking trouble. Nonetheless, as her attorney, I wanted her out of the house. As her friend, or whatever I was, I *needed* her out of the fucking house. Last night as I went to sleep, I caught myself thinking about her being in the house with that guy, and him sneaking into her room in the middle of the night, the way I wanted to do when I'd slept beside the room she'd been in. It drove me batshit crazy.

On top of that, my other client at the moment, Sam Weaver, had the same thing going, except in his case he was the Gabriel and his estranged wife was the Nicole. He'd been making living with him nothing short of hell for the woman.

We'd been to court once already, and she'd cried through the entire hearing, not because her children weren't getting the attention they deserved, but because she was being treated like shit in front of them. It was moments like those that made it difficult for me to represent "the bad guy," because Sam was most certainly the "bad guy." His ex had made her share of mistakes, most of which we'd uncovered throughout the divorce proceedings.

I knew I wouldn't be able to talk sense into Nicole. I could barely talk to her at all, which made my job insanely difficult to get through. Every time I saw her, though, I thought about the way her face looked at the peak of ecstasy and my concentration went to shit. I knocked on the door and waited. I needed to talk to Will before he left town.

"Come in," Will shouted. I stepped into his office slowly, taking in the dim lights and candles lit on the corner. "Meire's idea of relaxation hour. She says it's either this or I quit smoking cold turkey, so here I am." He sighed heavily and pressed a button to turn the lights back on. "What's going on?"

"I wanted to talk to you about Nicole," I said, undoing the button on my suit as I took a seat across from him. I put a hand up to keep him from jumping in. "I think she should move out of that house."

Will frowned. "The minute she moves out, she loses it."

"Not necessarily, Will, and she's fucking losing herself by staying there," I said.

"Explain."

"I went over there to take some papers for her to sign and apparently Gabriel had a party the night before. The only reason the place wasn't trashed was because Nicole had already cleaned up half the mess. His mess, while he walked around without a care in the fucking world, and the other day in Newport, she was upset over things with him. I just don't think it's good for her to stay there." My voice and fists shook as I said the words. I hadn't realized how pissed off that made me until I said it aloud. Will noticed, his brows rose as he appraised me. He stayed silent for a little while.

"Should I be concerned about this?" he asked, signaling at me. "I'm glad you've taken such an interest with Nicole and her case, but I've seen you lose your cool in here and keep it contained in court, and I want to make sure that's what's happening here. Because you know if you lose it out there, they'll have a field day with you, her, and this firm, and I can't make you partner if you have a shitshow surrounding your name."

I took a nice, calming deep breath. "I'm fine. I have court in a few hours with Sam Weaver's case and that has me riled up."

"How's that coming along?"

"Good. I think we'll be done with it today. He's giving her everything she's asking for, so I don't see why we wouldn't."

Will nodded. "Focus on that, in the meantime, I'll see what I can do about Nicole."

I looked at the man across from me one last time and nodded as I stood and walked out. I packed up my briefcase and left to pick up Sam before we headed to the courthouse. Nicole's issues would have to sit on the backburner for now. When I pulled up to the Beverly Hills mansion, I lowered my window, pressed the bell and waited until the two massive iron structures in front of me opened. I drove in, going around the ornate water fountain with the bronze mermaid in the middle, and parked in front of the steps that led to the house. I put my car in park and checked my email while I waited, and after sending out a few replies, I realized Sam hadn't come outside yet. I called his cell phone, which he answered on the first ring.

"I'm outside," I said.

"Going right now."

He was saying the last word when he stepped out of the house and closed the door behind him before jogging down the steps to the car. I was glad he was wearing a suit, even if it was orange as fuck and made him look like a Starburst.

"I thought you were gonna get out of the car," he said as he opened the passenger door and adjusted the seat so it was basically lying all the way back. I looked at it questioningly, but didn't comment.

"I'm your lawyer, not your prom date," I said, and started driving. Sam chuckled, rubbing his hands together nervously.

"Damn. I can't believe we're finally getting this done with."

"Let's hope so. We had to pull in a lot of fucking favors to get this done on a Saturday."

Sam exhaled. "I'm just glad this bitch will be out of my life forever."

I shot him a sideways glance as we reached a red light. "Not really. You have two kids with her, so you'll be stuck with her for life."

"But I'll only have to deal with her during birthdays."

I shook my head and started driving when the light turned green again. No use in bringing up school functions, sports activities, or basically any other life event that would technically include him. I didn't know what his goals or plans were for his family, and quite frankly I would rather keep it that way. One thing I learned about this job was not to get emotionally attached to anybody involved, and shit got complicated when minors were at stake.

We reached the courthouse with just enough time to spare, and when the media started huddling around my car, I was glad for that. I knew it would take us at least ten minutes to get from the parking lot to the front of the building if Sam stopped to chat as much as he liked to.

"Don't say anything negative about the divorce," I coached. "Don't say anything negative at all. Keep it positive. You're co-parenting. You're getting along. You're looking forward to sharing custody of the children."

Sam nodded and put on his megawatt smile and straightened his suit as he faced the first photographer. As expected, they started asking him questions about the divorce, his alleged affair, how he allegedly kicked his ex out of the house, and Sam answered everything like a pro. We walked with the cameras alongside us and took turns answering questions. When we got to the front of the building, we turned around and Sam said his final statement of gratitude that he'd surely practiced in front of the mirror.

"I'm so thankful to you guys, to my fans, to the team for standing behind me. I'm glad to put this behind me, and I'm looking forward to a good year on the field."

The cameras snapped, snapped, snapped.

"One last question," one of the reporters shouted. I squinted to see at the guy in the middle of the crowd.

"Last one," I said, glancing at my watch. We had five minutes to spare.

"Mr. Reuben, what can you tell us about Gabriel and Nicole getting back together?"

That made me stall. I was caught off guard, not only by the question, but by the way my chest tightened in response. My first thought was, "she wouldn't do that," and that scared me ten times more than the one that quickly followed which was, "I hate when clients don't keep me informed with the decisions they make."

In the end, I dreaded that my two seconds of silence would be misconstrued and used against that case, but I was able to compose myself. "I'm not here to comment on that case. I'm here representing Mr. Weaver. Thank you."

My phone rang the second we walked in, and seeing Corinne's name on my screen has never made me feel more anxious and relieved at once. Unfortunately, I had to put it on the dish and walk through the metal detector before calling her back.

"Why are these fuckers asking me about Nicole and Gabriel?" I said when she answered the call.

Her silence was telling. My heart sunk a little more.

"Don't tell me," I said when she started to speak. "I'll call you back when I get out of court. I can't deal with unfortunate news right now. Handle whatever you can handle without me." I hung up the phone before she could say a damn word. It must be the premiere. It had to be. There was no other explanation for it. Fuck if I liked the sound of it, regardless of the situation.

Chapter Ten

Pictures. Piles of pictures sat on top of my desk. In magazines, in newspapers, in print from what my buddy in the gossip industry was able to gather for me. Images of Nicole and Gabriel kissing on the carpet for the premiere of his newest blockbuster. Images of them gazing lovingly into each other's eyes. Images of her laughing at whatever he was telling the interviewers from major networkers. Was it an act? Was it real? If it was an act, she had a real future in Hollywood and it had nothing to do with costume design. I hated those pictures. I hated the way he looked at her. I hated that she looked at him—*period*. I wasn't a jealous man, but damn did that shit fester inside me.

"At least she only agreed to a premiere," my secretary said as she walked into my office with her laptop in hand.

"What do you mean?"

Corinne sat in the seat across from me, setting her computer on my desk. She turned it over and pointed at the headline of a popular gossip blog.

Gabriel Lane vows to work on his marriage.

"It's gossip," I muttered, running my hands over my face, feeling the exhaustion take hold of me.

"I know, but still. They look pretty freaking happy," she said, turning her computer to look at it again.

"Do you need anything else?" I asked. Corinne's eyes widened.

"No. You told me to show you whatever was being talked about, so that's what I came to do. I think this is it, though."

I nodded. "Thank you. Can you bring me coffee please? I feel like I'm about to pass out on my desk."

She stood. "Sure. You want me to hold your calls for an hour?"

I closed my eyes. That would be nice. An hour powernap on my couch. My eyes popped open, trained on the couch across from my desk, and suddenly all I could do was picture me sitting there and Nicole riding me. *Fuck.* I shook my head.

"No."

"Okay. I'll be back with the coffee," Corinne said in a singsong voice as she walked out.

I wasn't sure why I was suddenly picturing Nicole and me all over my office, but ever since she came in that day and I was assigned her divorce, she was all I saw. Originally, it had taken months to stop seeing her everywhere when I walked in. Back then, for concentration purposes, I'd had half a mind to trade offices with Bobby, but he had a shit view of the parking lot and the street, and I had the ocean, so I sucked it up and stayed. Now I wish I would've traded. I'd rather see grout than deal with thoughts of fucking my client. My beautiful, spirited, off-limits client.

Chapter Eleven

Victor

The second to last thing I needed was to see the news that Nicole was staying with Gabriel everywhere. Everywhere. Every magazine, every news outlet, even the major ones that were supposed to report *real* news were talking about it. Apparently they'd become the *it* thing to talk about since Nicole was being painted as the fan who caught the star. Bullshit. It was all bullshit. He wasn't a star when she met and married him, but I guess they'd forgotten that bit, or they didn't care since this sold more stories. I waited the week out. They'd gone to the premiere on Wednesday night and I'd been dealing with the gossip since, but I had more important things to do like finish up my other case, and it was like Corinne said, she'd only agreed to a couple of things, one being the premiere. As her attorney, I had no *right* to be upset about it. That didn't mean it stopped the feelings of annoyance and discomfort from spreading and sticking, though.

I liked to think I was pretty good about leaving my work in the office, unless I had something major pending, but this thing with Nicole felt like it was taking over my life outside of work. On Sunday, while I was straightening up my house, it was all I could think about. As if on cue, my phone vibrated in the pocket of my sweat pants. I stopped washing the plate in my hand and switched off the water when I saw Corinne's name on the screen. She rarely ever called me on weekends. If we had things to say to each other, it all went through email. I answered it quickly.

"Umm . . ." she said. "Are you watching the red carpet by any chance?"

It took me a moment to understand what she was saying. I didn't remember what was on tonight, but I reached for the control and switched on the TV nonetheless.

"No. What am I looking for?" I asked as I flipped through channels.

"Golden Globes," she said. I stopped on what I assumed was the event when I saw a woman wearing a fancy black dress holding a microphone and smiling. My heart dropped into the pit of my stomach when she held that microphone up to Gabriel Lane, who was standing beside her, looking larger than life, and then Nicole, who was standing beside him, wearing a red dress that hugged all her fucking curves, looking like she belonged in my bed.

"What the fuck?" I growled. The Globes wasn't part of the agreement.

"I wasn't sure if this was added to the original addendum," Corinne said.

"Fuck no, it wasn't."

"Okay. Well, I'll let you go. I just wanted you to see it just in case." She paused. "Do you think they're maybe getting back together and she's unsure?"

I swallowed back my impending growl as I looked back at the screen, back at Nicole, who was now holding Gabriel's hand as he looked down at her with a smile. I was going to kill her. I was going to fuck her and then kill her. What the fuck was she thinking? What the fuck did I want her to be thinking? I didn't even know anymore. I couldn't be sure. But the thought of those red lips on anybody else but me was enough to drive me fucking crazy.

"I don't know. I'll get to the bottom of it," I said.

"May I make a suggestion?" she asked just as I was hanging up.

"What?" I said, my impatience clear in my voice.

"Maybe ask William?"

"What a great idea, Corinne. Let me call her father, who happens to be my boss, and ask him if he knows what the fuck is going on with my client. I'm sure that will bode well with the whole 'maybe you can become partner when this shit is over, Victor' thing." I paused to take a breath. "I'll handle it."

I closed my eyes and started counting backward from ten. I felt like any moment a vein would pop out of my forehead, or my neck, or my fucking arm with the amount of force I was using on my remote control.

I called my sister to see if she was watching. Maybe I should watch this with other people present so I wouldn't end up trashing my entire fucking house.

"Mia and Jensen are here," my sister said upon answering the phone.

Shit. I'd forgotten our friends were coming into town.

"Are they there right now?" I asked.

"Yeah, they didn't bring the kids, though. We're watching the Globes.

Want to come over?"

"Yeah, I'll be there soon."

I'd picked up the keys, a bottle of wine, and started walking to my car before we'd ended the call. When I got to my sister's house the front door was slightly open, so I knocked loudly and stepped in, closing and locking it behind me.

"In here," Estelle yelled.

"Oh God," her best friend Mia groaned, and then caught sight of the bottle in my hands and perked up. "Oh. He brought wine."

I scoffed as I leaned over to kiss her cheek, and my sister's. "Now we know the way to Mia's heart isn't corny love stories, after all," I said, referring to her husband, and my other best friend, who was a writer and had made it his life goal to write stories about Mia, even when they weren't together. Fucking pansy. "Where is Jensen anyway?"

"Out back with Oliver, smoking a cigar."

My eyes nearly bulged out their sockets. "Oliver is smoking?"

"No. Jensen is. Oliver's probably lecturing him on how bad it is."

I chuckled, handed over the wine, and headed that way, but stopped when I got to the door and turned back around. "What do you guys know about Nicole Alessi and Gabriel Lane?"

Mia's smile widened. She tucked her short blonde hair behind both ears and sat up straight. "Well, aside from the fact that he's so hot," she said, and as soon as the words left her mouth Jensen opened the door behind me.

He looked at me and smiled, greeting me with our usual handshake and hug before looking at her again.

"I know I'm hot, babe, but you really need to stop telling everybody you see."

She rolled her eyes. "I'm talking about Gabriel Lane. He's so fucking dreamy.""He is. Did you see the pictures of his vacation in Mexico a few months ago? Holy shit. I mean, if his swimming trunks—" Estelle said.

"Would have gone a little lower. I know," Mia finished with a half shriek, half laugh.

I shook my head, making a distasteful face. "This is what you're married to?"

"We all have our vices," Jensen said with a shrug and a laugh.

"Hey," Oliver said, walking in. He frowned when he saw me. "I didn't hear the bell."

"That's because you psychos left the door unlocked and open again. I don't understand how you live. This isn't 1920, and you don't live in the middle of nowhere. Didn't you get the email about all the burglaries?"

"Oliver installed a camera system," Estelle said as she poured herself and Mia each a glass of wine. She paused. "Who else wants wine?"

"We need something stronger than wine to watch this shit," I said.

"So we save the cigar I brought you for later?" Jensen asked.

"When does this start?"

"Officially? In thirty minutes," Mia said.

I looked at Jensen. We had thirty minutes to spare. Once we were outside, we closed the door and sat on the chairs out in the porch. He handed me my cigar and the lighter.

"How's work?" he asked, blowing out smoke from his cigar.

"I need my drink, or something with a more calming effect than this for me to talk about it right now," I said, holding up the cigar. He laughed.

"I was going to stop at a shop on the way here, but Mia thought Bean would have a heart attack."

"Nah," I said, laughing because none of us had done anything like that since college, but loved to joke about it now that it was legal in California. "That shit is natural. He's good with the natural stuff."

"Noted."

"How's the book doing?" I asked.

"Pretty well," he said, putting his cigar down and swatting the air away, which meant he was basically blowing it all in my face. I put mine down as well and put it out slowly. I'd finish it another time. "How's the single life? Still not bored?"

I smirked. "How's married life? Insanely boring?"

"Fuck, no," he said, laughing. "Being with someone every day doesn't make it boring."

"We were once on the same page about that."

He shook his head. "We were once young and stupid. Some of us grew up."

"I grew up," I said defensively, taking the bait. He knew how much I hated when people put things like getting married and being a grown-up in the same box. "I have a house under my name. I have a car under my name. I'm hopefully about to make partner, if my client doesn't fuck it up for me."

Jensen's eyebrows rose, his eyes appraising me momentarily, dropping to my curled fists and back up to my face. He smiled. "Did I hit a nerve?"

I exhaled loudly and slumped back in my seat, looking out to the horizon. I focused on the water that was just a few feet away from us. Not that I could see it, but I focused on the sound of the waves crashing.

"I'm representing my boss's daughter in her divorce," I said. I looked at Jensen from the corner of my eye after a beat and caught his mouth hanging open.

"The one that you—"

"Yeah."

"The one you basically told things would never work out between the two of you?"

"Yes," I said, my voice growing more impatient.

I wasn't one to kiss and tell, but I'd told him and Oliver about our first wild encounter because even I'd had a hard time believing it had happened. This hot girl walking into my office and locking the door behind her to seduce me, and actually achieving just that. I just couldn't wrap my head around the way she went from having a regular conversation about the office to asking me if I'd ever fucked anyone on my desk and settling herself between my legs. And inching up her skirt . . . and licking her lips as she placed her legs on either side of me . . . and saying, *Do you want it, Mr. Reuben?* in that sultry tone of hers. Fuck. Me.

"Damn. Well, at least it only happened that one time, right?" Jensen said, cutting my thoughts short. I swallowed, suddenly feeling the need to drink a gallon of water. Or the wine I'd brought.

"Yeah, at least," I said, though my mind went to the second and third time she'd come by to visit, and then the last time.

That last time haunted me after I'd found out she'd gotten engaged. Will had told me she'd only known him a few weeks; that he asked her to marry him overnight and she'd agreed; that she was head over heels in love with him, and every single one of those things bothered me. At first I thought it was just weird for anybody, especially her, to agree to marry somebody that quickly. Then, I wondered if it had anything to do with me and the way I'd dismissed her. But she'd seemed so nonchalant about it, smiling and saying she knew it was just a good time and she'd enjoyed it as well. A part of me expected her to come back again, and when she didn't, and then I'd heard she'd gotten engaged, it dawned on me that it was really our last time together. And all I could do was hope she didn't visit me, thinking we could be just friends, because I really didn't know how to argue with her and not have it end in sex. And now that I knew she possibly felt more for me, I wasn't sure what I felt for her. This version of me felt like he was ready for that. For something more.

For something *real*. And as stupid as it fucking was, I thought maybe I could have it with Nicole. Maybe in another life. A different time. Our timing was complete shit. I sighed and looked over my shoulder, where Mia was waving at us to come back inside.

"I guess the show's starting," I said, standing up.

"So you're representing her?" Jensen asked. "In the divorce."

I nodded.

"You don't look too happy about it. Is it a tough case?"

"It's surprisingly easy, at least it was, but as usual women complicate the shit out of my life. We'll see."

Jensen laughed as we walked inside and sat around the television. I took out my phone to check my emails while the show started, but put it away when somebody turned up the volume.

"Oh my God! There he is. Isn't he hot? Like for real," Mia said. I looked at the screen and saw Gabriel as he spoke to another actor on the carpet. I didn't see Nicole anywhere.

"He looks gay," I commented.

The guys laughed. The girls scowled.

"You're just saying that because you're his wife's divorce lawyer," Estelle said. "Wait. What's going to happen now? Does all the work you did go out the window because they're back together?"

That was the question of the century, wasn't it? Nicole was on the screen shortly after, looking so fucking beautiful that the only thought in my head was that I wouldn't mind having her as a psycho ex-girlfriend. The thought surprised me. I tried to push it down.

"I'm saying it because he's an asshole, and they're not back together," I said. I wasn't sure if I added that bit for them or myself, but it felt like it needed to be voiced. Both Mia and Estelle shared a look before looking at me. "That's all I'm going to say about it."

"He doesn't seem like he's an asshole," Mia said. "Nicole is beautiful. Is she that pretty in person?"

I nodded, swallowing, trying not to think about just how beautiful she was. Just how good she felt.

"That's his mom," Mia said, pointing at the woman walking beside Nicole.

Gabriel's mom? Jesus fucking Christ. What a happy family. And that was just about when I decided to send Nicole a text message. If she wasn't going to answer my calls from the office or Corinne's calls and voicemails, I was going to start hounding her via text. And I hated anything that could be used in a court of law as evidence, which included text messages, but fuck it. Desperate times and shit, like my sister and Mia liked to say.

If I had to sit here all night watching them on screen, I was going to make sure her discomfort matched mine.

Chapter Twelve

Nicole

It was bad enough that I was stuck in this award show, and much worse that I'd given myself strict orders of staying one hundred percent sober throughout. The only good thing about the entire thing was that Gabe would most likely win the award he was nominated for, and it was for a movie filmed during a time when things were still . . . okay between us. Maybe they hadn't been okay then, but I still had hope. I guess that was the difference. Forgiveness always feels like a possibility in the presence of hope. Hope of which we had none now. Not enough, anyway.

The second good thing about this experience was that as I walked the red carpet with him and he joked around about the cameras flashing—the way he'd done when we'd attended our first red carpet event together—I realized I hadn't seen him as more than a friend or stranger for a long time. I think we lost that magic somewhere between picking up his vomit, dealing with his incoherent insults, and suspecting his infidelity. Despite all of that, I wished him well. I wished this guy, the one walking with me tonight—the sober and unassuming one—to have a good life.

His mom, Deborah, was with us tonight, so while Gabe went off to do his rounds talking to people, she and I found our seats. He joined us soon after, settling in the seat beside me, closer to his male costar in the movie he was being recognized for. Deborah kept pointing out the different celebrities that kept walking by, and when she wasn't doing that, she was begging me to stay with her son. It was such an uncomfortable conversation to have with someone who loved a person the way only a mother could.

She didn't know about the drugs, and that was something I couldn't bring to light. But she knew about the women, or at least as much as anybody could know about the women, which was that they were definitely around. If the tabloids had it right half of the time, he'd been sleeping around with more women than I could name. How he found the time to do it, I would never understand. How the women hadn't cared that he was married was intolerable. To Deborah, that didn't matter, because to her marriage meant standing by your man, even when he was off screwing everybody with a vagina.

I understood her standpoint, I really did, but it was something I understood the way I understood statistics in college. I got it, but didn't apply it in my life. *It shouldn't have to.* I grew up in a time when women didn't need men. We didn't need somebody to make money for us, or give us orgasms, or even impregnate us. We had the ability to make our own money, buy our own dildos, and go to a clinic. And fuck anybody who thought we needed to put up with the bullshit a man brought into our lives without questioning it. I was thankful when my phone vibrated in my purse and I was able to excuse myself from the conversation as I pulled it out.

I frowned at my screen when I saw an unknown number, and then a message that read: *We need to talk. - V*

My heart started to race. I shoved it back into my clutch before anybody around could catch the words. Who the hell would send me that? I looked at Gabe, who was being overly *friendly* with his co-star, Lina. It wasn't him. I thought about the people in my life, men and women, who would have been watching me, and looked around. Nobody seemed to be looking at me. My phone vibrated again.

323 8374949: *Anything I should know about? –V*

I typed back, *Victor?*

323 8374949: *. . . I asked you a question.*

Me: *And I can't answer that if I don't know who I'm answering.*

3238374949: *There's a reason I don't have conversations via text.*

I smiled, shaking my head. Definitely Victor. I saved his number under V since that was what he kept sending me messages under.

Me: *I've been busy.*

V: *Clearly.*

Me: *We can talk tomorrow.*

V: *Because you're planning to stay busy tonight?*

I held my phone in my hands as I thought of a response for that. Did he mean busy with Gabe? I was sure that's what he meant. I pictured him sitting at home looking all upset over that possibility and nearly laughed.

Me: *Depends on who's keeping me busy.*

V: . . . . .

Me: *What the hell does ". . . ." mean?*

V: *It means I don't know how to answer that.*

Me: *Which means you're thinking you should be the one keeping me busy?*

When he didn't respond for a couple beats and I didn't see the little cloud with dots that said he was responding, I put the phone on my lap and went back to looking around at the stars, so many of which I'd dressed. I said hi and caught up with some of them as they walked by and introduced them to Deborah, who was the ultimate fan, which I loved. The magic was still shiny in her eyes. Not that it wasn't in mine. It was hard not to be affected by the atmosphere at an event like this, no matter how many times you'd been.

My phone buzzed again, and I jolted a little, turning it over.

V: *Stop tempting me.*

I smiled.

Me: *I didn't realize you were tempted. You seem to be practicing control rather well.*

V: *Control? You're succeeding in breaking me down.*

Me: *Good ;-)*

V: *Are you wearing anything under that dress?*

The words made me shiver. I closed my eyes momentarily, picturing his deep-hazel eyes looking into mine as he said those words.

Me: *Are you trying to sext with me? I'm sober. I don't sober sext.*

V: *I don't sext at all. I'd much rather spend my energy fucking.*

I swallowed and took a sip of water, suddenly feeling very thirsty, and very hot.

"Hey, did you see Macie?" Gabe asked. I jumped at the sound of his voice and the mention of his current film director, and hid my phone again. He gave me a questioning look, but didn't comment. Macie was his current producer. "She said she's gotten good comments about us being together at the premiere the other day."

"Good. That's what I'm here for," I said, setting my glass of water back down.

"Thanks for doing this," he said, reaching for my hand over the table.

Trying to play the part, I smiled, though it was small, sad, and fleeting. My phone vibrated on my lap again, but I ignored it. I would have to ignore it for the rest of the night if I was going to stay sane, then I would read all the texts and kick Victor's ass for thinking it was a smart idea to send them in the first place. If this was how he wanted to get a response from me, I was already starting to miss un-communicative Victor.

Gabe's hand squeezed mine tightly and snapped me out of my thoughts. I glanced up at him and realized we were about to be the butt of the joke the host was telling.

"*I mean, if a divorce is how I'm going to get my wife to screw me again, I'm going to go file tomorrow,*" the host said. The crowd made all sorts of sounds and shook their heads. I was sure the camera was zooming in on Gabe's and my faces, so I fake-smiled and fake-laughed, when all I really wanted to do was hide my face inside Gabe's jacket. The evening continued on, champagne was poured, beer and wine were served. I touched nothing. Gabe touched my hand, my thigh. I wanted to punch his perfect veneers.

"Please stop touching me," I said through my teeth.

"I'm not drinking tonight, so my nerves are shot. I need something to touch so I don't lose it," he said with a laugh as he leaned into me.

"I swear to God, Gabriel, if you don't stop, I will lose it. I will go to the bathroom and pull a Britney in the middle of your acceptance speech."

He reared back a little, but left his hand on top of the fist I'd made with mine. "You really think I'll win?"

I sighed, shaking my head, my lips curling into a small, albeit real smile. "I know you will."

The first category was announced and we had to clap for the nominees and the winner. Again and again it continued until it was Best Performance by an Actor in a Supporting Role. I held my breath as Hannah, the presenting actress, read each nominee's name. Gabe was sitting beside me, looking like he wasn't fazed by any of it, but I knew he was freaking out. *I* was freaking the hell out.

"Oh my word," his mom said beside me when Gabe's name was read. I smiled, glancing at her with an *I know* smile on my face.

"The Golden Globe goes to . . ." talk about dramatic pause as she opened the envelope. I leaned forward in my seat. Gabe leaned forward in his seat. Everybody in our table was seemingly holding their breath. "Gabriel Lane in The Man Who Could Not Speak."

There was no way to contain my happiness for him. There was no way to mask the pride I felt. Everybody in our table stood as we clapped for him, and as he stood he turned to me, grabbed my face with both hands, and kissed me. He kissed me the way he kissed me on our wedding day. My heart did a little jump, but as he let go of my face and turned to kiss his mother on the cheek, and hug his costars, I remembered where we stood, and I wouldn't waver. Still, it was his moment. It felt like *our* moment. Like that gold statue should have shared custody. I'd been there for him when he filmed that movie. I'd been the one holding his head out of the toilet and cleaning up his mess. I'd been the one putting up with his rage the nights he came home when takes hadn't gone the way he'd wanted. I'd been the one who'd agreed to help fund the film when they'd thought they wouldn't be able to finish it.

Of course nobody would know any of that. It was our secret and ours alone, and I was okay with that. I'd never been in our relationship for the limelight.

He walked to the stage and smiled as everybody cheered, and he started thanking people. He thanked me for being there for him, and believing in the film, his mother for everything, yadda yadda yadda. The longer I watched him, the less I wanted to be there. It was as if the reel became focused on the screen in my head and suddenly I saw the full, clear picture. I realized that he was an actor, and I was just another observer in his life. When it hit me, I reached into my purse and took out my phone. The last text message Victor had sent said to meet him in his office at seven o'clock sharp. I frowned, but put my phone away and willed for the rest of the show to be over. When it was, Gabriel was as busy as I knew he would be.

"Are you sure you want to skip the after-party?" he asked before being escorted away for the third time.

"Positive. Thanks for the invite, though."

He walked toward me and leaned his face in. I thought he was going to kiss me again, but instead his lips pressed against my cheek.

"Thank you for coming. I'm really glad I was able to share that with you."

I nodded and swallowed, holding back the tears that welled in my eyes. This felt like goodbye. A real one. Like it was the last time we would share something like this. I thought of the good memories we'd shared, and a part of me felt like I didn't want to let go. It was hard, being with him like this, acting like he cared and believing once he actually had. I'd mourned our separation. I didn't want to mourn the loss again. I wanted to move on. I wanted to get it over with. But having him in front of me—this man I genuinely cared for—seeing him win so big . . . I remembered the conversations we'd had about it because I'd always believed he would be big. It felt like too much for me. And that's why when he wrapped his arms around me, I let myself feel the power in his hug. I let myself feel that he, too, was sad about us not working.

"I wish things would have been different," he whispered into my hair.

"Me too," I said, and stepped back to let go. I gave him one last smile before walking to where Marcus waited for me, leaving the glitz and glamour behind. And I would mourn this too. Not the lights and cameras, but the role of supporter, a role I felt I had done a fucking incredible job at.

"Home, right?" Marcus said once we got into the Escalade. I nodded, but suddenly hearing the word *home* and associating it with the life I once I had with Gabriel pained me, and I knew I needed to get out of there.

Chapter Thirteen

Nicole

It was still dark out when I got to the office, and Victor had to buzz me in. There weren't any paparazzi around this time, which was a plus, but Marcus stayed waited by the car in case they'd been tipped off and showed up. I assumed nobody would be in the office at that ungodly hour, unless my dad was there. On court days he also met people pretty early. During the elevator ride up, I fixed my messy hair and used the mirrored wall to check my reflection. When the elevator doors opened, my hands froze mid-finger comb as my gaze caught Victor waiting for me with his arms crossed. He wasn't wearing a suit like I expected. Instead he wore a pair of grey sweatpants, running shoes, and a white T-shirt that showed me just enough of his defined body to make my breath stop short. His hair was brushed back, but wet, and the expression on his face gave me a hint of just how much anger he was containing.

"Hi," I whispered as his eyes raked down my body slowly, sensually just once before returning to my face, and he gestured for me to step out of the elevator.

I blinked as I did so and tried not to visibly show how affected I was. I walked forward and followed him as he started down the hall. The light was off, but the light from the lobby illuminated it just enough. We stepped into the same conference room we'd met in before and he closed the door behind us. The blinds were drawn and the lights were off, so we were in the dark. A flutter of nervousness made its way through me.

"Are you going to turn the lights on?" I asked.

"Did you have a good time last night?" he asked, his voice low and close behind me.

I was afraid to turn around. I was afraid to move. Instead, I put my hands forward and held on to the top of the chair in front of me.

"I can explain that," I said, my voice as firm as my grip on the chair.

I blinked, letting my eyes adjust to the light of the projector in front of us as it switched on, giving the room a dim, orange glow. I turned around to face Victor, who was leaning against the wall across from me with his arms crossed. My eyes dropped to his defined arms and I felt my heart stumble on its own beats. I'd seen him in swimming trunks the other day, but he'd been wearing a wetsuit shirt, and while it showcased the toned ridges and definition I was already sure he had, I hadn't seen him completely naked. Now all I could do was stand there and wonder.

My imagination conjured images of myself clawing off that cotton shirt and tossing it aside as I went down on him. I shook my head and blinked rapidly to rid myself of my thoughts. What was it about being near this guy that made me so needy for him? I'd just been at a stupid award show with my hot ex, yet it was this man I lusted after. Always. It had always been that way. From the moment I met him, I'd known I'd wanted him. And now, standing in front of me with that darkened gaze trained on me—as if he could see the dirty film in my head that he was about to star in—I wanted him again, and again, but unlike the previous time we'd been together, I felt fragile. Like I could sense that I would get hurt. Maybe it was the sensitive state I was in. Maybe it was because when I spent time with him at my dad's beach house he was so different, so attentive, and I realized that underneath all that pissed-off exterior I knew there was a caring man, one who would comfort me even when I didn't want to be comforted. One that knew when to hold my hand and just shut up. I sighed.

"Nicole," he said, closing his eyes briefly and breathing out as if he was doing some kind of yoga meditation. "I am this close," he said, opening his eyes and demonstrating an inch of space with his long fingers. Long and skilled fingers. I blinked again. He exhaled again, this time pushing himself off the wall and walking toward me until he was inches away from me and I had to tilt my head to look at his face.

"I'm this close to losing my job, my license, and everything I've worked so fucking hard for," he said, his voice rough and low, and way too close to my mouth.

"Because you want me," I said, rather than asked.

"Because you keep looking at me like you want me," he said.

I pushed his chest with both hands, and he took a step back.

"You have to be the most self-assured person on planet Earth. You're the one calling meetings at crazy hours."

"And you're the one who's coming, no questions asked."

"That's how I usually like to come. No questions asked," I said with a smirk. He took in a deep breath, let it out slowly, heavily, loudly.

"Fine. Yes, I want you," he said.

His admission shocked me into silence. We both looked at each other, stared at each other, and I was sure my heart was bound to leap out of my throat and into his if he didn't break the silence. He didn't, so I finally swallowed and spoke.

"Why did you need to see me?" I whispered.

With the way he still looked at me, I was starting to feel really hot, like lava pent-up in a volcano dormant for too long, and I was afraid that at any minute this thing between us would make me completely explode. God knew it had been a while. For me, at least.

"What were you doing at the award show?" he asked. I could tell he was practicing restraint in keeping his voice reserved, and the thought of the way he held his ground and practiced control made me tremble.

"He asked me to go and I agreed," I said.

"That wasn't part of the agreement," he growled.

"I know," I said, my voice low as I tore my eyes from his and looked at the ground between us. "I'm sorry I didn't tell you. I thought you would try to talk me out of it."

"I would have."

"I know." My eyes snapped to his. "Why does it bother you so much?"

His eyes narrowed. "Because it does. And I want you out of that fucking house."

"Really? Out of my house?" My eyebrows rose at his tone. I'd already decided to get out of there, but having him demand it pissed me off. "And where would you suggest I go, Mr. Know-It-All?"

"Anywhere. Anywhere is better than living under the same roof as him. If I wasn't your attorney, which I swear to Christ I'm close to being just that, I'd haul your ass out of there and make you move into my house temporarily."

"Oh, temporarily," I said, narrowing my eyes as I took a slight step forward. "Until you got sick of me and moved on to someone new? Isn't that your MO?"

"My MO?" he asked. His voice suddenly dropped to a quiet seethe that made my heart drop into my stomach. "I'm not the one who fucks people and then goes off and gets engaged a few weeks later."

Oh my God. I wanted to strangle him. For a second I thought I could try, but then I would have to hop on a chair so we could be at eye level and that would tip him off. I took a breath and counted to five, then took another deep breath for good measure.

"In case you forgot our conversation the other day, you were the only one I did that with."

"That doesn't make me feel any better, Nicole."

"What does it make you feel?" I asked, tilting my face in challenge. "We had sex. Great sex. You broke it off, and I went and married another guy, one who wanted something more with me. Something more than just fucking me. Fucking sue me."

"I just might."

I laughed. "Oh. This is good. On what grounds?"

"Obliterating my fucking ego. Temporary insanity. Sucker punching my . . . my . . ."

"Your heart?" I asked in a whisper, and waited on bated breath for his response.

Damn him for thawing the shell I'd managed to start rebuilding around my heart with three simple, stupid incomplete sentences. His eyes widened slightly, as though he'd never even considered his heart in this, and I almost smiled. I'd never seen him look puzzled. Or unsure. It was endearing.

"Maybe," he said, frowning.

Sort of endearing.

"I don't think you realize how much I stand to lose here, Nicole. You keep making these jokes and—" I inched closer, pressing my chest against his. He sucked in a breath. "And doing this."

He stepped back again and searched my face. I hated it when he looked at me that way, like he was rummaging around in my thoughts, kicking shit around until he found something he could use against me. He licked his bottom lip, and I did the same, forcing his gaze to drop to my own lips.

"You can keep tempting me, but it won't work. Not after I saw you acting like everything was fine in paradise. Not after I saw you making out with your supposed soon to be ex-husband," he said.

"What do you want, Victor? You're like that goddamn Katy Perry song. I never know what I'm going to get with you. We talk, we argue, we fuck, and then you dismiss me because you have a client to tend to."

He shot me a glare. "Don't bring that up anymore. How the fuck was I supposed to know you wanted more? You were the one trashing marriage, bashing relationships left and right, saying you didn't want anything long-term."

"I said those things because I thought that's what you wanted to hear."

"What I wanted to hear? What happened to telling the goddamn truth? If it was a relationship you wanted, you should've said so."

"And you would have given that to me? You would have taken things to another level? Last I remembered you were married to this job."

He stepped forward so quickly, I almost lost my balance, but he held my hip to keep me from stumbling.

"Are you staying with him?"

I blinked. "What?"

"Are you going to stay with your husband?"

"Who's asking?" I whispered. "My lawyer or Victor?"

He closed his eyes briefly once more, and when they opened I knew where this was headed. "I can't represent you anymore, Nicole. I feel like I'm going fucking crazy over here."

"Why?"

"Because I want you," he said. I gasped as his fingers dug into my flesh. "I want you and I can't have you if I keep working for you."

"Says who?" I asked, surprised my voice was loud enough for him to hear me.

"I've worked so fucking hard and this case is going to blow it all to shit," he said, inching his face closer to mine. I stopped breathing. "All because I need this more than I've needed anything else in my fucking life."

His lips were so close to mine that I was sure he would kiss me. Was he expecting me to kiss him? Would he break the vow he made to the court over me? Was it fair for me to test his limits? He closed his eyes and leaned his forehead against mine, his minty breath hitting me as he exhaled. His hands were still on my hips. I was sure he could feel the rapid vibration of my heart there. I felt it everywhere.

"Have me," I said finally, unable to have him this close to me and not do anything about it. "Just . . . take me. You've done it before. You know I can keep a secret."

He shook his head, his forehead brushing back and forth against mine. "It's not that simple, Nicole."

"It was never that simple," I whispered.

One of his hands made its way up my back, stopping on my shoulder, then moving slowly, tentatively to my neck, my collarbone. My breath was becoming ragged, uneven, desperate for something, anything. I wanted to kiss him, touch him, fuck him, but more than anything I wanted him to want to do it. I wanted him to be the one to make the first move.

"You're right. It was never that simple." The way he said it made me wonder if maybe he'd felt something more than lust. "When this is over," he said, rearing back slightly to look at me, "when it's over, I'll have you."

"What if we see each other in private?" I asked.

"You want to sneak around?" he asked, his lip twitching into a smile. He shook his head and dropped his hands, stepping away from me. "Is that what you want?"

"Maybe."

He raised an eyebrow. "That isn't a maybe kind of question, Nicole. It's yes or no."

"Yes. I want to sneak around."

"Are the paparazzi still following you?" he asked, his voice serious.

"No," I said, and corrected myself when he shot me a look that said he didn't believe me. "Not as much."

"Let's see how it goes with them the next few days."

"And then we can sneak around?"

He looked down to try to hide his smile, but I saw it. "I never said that."

"Okay. Do you need anything else from me?" I asked, my eyes raking down his body to the half hard-on he was sporting.

"I need a lot of things," he said, eyes blazing.

"I would help you out," I said, pointedly looking at his hooded pants as I licked my lips before unlocking the door and holding the handle. "But you refuse to cater to my needs."

He slapped his hand on the door to keep me from opening it and pressed his hard chest against my back. I closed my eyes and tried to control my body to keep it from quivering at the feel of his breath on my ear.

"I don't want a time limit the next time I fuck you. I don't want a quick fuck where clothes don't even have time to come off. I want you naked and in my bed, and trust me," he said, lowering his voice as he pressed his lips against my neck, right under my ear, "I will cater to every one of your needs."

I had absolutely nothing to say to that, so when he put his hand over mine and opened the door, I stood off to the side and waited for him to brush past me. The light of the hallway had been switched on. Victor and I looked at each other, wide-eyed.

"Hey," Grace said, looking confused as she walked into the lobby with a big pot of coffee in her hand. "I didn't know you had an early meeting scheduled today."

I wasn't sure if she was talking to me or Victor, but he responded before I could.

"Yeah, I had to squeeze this in between my run and court," he said. "I'm going to get dressed. If anybody calls for me before it's time for me to leave, take a message and give it to Corinne when she gets here."

"Okay," Grace said, then turned to me. "Want coffee?"

"I've been wondering when somebody around here would offer me something worthwhile," I said, unable to hide my smile. Victor scowled as he turned and walked into his office.

Grace and I made small talk while I drank my coffee and she switched on the computer and did whatever she had to do to set up for the day.

"Well, I have to go. It's going to be a long day."

"What time do you go in today?" she asked. Grace was always interested in my job. It didn't matter how insignificant it was, she wanted to know about it.

"Today's a late night. Eight to eight."

"Wow, and you're here? I would be sleeping."

I smiled. "Yeah, that's where I'm headed." I paused and looked at the door to Victor's office. "Shit. I just remembered I had to give him something. I'll be right back."

She didn't even look up from the computer screen as I disappeared into Victor's office. My blood roared in my ears as I took off my sneakers, peeled off my yoga pants, slid off my panties, and quickly redressed. I walked over to his desk and stuffed them into his briefcase. I could only hope he looked inside it before he went to court. Of course, knowing Victor he probably emptied it and organized it more than I did when I switched handbags. I ran out of there before he could come out of the bathroom and catch me.

"Did you leave what you needed to leave?" Grace asked as I waved her goodbye and got into the elevator.

"I did," I said with a wide smile.

Chapter Fourteen

Victor

My misophonia was out of control. I knew this, yet I couldn't help the cringe that came every time Corinne took a bite of her sandwich. My skin crawled with every chew. I sighed and stood up to pace the conference room to distract myself from my agony. I fucking hated lunch meetings. Food had no place in the conference room. None. The only reason I'd even called a lunch meeting was because we had no time to waste and I was supposed to meet with Nicole in the afternoon to give her some papers.

"Everything's in here?" I asked, going back to the file Corinne had set on top of the table. She nodded slowly. "Did you file the paper I sent you? The last one?"

"The Golden Globe thing in the agreement she made with her ex? Yes."

I nodded sharply. I needed to keep that paper out of any file I gave her back, in case it fell into the wrong hands. The fact that it had been drafted and emailed was already making me paranoid. I hated the Internet. I started leafing through the pages, making sure each page was initialed and that the ones needed signing were marked for her. As long as Gabriel agreed to this, the divorce could be sped up. Normally I tried to make these cases as painless as possible for my clients, because I could only imagine how badly they must want closure, but with Nicole I wished I could jump through hoops and just get this shit done immediately.

I wanted her out of the house she shared with Gabriel Lane. I wanted him out of her life for good. I wanted her in my bed. It was quite simple, really. I wasn't an idiot. I knew the girl was a catch, and it would only be a matter of time before somebody else caught her. If she wanted to be caught, I wanted her to have the freedom to make that choice. But first, I'd have her. Maybe I was a fucking idiot, because every time the thought crossed my mind all I could do was imagine me catching her. Me being the one she stayed with. I tried to picture what my life would have been like if I'd been the one to catch her five years ago and not the guy she was divorcing. Would I have fucked things up? Would I have let her go? I had a difficult time believing I would have done the latter. Fuck things up, maybe. I'd been young and had more drive than I knew what to do with. While my friends were busy chasing skirts and getting married, I worked my ass off. I didn't regret it. I didn't wish I could turn back time and make more out of what Nicole and I had. The way I saw it, everything happened for a reason, and we just weren't meant to happen then.

How much had I changed during those years, though? Jensen seemed set on reminding me that I would be turning thirty-one soon, as if that meant I might as well start planning my funeral.

"Victor?" Corinne asked. I looked up from the papers.

"What?"

She shifted uncomfortably in her seat. "I was wondering how you felt about me taking time off next month?"

My gaze stayed on hers as I processed her request. When was the last time she'd taken time off? Had it already been a year? I flipped through my mental calendar, trying to remember what I had next month. There would be very little to do with Nicole's divorce by then. I would make sure of that. I had a meeting scheduled for later in the week with a well-known romance author, who was divorcing his wife, to see if they could settle out-of-court, so that shouldn't run over to the next month. I realized I was still staring at Corinne and blinked rapidly. I was in the habit of staring people down when I was lost in thought. I cleared my throat.

"Sure. Just put it on the Outlook Calendar so we can plan for it," I said finally.

Her shoulders sagged a little.

"Anything else I should know about?" I asked.

She shook her head, but I knew there was something she wanted to tell me. Women were so fucking annoying. Why couldn't they just spit it out? They would be a lot easier to deal with if they just voiced their thoughts instead of making us go on a goddamn scavenger hunt. I shook my head and went back to the papers in front of me. I didn't have time for that shit.

"It's just," she said quietly. I let out a breath. Of course she was going to start talking again when I was already trying to focus on something else. "I think my boyfriend is going to propose to me when we go on vacation."

I raised my eyebrows. "Well, that's good, right?" I asked slowly. One could never be too sure when he was going to hit a nerve when it came to women and these sensitive subjects.

"I guess," she said, shrugging. I rubbed my temple and looked at my watch. I had an hour to spare before I had to bolt to meet with Nicole, so I took a seat where I'd been before Corinne decided to turn into Bugs Bunny with her chewing.

"What's the problem? Haven't you been together for a while now?" I asked.

She started chipping at her nail polish. "Eight months."

Oh, wow. Her boyfriend really jumped into that one. I didn't comment, because nothing good would come out of my mouth. It wasn't worse than Gabriel Lane and Nicole. Fucking Nicole. Instead, I nodded for her to continue. She glanced up at me, her eyes welling with unshed tears. Jesus, fuck. I didn't do well with emotional females. How did I get myself into this mess?

"I just don't know if he's the one, you know? I don't know if he's my forever," she whispered, still chipping at her nails.

"Have you told him this? Maybe you should."

"He's a great guy. He makes me laugh, gets along with my parents, has a good job," she continued, ignoring me. "He has his own place, and he wants kids."

I tilted my head. So far I'd heard nothing but good. Throw in a vintage black Mustang, and I was about to marry the guy. I looked at my watch again.

"I'm assuming you're going to get to the bad part soon?"

She wiped her tears. "I don't know. I was with my ex-boyfriend for six years. I've only been with Daniel eight months. I feel like, I don't know." She shrugged. "Maybe I don't even know him, you know?"

"Corinne, as I'm sure you know, I am not equipped to give relationship advice." I paused and added, "At all."

She nodded and sniffled. "I know, but you date a lot. How do you know they're not the woman you want to marry?"

I let out a long breath and leaned back in my seat. That was a good question. How did I know? I frowned.

"I don't," I said with a shrug. She looked puzzled, so I continued. "I've never cared enough to continue any of those relationships, so I just assume they're not the one." She continued to stare at me at a loss for words, which made me keep talking. "I'll let you in on a little secret: none of us know what we're doing. We're all winging it. Your boyfriend? He's winging it. He's proposing to you because he hopes you're his forever. Maybe he believes it, I guess he must if he's taking the plunge, but if you're not willing to take it with him, you should probably pull him off that cliff before he does it, not when he does it."

She nodded. "You're right. Maybe I'm just having second thoughts because of all of these damn divorce cases we go through."

I laughed. "I'm pretty sure that was in the job description when you applied."

"People change," she said with a smile.

Right. *That* again. I shrugged.

"You don't think somebody will come along and change you?" she asked, frowning. I thought about that for a moment, my mind instantly going to Nicole. Again. I sighed, running a hand through my hair.

"I think the right person for me will want to keep me just the way I am."

Corinne seemed to be satisfied with my answer. I gathered the papers and put them back in the folder.

"Are you done having your moment?" I asked. "Because I really have somewhere to be."

Corinne laughed. "I think I'm done having my moment."

Picking up the folder, I stood and walked toward the door. I patted her back as I passed her. "Don't believe the hype, Corinne. Being single is overrated, especially when you think you've found someone you can stand to be with continuously."

The drive to the address in Manhattan Beach was brutal. The traffic was insane. Apparently there was some kind of street market being set up, which closed off the major street I needed to take, and further pissed me off. Who in their right mind would willingly shut down all of those neighborhoods so they could sell shit? By the time I got to the house, I was barely containing my rage. I used the street parking four blocks away, left my jacket and tie in the car, and rolled up my sleeves. There was no way I was going to walk through the pits of hell in a suit. Fuck that noise.

I walked down the steep street and used the folder in my hand to shield my eyes from the sun when I got to the house. Through the window, I could see Nicole, wearing a tight flower-print dress. Her dark hair cascaded down her back in loose curls that she must have had done earlier that day. I admired her from afar, her curves, the way her toned tan legs looked in the heels she wore, and I took a second to imagine how she'd look out of that dress, out of those heels, legs wrapped around me. I took a long, deep breath and walked up the steps.

I could hear her laughing at whatever the person she was talking to was saying, and I smiled at the sound of it. She had a good laugh, not high-pitched or low, or snorty, or crazy. It was just right. A guy opened the door, and I instantly tensed. He had straight, long blond hair that reached his shoulders and was wearing a suit. I could tell he worked out. I could tell he felt I was interrupting something special going on between him and my girl. My *CLIENT*. Not my girl. Not my anything. My eyes landed on her when I looked over his shoulder, and she smiled. She had this small, tentative smile she used sometimes. One that didn't give you the slightest inkling as to how fierce she was beneath it. She could claw her way into and out of anybody's life and leave you with the afterthought that it'd all started because of that one smile.

"Hey. Rick, this is my . . ." she said, pausing for a beat, the tentative soft smile blooming into a wider one, a little wicked, a lot sexy, "my attorney."

"Oh," Rick said, stepping out of the way with a frown on his face. "I didn't realize you were bringing your attorney."

Nicole laughed. "Not for this. He has some things to give me, but now that he's here, he might as well make himself useful and help me look at the place. Unless you have somewhere to be," she added, looking at me with those big blue eyes. If I hadn't already been convinced by that look alone, the way her realtor huffed under his breath at the mention of this sealed it for me.

"Sure. I had my schedule cleared since I thought we were actually going to be discussing this anyway. Lead the way," I said, firing off a text message to Corinne so she could clear my fucking schedule for the next two hours. I didn't have a face-to-face meeting scheduled with anybody, but I did have to be back at the office for a conference call. So they'd have to wait a little while longer for me to call them back. Big deal.

Rick pivoted and walked down the hall. Nicole winked at me before turning to follow him, and between that wink and the way her ass moved from side to side in that dress I was already regretting the decision to stay. Thank God I'd taken off my jacket and tie. Rick went over the specs of the house, the kitchen, the living room, the laundry room, the dining room, his eyes were on her the entire time. Every time she turned around, his eyes were on her ass. When she spoke to him, his eyes made their way down her body. Nicole had to notice it, she'd be an idiot not to, but she didn't goad him, and I was grateful for that because for some reason I wasn't sure how I'd react to it.

I'd never been the jealous type. The competitive type? Yes. But jealousy was foreign to me. I didn't have anything to be jealous of. With Nicole it was a little different, though. Maybe it was because I wanted her so much. Maybe it was because I couldn't have her, though if I was being honest with myself, I knew it wasn't just that.

"Let me show you the master bedroom," Rick said, giving Nicole a very pointed look as he said it. They started walking toward the stairs as I trailed behind. He looked over his shoulder to look at me for a second before lowering his head to her and saying, "The bed is still in there, but we have company, which is very unfortunate."

My heart picked up speed in my chest, but my feet stopped moving. Who the hell was this guy? Nicole looked over her shoulder to look at me with a coy smile on her face. She didn't comment, didn't laugh, didn't say anything at all to him. I made a face at her, nodding sharply toward the back of his head. She shrugged and kept walking.

"The steps are a little steep," he said. "But don't worry, I'm here to catch you if you fall."

I wanted to pull his ass down and toss him behind me. I exhaled and shook my head instead. I was forward when it came to telling women what I wanted, but I usually did that in a different setting.

"Is the master to the left or right?" she asked when she made it to the top of the stairs.

"Left," he said. "Or on top, whatever you'd prefer."

At that, Nicole laughed. Even I found myself letting out a laugh, though it was only because I couldn't believe what a fucking loser this guy was. I shook my head again. Thankfully, the douche got a phone call and excused himself, holding one finger up and saying it was an important client. Moron. Nicole opened the door to the balcony in the master bedroom and stepped out.

"This is nice," I said, joining her. The sand was on the other side of the sidewalk. It was a perfect beach house. "So did you finally decide to move out of your eight-million-dollar Hollywood Hills home and trade it in for this humble abode?"

She lifted her face to look at me, smiling. "It's half the price."

I chuckled. "You have expensive taste."

"I have good taste."

"I agree," I said, placing my forearms on the top of the balcony. My eyes made their way down her body. She really needed to stop wearing those dresses around me. She needed to stop wearing anything around me. She inched closer, moving so her forearm was against mine, her hip touching mine, and tilted her head back slightly so she could still look into my eyes.

"Wouldn't it be nice, though? For me to move in here. You can come over for wine night," she said, her voice quiet.

We were at eye level now, our faces so close I could smell her breath. She smelled like watermelon, like that pink marker in the scented pack my mom used to buy my sister and me when we were kids. So fucking good. Delectable. My gaze dropped to her mouth, which she licked.

"Yeah? When's wine night?" I asked, feeling myself gravitating toward her. It was unstoppable, this thing.

"Any night you pick."

My lungs squeezed a little, the air stifling at the pull I felt.

"You know," she said, beckoning my eyes to move up to hers again, "I called this guy because I remember him from a friend's wedding. He was hot and really, really knew how to move his pelvis, and you know what they say about guys who can move like that." She paused.

I felt everything inside my body begin to tighten. This burn began to form. It started in my ringing ears and made its way down to my toes. What the fuck was that feeling?

"So I called him up because I heard he was a good realtor and he liked to hook up, and I figured I'd get a two for one. Good house to rent and a hot fuck since I'm trying to maybe break the record of my one and only hot fuck being with you," she continued. The way she said it made my heart squeeze and made my dick hard at the same time. I didn't want her to break that record. Ever. Unless it was with me again. Only with me again.

"But then you showed up and I thought, damn." Her face was now even closer to mine. "That's a guy who definitely knows how to fuck, and I thought maybe I should forget about this realtor guy. Maybe I should go with the sure bet, you know?" she asked, a whisper against my lips.

For a second I didn't move. I let the wheels in my head turn some more. Pussy has ruined the career of a lot of highly successful men. I never thought I'd be on that list. Never thought I'd be anywhere near it, but there I was, headed down that path. The crazy part was that even as I thought it, I moved. I stood upright, pushing off the rail as I pulled her back inside by her wrist, and crashed my lips against hers. I kissed her with the desperation I felt for her, relinquishing all control, and she returned it equally as enthusiastically. Her hands flew to the buttons of my shirt, mine went around to her ass and squeezed.

"I want you so much," she said, pushing me back against the wall. I grabbed her ass harder and pulled her so she could feel just how bad I wanted her. She gasped against my lips, then pulled back to look at me. "Please, Victor. Don't make me wait."

I closed my eyes and loosened my grip on her, giving us a little bit of space, and let out a harsh breathy laugh. "I like to think that I'm good at practicing control, but when you're around . . ."

I didn't finish the sentence. I couldn't because her lips were on mine again, but even if they weren't I didn't have an adequate way of explaining what I felt, and it didn't matter. I could kiss her, I could fuck her once to get it out of my system, but I knew I would want more. And I couldn't have more. Not when my career was on the line, so fucking her out of my system was the only solution we had available, and even that one could be disastrous. In the end, I broke the kiss and gathered my wits. This was going to happen, but it wouldn't happen when a douchebag named Rick could walk in on us at any given moment. I needed to go home, figure out how much longer I had to exert self-control, regroup, and probably jack off, not necessarily in that order.

Chapter Fifteen

Nicole

That kiss. I couldn't stop thinking about it. I thought about it as I signed the lease. I thought about it as I held the keys in my hands. And I thought about it when I called Victor to tell him it was final. He'd agreed it was a good price and great location. He also went over the contract for me and approved it since it was a standard lease and didn't lock me in for more than six months at a time. It was something I definitely needed, because I wasn't sure where I would be in six months. Our conversation took a downward spiral when it went from my new place to the scheduled date I had with Gabe. At the mention of it, his mood changed, his responses became clipped and even though we were on the phone, I could practically see him running a hand through his hair roughly. I wondered what he must have been feeling. Whether or not my pretend being with Gabe affected him as much as he made it seem.

The ice cream shop we'd agreed to go to was one we'd frequented while dating, not as much once we finally married, but that made the story even juicier, apparently. His manager tipped off the paparazzi of our outing, so I dressed in sweats and a T-shirt, and he wore basketball shorts and a T-shirt, so it looked like we were having a completely "relaxed afternoon." It was such a strategic outing, that when I didn't have time to make it home, Gabe asked me to have Marcus drive me to the mall so I could jump in his car and go with him to the place.

He was on the phone with his assistant the entire ride to the shop.

"Lee says hi," he said, in reference to his assistant, when he finally hung up the phone. I looked out the window and stayed silent because Lee was on my eternal shit list, along with Darryl. "Did you hear me?" he asked.

"I heard you."

He let out a sigh. "Just because we're getting a divorce doesn't mean you have to push away our mutual friends, you know?"

"Mutual friends," I said with a scoff. "Lee is the last person I'd consider a friend."

"Wow." He shook his head as he drove down Hollywood Boulevard.

"Wow what, Gabe? In case you didn't know, the moment we separated Lee made it crystal clear he wanted nothing to do with me. Whenever I called you when you were on set . . ." I stopped talking and shook my head. "It doesn't matter."

"No, tell me," he said, his voice soft. He looked over at me when we reached the ice cream shop. The paps were already running toward us and we'd only been parked for a second. I ignored them and continued to look at Gabe, the way I always did when they were around, because I couldn't bear to look at that lens and the one-sided story it told.

"It really doesn't matter. Nine months ago this conversation would have made sense, but you were too busy getting high and screwing every girl in Hollywood."

He lay his hand over mine on my lap, his blue eyes searching mine. "I'm sorry."

A knot formed in my throat, because for the first time his apology felt genuine. I tore my gaze away from his and instantly regretted it when I looked out the window and into five different flashing lights.

"Let's just get this over with," I said, clearing my throat.

When he turned off the car and went around it to open the door for me, smiling for the cameras and laughing at one of their jokes, I closed my eyes and for the millionth time wondered if everything about him had been an act. I hated to belittle what we'd had. I hated to see it as if it were nothing more than a puppet show inside of a light box, especially when my feelings for him had been so real, but it was all I could think when he played the part so well. The sound of the door handle made my eyes pop open. I took his hand as he helped me out of the car and walked beside him, both of us with our heads down as we entered the ice cream shop.

"That wasn't too bad," he said, putting his arm around my shoulders. *Which part?* I wanted to ask? *The part where you pretended to care about me? The one where you made me fall in love with you, only to leave me high and dry when you decided you missed the single life?* I didn't voice any of it. I knew if I did I would go off on him and the entire charade would blow up in our faces. *New York*, I reminded myself. *Smooth mediation. Painless divorce.*

I smiled at Veronica when we got to the front of the line, but instead of smiling back, she kept looking at Gabe while he looked up at the menu. The way she looked at him and ignored me made an uncomfortable feeling settle in the pit of my stomach. That sixth sense women have was as much of a blessing as it was a curse in times like these. My mom used to tell me that men were like puppies. If you didn't keep them entertained long enough, they'd move on to the next toy. I never liked that idea.

I felt like we made far too many excuses for them just because they had dicks between their legs and we had vaginas, and really, if it's about anatomy, wouldn't the channel that they're birthed from be superior? But alas, women like my mom and Gabe's mom gave men the okay to be cheaters, and liars, and showed them that it was okay and that they could get away with it. All that aside, I remember when I was little and my parents were married, my mom had a private investigator tail my dad because she needed to know what he was up to when he left work. I didn't work that way. I always felt like you had to be willing to give a person enough trust to let them make their own choices. What they did with it was a different story.

"Do you want your usual?" Veronica asked, finally looking at me with an uneasy smile.

Gabe looked down at me, flashing me that wide grin that got me to agree to go out with him in the first place. "Cookies 'n' Cream?"

I nodded and smiled after a beat, when I remembered to. "In a waffle bowl."

"Got it," he said, still looking at me like I was something to be cherished. I hated him for it. I hated myself for even feeling anything at all, though what I felt wasn't the unrequited love I'd once felt. When he looked at the girl to order, he paused momentarily. A flirt smile bloomed on her face.

"You never called me back," she said.

I tried to swallow, but it turned into a cough, and soon after, I was slapping my chest and coughing. Gabe patted me in the back, but I jerked out of his touch. She spoke to him as if she had no idea who I was. As if she didn't know I was married to him. As if I wasn't wearing the gigantic rock on my finger that he'd given me five years ago. It wasn't her I was mad at, though. It wasn't her I'd given my trust to.

My skin began to prickle with a heated rage I hadn't felt since the day Gabe hit me with an onslaught of insults in the midst of his drug-induced state. I turned around and began to walk away. My idea was to sit down while he waited for the ice cream I could no longer eat, and breathe it out, but

Gabe's hand on my arm stopped me.

"That was a long time ago," he said.

I kept facing forward, toward the doors, where the paparazzi were still standing, aiming their cameras right at us, capturing the moment. I prided myself in being calm, cool, and collected when I wanted to be. I prided myself in being able to control everything that left my mouth, in being able to reel myself in when I was going too far, but I couldn't. I couldn't. *That was a long time ago? THAT was his excuse?*

"It was a long time ago?" I said, seething as I turned to face him. I pushed his hand off me with my other hand. "Long time ago when, Gabriel? When we were fucking married?"

"Don't make a scene, Nicole."

"Don't make a scene? Are you serious right now?"

"It was nothing serious," he said, lowering his voice and softening his gaze as if his sudden concern was going to be enough to keep me there.

I pushed back on his chest with both hands and turned around again. "Go fuck yourself."

He grabbed me by the wrist, hard, and pulled me back against his chest. His mouth was near my ear. "All we have to do is get out of here with smiles on our faces. That's all we have to do. I fucked up. I was a terrible husband. I'm sorry. I am, but doing this isn't going to solve anything."

I closed my eyes, surprised by the sudden need to cry. I felt sick. It wasn't surprising. It wasn't. I'd heard he was having sex with other women. This wasn't breaking news, but the heavy and unwanted feeling still settled in the pit of my stomach. I felt myself soften in his hold as I let out a long, deep breath.

"I have to go to the bathroom," I whispered. He let go. I didn't look at him at all, or in Veronica's direction as I disappeared down the hall and pulled out my cell phone.

"Hello?"

"I need you," I said, my voice hoarse with unshed tears.

"Are you crying?" he demanded. "Where are you?"

"I'm not crying," I said, even though it was clear I was about to. "Cold Stone in Hollywood."

"I'll be there in two minutes." He paused. "Four minutes. Fucking traffic," he yelled, then softened his voice. "Are the cameras still there?"

"Yes," I whispered, wiping my face. I hated crying. Hated it, and I had an aversion to crying in front of people, so I needed to calm down before he got there.

"Can you go out through the back?"

"Yes. I just have to tell Gabe first." There was a long silence. "Victor?"

"Yeah, I'm here. Okay. I'm at the light. I'll pull up to the back door," he said.

I thanked him, but realized he'd hung up the phone. I put it in my purse and looked at myself in the mirror. I looked normal, and it reminded me of how little we let people see of us. When I walked out of the bathroom, Gabe was standing in the hallway with our ice creams in his hands. He held mine out to me, and I took it.

"I'm leaving."

He flinched slightly, frowning. "Okay. I'll take you home."

I shook my head. "No. I'm leaving. Without you."

I could tell I caught him off guard when he lowered the hand he was holding his ice cream in and sagged his shoulders.

"Really, Nicole?" he asked, sighing. "It was a mistake. I was an idiot. It was one time—"

"I don't care. I don't care," I added slowly, sternly. "I haven't cared for a long time, Gabriel. I haven't, but for you to bring me here? How fucking insensitive can you be? And I'm here to do you a favor. I can't fucking believe—"

"You signed an addendum."

"And because I signed an addendum I'm supposed to stick around while somebody disrespects me and you *let* them?"

"I didn't realize you needed saving, Nicole. I didn't realize you were a damsel in distress."

He was *such* a bastard.

"I don't need saving. The only damsel in distress in this situation is you. And I'm sick of being your knight in shining armor," I said, pointing a finger at his chest before turning to walk toward the back door. I stopped when I reached it, hand on the handle as I tossed the ice cream cone into the waste basket next to me. "P.S. Fuck your addendum."

Victor's sleek black two-door Jaguar was parked right outside the door. I pulled the door open and got in. I hid my face in my hands momentarily before I even got a chance to look at him. Thankfully, he took that as a sign to start driving. As we reached the curb, the paparazzi started running toward the car with their cameras in tow. I hid my face, but I was sure they'd caught me in their photos.

"Where am I going?" he asked.

"Anywhere."

His fingers peeled away one of my hands from my face. I still didn't look at him, but I let him take my hand down with his and left it in his grasp when he threaded our fingers together.

"Having second thoughts on that stupid paper you signed yet?" he asked after a beat, squeezing my hand so I couldn't move it away when I tried.

"Something like that."

"What happened back there?" he asked, taking my hand with him as he shifted the gear.

I sighed. "Nothing out of the ordinary. We agreed to go for ice cream, and it was fine until the cashier, who I used to think was nice, basically told me she'd fucked him."

From my peripheral I saw him nod and mutter *he's an asshole*. He exhaled sharply and continued to drive down Pacific Coast Highway. Neither one of us said anything until we got to a house on the beach, where he parked his car right outside the garage. I swallowed, thinking about how quickly things could escalate as soon as I walked in the door. I'd wanted him for so long, but now that the moment was finally here . . .

"You brought me to your house?" I asked as he switched off the engine. He looked at me and smiled.

"Not my house. This is my sister's. I told her I'd come by to help her put up a TV. She wants to surprise her husband before he gets home from work."

I blinked. "Oh. Okay."

He reached out for my hand again and placed it over his open palm, looking at it as if he were measuring it.

"I've never seen you wearing this," he said, turning the bottom of my wedding ring in his fingers.

"Cameras," I said as way of explanation. There was turmoil in his eyes that made my stomach flip. "Does it bother you?"

He stayed silent for so long, just staring at me, reaching deep within me for something unknown to me, that I thought he wouldn't answer. I watched as his Adam's apple bobbed when he swallowed, and finally he nodded slowly.

"It does. A lot," he said, threading his fingers through mine and bringing his free hand up to my face. He used it to brush back some of the hair that had fallen out of my ponytail and caressed my jaw with his knuckles, those deep hazel eyes still on mine. I couldn't close my eyes even if I wanted to, and my heart felt like it was at the point of no return, kicking into overdrive as his hand continued to move down to my neck, my collarbone.

"I want to take you to dinner," he said, voice low. The only thing I could do was nod. I would have agreed to just about anything. "Somewhere public, where I don't feel like ripping your clothes off, but you know how the media will get if we do that."

I smiled at the thought. "And let's be honest, regardless of where we are, you'd still want to rip my clothes off."

His eyes darkened. "Who wouldn't?"

My smile dropped momentarily thinking of Gabriel. He obviously wouldn't. Not that it mattered. Not that I cared at this point. But, God, how many women could a man have sex with in order to stay satisfied? Wasn't one enough? I tried to lift my lips back into a smile before I gave my thoughts away, but Victor noticed. He brought my hand up to his mouth and kissed the back of it, his soft lips moving down to my wrist, over my pulse as he kept his eyes on me.

"If you were a cockatoo, your flock would've killed you already," he said, lowering my hand, but keeping it in his. I frowned, shaking my head as a laugh escaped me. I was glad for the distraction, so I went along with it.

"Random. Why's that?"

"They try to hide their ailments, but the flock usually notices, because they feel it, and they gang up on them and kill them off."

"That's harsh," I said, raising my eyebrows. "And you feel something? In me?"

He chuckled. "I can make a million jokes about that statement, but I won't. And yes, Nicole, I feel something, in you, for you. I thought that was clear."

His admission was so natural, so nonchalant, but my veins thundered at the words nonetheless. He picked up my hand and kissed it once more before turning to get out of the car. "But the flock still would've killed you."

I got out and walked beside him down the side of the house. I inhaled the smell of the ocean.

"You would let them?" I asked as I walked behind him. "The flock, I mean. You would let them kill me?"

"It would be one against a flock of birds, because you'd probably be crying in a corner."

"So you would let them kill me."

He shook his head and stopped walking. I could sense him smiling before he turned to look at me. "I wouldn't."

"Do you do this much for all of your clients?" I asked, trying to lighten the mood with a smile. I half expected him to joke about how much they pay him, but instead he brought a hand down and held the side of my face, dipping his closer. I felt like I was going to seriously combust right there if he set his lips against mine. He didn't, though. Instead he kissed my cheek, then the corner of my mouth before moving on to the other. He backed away from me slightly, gazing into my eyes with an intensity that made my heart flip.

"I think you know I don't," he whispered, still holding my face. "And I think you know this has passed the client boundary by now." He paused, dropping his hands from my face. "All jokes aside, I'd do anything to make sure you were safe, Nicole."

I felt his words roll through me as he turned around. It took me a second to get my feet to move and follow him down the side of the house, toward the door.

Chapter Sixteen

Victor

My sister's house was a mess. I should've called ahead of time and let her know I was bringing someone with me, but I didn't have any time to process the fact I was bringing someone with me. When Nicole called me I had just left the courthouse. I didn't have time to do anything other than haul ass to the ice cream shop and pick her up. Once I got there and saw the impending breakdown written all over her face, I thought she'd be a sobbing mess, but she wasn't. It surprised me and disappointed me, which caught me off guard. I hated dealing with emotions and shit. Why the hell did I feel so desperate for hers? Probably because she didn't give them to me.

"Estelle?" I called out, picking up the sweater by the door. I turned to Nicole, who was standing behind me, looking nervous. "Sorry. This place is a mess today." And almost every day since Oliver went back to work, really. I couldn't even imagine what it would be like when they started having kids. A shiver ran through me and I shook it off. Nicole laughed.

"Did you see something that creeped you out?" she asked.

"Hey," Estelle said, appearing in the hallway. "I didn't hear you."

I didn't say anything, I let my eyes do the talking as I looked at every surface of her crazy house. She rolled her eyes.

"Don't start with your shit, Victor," she said. "I need your help to set this up so I can pick up before Bean gets home."

"What you need is to hire somebody to help you pick up this insanity," I said, walking in all the way. "Oh, this is Nicole. Nicole, this is my messy little sister, Estelle. She's an artist," I said by way of explanation. It seemed like most artists were messy. Then it hit me. Shit. Nicole was in the fashion business.

Was she this messy?

"Oh," Estelle said, her eyes widening as she looked from me to Nicole and back to me. "That's fine. Sorry about the mess."

"Totally fine," Nicole said, waving her words away. "This is my house on a good day."

My head whipped to her. *What?* She shrugged in response, a little smile forming on her face. I sighed and looked back at Estelle, who was still studying the hell out of Nicole.

"She's—" I was going to explain to her who she was when I remembered my sister seemed to know more about Nicole than I did.

"I know who she is," Estelle said. I held my breath, waiting for her to start freaking out. "You're on TMZ right now, you know? I literally just saw you and Gabriel in an ice cream shop." She paused and frowned, looking at me momentarily. "Was all of that an act? Wait. Don't answer that. I don't want to know. Sorry. I'm sure you're sick of people asking you about him and stuff. Make yourself at home."

All I could do was stare. My sister was an idiot. Nicole surprised me by laughing.

"You'd be surprised how many regular people don't ask me about it. I only get questions from the paparazzi."

"Oh. That must suck so bad, being followed like that," Estelle said, walking over to the kitchen. "Do you want wine? Is it too early for you? Do you even drink? Sorry, I kind of assume everybody drinks."

"She does," I said. "She assumes a lot of things. Forgive her. I'm starting to think maybe my thirteen-year-old self had been right about her being adopted."

Nicole laughed. "I drink, and it's never too early for wine."

Estelle came back with two glasses and handed one to Nicole with a smile. "I hope you like Riesling."

"I do. I have a hard time discriminating when it comes to alcohol."

Estelle laughed. She looked at me, and I already knew what she was thinking. I glared at her so she would take that out of her mind, but she smiled wider.

"So, you're a costume designer, right? That sounds like such a cool job. How did you get into that?" Estelle asked.

"Umm . . . where's my drink?" I asked, raising an eyebrow. She shot me a look.

"You know where the kitchen is."

I shook my head and headed over there. Either way I was going to change my clothes before I started this process. I went to the guest room, where I kept some just-in-case clothes, for late nights drinking when I didn't feel like driving home, and changed into a pair of basketball shorts and the first shirt in the drawer, which happened to be a Born Sinner shirt from the J. Cole concert Jensen and I went to a couple years ago.

"I think my room is the neatest place in this entire house," I said, walking back to the living room, where Estelle and Nicole were sitting facing each other like old high school girlfriends reuniting.

The sight made me smile. It was like she'd been here countless times. My sister had met all of my past girlfriends, and some girls I dated briefly. I liked bringing them around her before I took them anywhere near my parents. I couldn't remember the last time she acted so comfortable around one, not that I was dating Nicole, but then again, my definition of dating differed from the rest of America it seemed.

"If you're so concerned about the mess, then pick it up," Estelle said. I caught Nicole's smile before she hid it behind her glass of wine. I held back my comment because talking about somebody's mouth on you in front of people was inappropriate, but there were a million things I wanted to do with that mouth of hers. *Stop thinking about her mouth. Stop thinking about her tongue and the way it feels against yours, and her soft skin beneath your grip.* Deep breath. I turned around quickly.

"Where's the box?"

"Right there beside the table."

I sighed, putting my hands over my head. This fucking girl. I let them continue to have their conversation about elastic and glass hearts and started to pick up everything in my way from a pair of flip-flops to a box of canvases. Once I was finished I realized it really wasn't as much as I originally thought. It just looked like a mess when it was in the way. I would keep that to myself, though. I took the TV mount out of the box and all the screws and stood up to get the drill out of the garage.

"You know I'm going to need your help after I'm done with this part, right?" I asked when I saw my sister serving more wine as I walked back to the living room with the drill in my hand.

"I know," she said, smiling. She blew me a kiss as she walked back to the kitchen with the bottle of wine, which I assumed was empty. "I love you, brother."

I made a face as I sat back down on the floor. Of course she loved me *now.* I heard Nicole get up from the couch, but didn't look up from the instruction booklet in my hands. She kneeled down beside me.

"You look hot with a drill in your hands," she said in a whisper.

My heart jumped. I tilted my face to look at her. Her cheeks were flushed from the wine, and her hair was falling out of her ponytail again. I reached out and pulled on her hair tie, letting it flow down her shoulders. I kept my hand at the nape of her neck. It was a beautiful sight. So beautiful that all I could do was picture all that hair splayed over my pillowcase.

"I always look hot. It's a curse I've had to live with all my life," I said. She smiled, a small laugh leaving her lips as she tilted her head to better meet my gaze.

"Are you going to help me set up my TV?" she asked, leaning forward, brushing her breasts on my arm.

I inhaled sharply, gripping her hair a little. Her eyes widened, darkened, her lids lowering at the move. It didn't help the situation in my pants. None of it did. I dropped my hand and stopped breathing for a moment, stopped inhaling her sweet scent. Maybe if I didn't breathe I could cut off some of my blood supply and I wouldn't get hard.

"I'll help with whatever you need," I said, swallowing thickly.

My eyes were on her breasts, which were covered in that stupid Mowgli's shirt she wore. I was a fan of the band, but not when I couldn't make out whether or not she was wearing a bra, though I'm pretty sure she was. I looked back into her blue eyes; they were soft and light, the color of a cloudless sunny day. Fucking perfect, like she was.

"Do you guys want something to eat? I have leftovers from last night," Estelle called out from the kitchen.

I cleared my throat. Nicole sighed and stood up. She leaned down and her hair cascaded over both sides of my face as she placed a kiss on the left side of my neck. I closed my eyes, wishing I was free to pull her onto my lap and kiss her.

"That depends," I said loudly so Estelle could hear me. "What did you eat last night?"

"Black bean burgers," she said.

"On bread?" I asked. Oliver had a thing about bread. They normally didn't keep any in their house.

"Lettuce."

I rolled my eyes, pivoting my torso to look at Nicole, who was typing on her phone.

"You want black bean burgers on lettuce?" I asked. She looked up, blinking. I repeated the question, and she nodded.

"Sure. That sounds great."

"We'll have some," I shouted as I went back to work. I stood up with the measuring tape and started to mark the wall.

"Okay, it's ready."

I set the pencil and tape measure on the floor. We walked to the kitchen together, playfully bumping at each other like high school crushes on their way to their next period. Before we reached the open doorframe that led to the kitchen, I put my arm around her shoulder and pulled her to kiss her temple. It was a quick move. I dropped my arm as quickly as I'd pulled her to me. She stopped walking, though. And I stopped walking. Her lips were parted as if she had something on the tip of her tongue, but instead she shook her head, blinked it away, and smiled as she stepped into the kitchen. I wanted to pull her against me and ask her what she was about to say. I wanted to slither my way into every single crevice of her mind and dig until I found her deepest thoughts, her darkest flaws. I couldn't, though. I couldn't, so instead, I followed her into the kitchen and sat beside her at the small wooden table in Estelle's kitchen.

Estelle and Nicole talked about food and wine as I ate and watched the animated way Nicole moved her hands when she spoke. I had to make a conscious effort to look away from her. I looked at my empty plate instead, but when Estelle brought up the subject of the media, my eyes found their way back on Nicole's face. I couldn't help but notice the way her smile dropped, and the light in her eyes dimmed. She shot a quick glance my way before giving a slight shrug and a little smile that upturned the side of her mouth just slightly.

"I don't think they'll follow me around anymore. I'm not that interesting. They only really follow me when I'm with Gabe anyway," she replied.

It was stupid that it bothered me when she called him that, right? She'd been with him for a long time. She could call him babe and I shouldn't care. But I did. And it irked me. Why the fuck did I care? It was a nickname. Then again, even if she called him by his full name at this point it would bother me. Maybe I wouldn't care if he was being amicable, but to get a call from her and know she'd been crying . . . I wasn't okay with that shit. We spent the rest of our time eating and talking about Nicole's new place on the beach. She took down Estelle's number and promised to invite her over. I excused myself from the table when I finished because I really needed to drop by the office to pick up some files before I went home for the night, and that had to wait until after I finished putting the TV up and dropped off Nicole.

I was almost finished drilling the stand when I heard footsteps approach. I glanced over my shoulder and looked at my sister, who had her arms crossed as she watched me. She came closer. I looked around but Nicole was nowhere in sight, and for a fleeting moment I panicked and thought she'd left.

"She's in the bathroom," Estelle said.

I swallowed and nodded.

"You look at her funny."

"Funny how?" I asked, lowering my arms.

She shrugged. "Just funny. Like how you used to look at Jenny Doherty."

I felt my lips twitch at the mention of Jenny. She'd been the only girl I'd dated for well over a year. I wasn't a player. Maybe back in high school I had been, but I'd had long-term girlfriends. It was just that my definition of long-term and my sister's definition of long-term differed. Jenny had been a catch, though. She'd been top of our class and once we graduated and I went to law school, she'd done the same in Connecticut. And then she'd met another guy and married him and started a family. We'd been broken up for years by then, but I still had fond memories of her.

I always thought if I settled down it would have to be with somebody like that. Not somebody who was as smart or as pretty, but somebody who cared about something other than her appearance or the amount of money in my bank account. Somebody who had a balance. That seemed like a simple request, but it wasn't. Not these days anyway, when everything was about Instagram follows and Facebook likes, and who thought you were pretty and who didn't. I would say that only extended to LA, but Jensen was in New York and had the same experience when he was dating, and I had clients who had more money than God and were in the same predicament.

"Vic?" my sister asked, frowning. I shook my head.

"Yeah. No. I'm her lawyer, and I care about her and want what's best for her, but she's not a Jenny." She was *better* than Jenny. I knew it because while I had loved Jenny, she hadn't made me feel like I was burning up inside. Nicole was a flame. And she wasn't going out anytime soon. I knew that. I knew that, but I felt so lost in this, in the way she made me feel and the way I couldn't control my feelings for her, and that scared me. She was my client first and foremost. I felt the need to reiterate that to myself when she wasn't around, because when we were in the same room, I could feel myself getting too comfortable for my own good.

Estelle patted me on the back and snapped me to again. "Whatever you say, Vic." She paused. "Thanks again for doing this."

"Sure. I just need to drill this right here just for extra support and then I'll need your help putting up the TV."

"Okay. I'm going to finish putting this shit away so you can stop glaring at every surface of my messy house," she said as she walked away.

Thank God for that. I went back to the drill.

"You look really good when you're doing housework," Nicole said. I smiled.

"I believe you."

She laughed. I could picture her rolling her eyes behind me, but then I felt the warmth of her breath on the back of my right shoulder and I stilled, gripping the drill a little tighter.

"Maybe I'll make an honest man out of you and you can quit your job and stay home while I go to work," she said in a low voice. I could tell she was having a hard time not laughing as she said the words.

I scoffed. "Fat chance."

"What? You wouldn't be a stay-at-home husband?"

My shoulders shook with laugher as I lowered my arms from the wall and turned around to face her. We were standing so close that if my sister walked in this very moment, she'd have a lot of I *told you so's*. Nicole had a huge smile on her face, her cheeks a deep pink from the wine, or her laughter, or a mix of both. Either way, she looked gorgeous.

"Are you proposing? Because in the state of California one needs to finalize one's divorce before jumping into another marriage," I said, raising an eyebrow. Her smile dropped a little, just momentarily before she rolled her eyes and smirked at me.

"If only you'd be so lucky," she said, backing away a little, her gaze lingering on my face, my eyes, and making their way down my body. She licked her lips as she appraised me, and my heart jumped. Thank God I could control my dick in situations like these, even though it was getting semi-hard from that look alone. I gripped the drill tighter in my right hand, but the only thing I could do was think about pushing her against the wall and drilling my dick into her.

"Yeah," I said, but I didn't even know what I was responding to anymore. I didn't care. Her eyes widened slightly. We looked at each other for a long moment. Too long for comfort. Too long for my lips not to be on hers and her legs not to be wrapped around my waist.

"When is the mediation thing again?" she whispered thickly.

"Not soon enough," I said, my heart hammering.

"God. I can't wait for this to be over. I just . . ." She sighed. "I really wish you had no morals."

I chuckled. If she only knew. "When it comes to you, my morals are very questionable, Nicole."

She looked wicked when she smiled and turned back to sit on the couch. She stopped walking suddenly, frowning when she turned around again.

"Don't you need help mounting?"

"I can assure you I do not need any help mounting," I said, my eyes raking down her body. She crossed her arms and laughed.

"The TV."

"What?" I paused. "Oh. Yeah. I need your help mounting that."

Nicole was still laughing when Estelle walked back into the room. She didn't bother asking and I was glad for that because the last thing I needed was another mental image fucking Nicole.

Chapter Seventeen

Victor

Days leading up to the mediation, I caught the flu. I was sick, pissed, and panicked. I'd never called out of work, but between the way I couldn't keep one pair of clothes on without sweating right through it, my eyes not staying open for more than two minutes at a time, and the pain in my throat, I had no choice. Thankfully Corinne passed by with the files I needed and I was able to call Nicole and speak to her on the phone about the mediation so she knew what to expect. I was in the bathroom, blowing my nose for the tenth time, when the doorbell rang. I really fucking hoped it was my mom. Fuck any man who can't admit that when they're sick they want their fucking mom. I opened the door and had to shield my eyes from the sun, and then blink to make sure my meds weren't playing tricks on me and it was really Nicole standing in front of me.

"Didn't we just talk on the phone?" I said. Fuck, it hurt to talk.

"Yes, and I brought you soup," she said, holding up a white plastic bag.

"Those words have never sounded sexier," I said, getting out of the way for her to walk into the house. "How'd you find my address?"

"I asked your sister for it."

I nodded. That's right. They'd exchanged phone numbers the day of the ice cream parlor drama. Nicole followed me into the kitchen and looked around.

"I was a little shocked when Corrine called me to cancel our meeting today, and I didn't like the idea of my lawyer not being on his A game in a few days, so . . ." She shrugged and held up the bag again as she set it down on the kitchen counter.

"That was nice of you," I said, my voice a croaked whisper. It was really fucking nice of her.

"Where are your bowls?" she asked. I pointed at the cupboard behind her. "And your spoons?" I pointed at the drawer beside me. "And," she glanced around once more, "I found your napkins." She smiled at me. "Okay, your majesty, go lie down. I'll be right there."

I groaned and did as I was told, going back to my living room and putting my feet up. I covered myself with the Chargers blanket Estelle and Oliver had gifted me for my birthday last year and let my eyes drift shut. I jumped a little when I felt a cold cloth on my forehead, and my eyes popped open to find Nicole's concerned eyes right beside my face.

"That feels good," I said, groaning. I tried to smile but I wasn't sure my lips were working.

"Your soup is getting cold," she whispered. I tried to sit up, but kept failing, and then I felt her hands reach under me and heard her groan as she pulled me up.

"You're strong," I said, and felt myself smile when she laughed.

"I try." She leaned down to pick up the bowl of soup and sat beside me. "Open your mouth."

"You're going to feed me?" I don't know why I was so taken aback by her gesture.

"You don't look like you're in any condition to feed yourself. Unless you want me to call your brother-in-law and have him put in an IV?"

My eyes widened. Did she know I hated needles? Had I told her that before? I frowned and asked her. She laughed.

"I didn't, but I'm glad I know now."

"Don't get any ideas," I said, opening my mouth to drink some soup. I closed my eyes. It was so good. "Did you make this?"

"Is it good?"

My gaze met hers. "Did you make it or not?"

She smiled and fed me another spoonful. "That really depends on whether or not it's good."

"It's better than good."

"Well, I didn't make it," she said, laughing. "My old housekeeper, Amelia, did."

I nodded, swallowing the soup in my mouth. "Well, tell Amelia I may want to marry her."

Nicole scowled, blinking away, her eyes trained on the soup. "I'm not sure I like the sound of that," she said.

"Why?" I asked, opening my mouth for another spoon.

"I thought you didn't believe in marriage."

I frowned. "I never said that."

She looked at me, one brow raised in a challenge.

"Okay, so maybe I said that, but I was a twenty-five-year-old idiot. People change."

"Not that much," she whispered.

"You did," I said. "But you're right, not that much. You were still willing to let me mount you the other day at my sister's."

She smiled. "Even if I had been willing to let you do that there, which I wasn't, you wouldn't have done it." She paused. "So I guess people do change after all. Twenty-five-year-old Victor would've done that anywhere I asked him to."

"Like I said, twenty-five-year-old Victor was a fucking idiot."

"You were pretty hot, though."

"Still am," I said.

She shook her head. "I think that fever is really getting to you."

I laughed, but stopped short because it hurt. I closed my eyes as Nicole stood and got the plate of soup, taking it to the kitchen. I heard the water behind me, but couldn't even tell her not to wash the plate. When I felt her presence near again, I opened my eyes. She had a glass of orange juice in her hand.

"You have to drink this," she said. "And then you're going to get up and shower."

I groaned. "Is this your way of telling me I stink?"

"No."

"Is this your way of getting me naked?"

She tried to stifle a laugh by pressing her lips together. "No."

"Is this your way of getting me in the shower and having your way with me because you'd have to give me a bath since I'm so weak right now?"

She laughed. "No."

I glanced up at her. She was so fucking beautiful. I hadn't really paid attention to the red dress she was wearing, or the way it curved out at her hips to accentuate her small waistline. I hadn't noticed she'd worn her hair loose or the way it draped over her shoulders and covered her tits.

"You're so fucking beautiful," I said before I could stop myself. Her eyes widened slightly. She took a seat across from me, placing the cup on her lap.

From the way the orange liquid moved in the glass, I could tell her hands were shaking.

"Thank you," she whispered.

"I don't tell you that enough, but you are. I never told you that enough," I said. "Before, I mean. Before I pushed you away and you married that fucking asshole. I should have told you how beautiful you were."

"Victor," she whispered, "just . . . drink this."

My head felt light, as if at any moment I'd pass out again. It was definitely the Nyquil.

"This isn't me telling you these things because I'm drugged," I said. "I'm not him." Not that I knew what he was like when he was drugged, but I felt the need to add that. "I liked you, Nicole. I really did."

"Before?" she asked in a low voice. I nodded. Before, during, after. I really fucking liked her.

"But your dad was my boss, and I couldn't . . ." I yawned. "I couldn't take that chance."

"I know. Priorities," she said and smiled.

She didn't seem upset about the admission. I didn't really expect her to be. Nicole never saw me as her long-lost lover. She'd been whole before I found her at the club, and whole after I left her at the office.

"I had no idea you wanted to get married," I said, yawning again.

"You wouldn't have settled down even if you had known," she replied, shrugging.

"It had nothing to do with you. That was all me," I said. She sighed.

"That was a long time ago. A lot has happened since." She stood from her seat and leaned down to place her hand on my forehead. I closed my eyes at the feel of it, tried to inhale the fresh scent she carried with her. "Do you just want to go to sleep then? Not shower? You should still drink this."

She brought the cup to my lips and I took a sip, cringing as the cold liquid hit my sore throat. When I was finished, she stepped away and put the cup down.

"I should probably—" she started, and I realized, to my horror, that she may be about to leave me here by myself, and I really wanted her to stay. I wasn't sure which one of those things was worse.

"Stay," I said. "Stay with me."

She let out a sigh and sat down beside me, and without a second thought, I put my head on her lap. She started running her fingers through my hair so softly, sleep didn't stand a chance.

"I have some designs to work on," she said. "Do you mind if I get my sketch book and do that here?"

"Please do. I want to see them," I said, looking into her eyes. She nodded and gave me a small smile as she continued to touch my hair. "I always liked watching you sketch." That was the last thing I remember saying before I fell asleep.

Chapter Eighteen

Nicole

Victor and I had been talking on the phone for the past few days. Ever since I left his house after taking him soup, he'd been calling me. It was mostly talk about the mediation and him apologizing for canceling our meeting, which led to him thanking me profusely for bringing him soup. Bringing him soup, which I wasn't sure was key word for a new page we turned or just literally bringing soup. It felt like a new page to me, though. With the late-night calls and the movie talk, and bowling challenges, and promises of surfing lessons, it felt like maybe we were becoming something. Something else. Something I wasn't sure either of us knew or wanted to label. But all of that was gathered in just a few days, and I'd married a man I barely knew within just a few weeks once before and look at how that turned out. The reminder left a bitter taste in my mouth. I washed it down with the cup of coffee in my hand, gulping it until it was all gone.

Victor called me at six thirty in the morning to wake me up and make sure I'd be ready on time. The meeting was scheduled for eleven thirty. Who the hell calls somebody at six thirty in the morning? Ever since the girl from the ice cream shop ended up on the tabloids with a tell-all about Gabe and her, Victor had been on edge, trying to figure out how we could really stick it to him during the mediation. My dad had been livid. Chrissy and Talon were furious. *"My wild night with Gabriel Lane"* was the title on the tabloids. It was definitely catchy, and if I was being completely honest with myself, I didn't care anymore. I was just . . . done.

Victor wanted to meet with me beforehand just in case I had any questions. I told him I didn't. He insisted I had to as way of apology for the missed meeting and I agreed just so I could get him off the phone. At nine thirty there was loud knock on my door. Thankfully, I'd gotten dressed already and had just finished drying my hair. I walked downstairs and opened the door just as he was putting his hand up to knock again.

"You have absolutely no patience," I said, gawking at him. He was dressed in a dark navy suit today, looking way too good to be my off-limits attorney. He gave me a quick, but thorough, once-over. I felt his gaze to the tips of my toes.

"You're not ready." He brushed past me and walked inside.

"I just need my shoes."

I closed the door and locked it, turning around to find him looking up at the ceiling with his eyes closed and his hands in his pockets.

"What's wrong?"

"Did you know there were photographers outside?" he asked, walking toward my kitchen.

"No." I paused, looking out the open windows in the front of the house. "Right now?"

"I was bombarded with flashing cameras on the walk from my car."

I rounded the counter and set up the coffee machine again before facing him, butt against the counter arms crossed. "Is that why you stormed in here like you were being chased by a White Walker?"

"A white what?"

"From Game of Thrones, you know?" I paused. "Didn't we talk about this last night?"

"Yes, and I told you I don't watch it."

I shook my head. "Have you tried to watch it and you just didn't like it? Because, I mean, this could very well be the moment I fall out of like with you, or whatever."

His eyes roamed over my face, a slow tease of a smile splaying on his face. "Fall out of *like* with me? Did I miss the middle school memo?"

"I'm just saying." I turned around when the coffee finished pouring in the first cup and replaced it with another. I held the cup in my hand as I walked over to him and extended it for him to take. "If I could go on any set for a day, it would be that one. Too bad I have no connections there."

Victor took the cup from my hand with one of his and picked out something in my hair before looking back into my eyes. "Have you tried applying for a job there?"

"Have I tried?" I scoffed. "Of course I've tried. They have the best costume designers ever, though. I mean, Michele Clapton is a freaking genius.

That's like if Prada hired Kanye West or something."

Victor chuckled, taking a sip of coffee. "So now you're throwing Yeezy under the bus too?"

I smiled, trying not to laugh along. "I'm just saying. I'm good at what I do, but I'm not her."

"I think you're good," he said, and added, "Really good."

His words were serious, though the crinkles around his eyes were still present from his smile. I was tempted to run the tips of my fingers along each line. I loved it when he smiled like this, as if he were giving me a private showing of the Victor not many were allowed to see.

"I think you're pretty good too," I replied, smiling. "And for the record, I would have hated you in middle school. And also, I like Kanye's music, I just think that when it comes to fashion, he thinks he's better than he actually is."

"Well, it doesn't matter what you think. You don't have the answers, Sway," he said. I started laughing. Hard. And he joined in, setting his mug down in front of him.

"You know, for somebody who's all business, and thinks his job is the most important thing ever, you can be pretty fun sometimes."

He appraised me for a moment, his eyes dropping to my chest. "I'm fun a lot of times."

"Sometimes," I said, my voice beckoning his attention back to my face. "And you haven't been much fun in that sense."

"With good reason. Let's try to get today out of the way."

"And then you'll be more fun?"

"Considering I'm just about ready to explode every time I hear your voice, let alone see you, I'd say that's a possibility," he said, his gaze heating the longer we looked at each other.

"Hmm." My heart did a series of wild pitter-patters as I put my mug in the sink and walked around the counter. We stood face to face, one of his hands gripping the side of the counter and the other in his pocket. I placed my hand flat on his hard chest and trailed it down to his stomach, stopping above his belt. His breath hitched. "A big possibility," I said.

"A very big possibility," he said, swallowing, eyes blazing.

I smiled and dropped my hand, stepping away just slightly. "I should probably go put my shoes on."

"You definitely should." From the way he was looking at me, the last thing I wanted was to put more clothes on. "You should probably go do that now," he added, stepping a little closer and bringing his thumb to my face to wipe at the side of my mouth.

My lips parted slightly, I felt my breath coming in tiny spurts as we looked at each other. His gaze held a promise, but more than that, there was a soft curiosity that hadn't been there before, and as his hazel eyes brewed and studied mine, I went completely still, my body anchored by his. An earthquake could have shaken, my door could have been pounded down by a million paparazzi, and I still wouldn't have moved, because his hand on my face and that gaze was the only thing I felt I needed.

We both blinked at the same time, his hand dropping as he cleared his throat.

"Yeah, let me . . . go get my shoes," I said again, and disappeared into the hall. By the time I reached the top of the stairs, I wasn't sure if my heart was galloping because of the steps I took two at a time or what had just happened in the kitchen. I didn't know what was happening, but I knew I needed to get to that courthouse and make this go away once and for all so I could at least explore the realm of possibilities between us.

When we got outside, Victor positioned himself on the side the paparazzi were standing and put his arm on my shoulder as he led me down the sidewalk. When the cameras started flashing, I was glad I had my sunglasses on.

"Nicole, what happened the other day at the ice cream shop?"

"Is the divorce back on? Is that why you moved here?"

"Are you still working on your marriage?"

I kept my head down, my eyes on my black Jimmy Choos, and kept it moving. The questions continued until we got to the car, and even after our doors shut, the flashes continued.

"I don't understand how anybody could live like that. It's like living inside a fishbowl," Victor said.

"With no water," I replied.

He glanced at me as he stopped at the red light. "Do you get used to it?"

"I guess in a sense it becomes the new normal, which is insane to admit. Once this whole thing is over I can go back to living life, though."

"You mean go back to partying without worrying about them trailing behind you?"

"Goals," I said with a sigh. I paused to think on that for a beat, though, and it didn't accurately portray what I wanted out of life. "As lame as it probably sounds, I kind of just want to be able to pump gas without being followed around and asked about Gabe. I'm assuming once it's over they won't feel the need to mention every woman he's seen out with."

Victor didn't take his eyes off the road, but nodded. "Does it bother you? Hearing about him and other women?"

"I think what bothers me is their need to throw it out there just to get a good picture of whatever face I make. The knowledge of the women . . . doesn't bother me anymore."

Once I saw him leave the club with the blonde, and survived, I knew that ship had sailed, and even though it had hurt a little, I realized rather quickly I was completely fine without him. I'd been without him for so long anyway.

"Do you read the tabloids?"

"Of course I do."

I was just as guilty as everybody else in Hollywood who *didn't read the tabloids*. I'd rather find out what they were saying about me firsthand. Victor didn't respond to that, instead he hit the steering wheel with his palm when we hit a wall of traffic.

"Fuck you, Los Angeles. Fuck you," he said. I couldn't help but laugh, and when he shot me a glare, I laughed harder.

"We're on time," I said.

He sighed. "I guess we are. Sorry. Court days make me crazy."

"Oh. Court days make you crazy. What's your excuse every other day of the week?" I asked, smiling. I could tell he was having a difficult time keeping a serious look on his face. He looked at me, his eyes dead set on mine.

"You."

My stomach flipped. "Me? How do you figure that?"

"You make me crazy every other day of the week."

"How?" I asked, hyper aware of the way my heart was pounding in my ears.

His hand reached out to grab mine. He put it on the shift and covered it with his as he moved it to another gear.

"Well, you're occupying my mind every day of the week, so my deduction is that you're the reason I'm completely crazy."

I swallowed. "Do all of your clients occupy your mind as much as I do?"

When we stopped at the next red light and he set the gear in neutral, he looked at me, and from the way his expression intensified, I was sure he was going to kiss me. Ravish me. I shivered slightly, and put my hand out to adjust the air vent so it wasn't hitting me directly. Victor smirked knowingly.

"Fuck, no," he said. "They don't, and that terrifies me."

I reared back slightly, taken aback by the sincerity in his tone. My heart was pounding so loudly now, I wasn't sure I could even say what I wanted to say.

"Why does it terrify you? Because of your job?" I asked in a whisper. He ran his thumb along the seams of my fingers.

"Not because of my job."

Our gazes were locked on each other. I wanted to ask so many things.

Because you like me more than you care to admit?

But I didn't want to ruin the moment. If he said yes to either of those things, I would be thrilled, but I still had to be mindful of his promotion. I wouldn't get in the way of him getting it. Yes, I wanted him. Yes, I thought sleeping with him again would douse this flame, but I knew we had to be careful. And the reality was that I liked him. A lot. He started driving again and I sat back in my seat. How messed up was it that I was feeling these things for another man? For the man who was helping me divorce my husband? If I was being honest with myself, I didn't really care how messed up it was. As far as I was concerned I hadn't been married for a long time, because even though we were on paper, the things that happened in that relationship over the past two years were things no respectful relationship should have to endure. I didn't blame Gabe on the matter, either. It was both of us. He changed. I grew. *Apart.*

When we reached the parking lot of the courthouse, he looked over at me.

"You ready?"

I gave him a small smile. "I think so."

He turned slightly in his seat with a serious look on his face. "No. You are. There is no think. There's only know. You're a hellion. Fuck what they say. Fuck what they want. This is about what you want, and whatever you want, we'll get."

His words filled me with a sense of serenity. I'd told Gabe I didn't need a knight in shining armor, and I didn't. I didn't need Gabe. I didn't need Victor, but it felt good to have somebody like him on my team. Fighting for me. Fighting *with* me. I told him as much, and caught a glimpse of a more tender Victor, one I'd seen more often than not lately. He looked at me for a long beat, with those beautiful eyes and just said one word. One drawn out, gravelly, deep voiced word that threatened to make my toes curl in my heels.

"*Nicole.*"

He gave my hand one tight squeeze before switching off the ignition. I took one last long breath before we got out of the car and headed toward the building.

Chapter Nineteen

Victor

I should be awarded a medal for dealing with imbeciles. First, the metal detector kept going off and I kept having to go back through it, even though Jean was the one securing the place and had seen me walk through these doors a million times. I wanted to say, "I'm pretty sure I left my shotgun at home this time, Jean." But with all of the mass shootings I couldn't really make a joke out of it. I told Nicole as much as I put my jacket back on and she laughed.

"That and your temper," she said.

"You're the only one who thinks I have a temper," I said, picking up my briefcase and glancing at my watch.

Nicole scoffed. "Maybe I'm the only one who *tells* you that you have a temper."

I waved at my friend Ezra as he walked by going the opposite direction with his client.

"Golf this Sunday?" he asked.

"And miss the Lakers game?" I shot back. He laughed, shaking his head.

"Maybe sometime next week then. I have a case I want to discuss with you."

I nodded and continued walking. "See? People like me."

We stopped outside the doors and I propped my briefcase on the piece of crown molding on the wall so I could look for the file I needed. As my fingers sorted through the tabs, I chuckled, thinking about the day I found Nicole's panties inside. We hadn't talked about it at all, mainly because there hadn't been a good time to bring it up. If I asked her about it when we were alone, we'd be charting troubled water. As it was, things were choppy, lines were blurring, if they'd even been there in the first place. When I found the file I was looking for, I took it out and shut my briefcase.

"Maybe it's because you only let them see one side of you," Nicole said. I frowned. What the hell was she talking about? I looked at her.

"Are you talking to me?"

She shot me a look. "No shit. Who else is standing here?"

I looked around, and sure enough, we were the only ones in the hall. I shook my head. "What are you talking about now? Your voice box hasn't taken a break all day."

She laughed and pointed at me. "You see? So grouchy. Like Oscar."

I rolled my eyes and put the file under my armpit. "Be an adult, Nicole. Stop talking about cartoons and fantasy shows for a moment."

"Oh yeah, let me just sit here and quote rappers so you can keep up with me."

I sighed. She wasn't going to shut up. Maybe it was her nerves. Everybody had a coping mechanism. As long as hers wasn't open-mouthed chewing, we'd be all right. Hell, as long as her mouth was on me, we'd be all right. I shook my head and blinked out of my thoughts.

"Nic," I said.

"Hmm?" She tilted her head slightly to look at me.

"Can you please be quiet for a little while? I need to think and I can't if you make me keep looking at your lips."

She smiled and put her hands up. "I won't even make a joke out of that."

I wanted to take her face in my hands and kiss that smirk off right there in the middle of the courthouse that was practically my second home. Instead, I walked until I reached the room and opened the door. Lewis was sitting at the conference table with the phone to his ear, taking notes of something. He looked up and nodded in greeting.

"I'll have to call you back. Okay. Sure." He hung up and stood, offering his hand for me to shake. "Good to see you again." He looked at Nicole and did the same. "Unfortunate circumstances, but good to see you."

We sat down across from him.

"Where's the prince of Hollywood?" I asked.

"Running a little behind. Thanks for agreeing to meet me here. I have a case ten minutes after this one and there was just no way I'd make it here with the traffic."

"The fucking traffic is unbearable. Is it me or is it getting worse?" I asked.

"It's getting worse," Nicole said.

Lewis smiled slightly. "We'll try to do this as fast as possible. Gabriel said you're amicable."

She scoffed. "Did he? We seem to have a difference of opinion in more things than I realized."

I looked at her. "This is off the record right now, but when he walks in here and we start our meeting, I can't have you jumping in when he says anything."

"So I just stay quiet?"

"If you can," I said, hoping she understood it was for the best.

I got along with Lewis, until we were put on a case against each other. Then the gloves were off, mainly because he was damn good at his job and I took no chances.

The doors opened and Gabriel walked in with a little kick to his step, looking like a man who was ready to be single. It gave me a vote of confidence because we'd be closing this sooner than expected, which meant soon I'd have his ex-wife in my bed. I'd always heard the saying, "One man's trash is another man's treasure" and took it at face value, but it was the first thing that came to mind. The problem was, now I was in the situation, I realized that in reality it wasn't one man's trash. Women weren't things you could discard. Much less a woman like Nicole.

"Sorry I'm late," he said, looking around the room. I didn't miss the way his eyes stayed on Nicole. A man walked in behind him. At first I thought it was the mediator, but I knew all of the mediators and I'd never seen him.

"Who's this?" I asked when the man took a seat beside Gabriel.

"I'm his manager, Darryl Cusack."

"And you're here because?"

"You're about to find out," he said, smiling smugly. He looked like a fucking caricature, his head not proportioned with his body.

Soon after, Marvin Harrison walked in. I could have leaped from happiness. From the smile on his face, I could tell Lewis was having the same reaction. Out of all the mediators, Marvin was the easiest one to work with. He was clear, to the point, and most importantly, fair. I rubbed my hands together as he took a seat. When I glanced over at Nicole she was giving me a funny look. *What?* I asked with a frown and a shrug. She shook her head, looking away from me.

Marvin started talking, and I shut all personal thoughts about Nicole out. He asked if they were both sure they wanted the divorce. They both said yes, though with the way he was looking at her, Gabriel didn't look like a man who was done. I looked away. We went down a checklist of things, the King Charles named Bonnie that Gabriel had kept (for now), the Hollywood Hills home, the Escalade, the Prius, the Porsche, the Bentley, the farm in Idaho, the stocks in a production company, and the New York condo. Darryl perked up at the mention of the condo. I kept the expression on my face impassive. Nicole made it clear that she no longer wanted the house in The Hills, but she did want to be compensated for the money she put into remodeling the kitchen and the guest house.

"The dog?" Marvin asked, looking at Nicole first.

"He can keep it."

"So there will no longer be a need to share it?" he asked.

From the corner of my eye I caught the way her hands gripped her thighs. I looked at her. "You sure about this?"

She nodded, her eyes watering. "I just want it to be over. I don't want to share anything that ties me to him," she whispered.

Across from us, Gabriel cleared his throat. "You can take her."

Nicole's gaze tore from mine and flew to his. She didn't speak, though.

"You can take her. It's fine. I'm barely home anyway," he said.

She blinked rapidly and cleared her throat before smiling. "Thank you."

"Of course."

I kept my face impassive, but couldn't bear to look at the moment they were sharing any longer, so I looked back at Marvin.

"Cars," he said.

"I want the Prius," Nicole told me.

I looked at Gabriel, who nodded. Lewis spoke up. "Done."

"And the Cayenne," she added. Gabriel's brows hitched, but he nodded. "Done."

"The house in Idaho?" Marvin prompted, looking at Nicole again.

"It's his."

"Done."

"The condo in New York," he said.

"My client and Gabriel came to an agreement on this," I said, sliding over the contract they'd signed. Marvin picked it up and read it quickly.

"Objection. She didn't uphold her end of the bargain," Darryl said. I could tell he was having way too much fun with this.

"She went to two events with Mr. Lane, er, Rogers," I said, unsure of which last name to use for somebody who evidentially acted like Dr. Jekyll and Mr. Hyde. "The contract doesn't state how many events she was to attend, so to the best of our knowledge she upheld her end of the bargain."

"The best of your knowledge isn't enough," Darryl said, slamming a hand on the table. I shot Lewis a look. His face was so red, I thought he was going to explode right there.

"Please let me handle my client, Mr. Cusack," Lewis said.

"Then do something about this, because she still needs to go to at least one more red carpet event with him after the scene she caused during their ice cream outing the other day."

I grit my teeth together. I took a deep breath. I clasped my hands together on the table in front of me.

"My client needs to process and think about it before she makes a decision. Is that all?" I asked. My patience was running thin, so for Darryl's sake it was best he kept his mouth shut.

"No, that's not all." But of course he didn't know when to shut the fuck up. "She needs to attend this event with him and we need to schedule another candid appearance."

I drummed my fingers on the table, and looked at Lewis again. He heaved out a heavy breath. "I'm going to have to ask you to leave, Mr. Cusack. We both want what's best for our client, and what's best for him right now is for you to wait outside."

He huffed and puffed, but did as instructed.

"As far as the appearances go, I'll speak to my client in private as well," Lewis said.

Marvin nodded and stacked up the papers in front of him. "Well, I guess we just need to come to an agreement on this and we should be able to put it behind us."

We stood with the condition that we'd figure it out by the end of the week. I shook Lewis's hand, then Gabriel's, and then stood off to the side with Marvin and Lewis as Gabriel and Nicole spoke. They were being very quiet, and I kept finding myself looking over to them frequently as Marv tried to set up a game of golf. Golf was a sport I didn't even like, but had learned to play because many successful business meetings tended to happen over a game.

The last time I looked over, Gabriel had his hand on Nicole's shoulder and she was nodding at something he said. A wave of jealousy crashed through me, and I didn't even know why. They were getting a divorce. They'd been married. They had history together. Maybe that last bit was what bothered me. She had history with him. That, and to my horror I realized, I wanted her to only have eyes for me. I glanced at my watch and excused myself from the conversation. I had a meeting in my office scheduled in an hour and I still needed to take her home.

"Excuse me," I said, walking up to where she stood with Gabriel. "I have a meeting scheduled soon."

"Oh," she said. "Oh. Crap. I'd forgotten we came in the same car. Will you be able to drop me off?"

"Sure, it's on my way," I said. It wasn't on my way at all, but I didn't want to give Gabriel the chance of offering.

"I can take you," he said anyway.

Nicole looked at me for a long moment, searching for something. I wished she would just ask me for it so I could give it to her. Then she tore her gaze away and looked at Gabriel. For as long as I could remember, even when I was back in elementary school, I'd always be the first to get picked for things. Soccer matches, kickball team, softball, basketball. You name it, I had been picked first. I'd never understood what the other kids felt like until this moment. That feeling of your heart dropping into the pit of your stomach and your gut filling with uncertainty? I was in my thirties, for God's sake. That wasn't a feeling I wanted to experience at this point in my life. But as with everything that came to Nicole, there I was, experiencing uncomfortable shit.

"It's fine. Victor can take me. Thanks anyway. I'll see you soon though, as I have to go pick up Bonnie," she said after what felt like an eternity.

Gabriel returned the smile she gave him, and for a fleeting moment I felt another pang in my chest as I caught a glimpse of what their life must have been like when they were good together—the laughter, the dreams they must have shared, the heartaches they'd endured. They were over, though. That seemed to dull the pain just enough for me to smile and shake his hand as I walked away with her.

Chapter Twenty

Nicole

I'd picked up Bonnie from the house I shared with Gabe and he'd asked me to stay awhile. Initially I said no, but he kept talking to Bonnie and scratching behind her ear, and I knew he'd miss her almost as much as I would have had he kept her instead of me, so I stayed. I was comfortable with it, until I wasn't, because as usual, we ended up back at: *where did we go wrong? What happened to us?* Those were topics I no longer cared to address. I told him as much, and he agreed it was unfair of him to revert back to them, but I could tell the thoughts lingered even as he stood by the door and watched me walk to my car with Bonnie.

"Are you still going out with Chrissy tonight?" Talon asked as she came into my work area. She was dusting off one of her makeup brushes against a towel as she watched me sew the black corset in my hands. "To celebrate?"

"Yeah," I said, smiling. "I feel like a celebration is in order in the form of getting intoxicated and dancing wildly."

Talon laughed. "That's a good way to celebrate. I would join you, but the girls are sick."

"Sucks," I said. "I won't even try to convince you then. Moms are the best medicine."

"Speaking of which, when are you going to go visit yours?"

I sighed, pushing away from the sewing table and running my hands down my face. I was dying to go see her, but with this whole ordeal, I hadn't even looked at flights.

"I don't know, but hopefully soon. She's finally done telling me the divorce was a mistake, and I really want to just go over there and lay low for a while."

"Is your dad still on his cruise?"

"Yeah, they come back next week. Meire emailed me pictures and said he was itching to get back to the office. I can only imagine what a pain in the ass he's being."

"These attorneys," Tal said, shaking her head. "That's probably why you like Victor so much."

I couldn't keep the smile that spread over my face. I rarely spoke to him during the day unless he had something to tell me about the case, which at this point he said would be white noise until we got the finalized papers, but our late-night calls continued and those were much more interesting than law talk. He'd told me about his first girlfriend. I'd told him about my first boyfriend. We spoke about our longest relationships and shortest, and weirdest, and sometimes we'd throw in things from our past together and laugh at the fact we still remembered.

"You really like him," Talon said. I shrugged a noncommittal answer, though I didn't make an attempt to deny it. I *definitely* really liked him. I always had, but this time it seemed like I liked him more. Like we were connecting on another level. As if we were becoming friends first. *Had that been what we'd missed the first time around?* I tried not to psyche myself out over it though. I knew him and his priorities were still intact.

On my way home, I called Marcus. He'd asked for time off to see his sick aunt a few days before the mediation. He said he hoped there was still a job for him when he got back, but he understood if I needed somebody else immediately. I told him he wasn't getting rid of me that easily. I'd gotten used to having him around. When Marcus didn't answer the phone on the second ring, I hung up and called Victor.

"Hey," he said. My veins thundered at the sound of his masculine voice. "Can I call you back? I just got to a restaurant where I'm meeting with a client."

"A woman client?" I asked. He chuckled.

"Hmm. No answer. Interesting," I said.

He paused for a beat. "Are you jealous?"

"Is she hot?"

"Not hotter than you," he said, his voice firm, but I could also feel a hint of amusement in it.

"Whatever," I mumbled. The entire time I'd been his client, I hadn't gotten the *let's go to a restaurant and discuss your case there* treatment.

He sighed. "Nicole, please don't be jealous. I can assure you that you have no reason to be."

"I'm not jealous," I said, and I wasn't. I just wished things would have been different. I wished we could go out and do things while we got to know each other instead of hiding our conversations behind late-night calls and stupid meetings, where our personal conversations were overshadowed by my past with Gabe.

"Good. I really have to go. I'll call you when I get out of here."

I mumbled a goodbye I wasn't even sure he heard before hanging up. I was stuck in traffic for twenty minutes before Marcus called back. After asking him how the ailing aunt he went home to visit was doing, I gave him the overview of what tonight would be like: club, girls, drinking, partying.

When I got home, Bonnie trotted to the door to greet me, her floppy ears dangling as she tilted her head for me to scratch. I did and picked her up as soon as I set down my bag, keys, and kicked off my heels. I held Bonnie on my hip and sorted through the bottles of wine I had placed on the wooden bottle holder on the wall and set her on the floor and poured some into a glass before putting on a pair of sneakers, and headed out back with her. I let her roam a bit while I sipped on my wine and took in the ocean breeze, watching her to make sure she didn't number two without my knowledge. There were few things I hated more than stepping on the shit an irresponsible dog owner left behind.

"Is that a cocker spaniel?"

My head snapped up to the shirtless guy slowing down from his jog. Perks of living on Manhattan Beach—hot shirtless guys jogging.

"Nope. King Charles."

He smiled, crouching down to meet Bonnie's excited little hop. "She's beautiful."

"Thank you." I smiled.

"She looks like you."

I felt my face heat up a little as I smiled. "Thank you."

"I've never seen you around here."

"I just moved from . . ." I paused. He obviously didn't know me as Gabriel Lane's wife, so he wouldn't know where I'd lived. It was the first time I realized I was starting from scratch. I was just Nicole Alessi again, and unless you were into digging into people's past and saw my socialite, wild child days, very few people knew who I was. "I just moved over here," I said, correcting myself.

"Oh. Where did you move from?"

"Like twenty minutes away."

"Oh. I moved here from Georgia a few months ago." He paused. "I'm Brent, by the way."

"Nicole," I said, bumping the fist he extended for me.

"My hands are sweaty," he said as way of explanation.

I heard my phone ringing inside and jerked out of my seat. When I looked at Bonnie again, I noticed she'd chosen that exact moment to take a crap. "Sorry," I said sheepishly. "I have to get that. Enjoy your run. I'm sure I'll see you around again."

"I hope so," he said, taking off again. I watched him leave for a second before Bonnie tugged at her leash, and I sighed, coming back to reality.

"What have I told you about using the bathroom in front of people?" I whispered, crouching down with the baggie in my hand. "So disgusting, Bonnie. So disgusting."

When I walked back in the house, I noticed the missed call was from Victor. I debated not calling him back, but I didn't want him to think I was being childish or jealous because he was out with a female client, so I called back.

"How was your lunch date?" I asked. The harsh breath he exhaled into the phone line made me shiver as if his face was on me.

"Meeting, Nicole. It was a meeting."

"Same difference."

"Not the same difference. I don't sleep with my clients."

I bit back a smile, tried to mask it from my voice. "That's too bad. I heard you have a client who was just about to touch herself thinking about that possibility."

"Fuck, Nicole," he groaned.

"Hmm?"

"You're killing me," he said, voice gruff. Butterflies ignited deep in my belly.

"What kills you more, Victor? Knowing you can have me and passing it up or thinking about me going out tonight and finding another man to satisfy this urge?"

He was quiet, but I knew he was there because I could hear his labored breath in my ear. I stayed quiet. I was never one to shy away, but I was afraid maybe I'd pushed the envelope and in turn pushed him farther away.

"I've been sitting outside, staring at the office building trying to get rid of the hard-on you've managed to give me, and now that's looking like it won't be going away any time soon, which means I'm going to be late to a fucking meeting I arrived twenty minutes early to," he said, pausing. I smiled. "To answer your question, both of those options fucking kill me, but when I fuck you again, and I will have you again, it's my name you're going to be screaming."

"We'll see," I said, trying not to sound as affected as I felt.

"Yeah, we will see." He let out a breath. "I have to let you go so I can see what to do about my . . . problem."

I laughed. "Sorry. Sort of. Good luck in your meeting."

"Thanks. I'll call you tonight."

"Oh. I won't be home," I said. His silence told me he was expecting me to expand on that, but I didn't. I wanted him to be the one to ask.

"Where are you going?" he asked finally.

"Out with Chrissy."

"Chrissy . . . the friend you go club-hopping with?"

I laughed at the fact that he knew Chrissy as the club-hopper. "We don't club-hop. We're not twenty-one. We just go to one."

"Still sounds like trouble," he said, but I could hear the smile in his voice as he said it.

"You know me, always up to something."

"I do, and I like that. I'll call you when I get home. Maybe I'll catch you before you head out."

After I hung up with him, I drank two more glasses, soaked in a bath, ordered sushi, got dressed and put on my makeup before Marcus knocked on my door. I opened it and welcomed him inside while I walked around making sure I'd blown out all the candles I'd lit during my hour of relaxation. Rather than her picking me up, I promised Chrissy I'd meet her at the club.

"Let's go, Marky Mark. If I don't leave now, my buzz will be gone by the time I get there and I won't be brave enough to walk into the club by myself."

"Didn't you just tell your friend to put me on the list so I could escort you in?"

"You know what I mean."

"I don't, but it's okay, I don't want to know."

It took us a bit to get to the club, and then a little longer to park in the back. Marcus suggested valet, but I said no. There was no way I was letting a valet drive my Cayenne. And there was no way I was getting out of the car with the paparazzi around. I wanted to wait for at least some of them to scurry out. Once they did, we got out of the car and walked to the back door. We got inside with no hassle at all. The bouncer looked at me and let me go in, and then did the same to Marcus.

"I'm surprised they didn't card you," I said loudly, over the music.

"Why?"

"Baby face," I said, raising a hand and slapping him playfully. He shook his head.

We made our way upstairs, where Chrissy was waiting with Cass and a few other friends again. The minute she saw me, she bolted out of the chair and pulled me into a hug. But the moment she saw Marcus she let go and gave him all her attention. I couldn't stop laughing at the look on his face. He came over and told me he was going to stand by the foot of the stairs just in case I needed anything. I was sure he was doing it to get away from Chrissy and her forwardness.

I joined Chrissy and let her pour me a drink from the bottle she'd ordered.

"How's the hot lawyer?" she asked.

"He's . . . there. Being hot," I said as I took a sip of champagne. I really didn't want to get into it, especially not at a loud club.

"I'm pretty sure I saw him here," she said, looking around. "I mean, it's dark, but I could swear it was the same guy."

My stomach dipped. Victor. *Here?* I looked around and did a double, then triple take when my eyes landed on Victor. Even though his upper body was facing away from me as he spoke to the people beside him, my heart raced. And when he turned toward me, as if he were looking for me in the crowd, and his eyes met mine, unblinking, I felt the breath whoosh out of me. He stood, and even though it was too dark to see his eyes, I could read the lines of his face and followed suit.

"I'll be back," I said to Chrissy, who was now enthralled in conversation with one of the girls sitting in our table.

Victor turned and started walking in the direction I'd come from, and I followed. I saw Marcus when I got there and told him I would be right back. He saw Victor, looked at me, and nodded.

"I'll be right here," he said as I walked away.

Victor didn't stop walking or go outside like I half expected. He didn't go toward the bathrooms either. Instead, he walked to the right, toward the huge dance floor. My head was pounding with the music, my heart with excitement, trepidation. He stopped walking and stepped off to the side, toward a dark corner where nobody could bump us, and pulled me with him. He leaned back against the side of the bar, his forearm on it so the drink in his hand was dangling.

"What are you doing here?" I asked, stepping forward and speaking up so he could hear me over the music.

His eyes made their way down my body slowly, he licked his lips as they made their way back up and suddenly, despite the vodka in my system, I felt parched. I swallowed and reached out for the drink in his hand, taking a sip of it and making a face at the unexpected bite of alcohol. Victor's lips bloomed into an amused smile. When he extended his arm, I thought it was to take the drink back from me, but instead it went around my body and pulled me close to him so we were almost chest to chest and the heat of his gaze wasn't the only thing warming me.

"Isn't that obvious?" he said, his breath tickling my ear. I shivered and shook my head. His chuckled vibrated into me. "What are you doing here?"

"Dancing," I said, tilting my face slightly so my nose brushed against his light beard.

"So dance," he responded, setting his hands on my hips. I leaned forward, brushing my chest against his arm as I set the drink down behind him, smiling when I felt his grip tighten a little. I started to move my hips side to side, quirking a smile at the way his gaze smoldered on mine.

"Well, I'm not going to stand here and give you a private show," I said, raising an eyebrow. "I charge for those."

His grin was dark and full of mischief as he pushed himself off the bar and began to move with me, his hips in perfect tune with mine. "I'd pay a fuck ton of money to see it."

I smiled, running a hand through my hair to push it away from my face. I tilted my head slightly with the movement, and gasped when his lips came down and sucked me there.

"Did you find what you were looking for?" he asked, his lips making their way up my neck, to my chin, my cheek, my earlobe.

"Did *you*?" I asked breathily, still moving along with him.

He reared back, cupping the side of my face as he gazed down on me with those dark, lust-filled eyes. He nodded.

I stopped breathing.

Stopped moving.

I looked at him, eyes wide. "What?"

"Come home with me," he said, his mouth brushing the edge of mine. "I'm sick of playing games. Come home with me, Nicole."

"Why now?" I asked. I tried to swallow that thought before I vocalized it, but it was no use. I had to know. I had to know he wasn't the one playing games with me.

"Because I want you too fucking much. Because the thought of you coming to this place and hooking up with some other asshole is just too much for me to bear."

I felt myself smile. "So you want to be the asshole that takes me home?"

"More than anything."

More than anything. I didn't dare question him further. There was no point. I could see the resolve in his eyes, and that alone assured me that this was happening. I could've just brought up the reasons he'd been turning this idea down, but I wanted it more than anything, so instead, I went for light.

"No bathroom sex?" I asked, gazing up at him. His smile was slow, wide, and sensual as he shook his head as he brought his face close to mine again.

"Fuck. No. Definitely no bathroom sex, unless it's one of our bathrooms," he said, his mouth near my neck. He dropped a kiss there. "People change."

All I could do was nod and turn around, ready to bolt out the door, but suddenly his arms were around me body, pulling me back to him, and I gasped at the feel of his hard body pressed up against mine. God. It'd been so long.

"Do you remember where I live? Have Marcus drop you off there," he said into my ear before nipping the tip of my earlobe. I rocked against him. "We need to be careful until everything is finalized."

I nodded and stumbled a bit when I felt his mouth on my neck again. *What I would do for him to just fuck me right there on that dance floor. In that stairwell. In the club bathroom.* I was past the point of caring. He let go of me and walked at a normal distance once we reached the top of the stairs and into the VIP section. I introduced him to Chrissy, formally. They already knew each other from the first club experience Victor and I had, and then from the whole *the guy I fucked in the bathroom on my birthday works for my father! What are the chances?* fiasco.

"I saw you on TV when you represented Harlow Winters in her divorce. You look hotter in person," she said. Victor gave her a *tell me something I don't know* smile.

"Let me go tell Bobby I'm leaving," he said after I told Chrissy I was leaving. At the mention of my Bobby's name, I paused. Victor shot me a confused look, so I pulled down on the sleeve of his suit jacket so he could lower his head.

"Isn't it going to look weird if we both say bye to him and leave together?"

He straightened and looked at me for a long moment. I could practically hear the wheels in his head turning, trying to think of a solution. Finally, he nodded in agreement. I walked back to where Marcus was instead, and left while Victor went back to his table. When we opened the back door to go outside, the paparazzi snapped pictures, probably hoping to catch their newest juicy story, but stopped quickly when they saw it was only me, though they did ask their usual questions. *What are you doing now that Gabriel is filming in Canada? Do you miss him? Will you visit him on set?*

I let out a relieved breath once I got into the passenger seat.

"They are so fucking annoying," I huffed when Marcus got into the driver seat.

"Where to now?" he asked. I hated when he ignored my remarks. *Didn't he understand that I wanted to rant?*

I pulled up Victor's address from the text message Estelle had sent me the day he was sick and instructed Marcus to drive me there.

"Drop you off?" he asked when I said that.

"Yes." I leaned back into my seat as I sent a quick reply telling Victor I'd be there. "I'll get a ride home."

Marcus looked at me for a beat. I didn't acknowledge it, but I felt his stare on the side of my face before he sighed and started driving. I kept quiet the entire time. My hands on my lap shaking slightly. My nerves making it difficult to breathe calmly. I'd done this before. I'd done it often, but I couldn't escape the fact that I'd never completely planned for it. The ride was long enough for me to have no choice but to think about the decision I'd made. I wondered if he'd purposely sent me there in a different car for that reason, to see if I chickened out and decided I couldn't follow through with it. I took a breath and let it out slowly when the car slowed into a stop as we reached the quaint two-story beach house that I'd fallen in love with the day I came to visit.

"I'll wait here," Marcus said when he put the gear in park behind Victor's Jaguar.

I swallowed. I could have him wait there. It would be the perfect scapegoat. But I didn't want a scapegoat. I didn't want a way to leave. If he wanted me to stay, I'd stay, and if he pissed me off, I'd Uber home. I took a deep breath.

"No. Just go home. I'll call you when I need you to come pick me up." I put my hand on the door handle and looked at him. I could tell he was still having a difficult time with the idea of just dropping me off. "I know I don't have to say this because you signed non-disclosures, but—"

He put a hand up, and I stopped talking. He didn't say anything, but his clear-blue eyes were sharp and serious, and I knew I was understood. I got out of the car, made my way up the gravel driveway and the few steps to the door. My hand went up in a fist to knock, but the door opened before I could. Victor didn't peek out, he just opened it wide enough for me to step in and closed it right behind me. The house was dark, only the glow of the kitchen light seeping through.

"Hi," I whispered, suddenly feeling shy as I tilted my face to his.

"Hi," he whispered back, grasping my wrist with one hand and pulling me a little closer, until his minty breath was over my face, and bringing his other hand up to the side of my face in a slow caress.

"I don't know if I already told you this, but I really love your house," I said.

I could barely make out his smile, but I knew it was there. In this kind of lighting I could barely make out his face, but I knew his features so well it didn't matter. If I went blind in that instance, I could perfectly describe him for a sketch.

"Wait until you see my bed," he said, his voice still quiet as if he were afraid to burst the bubble we were in. I smiled.

"Were you followed?" he asked, bringing his lips down to my jaw. "I don't want the media assuming things about you." His mouth worked its way up to my ear and back down slowly. I sighed against him.

"You mean about us," I said. He pulled back slightly, his hand still on the side of my face, the other making its way down to my ass.

"I wish I cared about that. I should, but I want this to happen too much to let that stop me," he said squeezing my ass. "I don't know if you were serious about finding another man to satisfy your needs, or just saying it to push me over the edge, but fuck that idea, Nicole. Fuck that idea. I need you. I want you, and I always get what I want."

"So spoiled," I whispered, leaning into him and tipping my face a little more until our lips brushed against each other's.

"Hard working," he replied as his hand slid to the back of my neck and his lips molded against mine.

They were soft and tentative, tasting, his teeth teasing as he tugged on my bottom lip, his hands making their way down my body and inching my dress up slowly. So slowly. I started undoing the buttons of his dress shirt quickly, and he chuckled against me, the sound vibrating through me and making me shiver.

"We're not rushing this, Nicole," he said, a whisper against my lips. I felt like I was on fire, burning for him, desperate for anything he'd give me, my breath fast and erratic.

"A quickie is fine by me," I said when he successfully pulled the dress over my head. His gaze alone made me feel like I was off balance. The way he looked my body up and down, slowly, as if savoring me. He shook his head.

"No quickie."

I reached for his shirt again, tugging it open and planting my palms on his hard chest, making my way to his shoulders and down his sculpted arms, taking the shirt off with my touch. My heart was beating wildly as I studied the sight in front of me, his lean frame, the six-pack I had no idea he had beneath his work clothes. I swallowed thickly as my gaze made its way back up to his eyes. The fire in them made my stomach flip. He took his shoes off, kicking them off to the side before stripping out of his socks, then he pulled me back to him and took my mouth in his again, his hands groping my ass, my waist, my breasts. His hands went around and unclasped my bra, tugging it down quickly and throwing it to the side. His hands cradled my face as he gazed down at me and my heart began to thunder inside my chest. He opened his mouth like he was about to say something, but didn't, instead lowering his mouth to mine once more.

He walked backward, bringing me with him as he held me by the waist, his mouth all over me—my mouth, my neck, my shoulder, my collarbone. I held on to his strong forearms so I wouldn't trip over my feet or his. He pushed a door open and I gripped on to him when I opened my eyes and realized I was standing inside Victor's bedroom. The young version of me did a backflip. Never in a million years did I ever think my life would take me there, to his intimate lair. And never in a million years would I have thought it would be so normal, so cozy, unintimidating. It was a very manly room, from what I could see—large bed, dark sheets, dark décor. He pulled me toward the bed and pushed me down so I landed on my back, the plush mattress catching me and springing me up slightly.

I laughed as I looked up at him, towering over me, looking all serious wearing only his slacks.

"You look like you're about to punish me," I said.

"Be careful what you wish for."

His gaze made its way down my body as he said the words, licking his lips in the process. I shivered against the soft sheets beneath me. He came closer, putting a knee between my legs to push my legs farther apart. In only a black silk thong and matching pumps, I was exposed. I would have felt shy, had it not been for the way he looked at me, like I was the most incredible thing he'd ever seen. I opened my legs farther as he stood up straight and started working on taking off his belt. As he unbuttoned his pants, I fondled my breasts, and he groaned at the sight. My hands trailed over my stomach. I laid them flat against my abdomen, tucking them into my panties.

"Fuck. Yes, Nicole," he said, his voice raw as he stripped out of his pants, taking his boxer briefs with them. My heart stopped for a second as I looked at his erection and just how ready he was for me. His hand closed over it as he pumped and watched me. I moaned, slipping my fingers along my folds, remembering what he felt like inside me.

"You look so fucking beautiful right now," he said. "I wish you could see yourself."

"You look so fucking beautiful right now," I said, biting my lip to stifle another moan. "I wish you would touch me instead of yourself."

His jaw clenched as he stepped toward me. It was as if his self-control snapped in that instance.

His hands gripped my panties and pulled, the thong biting into my ass as he ripped them off me.

He brought his face down to my chest, making his way to one of my nipples and licking, biting, tugging before sucking the entire thing into his mouth. My hands flew to his hair and pulled.

"Holy shit," I said, feeling the sensation everywhere. "Victor."

"Yes," he said against my other nipple. "Keep saying my name. Tell me how much you want this."

"I want this so much," I said, a gasp when he made his way down my stomach, licking, biting, dragging his teeth all the way to my clit and sucking it into his mouth. "Oh my God." He licked the seam, up and down, not leaving any bit of it untouched by his tongue, before focusing on my clit again.

"Tell me, Nicole," he said, tugging at my lips. "Tell me how much you missed this."

I groaned, my pelvis jumping at how good his mouth felt on me.

"Tell me how much you need this," he continued as he groaned, putting more pressure on that spot. I felt my eyes rolling to the back of my head, my toes curling, a burn gradually moving from the tips of my toes to the top of my head as an orgasm began to wash over me. He kept licking me, sucking me, even after I screamed out his name. I shook my head, pulling at his head.

"I can't," I said in a whimper. He kissed the inside of my thighs and re-placed his mouth with his fingers as he made his way up my body, his eyes right in front of mine. "Victor," I cried out again when he pushed his fingers inside me. He didn't do it slowly. He didn't let my body acclimate to anything.

He wanted me to feel it.

And I did.

Everywhere.

"I am going to fuck you so hard," he said, lowering his face to suck on the side of my neck.

"I thought you said no quick—" I said, gasping loudly when his fingers began to move against my clit and inside me all at once.

"Does this feel like a quickie?" he asked as the tips of his fingers stroked my clit, bringing another orgasm out of me. I cried out again and again.

"No," I said, my voice barely containing the shrill behind it. He took his fingers out and licked them one by one as he looked down at me. My head was still clouded with what had just happened, but the sight of him licking his fingers, and knowing it was me he was tasting—*savoring*—with a look of ecstasy on his face that made my core tighten more than it already was. Victor didn't let me take breaks. He didn't give me time to sit up and try to please him. Instead, he propped a hand on either side of my head and pushed himself inside me. I screamed, my back arching off the bed. He was so big. I felt so. Fucking. Full.

He paused his movements. I shot him a confused look.

"You okay?" he asked. I nodded wildly.

"More than okay."

"You sure? You look like you stopped breathing there for a while."

"I don't need to breathe. I just need you to fuck me."

"Yeah?" he asked, his mouth coming down to my ear. "How would you like to be fucked? You want me to go slow?" He pushed in and pulled out slowly. So. Slowly. In and out. In and out.

"Fuck," I said. "Fuck." It was the only thing I could make out. It was the only word I could even think.

"You like this?" he asked, his hips moving in and out in a slow, long tempo that had me searching for my next breath.

"Fast." I gasped. "Hard."

He groaned, pulling out of me completely, and flipped me over. "Get on your knees." I did, and shrieked when he slapped my ass hard. "You like that?" he asked, his voice raw. "You like it when I slap your ass like that?"

I whimpered. It's not that I hadn't had someone slap my ass before, but the way he did it, the things he said while he did it? I felt like I was going to come right there. I pushed my hips back, wordlessly begging him to fuck me. He grabbed my hips and pounded into me. I shrieked again. This time, he didn't go slow. He fucked me hard, pumping inside me hard, reaching for my hair and tying it to his hand as he pulled me up. The bite of it felt good. Everything felt so good. I couldn't even remember what my sex life had been like before that instance. I couldn't remember how another man felt inside me.

"I'm going to make you come again. And again. And again," he said as he pulled my hair harder, until my ear was by his mouth. "You're never going to be able to forget who makes you feel like this."

"Oh God," I said, feeling myself tighten around him, feeling the familiar burn of another orgasm forming. "I'm going to come, Victor."

"You're fucking mine, Nicole," he said, thrusting harder.

I groaned, nodding as I tightened around him. "Yes."

"Say it."

"My . . ." I gasped when he slapped my ass again. Hard.

"Say. It," he said through his teeth, slapping my other ass cheek. "Your ass is mine. Your pussy is mine. Your tits are mine. Fucking say it."

I did, though my voice was hoarse and my words were quiet. I couldn't remember him pulling out, or the way he pulled my back to his chest once he came back from throwing the condom away. I couldn't remember how we fell asleep or what he said to me, but I remembered those words, because I felt him inside me when I woke up before the sun came up and called Marcus to pick me up.

Chapter Twenty-One

Nicole

Marcus's silence on the ride home made me uneasy. I could only imagine what a straight-laced guy like him was thinking, and I wasn't sure I wanted to know, but of course I asked.

"You think I'm a slut," I said finally, unable to stand the discomfort any longer.

He didn't respond, not even when I looked over at him and caught him glancing at me quickly.

"You think I'm a slut because I didn't even wait to finalize my divorce before hooking up with another man."

At that, I saw the corner of his mouth tilt. "I don't think that."

"Why are you so quiet then?"

"I'm always quiet, ma'am."

"No, you're not, and you never call me ma'am."

"Okay. Miss Alessi."

I glared at him. He didn't acknowledge me. "Just Nicole, please, unless you've decided to go back to being all proper because you think I'm a slut." Again, no answer. Finally, as we were getting close to my house, he sighed.

"What you do is your business. I don't think anything less of you."

"So you're not mad that I called you before the sun came up?"

He laughed. "That's my job."

"Okay." I nodded. "Thank you, and thank you for not judging."

"That's also my job."

I shook my head and smiled as I climbed out of the car. I practically stumbled into my house. My legs were tired, my thighs were burning, my vagina felt like it had been pounded . . . which, it had been, but I hadn't expected to feel it as much as I did. I hadn't done the walk of shame in a long time, and I felt a little excited, like I was back in the game. Along with giving me the best sex of my freaking life, Victor had also made me feel desired. I hadn't felt that way in so long, I'd forgotten the power it held. I stripped off my clothes, showered, and slept like the dead. The only reason I woke was because of Bonnie's whimpers.

"I know. I know," I said as I got out of bed and wiped my face. Back to the bathroom I went to brush my teeth and make myself semi-presentable for my new neighbors before I went outside with Bonnie.

I was holding on to her leash with my eyes closed, face tilted to the sun, when a shadow suddenly set over my face. My heart jumped as I sat upright.

"You scared me," I said. Victor's face was serious as he looked at me. He turned his face toward Bonnie, who was now trotting toward him. Without saying a word to me, he crouched down and started to pet her. He took her nametag in his fingers and smiled.

"You left," he said, still looking at my dog. "I wanted to take you to breakfast."

"I left because I didn't think it would be smart for me to be there and do the walk of shame in front of photographers."

He appraised me for a moment. I wondered if he was thinking about what we'd done last night. My stomach clenched at the memory: his mouth on mine, his head between my thighs, thrusting his dick inside me like he was afraid it would never happen again. I felt a blush creep over my face and had to look away.

"That is smart," he said, finally.

"I thought you'd appreciate it."

He opened his mouth to say something, and closed it again.

"I had a good time last night," I said.

Understatement of the century. I wanted to tell him that it was a night so memorable, I'd be sure to have fantasies about it continuously. I wanted to tell him how much my ass hurt when I sat down and how I kept smiling at the recollection of why. I wanted to ask him what his possessive chants meant. *You're mine.* Was that just something he said during sex or was it something he said during sex with *me*? The thought made a flush creep into my face. I ducked my face to hide it.

"I wasn't sure you did," he said, "with you leaving before I woke up and everything."

"Was that a first for you?" I asked, smiling at his handsome, serious face.

He smiled slightly.

"You could say that."

"How are we supposed to go to breakfast without it looking like something is going on?"

He was dressed in jeans and a button-up shirt, looking hot as fuck, especially now that I knew what was beneath his clothes. Despite the burn in my inner thighs, I wanted to strip him and climb him again.

He looked thoughtful for a moment and sighed, running a hand through his hair. "You're right."

"I'm beginning to sense a theme here," I said, smirking. "Me leaving, me being right . . ." His scowl encouraged me to continue. "You know what's funny? The world seems to think that women are the chasers after a one-night stand. That we go along with it and then are all broken-hearted when the guy doesn't call, because God forbid we use what's between our legs to have fun the way guys do." I paused to smile. His ears were red, which made me smile harder. "So I think it's funny that you, Mr. *I Have Work to Do* came over here to chase me down."

He was quiet for a beat before reaching down to pick up Bonnie and going inside my house. I followed, confused, but still feeling like I had the upper hand, until I shut the door and curtain and turned around to find Victor taking long strides toward me. I took a step back, my heart rate spiking at the sight of his narrowed eyes on mine, his head slightly tilted as he appraised me. When he reached me and placed both arms on either side of me, caging me in, I swallowed as I looked up at him.

"Like I said, people change. Besides, that's how it works in nature," he said, his eyes on mine. "Most of the time, males chase until the woman is forced to cave."

"And that's what you're trying to do? Force me to cave?" I asked in a whisper.

"I'll do whatever it takes if it makes you cave to this," he said, lowering his voice.

"You're not afraid of the consequences anymore?" I asked.

"I am." He paused, his eyes searching mine. "I think you might be worth it, though."

Even if my galloping heart would have let me speak, I had no response for that. This careful man who cared about his job more than anything else had taken a chance and chased me down, and it thrilled me.

"Come to breakfast with me," he said. "I'll leave through the back. We'll take separate cars, but come."

I nodded, in awe of what was happening, and when he lowered his face and brushed his lips against mine, I reached out and pulled him closer into me, taking his mouth in mine, and kissing him deeply. He groaned against my lips before pulling away.

"I'll text you the address."

"Okay," I whispered.

I fed Bonnie before I walked to my car. On my way there, I sidestepped a jogger, almost losing balance because I was looking down at my phone screen.

"Nicole," he said. My head snapped up from my phone, where I was typing a response to Victor, letting him know I was on my way.

"Hey," I said, smiling at the hot jogger I'd met the other day. I couldn't for the life of me remember his name. It must have been apparent from the face I made because he chuckled and said.

"Brent."

I smiled. "Brent. Sorry. How are you?"

"Better now," he said, eyes glimmering as he gave me a once-over. "I'm assuming you're not headed to the beach."

"Not today. I still haven't been able to enjoy the perks of living here." I sighed. "I work all day tomorrow, so that's not looking promising either."

"On a Sunday? Tough job."

"You can say that." I looked up and down the sidewalk. "It was nice seeing you again."

"Maybe Monday?" he said. I looked at him with a frown. "The beach?"

"Oh." I thought about it. "Maybe."

He smiled. "I'm going on my run at noon. It's the perfect time to catch rays."

"Maybe I'll see you then," I said with a smile.

I watched him jog away. He was really freaking hot. Twelve months of zero interaction by any straight male and suddenly I had their attention. Unfortunately for the rest of them, my heart was set on one. I shook my head and sighed as I walked toward my car.

Chapter Twenty-Two

Victor

I got to my parents' house earlier than usual and dropped the bomb about Nicole coming over. My dad didn't say anything, only raised his eyebrows. My mom, on the other hand, gasped and covered her mouth as if I was announcing my engagement.

"She's just a friend, Mom," I said. "A friend who I also happen to be representing in her divorce."

"Oh. Dammit, Victor. I thought you were bringing a girlfriend," she said, sighing. "Maybe she has friends."

"Please don't talk about my love life, Mom."

"What love life?" she asked. "You have no love life. Even your friends are somehow involved in your work."

I groaned. I really wished I could just be straight and tell her how I felt about Nicole, but *I* didn't even know how I felt about Nicole. I felt this overwhelming sense of needing to see her again after last night. So overwhelming that I panicked when I realized she'd left. Panicked and chased her down. I had to. And then she'd tried to treat it like a one-night stand, as if I would jeopardize my job for a fucking one-night stand. I wanted to tell her to pack a bag and go away with me, but she'd mentioned that she had to work Sunday, so I knew she wouldn't do it. Restaurants were out of the question because they were so public and I really wanted to touch her. I wanted to talk to her and look at her openly.

My phone rang in my pocket, pulling me out of my thoughts. I looked at it and frowned at Quinn's name. Quinn was the founder of one of the biggest gossip blogs in the world, so big they'd turned it into a television series. He only called me on a weekend when something important was going on.

"What's up, Q?" I asked upon answering.

"Dude. I was going to call last night, but then I got busy. How's every-thing?"

"Everything was good until I saw your name on my phone screen."

He laughed. "Yeah. Well. Yeah."

I raised an eyebrow. My parents were watching me, so I put a hand up and excused myself, walking outside. "What's up?"

"Somebody has been contacting one of my photographers and having him follow Nicole Lane."

"Alessi. She never changed her name," I said, my blood simmering at the mention of her name. "We knew she was being watched."

"Hmm."

"What?"

"I'm going to text message you some pictures right now. Look at them while we're on the phone."

At the sound of the vibrate, I pulled my phone down and looked at the text. It was a picture of Nicole and me on her balcony. I recognized it as the day she was inspecting it. In the photo we were standing very close to each other, looking into each other's eyes. To an outsider it looked like we were about to kiss. The next picture was more of the same. Close. Almost kissing. My heart hammered. The way she was looking at me in those pictures was so fucking intimate. From the look in her eyes . . . from the look in *my* eyes, there was more than just lust going on there. We looked like we were . . . *holy shit*. I couldn't even bring myself to admit that, even though for the first time in a long time I wanted to explore the possibility. Under different circum-stances, I would have. *Could have.*

"Your photographer took this?" I demanded.

"That's the thing, Vic, he didn't take these. These were brought to me. The ones he's taken of her have been just her doing everyday things."

"Who brought these to you? What did they say?"

"You know I can't give you my source. I'm showing these to you because you're my friend and I'm not going to put them out there, but I can't promise you that other blogs will extend the same courtesy."

Fuck. I sighed and closed my eyes. We were just talking. Just talking, but I knew they could potentially turn it into something more.

"I have more coming in tomorrow morning. I'll call you if I feel like it's anything you need to see."

"Call me if it's anything with her at all."

"Will do."

"Thanks, Q."

"Of course."

As we hung up, my parents' gate opened. I watched Oliver's black Cadillac pull up and Nicole's white Prius follow behind him. I felt a pang in my heart at the sight of her. She was so beautiful. I thought about the images on my phone. I remembered the very moment they were taken. I remembered my desperation and how badly I'd wanted to kiss her, touch her, hold her, fuck her. Make her mine. I'd gotten just a taste that day. Just a hint of what her lips felt like against mine. Our fate was set that day. Maybe even before then. Maybe it'd been set the day she stepped into that goddamn conference room wearing that tight-fitting dress and looking at me with her *fuck me* eyes. Whatever the case was, I would take care of this. I wouldn't tell her about the pictures. Not yet. Not until I had more information. The last thing I needed was a worried Nicole.

"Hey Chicken," I said as my sister walked over to me. She rolled her eyes and gave me a hug.

"Hey Vic. I see you invited Nicole."

"She can't go out to breakfast without being hounded. It was the least I could do," I said. Estelle shot me a look that said she didn't buy my story. I shrugged.

"Who's the girl?" Oliver asked as he greeted me.

"Nicole."

"The one married to that guy?"

"The one who *was* married to that guy," I said, at the same time as Nicole walked up and smiled at my words. She looked so fucking good in that long black dress she wore. I wanted to peel it off her and discover what she had underneath.

"Oliver," he said, offering his hand for her to shake. I wanted to kick his ass when he smiled at her like he was trying to flirt with her. "I hear I owe you a thank you for helping my wife and brother-in-law install my TV."

Nicole laughed. "Victor did most of the work. I just sat back and watched him *mount* it and drank the wine Estelle offered."

My heart hopped when she looked over at me with that flirty gleam in her eyes as she said it. Fuck. This girl did things to me. She did things to me and I realized something.

The woman I would have to let go of if I wanted to keep my career was the same woman I didn't want to live without.

How's that for life issues? I was half tempted to write a letter to Jensen Talks and see what my friend had to say about this fucked-up situation in the newspaper column he wrote. Oliver went inside and Estelle followed after she exchanged a tight hug with Nicole.

"Where did you bring me?" she asked, looking at the house.

"My parents' house."

From the look of sheer panic that crossed her face, I thought for a second time that maybe bringing her here was a bad idea. It was a good idea before I'd gotten that call, but now I knew what was to happen, I felt every part of me breaking down slowly, like a car running out of gas. I hated that feeling, and when Nicole's smile dropped and she frowned, I felt it punch me in the gut.

"You really need to come with a warning label," she said as she stepped in front of me. "A serious warning label. Are you regretting your decision? I can still leave." She brought her hand up to me face. She was so fucking sweet, thinking of my feelings before her own. Comforting me even though she had no clue what I was thinking. I closed my eyes and leaned into her touch; it was so soft, warm and inviting. I never wanted to leave. I never wanted to let go of this moment. I cleared my throat and straightened. What the fuck was going on with me?

"I'm fine," I said with a smile. "Come meet the people responsible for making the hottest man you've ever laid eyes on."

Nicole laughed beside me. "Oh my God."

I shrugged. Before I could say anything else, my mother walked toward us with a huge smile on her face, light eyes trained on Nicole.

"Hi. I'm Hannah, Victor's mom. It's so nice to meet you, Nicole," she said, walking up to her and giving her a hug. Nicole smiled, a little blush on her cheeks when she pulled back. She gave me an embarrassed glance that I'd never seen and wish I could record and watch forever.

"It's nice to meet you. Thank you for having me over," she said.

"Of course. Make yourself at home. Thomas. We have a guest," my mom shouted, taking Nicole by the hand and dragging her forward.

"Mom, she's not going to run away, you know," I said.

My mom looked over her shoulder and shot me a pointed look, mouthing the words "shut up." I couldn't help the laugh that escaped me. I mouthed the word "client" as a reminder, and she shrugged. I walked behind them and into the kitchen, where my dad also greeted Nicole with a hug.

"Where are you from?" he asked.

"Argentina," she said, smiling.

"Argentina. Beautiful place. Hannah and I have been there a couple of times. Great people. I'm Puerto Rican, and when I lived back home I made some connections in Argentina," he said as way of explanation.

"Oh, that's so cool. What do you do?" Nicole asked.

"I'm an orthodontist. It was cooler before I decided to slow down and stop traveling." He laughed when my mom nudged him in the ribs. "But of course that means I get to spend more time with my lovely wife," he said, pulling my mom into a side hug.

"You guys are gross," Estelle said. "Also, I set the table."

"Let's eat," my mom said.

We sat around the table, Oliver and Estelle on one side, me in my usual seat across from them, and Nicole in the normally empty seat beside me, while my dad sat at the head and my mom at the other end.

"I hope you eat carbs," my mom said, bringing out the first dish: waffles. Estelle stood and went to help her.

"I eat everything. Do you need help?" Nicole replied.

"No, no. Stay right there. I don't want Victor to have an early heart attack because we made one of his girl . . . friends work the first day he brought her over," my mom said.

I tucked my hand under the table and reached for Nicole's hand over her lap. She jumped at the notion, and I ran my thumb over her soft hand. I wanted to pull her close and kiss the hell out of her. Our fingers threaded around each other as if on autopilot, as if we held hands every day. It felt . . . right. It reminded me of what I had told Corinne about why I had never settled down. I couldn't deny that the ease I felt with Nicole by my side, with my family, *felt* right.

"What time do you have to be at work tomorrow?" I asked.

"Eight in the morning. It's supposed to be a twelve-hour day," she said. I leaned closer to her.

"Would you mind leaving your car here today and picking it up tomorrow after work?" I whispered in her ear. Her eyes widened as I backed away. She shook her head, then leaned in and whispered in mine.

"I don't have extra clothes, though."

"Neither do I. We can stop somewhere along the way."

She smiled, a big, happy smile. "Okay."

Breakfast was great. Oliver talked about the kids at work. I tried not to talk about work at all, which brought on a conversation about what a work-aholic I was. Nicole talked about her job, which had Estelle and my mom enraptured. My mom practically begged her to design a dress for a friend's daughter's wedding.

"She's been looking everywhere for somebody. Don't you think this is the perfect solution?" she asked when I told her to please stop.

"That's not what Nicole does," I said defensively.

"I can," Nicole said. I looked at her, trying to read her and make sure that she was okay with it. She didn't know how annoying my mom could get about things she wanted to get done.

"She can be difficult to work with," I said, squeezing her hand a little. "You have a lot on your plate."

"I can handle everything on my plate."

That smile accompanying the words with made me want to *be* every-thing on that goddamn plate. Once we were done eating, my mom, Nicole, and Estelle went off to the office room to talk about the dress, and my dad, Oliver, and I went to the living room to watch college football.

"Are we on for tomorrow?" Oliver asked every weekend and every weekend for over ten years I'd always responded a solid yes. This time, I hesi-tated. Sure, I'd have Nicole back in time for work, but I also had to meet with Quinn, and that was a priority to me.

"I'll have to let you know in the morning," I said. Oliver balked.

"You're . . . kidding."

"I have work to do tomorrow."

His eyes widened. He looked around, at my dad, who was dozing off on the recliner, the television, as if Lee Corso had the answers to whatever ques-tion he had, and finally he looked at me again, jaw still dropped.

"I've known you most of me life, Vic. We've been through some real shit together," he said, pausing. "And I . . ." he sighed, shaking his head, "I'm not going to say anything. I'm not going to get involved. I just hope you're thinking this through."

"Nothing is going on," I said. He shot me a *don't give me that shit* look.

"Tell that to someone who doesn't know you. Actually, forget it. Even a goddamn blind man can see that something is definitely going on. You better be fucking careful."

I groaned, but didn't respond. I knew he was right.

"Like I said, be careful."

I *was* being careful. I was about to take the girl to Newport Beach so that we could be together without worrying about getting caught. How was that for careful? Though the more I thought about it the less I knew if I was being careful or just needy for wanting her this badly. But I wasn't a needy guy. Just careful. I wasn't an idiot. I knew I couldn't have both. I knew that if those pictures got out, I would have to let her go until she was no longer my client. We would be fine. We'd done it once before. *But she moved on that time.*

Thinking that made me feel sick.

She'd moved on and got married.

I'd told her she was mine—pounded that into her—as if that alone could keep her around.

From every which angle I thought about it, *I was fucked*.

Chapter Twenty-Three

Nicole

"Your parents are the sweetest people ever," I said, smiling as I waved to his mom while getting into the passenger seat of his car. "I don't know how they ended up with a grouch like you."

I inhaled, like I usually did when I was in his car. It had a new-car smell. How? I didn't know. Mine lost that smell after two weeks. Probably because I ate so many In-N-Out burgers in it. Victor didn't say anything, instead he reached for my hand and threaded his fingers through mine. My heart skipped a beat every time he did that. Every time he touched me. Every time he freaking looked at me. I felt like a ridiculous junior in high school who had a crush on the star quarterback. I just couldn't get enough of him.

Victor chuckled. "They really like you."

"I really like them."

"*I* really like you."

My heart summersaulted into my stomach and back up. Oh my God. I was going to die via sweet nothings from Victor Reuben. I really was, and damn what a beautiful death it would be.

"I like you too," I whispered. I felt my cheeks burn as I smiled and looked over at him. We were stopped at a red light that changed to green and he was just looking at me without a care in the world. He leaned in as if to kiss me and I said, "The light is green. People are honk—"

"Fuck them. Let them honk," he said, his lips grazing mine.

I forgot how to breathe, let alone how to complain. I grabbed his face and kissed him back amidst the honking behind us. He pulled back slightly, gaze tender on mine, as if he were seeing me for the first time. As if he were just now realizing his words about liking me were actually true. I smiled softly, and he mimicked it as he pulled back. Somebody else honked and Victor stuck his middle finger up.

"Idiot."

I slapped my palm on my forehead and lowered myself into the seat. "Victor."

"What? People act like they can't wait three seconds. Like they have somewhere important to be on a Saturday afternoon."

I laughed. "Maybe it's a doctor."

"Well, they should've left their house ten minutes early so they wouldn't have to deal with assholes like me."

"Oh my God. You are so fucking crazy."

Without looking away from the road he lifted my hand and brought it up to his mouth. "And you love it," he said, kissing my palm lightly before nipping it with his teeth.

I yanked it away. I really did love it, but I would never in a million years tell him that. "So, where are we going to stop to buy clothes? Target?"

"I was going to take you to Nordstrom, but if Target is good with you, let's go there."

I laughed. "Well, I'm not going to pass up Nordstrom."

"Nah, Target was your first choice."

I poked him in the ribs and he laughed, taking his hand off the gear to catch my hand and bite the tips my fingers until I yelped. He let go and shot me a look, raising a brow in challenge. I smiled and looked out the window. He turned the radio up a little and started bobbing his head to the Bryson Tiller song playing.

"I like you like this," I said after a while. He lowered the music a little.

"How?"

I shrugged. "Not cautious."

He looked over at me quickly, tilting his head a bit before looking back at the road ahead. He didn't acknowledge my statement, instead turning up the radio again and singing along. We talked and sang and scrolled through different songs on the playlist he had set up in the memory of his car. I made fun of him for having Justin Beiber on there, and he assured me that it was Estelle's doing.

"Liar," I scoffed.

He shrugged. "Maybe I like some of his new songs."

"I knew it," I said and paused as I continued scrolling. "You know, for a half Puerto Rican guy who doesn't speak Spanish, you listen to a lot of Hispanic artists."

He chuckled. "I never said I didn't speak Spanish."

"Do you?"

"Un poquito."

I smiled wide. "My mom will be pleased to hear that."

"How often do you visit her?"

"Not as often as I would like," I said, sighing. I put my hand over his on the gearshift. "I'll probably go over there in a month when we're done filming this movie."

He gave me a sharp nod, opening his fingers to hold on to mine. "I would offer to go with you, but your Spanish is completely different than mine, and I probably wouldn't understand anything you guys are saying."

I laughed. "I'll teach you."

"I'll hold you to that."

I felt my heart expand. Was he serious? Gabe never cared about any of that, though he did go with me to see my mom a couple times when we first got married. I smiled at the memory of him eating a ridiculous amount of steak and getting a stomach ache for the rest of the trip. He was so funny then. So willing to please me. I sighed, looking out the window again. There was construction in the canyon we were near and I was grateful we were driving along it during the day. I always had a fear of driving so close to the edges of the canyons, despite the barricades that were supposed to keep the car from actually falling into it.

Victor pulled into the parking lot of Target a few minutes later. I couldn't even imagine this Armani-suit-wearing man's man at Target, and I couldn't wait to experience it with him.

"Let's get what we need first, like body wash," he suggested, steering the cart to the right.

"Okay. Should we get snacks?" I asked, eyeing the chips on the way over.

"Are you planning on kidnapping me for more than a day?" he asked, looking over at me. I shook my head, smiling. *I totally should, though.*

"Then no snacks needed. We'll go to dinner at the hotel."

The hotel. Oh my God. I was going to stay at a hotel with this man. I had to bite down on the inside of my cheek to contain my giddiness. Much to Victor's amusement, I sent Talon a text message and asked her if she could watch Bonnie. *That's why I don't have pets,* he'd said. *I don't have time for more stress.* Shopping with Victor was worse than shopping with Talon or Chrissy. The guy took forever to decide what shorts he should buy: cargo or not. Then, button-up or polo. Then, socks for the shoes he had on or flip-flops? And all the while, he was acting weird, looking around, keeping his distance from where I was standing, not looking me in the eye. Somewhere between the men's underwear and the pajamas, I got sick of it.

"Why are you acting so weird?" I asked, pivoting to face him with my hands on my hips.

"What do you mean?" he asked, picking up the bottom of the oversized Batman footie pajamas in front of him. Still avoiding my eyes. "Who the hell buys this?"

"Victor."

"Really, though, who over the age of twelve months wear this?" he said, ignoring me.

"Victor," I said, raising my voice. I felt my face burning with anger. "Stop looking at the ridiculous pajamas and look at me right now."

He whipped his head to look at me, letting his hands drop to his sides. Now that I had his full attention, his eyes on mine like that, I lost my train of thought.

"What?"

"Why are you acting distant?" I asked, lowering my voice and stepping closer to him.

He let out a heavy sigh and stepped even closer, until we were toe to toe and reached his hand out to take mine.

"My mind is just . . . occupied."

"Occupied," I repeated, taking his hand and wrapping it around my body so he was holding me against his chest. He dropped his face into my hair and inhaled deeply.

"Occupied," he murmured against my ear.

"We're far enough from home that we can act like we know each other, Vic."

"I know, baby. I know," he said, dropping a kiss on my temple, and another on my cheek. "For the rest of the weekend, you're the only thing occupying my mind, okay?"

I pulled back to look at him. "Only this weekend?"

He looked at me for a beat. "Oh, Nicole. What am I going to do with you?"

He pressed his lips against my forehead as he dropped his hands and started to walk toward the T-shirts, shaking his head as he did. I smiled when I heard him rambling about how much time I occupy in his mind. He went back to looking at every piece of clothing in the men's section. What shorts should he get? Cargo or not? Khakis or denim?

"Are you kidding me, Victor?" I demanded, finally. I took the cargo shorts, the non-cargo shorts, the polo, the button-up, the socks, and the flip-flops and threw it in the cart. "You act like you can't afford all of it."

He pointed at me. "That's the kind of mentality that makes people Target's bitch."

"Yeah, well, I was put in that category a long time ago. I don't plan on getting out of there any time soon. Besides, Red Card."

He shook his head, but kept walking toward the women's section. I took two seconds while he was on the phone to get what I needed before moving to the underwear. Suddenly Victor told his caller that he "needed to go because he had something important to do." I rolled my eyes as I sorted through the bras.

"This one's nice," he said, holding up a bra a row over. I frowned.

"That's like . . . a D."

He examined it better. "Yeah, you're right. How'd you know?"

I raised my eyebrows and shook my head, going back to my section.

"What about this one?"

"Thank God we're not in Victoria's Secret," I muttered, looking over again. He was holding up a sheer bra. I laughed. "That one's good."

"34 C, baby," he said loudly. I felt my face turn a shade of red as a woman walked by us. She shot me an amused look.

"Excuse him, he doesn't Target much," I said with a smile.

The woman laughed and walked away.

I gasped when Victor came up behind me and wrapped his arms around me. "You're having way too much fun with this," he said into my ear.

"Just a little," I said, smiling. "Did you get my bra, honey?"

"I sure did, baby."

"Let's go," I said, starting to walk. He held me tight in his hold so I couldn't move and kissed my cheek.

"You make me this way," he said. The tone of his voice made my insides rattle. I tilted my head to look up at him.

"Like what?" I whispered.

"Not cautious," he said, snuggling into my neck. "I feel free when I'm with you."

I closed my eyes and leaned into him. It felt so good to be in his arms like that, away from it all, without fear we'd get caught. He pressed his lips against the side of my temple and dropped his hands.

"Let's go. I'm only getting you underwear because you'll need them for work tomorrow. Don't even think about wearing them to bed tonight," he said, slapping my ass as he walked away. I laughed as I followed behind him.

When we got to the front of the line, the cashier tried to talk Victor into signing up for a credit card, and he started rambling about credit lines and stores that want to lock you in and keep you in debt. The woman laughed.

"All right then," she said, shaking her head as she looked at me. "Good luck with this one, hon."

"Oh, no. We're not together," I said, wrinkling my nose. "Too straight-laced for me."

Victor narrowed his eyes at me. I smiled at him and shrugged. The woman laughed again. We left and on our way to the car Victor held the bags in one hand and wrapped his free arm around me body, lifting me off the ground.

"Straight-laced, huh?" he growled. "I'll show you straight-laced."

I laughed the entire way to the car. When he set me down I reached up and kissed him. "I was just kidding."

"Too late."

I smiled. "You should let me drive."

He balked at me, pausing as he put our things in the trunk. "You've completely lost your mind."

"Why not?"

"Because it's my car and nobody drives my car."

I jutted my bottom lip out. "Please?"

His gaze dropped to my lips. "No."

"You really wouldn't let me drive your car?" I asked, putting my hands on my hips.

Victor looked at me for a long, quiet moment. He sighed. "Do you know how to drive stick?"

"I'm very good with a stick," I said with a wink. He wasn't having it.

"I'm serious."

"Yes, Victor," I said, rolling my eyes. "Give me the damn keys. I'll take care of your baby."

He wasn't happy about it, but he handed over the keys. I was sure he regretted it instantly when I jumped up and cheered, doing a little dance as I made my way over to the driver's seat.

"God help me," he said, making the sign of the cross as he sat down in the passenger seat. I laughed.

"He gives a girl his car keys and suddenly he becomes a born-again Christian."

He huffed, looking out the window. "I'm Catholic."

I laughed harder. I started the car and pushed down on the petal, clapping at the sound of the purr before I took off.

"You need to tell me where to go."

"You need to stop talking and focus on driving."

"I can drive and talk at the same time."

"I don't care."

"Why don't you go back to praying? You were much less annoying," I said, but I couldn't help my smile. He was kind of adorable when he was like this.

"Nicole," he groaned, "just . . . please stop talking. You're making me nervous."

I laughed. When I reached a stoplight, I turned the music up. "Is Selena Gomez also on your playlist?"

He sighed. "No, Nicole."

"Straight-laced."

"Wait 'til we get our room," he said. "I'm going to fuck you until you can't talk anymore."

I sighed. "Goals."

He stayed quiet for a beat. "What's up with that?"

"What?"

"Goals. You say that all the time. Why?"

I smiled. Of course Victor didn't know what that was about. "You mean you can't deduce what it may mean?"

"I can deduce it, yes. I just don't know if my deduction is correct."

"Tell me what you think it is."

"I don't know. When you like something or you want to do something, you say goals? Is it like a bucket list of sorts?"

"Yeah, I guess."

"Hmm."

I looked at him from the corner of my eyes. "Do you have any goals?"

He was quiet for a moment. I thought maybe he hadn't heard me over the music, but then he said quietly, "I do have goals." He didn't elaborate, so I didn't push him.

We got to the hotel, checked in, went to dinner, laughed our asses off as

Victor came up with a story for every old man in the restaurant. I'd missed this. Fun. Laughter. Feeling carefree. I realized in the last eighteen months, I'd become a reclusive, introverted side of myself, one I couldn't entirely get used to. With Victor, I slowly felt I was getting myself back. *Finding me.*

"So basically all of their wives married them for money," I said, taking a sip of my Riesling.

He shrugged. "Basically."

"Do you ever want to get married?" I asked.

His eyes snapped to mine, and for a moment I got lost in their intensity, the greens mixing with the browns, and the blue undertones swirling around.

"Maybe . . . probably."

My eyebrows rose. "Really?"

"Yes, really. Why is that so hard to believe?"

"I don't know. I just didn't take you for the married type."

His lips twitched. "You only took me for the random hookups in his office type?"

"I guess so?" I smiled. "At least I didn't assume you'd hooked up with any previous clients."

His eyes dropped to the table, and my stomach went with them.

"Have you?" I asked. I wasn't sure why it bothered me. Suddenly, I felt disgusted. The way I felt when I found out Gabe had potentially cheated on me. My stomach turned at the thought of Victor with another woman, driving her away like this to not get caught. He was quiet for so long, that my mind threatened to run off into the realm of visualization. Victor with some prissy redhead, or skinny blonde, everything I wasn't. His deep chuckle cut through my thoughts.

"No, Nicole. You're my first. And last."

My heart pounded loudly at his admission, at those words and the way he said them. I narrowed my eyes at him despite the way I was feeling.

"Asshole," I said. He laughed harder, and even though I was laughing along and felt a sense of ease at his words, I wondered if he felt the same. I cleared my throat. "Would it bother you if somebody asked me out on a date?"

His laughter stopped instantly. "Why? Who asked you out? That asshole realtor?"

That made me laugh. "No. You know there are more men in the world, right?"

"Who asked you out?"

"Some guy. A neighbor of mine."

"What's his name?"

"Why do you need to know his name?" I asked, frowning. "It's not like you know my neighbors."

"You can tell a lot about a person from their name."

I laughed. "Brent."

He shot me a look. "You're going to go out with a guy named Brent?"

"What's wrong with that?"

"Everything." He stood up and folded his napkin on the table. "Ready?"

By the look in his eyes, the thought of me on a date wasn't sitting well with him. He looked . . . demanding. Intense. *Sexy*. Irresistible. I put my hand in his and stood. He brought it up to his lips and kissed it before pulling me closer and walking toward our room. I expected him to throw me against the door the moment we walked in. Instead, he'd said he was going to shower first because he needed to make a phone call to follow up with a client. I couldn't say I wasn't a little disappointed, but I took it in stride. He'd brought me here to spend time with *him*, away from prying eyes. I'd seen the desire in his eyes. I knew he wanted this as badly as I did, but I also knew work was a priority, and I wasn't going to act like a child over it.

The shower switched on as I was unpacking our things and removing the tags. I tried not to picture him naked on the other side of the door, but it was difficult not to visualize the water dripping down his hard body. I groaned, and when he walked out of the bathroom wearing a white bathrobe, I had to take a calming breath to regain composure.

"I'll only be fifteen minutes," he said, kissing the top of my head. I wanted to tuck my hands inside the robe and climb him like a fucking tree, but I nodded and brushed past him instead, taking my new underwear with me.

When I walked out of the bathroom wearing a white fluffy robe, I found Victor sitting at the edge of the bed with his phone in his hand. As soon as he sensed me come in, his head snapped up. He took in my appearance and pushed a button down on his phone, slinging it to the couch beside him. I untied the robe and parted it to show off my new lingerie.

"You like me in my sexy Target bra?" I asked, placing a hand on my hip and jutting it out as I modeled for him. He nodded, eyes hooded as they raked over my body.

"I like you in any bra. Every bra. But I prefer no bra," he said, voice raspy, eyes darkened with desire. "Strip for me."

My stomach flip flopped at the command in his voice. *Strip. For. Me.* I swallowed and started to lower the shoulders of the robe, letting it drop and pool at my feet. My bra came next; I unclasped it and took it off slowly. Victor spread his legs farther apart. He was wearing his own robe and a devilish grin that made my knees quiver.

"What are you wearing under that?" I asked, tossing my bra aside. His eyes fell to my naked chest.

"Why don't you come find out?"

I walked forward, stopping right between his knees, close enough for him to reach out and grab me, but far enough that he couldn't put his mouth on me without pulling me to him, which was what he did, his arms circling around my waist and tugging me. He placed his mouth on my stomach, kissing me lightly. I felt the effect of his mouth everywhere.

"Are you ready for me, Nicole?" he asked against me, his mouth moving lower, to my belly button, his light beard grazing my panty line. "If I keep going down, will you be wet?"

My breath hitched. I nodded.

He glanced up, his eyes locked on mine. "Tell me."

"Yes."

"Yes what?" he asked, licking along the top of my panties. I repressed the urge to shiver, my hands shooting out to grab his hair.

"Yes. I'm wet," I said in a shaky whisper.

He groaned, letting his forehead fall against my stomach for a beat before hooking his fingers on either side of my panties and sliding them down. He grabbed my thighs and made a groaning sound in the back of this throat.

"I fucking love your legs, Nic," he said, gripping the backs of my legs and biting the front. I cried out. "Do you like that, baby?"

I whimpered out, "Yes."

"You like it when I'm rough with you?" he asked, sliding his fingers between my thighs, gliding along my folds. I pulled his hair tighter and moaned. "Do you want me to go slow?" He tilted his face to look up at me as he leaned in and sucked on my clit. My knees buckled.

"Oh my God, Victor."

He smiled against me. I couldn't see his lips on me, but I could see it in his eyes. "Say it again," he said, licking me. "Say my name, baby."

"Victor," I said, throwing my head back in a moan when he inserted his fingers into me and continued to lick my clit. "Victor." I said his name again, and again in a whispered chant. "I'm going to come."

He groaned deeply, and I felt it vibrate everywhere. "Come for me, baby.

Show me how ready for me you are." His fingers worked faster inside me, his tongue lashing against me until my eyes rolled back and my knees gave out and I was only standing upright because he'd grabbed my hips. He was reaching for the condom beside him when I caught my breath and opened my eyes, and I stopped him, kneeling between his legs and parting his robe to expose his hard, thick cock. My heart skipped a beat at the sight of it. I licked my lips and looked from it to his face.

"Nicole—" he started to say, but I cut his sentence short by licking the tip of his cock and taking him into my mouth. His hand gripped a fistful of my hair as he muttered a string of curse words. "Fucking shit, that feels so fucking good. Oh my fucking God. Your mouth. Your fucking mouth." His words became unintelligible as I continued to suck, bobbing my head up and down, his dick popping in and out of my mouth loudly. His breathing was labored and loud, and I loved the look of awe on his face when my eyes met his momentarily. He pulled my hair hard and successfully popped out of my mouth and leaned down to crash his lips against mine.

"I need to fuck you," he said, reaching for the condom and sliding it on. "I need to feel you."

I nodded and stood, putting one leg over each of his and pushing his chest back so he was lying flat on his back. "I'm going to ride you," I said. "And you're not going to remember any woman you fucked before me."

His lips tilted into a slow, tantalizing smile as he gripped two handfuls of my ass, helping me climb on him and settle myself on the tip. "Show me, baby. Make me scream your name."

Oh, I would. As I placed my hands on his shoulders and lowered myself onto him slowly, I wondered if he realized how sexy those words sounded to me. I held my breath as I let myself acclimate to his girth. I was still sore from yesterday, and I remembered it as I completely sat on his lap. I cringed and gasped.

"You okay?" he asked in a quiet voice, as he sat up again, his hands pushing my hair out of my face. I nodded, though my eyes filled with unshed tears. It was too much suddenly, having his face in front of mine, his heart beating against mine, his eyes trained on mine. In that one instance, where he was looking at me like I was the only woman he'd ever really seen, I felt everything.

Everything.

This was so much more than the last time. So much more than the times before that. And it was terrifying.

"Nic, are you okay?" he asked, his voice a whisper.

I nodded, blinking rapidly. "I'm fine. Just a little sore, but this feels good. I'm fine."

He looked at me for a beat, until I started to grind against him and he threw his head back with a loud growl. "You feel so fucking good."

I kept moving, up and down, slowly at first, and then picked up the pace. I tried not to look into his eyes. I tried to focus on the shape of his muscular arms, the definition of his chest, the way he bit his bottom lip every time I clenched. He gripped my ass harder, moving me up and down with ease as if I weighed nothing. His eyes snapped open at the sound of my moan. When he lifted me, his mouth closed over my left breast, his tongue teasing, his lips grazing against me.

"You make me desperate for you, Nicole," he growled, cradling the back of my head and crashing my lips to his. "You're fucking mine."

I nodded, slowing my pace and closing my eyes to hold back tears. "Yes."

"Say it. Tell me," he said, his lips against mine, his tongue doing a slow sweep of my mouth, playing with mine, teasing, sucking. "Tell me you're mine."

"I can't," I whispered. I felt the familiar burn building inside. "I'm so close. So close."

Victor gripped my thighs, trapping me so I couldn't move. "Look at me."

I opened my eyes and my heart skipped.

"Tell. Me," he said, pumping me up and down once. I moaned.

"Please, Victor."

"Tell me." He moved again, standing up and pumping me up and down as he stood, my legs wrapping around his waist. He was so deep like this.

So deep.

So good.

I grind against him, trying to reach my resolve. "Why won't you say it?"

I grabbed the back of his head and pulled him into a kiss, making him forget for a moment. He walked and thrust deeper, walked and thrust harder, biting my bottom lip as he did it. My moan was deep and long, a mix of a growl and an *I'm yours* as I reached my climax. He thrust inside me a few times more, long and deep, growling a "fuck, yes," as he reached his own.

Chapter Twenty-Four

Victor

I know when a woman is falling for me. I know because I usually leave right before it happens. Right before she gets that look in her eyes that says *this could be us* when I'm fucking her. Nicole had that look tonight. I saw it. She'd had that look while we were at my parents', while we were out shopping, and as she'd handed my keys to the valet when we'd arrived at the hotel. And I couldn't fathom leaving her, even though I had to. I had to. I should. Not because I wanted to, because for once *I didn't*. For the first time that look on *her* face most likely mirrored mine. But my career was on the line as well as her reputation, and those were two things I wasn't willing to mess with. I sighed and ran my fingers through her hair. Her face was on my shoulder, her lips slightly parted as she slept peacefully. It looked like a scene right out of a goddamn romance movie. Me watching her like a total creeper while she slept peacefully.

"I think I'm falling in love with you," I whispered as she slept. "And I really don't fucking want to. You probably don't even want a serious relationship right now. You probably just want to have fun." I sighed. "But the thought of you having fun and being like this with anybody but me . . . kills me."

I stopped talking when she groaned and moved against me, leaving some drool on my shoulder as she moved her head. I chuckled. That was a first. That's what I get for letting her snuggle up on me and shit. She was so cute when she slept, though. Probably because she wasn't talking or taunting me. Most likely because she was on me, though. Nicole Alessi on top of me was my new favorite sight. Nicole Alessi anywhere near me was my new favorite sight. On me, under me, next to me . . . This was bad. Really fucking bad. I was starting to think like Oliver . . . or worse . . . Jensen. Fuck. I couldn't possibly have the same love-struck fool look on my face as those two did when they looked at their wives. I adjusted her so she was on the pillow and no longer on me, but I kept my fingers running through her hair because it was soft and doing it soothed me.

"Just . . . promise me that when I let you go you won't run into another man's arms. You're mine, Nicole. We just need to get through this. We need to sort this out and let it blow over. It's just a break. Just a short break," I said, sighing and pulling her closer to me. "Good talk."

Fuck my life. I finally had somebody I wanted to keep in my life, and she had to be the only one I couldn't have. I knew letting it get this far before finalizing everything in her divorce made me a complete idiot, but there was no stopping. And having her, kissing her, fucking her, being beside her like this made that clear. The issue now was that I wasn't sure my heart could take it if she didn't believe a short break was all it would be. I'm not sure I would believe her if she said she'd wait for me. That hadn't been the plan before, but I needed it to be this time. Fuck all of this.

The phone rang way too fucking early, but I'd set the call an hour earlier than we needed just in case, and I was glad. Nicole kept rubbing her ass on my hard-on and there was no way I wasn't going to take advantage.

"Hmm . . . that feels good," she said, moving her hips when I tucked my fingers between her legs and started strumming on her clit.

"I'm going to make you feel very good," I said against her ear as I thrust inside her. She yelped.

"Holy . . . Victor."

I chuckled, biting down on the skin between her neck and shoulder. "There's nothing holy about Victor."

I moved us so she was on her knees and I was bent over behind her, holding her hips to meet my thrusts. I wanted to slow down for her, but everything about her had me on overdrive. I couldn't be near her and not go full throttle. She pushed back onto me, and I groaned at the feel of her clenching around me. I slapped her ass.

"Fuck," she said, clenching harder. She was so wet for me. I slapped her ass again. "Victor."

I couldn't take it anymore. I reached for her hair and looped it around my hand, pulling her toward me as I pounded into her. I was sure between the two of us, we alerted everybody within a fifteen-mile radius that we were fucking, but I didn't care. My only regret was that I was wearing a condom. I wanted to feel her on me. And I would. Not today, but soon. *I hoped.*

We took a long time in the shower, because the way the soap ran down her curves and her tits as she washed her hair distracted me.

"Stop touching me," she groaned when I pushed her against the wall. "I'm going to be late."

"Fuck that job," I said, taking her lips in mine. She laughed against me.

"Would you say fuck your job and skip work tomorrow if I asked you to?" she asked.

I pulled back, grazing the pad of my thumb over her nipple. She groaned and pushed onto me. I held her gaze.

"I would. If you asked me to, I would," I said, and I meant it. If she asked me to take a day off, I'd do it. She looked as surprised as I felt. Without another word, she lifted herself up and wrapped her legs around my waist, clinging on to me.

"I'm really sore," she whispered. "Really sore. But I want you."

I shook my head, holding her in place. "I don't want to hurt you."

Her blue eyes searched mine. "Rain check?"

I nodded with a smile. She must have sensed my uneasiness, because she narrowed her eyes.

"Promise?"

"Promise."

She looked at me for a beat longer before putting her legs down and turning around to finish washing. My heart dropped to my stomach. I felt like shit. I didn't make promises I didn't keep. Ever. And that was one I wasn't sure I could keep even if I wanted to. I tried to put it out of my mind. No use in thinking about it now. I'd deal with it when I had to. I needed to meet with Quinn before I jumped to any conclusions. We ordered breakfast and took it on the road. We were both quiet, contemplative, as if we'd been changed by our little outing. Maybe we had been. Whenever I looked over at her, she looked like she was lost in thought. In an effort not to rock the boat, I didn't say anything at all.

We kissed when I dropped her off in front of the lot, and she thanked me.

"I'll get a ride to your parents' house," she said. "I have your mom and Estelle's number, so I'll be fine if you're busy."

Why would I be busy? I wanted to ask, but didn't. Instead I nodded.

"Thank you," she whispered as she got out of the car, her back facing me.

"Thank you," I whispered back, wanting to reach out to touch her. Instead, I let her go. I wasn't sure I could watch her walk away again, so I turned my face and looked the other way. And I think we both knew it was more than just a drop off.

"Who did you piss off?" was the first thing Quinn asked upon my answering my phone the following day.

I'd heard from Nicole late last night when she was still at work and I could hear the exhaustion in her voice as we spoke, so I kept the conversation short. Short and sweet, though it didn't feel that way, because after we hung up I felt like I couldn't bear to listen to her voice again until this thing with the pictures got resolved, which was what I hoped to do today.

"I'm assuming you're going to spit it out and not make me beat it out of you," I responded. Quinn laughed.

"Are you in the area?"

"I actually am," I said as I drove past the café he and I frequented. "Usual spot?"

"Be there in five. Bring your laptop."

The call ended and my Bluetooth shut off, the sound of classical music circulating the airwave of my car again. I turned the steering wheel and made a U-turn at the light, going back to the café. We pulled up at the same time, me in my Jaguar, and Quinn in his Mercedes-Maybach S600. The guy had made a killing exploiting celebrities and reaped the benefits quite openly with his extravagant purchases. He had a different car for every day of the week and mansions in three different countries; all of them worth more money than I'd probably ever see in my lifetime. He gave his keys to the valet, walking around the back with an oomph in his step that made women's heads turn. He was a cocky motherfucker. Rightfully so. His smile was wide as I approached and he leaned in to give me a side hug.

"My man," he said.

"Just when I was starting to think the world may be a peaceful place," I said, backing out of the hug. "The devil himself calls me up."

Quinn chuckled. "Gotta keep you on your toes."

I shook my head, smiling as we walked into the café and walked toward the table in the upper right corner. We always sat at the same one. Even when I came in without him, I saw him at the same one.

"Do you lease this table?"

"Basically," he said, smiling. I could tell there was something more to his smile, but didn't ask. Quinn had a don't-tell policy, and while he'd shared private things about his life with me in the past, he tried to avoid getting personal with anyone.

"What do you have for me?" I asked after we each ordered our food and drinks.

His brows rose as he sat back in his seat, and lifted the glass of water to his mouth. "How many clients do you have right now?"

He loved playing a game of cat and mouse before handing out cheese. I ran through my mental catalogue, knowing he wouldn't meet me to give me bullshit stories about closed cases. He knew what high-profile divorces I was working on. With the media, it was impossible for anybody not to know. Something about the gleam in his eyes made me uneasy. I narrowed my eyes a bit.

"I'm not in the mood for games today. The pictures you sent me the other day were nothing."

His expression turned serious as he set the glass of water down. "How much is Nicole Lane worth to you?"

My heart dropped. I stared at him for a long moment. "Her name is Nicole Alessi, and she doesn't have a price tag." I paused, feeling at odds with the situation for once. "Are you printing a story?"

"Not yet. I knew she was yours so I wanted to bring it to you first."

Mine. Clearly he didn't know the half of it if he was so nonchalant. I intended to keep it that way. He reached into the pocket of his jacket and took out a USB, setting it on the table and sliding it across.

"What's this?" I asked.

"Compromising pictures."

My throat tightened. I swallowed past the knot sitting there. I didn't want to ask what kind of pictures they were. I took the USB from the table and put it in the pocket of my jacket. My chest burned in that spot.

"How'd you get it?"

Quinn shot me a look. "How do I get anything?"

"Who's shopping this?"

"You know I can't give you a source."

Slow, hot anger started to burn through me. "This isn't . . ." I stopped talking when the waitress came by and put the plates on our table. "I can't have somebody shopping naked pictures of her right now."

"It's not just her that's naked," he said, taking a bite of the steak he ordered while I nearly choked on mine.

"What?"

Quinn nodded slowly. "I wanted to bring it to you first."

"Who else has seen this?" I asked, taking the USB out and reaching for the laptop in my briefcase.

"No clue," he said, shrugging. "As far as I know, I'm the only one. I usually get first dibs on things like this."

I inserted the USB and waited for the items to load. Without even clicking and enlarging, I could already feel the burning anger returning. My ears felt like they were on fire. I was undoubtedly staring at a semi-naked Nicole sitting in front of Gabriel Lane. In the next picture, her head was thrown back, his mouth on her neck. I felt bile rise in my throat. I hadn't expected for it to bother me as much as it did, but the longer I stared at the image, the hotter my blood simmered. I knew it was her ex-husband. I knew she was with me now. Sort of. But fuck, it hurt seeing her with him. It hurt knowing her lips, lips that belonged to *me*, were on his just short days, maybe weeks before they were on mine.

In the next frame, she was looking at the camera with a look of shock on her face. And in the next she'd stood up and was fixing her shirt. I felt sick. Physically ill. My stomach was turning in disgust. The shots were grainy, no doubt taken on a cell phone, but it was her. It was her curvy frame and her perfect tits, and that incredible mouth of hers. I took a deep breath. I needed to stop thinking about it before I made myself sick.

The next photo was one of her and me on the balcony of her house. It was similar to the one Quinn had texted me before, but these were less grainy, sharper, and from the angle they were taken it definitely looked like we were kissing. My heart pounded as I looked at them, at the way she was looking at me in the picture. I was uneasy about the way I was looking at her. It was as though nothing else in the universe mattered but us. If anybody got hold of it, there would be no sense in denying what was going on between us. Nobody would believe it. I cleared my throat.

"I'll buy every copy of this. Every single fucking copy. And I'll throw in a bonus if you give me your source."

"Vic, you know I—"

"How long have we known each other, Q?"

He sighed, running a hand over his face. "People will want to see this. This is huge. They're supposed to be getting a divorce, and they've been popping up everywhere together and now these pictures . . . this is the type of thing that breaks the Internet."

I propped my elbows on the table and buried my face in my hands, closing my eyes to try to forget the image of her half-naked in front of another man. I needed to think of her as my client, not the woman I felt I could say anything to without second thought. Not the woman I'd had the most meaningful sex of my life with, because that's what it was. Meaningful and hot as fuck.

"What's going on with you and Nicole?" Quinn asked. My head snapped up. "Off the record."

"Off the record, I want you to give me your goddamn source and help me make these pictures go away," I said, shutting my computer. He studied me for a long moment.

"Yours or all of them?"

My eyes narrowed. "Every single one of them."

Quinn smiled. "This one's special."

"Don't start with your shit, Q. I don't have time for it."

"I'm not judging. She's beautiful," he said, raising his hands.

"Keep your fucking opinions to yourself. I'm having a hard enough time accepting that other people have seen this shit. And I don't think you want anybody to know how much you've been visiting an unnamed married woman. We should probably keep that between us," I said. "For now."

His eyes widened, but his smile stayed intact. The reason Quinn and I got along so well is because we respected each other, and we knew not to call each other's bluff. We were both ruthless. We'd claw the shit out of anybody who stood in our way, regardless of who it was.

"I don't understand why you don't come and work with me," he said.

I chuckled at the thought, but got serious quickly. "One of us would be dead by the end of the first week. Now, give me the fucker's name, and while you're at it, I'm going to need a favor from a mutual friend of ours."

Chapter Twenty-Five

Nicole

Normally I wasn't one to dwell on reasons guys hadn't called before their three-day quota, but with Victor it was all I could think about, mainly because he wasn't the type of guy who played by any rules. I'd spoken to him just briefly after our weekend together and I'd been busy when he called, so it couldn't even be considered a conversation. Over the weekend, half of the wardrobe on the movie set had been messed up, and luckily I was insanely busy working with two seamstresses to get caught up in making everything. Still, when I got home and soaked my hands in ice-cold water because they hurt so much from sewing non-stop, all I could think about was Victor. My phone finally rang with a call from him when I got home from work that night. I was soaking my hands in iced water, stumbling and spilling it everywhere to answer it.

"Hey," he said, his voice making me lose my breath momentarily.

"You really stuck to the three-day rule," I said. He was quiet for a beat.

"Sorry. I've been busy."

"So have I."

"Yeah, my mom said you left the car there until the next morning because you'd gotten out of work too late to call," he said. "I need you to come into the office to sign the final papers so we can put this divorce behind you. Are you free tomorrow morning?" His voice was serious, all business, all Victor. I sighed.

"Sure. What time?"

"Nine?"

"I'll be there."

"Good," he said, pausing to clear his throat. "And . . . you're good? Everything is going okay?"

I made a face. He couldn't see me, but he was acting really fucking weird. I chalked it up to his fear of everything being recorded. The guy swore he was Richard Nixon or something.

"I'm fine. See you tomorrow, Victor."

"Looking forward to it, Nicole." The way he said that made me stomach flip. Maybe I was just worrying for no reason. We were good. We were fine, and he said he was looking forward to seeing me.

When I woke up the following morning, my entire body ached. My hands, my head, my throat, and I was pretty sure I had a fever. I could barely open my eyes, and when I did I realized it was eight forty and I was going to be late. Before showering, I called Marcus because there was no way I could drive like that. By the time I finished getting ready, he was standing outside, his mouth dropping when he saw me.

"You look tired."

"Thanks," I muttered. At least he found a nice way to tell me I looked like crap. "We should be quick, and the quicker we go, the quicker I get back to bed."

"Okay."

He didn't make small talk. Shocker. And for once I was completely glad for the silence in the car, which I think was a shock to him. He kept looking over, probably to make sure I was okay, but I was too busy blowing my nose and trying to keep my snot from going everywhere to care. I'm pretty sure he was completely disgusted by the time we reached Victor's office.

As soon as we got there, paparazzi swarmed my car.

"What the hell happened now?" I asked, my voice nasally in my own ears.

"Stay in the car. I'll go around," Marcus said.

I did as I was told and kept my head down as he walked me to the front door. I couldn't even make out their questions because of the pounding in my ears, but I did catch Victor's name, which further confused me.

"What were they saying?" I asked Marcus as I buried my nose in a tissue.

He frowned. "I didn't really understand them."

"Me either."

When I stepped out of the elevator, Grace looked at me with wide eyes and an open mouth. The last time she gave me that look was when rumors about my divorce began circulating. I smiled and waved at her as I walked down the hall, because even if I had time for her crap, I didn't feel like dealing with it today. Marcus stayed behind as I walked up to Victor's door and knocked. It opened and Corinne stepped out. She gave me a quick once-over and smiled.

"He's on the phone, but you can go in."

"Thanks," I said, stepping in as she stepped out.

My blood was vibrating with nervousness. I'd been there a million times, but it felt different, though I couldn't quite put a finger on why. Was it because of what we'd shared? Would things be weird now? Would he be weird toward me? Would I be awkward? We'd had sex, yes. Like in the past. But not like in the past. It felt like more. Something about what had been going on between us even before we hooked up this time felt like more. And he'd said he had the final papers. The *final* papers.

Victor straightened in his chair when he saw me. His eyes searching my face, wandering down my body and back up in a slow caress that made my breath hitch. Whatever Mr. Perfect saw now when I was makeup-less and wearing sweats was definitely good, because he was eyeing me the same way he did when I was in a skintight dress. I plopped down in the chair across from him and put my arms on the table to lay my head down, hoping to relieve the pounding in my head, because despite his very wanted attention, I felt beyond sick and very exhausted.

"I'm going to have to call you back," he said into the phone and hung up. I heard the squeak of his leather chair as he stood up and walked around his desk, and felt his hand on my hair as combed it with his fingers. I moaned a little. "What's wrong?" he asked, his voice soft as he crouched down beside me.

"I think I caught whatever you had." I sniffled and shivered.

His hand stopped moving. I lifted my head up as he stood. "You should have told me. I would have come to you."

"Maybe if you would have called," I said. I closed my eyes momentarily, trying to regain composure. *What was it about this guy that made me revert to my teenage self?* "Just . . . let's get this over with so that I can go back to bed."

He sighed and took a seat beside me instead of going back behind his desk. He was quiet for so long, I accidentally dozed off in my chair. When I woke, it was with a start, blinking rapidly.

"I'm so sorry," I said. "Please, just . . . do I need to sign something?"

"I should have called. I'm sorry. I just," he paused to take a long, deep breath, his eyes looking pained, "just this." He handed over a paper similar to one we'd gone over in the past. I signed and handed it back, when I did he held my gaze. The seriousness in his eyes made my stomach dip. "Nicole, we need to talk."

An array of possibilities crossed my mind in a split second, and if I wasn't already on the verge of crying because of how sick I felt, I would have cried over what he was insinuating. I closed my eyes. Those words were never a good sign. Flashbacks of how this had happened the first time assaulted my thoughts. *We can't do this anymore,* he'd said then. If he said that now . . . God. If he said that now I wouldn't know what to do, what to say, how to react.

"About what?" I whispered.

"This. Us," he said, his voice firm, though his eyes looked anguished, and I knew he wasn't thrilled about the talk either.

I swallowed, even though it hurt. "Are you kidding me?"

"I wish I was," he said, letting out a sigh. He reached over his desk and placed some pictures in front of me. I squinted to look at them, and gasped when I saw the one of me on Gabe's bed. It was from the drunken night when that girl had interrupted us. Bitch.

"Nothing happened," I said, looking at Victor. They were taken before we got together, so I didn't have to explain myself to him, but I still felt the urge to. "I mean, we made out, but I swear nothing else happened."

He closed his eyes momentarily and breathed out. When he opened them back up he looked as torn as he did before he took a break to think.

"It's . . . it doesn't matter. It's not about that."

He paused, reaching out and flipping to another picture. The picture was one of him and me on my balcony. Before I signed my lease. The *day* I signed my lease. My eyes snapped up to meet his. This was the reason for the *we need to talk* speech. The sinking feeling threatened to return. It was his biggest fear come to life. We'd been caught and now anything said about him, about us, about this case, would come back and haunt him when the time came for his promotion. *His promotion.* Dammit.

"Can we make it go away?" I asked, my voice a croak.

"I'm working on it. Trust me, I'm working on it. These," he said, pointing at the ones of Gabe and me, "will never see the light of day." He pointed at the ones of us. "These, unfortunately, are already circulating. My guy couldn't stop them. I'm trying to get to the bottom of it."

My heart squeezed in my chest.

We'd had our fun.

I kept telling myself that to keep the tears at bay, because despite going through this once before, it felt different this time. It felt personal. It felt . . .

wrong. I didn't feel just a little crushed by this. This felt like a boulder was sitting in my throat, making its way to my heart.

"We can't see each other anymore," I whispered, meeting his gaze. "I get it. This was just a fire we needed to put out. And we did that."

I wiped my nose with the tissue in my hand.

But I didn't get it. I didn't get it and I felt the intense urge to cry. I was losing him. I was losing him and there wasn't anything I could do about it because now there were pictures of us together. Proof of what was happening between us. Things that could rip apart his career and mess up my divorce. I expected to feel something when we ended it. Last time, I'd felt hurt. This was worse.

Annihilated.

I never expected to find a man so soon after Gabe. I hadn't. I'd set my mind to having fun and working on myself, which I did. But I also hadn't expected for my life to collide with Victor's again or to feel so connected to him.

"Nicole, please don't," he said, his voice quiet, his eyes pleading. "Don't belittle this."

I blinked, trying to stop impending tears. Blinked again when I felt one escape through my lashes. I wiped it quickly.

Don't belittle this.

"It's okay," I whispered, standing from my chair. I took one of the pictures with me and shoved it into my purse. "I know how this goes. I hope you know that even with these pictures, I'll deny it. You don't have to worry about me. I would never do anything to jeopardize your job."

He stood up and reached for my wrist, squeezing. I yanked my arm quickly. I couldn't bear his touch right now. Not when it hurt this much. His eyes widened, his broad shoulders sagged a bit.

"I'm sorry. Had this happened under different circumstances—"

"Stop apologizing. It's fine," I said, interrupting him. "Been there, done that, bought the shirt."

"That's not funny, Nicole," he said, his face serious. I dropped my head, unwilling to look at him anymore.

"I've learned to deflect."

Despite how weak I felt, I started walking toward the door, and he followed, holding me by the shoulders possibly when he saw me sway a little. I tilted my face to look at him, and cursed the stir in my heart when I realized our faces were so close.

"Please don't touch me," I whispered.

"I don't know how to stop," he whispered back, dropping his forehead to the back of my shoulder.

"You'll learn."

I left his office, heard him follow behind me, and when I reached Marcus, I could barely keep my legs moving. I practically threw my arms out for him to catch me. Thank God he did.

"Let's get you home," he said, looking over my shoulder.

I turned my head and saw Victor standing in the hall with his hands in his pockets looking as defeated as I'd ever seen him. I tried to smile, tried to reassure him that he was doing the right thing, but I couldn't find the energy to do it. I let Marcus lead me away, back to the car, and drive me home. On my way there, I got a call from Meire and answered straight away, which I rarely did.

"I saw the pictures," she said upon my answering. "Are you crying?"

"No," I sniffled. "I'm sick."

"Come stay over here. You shouldn't be by yourself right now."

"Okay," I said, and agreed to drive to their house later on, after I'd showered and napped on my bed. I needed to be by myself for a little while. Needed time to process everything that had happened earlier.

Later that night, when darkness had fallen over, there was loud knocking on my door that startled me awake. Fuck. Shit. I was supposed to go to my dad's. I checked my phone and saw the missed calls from Meire and Dad as I walked to the door and opened it. Victor was standing on the other side dressed in jeans, a Dodgers cap, and a black hoodie. I knew it was him because I knew him, but you could barely make out his face with that thing over his head.

"What are you doing here?" I asked, my voice a croaked whisper. It was getting worse.

He held up a bag. "Soup."

I closed my eyes and stepped back so he could walk in.

"Didn't we break up? Did I imagine that?" I asked, closing the door and following him down the hall.

Bonnie jumped on her back legs and wagged her tail when she saw him. Stupid dog. Hadn't I spent an hour crying over him to her? Why was she being nice to him?

"Get comfortable while I heat this up," he said, rounding my kitchen counter and tearing the bag open.

I looked at him for a long moment, studied his face now he'd taken the hood off: the planes of his chiseled jaw, the light scruff, the light brown hair curling under the baseball cap, those hazel eyes that made my knees go weak, his long fingers as he popped the lid on the plastic container. Each second that passed made my heart hurt a little more. I turned around and left the kitchen, opting to sit in the living room and switch on the TV. Maybe if I had a distraction I wouldn't have to think about how over we were.

Victor returned with a bowl of soup and a glass of orange juice and sat beside me. He put the juice and a napkin with two blue pills down on the coffee table and turned to face me. He was too close.

I could smell the scent of his body wash and shampoo.

So close.

I could see the lines of brown on his greenish eyes.

Too close.

I could practically taste his lips against mine. I swallowed and cringed at the pain, and when he lifted a spoonful of soup up for me to drink, my eyes widened.

"You can't feed me," I whispered. The dip in his brow, and the look in his eyes told me he was crestfallen.

"Please, Nic," he whispered, a plea. I'd never heard him plead before. It made my chest squeeze, my eyes water.

"I can't, Victor. It's all or nothing, and you know it can't be all."

The spoon clinked against the bowl as he closed his eyes. "It can be," he said, opening his eyes again, "just not right now."

"I get it."

"I really . . . this . . . it wasn't just for fun," he said.

"I know." I swallowed. "But we still have to keep our distance. You being here isn't helping anything."

He nodded slowly. "I couldn't just . . ." He sighed. "I wanted to make sure you were okay."

"I am, Victor. I'm okay. I'll be okay, but you can't be here. You can't say no to me and tell me this isn't good timing and then show up in my house with soup. I'm strong, but I still have feelings."

Feelings that were overwhelming me.

"I know. I'm sorry," he said, sighing. "I really am."

"Thank you for the soup."

"You're welcome." He paused, taking his cap off with one hand to run his hand through his hair. "I'm going to leave now."

I nodded. He glanced at me again.

"I'm going to leave because this is the responsible thing to do," he said. "If I was careless, I'd stay."

"That's . . . good to know," I said. And it was. Maybe not now, but someday there would be a future for us. Maybe someday we'd work out.

If I was careless, I'd stay.

When he left, I drank my soup, picked up Bonnie, and then headed to my dad's. Meire didn't even let me knock before she opened the door and pulled me into a hug.

"Your dad is not very happy. He's not even going to the office tomorrow."

My heart dropped. I was afraid of that. I let go of Meire and started walking toward his study, where I knew I'd find him.

"There's soup for you in the kitchen. I'll warm it up," she called out. I didn't bother to tell her I'd already had some. I could have another bowl.

"Thank you," I called out, cursing my teenage self for all the times I'd talked shit about her for marrying my dad. I wasn't one to welcome new people with open arms. I was always cautious about letting people in because I'd seen so many people get burned by loved ones, and I just never wanted that to be me. The irony.

I knocked once on my dad's office door before walking in. He was sitting behind his desk with his hand on his forehead.

"Hey, Dad."

His head snapped up. He smiled softly. "How are you feeling?"

I shrugged. "Like shit."

"Nicole."

"Like crap," I said. I never understood why crap was accepted while shit was frowned upon.

"Can you please explain these to me? I'm having a hard time understanding them," he said, waving the pictures of Victor and me around. I took a deep breath and let it out as I sat across from him.

"There's nothing to explain. It was windy and we were trying not to be loud so the realtor wouldn't hear what we were saying about the house. End of."

His brows rose. "You're sure?"

"I'm positive," I said, but the more his blue eyes searched my face, the more nervous I felt. Every time I lied to my dad I felt like I was going up against the Supreme Court justices and pleading my case. Technically I wasn't really lying. There was nothing going on between Victor and me anymore.

"Okay," he said with a sigh. "I was worried I'd have to let him go."

My heart lurched. I leaned forward in my seat, suddenly feeling all the energy come back to me at once. "Let him go? Why?"

"It doesn't look good if a lawyer is involved with his client. I'm sure I don't need to explain that to you."

I tried not to roll my eyes. He'd met Meire when she'd hired him as her estate attorney after her husband died. Not the same, but close enough, and Dad had made it very clear that their relationship didn't start until after her things were taken care of and she was no longer his client.

"I know, Dad. Like I said, nothing is going on. We are friends, though. I don't think that's against the law."

"It's not, but you need to steer clear until this blows over. Victor is very serious about his job and I don't want anything interfering with my making him partner."

"I won't."

"Are you dating somebody?" he asked suddenly.

"No," I said, and it pained me to say it. Physically pained me as I thought of Victor and his smile and his grouchiness.

"Well, find someone." He paused. "Well, that's probably a good thing to be single at this point. Probably good for you too. I'm having a company party to announce Victor's promotion in a couple weeks." He paused. "I'm not trying to pimp you out, love, but if you want to bring someone as a friend, do so. I'm just trying to make *this,*" he holds up the pictures again, "go away for everybody's sake. I'm sure he will bring a date, so I won't have to worry about him. People will see you guys with other people and this will be erased."

"I hear you," I said.

And I wasn't lying. I heard him loud and clear. It still didn't help the deep cut I felt at the idea of Victor dating another woman. *Someone he didn't have to worry about being careless with.* I excused myself and left his office, not even bothering to get my bowl of soup before I went to the guest house. I face-planted onto the plush queen-sized bed and let out a single sob before I fell asleep.

Chapter Twenty-Six

Victor

"Why would you invite her to your birthday party?" I asked my sister, who looked at me like I was an idiot. It had been a couple weeks since I'd seen Nicole and I was doing pretty good at avoiding her as a whole. The only time I communicated with her was through Corinne, and it was solely about the divorce and the agreement she had with Gabriel to attend an event with him.

"Because I like her, and I was handing out invitations the day I met up with her to talk about Sunny's wedding dress. Or did you forget that you practically begged me to call her to see how she was feeling when she was sick?"

I blinked. That was beside the point. I couldn't call her after I took the soup to her house. I was being a pussy but I was man enough to admit that the sound of her voice would break me if I wouldn't be able to touch her or see her. Estelle waved an envelope with my name on it and jerked me out of my thoughts.

"Are you five? Is this your fifth birthday party? Who the fuck hands out paper invitations?"

She rolled her eyes and flung an envelope across the table. It hit me in the chest before I could catch it. "If you don't want to go, don't go. Nobody told you to act like an asshole to a perfectly perfect girl."

I let out a breath and shook my head, trying my best not to roll my eyes right back at her. I hadn't seen or spoken to Nicole in a couple weeks. That was nothing. It wasn't even enough time to miss a person, but there I was, missing the shit out of her and thinking about her every time I closed my damn eyes.

"When is that party your boss is throwing for you?" she asked.

I ran a hand through my hair, closing my eyes momentarily. "After he tells everyone about my promotion. When is your adult-child party?"

She glared at me. "Do you think Nicole will go to the office party?"

"I doubt it." I hoped not.

"Are you taking a date?"

I looked at my sister. "What are you getting at?"

"I'm just curious."

"I'll probably take somebody. I need to make sure people understand the pictures circulating aren't what they've made them out to be."

"Aren't they?" she asked, raising an eyebrow.

"Are you done?" I paused. "I know you're dying for me to find the love of my life and all, but some of us don't think love is the end-all be-all of life."

It was a good thing I was a good liar.

"Some of you are idiots."

"Thanks."

"You're welcome." She took a deep breath. From the way her ears were turning red, I could tell she was getting upset about this. I tried not to smile. She was so funny when she got upset. "It doesn't matter. Even if she goes and you take someone it'll be fine. She's dating this really hot guy."

Until she wasn't so fucking funny. "What guy?"

She shrugged. "Some guy named Brent that lives by her house. It's pretty convenient, really," she said, her smile widening as she looked at me. "He's gone over a few times. She says he has an incredible body. I mean, I know he does. She showed me a picture."

I felt like there wasn't enough room in my body for the air that I needed. I clenched my jaw, trying to rein in my anger and keep all the words in, because the last thing I needed was to give her more ammunition. I thought about the cases sitting on top of my desk and looked around the coffee shop, my eyes everywhere.

"Good for her," I said when I felt like I could speak without sounding like I wanted to murder whoever the guy was.

"That's what I said," Estelle said, lifting her cup of coffee and taking a sip. My eyes focused on her paint-stained hands. I was dying to get out of that place already. "I think he's a producer or something."

I exhaled. What the fuck, Nicole? *What the fuck?* Did she completely ignore the *we just can't be together right now* part? Was she really moving on? A sense of déjà vu fell over me, when I'd asked her to leave the first time, and she had, and three weeks later she'd gotten engaged.

Fuck.

My.

Life.

"Like I said, good for her," I repeated.

Estelle smiled as she stood up. "I have a class to teach in twenty minutes. Let me know if you're going to make it to the party."

"Obviously I'm going," I said, giving her a kiss on the cheek.

I started opening the envelope as I walked away and reading the invitation, but she was too far for me to say anything to. A costume party. She was turning twenty-eight and was having a costume party for her birthday. I hated themed parties. They meant going out and looking for specific outfits and spending money on those outfits and then keeping them on at the actual event instead of just wearing whatever was already in your closet. And a fucking pirate-themed party?

"You're fucking kidding me," I muttered, putting the invitation away and tossing it to my passenger seat. Oliver wasn't going to hear the end of it when I saw him on Sunday. I'd have to buy something online. Once that was out of the way I could figure out who I was going to take as my date to the office party going on in my name. They were honoring me and I was already dreading it. Under normal circumstances I'd be glad to go and stand up there, thanking the people who'd helped me get there. But under normal circumstances, Nicole *would* be on my arm and we'd be able to walk around openly. Under normal circumstances, she wouldn't be dating producers named Brent.

A few days later, I couldn't stop thinking about it and I realized I was running out of options, and I didn't like running out of options. I wasn't the kind of man that could just sit back and take a punch. I liked to be the one punching. I knew it wasn't right, I knew it wasn't necessarily professional, but I was in the business of not giving a fuck. If Nicole wanted to go off and date other guys, I couldn't stop her. I actually appreciated it. That way the spotlight was off of me for the time being and I could take care of unfinished business.

For two weeks I had been okay showing up at the office and getting patted on the back by Will and pretending the story about his daughter and me was fabricated. It was easy enough to go in, get lost in work, meet with clients, look into their cases, go to court, defend them, and close a case. I was on autopilot. No. I was back to where I was before Nicole ambushed her way into my life. I was back to being me. The difference was that I was an unhappy version of myself. I'd tried to get in touch with the douchebag that was Darryl

Cusack, who happened to be the source Quinn gave me for the "leaked" pictures, but he hadn't responded to any of my messages. The guy clearly didn't want me to find him. Gabriel Lane was my last resort, and I didn't intend to use that card at all if I could help it. My last resort was to exchange information with some of Quinn's photographers.

They'd tell me where I could find him, and I would give them a few pictures they were after. The day after I put that out, I got a call from one of them letting me know Darryl was eating at a popular Italian restaurant in West LA. I showed up there with an old friend of mine, Jessica. She was the kind of friend I used to take on group dates, one of the girls my sister couldn't stand, but she was also always down for whatever, whenever, wherever. As soon as she heard there would be paparazzi there, she agreed. She owned a hair salon, so I assumed she thought it would be good for business. I figured as soon as they got pictures of Jess and me hooking up, they'd move on and bury the story about Nicole and me. Who liked old news anyway? Jess and I played it up outside, holding hands, kissing right outside the restaurant, laughing at some stupid comment she made about possibly having gum under her shoe but not being able to bend down because of her short dress, and basically doing shit people who went on dates did. I hated every second of it. Her lips felt wrong against mine. Her hand felt wrong when I held it. It was just . . . wrong. I hadn't even thought about giving Nicole a heads-up about the photos, but I hoped she never saw them, and if she did, I hoped she had enough sense to know it was all for show and that I'd done it with her best interest in mind.

From my seat I had the perfect view of Darryl's table. He was there with a known actress and a couple of her friends. When I saw him get out of his seat and head to the bathroom, I excused myself and did the same. When I got back there, my friend Sergio, one of the waiters, handed me a pair of gloves and I asked him to block the entrance of the bathroom with a sign. I waited for the other man in there to walk out and put the gloves on before turning around and locking the door when I walked in. Darryl did a double take when he saw me.

"You know what I appreciate about you, Darryl? That you stay true to yourself," I started. I took a baseball out of the pocket of my jacket and started throwing it up and catching it softly. "I don't know if you know this, I'm sure you do because it seems you've taken a liking toward me." I raised an eyebrow. "And I'm flattered, though I don't bat for that team." I shook my head. "Before I got into divorce, I practiced criminal law. It only lasted about two years." I tilted my head as I thought about it. "But in those two years I earned the trust of a lot of criminals. People you wouldn't think I'd know. I don't have to tell you how shady people can be, and I'm sure I don't have to tell you the lengths people go through to make sure they stay out of jail." I paused for dramatic affect. His eyes were a little wider now as he looked at the ball I was throwing up.

"Where did . . . is that my . . ." he started, frowning as he looked at the ball in my hand, recognizing it from his home office, where it was taken from.

"So this is what you're going to do next," I said. He looked more concerned about the ball than he did scared, and that was fine. I didn't want him scared. Scared people went to the cops. Nervous people went to bed with their secrets.

"You're going to pull whatever photographers you have following me and Nicole, and you're going to give me their names. That's all you have to worry about. I'll make it all go away."

Darryl scoffed, pushing his oversized glasses higher on the bridge of his nose. "In exchange for what?"

"In exchange for me not having some old friends of mine who owe me some really big favors pay you a visit."

"I'm not doing anything," he said, his voice firm. I knew he was calling my bluff. I knew he was probably thinking that a clean-cut guy like me was ruthless in the courtroom, but the courtroom and real life were two completely separate things. I appreciated that seed of doubt. I kept calm until he started screaming.

"Nicole is nothing. Nobody cares about her. Fuck you. You're just mad because she's still hung up on her ex. And guess what? She will be forever because you're not a multi-million-dollar earning actor," he said, his face turning red. "And if you want juicy pictures, I can show you the ones of her and her new boyfriend. Those make your balcony pictures look like a walk in the fucking park."

I breathed one more time, but the burn of fire inside me was stronger than the breaths I took. Finally, I pitched the ball, the way I did when I played baseball with the guys the seldom times we were all free. I pitched it so that it hit the mirror beside him and shattered it, the pieces flinging off it and going in every direction. One nipped me in the side of my face. I felt the sting, but not enough to care.

"You're a fucking lunatic," he screamed, holding on to his head. "Security!"

I stood, arms crossed, waiting for the security I knew wouldn't come, as he kicked the glass on the floor, his eyes wild, glasses falling, head turning in every which direction as if he didn't know what to do with himself. Finally, his eyes landed on the ball. He gaped at it as he lifted it out of the sink.

"Where the hell—?" He looked up at me. "Is this from my house? You were in my house?" he yelled.

"I would never step foot in your personal property," I answered calmly, feeling much better after my outburst. I hadn't. I hadn't been to his house or made the call for the guys to go there. I'd been very calculated with my orders and made sure nothing could be traced back to me.

"Who the hell do you think you are?" he demanded. I smirked. I'd been waiting for that question.

"You're about to find out," I replied, and turned around to walk out.

I unlocked the door and looked over my shoulder to where he was still standing with the Babe Ruth baseball in his hand. "My professional opinion? Don't fuck with me anymore."

I walked out of there, thanked Sergio and Lazaro who was now also standing there.

"Sorry about the mess, guys. The man in there went crazy over the empty soap container," I said. Both of them looked at each other before looking at me and shrugging. I handed Sergio two wads of bills. "Please give this to Ignazio. That should cover it. The rest is for you guys."

"It's the wine, dawg. That makes these old men go crazy," Sergio said with a tsk. I smiled as I walked away. I went back to where Jessica was sitting and she gasped.

"Holy cow. What happened to your face?"

I brought my hand up and felt liquid covering my left cheek. I looked at my hand, now wet with blood.

"I think we're going to have to cut this date short."

She nodded, eyes wide. "Of course. Let's go. You probably need stitches."

As soon as we stepped outside, there were photographers everywhere. What wasn't supposed to be a money shot, became one. Me dating a different girl wasn't news anymore. It was me dating a different girl and the blood all over my face. I doubted they'd put them up anywhere. I wasn't a celebrity.

"I hope they don't think I did that," Jessica said with a nervous laugh as we climbed into the car. "Wait. Let me drive."

I gave her a side-eyed glare. "Are you out of your . . .? You think I would let you drive my car? I'm dropping you off at home."

She protested the entire way there, saying I was an idiot—an asshole—

that she didn't understand why I couldn't just be like a normal human being and let her take me to the hospital. By the time I parked outside her house, I had a migraine.

"Jess, I've had a really rough night, so I hope you don't take this the wrong way, but, get the fuck out of my car."

"What about your office party? Aren't we supposed to be taking pictures that make you look like you've found a girlfriend?"

I groaned. She was right. "Meet me there please. Just . . . meet me there. I'll pay you. I'll send a celebrity to your salon. I don't care. Just meet me there in two hours."

I drove to the hospital, got three stitches on my face, and was parked outside the office building a little past nine o'clock. My heart lurched at the familiar white car parked outside the office building. Would she be here?

Chapter Twenty-Seven

Nicole

By the time Victor walked in, looking like every sin I was ready to commit, in a black suit and navy tie, I was on my third glass of champagne. He came solo. I smiled at that, but my smile quickly faded when I saw the bandage on the side of his face. I gravitated toward him as if on autopilot, only stopping when I remembered I was supposed to keep my distance. I was furious with myself, with my dad, with the media, with Victor. I'd gone from sad and understanding to angry and bewildered, like a rabid dog on a leash wanting to attack the postmaster. I hated it. Hated him for making me yearn for him this badly. Hated me for putting myself in this situation. Hated the stupid laws in place that prevented us from being together.

"I got you an hors d'oeuvre," Brent said, walking back to me. He also looked great in a suit and tie, opposed to the running shorts I usually saw him in, but he wasn't Victor. I'd invited him as my date because sadly I had nobody else to bring, unless I brought Marcus and everybody knew he was my security detail. He wouldn't really pass as my sudden boyfriend. Well, with my track record, he might, but that would have been awkward for both of us. Brent stuck out the tomato and mozzarella skewer in his hand and brought it up to my mouth for me to take a bite. I complied and thanked him.

When I looked back up, Victor was looking right at me and I felt the air swoosh out of my lungs. I tried to look away, but I was a prisoner to his gaze, and couldn't until I felt Brent's finger on the side of my mouth and was jolted out of the moment. My eyes snapped back to Brent.

"You got some olive oil here," he said, wiping it off.

I couldn't formulate words as I watched Victor move toward us, his jaw clenched, eyes narrowed. My heart dipped into my stomach, and when he stood right in front of me, I could only swallow it all down and tilt my head to look at him.

"Hi. Congratulations," I said.

"Thank you." He paused, looking at Brent. "I don't think we've met. I'm Victor Reuben. Nicole's attorney." The way he said it, almost as if he loathed the introduction, made my heart gallop.

"Brent Thomas. Nice to meet you."

They shook hands, and all I could do was look at Victor's face and wonder what happened.

"I need to speak to you before you leave," Victor said to me, lowering his voice. "Alone. In my office."

I was sure everybody in the room could see through us, hear the promise in his statement, feel the tension we created. His eyes raked up and down my body slowly, without a care in the world, as if there weren't at least forty eyes on us. As we stood there, a tall blonde woman came up to us. At first I smiled at her, thinking she was one of the guy's wives, but then she put her red nails on Victor's face and touched his cheek, and my smile disappeared.

Victor's lips twitched at whatever expression I must have been making, and it became clear that we were playing a game. A stupid, annoying, childish game I had no interest partaking in. My life was already a damn game with the media attention and Gabriel. I didn't need that to bleed into this part of my life. *Why the hell would he do this to me?* He knows how much I hate the games I've had to play with Gabe.

"Does it hurt?" the blonde asked. Her voice felt like nails on a chalkboard, and I knew it was just me that felt that way.

"It's fine," he said. I wanted to punch him for not moving away from her touch.

"I can't believe you didn't let me drive you," she said.

"I don't let anybody drive my car," he said. I hid my smirk behind my glass of champagne as I took a sip.

"I feel you," Brent said beside me. "It takes a real special girl for me to take things to that level."

"I feel the same. Only Marcus drives my car," I said, feeling the need to chime in.

Marcus, who I needed to call so he could take an Uber here at some point and drive me home. Unless I just took one myself. Brent laughed and draped his arm around me. The way Victor was glaring at him, I was surprised lasers weren't shooting from his eyes. Maybe this game would be fun after all.

"Maybe tonight will be my lucky night," Brent said, clinking his glass of water with my nearly empty champagne flute. I raised an eyebrow, looking at our glasses.

"Maybe you're right."

"It was nice to meet you," Brent said to Victor. "Congratulations. Nicky, aren't you going to introduce me to your father?"

"Right," I said, looking at Victor's date, who he still hadn't introduced. She was smiling at me though, so I felt obliged to return her smile as I walked away. My gaze got caught on Victor's again. "See you around."

While I introduced Brent to my dad, I checked my phone and veered off to the side to look at the text messages Chrissy had sent me.

CC: *Did you see this?!?!*

I opened up the message and clicked the link she'd attached, my stomach instantly dropping and curling in disgust as the pictures of Victor and the blonde girl appeared on my phone. They were holding hands, laughing, kissing, acting very together. *Today.* I felt the heat hit my ears first, and then spread quickly through my body. I'd hung out with Brent a few times outside my house, but that was all it was. Hanging out. It had never gotten to the point of kissing. He'd tried, but I'd shot him down and told him my mind was on someone else, because it was. I'd been too busy thinking about Victor, and that asshole now seemed *too* busy, actually playing the part a little *too* well.

Unless he wasn't playing the part at all.

I narrowed my eyes in his direction, and sure enough, there he was, holding hands with the blonde.

Holding. Hands. With. The. Blonde.

I glared so hard, trying to make his head explode first, then hers. One of the waitresses passed by with more champagne. I set down my empty flute and took another.

"What is that? Number four?" Brent asked, joining me. I was too mad to smile, but I nodded as I took a sip. "I would say tonight might really be my lucky night, but I'm not into taking advantage."

I looked over at Victor again, his broad back facing me, his hand on the blonde's shoulder, and something inside me snapped. I took a deep breath, walked into the dimly lit hallway, and pulled Brent by his tie. The last thing I saw before my lips crashed on his was the confused look on his face. Luckily his confusion didn't translate into his kiss. I tugged his tie a little harder, wishing he'd drop the good-guy act and kiss me. I wanted to be kissed like

I was needed, but he was cautious, nice, his lips soft, his tongue coaxing. I ended the kiss and he leaned away with a huge smile on his face, his brown eyes glinting.

"That was . . . unexpected."

I smiled, trying to work up some excitement, and took another sip of champagne.

"Nicole."

I gasped at the sound of Victor's voice saying my name. Brent's smile dropped as he turned around, wiping lipstick off his mouth. Victor's eyes jumped from me to Brent and back to me.

"Am I interrupting anything?" he asked, his voice a quiet storm that made me uncomfortable.

"No, we were just . . . talking," Brent said slowly. He turned toward me again and smiled over his shoulder. I forced myself to meet his gaze and smile back, because fuck Victor. The only thing I could picture was his lips on that girl. It was driving me crazy. Why? Why was such a stupid thing driving me crazy?

"I need you to sign some papers. I won't take up too much of your time," Victor said, beckoning my attention. I cleared my throat and walked forward, brushing past Brent.

"You're going to make me snap," Victor said, his voice dangerously low as I walked beside him. I plastered on a fake smile for whoever was looking at us.

"Already beat you there," I said, continuing to walk toward his office. "Where's your girlfriend?"

"Is that what this is about?" he asked, closing the door behind us. I inhaled the smell of him. His office was coated in it. I exhaled, walking to the front of the desk as he stepped behind it.

"No, I just act like a fucking child for absolutely no reason."

"I thought you weren't jealous," he said, his voice hard.

Did he not want me to be? I looked down at the desk between us, unwilling to look at him. "I thought you weren't jealous either."

He scoffed, and at the sound, I lifted my head. Our eyes locked. My gaze held a challenge. Daring him to let me go home with Brent. His eyes seemed to hold the same challenge. Or something. I didn't even know anymore. Maybe I'd had too much champagne, but I knew that no amount of alcohol was going to dull the fire inside me. I was burning for his touch, for his kiss, for *him*. After a moment, he punched the top of his desk, making me jolt.

"Apparently I fucking am," he muttered, and cleared his throat as he slid two papers across the table.

My mouth dropped. I couldn't even respond. I just reached for the papers and looked at them, though I couldn't even make out the words.

"One is just finalizing the terms, the other is the agreement that you'll go to that red carpet event with Gabriel."

I put my left hand on the paper, my right hand reaching for the pen he offered. He held it until I acknowledged his gaze on mine. Our faces were close. So close. Too close. My heart jumped.

"Don't go, Nic," he said, his voice so soft I had to swallow the lump forming in my throat.

"I saw the pictures of you and the blonde," I said, licking my lips. His eyes dropped to my mouth momentarily before he looked back at me.

"Nicole," he said, sighing as he ran a hand through his hair. "You know why I'm with her."

"For the media? So that people will think we're not together? To make those pictures go away?" I posed, my voice rising with each word I said. "Do you forget I was married to a celebrity?"

His jaw clenched. My eyes shot to the Band-Aid on his face. "I can't forget you were married to a celebrity. I'm reminded of that every time I fucking turn around. You're not the only one being harassed by the paparazzi."

"Oh. I'm sorry I've made your life so difficult," I said, yanking the pen from his hand and signing both papers. I dropped the pen and glared up at him. "Is this it?"

We both stood up and looked at each other. I could tell he wanted to say a million things, but I knew he wouldn't, and I was sick of that. Despite the stupid paper I'd just signed, I was sick of men acting like *I* had to cater to their needs. I was okay with bending over backward for somebody who would return the favor, but I wasn't going to do it for somebody who wasn't willing to reciprocate.

He walked around his desk and stood in front of me. I took a step back, but didn't stop his hand from circling around my waist, or his lips from crashing down on mine. I got lost in that moment, with our lips locked and our hearts pressed against one another. It was a slow kiss, not urgent, but it held the sparks that Brent's hadn't. Victor's lips were meant to mold against mine. They were meant to push me over the edge. But they shouldn't. They couldn't. *We* couldn't. And that was the realization that made me break the kiss.

"Don't go to the premiere," he said, a hard breath against my lips.

"Are you telling me this as my attorney?"

He took a step back, raking his fingers through his hair as he looked away. I felt my heart sink as I followed his line of vision from the floor to the large window in his office. We couldn't see the ocean in the dark, but the sound of the waves was soothing enough.

"No," he said finally, his voice low.

Our eyes met again. "Are you staying with the blonde?"

"I'm not *with* the blonde."

I rolled my eyes and took out my phone, holding up the pictures Chrissy had sent me. Surely he would understand how much it had hurt me to see these. "Your tongue down her throat tells a different story."

"Jesus Christ, Nicole. It was a fucking picture. Pictures hold more lies than they do truths. You of all people should know that."

"I can't erase what I saw."

He let out a laugh and muttered, "Tell me about it."

"What's that supposed to mean?" I said, knowing he was thinking about the pictures of me and Gabe. "Those were taken before . . . before *us*!"

"And these were taken *because* of us," he shouted, pointing toward the door.

I knew he was right, but it didn't change anything. Unless it did.

"Will me not going to the premiere change anything? Between us?" I asked. He closed his eyes, and didn't open them as he shook his head slowly. I closed mine as well, trying to rein in the pain. I didn't do pain publicly. I swallowed and crushed it.

"Okay. I'll see you around, Vic," I whispered, walking out and heading to the bathroom. On my way there I let Brent know I was ready to go as soon as I got out. In there, I was hoping to calm myself, but then ran into Grace, who seemed startled to see me.

"I thought you'd left," she said. "Did you see my dad out there by any chance?"

I frowned, trying to think about when I'd spoken to my uncle. I was pretty sure it was when I was having my first glass of champagne. I'd been pretty good about going around the room and talking to everybody, introducing them to Brent, but once Victor got there it all became a blur. He seemed to have that effect on me.

"I think he left."

She sighed. "My boyfriend is picking me up here, but Dad hates him."

"Oh. Okay," I said, walking into a stall and closing it behind me.

"So, what do you think of Victor's date?"

I blinked rapidly, trying to sober up quickly. "Nothing. What am I supposed to think?"

"Corinne hates her."

I half-laughed, half-snorted as I flushed the toilet and fixed my little black dress. I looked at Grace in the mirror when I went to wash my hands.

"Corinne hates everybody that gets near Victor. I'm sure she hates me too."

Grace smiled. "I don't think anybody hates you."

She was so young and innocent, probably thinking I was the nicest person ever. I dried my hands and looked at her one last time. "Have fun tonight."

"Thanks. Are you leaving?"

"Yep. My time is up. I came, I saw, I stirred up shit." I shrugged. "Now it's time to go home."

Grace laughed as I walked out of the bathroom. Brent was standing in the hall, waiting for me.

"Ready?" he asked, offering me his arm, which I tucked mine into. Instinctively, I looked for Victor. He was off to the side, talking to the blonde. I was so not waiting to talk to him in private.

"So ready. My feet are killing me."

"I can carry you."

I smiled, but didn't say anything. Brent was hot. He had an incredible body, a great smile, a nice personality, but I was his height when in heels. Not that it meant he couldn't carry me. I was sure he could. But I didn't even want him to try. I sighed. I should probably just have sex with this guy and see if I stopped thinking about Victor. Unfortunately for me and my vagina, I was just not that kind of girl. Once I had my mind set on one guy, it was set on that guy until I was over him. Despite walking straight into Gabe's arms all those years ago, I had to move forward. I wanted to be cherished, but I wasn't that needy girl anymore. I didn't *need* a man to sweep me off my feet. Maybe I should go back to just having a little fun.

Whether Victor was over me or not, I didn't know. What I did know was that he wouldn't act on whatever he felt. I could read him enough to know that his resolve was steady again. Maybe because he got his promotion. Maybe because I gave him what he wanted of me. It hurt to admit that to myself. It hurt because I gave him more than just a hookup. I gave him me, and he didn't even know it. Or maybe he just didn't care.

I looked over at Brent again, who was there and available and willing to try to make me forget things that could be hidden but not forgotten . . .

Chapter Twenty-Eight

Victor

What bothered me most about Nicole going home with the guy named Brent was that she didn't go home. I knew because I went to her house after I left the office and her car wasn't in the driveway and all her lights were off. If she wasn't there, it could only mean she was still with him. Spending the night with him. The thought made me crazy. Fucking crazy. I knew then, while I was standing outside her house, listening to the sound of the waves crashing, that I would willingly go insane for her love. It was more than just desire that I felt. It was deeper than that, more serious than that. In that instant, as I thought about her in bed with another man, the rage that ran through me was aimed toward myself for being an idiot. For not opening my eyes sooner. For not handing the case to somebody else when I should have. For not realizing the kind of woman I had and now had probably lost. No, fuck that, I hadn't lost her. Not yet. But worse than losing her, I was now sharing her. And I didn't share. Ever.

Chapter Twenty-Nine

Nicole

"Yes, Dad," I said for the tenth time. I was definitely going back home. I'd stayed a week longer than anticipated because when I went to get clothes the day after the promotion event, the media frenzy outside my house had been too much for me to handle. *Why were they still on my case?* During my week at Dad's, I managed to stay away from the cameras, aside from the day I went to the premiere with Gabe, which was when he asked me if I wanted to fly to Argentina. *To visit your mom,* he'd said. *I'll pay for your flights. It's the least I can do.* And I had agreed. It was the least he could do, and I was dying to see my mom.

"I just want you to be careful over there. Are you staying with your mom?" Dad asked. He knew I would. I never went to Argentina and stayed anywhere else. I responded anyway. "Good," he said. "What time is Gabriel picking you up?"

"At four. No need to get up and ready your shotgun at such an ungodly hour," I said.

"And you're sure you won't be with Gabriel?"

"No, Dad. We're over."

I told him I wouldn't go to the actual press events with him, but I would go on the same flight. He seemed okay with that. Gabe was definitely being cautious around me. Good thing, too, because despite my agreement, I still hadn't forgotten about our ice cream shop experience, or that girl's tell-all. Despite that, I wasn't going to turn down a free trip to go see my mom.

"Okay, sweetheart. Good night. Call me when you land," Dad said.

"I will."

I gave him a hug and went out to the guest house to finish packing. I couldn't sleep, so I went online and looked through gossip sites, because I needed to see what they were saying about me now. I'd kept a very low profile since the night of Victor's promotion, so I couldn't imagine they had much to say, unless Darryl fed the media things about Gabe and me. One of these days I would wake up and not find anything posted about me, and no cameras following me. *Goals.* One day soon. I just needed to get through one last media frenzy first.

I woke up at three and got ready, and Gabriel pulled up at the gate just as I was lugging my suitcase to the front of the house. He opened the backdoor of his Escalade and jogged toward me with a smile on his face. He looked like the man I'd met all those years ago, willing to help, excited to be going on a trip with me. Excited to see *me.* He leaned down and kissed my cheek as he reached for my suitcase.

"Thanks for coming," he said.

"Thanks for inviting me," I responded. As I looked at what he was wearing, which looked very similar to what I had on, I laughed. He gave me a once-over, taking in my black sweats and white T-shirt, and did the same. My shirt was a tank I'd tied at the bottom so it fit more like a crop, and his was just a regular white tee. We were both wearing the same black Nikes. Gabe laughed.

"Great minds, huh?"

"I guess so."

On our way to the airport, we both kept yawning, and at some point I dozed off with my head on his shoulder. I was startled awake when he moved, and I felt a flash of light on my face.

"Holy crap," I said, wiping my eyes and fixing my hair. "How the fuck do they wake up so early?"

Gabe groaned. "I don't know, but I swear Darryl didn't call them."

"Where is that asshole anyway?"

"He's in Argentina," he said.

"Oh. Fun."

Gabe chuckled, but didn't reply. A mob of paparazzi surrounded us as we stepped out of the car, security in tow. They started with their usual onslaught of questions, and we ignored them, both of us keeping our heads down. Gabe pulled me into his side just as we were trying to step inside, and in that moment, I was grateful to have the bit of comfort he provided.

The moment lasted all of two seconds. Once the doors closed on the cameras, I pulled away and waited for him to hand me my ticket. I was surprised his manager wasn't traveling with us and said as much as we went up the escalator. We both slept throughout the flight, not even bothering with the food they served, and by the time we landed we were starving. My mom had offered to have food ready for us, and I felt the need to extend the invitation to him, though I was hoping he turned it down. He didn't.

"I feel like I owe it to her to see her before . . ." He let his words hang. Before the divorce is final, I guessed. Before he never sees her again, I assumed. I didn't care enough to ask, and I didn't mind him going. "You know, I've never been to a red carpet event without you," he said as we waited for the security detail to sort things out so we could exit the car.

Similar to the U.S., the paparazzi didn't stop in Argentina. Once they caught wind that we were there, they were relentless. I was sure Darryl played some part in that.

"Yeah, well, you've done a lot of other things without me," I said, shooting him a pointed look. He flinched.

"I'm sorry."

"Stop apologizing. It's fine." I paused. "It's not fine, but it's over, and I'm over it. I'm just glad the LA premiere is over with."

"I really am sorry, Nic. I feel like . . ." He sighed. "We really had something good going for us. You were the only normal thing I had in my life, and I completely fucked it up."

"You definitely did. Maybe we both did, though," I said.

He shook his head. "It was all me."

"Maybe you were right, though. I just couldn't handle sticking around when things got tough. That's on me."

"Things got tough because of me," he said. "I let this," he waved his hands around, "change me. I let it change me. I see that now. I'm sorry I realized it so late."

I shrugged. It is what it is. You can't turn back time. "I wish you well, you know that, right?"

"Same goes for you." He stayed quiet a long time. We got out of the car and were escorted to the front of the house, and he put his arm around me to shield me from the overzealous cameras that were nearly in my face. When we reached my mom's door, he sighed and turned to me. "I've been dying to ask you something. Is something really going on between you and your lawyer?"

My mouth dropped. "I'm going to pretend you didn't really just ask me that."

My mom opened the door before he could say anything else, and my heart soared at the sight of her. People said we looked like twins, more than we did mother-daughter. I used to hate it when I was young because all the guys in school would tease me about wanting to bang my mom, but now I appreciated it. We had the same long dark hair, dead straight unless we attempted a curling iron, and the volume was always short-lived, the same blue eyes, and the same curvy body. Hers was a little fuller than mine, but she still looked incredible for her age.

"Hija," she said, throwing her arms around me. I squeezed her so hard, I was sure I cracked her back. She backed away and held my face in her hands as she looked at me. "Te vez cansada," she said.

"I am tired. I woke up at three in the morning and flew twelve hours," I said, stepping aside so she could greet Gabe.

They hugged as if we weren't waiting for the final papers of our divorce. My mom was like that, though. Forgiving, caring, always willing to give people a second chance until you fucked up again, in which case she'd put you on her shit list. With Gabe it was different though. She felt she saw him grow up, and she felt sorry for him. I also hadn't filled her in on just how many women he'd evidentially cheated with.

The three of us sat around the dinner table and chatted while being catered to by the cook and housekeepers, and I felt myself relax. Of course, that was until I saw the pictures of Victor leaving a nightclub with another woman. Then, I was raging and actually glad I'd agreed to go to the premiere with Gabe and wasn't back home in LA where these pictures would've been pushed down my throat. I needed to stop looking for things I had no interest in seeing. All I was doing was forcing the knife deeper into my heart, and I couldn't bear it anymore. I hid my pain behind a bright smile. It was the only way I knew how to cope. I hid. I hid my pain behind a bright smile. But inside, I also cried. Inside, my heart broke a little more, as if I hadn't experienced enough pain over the last two years. He was moving on. Despite that kiss in his office—our last kiss—he was really moving on.

At least I knew I was going to spend the week with my mom and not in public with Gabe. I was finally done with that life. Still, it didn't mean when Victor actually did text message me that it didn't bother me. I knew the game. I knew he was trying to make it seem like he was never with me, but those pictures, seeing them, seeing his smile, seeing him shielding the blonde with his arm so the camera's flash wouldn't get her . . . it hurt. It hurt, and I knew I couldn't talk to him. I wouldn't talk to him. Not unless he was ready to actually be with me. Not until after all of this was over. Not unless he was ready to actually be with me. I deserved better than to be somebody's dirty little secret. I deserved to be number one in somebody's life.

Chapter Thirty

"Look at this one," Estelle said.

While we'd been watching the Golden State game, she'd been scrolling through her phone, showing Mia the latest on TMZ's update about Gabriel and Nicole. Did she not realize how sick to my stomach I was over it? Did she not comprehend to what extent the whole thing angered me? Thankfully, I was holding Greyson in my arms and it was hard to rage while you were holding such an innocent little thing. I smiled, looking down at him.

"Women suck, Grey. When you grow up all you'll hear about is how much men suck and how terrible we are, but remember, they make us this way. They drive us crazy and make us want them and then they go fuck everything up," I said in a coo while I kissed the top of his head. He smelled so fucking good.

"What are you saying to my kid?" Mia asked. I lifted my head up to look at her.

"Nothing. Guy talk."

She shot me a dissatisfied look. "I'm not sure I want you having guy talk."

"Why not?"

"Because you're a bad influence."

"What?" I paused, frowning as I adjusted Grey in my arms. "I'm not a bad influence."

"Every time I look at this," she said, waving her phone around, "you're with a different girl. Weren't you supposed to be with Nicole?"

I groaned. "I'm not *with* any of those women."

"Yeah, good luck convincing Nicole of that," Estelle said.

"She doesn't care. Aren't you looking at pictures of her and Gabriel, looking like they're back on and about to go to the courthouse and get re-married and shit?" I asked, not caring how pissed off I sounded. Greyson cooed in my arms, and I stuck the pacifier back in his mouth with my finger.

"Can they do that?" Mia asked, gasping. "That would really suck."

"It would really fucking suck," I said. The thought alone made me feel defeated.

"Is she wearing . . . an engagement ring?" Estelle asked slowly, quietly, almost in a whisper.

I walked toward her and handed Grey over to Mia, and as I did, I caught a glimpse of the picture they were looking at. She picked him up and I took the phone from her hand. It was a video of Nicole and Gabriel. I clicked on it and brought the phone closer to my face. They were walking through a street market, and she was smiling up at him. His arm was casually draped over her shoulder. At the end of the video, the camera zoomed in on her hand and the voice-over made mention of the ring she wore. Nicole wore a lot of rings, though. She wore bracelets, and rings, and necklaces of all lengths.

"She wears a lot of rings," I said. I knew it wasn't her engagement ring because it looked much smaller. Seeing it on that finger didn't make it hurt any less.

"Let me see," Jensen said, reaching for the phone. "On that finger, though?"

I tried to shrug nonchalantly, but the lump forming in my throat spoke volumes. I looked at the television, so I wouldn't have to witness the compassionate looks they were surely giving me. I might actually break down right there in her living room. The truth was that when I told Nicole that she was mine, I'd meant it. I couldn't bear the thought of Nicole with anybody else in any capacity, much less in such a serious one. It physically pained me when I thought about it.

"When are you going to admit to yourself that you're in love with her?" Estelle asked suddenly.

Her words came at me hard, pushing a boulder of pressure against my chest. *Love.* I'd told her I thought I was falling in love with her when she'd been lying in my arms. All this time apart did nothing to diminish my feelings for her. Nothing. If anything, it made me realize how much I was missing. No late-night talks about our days. No humorous discussions. No kissing. No fucking. No . . . light. No Nicole. Fuck. And I realized Estelle was fucking right. *How did that happen?* There was no way around it. No point in denying it. I was in love with her and there was nothing I could do to stop it. I'd known it in that hotel room. I may have known it before then. Who knew? Love was a strange thing. But the more time that passed without seeing each other, and the longer she was in Argentina, the clearer it became that I'd lost her. Probably for good. Maybe I'd have to come to terms with the fact that I let go of the one woman who made me want to settle down once and for all.

"I . . ." I started, but stopped.

"Dude. She's right," Oliver added.

I closed my eyes, but it was useless, because all I could picture was Nicole's smile when she looked at me, her laugh when she made fun of me, the way her blue eyes lit up when she saw me walk near her. And fuck, I loved all of that. I loved the way she tried to hold back her emotion from the world but let me see it. I loved the way she let me see all of her, unfiltered. And my sister was right. I was in love with her.

"This is you admitting it?" Jensen asked with a laugh. I opened my eyes and looked around the room, at him, at Mia, Oliver, Estelle, and finally, at baby Grayson.

"I . . . it doesn't matter. I can't . . . it doesn't matter what I feel," I said.

"Shit. Victor stuttering and at a loss for words. This is big," Mia said.

"I fucking lost her," I said quietly. "The one girl I could stand to be near when she chewed her food and got all emotional and shit . . . and I fucking lost her." *Again*, I wanted to add, but didn't.

"You haven't lost her yet," Estelle said with a small smile.

I loved my sister. She was a pain in my ass most of the time, but she encouraged me when I needed it. I haven't lost her yet . . . but it didn't take away from the fact she was still in another country with her ex. I decided to call her. What else could I do? But her phone went straight to voicemail. Once. Twice. Three times. Finally, I sent her a simple three-worded text message in hopes she'd get it. Thankfully they hadn't pushed me for more, because there wasn't much I could offer. I wanted to fight but I had no idea how. The only thing I'd ever had to fight for was my career. My love life always sorted itself out. Fuck.

Later that week in the office, I snapped at everybody. Corinne cringed every time she walked into my office to drop off a paper, and I didn't blame her. I was sick of her, William, Grace, Bobby, and everybody else I had to see. The next time somebody knocked on my door, I growled a loud, "What?"

Bobby.

"Did your promotion come with a pissy attitude?" he asked as he stepped in.

I took a deep breath and put down my pen so I could massage my temple. When I knew I wouldn't snap, I dropped my hands and looked at him.

"What's up?"

He raised an eyebrow. "You wanna talk about it?"

"Not really," I said, letting out a breath. The last thing I needed was to talk about it. I went from being upset at myself for letting her go, to being pissed off at her for going and going with him. *Him.* The guy who had treated her like shit, cheated on her, let himself be seen in public with other women, and then there was the ice cream parlor thing . . . I just . . . I couldn't understand. I couldn't.

"Okay. You want to go watch the game, have a drink? Maybe it'll help you sort your shit out."

"I'm fine," I growled. "Nothing to sort out."

"Dude. Everyone in the office is fucking scared to talk to you right now. This has been going on for a week. You really don't think we realize you have a problem?"

My hands formed fists. I ground my teeth together to keep myself from lashing out. The moment I felt my heart tighten and thought of the heart attack scare my dad went through a couple years ago, I realized I couldn't do this anymore.

"I have to go talk to Will," I said, standing from my chair and heading toward his office. I knocked once, twice, and raised a hand to knock once more before he shouted for me to come in. He was sitting on the other side of his desk with his eyes closed, the lights dimmed down as he listened to one of those relaxation podcasts he'd been into as of late. He'd even gone as far as to email one of the links to me, which I deleted without opening.

"Hey. What can I do for you?" he asked, straightening in his chair and pushing down on his phone to shut the Zen bitch up.

I took a deep breath and sat down across from him. This man had given me the opportunity of a lifetime twice now. First, when I came to him looking for a job in divorce law and he took a chance the moment I sat down and went over the reasons why I thought I'd be a good fit in his firm. Second, when he named me partner. *Partner.* My fucking name had just been painted on the outside of the goddamn building. Alessi, Cohen, and Reuben, Esq. I wasn't ashamed to admit tears were almost shed when I saw that. And there I was, about to let it all go. Or most likely let it all go, because if he told me I needed to quit, I'd do it and start from scratch at a different firm. The thought alone made me want to throw up, but the thought of my life without Nicole in it was unacceptable.

"I'm in love with your daughter," I said, surprising myself. That wasn't the way I wanted to start the conversation, and from the way his eyes nearly bulged out of their sockets, I could tell I took him by surprise as well. He cleared his throat, blinking.

"I'm sorry, what?"

"I'm in love with your daughter," I repeated. "I'm in love with her, and I don't know when it happened, but I do know I should have passed her case along to someone else when we were well underway with it. It was wrong of me, and I'm willing to take responsibility for all of it."

Will stayed quiet for a long moment, just staring at me. He was going to ask me to pack up my shit and leave. I knew this, because he was giving me the same look he gave Roger Petit when he fired him in front of the entire staff.

"Does she know?"

I swallowed, nodding, and then shook my head. "Not . . . no. I don't know. She should know. It's obvious."

At this, his mouth twitched. "Obvious to whom?"

"Everyone, apparently," I said, shrugging.

He put a finger up as if telling me to hold on, and pressed the intercom button on the office phone. "Corinne, will you come to my office?"

I frowned. Maybe he would tell her to pack up my shit for me. At least then I wouldn't have to do all the work. That may be a good idea. But then she wouldn't know where to put what and she'd probably mix up my boxes and I'd have to work double. Fuck.

"Yes, sir," she said behind me. I didn't even turn around to acknowledge her.

She probably still had the mustard stain on her ivory top anyway, and my eyes would get glued to that and she'd think I was staring at her tits and get the wrong impression.

"Come here for a second," he said, signaling for her to come in. I finally looked up at her when she stood beside me, and sure enough, the mustard stain was still there. "Have you heard anybody say that Victor is acting a little . . . off lately?"

I examined the side of her face. Her cheeks flushed. She shot me an embarrassed look before looking at Will again. "You mean, more off than usual?"

My mouth dropped. "What the fuck is that supposed to mean?"

She shrugged, cringing. "Just . . . you've been in a bad mood."

"Says who?" I asked.

"Everyone," William answered. "Everybody here has made mention about your mood, and it started the day after your promotion went through." He looked at Corinne. "Thank you. You may go now."

She scurried off. I narrowed my eyes at the betrayer as she left the room.

"That's bullshit," I argued.

"It's not, and now you come in here telling me that you may have feelings for my daughter," he said, raising an eyebrow as if to say *what the hell am I supposed to think?*

"I don't think I have feelings for her, William. I fucking know it. If I didn't know it, I wouldn't be sitting here telling you, and if I wasn't absolutely certain I was in love with her, I wouldn't risk my job."

I decided that if I was going to get fired or demoted, I was going to go out with a fucking bang.

And that's pretty much how my two-hour meeting, later known as *The Big Debate* with William started . . .

Chapter Thirty-One

Nicole

"And you just let him go?" I whispered, my heart and head pounding simultaneously.

"I had no choice," my dad said.

I closed my eyes, sagging down to my living room floor. Bonnie climbed on my lap and nuzzled herself between my legs.

"He was okay with that?" I asked, running my fingers through Bonnie's soft hair.

"He had no choice."

Sadly, no choice seemed to be the only choice we had.

"Okay, Dad. I have to go. I'll see you soon."

"I'm sorry, pumpkin. I love you."

"Yeah. Love you too."

I hung up and tossed the phone on the couch behind me. I felt sick to my stomach. He'd acknowledged us? To my dad. Why would he do that? Why would he even . . . I didn't understand it. Clearly he hadn't told my dad because he wanted me. He'd told him because he wanted to come clean about having supposed feelings about me. Because he couldn't live with himself, knowing it was something that was against the company policy and not telling my dad about it. But it wasn't for me. It wasn't because he wanted me.

I twisted and picked up my phone again, texting Estelle to thank her for inviting me to her party, but sending her my regrets for not being able to attend. Victor had sent me a text message while I was in Argentina. Three simple words that set my soul aflame.

I miss you.

I hadn't responded because I was shocked he'd do that, especially with his paranoia of having things traced. I hadn't called because what I wanted to say to him couldn't be said over the phone.

My phone rang a few seconds after I'd tossed it.

Estelle.

I almost didn't answer, but then figured it wouldn't be fair to her. She seemed like a planner and probably had something specific for the attendees.

"Why aren't you coming?" she asked.

"I just . . ." I sighed. I could lie, or I could just come out with it, and because I was a shit liar, I came out with it. "I think it will be awkward to see your brother. I need to see him, but I don't think your party is the right setting."

"Who cares about him? I invited you, not you and him together. You. Please come. I already made you a heart."

I closed my eyes, feeling impending tears form behind my lids. "You made a kaleidoscope heart for me?"

She made *me* a heart, made of broken glass that represents broken hearts and pain and how beautiful the brokenness we carry inside makes us. *Why did she have to be so nice? How could she have known how badly I needed something like that right now?*

"Of course. You said you liked them," she said.

I swallowed. "Okay. I'll just pass by."

"Yay. See you tomorrow. And remember, pirate."

"I remember," I said, smiling as we hung up.

I called Marcus and asked him to pick me up, not because of the media—as I hadn't seen any—but because he was still on the payroll and I didn't want to park anywhere. He showed up much sooner than expected.

"You must have been dying to see me again," I said, opening the door.

He shook his head, but smiled a little. "If Gabriel didn't pay me so well, I would have taken twenty minutes longer."

I hid my smile by turning around and locking the door. "You're getting better at jokes," I said.

"I'm not sure that's a compliment coming from you."

"It's a very big compliment coming from me. I'm the funniest person you know."

"I worked for Martin Lawrence once," he said as he turned on the car.

"Ah. So he will tell me who he's worked for in the past."

He shrugged and went back to silence while I sketched out some pirate outfits I thought I could make by tomorrow night. In the end, I decided to buy most of the materials already done, like a white frilly blouse and tall black boots. I'd figure out what I could do with the elastic, black chiffon, black lace fabric, black latex, and basically any black material I could find. After I bought what I needed and got back in the car, I started feeling nervous again. I was going to the party, and I was going to see Victor, and I hadn't even spoken to him. I'd have to call him. Right? I'd text. He'd texted, so I'd text back. Tonight. Or maybe when I got home.

"Marcus, let's say you were going to a party, and you knew a girl you used to . . . have something with was also going . . . would you take a date?"

"Maybe. Are you taking one?"

I blinked. "I'm not talking about myself."

Marcus's eyes slid toward me. "You're asking for a friend?"

I pursed my lips. "You know, I didn't ask Chrissy to come shopping with me because I thought we could use this time to do some quality bonding, but if you'd like me to call her . . ."

His eyes widened. "I wouldn't."

"She really seems to like you," I said, smiling.

"No. I mean, I wouldn't take a date," he said, frowning.

"Oh." I paused. "Well, he's been seen with a lot of blondes lately."

"You've also been seen with more than one man."

"That's different."

Marcus shrugged.

"It's different. I didn't hook up with either of them. I kissed Brent because I was tipsy and Victor was pissing me off, and then I went with Gabriel because I had to," I said defensively, and looked out the window when Marcus stayed quiet. "And I went to Argentina because I needed to get the hell away. I mean, who the fuck tells somebody's dad they have feelings for his daughter after they get a promotion? I'm not taking responsibility for his stupidity. I kept our secret."

Marcus parked in front of my house and left the car on. We stayed quiet for a long moment. It was so quiet, but all I could hear was noise. My dad's conversation kept replaying in my head, the pictures of Victor flashed in and out in between . . .

"Don't take a date," he said after a long time.

"Huh?"

"Don't take a date to the party. Go by yourself. You're a fun girl, you can party by yourself, can't you?"

"Of course I can," I scoffed. "I don't need anybody's help to have fun." I paused. "Will you go with me?"

Marcus laughed. "Definitely not."

"I'm scared," I whispered.

"That's usually a good sign."

I rolled my eyes, picked up my bags, and got out of the car. "Pick me up tomorrow at eight."

As soon as I was in the house, I went to work, but when I took a break to feed Bonnie, I felt myself gravitating toward my phone. I typed quickly, before I could change my mind. He was probably out anyway. It was Friday night, after all.

Me: *I miss you too.*

I set the phone down as if it were burning me and walked away from it before I could do anything crazy, like call him. My phone buzzed a few seconds later.

V: *Did you have a nice vacation?*

Me: *Yes.*

He didn't respond after that, and I developed a sinking feeling in the pit of my stomach. I went back to my costume and tried to ignore the phone and the way it wasn't buzzing.

⁕

Marcus knocked on my door at seven fifty, and I could tell he was having a hard time not looking at what I was wearing when I opened the door.

"It's okay, you can check me out. I look hot," I said. "Unless I look slutty, then I have to wear the other outfit."

"You look fine."

"Not slutty?"

He shrugged. "I thought you didn't care if you looked slutty?"

This guy. I shook my head, grabbed my purse, and followed him to my car. Thankfully there was still no sign of photographers, but as we were about to drive off, there was a knock on my window that startled me. I looked and saw Brent standing outside.

"Hey," I said, lowering the window.

"Hey. I haven't seen you around. Are you back with Lane?"

Evidentially, I'd used Brent as my sounding board one too many times. Thankfully I never said Victor's name, so I guess he thought my rants about men were all about Gabe. I tried not to laugh at that thought.

"No. Definitely not."

"Oh, good to know," he said with a smile. "Maybe we can have dinner one of these days."

"Sure. I'm running late though, so I'll have to get back to you."

"Of course," he said, stepping away from the car. We waved at each other and Marcus drove away.

"Good thing you didn't invite him," he said after.

"Funny."

We were quiet on our way to the party, which was at Victor's parents' house. Even that made me nervous. I'd be seeing them again, and I really, really liked them. The funny thing was that this was reminding me of a divorce in itself. A divorce where instead of the dog, I wanted shared custody of his family. The gates were open for us to drive in without ringing the bell, and we were able to pull up to the door. I stayed in the car for a while, breathing in and out.

"Call me when you need me to pick you up," Marcus said.

I took one last long breath before stepping out of the car and telling him that I would, then walked up the steps with the bottle of wine I'd brought along and rang the doorbell. My heart pounded and shook in my chest, and when Victor opened the door, I was pretty sure I was close to fainting. I swallowed, registering the look of surprise on his face, his gaze skimming over me slowly. I felt the charge everywhere, and realized that despite the time we'd been apart, nothing had managed to numb what I felt for him, let alone make it vanish.

"Hi," I managed to say, clearing the croak in my throat.

"You look beautiful," he replied. My heart leaped again. I was finding it impossible to breathe with the way he was looking at me.

"I . . . thank you. You look . . ." My eyes followed the length of his body. He was wearing a legit pirate costume.

"Ridiculous," he said. "I know."

I smiled. "I was going to say hot."

He tilted his head a bit and smiled. It was so sexy, and real, and unexpected, that it made my heart squeeze in pain. "I'm glad that wasn't lost under this ridiculousness."

I laughed as he stepped aside for me to walk in. The house was decked out in pirate paraphernalia. I felt like I was on the set of Pirates of the Caribbean. "You guys really know how to throw a party."

"Yeah, my mom and sister have no life."

"I heard that," Estelle said, appearing from where I knew the dining room was. She looked like a sexy Captain Hook, with a hook on one arm and a parrot on her shoulder. She walked over to me and pulled me into a hug. "Hi. Oh my God. I love your costume; did you make it? I'm so glad you came."

Victor's lips twitched when she said that, and I found myself smiling as my stomach flip-flopped again. I wanted to stop looking at him, but I couldn't. I knew I missed him, I guess I hadn't realized just how much until I saw him again.

"I made most of it," I said. "Pulled an all-nighter."

"Vic, can you help me get this?" a woman said, and when she walked in wearing her own sexy pirate outfit, I recognized her as the blonde in one of the pictures I'd seen of him. My smile instantly vanished and I started to feel like I couldn't breathe.

"Victor," she said again, more demanding.

"Chill out, woman. I'm coming," he responded, looking at me momentarily. "I'll . . ." He walked away without finishing his sentence, and I didn't even know what to feel. I just knew my heart felt like it was too big for my chest and would possibly climb up my throat and spill out of my mouth at any moment.

"They're planning something for me," Estelle said in a quiet voice. "They think they're slick, those two."

I tried to smile at her, but couldn't, so I just nodded. "Everything looks great."

"Thank you. My mom did most of it," she said.

"And me," the blonde said, coming back to where we were still standing. "I helped. A lot."

"You did a good job," I said, catching Victor's gaze over her shoulder.

He was looking at me with an intensity that wasn't appropriate while out in public, much less with his girlfriend standing right there. However, I felt the heat of his gaze everywhere.

"Oh my God. I'm sorry. I've been staring at you since you walked in and haven't even introduced myself. I'm Mia," she said with a huge smile.

"Nicole. Nice to meet you," I said, returning her smile, though mine was much smaller, not as excited.

"Hey, can you help me carry the drinks outside?" Estelle asked Mia.

Mia gave her a sharp look. There was an exchange in their gazes, and Mia finally seemed to get whatever it was that Estelle was trying to tell her.

I felt another pang in my chest. They were really, really familiar with each other. Clearly Mia had either been a part of their life a lot longer, or really hit it off with Estelle, much more than I had.

"I'll see you later," Mia said, shooting one more smile my way before she turned around and punched Victor in the arm playfully. He rolled his eyes at her before looking at me again.

"She's really pretty," I said once they walked away.

"Not as pretty as you." He took a step toward me. I swallowed.

"You shouldn't say things like that," I whispered, tilting my face to look at him when he stood right in front of me.

"I only speak truths," he said, his voice low, making my heart stutter.

"Stop."

"Hey, is that Nicole?"

Victor groaned. "I'm in a house full of cock-blockers."

I sidestepped him until I reached his mom. She wrapped her arms around me. "Hi, Hannah."

"I've called you a couple of times so you could come over and see the dress. I can't wait to show it to you. The seamstress was very, very impressed with your design. She really wants to meet you," she said, her words fast and close together.

"Mom, she just got here," Victor said.

"I was in Argentina for a little while."

"Oh, you visited your mom? How was it? Did you have fun?" She pulled me toward the back of the house, and I was glad for the intrusion of whatever moment it was Victor and I were sharing. We couldn't have those anymore, especially now that he'd clearly moved on. I hated my dad right now. Why would he call me and tell me all those things if Victor had clearly moved on? He should have just kept his mouth shut, then I would have never known that Victor had thought about me at all.

Hannah took me around the yard, introducing me to the people there, which was interesting in and of itself. Some of the people were artsy, painters and such, others were doctors, architects, housewives, you name it, they were at the party. I'd already met Oliver, so I said hi to him, and he introduced me to some of his friends. At least there were hot guys there. Maybe they'd help me keep my eyes off Victor.

I excused myself and walked back to the drink table to pick up a glass of wine.

"I'm assuming your dad told you we spoke," Victor said, his voice making me shiver. I took a long sip of wine, hoping it would calm my nerves.

"He did."

He put his right hand over the handle of the pirate sword sticking out of its holster. I couldn't imagine how he thought he looked ridiculous. I'd never seen a sexier pirate in my life.

"What did he tell you?" he asked. I tore my gaze away from his hand, those long fingers of his, and looked back into his eyes. Big mistake.

"Are you going to cut off my tongue if I don't tell you?" I asked, smirking. His gaze heated as quickly and my breath caught in my throat.

"I can think of more than a few things I'd like to do with your tongue. Cutting it off isn't one of them," he said, bringing the hand he had on the sword up to my hair, pushing some of it behind my ear. I closed my eyes as he adjusted the bandana I had on.

"I really don't think it's nice for you to say things like that," I whispered, eyes still closed.

"Why?"

"Because you have a girlfriend, and I don't think she'd appreciate it," I said, opening my eyes to look at him. He frowned.

"What the hell are you talking about?"

"Really? You're going to the 'let me pretend I don't have a girlfriend' route while she's here?" I paused to take another sip of wine and tipped my head a little to glare at him. "I'm not a good candidate for bullshit, Victor. I see right through it."

He balked at me. "And as you know, I'm not good at practicing patience. What the fuck are you talking about, Nicole?"

"Mia," I said, a little louder than anticipated. His face morphed from confusion, to amusement, to anger, and back to amusement as he started to laugh.

"You're fucking insane."

"Yeah, well—" I started. Before I could finish, he was pulling my hand and practically dragging me to where Mia was standing with Oliver and the hot guy crew. "Victor."

"No," he said, stopping in the middle of the yard to look back at me. "If you're going to accuse me of something, you should have the sense to get your facts straight. Do you know how fucking mad I am at you? Do you know . . .?" He stopped to take a deep breath before pulling me again. "We'll discuss that later. Just . . . come."

Oliver, Estelle's husband, turned around with a frown. He pushed his long hair out of his face and looked between Victor and me.

"Everything okay?" hot guy number two said to our right.

"Mia, why are you here?" Victor asked, his voice strong.

Mia pulled a face. "I'm not sure I'm understanding the question."

Hot guy number two, I was pretty sure his name was Jensen, hid his smile behind the bottle of beer in his hand.

"Jensen, stop fucking laughing. Tell Nicole why Mia's here," Victor said.

Jensen started laughing and shaking his head, then Oliver joined in, and the other guy they were talking to followed.

"I told you," Jensen said when he finally stopped laughing.

"No, I told you," Oliver said.

"Fuck you. I said it first." He paused, wiping his eyes and looking over at Mia. "Babe, what did I say about Victor last week?"

Babe? My eyes widened. Oh fuck. *No.*

Mia frowned. "I don't know, Jensen."

"You need to remember."

She rolled her eyes. "Are we done here? I need to go see if Grey's still sleeping."

"You have the video monitor attached to your ass. I'm pretty sure he'll alert you when he wakes up," Victor said. "Can you answer my fucking question before I punch your husband?"

Oh motherfuck. She was *not.* And she was a mom?

"Estelle's my best friend. I'm not going to miss her birthday," Mia said.

"Okay, and who did you come with?" Victor pressed.

"Jesus Christ. With this idiot," she said, pointing at Jensen, who started laughing again. "Why?"

"She thought you were my girlfriend," Victor said, his eyes cutting to me. I wasn't looking at him, but I could feel them on me.

"What?" Mia said, laughing now. "Oh my God. That's disgusting." She paused and looked at me. "No offense or anything."

I opened my mouth to say something, but there was absolutely nothing I could say.

"Don't worry, this one right here is your brand of crazy," Jensen said, pointing at Mia with his thumb. She pushed him.

"Shut up," she said, then looked at me again. "Why . . . oh. Is it because our pictures in the tabloids? I told you we were famous. I'm a huge fan of yours. Well, I was a huge fan of Gabriel, but then all that . . . stuff happened, so I'm not as big a fan as I used to be, but I still like him as an actor because he's really good."

Jensen wrapped an arm around her shoulder and pulled her to him. "Babe."

"What?"

"Your fangirl is showing."

She buried her face in her hands and took a breath before looking at me again. "I talk a lot when I'm nervous."

I smiled. "That's fine. I'm sorry for probably giving you the biggest bitch face earlier. I really didn't know you guys were just friends."

"Totally fine. Totally cool," Mia said. I smiled at her and everyone else before excusing myself once again. As I walked away, I heard Mia say, "She's officially my new best friend," and I had to laugh.

"You thought I was dating someone?" Victor asked when he caught up to me. "And you didn't even fucking think to ask?"

"How would I ask?"

"You could have called."

"You broke up with me." *And it broke my heart.*

He narrowed his eyes, jaw set. I raised an eyebrow, daring him to take a different approach. "You're going home with me."

"What?"

"Tonight. You're going home with me, and we're going to have this fucking conversation. Either you go with me, or I go with you. You pick, but I swear to God if that Brent guy shows up at your house I'll get arrested, and you'll have to bail me out of jail."

I bit my lip to keep from laughing but was unsuccessful. "You're the lawyer."

He scoffed. "If I get to keep my license."

My smile dropped. "What do you mean?"

"Your dad didn't tell you?"

I blinked and shook my head slowly.

"We're having a meeting with the associates on Monday to see if they want to keep me on board as partner."

My stomach dropped. "What?"

"What did he tell you?"

"That you told him you had feelings for me."

"He didn't tell you what we argued about?"

"No," I said, frowning. "What the did you argue about?"

"You."

"Me?" I asked. My head was spinning. I needed to sit down for this. I needed an entire bottle of wine for this.

"Come home with me," he said. "I'll tell you everything."

"Okay." I paused. "Okay, but I need to call Marcus."

Victor growled. "Always calling some guy."

"He's security detail, and a friend," I said, rolling my eyes as I took out my phone and dialed. "Marcus, you don't have to pick me up tonight."

Before I could explain anything, Victor snatched the phone from my hand. "Marcus, this is Victor. If you must know, she's coming home with me, and she's staying until, and if, I let her go. If I let her go, I'll be the one driving her home, so if she fucking calls you before five in the afternoon tomorrow, ignore the call. Thanks. Bye."

He hit the end button before handing the phone back to me and all I could do was stand here, holding my hand out to take it.

This. Fucking. Guy.

Chapter Thirty-Two

Nicole

We stayed at the party long enough to sing happy birthday. Long enough for Victor's friends to tell him he was whipped and make fun of him. Long enough for him to send them all to hell. And long enough for me to witness Victor holding a baby with so much care and love, I was afraid my ovaries would explode right there. Neither one of us said a word on the drive to his house, me because I was afraid I would say the wrong thing. I wasn't sure what his silence was about, but it was making me nervous. He hadn't touched me either. Not since we were outside, when he would do the occasional drift of his fingers along my bare shoulder to call my attention. It made my stomach dip every time and even though I tried to focus on the wine, after two glasses I didn't even want any more.

His house was dark except for the porch light when we got there, and I was so worked up I was sure if he touched me I would jump out of my seat. He switched off the engine and sighed as he glanced over at me.

"Let's go."

I nodded and stepped out of the car, taking caution with my heels in the gravel of his driveway. He seemed to notice, or maybe he'd had many women in heels over, because he came over and grabbed my arm to steady me and help me inside. I thanked him and let him open the door and switch on the inside light for me. I looked around and crossed my arms as he locked the door behind me and gasped when he walked back over and dropped a kiss on my shoulder.

"I've been wanting to do that all night," he said, his voice a rasp behind my ear. I closed my eyes to savor the moment. "Turn around."

I opened my eyes, my heart pounding in my throat as I did.

"I'm so mad at you, I don't . . ." He sighed. "Maybe we should talk in the kitchen."

I felt like I was being sent to the principal's office on the first day at a new school, like everything was riding on this conversation. My nerves were shot to hell because whatever I'd done would never truly be forgiven. But I hadn't done anything wrong. Not really, anyway. I'd tried to save his job, and he was possibly being demoted anyway. We sat beside each other on the barstools after he served us each a glass of water.

"So you're meeting with my dad and the other guys on Monday," I said, figuring I'd start where he left off earlier.

"Right."

"How'd that come about?"

Victor looked down at the floor for a long time before tilting his face to lock eyes with me. "I'm not sure I want to start at that part."

"Okay," I said, lifting the glass of water to my lips to take a sip and setting it down. "Start, then."

He clasped his hands on his lap, his leg bobbing rapidly. "What's going on with you and Gabriel?"

"Nothing." I paused. "You're handling my divorce. Why don't you tell me?"

His eyes narrowed. "It wouldn't be the first time you kept something from me."

"That was different, and there's nothing I'm keeping from you. Everything's on paper," I said.

"Him holding your hand, putting his arm on your shoulder, hugging you, kissing you, that shit is on paper?" he said, his voice rising.

"He didn't kiss me," I said, but he ignored my comment and stood suddenly, the top of the chair hitting the edge of the counter with a little bang. I flinched. He started pacing, taking off the pirate sword and vest, and I watched.

"If I knew that shit was going to be part of the agreement, do you really think I would have let you sign? What else was part of the fucking agreement, Nicole? Did you fuck him too? How does one get into that kind of contract with you? Is being an asshole a requirement? Cheating on you? Being a drug addict? Treating you like shit? Tell me. Tell me because I wanna know where the fuck I'm going wrong."

I blinked. And blinked. Trying to make the stupid tears I felt forming in my eyes go away. I swallowed the lump in my throat and swung my legs to and fro to distract myself from crying, because I wouldn't do that. I wouldn't cry.

"Tell me," he seethed, walking over and placing his arms on either side of me, his face at a reachable distance from mine. I swallowed again.

"If those are the requirements, I'd say you fit at least two of those categories," I whispered. His eyes widened as he stood straight and rubbed his face with both hands. "You know what? Fuck you, Victor. Fuck you for putting this on me when you pushed me to it." I seethed, feeling hot tears burning my eyes.

"Just like I pushed you to marry him five years ago?"

I flinched again. I'd seen Victor angry. I'd seen Victor annoyed. I'd seen Victor let loose and have fun. I thought I'd seen Victor in all of his elements, but I'd never seen him like this. I wasn't sure what to do with this version of him, so I stayed silent and let him work out his issues in front of me. If this was his ugly, I wanted to see it. I wanted to see all of him. I needed to see all of him before I could decide whether I would stay or leave. He closed his eyes and took a deep breath before coming over to me again and standing in front of me, farther than before, but still close enough for me to reach out and grab him. Or slap him. I took a deep breath. Long, deep breath.

"What happened to your face?"

I hadn't asked him when I saw him last. Whatever it was looked like it was almost healed, but the scar was still there. He let out a chuckle, although it sounded anything but amused.

"I had a difference of opinion with someone."

"A difference of opinion . . . Care to expand on that, or are we here to keep harboring secrets?"

"I don't know, Nicole. You tell me. You tell me what we're harboring."

"I flew to Argentina with Gabriel because he was going and I wanted to go see my mom. I only saw him that one day. After that I spent the rest of the time with my mom. Look at the fucking pictures. We're wearing the same thing in all of them." I paused, taking a breath and letting it out, trying to calm down.

"I'm here because you asked me to come. I'm here because I want to know what happened with you and my dad and your job, because the only thing I'm guilty of is helping you keep your goddamn dream alive."

He moved closer, standing between my legs. "My dream? You don't know anything about my dreams. You never asked me what I wanted."

"You never asked me. You broke up with me. You broke things off because you were afraid you'd lose your precious career."

He closed his eyes and let out a harsh breath that caressed my face.

"You made me think that us being with other people was the right thing to do, so I went and saw other people, like you did," I added.

"I didn't see anybody else, Nicole. All I ever saw was you."

"I saw the way you kissed that blonde. Not Mia, but that other one, the one you took to the office party."

He growled. "Fuck that girl."

I tilted me head and shot him a look. "Did you?"

"No! Christ, Nicole. How could you even ask me that?"

"How could I not?" I said, my voice breaking a little. "How could I not, Victor?"

He placed his palm against my cheek and tilted my face so I could look into his eyes. "I would never do that to you. *Ever.* Did I kiss her? Yes. For pictures. That was all."

"It hurt," I said, swallowing back that damn lump of emotion. "It hurt a lot."

His gaze fell over my features, appraising me for a long moment, and during those seconds I saw his expression thaw and his posture relax. He lowered his forehead to mine.

"I'm sorry, baby," he whispered. "Seeing you with Brent at the office hurt too. So did seeing you with Gabriel fucking Lane in every news outlet available while you guys were off in Argentina visiting your mom. Did you think that would be easy for me?"

"I didn't know what to think," I whispered. He held my face with his hand.

"It was fucking brutal," he said, lowering his hand and setting it over the elastic corset I'd made. He tucked a finger underneath it and snapped at it. "I'm not this," he said. "I don't stretch. I don't mold. I don't conform, and despite what people say about my career, I'm not a liar. So when I tell you I'm in love with you, Nicole, it's because I'm in fucking love with you. And when I barge into your dad's office to tell him I'm more in love with his daughter than I'll ever be with my career, it's a big fucking deal."

My heart stopped as I processed his words, and I found that no amount of swallowing or blinking was going to keep my tears at bay. He cradled my face with both hands and wiped my tears away with his thumbs.

"You said that to my dad?" I whispered. He nodded, bringing his mouth down to mine and placing a chaste kiss on it. I leaned forward to try to get another, but he moved. "So they really might demote you because of me?"

"Not because of you, baby. It has nothing to do with you," he said.

"But you just said—"

His lips curled into a small smile. "Okay, it has everything to do with you, but it's not your fault. I made my choice. I'm surprised your dad didn't tell you when you spoke to him."

"Well," I said, eyes wide, "he asked me if there was anything going on between us and I denied it, and then he said you argued and left and . . . yeah, I don't know. He didn't make it sound very good." I paused, searching his face. "I am so sorry."

"Not your fault."

"I can talk to him."

"I have a meeting on Monday. I'll plead my case and see what they say. If they don't want me as partner, then it wasn't meant to be."

"How can you say that?"

He didn't answer me. Instead, he bent down and kissed my temple. Just once, but the gesture somehow gave me the answer I needed.

"Are you staying?" he asked. "For good?"

"What does for good mean?" I asked.

"It means for good. That you're mine and no one else's. No more fucking around."

"Are you mine and no one else's?"

He smiled, caressing my face with his thumb as he brought his lips down to mine. "Always yours. I was never anybody else's." That tone. It made me think of the time he'd begged me to scream that I was his. When he'd pounded into me with a ferocity I'd only experienced with him. Just thinking about it had my heart racing. He loved me. He was *in fucking love* with me.

"Hmm," I said, moaning when I felt his mouth on my neck, his hand crawling up my leg and under my skirt. "You mean I finally caught the untamable Victor Reuben?"

He chuckled against my chest, his other hand pulling my panties hard and ripping them off. I gasped, startling a little, and when he started moving his fingers inside me and using his thumb on my clit, I threw my head back.

"The untamable Victor Reuben," he said, nipping my cleavage. "Take your tits out and I'll show you how tame I am."

I pulled the top of my bustier down, and uttered an unintelligible "oh my God" when I felt his mouth on my left nipple as his fingers moved inside me. I was all nerve endings, all feelings, no holds barred as he played my body with his fingers, his tongue.

"I'm going to fall," I said, feeling my toes curling with an impending orgasm. "I haven't . . . oh my God . . . that's so good . . . you're so good . . . oh my God. Victor!"

"Say my name. That's right," he said, biting my other nipple.

"Fuck."

"That's right, baby."

And then, on his kitchen stool, I orgasm, eyes closed, toes curled, head thrown back. He pulled me off the stool and turned me around, pushing my torso down, my breasts on the freezing cold granite as he spread my legs. I tried to brace myself, but it was no use. When he thrust inside me I took in a huge gasp of a breath. He yanked the bandana off and threw it on the counter.

"I should use it to tie your fucking hands." His voice low and in my ear as he fucked me. Hard. "I should blindfold you." He leaned back and pulled my skirt up, his hand coming down on my ass in a hard slap. "I shouldn't even fuck you right now," he said, pulling out of me completely.

"No. No. No," I shouted, pushing myself back. "Please."

He thrust in just as quickly and hard as he pulled out, and I yelped at the feel of his girth and the slap of his hand on my other ass cheek. "I should make you fucking beg for it. If I wasn't so desperate for you, I would."

"Oh my God," I said, feeling another orgasm surfacing.

He grabbed a fistful of my hair and brought his other arm around my body to play with my clit. "You make me feel desperate for you, Nicole. I can't stop thinking about you. I can't bear the thought of you with another man."

I gasped, my eyes rolling back. "You're the only one." I gasped again, the strumming of his fingers on my clit was increasing and I knew I'd lose it in a second. "Never anybody else. I swear."

"Good," he said, pushing my face down so I was flat on the surface as he increased his pace and started to fuck me wildly. I squeezed my eyes shut and screamed when the orgasm finally ricocheted through me, and gasped at the feel of him emptying himself inside me in three slow, long thrusts. "Fuck, baby."

"Hmm," I gasped. It was the only thing I could say.

He helped me upright after a couple seconds and pulled me to his chest, holding the back of my neck. "I missed you so much."

I looked up at him. "I love you too." His smile was slow forming, but huge.

"I know."

I laughed, pushing his chest. "*You know?* This isn't Star Wars."

He shrugged. "No, but I know. I think you fell in love with me the last time I fucked you in my office, before you got married."

"That makes absolutely no sense, but let's say I did, what took you so long?" I asked. He bent his knees and lifted me into his arms, carrying me toward his room.

"I was a fucking idiot."

Chapter Thirty-Three

Victor

Having Nicole in my bed, fast asleep, for two days in a row when I woke up was perfect. I got up and headed to the bathroom to brush my teeth before putting on a pair of board shorts and heading outside. I hadn't stepped foot in the ocean since I brought her home on Friday night, and I needed to clear my mind before I headed to the office for my meeting. We'd talked, fucked, and argued the entire weekend, and I wouldn't have traded it for any amount of promotions or money in the world. I ran out with my board and caught some waves, and on my way back in, I smiled when I saw her standing outside with a cup of coffee in her hand. Bonnie was running around my grass, probably taking various shits, but that was fine. I'd deal with the dog later. At least she was potty-trained. I unzipped my wet suit and grinned when I caught Nicole licking her lips, her eyes dropping to my exposed chest. I couldn't stop fucking smiling.

I took it off and tossed it in the basket I had outside and put my board down as I ran up to her and swept her into a hug.

"Victor. You're going to get burned," she said, laughing as she tried to balance her cup of coffee.

"I'm sure you don't have any left in there," I said, looking in. Sure enough, there was only a drop left.

"I could have just poured it," she said when I let go of her. My eyes drifted down to her white shirt, which was now completely wet and see-through. She had no bra on. She slapped me on the chest and my eyes snapped to hers.

"What?"

"Stop looking at my boobs."

I put my hands out and grabbed them, playing with her nipples over her shirt. She moaned. "You want me to stop?"

"No," she said, gasping when I pinched them. "Let's go inside."

We went inside, stripping clothes off until we were both naked. I propped her up by the wall and started closing the sliding glass door, my lips on hers. She broke the kiss and gasped out a, "Bonnie's outside."

Of course. The shitting dog.

"Bonnie. Get the fuck inside the house," I yelled. Nicole laughed until I pinned her with my stare and pushed the tip of my dick inside her, and then her laugh turned into a series of gasps and oh fucks. Those were my favorite.

"You have to leave soon," she said, moaning when I grabbed two hand-fuls of her ass and started driving into her. Fuck. She felt so good. She was so fucking wet. So. Fucking. Wet. I threw my head back, increasing my pace.

"I know."

"I'm going to come. Fuck. Victor. Victor," she shouted. "I'm going to . . . oh my . . ."

And then I shattered inside her. I caught my breath and let her catch hers before I helped her stay steady on her feet.

"I'm pretty sure the entire beach heard us," she said.

"Good."

She laughed and went back to the kitchen while I ran to my room and into the shower. I had thirty-five minutes to get to work. Fuck.

I was finishing putting on my tie when Nicole walked into the room.

"I brought you coffee. Do you have time to eat?"

I looked over my shoulder at the clock on the nightstand. Eighteen min-utes. "Nope. I'll have Corinne get me something on her way."

"You look hot."

"Thank you."

"Really hot," she said, lowering her voice. I closed my eyes.

"This is going to be a problem," I said, looking at her.

"What?"

"Me having to go to work and wanting to stay home to fuck you instead."

She smiled, looking at the floor between us. I walked over to her and lifted her chin.

"No matter what happens today, I love you. That's not going to change, and I want you here, that's also not going to change."

She swallowed and looked at me. "I'm going to have Marcus pick me up. I should probably stay over there a couple of days. I do pay bills, you know."

I let go of her chin. I didn't like that idea at all, but I understood why she felt the need to go. I'd have to find someone to take over her lease so she could move in with me. That topic hadn't been discussed as of yet, but it would be soon, and that was a battle I'd win.

In the office, everybody greeted me a little warily since I'd been a complete ass for a few weeks. It made me wonder if they hadn't been informed of anything. When I got to the conference room, only William was there, sitting at the head of the table. He looked up from his phone when he heard me come in.

"Have a seat."

"Where's Bruce?" I asked as I unbuttoned my suit coat and sat down where I normally did, beside him. Bruce was the other partner.

"I decided not to call anybody in for this." He paused, setting his phone down. I looked at it, wondering if he'd set it to record. As if reading my thoughts, he chuckled and lit it up so I could see the home screen. "So paranoid about some things, so careless about others."

I let the jab slide. He was right.

"How's Nicole? Did you speak to her about . . . your situation?"

I tried to keep my face impassive, but my lips twitched into a smile. If he only knew how many situations his daughter and I got into over the weekend . . . "I did."

"And?"

"I already told you. I wouldn't have gone through the trouble with her if I didn't know it was the real deal."

"And how do you know it's the real deal? How do you know that in five years you won't be in this office talking about your own divorce? I know your track record."

My brows rose. Good questions. Fair questions. How did I know . . . how could I explain that?

"I don't," I said. "I have no idea what will happen in five years. I came in here thinking there was probably more than a fifty percent chance I'd get fired, or demoted, and I still haven't been able to stop fucking smiling, and that's the only way I know that. Who knows?" I shrugged. "Maybe it won't work out the way I want it to, but I sure as hell want to try, and when I think about my life five years from now, the only thing I see with sureness is Nicole."

Will tilted his head, his eyes assessing me. "When do the finalized papers get here?"

"They should be here soon. Possibly next week. I rushed Judge Matthews."

Will nodded. "You know how I feel about you as a person and as an employee. You're like a son I never had, and that's one of the reasons I'm being hard on you about this, because as much as I love you, I love my daughter more."

He picked up his phone and pushed a couple buttons, turning on the speakerphone. Three rings later Nicole's voice seeped through the room. My breath caught in my chest. I glanced up at him, and he shrugged as if to say let's see what she says about this.

"Hey, Dad," she said. My heart gripped at the sound of her voice.

"Hey, sweetheart. I have a question for you, and I need you to answer honestly."

Nicole groaned. "What now?"

"Promise?"

She stayed silent for a second. "Promise."

"Are you involved in any way with Gabriel?"

She stayed quiet again. My heart constricted. "No. Argentina was the last thing I was going to attend with him. Why?"

"I mean romantically, Nicole."

"No."

"That's a definite no? What about in Argentina?"

My heart squeezed again. I didn't want to hear this. I didn't want to know. Out of mind, out of sight. That had been my motto.

"No, Dad. Why are you asking weird questions?"

"What about Victor Reuben?"

"What about him?" she whispered.

"Last time I asked you, you said nothing was going on with you guys. Were you lying?"

She breathed into the phone.

"Promise, Nicole."

She breathed into the phone again. "Yes."

"Yes you were lying?"

"Yes."

"Why?"

"Because I thought if I told you the truth, you'd fire him," she said, and I could tell she was crying. I saw her cry the other day, but hearing her like this and knowing I wasn't there to comfort her made my heart physically ache.

"Why would I fire him?"

"Because he's my lawyer," she said, crying openly. "Please, Dad. Please don't fire him. It's my fault. I pushed him and pushed him."

I closed my eyes, burying my face in my hands. I couldn't do this. I couldn't sit there listening to her plead for me like this.

"He's not getting fired," Will said. My head snapped up.

"Oh, thank God," she said, sniffling. "Thank God."

"He said he told you he's in love with you."

"He did." She sniffled. "And I love him."

Will stayed quiet for a moment, his eyes appraising me. I kept my face neutral because I wasn't sure I wanted him reading into my relief. I didn't want him to know I felt like celebrating. He smiled after a couple beats. "Okay, sweetheart. I'll let you go now."

"Okay. Talk to you later."

He ended the call and drummed his fingers on the table. "So . . . that happened."

"Like I was saying, when I met you, I saw myself twenty years prior. I didn't have a mentor or anybody to walk me through things or help me when I fucked up, and I really wanted to be that person for you," he said. "But then I hired you, and I never really had to do that. You were like a newborn child who was already potty-trained. I've never seen anything like it. I didn't assign you to take care of my daughter's divorce so you could make partner. You were going to make partner anyway. That promotion has been yours since you stepped foot in this office." He paused.

To know I had his support for the role was incredible. While gaining Nicole in my life was a far greater reward, I couldn't deny the way hearing those words made me feel.

"I wanted you to represent her because I knew you'd do right by her, and I know you'll do right by her now as well."

I let out a breath. "Thank you. That means a lot." More than he could ever know.

"You wanna know how I know you're right for her?"

I swallowed. "How?"

"Because I don't even feel like I need to give you a warning, or tell you the things I'd do if you fuck things up, though maybe I should warn you that she can be a little difficult."

I chuckled. "I got that part."

"So then you're good," he said, smiling. "I couldn't have picked a better man for her."

"Thank you," I said, because I didn't know what else to say and fuck me, I was feeling emotional. "I'll always do right by her, Will." I took a deep, relieved breath. "Does this mean I'm not getting demoted?"

Will laughed. "Yes, but you will need to take time off until Nicole's papers come in."

"And not work?"

"And not work."

My jaw dropped. "What the fuck am I supposed to do?"

"You'll figure something out."

I sighed. I guess I would have to.

On my way out, I took a pit stop to Corinne's office to let her know. She looked at me like she wasn't sure what to do with the information.

"You're serious?"

"Yes, I'm serious. Why would I joke about that?"

"But you never take days off."

"Maybe I was waiting for my vacation to accumulate so I could take a longer break."

She frowned. "Six years later?"

"Corrine," I said, sighing. She closed her mouth when she realized she was pushing my buttons.

"Sorry. I just . . . I'm shocked. Does that mean we'll be on vacation at the same time? Does that mean I won't be able to take my vacation?"

Why did she have to get so shrilly? I let her have her moment, but instead of getting over it, she continued to look at me like I had some kind of answer written on my face. Finally, I cleared my throat.

"You put in your vacation and you'll take it. There are five other attorneys in this office, Corinne. Go get engaged, or married, or whatever," I said.

"What will you do?"

I made a face. How was that her business? "Not go get engaged or married or whatever," I responded. She smiled.

"I heard," she whispered, leaning into the desk as if she were sharing a great secret with me, "that you're in a very serious relationship."

I opened my mouth and closed it immediately. Whatever I said would be used against me for life around the office, and taking time off for what I'd done was the most lenient form of punishment for most people. Even though being without work for more than a couple days was like walking through the pits of hell, I had to be grateful it was all I got. That said, being out in the open with Nicole right now wouldn't be the smartest thing to do for either of us, and I knew that. Instead of answering her question the way I wanted—which was: I am in a very serious relationship—I just shrugged.

"If you need anything, call my cell phone," I said as I walked off. "Good luck on your vacation."

"You too."

I knew Nicole wouldn't be at my place when I got home, but it didn't keep me from missing her as I walked through the house, looking for any sign that she'd been there. The only sign was a navy blue blanket on the living room floor where the dog had slept. I'd never cared to have a dog, but I'd definitely have to get used to it being around. I looked at the blanket for a long time, debating whether or not I should pick it up. Itching to pick it up, really. In the end, I took a breath and made myself walk away. I went upstairs, changed into something comfortable, and smiled at the sight of my shower still being wet with her handwriting on the foggy mirror that read, *I love you*. I took my phone out and snapped a picture of it before I decided to call Quinn to ask him for a huge favor before heading to her house. I only hoped what I had planned would work and that she'd be able and want to go with me.

Chapter Thirty-Four

Nicole

I was sitting outside with Bonnie, enjoying a cup of cereal, when Brent jogged by. As much as I appreciated the eye candy, I was seriously starting to wonder if he had a job.

"Hey, you want to grab lunch today?" he asked, stopping to catch his breath in front of my porch. I put my hand up to shield my face from the sun as I looked at him.

"Nah. I kind of—"

"Have a boyfriend," Victor said, his sudden presence making me jump an inch out of my seat.

Brent's and my head whipped toward him. My heart leaped at the sight of him, standing there in a pair of jeans and a polo. The fact he wasn't at work and had changed from his suit to this was not a good sign.

"What are you doing here?" I asked, blinking rapidly.

"Aren't you her lawyer?" Brent asked, frowning.

"Was."

My stomach dropped. *Was?*

"Yes. Was. Do you have any more questions for me or are you going to finish that run now?" Victor asked. I wanted the ground to swallow me whole.

"Maybe another time," I said to Brent, who nodded slowly.

"I'll catch you later," he said as he ran off.

"That was so mean," I said as soon as he was far enough away. I took a handful of cereal and began to chew.

Victor eyed the cup in my hand as he sat down in the chair beside me and patted Bonnie on the head. "Fuck that guy."

My eyes widened. "He's a nice guy."

"A nice guy who wants to fuck you."

I smiled, shaking my head. "Can you blame him?"

He had this wicked gleam in his eyes as he gave me a slow once-over. "Fuck, no. Doesn't mean I want to see him try, though."

"Now I know why you never have a girlfriend," I said, raising an eyebrow. He lifted my foot from the little table I had it on and placed it on his lap, massaging it. I closed my eyes and tossed my head back, putting down the cup of cereal on the floor beside me.

"What were you saying?"

"Huh?" I asked, opening my eyes to look at him. He was still smiling as he lifted my foot and bit down on my toe. "Ouch! Fuck."

He chuckled. "You were saying that you knew why I never had a girl-friend."

"Oh." I straightened a bit in my chair. "Your controlling tendencies. I don't know if women can handle that."

"Can you?" he asked, raising an eyebrow.

I looked at him for a beat, unable to keep myself from getting lost in the intense look his eyes held. The challenge. I freaking loved it. Loved *him*. I realized, as he massaged my feet, clearly not at work like he would have been if he'd worked his magic on my dad and whoever else he met with, that in a world full of Gabriels, men like Victor came a dime a dozen.

"I think I can," I said quietly. I smiled when he dropped my feet and stood, towering over me with both hands clutching the armrests on either side of me.

"If anybody can, it's you," he said, dropping his lips to mine and kissing me deeply, his tongue delving into my mouth in a way that took my breath away. He broke the kiss and backed away slightly, still holding the armrests. "I have a surprise for you, but now that you're being so sassy, I'm not sure I want to give it to you."

"What are you going to do? Spank me?" I asked, smirking.

His gaze heated instantly. "Don't tempt me."

"Maybe I want to," I said, bringing my foot up and brushing it against his crotch, which was already hardening. He breathed out harshly.

"You love playing with fire, Nicole," he said, his voice a low rasp as he placed his forehead against mine.

"I love playing with you," I replied, pressing my lips against his.

He reached down and carried me, my chair making a screeching sound against the concrete as he lifted me and pushed it aside.

"Wait," I said as we waited for Bonnie to walk in before closing the door behind us. "Did you get fired?"

He chuckled, setting me down on the couch. "You wait until now to ask me that?"

"I was distracted."

"By how handsome and controlling I am?" he asked, grinning.

"You are so full of yourself."

"So I've been told," he said, grabbing his crotch in his hand. I nearly moaned at the sight of it.

"Did you?"

"No, I'm on leave until your divorce papers come back."

"So . . . you're still partner?" I asked quietly.

He sighed and took a seat beside me on the couch, putting an arm around me. I put my legs on his lap and scooted closer. "I am," he said, running his fingers through my hair. If he kept this up, the massages and the hair touching, I'd definitely keep him. "I was there when your dad called you."

My eyes widened, meeting his. "Did I . . . well, obviously he kept you on board so I didn't mess anything up, but . . ." I groaned. "I hate that he put me on the spot like that."

"You did great, Nic." He pulled me closer to him. "You did great, and," he let out a breath, "you were fine. It was fine. Will just doesn't want any more attention around this until it's clear the divorce is over. I really can lose my license. That's not a game."

I blinked. "We were just outside kissing. You just told Brent that you were my attorney and insinuated you were my boyfriend."

"Fuck Brent. He's not a threat."

"You don't know that."

He shot me a look. "If he becomes one, I'll take care of it."

"Like you took care of Darryl?" I asked, raising an eyebrow. I knew I'd caught him off guard because of the way his eyes widened and he reared back slightly. "I saw him in Argentina. His face was all cut up the same week you had a bandage on yours. Coincidence?"

"Probably. I'm sure a lot of people want to cut his face," he said.

"You're going to sit here and lie to me?"

He sighed, running a hand through his hair. It was telling.

"You can't just go around beating people up because of me," I said. "Isn't that worse than us being out together?"

Victor let out an unamused chuckle. "Not in the state of California."

"He can press charges."

"Let him try," he scoffed, then looked at me. "You don't have to worry about any of that, Nicole. Trust me."

"I do. I just don't want to be the reason you go through all this trouble and lose a great job."

His gaze held a seriousness that made my heart dip. He didn't say anything else, instead he reached for my hand and brought it to his lips. I leaned the side of my head on his shoulder, and we sat in silence for a little while, just silence. A comfortable, beautiful silence.

"I have something for you," he said, arching off the couch to pull something out of his back pocket. He handed over a folded packet, which I took as I sat up. I opened the papers and read through it, gasping, my heart beating uncontrollably. Tears started to form in my eyes before I even finished reading the entire thing.

"We're going to Iceland?" I asked in a hoarse whisper.

Victor smiled softly. "We're going to Iceland."

"You know that's where they film—" I started, but he snatched the papers from my hand and turned the page before I could finish. I screamed. Loud. And bolted out of the couch. "Oh my God! Oh my God! We're going? We're really going? But how?"

Victor laughed and pulled me onto his lap. "I know people."

"Did you tell your sister about this?" I asked after long quiet minutes, in which I read everything on the pages he'd given me.

"Hell, no. She'd kill me. We can send her a picture when we get over there. We leave in a week by the way," he said, kissing my forehead.

"A week." I paused, eyes wide. "I have to find out if we're still on shooting break."

"You are."

"How do you know?" I asked, my veins still drenched in adrenaline.

"Your friend Talon told me."

"What?" My mouth dropped. "How did you get in touch with her?"

He chuckled, pulling me so I could straddle his lap. "I already told you, I know people."

I wrapped my hands around his neck and smiled. "I really do love you."

"You better," he said. "I don't even watch that fucking show."

Chapter Thirty-Five

Victor

Iceland was fucking freezing, but the permanent smile on Nicole's face made the trip worth it. We were on set, and even though she said she was a huge fan of the costume designer, all she did was check out the guys.

"You're drooling again," I whispered in her ear. She shivered, wrapping her arms around herself.

"I'm sorry. I know it's in bad form to check out another man in front of your boyfriend, but oh my God," she said, her teeth rattling. I laughed, wrapping my arms around her.

"I'm not worried."

She smiled, tilting her head to look up at me. "You're so sure of yourself."

I shrugged. No point in denying it. She wasn't going anywhere, and neither was I. Even if I wanted to leave her, my family would probably disown me at this point. In the week we had between our reconciliation and the trip, we'd been inseparable, which meant everywhere I went, Nicole was there and vice versa. One of those days, we'd gone over to my parents' house for dinner, where Mia, Jensen, Oliver, and Estelle joined us. Whenever Nicole wasn't in the room all I heard was, "put a ring on it" and "you better marry that girl." Every time I reminded them her divorce wasn't even officially final, they shook their heads as if it was somehow my fault. But when I admitted I would marry her someday, Jensen and Oliver didn't shut the fuck up about me being in love.

I let them have their fun because every time the subject was brought up they ended up arguing about who won whatever bet they had going. It was amusing to watch.

"I'm glad you've taken such an interest in my personal life," I said when we were sitting outside having a drink.

"We bet five hundred dollars and this asshole won't admit he was wrong," Jensen said, nodding at Oliver. I gaped at them. Five hundred dollars?

"What the fuck was the bet?"

"That you were involved with a client," Oliver said.

"No. That you would become involved with a client and actually fall for her," Jensen corrected.

"No. He only had to fuck one of his clients, and he told you he was representing Nicole before we made the bet, so it should be thrown out the window," Oliver said, raising an eyebrow.

"You should have bet for Jensen to get a tattoo on his ass and for you to cut your fucking hair," I said.

They scoffed.

"All I'm saying is I won," Oliver said. "Did you or did you not fuck her before you became her attorney?"

My jaw twitched. I didn't want to talk about my sex life with Nicole, and I couldn't even throw anything back at him about his because I really didn't want to talk about his sex life with my sister. I took a gulp of Jameson and looked at him over my glass. "Fuck you, Rapunzel."

Jensen laughed loudly. "You do need a haircut."

"Fuck you both," Oliver said, running a hand through his hair. "The kids like it."

They probably did. I'd heard from a friend of a friend that the pediatrics office where he worked boomed after he'd gotten a job there. My sister seemed to be amused by the whole hot doctor thing he had going on at work. I shook my head.

"Both of you are assholes," I said, standing and stretching. "Now let me go get ready. I have a long flight and I hear Game of Thrones shoot is pretty epic, so I don't want to be tired when I get there."

That shut both of them up for all of three seconds before they started with an onslaught of insults. *You bastard! I can't believe you're going! I hope they hire you as an extra and kill you off!*

I chuckled and raised my middle finger up as I walked away from them. "They only kill Muggles."

"That's not even the right series," they screamed.

"Keep betting against me. You'll never win," I shouted back.

"You're an asshole. Send pictures."

"I'll think about it."

Now we were here and I realized just how impressive the set actually was, I'd sent short of a thousand pictures. Nicole was just in awe of everything, the way I probably would have been if I'd actually watched it on television. I'd always avoided things when my clients worked on shows I enjoyed because I thought they'd take away from the fantasy of what I liked watching on screen, but this was the real deal. The set was Iceland, and Iceland was breathtaking. And I'd probably never set foot back here again, so I tried to enjoy every second of it and openly being with Nicole.

My phone buzzed in my pocket and I took it out. Nicole rolled her eyes.

"I thought you were off work. You check your phone every two seconds."

"Some of us need to stay employed, baby," I said, scrolling through my email. My heart stopped when I saw it was from Will and had a smiley face on the subject line. A fucking smiley face from Will could only mean one thing. I opened it up and noticed the attachment. Above it, the email said, *Good to have you back, partner.*

My heart leaped, soared, in a way that only rivaled what Nicole made me feel when she looked at me.

"Your hands are shaking. You need better gloves," Nicole said beside me. I shook my head.

"No. I'm not cold," I said, and meant it. As I opened the attachment on the email, all I felt was warmth. I let out a long, relieved, icy breath. "Thank. Fucking. God."

"What?" she asked. I turned the phone so she could see, and smiled when she gasped. She stayed quiet for so long, that I had to look at her. I noticed she had tears in her eyes. Tears that would probably freeze before they fell onto her face. I pulled her head and crashed it onto my beating heart. "It's over," she whispered. "It's really over."

I wasn't sure if she was sad, happy, relieved, and I didn't know if I had it in me to ask. I faced things head-on, but if she told me she was sad about her divorce finally being completely over, I wasn't sure how I'd feel. Probably broken-hearted. Probably crushed. I decided I need to man up and took a deep breath, rearing back slightly and tilting her face to look into her eyes.

"You okay?"

She nodded, blinking slowly. "I am." Her smile was slow, but wide. "I think . . . I really am." She let out a smoky breath. "I feel . . . free."

I smiled, bringing my lips to hers in a soft, chaste kiss. "Sorry to break it to you, but you're kind of stuck with me."

She laughed. "I'm okay with that."

"You better be, or I'll go tell that guy with the black feather cape to lend me his weapon," I said. Her eyes got huge and she completely froze for a beat.

"Is he behind us?"

I looked over her head. "Not right behind us, but yeah."

"Oh my God. I think I'm going to faint."

I laughed. "You haven't even seen him. He's not that big a deal."

If possible, her eyes widened more. "Jon. Snow. Is. A. Huge. Deal."

I groaned, remembering Mia and Estelle and everybody else I knew talking about him. "That's the fucking famous Jon Snow?"

Nicole turned around and let out a little silent excited shriek. "Yes."

I wrapped an arm around her and pulled her to me. We were on top of a little hill as we watched him walk with a heavyset guy. He was not a big deal. He looked short. I was sure his hair made Oliver jealous, though, so I snapped a picture of him and sent it, knowing I wouldn't get a response until later on.

"Are you happy?" I asked, my mouth near her ear. She nodded.

"So happy," she said, turning in my hold and wrapping her hands around my neck. "I really, really, really fucking love you, Victor Reuben. Despite your aversion to marriage."

I grinned. She was so clueless. "I don't have an aversion to marriage."

"I heard you talking to your parents the other day." She paused, her blue eyes searching my face. "I'm okay with that. I don't need to get married again. Been there, done that, bought the shirt."

"Fuck that shirt."

"You say that about everything that has nothing to do with you," she said, laughing. "I'm just saying, you have a really great life. I'm not here to disrupt your organized, meticulous lifestyle. I just want to be part of it."

I sighed and bent my knees, pulling her down to the warm blanket we'd been given when we got here. I held her gaze as I spoke to make sure there was nothing I said that would escape her realm of comprehension.

"You once said this was a goal for you," I said, waving a hand around the set around us. "My goals were always career-driven, and when I attained those, I realized my goals had changed a little and that somewhere along the way you became my goal. I'm in love with you. I've achieved a lot in my thirty-one years, and I'm proud of those accomplishments, but none of them make me feel the way you do. When we go back home, my next goal will be to get you to move in with me, and later on down the line it'll be to get you to agree to marry me, because I love you and I never want to be without you."

It took a moment for my words to sink in, and when they did, she blinked, and blinked, and the tears forming in her eyes began to fall. I caught them as they did, brushing them away.

"*I'm* goals?" she whispered, smiling.

"You are *every* goal I never knew I wanted."

Our lips met in a slow, sensual, long kiss that made me want to run back to the hotel and fuck her in our hot tub. When we broke apart, we smiled at each other.

"You know, this is the second time you've proposed to me," I said. "That's a record for somebody who says she doesn't care to get married again and just finalized a divorce."

She blushed, looking away. "I never said I was against marriage just because it didn't work out for me before."

I caught her chin and made her look at me again. "Good, because I'm going to marry you."

"You say that as if you know I'll say yes."

"Haven't you learned by now?" I asked, pulling her bottom lip into my mouth and letting it go with a pop. "I always get what I want."

She was it for me. I'd never in my thirty-one years wanted anything the way I wanted my beautiful, feisty, and sexy Nicole Alessi, and I knew I never would.

Epilogue

Nicole

Two years later

"You should just quit your job and design wedding dresses for a living," Talon said as she did my makeup.

"Maybe one day I will," I said, looking up as she applied eyeliner.

"You're going to look incredible. Victor is going to wish he'd asked you to marry him eight years ago."

I smiled. "I wasn't ready for him then."

"He is pretty intimidating," she said, smiling.

"A little." I paused. "Are the girls ready?"

"If by ready you mean dressed, yes. Mike said they're picking up all the flowers they scattered during their practice session, though."

I laughed.

"Stop moving."

"Sorry."

There was a knock on the door, followed by the loud voices of Hannah, my mom, Mia, Estelle, and Chrissy. Mia and Chrissy hadn't stopped talking since they met at the bachelorette party last week. They were highly entertaining to be around. I think all of us agreed on that. All of us except Victor, who groaned every time they walked into a room together.

"I *so* hope you guys have daughters," Estelle said. I smiled and reached to touch her pregnant belly when she stood beside me.

"So your brother can have a heart attack by the age of forty?" I asked.

Estelle laughed.

"He'll be a great dad," Hannah said. I completely agreed with that sentiment.

"He would be, and they'd make beautiful babies," my mom agreed. When I first told her that instead of moving into another place when my lease ended, I was moving in with Victor, she flipped out, but then she came to the U.S. and met him, and they instantly hit it off.

"I completely agree, and so will you," Meire added as she walked into the room.

Mom's head whipped around quickly. We'd all gone out to dinner numerous times through this process and it had given Mom and Meire a chance to get to know each other. I doubted Mom would approve of anybody Dad married, but she seemed to have a lot of respect for Meire.

"You look incredible," Chrissy said.

"I know, right? I wanna marry you right now," Mia added.

I laughed. I was already feeling overjoyed, but having these people in my life, on this day, took my excitement to another level. I didn't want a big wedding this time around, but once we started adding up our family members and friends, we ended up with two hundred people on our list. I put eloping on the table, but Victor turned it down as quickly as I said it. He didn't say it in so many words, but I knew he didn't want me to compare this wedding with Gabe's and mine. Not that I ever would. Victor made me feel stable, and cherished, and loved, and even though I could make a million comparisons and give a million reasons as to why this marriage was a one hundred percent sure thing, I didn't. It wouldn't have been fair for me to diminish *the good* I'd once had with Gabe just because we hadn't worked out.

I'd seen him a couple times when he'd met up with me at the dog park to see Bonnie. Something the paparazzi loved to speculate about, much to Victor's annoyance, but he was okay with us maintaining a friendly relationship.

"I don't expect you not to be friends with somebody you were with for that long, but it doesn't mean I like the attention it gets," he'd said. *"And I still think he's an asshole."*

He did appreciate Gabriel sending him a box of Cuban cigars and a bottle of Blue Label as a congratulatory gift for our wedding, though.

"That was a nice thing to do. He owed me for keeping you from me all those years," he'd said when Marcus dropped off the present at his house, which we'd been sharing since we came back from our trip to Iceland.

Marcus no longer drove me around. Well, not all the time. I definitely didn't need security anymore, but we'd kept in touch and now he had to deal with Victor's and my rants. He seemed to be totally okay with both, but preferred Victor's, probably because the rants usually happened over basketball, baseball, or football games, which were a thing in our house. I hated sports, so how I ended up marrying somebody who was so obsessed with them was just . . . crazy. I loved it, though. I loved having a house full of people.

He'd brought up marriage a few times, but I never imagined him getting down on one knee. I never imagined him pulling me into his arms one night as I'd walked through the door after a long day at work and holding me for the longest moment. Just holding me and breathing into my hair. When he leaned away from me just slightly and wordlessly searched my face, I began to worry. I was going to ask what was wrong, what had happened, when he dropped down on one knee and took a little black box out of his pocket as he looked up at me.

"I've had this ring for a few months, but there hasn't been a right time for me to ask, with work, and everything else we've had going on. There's never a right time because that's how life is. It's always chaotic, it's always hectic, and work will never stop, and I love sharing that with you. I love being able to come home and have you as my sanctuary. You've built that for me, with me, and I want us to have it forever. I don't want to imagine a life without you, Nicole Alessi. Marry me."

I still got teary-eyed thinking about it. Estelle saw the look on my face and slapped my arm playfully, snapping me out of my thoughts.

"Stop it. You can't cry," she said.

"I know. I was just thinking about Victor."

"Ugh. Yeah, I'd be crying too," Mia said, making us laugh.

"Are you ready?" my mom asked.

I nodded. "Yes." And I had been.

My dad's eyes widened when he saw me, a huge smile spreading over his face. I remembered the last time we'd done this and how serious he'd looked. Today he looked carefree, happy, as if he'd been waiting to give me away his entire life instead of wanting to grab me and lock me in my room forever. I asked him what changed, and he chuckled.

"I don't know. Maybe the fact that you've already done this?" he mused, and locked eyes with me. "Or maybe it's the man you're marrying. I see the way his eyes light up when he hears your name, and the way he takes care of you and puts you over everything. Not many things can drive him out of the office, you know? You did good, Nic. He's one of the good ones."

I smiled, feeling myself tear up again. Shit. I needed to stop doing that. "I know."

When the church doors opened, our friends stood up along the aisle, but the only man I saw was Victor, who looked fucking edible in his sharp tux. Victor, who didn't look at me like I was the end of something, but rather, the *beginning* of everything. I loved that man. So much. When I reached him and he shook hands with my dad, I felt my heart nearly jump out of my chest. This is what it felt like to be complete. This is what a fairy tale was like. This feeling right here. *This* was goals. This moment.

We looked at each other for a long, quiet moment, one filled with endless possibilities, the way our future together felt.

"You look beautiful," he whispered as the priest started the mass.

"So do you," I replied. His lips curved up.

"I know."

I shook my head, rolling my eyes.

"You already signed the paperwork, Nicole Reuben. No going back now," he said, his eyes twinkling.

He was so keen to mention that every five minutes since the day we'd gone to the courthouse. His face had been priceless when I'd reached for the name-change form and filled it out. I'd not taken Gabe's last name. I didn't really want to change mine, as I loved the name Alessi, but I knew how much it meant to Victor, and the more I thought about it, the more I liked it. Nicole Reuben had quite a nice ring to it.

"I would never," I said.

"Not even if I was richer?" he asked. "Not even if I was famous?"

"No way. Been there, done that, bought the shirt."

His eyes darkened. "I tore that shit up."

"Victor," I whisper-shouted, giving him a pointed look. We were at church.

"I'm just saying, my shirt's better," he whispered with a shrug, then smiled. "And much bigger."

Note from Claire:

Thank you so, so much for reading!

The characters in this series will forever have a part of my heart. They've been there for me when I needed to focus on the lighter things in life and believe in love so powerful, it could pull you out of any funk life wants to bury you under. I hope they did the same for you!

If you can take a minute to write a quick review, I would be incredibly grateful!

Also, if you'd like to receive a bonus scene from Victor and Nicole, fill out this form:
http://goo.gl/forms/aWqhuRGhxz

Xo,
Claire

Acknowledgements

I'm not going to name <u>everybody</u> because publishing a book takes a village, and my village has so many wonderful people in it that I'm afraid I'll forget to name some of them, like the bloggers who share my things, the authors who support me, and the readers who continuously tell their friends to buy my books. You're the ones who matter most, so thank you, from the bottom of my heart.

To my SQUAD. I love you. #SQUADGOALS

MY FYW girls. I'd be lost without you.

B.B.F.T. & the incredible girls in my FB group–YOU ROCK.

Willow A., Jenn W., Rachel K., Yvette V., Tiffany C., Michelle K., Lisa C., Julie V., Clarissa L., Sandra C., Priscilla P., Jen G., Jessica S., Katie R., Bridget P., Toski C, Karinna B., Anabelle, Diana, Barbie, Mimi, and the list goes on and on! – you guys are incredible and deserve a medal for putting up with me.

Every single blog who has shared my cover, read my books, reviewed them, and spread the word– I appreciate you more than words can say.

TRSOR- THANK YOU for putting together my tours.

Sarah at Okay Creations- thank you for putting up with my anxiety and designing the most amazing covers on my shelf.

Marion Making Manuscripts & Karen Lawson- The dynamic duo! I love your eyes.

Stacey Blake- you're a queen. I love you.